MIXTAPE SERIES TRACK 3

FOUNDED ON *DECEPTION*

KAT SINGLETON

EPIGRAPH

LOVE IS BEAUTIFUL, A
BEAUTIFUL DECEPTION.
ONE FALLS IN IT TO DECEIVE
THE OTHER.

-AMIT ABRAHAM

DEDICATION

To the misunderstood. The ones overlooked when it comes to falling in love, yet often, the ones most deserving of love.

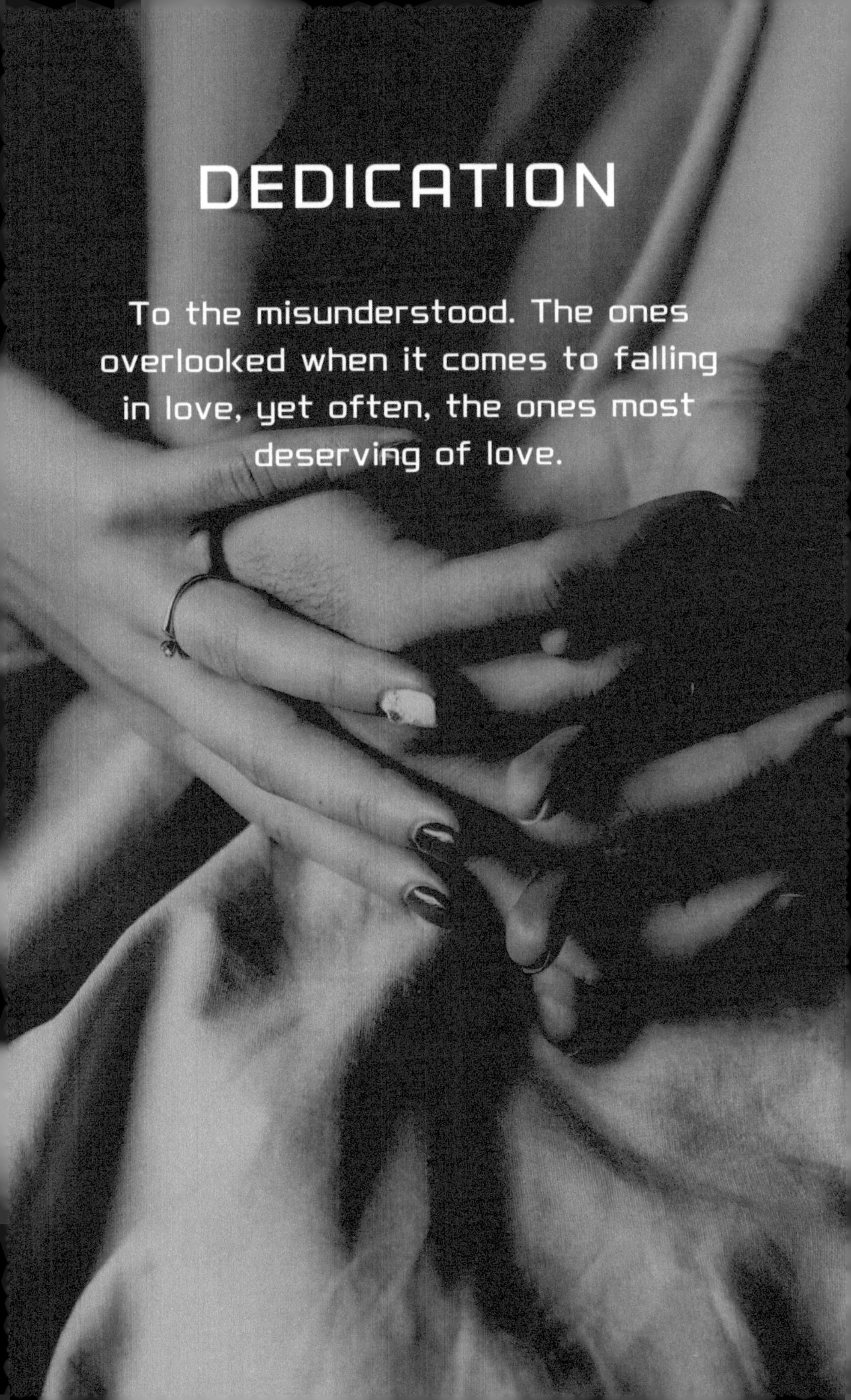

1
MONICA

I'VE NEVER BELIEVED in mistakes—you make a choice, and you live with it. The word *mistake* was created by people that dwell on the past. I'm not one of those people—or at least, I didn't used to be.

Two years ago I made a choice. A decision that would stick with me to this day. I'm still not sure it was the *wrong* choice, but it is one I constantly think about. I tell myself that I did what I had to do to protect someone I care about.

Right now, I'm wondering more than ever if that choice was actually a mistake. A big one.

I'm standing in front of a towering tour bus as the Los Angeles sun beats down on my skin, probably causing wrinkles I'll have to pay thousands to erase. The bus is one of several in a row spanning the expansive lot. People bustle around me, preparing to embark on another Nash Pierce world tour. Tyson, Nash's publicist, stands to my right, jawing on about securing another interview for Nash and his fiancé, Nora, before their impending nuptials.

I ignore every single word out of his mouth. As Nash's manager, I should be focused on the conversation, but my attention lies elsewhere.

Tyson follows my gaze to the man sauntering our way as if he doesn't have a care in this world. He's got a black leather jacket draped over one of his shoulders, the fabric hanging loosely from his grasp. There's a certain swagger to his step, as if he's the most popular kid in high school walking down the hallway. His messy brown hair blows in the slight California breeze, brushing against a pair of sunglasses covering his eyes.

Even with his eyes concealed, I know who he's focused on—unfortunately, that would be me.

Aiden Pierce. Nash's loud, obnoxious younger brother who I *thought* I had the absolute pleasure of avoiding for the duration of this tour.

"What the f—" I start, before getting cut off by Aiden.

"Aw, Monica, did you miss me that much? I thought cussing was so *beneath* you." He reaches out to tap my nose, but I swat his hand away before he can follow through.

Cussing *is* beneath me, but for Aiden I'll make an exception.

It wasn't always like this. My past choices have complicated some things. Nash could have fired me for them. He probably should have—Aiden practically begged him to. But he didn't, and now Aiden has made it his mission to berate and annoy me any chance he gets. A mission that he is succeeding at more and more every time I see him, though I would never admit it.

"Does Nash know you're here?" I clip, taking a step toward him. The sun is hot against my forehead as I refuse to break eye contact with the menace.

He smiles down at me, showing off his staggeringly white teeth. The creases of his smile lead up to his high cheekbones. I don't recall ever knowing anyone with a face so sculpted, but that's just Aiden. I've always thought it was such a waste to give someone so intolerable *that* face. His sharp features pale in comparison to his razor tongue—and the blade is always aimed at me.

"Does it matter?" he snaps back, seeming to just notice a

cowering Tyson standing next to me. He looks him up and down, before handing him his jacket. "Could you put this on Nash's bus? He knows I'm coming."

"We don't have room for you," I interject. My phone vibrates in my hand, but I pay it no attention. Nash's team, including me, spent weeks planning the accommodations for this tour. We didn't account for Nash's disaster of a little brother joining us.

His lip twitches upward. "Nash seems to have a different idea."

I try not to let my face show any form of reaction. *Surely* Nash would've told me if he was allowing his brother to come on tour. Last I'd heard, Nash didn't want to deal with Aiden's antics.

"He's wrong," I counter. "There's no bus for you."

He takes a step closer, crowding my personal space and forcing me to take in his scent to avoid giving ground.

"Sure there is, Monica. Just give me the furthest one from yours."

"I've got to go," Tyson mutters quietly, jumping at the opportunity to get away from the two of us.

"Fine," I respond, dismissing him with a wave of my hand and looking down at my phone. It lights up with the caller ID for the head of Nash's label, Roy Goodman. Taking a deep breath, I swipe to answer, silently dismissing the nuisance in front of me to take the call.

"This is Monica," I answer, swiftly weaving through crew members until I find a semi-quiet place.

"I don't see any recording sessions on Nash's calendar, Monica," Roy says, his voice bland. Every time we speak he talks as if I'm a child, and not a fully capable adult who has helped line his pockets with money for years.

"I'm going to speak with Nash," I inform him. The tip of my heel kicks away a discarded cigarette. *Gross.*

"I seem to remember hearing that before," he quips.

My shoulders stiffen, recalling what he's talking about. "I'm not sure if you remembered, but we're starting our tour today. We've both been preoccupied. I'll talk to him when I get the chance, Roy." Pulling the phone away from my ear, I hit 'end'. My hand finds the side of the bus I'm standing next to. Steadying myself, I take a deep breath.

There are few people on Earth that I tolerate less than Aiden, and Roy might be one of them. If he didn't have such a stranglehold on Nash's career, I'd never answer another call from the man.

Maybe one day, I hope. But that problem can wait. Today, I'm stuck in an entirely different hell. Just when Nash and I were starting to get back to normal, his devilish brother had to swoop in and throw a wrench in my plans.

A twenty-two-year-old wrench who hates the mere sight of me.

This next year on the road just got a whole lot longer.

2
AIDEN

THE HOT METAL surface of the bus door radiates to my knuckles as I knock on it. For a moment, I wonder if my plan is going to fail before it's even begun.

I let loose a breath I'd been holding as the door swings open. Standing in front of me is a smiling Nora, Nash's former backup dancer turned fiancé. Well, at least she *was* smiling. Now that she's seen me, her smile has faltered a bit in surprise.

"Oh," she says quietly, taking a step back until her calves hit the stair of the bus. "Hi, sorry," she lets out quickly, "I just wasn't expecting to see you here."

"Good to see you too, sis." I take a step into the bus, forcing her to retreat up the stairs.

"Rose?" I hear my brother yell from deeper in the bus, using the sickening nickname he gave her. "Who is it?"

"Uhhh," Nora drags, looking over her shoulder at me as I ascend the stairs and stop next to the captain's seats at the front of the bus.

"Honey, I'm home!" I cheer, my arms outstretched wide.

Nash stares at me from the doorway of the back bedroom. He's shirtless, but not for long. Reaching for something out of sight, he pulls on a t-shirt.

"What are you doing here, Aiden?" he questions, pushing his arms through the armholes.

"Well, what do you think, big bro? I'm going on tour with you, obviously."

My feet take me down the narrow pathway of the bus. On one side there's a small kitchenette and the other houses a leather couch piled with bags of various sizes.

Hitting one of the bags, I look at my brother. "I gave my things to one of your people. I'm all packed and ready to hit the road. My stuff just needs to find its way to the right bus."

Movement out of the corner of my eye catches my attention. Nora leans against the counter, her eyes bouncing from Nash to me, and back again.

"All I said was that you could *maybe,* come on tour," my brother points out. "I never said yes."

I swat at the air. "You implied it was a yes."

Nash laughs, shaking his head and walking in my direction. "No I didn't. You're in school, Aiden. You can't drop everything and come on tour with me."

My eyebrows narrow. "You didn't even go to college. Who gave you the right to lecture me on school?"

He shakes his head. "It's *because* I didn't go to college that I want things to be different for you."

I sigh, moving bags around until I can make room for myself on the couch. My body falls to the cushions with a soft *thud.* "I'm not *never* going to go. I've told you this. I'm just taking a year off. Plus, I haven't learned shit yet. I'm too busy dodging classmates—and professors—that are asking questions about *you.*"

"I think it would be great for him to come along," Nora interjects softly. She doesn't look at me, instead focusing on Nash. Her fingers nervously flutter against the kitchenette countertop as the two of us wait for his response.

"Do you?" he asks sarcastically. I smile, wondering if Nora is actually on my side instead of his.

She nods. "It'll give you the chance to spend some time together."

"What happened to *us* spending time together?" he questions her, a playful tone to his voice.

"You know I want to make sure I spend time with Lennon on this tour. Now you have the chance to spend time with your brother as well. It's a win-win situation."

Lennon is Nora's younger sister. I don't know all the details, but I do know that Nora is trying hard to mend their relationship. Apparently, that's why she was invited and I wasn't. Well, that and Nash couldn't stand a year of Monica and me at each other's throats.

He doesn't understand that I'm only looking out for him by trying to expose what a conniving *bitch* Monica is. If he would just fire her ass, I wouldn't have a reason to misbehave. Hell, I'd even hold the door for her on the way out. I'm a gentleman, after all.

"I wasn't aware my tour was a family reunion," Nash groans, finding the spot next to Nora. He pulls her into his side effortlessly. Never did I imagine my brother being a lovesick puppy for a woman, but if he's happy, I'm happy...as long as Nora treats him right and doesn't break his heart again.

"So, is that a yes?" I say, grinning. My knuckle runs over my bottom lips as I watch him carefully.

Rolling his eyes, he sighs. "Like you'd even taken no for an answer."

Leaning forward, I clap my hands together. "Hell yeah!"

Nash cuts off my celebration. Closing the distance between us, he stops in front of me, the toes of his sneakers coming to rest against the toes of my combat boots. "Under one condition."

"Lay it on me," I say.

"You leave Monica the hell alone," he responds instantly.

My jaw tightens. I don't argue with him because I know he's serious. So I keep my mouth shut for now, knowing that'll be the last thing I do.

3
MONICA

Stopping in front of Nash's bus, I take a long, deep breath in. Slowly, I let the air back out and repeat the process. I started my morning with a long Pilate's session followed by some restorative yoga. I was zen—as zen as I can get—until I showed up at work and all went to hell.

We're set to hit the road soon and I haven't even had time to give Nash his schedule for the next three days. I'd planned on using the long road ahead of us to catch up on some meetings with him. Judging by the amount of voices filtering from the door, I'm not sure if I'll have enough of his attention.

Taking one last deep breath, I pull the bus door open. The start of the tour is always a disaster to begin with. Add in skeevy Roy breathing down my neck coupled with Nash's vulgar and impulsive little brother, and I might just have to bring my therapist along with me.

My heel scrapes against the steps, barely audible over the symphony of voices coming from the living area. I find Nash sitting at the corner of one of the couches with Nora laying against his chest. The rest of the occupants pile in around them. Next to Nora is her sister Lennon, who has her nose too deep in a book to be paying attention to the loud voices around her.

Beside Lennon sits Poe and then Landon, two members of Nash's band. On the opposite side sits Matt, the head of Nash's security for tour and Nash's new personal bodyguard, Monroe.

"Did you come to ruin the party?" a voice asks from my side. Turning my head, I find Aiden lounging in one of the seats.

"Not much of a party," I say, stepping over the large boot he deliberately placed in front of me.

"It was before you got here," Aiden fires back.

Nash groans from his spot. He leans forward, causing Nora to have to readjust her position. His shoulders look tight as he pinches the bridge of his nose to release tension. "The two of you haven't been in the same space for more than a minute and it's already begun."

"I'm sorry, Nash," I offer, keeping my cool. I'm under no impression that Aiden will somehow grow up and learn to leave me alone. I'm the adult in this situation. I just need to stop engaging with him. "I came to discuss your schedule for the next three days."

"Oh hell yeah," Landon says excitedly. He jumps up from his position, swiping one of the printed schedules from my hand.

"I was going to pass them out if you would've given me the chance," I tell him, annoyed.

All he does is give me a wide smile before ungracefully plopping down in his vacated spot. The quick movement causes Poe to bump into Lennon, knocking the book out of her hands.

Poe bends down and snatches the book from the floor before Lennon can grab it. Handing it to her, he says, "Sorry about that."

Lennon stares at him, timidly taking the book without saying a word. She holds his wide-eyed stare for a moment before finally looking away. When I first met Nora, she was timid as well. She almost refused my offer to come on tour as a backup dancer for Nash. Admittedly, there's more to that story, but her eventual acceptance changed the trajectory of a lot of our lives.

Typically, I don't get along with soft-spoken women. I've never been soft, and I don't understand it. But the way I understand it, Lennon has had a bit of a rough go in life. She mostly keeps to herself, so I don't mind having her here. She's much easier to tolerate than the *other* sibling joining this tour.

Continuing with my route, I walk past them until I land in front of Nash.

I lick my index finger and separate the top piece of paper from the rest of the stack. Handing it to him, I wait for him to look it over and offer his thoughts.

"I'm going to be exhausted as hell, but it looks fine to me. Only two interviews?" Quirking an eyebrow, his gaze fixes on me.

I shift my weight. He knows typically we do triple the amount of press at the beginning of a tour, but he's been more vocal as of late, so we've had to compromise in places. For example, he *hates* interviews. "If it were up to Tyson, you'd be booked for another one—with Nora. Roy wants more publicity on your engagement. Tyson agrees."

My words make Nora anxiously bite her lip. If anyone could be less of a fan of interviews than Nash, it's Nora. I don't blame the girl. She got put through the wringer a while ago by some soulless reporter looking to turn past trauma into a juicy story. A reporter whose career I promptly ended. Since then, it's been hard for her to trust the press.

Which is good. She needs to learn that there's *nobody* she can trust in this business.

"Damn, what else do these people want to know?" Nash says dejectedly. "It's not like we'll ever disclose the date or venue."

"That's *exactly* what they want to know," I point out, taking the opportunity to pass out the schedule to the rest of Nash's team on the bus. I also emailed the schedule to every single crew member, but I live and die by a schedule and having a hard copy never hurt anyone.

Nash and Nora are getting married mid-tour. There's a break in the schedule for the wedding and honeymoon before the LA show and then we'll start the second leg, which will take place overseas. The guest list started out small, but it's grown so much overtime that it's becoming a full-time job trying to keep the details of their marriage a secret.

"Do you think we should do it?" Nash looks at Nora, waiting for her to answer.

"I think we should hear more about our options," she offers.

Looking at me, Nash runs a hand over his chin. "Do you think we should do it, Monica?" He watches me carefully for an answer.

I used to think every opportunity for press was something we should take. That's when I was naive enough to believe things like *no press is bad press*. Maybe for socialites or washed-up reality TV stars that's true, but when you're a top selling, award winning music artist in his prime, you don't take every interview.

"No," I say boldly.

A laugh erupts from over my shoulder. "Bullshit," Aiden barks, pretending to cough.

I don't react, even though every part of me wants to.

Nash gives his brother a look that could kill. "Aiden," he warns, holding eye contact for a beat longer before looking my way once again. "Elaborate," he says.

"I think it's unnecessary to take away from your music right now. If someone wants an interview, we should be discussing your tour. While I think the all-American love story you've got going with Nora has done nothing but improve your image, I don't think it should be the *only* thing people get from you anymore."

From the corner of my eye, I see Poe whisper something to Landon. Whatever he says has Landon stifling a laugh. Nash's eyes flick in their direction for a moment before he speaks again.

"So I'm not supposed to talk about the woman I'm going to marry?"

An annoyed sigh passes through my lips. Trying hard not to roll my eyes, I disperse my weight on my heels. "I didn't say that at all. Don't be so dense."

"Oh, Monica," Nash says slowly, wiping his hands down his dark jeans. "I've known you long enough to know that you already had a plan in your head on what I *should* do before you even told me about the interview Tyson wants. Care to share with the class what that is?"

I smile. My mom always taught me you're nothing without a plan—and she was right. I didn't get where I am in my career, or life, without a Plan A, B and C.

"So here's what I think you should do…" I begin, turning around to sit down at the small kitchenette table. I take a seat across from Aiden. He raises his eyebrows, surprise written on his face.

Pulling out my work laptop, I set it down on the table and open it up. My fingers fly across the keyboard as I type in my password and pull up the document I need. My eyes scan over the document of my carefully laid plans. "For the next two weeks, we *do* continue to sell the Nash and Nora love story. But we don't talk about your wedding, we talk about the music."

"Genius," Aiden cheers, clapping his hands together. "We talk about the music of the man who is starting an international music tour. *Brilliant,*" he adds sarcastically.

I cross my legs underneath the table, accidentally kicking him in the shin. "The first thing we do is have Nora post a video of her dancing to one of your new songs on her Instagram."

"Like dancing on tour?" Nora asks, her eyebrows pinched together. Even though she doesn't dance on tour anymore, she used to be a backup dancer for Nash during our last tour. Well, for half of it. There was a little misunderstanding that may have caused some issues between them and eventually lead to their breakup and Nash going to rehab. I may have been partially responsible. It's *complicated.*

"No. Like just a snippet of you at a studio or even outdoors dancing to one of his songs. Get *your* fans, which are in return *his* fans, excited about the music. We then repost it from Nash's account, and you get the hype for the two of you, but it actually involves his music."

Cocking his head to the side, Nash nods. "I see where you're going with this."

"Damn Monica," Landon drawls. "It's kind of scary how good you are."

"I believe the word you're looking for is calculating—manipulative," Aiden points out from across the table. He reaches into the small cup holder next to him, pulling out a piece of hard candy and popping it into his mouth with a sinister smile.

"That's the nicest thing you've ever said to me," I say, not bothering to give him any more of my attention.

"When we get you back into the studio, which needs to be soon, by the way," I add casually, flashing back to my earlier conversation with Roy. "We need to get some footage of you and Nora both there. Her cuddling into you, watching you sing, all that boring intimate stuff your fans eat up. We'll have one of our videographers make a highlight reel of it and we'll have the two of you post that. Maybe they can make a lyric video out of one of your singles and we can have the highlight reel playing in the background."

My gaze finds Nora, who's attention has turned elsewhere instead of focusing on the conversation. At least, I thought she'd grown tired of the conversation, but she surprises me by saying, "I'd do almost anything if it meant I didn't have to do an interview."

"Should've dated a band member then," Landon says, his lips pulled into a lazy smile. "No one cares about us."

"Aw don't say things like that, Landon," Aiden jokes, holding a hand over his heart. "I care about the band. You're the most underrated part of Nash."

"You take your brother on tour for the first time and all of a sudden he's choosing your bandmates over you." Nash shakes his head.

"All I'm saying is if I would've been old enough to perform at that middle school show with you and the guys, they would've much preferred this," Aiden gestures to his face, "over that," he points to Nash's face.

Standing up, Nash quickly closes the distance to his brother. Wrapping an arm around his neck, he puts his cheek against Aiden's. "You can't sing worth a shit." He flicks his brother's temple, "And keep dreaming, bro."

I watch the two of them carefully, absentmindedly wondering what it's like to actually *care* for your sibling. My older sister never cared about me—a product of our strict upbringing. In fact, my entire childhood was just a long, drawn-out competition with her. It partially still is one, just not in the ways my parents had expected. Maybe that's why even though Aiden is sure to get on every last one of my nerves—and then some—on this tour, I can't blame him. He loves his older brother. He's a fierce protector of him, and in his mind, I'm enemy number one.

The goal is to stay the enemy in his eyes. If Aiden ever found out who the *real* threat was, I'm scared for what he'd do to avenge his brother. I'm already working on a plan to protect Nash, and his career, but Aiden could blow everything up with his temper.

So I'll keep playing the villain. It's what I'm good at. And behind the scenes, I'll take down the real enemy. The one who forced me to make the decisions that put a target on my back to begin with.

4
AIDEN

MY LIFE HAS ALWAYS BEEN FAIRLY normal, considering my brother is one of the most famous people in the world. As his fame grew, Nash slowly started distancing himself from his former life—his normal life—which meant Nash left me behind as he followed his dreams. I don't blame him…I never have. In fact, I've always idolized him.

He took all of the heat from my father, leaving me to be the favorite son without resenting me for it. As I got older, I realized how much Nash had done for me growing up. Even when he wasn't nearby, he always had my back.

He'd send me tickets to attend cooking classes with world-renowned chefs, knowing that cooking had become a passion of mine. He was a good big brother to me, but as time went by, I missed the brother I grew up with. The best friend that used to be my taste tester when I was cooking up new meals, even when I knew they tasted like shit. He'd always sent me money, making sure it came to me so mom and dad couldn't spend it on themselves.

Staring at him right now, he feels like a stranger.

I know the version of Nash in the media and the version he shows his team, but I don't feel like I know him well enough to call myself his brother anymore. He's my blood, I should know everything there is to know about him, yet I know almost nothing of the man he's become over the past few years.

Recently, we'd both made more of an effort to see each other, but it still felt forced. So, I'd decided it was time to take matters into my own hands and really commit to this relationship. To accompany Nash on tour and spend as much time with him as I could.

College wasn't really for me anyway. I knew it the moment I paid more attention to the teacher's puffy lips than the things she was trying to teach me. I gave it the ol' college try for over a year before deciding I could learn more about world studies by just experiencing it rather than confining myself to the four walls of a lecture hall.

What better way to experience the world and bond with Nash than go on an international tour with him? I've been desperate to get to know my brother better. To know who he is deep down. To know why he'd ever fall back in love with a woman who hurt him like Nora did. Most of all, I needed to know why he seemed closer to his wicked manager, who back-stabbed him for profit, than he was with me.

Why does a little liar like her get to know him better than I do?

It's unacceptable.

Sitting in the corner, I watch Nash interact with Monica carefully. It's the first night of his tour, and makeup artists and stylists rush around him, putting together finishing touches on the 'look' they've fussed over for the last hour. Lennon sits on the couch next to me, but she's too deeply invested in the book she's reading to pay any attention to the bustling world around her. Nora is deep in conversation with Tyson, looking like she's two seconds away from rolling her eyes at whatever he's telling her.

Over a year ago, I'd watched my brother fall apart on national TV because of Nora. I'd barely known anything about his relationship with her then and I had to witness him hit his lowest point along with the rest of the world. I should've been there for him. I should've known that he was in love, but I had no idea until after the fact. He'd fallen madly in love with one of his backup dancers—something he swore he'd never do.

Nash had given Nora his heart, only to find out that the reason Nora was on tour was because Monica had hired her to break it. Apparently Nash needed a muse, someone to break his heart, in order to write better music. Monica viewed him as a tool to make her money and didn't care about the consequences. Nora had fallen for him by then, but the discovery was too much.

No one had been prepared for the downward spiral of Nash afterwards. I was states away when I learned of how deeply in love my brother was with a girl who had broken his heart. I tried to contact him—but he was too busy with his benders, coping with his hurt in the only way he knew how—to answer me.

Fast forward a few months, and somehow Nash forgave Nora. They appear happier than ever, which is all I really want for him. I've accepted that Nora has made up for her mistakes with Nash. What I *can't* get past is how Nash ever forgave Monica for her part—her scheming—in all that transpired.

Looking away from my surroundings, I focus on my brother—and *her*. The mere sight of Monica makes me angry, but there's also something else I can't put my finger on. Maybe it's jealousy. She's done the worst to my brother and somehow she's still one of the first people he goes to—one of the people he trusts most in this world. Maybe it's that my insults don't seem to faze her like I want them to. Or maybe it's because despite everything, I'm finding myself drawn to her for reasons I cannot begin to understand.

She wears a long black skirt that hugs her slim figure, paired with a white button-up shirt and black blazer. Fitting, since that's probably the same color as her soul.

This morning, I'd woken up to hear her yelling at someone outside my bus window. The sun was barely up in the sky and she'd already found time to lay into some poor soul.

She and Nash both hover over something on her iPad until she pulls her phone out of her blazer pocket. She stares at her screen for a moment, frowning before saying something to Nash. Walking away, she puts the phone to her ear. I watch curiously as she steps into the corner opposite me. Monica faces the wall, her shoulders rigid as she speaks to somebody on the other line.

Whoever she's talking to, it doesn't seem like a conversation she's thrilled about. She holds her phone in one hand as she waves the other around manically. One of her feet taps, clearly annoyed by whoever is speaking on the other line. The conversation gets heated enough that she leaves the room to finish it. I itch to follow her, to find out what's being said on the phone, but I can't be too obvious. Eventually I'll figure out what's going on in that calculating mind of hers. But it's a long tour...I can be patient.

I have two goals on this tour—get to know my brother and get dirt on the woman who betrayed his trust.

"You really should stop staring," Lennon whispers quietly from my side. My head whips to the side to look at her. I don't know how she even knows what direction I'm looking in, her eyes still scan over the words in her book.

"I don't know what you're talking about." Lifting my hips, I adjust my position on the couch. She's far enough away that the change does nothing to disturb her. Her feet are tucked delicately underneath her body. She's managed to tuck some unruly pieces of wavy hair behind her ear, but one side of her hair billows around her, acting like a curtain to shield her from the world.

Lennon sighs, as if she's annoyed by my answer. "They

might all be too busy to notice, but I do. You watch her with hate in your eyes, but also with…"

"With?" I ask, biting the inside of my cheek.

Finally, she looks up from her book. It's odd how much she resembles her sister, but also looks so incredibly different. Those large eyes seem like they know more—see more, since she's always quietly observing people from the outskirts. "With interest," she mutters.

Pausing, I mull over her words. "I *am* interested. I'm fascinated by how she managed to keep her job after everything she did."

Closing her book, she sticks her fingers in between the pages to keep her place. Her knowing eyes scan over my face, making me feel uncomfortable. I barely know her and I feel like she can see more than I'm willing to give. Finally, she speaks. "Be careful. An obsession is an obsession, whether it's good or bad."

My jaw clenches. Her point is valid, I just don't give a shit. Call it what you want—obsession, hate, fascination—all are words that fit. I'm just tired of being called out for it. "If someone betrayed your sister like that, but she still forgave them after it all, wouldn't you want to know more?"

Shrugging, her attention returns to the book on her lap. "I wouldn't pay them any mind. People like attention, whether good or bad. No one likes being ignored. Just a thought."

Just then, Nora makes her way to the two of us. She stops a few feet away from the couch. "The two of you look cozy over here."

Smiling, I scoot closer to Lennon. My cheek finds her shoulder. She stiffens slightly underneath me. "Oh yeah, we're besties now," I joke.

"Hardly," Lennon says quietly. I'd be offended if she didn't have a slight smile on her face.

"We'll be best friends by the end of this tour," I say, looking up at Nora. "Just wait."

Shaking her head, she steps forward and separates me from Lennon. Pushing against my shoulder, she attempts to move me on the couch. I humor her, scooting over until I'm up against the opposite armrest.

Nora falls down in the empty space between Lennon and me. "I think this tour will be good for all of us. A way for us to get to know each other—be a family."

5
MONICA

THE GROUND beneath my feet shakes as I watch Nash from the side of the stage. He's performing his encore song, the crowd eating straight from his palm. This may be the loudest I've ever heard an audience. He convinced Nora to go out on stage and sit on a stool as he sings one of the songs he wrote about her when they got back together.

The fans roar wildly when Nash stops singing. He swings the guitar around on his body, getting it out of his way and onto his back. Leaning in close, he pulls Nora's face to his, making the fans in the stadium erupt in cheers.

I feel the body behind mine before I hear him speak. "Hate to break it to you, Monica, but it seems that your scheme ended in a real love story."

I don't have to look over my shoulder to know who's behind me. His voice is recognizable even over the boom of the people around us.

No part of him touches me, but he's entirely too close for me to feel comfortable. "I don't know if I've seen two people more in love than them," I answer.

His shoulder bumps into mine as he takes the spot next to me. Aiden watches Nash and Nora carefully. He takes in every move they make. "Would you do it again?" he asks, anger and curiosity intertwined in his tone. I don't have to ask to know what he's talking about.

Confused, I look in his direction, trying to figure out what his play is here. This conversation seems too normal given all of our previous encounters.

"Well?" he says, agitated. "Would you?"

I watch the way Nash runs his fingers through Nora's hair, looking at her as if she's the only person in this world, even as thousands of people surrounding them chant his name.

"If I would've made a different choice, they wouldn't have each other," I answer honestly, my voice tight. I'm waiting for Aiden's rubber band to snap, for him to say something hateful. This is the most normal conversation we've ever had, and I don't expect it to last long given my answer. Soon, he's bound to try and hurt my ego by lashing out. It's a shame he's too naive to realize my ego has been bruised so many times throughout my life that I've learned to make it impenetrable.

From the corner of my eye, I see him reach up and run his fingers through his hair. The long strands fall in new directions, still looking just as messy as before.

"True. But, you didn't know that before you did it."

I make sure to look him dead in the eye. I want to make it obvious I won't back down. That no matter how many times he tries to make me feel shitty about my past decision, I don't regret it. "No I didn't, Aiden. And it's a choice I have to live with. I did what I had to do—for *your* brother."

He laughs, a sound I can barely hear over the noise around us. "Keep telling yourself that so you can sleep at night."

The screams coupled with the shaking bass underneath my feet—and the fact that I've been up since way before the sun rose this morning—have all started to wear on me. There's a dull ache forming between my eyeballs, the pressure building quicker from Nash's annoying egotistical little brother. I'm supposed to be the mature one, but he finds ways to get the best of me, and I can't help but retaliate.

Turning around, I close the distance between us, not stopping my stride until I'm standing chest to chest with him. Craning my neck to look at him, I jab my finger into his chest. "I won't make excuses for the shitty things I did. But maybe you should aim some of this hatred toward yourself. I vividly remember trying to pull your brother out of countless bars when he was drunk or high off his ass. Where were you, Aiden?"

My words stun him for a moment before his eyebrows furrow and he regains the fiery look in his hazel eyes. "I tried. He wouldn't let me help. There was nothing I could do," he spits back angrily.

"You can fool yourself, Aiden, but you won't fool me. I'm in charge of so much of Nash's life. I know everything that goes on. I know he'd call you when he was spiraling out of control and you wouldn't answer. Too busy to pick up the phone, Aiden? Funny, you know what you didn't miss? The payments that always came your way."

His eyes widen at the same time the muscle in his cheek begins to tick. If I'm not mistaken, he looks a little shocked. Maybe he wasn't expecting me to throw insults back at him.

"I was away at college. Every time I tried to contact Nash, he wouldn't answer. It wasn't like I was ignoring him…" His words break off as he looks at his brother on stage. Nash takes his final bow, pulling Nora in close to him. Nash tells them goodnight before running offstage, right in the direction of Aiden and me.

Aiden looks at Nash as if he's seen a ghost. He opens his mouth as if he's going to say something, but instead he turns around and disappears into the throng of people gathered backstage.

"What's his deal?" Nash asks me, taking a towel from an

assistant to wipe his face. He pulls each one of his earpieces out of his ears, letting them fall to rest on either side of his neck.

I stare at the group of people he disappeared behind, wondering the same thing as Nash. I let myself ruminate on it for a few seconds before shaking my head, upset I'm even giving an ounce of my time to it.

Looking back to Nash, I roll my eyes. "He's your brother, you tell me."

"Your guess is as good as mine," he laughs sarcastically. A sound engineer runs up to us, unclipping Nash's mic-pack from his jeans.

Nora looks up at Nash lovingly. "Wasn't that show great?" She intertwines her fingers with his.

Stealing a water bottle from a passing assistant, I hand it over to Nash. "They loved you out there, Nash. I think this tour is going to do so much for you."

Nodding his head, he leads the way back to the dressing rooms. The crew is efficient at breaking down all the tour equipment and getting it on the semis so they can do it all again somewhere else. Typically, we don't linger after the concerts, allowing them to rush around without us getting in the way.

"Being out there again was incredible." Nash's words are filled with excitement. I remember the days when the moment he came off stage, he'd be yelling for a drink. The dejected tone of his voice back then is a far cry from his now excited one. It's nice to see him having fun touring again.

"I'm happy to hear that," I say, my feet working tirelessly to keep up with his fast pace. "Keep that same excitement for the meet and greet tonight. You've got double the amount of people."

Nash gives me a look. *"Double?"*

I smile, reaching into my purse to grab an extra copy of the itinerary for today. Handing it over to him, I run my finger across the bottom line. "Yep. It's written right there. See?" I tap the time slot we're coming up on.

Nash groans, looking over at Nora. "Well, there goes all the plans I had for us on the bus."

Nora blushes at the same time I try not to throw up in my mouth. "Spare me the details on that," I respond in disgust, doing my best to rid any pictures of what has been done on the surfaces of his bus from my mind.

"Oh loosen up, Monica," Nash jokes. "I'm almost a married man. What did you expect?"

We continue down the long hallway underneath the stands of the stadium. Workers pass us on both sides, congratulating Nash on his opening show.

"Do what you want. Just don't tell me about it," I beg, stopping in front of his dressing room. Inside, his team waits to freshen him up for the meet and greet. I can hear his rowdy bandmates already in there, being incredibly too loud for my taste. "And for the love of god," I clench my eyes shut before continuing, "please don't let any paparazzi catch you doing it. You got it?"

Nora nods in embarrassment, her cheeks almost as red as the lipstick she has on.

"Aye aye, captain," Nash says, mocking me by putting his hand to his temple and doing a salute.

"Now get cleaned up and get ready to meet all your fans. I'll see you soon," I finish, turning around to head to the location of his meet and greet. It's called the Rose Lounge, and there's no doubt that by now there's a line of people waiting outside it to meet Nash.

6
AIDEN

I'M elbow to elbow with Nash's entourage as he sits in the sound booth taking direction from some guy that says 'brah' way too many times to be a functioning adult.

Lennon sits on the left side of me, for once her nose isn't buried in a book. Instead, she watches Poe, Nash's bassist, closely. He takes direction from Nash, adjusting something on the instrument before nodding. On my other side is Matt, who is too busy thumbing through something on his phone to pay much attention to what's going on in the sound room.

There are two guys sitting in front of the soundboard. The 'brah' dude and some other guy who is so laser focused on pushing the buttons in front of him that he's barely said a word to anyone.

Monica stands in a corner off to the side. She rests her shoulder against the wall, watching what's going on around her carefully. I'd love to know what's going on in that scheming mind of hers. She listens to the conversation between Nash and the sound guys intently. They're using language and acronyms I can't even begin to understand, yet she seems to understand all of it.

Occasionally Monica will leave her corner and have a hushed conversation with 'brah' dude before she retreats right back to where she started.

Fidgeting in my chair, I try to get comfortable. I'm here to support Nash, but I do wish there was more going on. When he'd asked me to come, I'd jumped at the idea. I'd never seen this version of my brother's life—or the inside of a recording studio. It turns out, it sounds a lot cooler than it actually is. I don't know what I expected, but it wasn't hours of hearing the same line over and over again until they got it perfect. Another hour in this room and I'd be able to perform the song in front of an audience. Not that anyone would want to see that.

I'm contemplating leaving the studio and wandering around the block while Nash finishes up recording for the day. I've always loved to travel and explore different places. You can learn a lot about a place just by exploring the different restaurants in the area. I barely remember what city we're in, but I know I'm itching to leave the confinement of the tour buses and hotels and actually have some local cuisine. More than that, I'm desperate to get my hands in the kitchen. It's been forever since I've cooked for myself, and even longer since I've prepared food for others.

My mind wanders far away from the studio I'm in, wondering if I can convince Nash to let me do some cooking for the crew. Shit, I'd settle for using the tiny kitchenette on the bus if it meant I got to be useful somehow. I didn't think mooching off my brother would get old so quickly—but not being able to contribute anything but my good looks and personality is overrated.

My daydreaming halts when the door to our room swings open, an imposing figure filling the doorway.

Monica pulls away from her perch against the wall instantly. She scurries across the room quickly, despite wearing her signature heels. "Roy, what are you doing here?" Her voice is tight. She stops in front of the new arrival. He wears a full three-piece suit even though it's hotter than hell outside. Everything about him screams money, from his polished leather shoes to the gigantic watch on his wrist.

His arms lift in the air, gesturing to the room around us. "Tell me how my top star is set to record new music today and I wasn't made aware?"

Monica runs the palms of her hands down her skirt. "It was sort of a last-minute thing."

He gives her an uninterested glance before looking over her head at Nash. A slight, "Mhm," leaves his lips before he dismisses her completely and walks right up to the sound guys.

For a split second, Monica's eyes light up with rage. I'd recognize it anywhere because I've had that same look aimed my way before.

But why is it aimed at him? Who is this guy?

The look disappears as quickly as it appeared.

"How's it going?" the man questions, his tone commanding and straightforward. I don't know anything about this man and I'm positive I don't like him. It's the way the air has shifted since his arrival. Even Monica's demeanor has changed significantly, and typically nothing fazes her.

Her back is ramrod straight. Her eyes piercing a hole into Roy as he asks one question after another to the sound engineers.

Nash has been busy re-recording the vocals to the song since Roy walked in. His eyes are closed, his mouth pressed against the microphone. He waves one hand around in front of him as he performs the song, incorporating feedback from the sound guys in this version. Nash's eyes slowly open as the song comes to an end. His eyebrows furrow when he notices Roy.

"What's this?" Nash asks into the microphone. His tone has

changed. Earlier he was joking around with everyone in the room, now he seems annoyed—on edge.

Quickly, Monica makes her way to the counter with different buttons. Bending over, she presses a big red button. "It looks like the label wanted to check in on your progress for the album." Monica looks through the glass at Nash, faking a smile. "Isn't that great?" she finishes.

"I don't remember asking for any more of an audience," he protests, his voice cold.

My eyes bounce between Nash and the people gathered at the sound board, wondering what is happening. It's clear that there's some bad blood between Nash and this Roy guy. I may not know my brother as well as I used to, but I know that look.

Roy leans down next to Monica, his large frame edging her to the side. Pushing the same button she did, he grins deeply. "Nash, buddy, I wanted to hear for myself what my favorite superstar is cooking up."

"I'm not your *buddy*," Nash seethes. Behind him, Poe's eyes widen while Landon snickers, clearly enjoying the show in front of him.

"Don't mind him," Monica apologizes. "We had a long day of traveling yesterday."

Lennon squirms next to me, her elbow coming close to jabbing me in the stomach. Her nail taps nervously on the cover of her book. Everyone has their eyes trained on the drama playing out in front of us.

"Who is this guy?" Lennon leans close to me, whispering softly next to my ear.

Looking at her, I shrug. Judging by the way he walked in here like he owned the place, and the way he keeps calling Nash *his* artist, he's probably someone high up at the label.

Roy stands to his full height, turning to look down at Monica. He still wears a fake smile, but his face has turned a slight shade of red. "A word?" he asks, his voice low.

Monica looks into the sound booth, exchanging a look with Nash. Nodding, Monica looks back to Roy, her arm outstretched toward the door. "After you," she murmurs.

Nash removes his headphones once he notices Monica and Roy leaving. One of the sound guys quickly distracts Nash by asking him to try something different on one of his verses. It's clear that Nash wants to follow Monica and Roy out the door, but he stands down. Sighing, he straightens the headphones on his head. He turns to his band, waving a finger in the air. "From the top," he demands.

The tension in the air is still thick as they re-start the song. As everyone attempts to focus on Nash again, I can't seem to shake the feeling from a few minutes ago. There's clearly something going on between Nash, Monica, and Roy. I've been waiting for an opportunity to catch Monica scheming again, and this might be the perfect chance.

Slapping my hands on my knees, I look at the people next to me on the couch. "Well shit, I need some air after all of that." I stand up, stretching my arms over my head.

No one questions me as I slide through the door and disappear from their sight.

The hallway is eerily quiet. Monica rented out the entire studio, not wanting anyone to catch wind that Nash was here—or worse, get a glimpse of what he's currently recording. I know Monica and Roy can't be too far, though, so I meander through the hallways in search of them.

Silence greets me as I check room after room. I've nearly made it to the other side of the building, moments from giving up, when a loud whisper catches my attention.

"What the *fuck* was that?" the voice seethes.

"I can explain," a familiar voice answers. Monica.

My footsteps are light on the carpeted floor as I draw closer to the hushed voices. Peeking through the slight crack in the doorway, I find Monica and Roy standing in what appears to be some kind of lounge. The hums of two large vending machines to their left threaten to drown out their hushed voices. An array of open chairs sprawls out to their right, but neither person is sitting.

Monica stands in the middle of the room, her arms folded defensively across her chest. She looks up at Roy with an emotionless face.

"You better get to it, Monica. I've been on your ass for weeks, telling you to get Nash in the studio. And when you do, you don't bother to let me know?"

I'm staring at both of their profiles, trying to make sure I only peek around the corner slightly. The last thing I need is for either of them to see me. If I weren't so desperate to get dirt on Monica, I'd turn around and go back to the room. But Nash needs to know the truth. *I* need to know the truth. And I'm too far in now not to figure out what Monica is up to with this man whose face looks more rat than human.

Monica takes a calming breath. Her posture seems to loosen slightly. "Like I said, it was last minute."

"Last minute my ass, Monica," Roy scolds, spit coming from his mouth. Monica steps lightly to his left, dodging the spray of saliva. "Nothing you do is last minute."

"Perhaps. But I don't always make the rules. Nash finally wanted to record. Was I supposed to say no?"

A dry laugh escapes his mouth, the sound void of any genuine humor. "No. What you were *supposed* to do is call me the *minute*—no, second—Nash decided to get his lazy ass in the studio."

"Noted," Monica responds sarcastically.

The tone of her voice takes Roy by surprise. His head rears back, looking at her as if she's done something completely out of character.

"You've disappointed me, Monica. I don't like that this is slowly becoming a habit of yours."

"I'm truly sorry for the miscommunication today, Roy."

He puts his finger in her face. I'm shocked she doesn't slap it out of her way. If it had been my hand that close to her mouth, she may have bit my finger straight off. "You better not let it happen again."

Dropping his hand, he waits for an answer. When she nods, he takes a small step away from her. I'm about to hightail it back down the hallway before I'm discovered when Roy speaks again. "And while we're at it, I don't appreciate the way Nash spoke to me in there. Fix it."

It's Monica's turn to laugh. Her head shakes. "I can't control what comes out of Nash's mouth, Roy. You and I both know that."

Her words enrage him. His cheeks puff out and he steps closer to her, leaning down so he's right in front of her face. "You better figure it out. We've been here before, Monica. Put a leash on him or you know what I'll do to him."

Woah. What does that mean?

I'm staring blankly at them, wondering what he could be insinuating, when he rushes right toward me. His steps are angry, his leather shoes pounding against the carpet as he leaves Monica standing there alone.

Breaking out of it, I hurriedly find an empty room to hide in before he can catch me spying on them from the hallway. Just as I slide into what appears to be a dark storage room, I hear him make his way into the hallway. The sound of his footsteps retreat down the hallway until I no longer hear anything.

Sticking my head out into the hallway, I look in both directions. I didn't hear Monica leave the room at all, which means she must still be where he left her.

Perfect.

Now I have the opportunity to ask what the hell he meant with those parting words of his. Not bothering to hide my footsteps, I make my way toward the room, stopping in the doorway Roy just exited.

Grabbing the door to the lounge, I slam it angrily. The sound makes Monica jump, her eyes focusing on me.

Leaning against the cold metal of the door, I speak slowly. "Now Monica, tell me exactly what the fuck just happened."

7
MONICA

I'VE BARELY HAD enough time to get my pulse back down to a reasonable level when the door to the lounge slams shut, sending adrenaline shooting back through my veins. Looking up, I see the last person I expect to find in this room with me—Aiden.

"Now Monica," he says, his voice low and controlled. "Tell me exactly what the fuck just happened." His back rests against the door, his eyes raking up and down my body like a predator seeking out their prey.

Rolling my eyes, I run my hands over my forehead. "This is the absolute *last* thing I need to be dealing with right now, Aiden."

Shaking his head, he pulls his body off the door. His movements are fluid. "That answer isn't going to cut it."

Turning around, I retreat across the room to try and get a moment to gather my thoughts. The last thing I was expecting was for Roy to show up today. Nash had decided at the very last minute that he wanted to record. I knew he wouldn't want Roy involved, so I consciously made the decision to forego telling anyone at Coleman Records.

I knew eventually Roy would find out—he always seems to. I

just didn't expect it to be in the middle of Nash's session. There aren't many people on this earth that Nash despises more than Roy, and I don't blame him. The guy doesn't have many redeeming qualities. But he's still the head of one of the biggest labels in the business. He isn't someone we want to piss off—at least not *yet*.

Roy has been bullying and threatening me for years. It isn't out of the norm. What *is* out of the normal is Nash having to interact with him. Over the years, I've meticulously planned out every interaction with Roy so Nash *wouldn't* have to deal with him. As much as I love Nash, his temper is like his brothers, and I can't have him doing something reckless to spoil my plans.

I stop in front of the wall, entirely too aware of the piercing gaze hot on my neck. Closing my eyes, I try to think of a way to explain what Aiden heard without divulging too much. As if I didn't have enough on my plate, Aiden had to go and bear witness to a conversation that was never supposed to reach his ears.

"I'm waiting," he says, his voice closer than before.

Still staring at the wall, I take a deep breath. "For once in your life, can you just do as you're asked? Can't you just pretend you didn't hear any of that?"

A large hand grabs my shoulder, turning me around in one straight motion. "Not going to happen. Now stop the games and tell me the truth. What. Was. That?"

I shouldn't have come to this side of the room. It wasn't a good idea to allow myself to be cornered. I know if I were to take one baby step backward, my calves would hit the wall. His body towers over mine, caging in the light, dousing me in his shadow. I stare blankly ahead of me, my gaze turned slightly upward to the point on his neck where I can see the strain of a vein. Following that vein up, I take in his clenched jaw.

That strong jaw opens, but I still don't look him in the eye. I haven't yet thought of what lie I'm going to tell him to make him forget about everything he just heard. "Tell me what he has on my brother—what his threats mean," Aiden says.

"I can't," I answer truthfully, my mind spinning with words I could say. I remember a very similar conversation I had with his brother. It feels like it was just yesterday...but also somehow like it was ages ago. I finally had to come clean to Nash about everything I did to keep his career alive and thriving and that same day, Nash made me promise we wouldn't speak of it again.

It was a promise I'd intended to keep. What I hadn't ever seen coming was his snooping brother. I never prepared for Aiden's personal vendetta against me to result in stalking. I didn't expect his distrust in anything I do to fuel his persistence.

Strong fingers grasp me by the chin. I try to pry his iron grip away, but my efforts are futile. He brings his face to my level, no longer allowing me the luxury of avoiding eye contact.

"My patience has worn thin," he hisses. I can feel his breath hot against my cheek and I hate the way my heartbeat quickens. I should despise the way he's currently manhandling me. If it were any other time or person, I'd have clawed his eyes out.

But yet—I haven't. Instead, I'm left staring into the greens of his eyes, wondering why I don't *want* to have to lie. It's the best and worst feeling all at once.

"It isn't my place to tell," I whisper. His fingers push even deeper into my jaw. Deep enough I know there will be perfect fingertip prints on my chin the moment he removes his hand. The pressure on my chin has me taking a step back, my shoulders and spine pressed firmly against the wall.

He presses up against me as he rakes his gaze over every inch of my face. He's inspecting me—trying to call my bluff. For once, I don't have one. I'm telling the truth.

He sighs, annoyed by my unwillingness to share anything with him. "I'm not surprised. You're just a pretty little liar. I wouldn't be able to trust a thing from that mouth, anyway."

Ever so slightly, his eyes drop to my lips for a fraction of a second. "This isn't over, Monica," he threatens, finally releasing my chin. "I'm going to find out what's going on—one way or another. And if I find out you had *anything* more to do with it," he snickers, lips pulling into a sinister smile that doesn't reach his eyes, "you'll have a lot more to deal with than that asshole."

He retreats from the room, leaving me staring after him, wondering how the hell I'm going to keep Aiden from ruining everything.

8
AIDEN

The stifling heat hits me in the face as I push the door open. My lungs eagerly take in the fresh air while my mind reels from everything that just took place. My shoes scratch against the chipping asphalt of the alleyway as I begin to pace.

What had Roy meant with his threats?

Put a leash on him. My pulse thumps angrily against my neck as I recall his words and quickens when I remember Monica's unwillingness to tell me what those words meant.

It was my *brother* he was threatening. I deserve to know. Nash deserves to know. But Monica made it sound like he might already know something…

The way she spoke paired with the looks exchanged between her and Nash in the studio, I'm wondering if he knows more than he's letting on.

My mind spins. Surely if Nash knew Roy was threatening him, he would just leave the damn label. It seems simple to me but judging by Monica's reluctance to share a single detail, there must be more to it.

That wasn't the same calm, confident Monica that I'm used to seeing. Roy had her shook. And when I confronted her, I saw something in her eyes I hadn't ever seen before—fear. She was afraid. But afraid of *what?* I'm starting to realize her lies—her schemes—may go way deeper than I'd imagined. Maybe Nash knows more than I give him credit for. Maybe that's the reason he didn't fire her when she did the unthinkable. Maybe there's a good reason for the things she's done…

No. There's never a good reason to *want* to break somebody's heart. Decent people don't just *hire* someone to break the heart of someone they're supposed to care about. It just doesn't make sense.

And yet, in that room, I couldn't help but aim a sliver of my anger at someone else for a change. *Roy.* I have a feeling I'll be seeing more of him in the near future.

Out of the corner of my eye, movement catches my attention. A pile of trash bags rustle beside a dumpster. There's a slight whimper before a furry tail pops out from underneath one of the bags.

Interested, I walk toward the pile of garbage. Carefully, I use my shoe to shift the bag in front of the long tail out of the way. The back end of a small dog protrudes from inside a trash bag as the front half scavenges for food.

Puckering my lips, I gently whistle, catching the attention of the dog. It freezes for a moment before scrambling out of the bag.

I move slowly as I crouch down to the dog's level, trying my best not to startle it. "Hey little guy," I say softly. I gently stretch my arm out, allowing him to sniff the back of my hand.

The dog is cautious—its cold, black nose brushing against my knuckles. It's clear by the matted fur and how thin the dog is that it's a stray. His body has wiry, tan fur, but the fur around his eyes and nose are black. By the huge size discrepancy between his paws and the size of his body now, I'm also guessing that the dog is young—still a puppy, and nowhere near full-grown.

Warming up to me, the dog takes a step closer. His snout

nuzzles into my hand. My fingers go to scratch the dog's chin, which only makes the pup warm up to me more. He practically crawls into my lap, lifting his head and giving me better access to his chin.

"What are you doing out here?" I question, moving my hand to scratch beneath one of his floppy ears.

The dog answers by letting his large tongue hang out one side of his mouth. Stretching, he turns his body in my lap to give me access to his belly. I rub over it, my fingers getting stuck in the mats of his fur. When my fingers brush over his ribs, I'm taken aback by how many of his bones I can feel.

"You must be hungry." My eyes take in his fragile frame, wondering what I should do. I can't just leave the dog out here to starve. It doesn't appear that he has a home or that there are any other animals with him.

Forming a plan, I stand up, keeping the dog in my arms. At first he panics, pivoting so he's no longer on his back and his chest rests against my shoulder.

"You're okay," I tell him, running a hand down his spine. "We're just going to get you some food—and maybe a bath," I finish, the smell of him reaching my nostrils.

Grabbing the handle of the backdoor to the studio, I crack it open, sticking my head in to make sure the hallways are empty. I'm not sure about the pet policy of this recording studio, but I'm also not trying to find out. My only goal is to find this dog some food and water and get him cleaned up.

I retrace my steps from earlier, finding the lounge empty. *Thank fuck.* The last thing I need is for Monica to catch me bringing in a stray.

The dog in my arms takes in his surroundings carefully. When I walk up to the vending machines, he twitches slightly, the loud hum of the machine seeming to spook him at first.

"You're okay, little guy," I whisper. "We're trying to be very secretive, so if you could just keep your cool for a moment while I get you some food, I'd appreciate it."

Oddly enough, it seems like the dog understands me. Taking a deep breath, he rests his head on my shoulder, his body going lax in my arms.

"You're a cool dude," I compliment, my eyes raking over the choices in the vending machine. I'm wondering what the best thing to feed him is. Any of these options would be better than the garbage he was just trying to make his lunch.

"What are your thoughts on potato chips?" I swipe my card, pressing the keys for the chips. I also decide on a thing of peanut butter crackers and a stick of beef jerky. Bending down, I grab the items from the bottom of the machine. I stop in front of the next machine, paying for two water bottles as well.

The fear of vending machines seems to have passed quickly for the puppy. He sits calmly in my arms as I balance him with the food and water.

"Now," I mutter under my breath, "we've got to find a private bathroom for you. We need to get you all cleaned up."

I sneak around the hallways like I'm a damn spy, making sure I don't run into anyone as I finish my mission. I don't know how I'd explain the dog. Luckily, I don't have to because not only do I find a bathroom, but I find a *suite* when it comes to bathroom standards. There's a large fluffy chair in the corner with different kinds of toiletries. Across from it sits a large counter with a deep trough-like sink that reaches from one end to the other.

"Bingo," I say, putting the dog down on the tile. His nails scratch the floor as he walks around and sniffs his surroundings. I switch the lock to the bathroom, ensuring no one will catch us in here.

"Alright, little guy. Let's get you some food." I walk over to the chair, sitting down and working on opening the food. The dog eagerly sits down in front of me, his tail *swishing* against the tile.

First, I give him the beef jerky stick. He scarfs it down in two seconds flat. I'm not sure he even had enough time to chew it. "Slow down," I tell him, reaching to pat him on the head. "You don't want to get sick."

He answers by bumping his nose against my knee, seeming to tell me to give him the next thing. "Alright, alright. What do you say?" I ask, holding up the bag of chips and package of peanut butter crackers. "Are you in the mood for chips or crackers?"

The dog paws at the bag of potato chips, letting out a small whine when he goes to sit back down.

Reaching into the bag, I hand the dog a chip. He takes it from my hand excitedly. We repeat those steps until he's cleared the entire bag.

Tipping the bag over, I show him that there's nothing left. He checks it for himself, sticking his snout in the bag and licking every single crumb out.

"Now let's get you some water. You just had a shit-ton of salt." I look around the bathroom, trying to see if there's anything I can use as a makeshift water bowl. On the table next to me, there's a marble bowl full of different toiletry items. I remove all the items and set them on the table, emptying the bowl completely. Twisting the cap off of the water bottle, I fill the bowl up and set it on the floor.

The dog eagerly drinks the water as I stand up and throw away all of the vending machine trash. As the dog continues to drink, I look at the sink, wondering if it'll be possible to wash him in it. It's a fancy sink, definitely not made for washing dogs, but it'll do the job.

A wet nose rubbing against my jeans alerts me to the fact he's had his fill of water. Looking down, I find the dog happily staring up at me. His tongue hangs out of his mouth, and he already looks better than when I found him.

Bending over, I scoop the dog up into my arms. "Now I don't know if you're going to like this," I begin, setting him down in the sink. "But you fucking reek, and we need to wash you off. I found you in the trash, my dude."

His tail folds against his belly, his posture making it clear he's unsure of what's going on. I turn the knob of the sink, letting the water wash around his paws to get him used to the feeling. Once he seems a little more at ease, I quickly grab the water bowl from earlier to help me get the rest of his body wet.

The dog is calm as I scoop water over him repeatedly. His wet fur clings even more to his body, showcasing more of his bones. "Good boy," I praise, wondering if I should soap him as well.

I keep one arm on him as I pick up the bottle of soap on the sink. Reading over the label, I check the caution label to see if it'll be safe for a dog. "Surely this fancy shit wouldn't be toxic to you. Right?" I ask him. All he does is look up at me wide-eyed, as if to say *how would I know?*

"Should be fine," I mutter, flipping the bottle over and putting a heaping glob of the liquid in my palm. My palms rub together as I get the soap nice and sudsy.

I'm working it into his fur when the dog shakes, soaking me. "Oh shit," I yell, wiping soap and water from my cheek.

A knock sounds at the door as I start washing the dog again. "Aiden?" Monica says from the other side.

"Double shit," I whisper to the dog, holding him in place as I wonder what the hell to do now.

I try to stay silent, hoping she'll just go away if I don't answer. The doorknob rattles, making the dog in front of me jump and let out a yelp.

"What was that?" she asks from the other side, rattling the doorknob even more.

The dog apparently has it in for me, even after all the help I've given him, because he barks—loud.

"Is that a *dog?*"

"What can I help you with, Monica?" I shout. "Can't a man get some privacy in the bathroom?"

"Nash sent me to find you. He's ready to go."

"You guys go ahead," I say, trying to quickly wash the soap from the dog. "I can catch a ride later—when I'm done, you know…"

A large *thump* sounds against the door. "Open this right now."

The sound makes the dog bark again.

"Really, dude?" I ask the dog, wiping my forehead with the back of my hand.

"Aiden!" Monica yells.

I sigh, leaving the dog in the sink to open the door. I quickly unlock it, not bothering to open it for her. She must hear the click of the lock because the door swings open immediately after. Her eyes land directly on the sopping wet dog in front of me. Unbothered, he lets out an excited bark at her entrance.

Monica steps into the bathroom, letting the door swing closed behind her. She watches the dog for a few moments before looking at me, her mouth hanging wide open.

"Where in the world did you find a mangy dog?"

9

MONICA

THIS DAY COULDN'T GET any worse. Just when I finally thought Nash was going to get a good start on his new album, Roy shows up and ruins everything. After the altercation with Roy, Nash called off the rest of the recording session, claiming he was no longer in the headspace to record.

I'd wanted to plead with him, to have him at least finish the demo for this *one* song, but I decided against it. I couldn't blame him. His distaste for Roy runs almost as deep as mine. But we still need him—for now. I still need time to formulate a plan before we go and blow everything to hell. We have to play our cards right and running out on the recording session is not the way to do it.

Adding to this disastrous day, Aiden had to overhear what was supposed to be a private conversation between Roy and me. As if he needed more of a reason to distrust me, overhearing the guy in charge of Nash's music telling me to put Nash on a leash —or else—doesn't do much to help things.

I need to have a private moment with Nash. To tell him to control his own brother and that mouth of his if he doesn't want drama with the label.

Unfortunately, Nash isn't in the talking mood right now. As

he was storming out, he asked me to go find his brother so we could leave. That's what I'd been doing when I'd heard odd noises coming from a bathroom near where Aiden had last confronted me.

Which brings me to the last reason this day has been an absolute dumpster-fire. Aiden has managed to find a stray mutt and is *bathing* it in the bathroom sink.

Staring ahead of me, I wonder how many breathing exercises it'll take to find my *inner peace* after a day like today.

Aiden stands in front of me, his fingers tangled in the matted fur of the creature. "I can explain," he begins, looking incredulously at the panting dog in the sink. The animal appears to be having the time of their life. A large, pink tongue dangles out of its mouth. Its tail wags back and forth vigorously, further soaking Aiden's already drenched clothes.

Nodding, I walk to the furthest point in the room away from the dog. The last thing I want is for that thing to shake water on me and ruin my clothes. "Explain. Now," I clip, setting my bag on a small table next to a chair. My bag accidentally knocks a sealed package of peanut butter crackers to the ground.

Aiden looks back at the dog in front of him. He uses a marble bowl to pour water over the dog, his fingers wiping away the soapy suds from the animal's fur. "I'd stepped outside to get some air after overhearing your conversation with that prick. While out there, I found this guy rummaging through the trash. He was skin and bones and smelled horrendous. I couldn't leave him out there..."

"His name is Roy," I tell him. "And he's the head of the label that controls the music your brother gets to release. You probably shouldn't call him names."

Aiden grunts, running more water over the dog. "Well, he's a prick, and I trust you even less if you don't have the same viewpoint of him."

I try to hide the smile on my lips. "I don't think it's possible for you to trust me any less. Nor do I care."

He doesn't answer. His focus stays on continuing to wash the mangy mutt in front of him.

"I didn't say he wasn't a prick. But that *prick* has your brother's career by the balls. Best not to piss him off."

"Then Nash should just leave. Any label would take him on."

Sighing, I tuck a piece of hair behind my ear. "It's not that simple, Aiden."

"To hell it isn't," he responds immediately. "Will you hold him for a second? I need to find a towel."

I shake my head, my nose scrunching. "Absolutely not. I'm not touching that thing. How do you know it doesn't have some disease? Or fleas?"

Aiden laughs, wiping bubbles from his brow. "I don't know why I even asked. Of course you hate dogs."

"I don't *hate* dogs. I'm just not coming near one you found in the trash. What exactly is your plan here?" I walk to a tall, thin cabinet, careful to avoid the puddles of water on the bathroom tile. Opening it, I find extra soap, toilet paper, and towels. I grab a few towels, letting them drape over my forearm.

"I didn't have time to think of a full plan," he says, taking one of the towels from me.

The dog tries to lick Aiden as he attempts to dry the head of the animal.

"You can't keep it. I can find a nearby shelter," I offer. I've never been a fan of animals, but I don't think suggesting we throw him back in the trash would get me very far.

Aiden affectionately rubs the dog's ears with the towel. "I don't want to abandon him," Aiden says, lifting the dog out of the sink and placing him on the floor. Before he can get another towel on the dog it shakes violently, causing water to spray everywhere.

"Aiden!" I shriek, my hands waving in front of me to block the shower of water from hitting me.

The dog continues to shake, so I try to outrun the barrage of water droplets. My heels slip on the soaking wet floor as I retreat, my arms flailing as I try to regain my balance. Instinctively, I clutch onto Aiden's arm, pulling him over and sending us both tumbling to the ground.

Luckily, I land partially on top of Aiden, my chest pressed up against his face.

"I'm going to kill you," I threaten through clenched teeth, pushing myself up off of him and resting on my elbow. Looking down, my entire outfit is drenched. The suede fabric of my skirt is guaranteed to be ruined, and the soapy droplets on my silk blouse don't give me hope it will fare any better.

As if to add insult to injury, the dog walks right up to me and, before I can stop him, swipes his tongue across my cheek in one long motion.

"Disgusting!" I yell, scrambling to push the dog away from my face.

"Good boy," Aiden chuckles, not bothering to help get the dog off me. "Except I'm not sure he's got the best judgment of character." Patting the back of the dog, he says, "She's evil, little guy, don't get too attached."

I scoff. "*You* shouldn't get attached to that beast. There's no way you're keeping it."

He throws a towel over the mangy mutt, pulling the dog toward him as he dries it off. "He could be a tour dog."

"First off," I start, pointing to the abdomen of the dog. "I think your *he* is a *she*. Second, you can't take a dog on tour. Look at the size of those paws! She's going to be massive. That thing doesn't belong on a tour bus."

Aiden looks at the belly of the dog inquisitively. His eyebrows pull together on his forehead, creating two deep lines between his brows. "I swore you were a boy," he says in shock.

"I know you may not be familiar with female anatomy since I can't imagine any woman ever tolerating you long enough for that. But I can assure you, it's a girl."

He throws a cocky smirk my way. "I don't know, I got you wet didn't I?" He points to the dark, wet marks on my clothing.

I grimace. "Grow up."

Aiden finishes drying her off. Her fur sticks up in all directions as she excitedly grunts. She runs around the bathroom, rubbing her body against the different surfaces as she passes them.

Both Aiden and I watch her for a moment from the floor. Aiden sighs, adjusting from crouching down to sitting on the floor completely. Outstretching his long legs, his boot lands next to my hip.

His new position excites the dog. She gallops over to him, nuzzling her wet face into his neck.

Sighing, I realize that getting him to drop her off at the nearest shelter may be a battle I'm too exhausted to win right now. Not after the day that I've had. I reach out for the counter, using it to help steady myself as I stand up. The entire bathroom is covered in water—it looks like someone took a hose to the room.

Once standing, I try to wipe as much water from my clothes as possible.

Watching Aiden cradle the animal, a thought pops into my head. Maybe this dog is exactly what I need to keep Aiden off my butt. At least then he'll be preoccupied. Dogs are a lot of work, and he can't pester me if he's busy taking care of it.

"I'm going to let you be the one to ask your brother to bring this mutt on the road. I think it's the worst idea on the planet, but it isn't up to me."

Aiden looks shocked by my words. He moves a wet, brown piece of hair out of his face. "Did you hear that, girl? The

Wicked Witch of the Tour gave you permission to come with us. Maybe she has a heart after all—even if it's cold, and black."

The dog answers by wagging her tail and licking his face aggressively.

"If it were up to me she'd be back on the street, but you've caught me on a day where enough has gone to shit already. I don't have it in me to argue with you about a dog. Get control of her and go ask your brother," I say, carefully walking across the floor to grab my purse.

Stopping at the door, I turn around to look at Aiden. He cuddles the dog on the floor, not giving a care in the world that the dog is still damp and soaking his clothes through even more.

"Oh and Aiden," I start, opening the door to the hallway. "Things with your brother—and the label—are far from simple. Don't push it, and don't do anything stupid. You got it?"

Aiden doesn't answer me. All he does is give me an unreadable look before burying his face in the crook of the dog's neck.

Walking out the door, I make my way back to our ride. I have no doubt in my mind that Aiden won't drop what he overheard today, but maybe this dog will be the distraction I need to buy more time.

10

AIDEN

"YOU'VE GOT to be kidding me," Nash mumbles, looking at me as if I've grown a third arm.

I shift the puppy in my hands, putting my face close to hers. "Look at this sweet little face." I push my lip out in a puppy dog face. "How can we just leave her on the streets?"

"I told him to take it to a shelter," Monica pipes up from inside the SUV, the black tint of the windows making it impossible to see in. Matt sits in the driver's seat of the car, with Nora, Lennon and Monica sitting in the third row waiting for the rest of us to get in. Monroe takes the seat next to Matt, leaving Nash and I standing next to the black exterior of the vehicle.

I go to give Monica a dirty look through the open door, but she isn't even looking in our direction. She's typing madly away at her phone, only paying attention enough to give my brother bad ideas.

"I'm not taking her to a shelter," I state. Now that she's bathed and fed, she's calmed down. Her body relaxes comfortably in my arms, unaware that I'm fighting to keep her.

"Have you thought this through, Aiden?" Nash asks, reaching to pat the scruff on the dog's neck.

Shrugging, I watch my brother find the spot the dog loves. The instant he scratches her chin, one of her legs thumps excitedly against my chest. "I'll figure it out," I promise. "You'll barely know she's there."

Nash looks at me dubiously. "Somehow I feel like that isn't true," he laughs.

"She'll be a good dog," I counter. "I'll train her so she doesn't get in anyone else's way. I can't just leave her here to fend for herself again. And leaving her at a shelter...what if she doesn't go to a good home?"

I feel like a child pleading my case to keep the dog. I used to beg as a kid to have a dog. The best my parents did was get me a rabbit. If I wasn't on tour and was living on my own again, I wouldn't have to be begging my brother to keep her. If he says no, I could decide to forego the tour, find a flight home, and keep her. I'm hoping it doesn't have to come to that. I want to continue to get to know my brother, especially after what I overheard today, but I also don't want to abandon this dog.

Nash sighs, sharing a knowing look with Nora. She smiles softly, nodding to him encouragingly. He looks back at the dog in my arms. I'm getting nervous at his silence, but finally he speaks. "I think Nora would have my balls if I told you no."

The corner of my lips twitch. "So, is that a yes?"

Letting out an exaggerated breath, he nods his head. "Yes, you can keep that dog." He holds up one finger. "On one condition..."

I look at him expectantly, waiting for him to continue. "Okay."

"You don't name her after somebody famous."

I groan. "I was like *five* when I named the rabbit."

His smile is taunting. "It was such a unique name, brother."

You name a rabbit Britney Spears when you're five and fifteen years later your brother still won't let you forget it.

"So is it a deal?" Nash prods.

Laughing, I nod my head in agreement. "You've got a deal."

"Good. Now let's get the hell out of here. I'm starving and it looks like we need to make a stop to get some pet supplies."

"I'm already on it," Monica says from the back row, waving her phone in the air. "Someone will be delivering them to the stadium within the next two hours."

Climbing into the captain's chair adjacent to hers, I give her a confused look. She didn't try to hide her distaste for the dog earlier, so I'm shocked by her willingness to suddenly order supplies for her.

Monica rolls her eyes at me as Matt backs out of our parking spot. "Stop looking at me like that. I couldn't let you feed that thing potato chips and peanut butter crackers. I mean seriously Aiden, do you know what's in those?"

"She didn't seem to mind. Besides, I didn't give her the crackers," I add, remembering I left the unopened package in the bathroom.

Monica hums disapprovingly. "My point stands. You filled that dog full of toxins and preservatives."

I hold the dog in front of her, waving her in the air gently to annoy Monica. "She didn't seem to care, did you girl?" I ask. "It was an improvement from the trash she was eating when I found her."

Monica sighs, plastering her body against the car window to try and get as far away as possible from me and the dog.

11
AIDEN

The following day, we're back on the road to our next destination. So far, my new travel companion has made an excellent road pup. I can't say I've been the best owner, though, since I'm still figuring out a name for her. That may be largely because all I can really focus on is the conversation I heard between Roy and Monica. I'm trying to piece together the small scraps of information I've been given or overheard to figure out the bigger picture.

Most of all, I want to know what my brother knows, and what's at stake for him right now. With my mind focused elsewhere, the dog has remained unnamed.

She lays at my feet, every now and then letting out a loud snore. Nash and I lay beside one another in the small bedroom he shares with Nora. We're locked in here while Nora and Lennon speak to Nora's best friend, Riley, over FaceTime in the front half of the bus. Apparently, they're going over some top-secret photos they'd taken of Nora at her wedding dress fitting earlier.

I don't mind the rare alone time with my brother. Moments with just the two of us on tour have been far and few between. It reminds me of when we were kids, before he made it big around the time he was in middle school. The two of us have one hand behind the pillow supporting our heads, watching some random daytime game show.

My mind wanders back to the time when Nash and Nora were broken up, and I feel guilt swell inside me. In the months after she broke his heart, it was hard to watch my brother fall victim to his own recklessness. It's even harder to remember my part in it. Instead of encouraging him to get himself help, I'd been downing shots like it was my job right along with him. I hadn't realized how bad he'd gotten, too caught up in enjoying a lifestyle I wasn't used to at the expense of my brother.

I have many regrets. Fueling the fire of my brother's addiction is one of my biggest ones.

"Have you talked to mom and dad recently?" Nash breaks the silence, taking a sip from his water bottle.

I remember a time when he'd have some sort of clear liquor in his water bottles instead, but now I know differently. He hasn't had a drink since before he went to rehab.

"Are you awake?" Nash asks, leaning forward to look at me. I'd been blankly staring at the show ahead of me, too lost in my own thoughts to remember he'd asked me a question.

"Sorry, I don't know where my head was at," I lie.

Stretching my legs out, I accidentally bump into the puppy, causing her to wake up. She stands, circling around on the bed before laying back down with a big sigh.

"It's been a while since I've talked to them," I answer. "I've been caught up in everything with the tour, it slipped my mind to call them."

Nash nods, picking at a sticker on his water bottle. "You know, they're the parents. They could reach out to you…"

Growing up, Nash and I didn't have the picture-perfect parents. They weren't awful. We were always fed and never abused, but they just weren't loving parents—especially to Nash. My dad was always on Nash's case for something. I don't remember much before Nash was famous—I was too young to realize how much Mom and Dad favored me. Once he hit it big time, it wasn't hard to miss how they suddenly wanted to pretend they were parents of the year to him.

As a kid I wanted to pretend that my Mom and Dad were perfect, but as I grew up and spent the night with friends, I could feel the *love* their parents had for them. That was something I never felt. Moving out and going to college was one of the best things I could do to get away from them. To find my own identity—or at least attempt to.

"I'm sure they'll call soon," Nash offers, filling the silence.

I grunt, realizing how long it'd been since I spoke with them last.

Nash and I fall back into silence as we watch the show for a while longer, but my mind won't stop racing with what I overheard yesterday. I need to talk to him about it, even if I know he won't like how I found out.

"Hey, Nash?" I ask hesitantly, staring up at the ceiling.

"Hm?"

"I need to tell you something, but I need you to not get mad at me. Okay?"

Nash gives me a look. "I'm not sure if I like where this is going."

"Yesterday at the studio..." I begin, trying to figure out exactly what I want to say. "What was up with that Roy guy?" I decide to fish for answers from him first before I tell him what I overheard. I'm interested to hear what he'll divulge.

A low growl starts in Nash's throat. He picks up one of the decorative pillows at his side, putting it on his lap to give him something to do with his hands. "I don't want to talk about that asshole."

"It just seemed like everyone was on edge when he dropped in on your recording session. What's going on there?"

"Don't worry about it, Aiden. I should've acted more professional in front of everyone. I just…" He shakes his head.

"You just what?" I press.

Sitting up, Nash moves the pillow to his side. He trains his eyes on me. "I just lost my cool. It was something I shouldn't have done but it's also something you don't need to worry about."

"I overheard a conversation between Monica and Roy," I blurt out. My stomach tightens as I observe him, waiting for him to give any kind of reaction to my words.

Nash rubs at his forehead. "*Overheard,* huh? What exactly did you hear?"

"I heard Roy tell Monica to put a leash on you."

He snickers. "That's something he's wanted for years. Monica wishes she could have a leash on me too, I'm sure. It would make her life much easier."

"This isn't funny. He seemed serious—like he was threatening you both. He told her that she knows what he'll do to you if you don't listen. What does that mean? And why is Monica just bending over for him?"

"It's complicated," Nash answers. "And like I said earlier, you don't need to worry about it. We've got it under control."

"I don't get why you guys won't just tell me what the hell is going on."

Nash purses his lips. "You *guys?*"

Whoops.

"I may have cornered Monica after I heard that conversation between her and Roy. She basically told me to ask you. I don't trust him, Nash, and I don't trust her, either. I'm confused as fuck about why this seems like a game to you."

Nash's hand slaps the bed next to his leg. "For fuck's sake, Aiden. Will you just drop it? I told you it's fine. I don't like Roy, but I need him right now to do the thing I love. And you need to leave Monica alone—she's on our side."

My jaw clenches in frustration. Staring at my brother, I can't help but wonder what he won't tell me.

"I'll drop it when I figure out what the hell is going on here. You're so cagey when it comes to talking about him. And Monica…"

Nash cuts me off. "Is none of your concern. None of this is. If I told you, you'd just end up doing something reckless. I'm sorry, Aiden, but you need to trust me that it's fine. Drop it."

Grunting in annoyance, I lean back on the bed. There's no point in prying further with my brother, he's as stubborn as I am. I'll just have to figure out what's happening on my own.

And if Nash won't give me the information, I'll get it out of Monica one way or another.

12
MONICA

STARING at my reflection in the hotel mirror, I wonder how the hell I'm going to get through tonight. Typically, I don't put my energy into dreading things. The negative energy in my life is something I've worked extremely hard to get rid of over the years. I've read countless self-help books and have been to numerous seminars learning from the best in the industry on how to maintain a healthy mind. Unfortunately, not many books cover how to handle being forced into a room filled with greedy, self-absorbed pigs.

Tonight is a black-tie event for Coleman Records. It'll be filled to the brim with some of the most influential people in the industry, but it'll also be full of all the people that wanted to hurt Nash in order to get better music and line their pockets. The same people that hold the rights to his music and use it as a threat to try and control him.

A few years ago, I was naive. I didn't know what I know now. When they told me they'd drop Nash from Coleman if he didn't get another album out, I had figured out a way to stop that from happening. I didn't realize they'd never stop.

At the time, Nash had been on tour. Dropping Nash mid-tour would mean having to cancel all the remaining shows. That alone may have ruined his image, but it's not the only detriment to being dropped. They also would have remained in full control of all the masters from his albums. He wouldn't have control of his past music, which means he also wouldn't be able to profit or perform the songs he had poured his heart and soul into—the songs that had helped heal so much of his pain and continue to give him purpose.

I'd propositioned Nora because I thought it was the only way I could get us out of the situation we'd found ourselves in. His lack of new music was catching up to him. The label was going to drop him or try to force him to record music that wasn't his —music he wouldn't be caught dead recording. Nash was already holding on by a thin thread mentally, and I knew both things could send him over the edge.

Hiring Nora was a last resort—one I didn't think would have the effect it did. I wanted him to develop a crush on her—an innocent *fling*. Back then, Nash was known to move from one woman to another easily. I thought Nora would be the same thing. I just wanted her to pique his interest enough for him to get inspired—to write good music again. My attempt to save Nash's career almost ended it for good. I still haven't forgiven myself for it, despite having his best intentions in mind.

After all that had happened, I thought Nash would surely drop me as his manager. I was fully prepared for that to happen. If Nash was going to fire me, I wanted to make sure he knew what he was up against. Despite having my own sibling, Nash was the closest thing I'd had to a brother in all the ways that mattered. I couldn't let them continue to bully him.

Roy has been salivating at the mouth to ruin Nash long before the label threatened to drop him. He didn't care that Nash was the reason Coleman Records was as big as it was. He had no appreciation for the work Nash did to put them on the map and bring in countless new artists.

Roy didn't—and still doesn't—care. Nash is one of the only

people who doesn't bow down to the man. It's quite the opposite. From the very beginning, even as a new solo artist, Nash didn't let Roy control him. He pushed against Roy all of the time on decisions, and over time, it led to a tumultuous relationship between the two of them, and Coleman in general.

Nash needs out of his contract. He needs to get away from Coleman Records. The problem is, he signed on for three more albums with them. They've made it impossible for him to buy his way out of the contract. Nash's net worth is high, even by musician standards, yet the money they want for him to buy his own contract isn't even close to feasible. Roy has made it his personal mission to fuck Nash over.

The last album, fueled by Nash's breakdown over Nora, was enough to satisfy most of the label executives temporarily. The record had sold more than any in the past. Combined with the number of streams it had after its release, it more than doubled his previous sales.

His heartbreak was heard around the world—and they loved it. Again.

That album was the reason Coleman kept dealing with him, but it didn't last long. Their happiness with him was directly related to his album sales. They wanted him to be a machine and pop out another instantly. All they cared about was the money.

When Nash called me into his office after discovering that I'd hired Nora to break his heart, I'd told him everything—Roy, the threats they made, all of it. I braced myself for a verbal onslaught, but he only said one thing. I remember his reaction like it was yesterday instead of years ago. He sat up straight in his chair, looked at me, more sober than I'd seen him in a long time, and said, "So what are we going to do about it?"

I was confused at first. No part of me thought I'd walk out of that room with my job. I'd been prepared to find something new. I just needed him to know what battle he was fighting.

Nash had other plans. Instead of firing me, he put his trust in me even further. He gave me a second chance, and I won't mess this one up. We knew that somehow we had to find a way to break his contract and get ownership of his music. Easier said than done, but we've managed to find some breadcrumbs that are slowly starting to add up. The lawyer route hasn't proven very useful thus far, but I'm making progress on my own in another, slightly less clean way. It's slow—but I'm closer to freeing him than I've ever been before.

If his stupid brother doesn't ruin it all for us.

Tonight, we're dancing with the devil. We'll be in a room full of the people who only see Nash as either a dollar sign or a nuisance. People who only want to see him succeed on *their* terms, or not at all.

Nash will have to be on his best behavior tonight. We all have to. If Roy gets a whiff of what we're up to, it could spoil everything. Nash leaving has to be a surprise. We won't be able to do it until our lawyers find some miracle loophole, which isn't likely, or I can find a way to take down Roy—which is my current plan. I haven't divulged much of my current plan to Nash. I don't want him to have to worry about my tactics. I'm willing to do whatever it takes this time to help Nash, even if it means getting dirty.

The corset of my dress is tight around my ribcage. I had my seamstress take it in significantly, wanting it to dig into my flesh until I could just barely breathe. The hard seams bite into my skin with every move I make. I had the dress custom made, knowing I needed to dress to impress tonight. Tonight I'm playing the part of the dutiful manager. One *eternally* grateful to Coleman Records for keeping Nash on despite his scandals over the years—and the lull in between records. I'm playing a part, ensuring they don't catch on to the scheming going on in my head.

I hate to admit it, but every new pop artist wants to work

with Roy, which means they want in with Coleman Records—at least for now. Once I'm done with Roy, he won't be able to get a job selling burgers and fries.

"I'm going to burn the label to the fucking ground," I say to my reflection in the mirror.

Taking in my appearance, the dress seems fitting for this evening—for the foundation of destruction I'll be laying. The satin fabric is a fiery red, a perfect combination of red and orange. The fabric is cold against my chest. It billows loosely over one of my shoulders, the other strap hangs loosely over my bicep. The beautiful, ruched material runs into the corset at the peak of each breast. The corset hugs every inch of me all the way to my hips. There the ruched fabric begins again, billowing all the way to the ground except for the slit that begins at the bottom of the corset over one of my hips. I paired the dress with my favorite black Louboutin's.

Next door, a team of people prepare Nash and Nora for the event. According to the schedule I'd handed them this morning, they should be finishing up their last-minute touches with the makeup team.

I check my appearance one last time in the mirror. Two diamond clips pin my short, blonde hair away from my face, bringing more attention to the dark shadow on my lids, the hues making my brown eyes appear brighter. The look is finished off with deep red lipstick. Satisfied, I toss the lipstick into my ring-clutch and get ready to check in on how it's going in the other room.

Even though this event is in LA, we elected to book rooms for the people of Nash's team that are attending, as the event is being held in one of the ballrooms of the hotel. Most of the artists attending have elected to do the same thing since Coleman Records booked a block of rooms for that reason. The caliber of artists attending all but ensures there will be tons of fans and paparazzi outside, which means there'll also be a ton of security. Getting here early and staying in the hotel was our best option.

Luckily, there's no red carpet for the night. Red carpets are something I always have to battle with Nash on and I'm glad tonight we won't have to go there.

I check my curling iron, ensuring that it's no longer on before turning the lights off. Grabbing my keycard from the nightstand next to my bed, I place it in the clutch along with my phone and my ID for the party. Once I've gathered everything I need for the evening, I make my way next door, fully prepared for what tonight will bring.

13
AIDEN

I DON'T KNOW how my brother manages to kiss ass so much. It must be tiring having your lips puckered, ready to move from one douchebag to another—pretending to care about any of this.

We haven't been here for ten minutes and I'm already exhausted for him. We've barely made it ten feet into the large event ballroom and Nash has already been stopped by five people, all look fake as fuck as they pretend to dote over him. I know my brother can't possibly believe a word they say, yet he plays right along. He politely shakes their hands, laughs at their awful jokes, and expresses gratitude when they pretend to be excited for his wedding.

Boring.

I hide my yawn behind a closed fist, trying not to voice my boredom. I need a drink or *something* to make this night more tolerable. There's no way in hell I'm going to survive following my brother around all evening, watching him pretend to give a shit about any of these high-class wannabes. I'm starting to regret working so hard to convince Nash to let me come tonight, but I couldn't miss this opportunity to do some digging. What better place to figure out what's going on with Nash than here in the den of the enemy?

Finally, our group gets a moment of reprieve as we make our way toward our table. I round out the back of the group, my footsteps slower than those in front of me. My eyes are trained on Monica's back as she leads our pack through the throng of people. I have to calm my conscious down as it has a visceral reaction to Monica. For the first time, looking at her in her skintight red-as-a-devil dress, my entire body burns with new desire. One I try to bat the fuck away because it's *Monica*. The lights from the chandeliers hanging above us illuminate every delicious curve of her body, simultaneously sending shockwaves through me—shooting right down to my dick. I gulp down incessant, filthy thoughts as I remind myself what a little liar the woman is. Suddenly, she slows, allowing Matt and Monroe to take the lead as her steps come to a halt.

Nash gives her an inquisitive look as he passes her, but he continues on, following in Matt's footsteps.

Before I know it, Monica is standing next to me. Her brown eyes look up at me. "A word," she demands, arching her head to a small alcove.

My eyebrows raise. "To what do I owe the displeasure?" I ask. Intrigued, I follow her the few footsteps it takes to fit ourselves into a small corner of the ballroom, hidden from the view of others.

"The *displeasure* is all mine," she hisses, looking down to adjust one of the straps of her dress. The strap had fallen dangerously far down her arm, weighing the loose fabric of her dress down and showing off the rounded top of her breast. My gaze stays fixed on the spot, wondering if it would be ice cold if I were to touch above it, her chest void of a beating heart.

My tongue clicks. "Well that depends why you wanted to be alone, Monica." I tease, still looking at her cleavage. Nothing seems to frustrate her more than pretending to flirt.

A hand hits my cheek. Not hard enough to hurt, but enough to catch my attention.

"Pay attention, Aiden. I'm only going to say this once," she says harshly. If looks could kill, I'd be dead. If words could slice through skin, I'd be bleeding out onto this ballroom floor. Anger flashes in her eyes when she looks at me, realizing that I'm not taking her too seriously.

"And what is that?" I ask, annoying her by adjusting the fallen strap all over again.

She slaps my hand away, shaking her head. "You are to be on your *best* behavior tonight. Understood?"

I can't hide the smile her words elicit from me. "Aw, Monica. I think it's cute that you think I'd ever behave." Placing my lips by her ear I whisper, "It's never been my style."

Monica pushes me away. Her urgency to get me away only strengthens my need to annoy her further by encroaching on her personal space. The way my pulse hammers under my skin reminds me of how much I'm enjoying this.

"You're appalling," she seethes, her voice barely above a whisper. She doesn't have to raise her voice to elicit power, she carries it in even the quietest movement of her lips.

But unlike the rest of the world, I'm not intimidated by her.

"I could say the same thing about you, you know," I fire back. "Well, at least the choices you make to *help*," my fingers make mock quotation marks between us, "your clients."

She rolls her eyes, backing away from me as much as she can. "This night is important. Don't do anything to jeopardize your brother." Monica doesn't give me time to respond, just as quick as she pulled me into this private corner, she leaves it.

For the next two hours, I'm left to my own devices. I've watched Monica carefully for the entirety of the night—something I know she's noticed. I want her to know that I've got my eyes on her. That whatever she's up to, I'll figure it out. I've cataloged each person she's spoken to, trying to piece together this puzzle.

Occasionally, I'd let my focus move from her to Nash. It

was refreshing to see him speaking with a group of other artists from Coleman—with peers instead of the phony label execs.

Now, scanning the room again, I try to find Monica in the crowd. A waiter in a crisp white button up and perfectly tied bow tie stops in front of me. "Would you like a drink?" he asks politely, lifting his tray of champagne flutes.

Shaking my head, "No thanks," I say. Even though I'm freshly twenty-two, and all of my college buddies are probably out getting shit-faced tonight, I want to stay clear-headed. Seeing Nash go through what he did, and being there to push him further, has stifled my desire to drink too often.

The waiter nods. He begins to walk away before he stops and turns around. "Yo, where did you get the suit? I've been looking for something just like that," he explains.

"I honestly have no fucking clue," I answer. "It was some fancy place my brother took me to."

He looks disappointed for a moment. "Damn," he says. "Thanks anyway."

I watch him disappear behind a group of people. Looking down, I take in the suit I'd picked out with Nash a few weeks ago. Once I convinced him to let me attend, I realized I'd need something to wear. His stylist had lit up like a damn Christmas tree when she thought she'd have the opportunity to dress me, but I'd politely declined, deciding to pick something out for myself.

I'd settled on a matte black suit jacket and pants. The lapels are made out of black velvet. His stylist had picked out a velvet tie to match, but I'd vetoed it. I'd fought wearing a tie to prom in high school and I'm not planning on starting to wear one now.

Instead, I'd opted for a black button up underneath the jacket. I hated the feeling of being buttoned up all the way to my neck. It was stifling and uncomfortable. When we were getting on the elevator, I'd undone the first few buttons so I could breathe.

I'd been distracted by the waiter long enough to lose track of both Monica and Nash. I canvas the room, finally spotting my brother and Nora speaking with a girl in a tight gold dress. I vaguely remember her as someone that Nash once released a single with. The more I think about it, I remember sitting in front of our living room TV and watching the two of them perform at an award show. At the time, I'd thought she was someone he was hooking up with. The way their conversation seems cordial, even friendly, it doesn't appear like they had. Any woman that Nash hooked up with seemed to always be left in a pissed off mood—or became a bitch. Her friendly smile to Nora doesn't suggest any hint of jealousy.

Looking away from them, I take in the bustling party around me. I don't know if there's been another time that I've been surrounded by so many famous people. I should think it's cool. Part of me wants to flirt with the group of girls who keep whispering to each other and looking my way—to forget about why I came here and let loose. But I'd be lying if I said tracking Monica isn't the most fun I've had in a while.

The lights have dimmed in the last hour, bringing more attention to the illuminated dance floor. There's a large stage with a live band performing atop it. The dance floor has filled substantially since we got here. It's the last place I'd expect to find Monica.

Except, that's exactly where I spot her. She's hard to miss in a dress like that. Toward the middle of the dance floor, with her back to me, Monica sways in time to the music, a man's hand snaked around her waist. Her dance partner's face is obstructed by some gaudy flower arrangement hanging from a pillar.

Fascinated, I leave my private corner and head toward the crowded area. People keep stepping in my way, and I fight the urge to run every single one of them over en route to her. I want to see what kind of creature it takes to get Monica on the dance floor—whose hand is placed so dangerously close to the top of her ass.

Circling the dance floor, I'm both shocked and disgusted to find the identity of her dance partner—Roy. He's got one meaty hand placed on her lower back, the other one holds her arm in the air as they drift around the floor.

What the fuck.

They seem deep in conversation. He says something to her that makes her straighten her spine. Whatever he said, he must find himself hilarious because he laughs, his head falling backwards. Monica looks sideways, as if to avoid making eye contact with him.

Or because his breath probably smells.

Even on the opposite side of the room I can tell that Monica isn't a fan of the conversation. She has that same tense look to her face that she gets when I'm throwing crude remarks her way. I can tell she's biting her tongue, the way she's done many times with me before.

I'm content with watching the encounter. I want to see if I can read their lips and body language to discern new information. He tries to pull her body into his further, letting his hand drift even lower on her body—somewhere he has no business touching. The look on her face is one of revulsion. Her body shifts slightly, moving his hand without making it too obvious. The attempt at keeping his hand in a safe territory doesn't last for long. His hand travels back down again immediately, even lower this time.

Something in me snaps, and before I know it I'm weaving in and out of bodies, heading right in their direction.

Her face is bright red when I find them.

"My turn," I announce sharply, catching both of their attention.

"Actually, we aren't done here," Roy says smoothly, trying to turn his back to me. "You can cut in after the next song."

He looks toward her, trying to dismiss me as if I'm a pesky fly. Too bad for him I've never been one to back down. Both of his hands go to her waist, still clutching her tightly to his body.

"No can do, asshole," I say through gritted teeth. My hand comes in between the two of them. I'm not gentle as I push on his chest to get him away from her.

"Aiden, it's fine," Monica says through a tight-lipped smile.

My head swings in her direction, my eyes narrowing. I know Monica well enough that Roy should be bleeding right now for his antics. She doesn't take shit from anyone, especially some creepy old guy trying to manhandle her in front of all of their colleagues. Yet there's no action supporting the fire in her eyes. She bites her tongue. And I want to know *why*.

A large hand pats my shoulder. "Leave the adults to speak," Roy says, not bothering to hide the condescending tone of his voice.

"I'm afraid it's my turn for a dance," I retort, carefully taking Monica's hand in mine. I don't give Roy—or Monica—the chance to object. My hand finds the arch of her back as I guide Monica further into the crowd, letting Roy disappear behind the other dancers.

I glance over at Monica as we make our way to the edge of the dancefloor, the fire in her eyes now burning a hole in me. Even though I despise her, I couldn't let Roy have his way. No woman deserves that, not even her.

She has some explaining to do, and I'm not letting her off this dance floor until I've figured why she just allowed all of that to happen.

14
MONICA

I'M GOING to fucking kill him. It's settled. Everything was going according to plan. I had Roy thinking that I was meek—that he could throw threats my way and I would bow down to him. That he could do whatever he wanted and I would just accept it as his humble servant. I had him eating from the palm of my hand.

And then Aiden had to step in and potentially ruin everything—coming in like he's a white knight, surely blowing whatever progress I'd made with Roy tonight.

Aiden ushers me to the edge of the dance floor, away from Roy. His hand on my back is warm compared to the cold clamminess of Roy's, while his other wraps tightly around mine. It's as if he can sense that I'm about to run, his firm grasp keeping me on this dance floor.

"Are you done planning my murder in your head yet?" Aiden questions, letting his hand apply more pressure at my lower back. His touch doesn't make me want to crawl out of my skin like Roy's did, but I don't exactly enjoy being held here. I'd prefer to be off this dance floor entirely.

"I'm still trying to come up with what would be the most painful way for you to go. I was thinking, perhaps…castration?"

He gasps, his jaw finally relaxing from the earlier encounter. His eyelashes flutter against his cheeks as he looks down at me. "If you wanted to play with my dick, Monica, all you had to do was ask." His tongue darts out, wetting his lips before they break out into a wide grin.

I don't bother to hide the look of disgust on my face, fighting the urge to smack the cocky smile right off his face. "Grow the hell up," I scoff, shaking my head to rid it of the mental picture. "Does that really work with girls your age?"

Before I can catch on to what he's doing, his chest comes against mine. His forearm digs into my back as he quickly dips me backward. My shoulders are only a few feet from the ground as he leans over me. His lips form a predatory smirk. "Couldn't tell you," he says confidently. "I've never been too keen on girls my age." His eyes flick to my throat.

What the fuck is happening, I think, having to dig my nails into his arms to steady myself. The asshole dips me even lower, his grip on me loosens and I'm wondering if he's going to drop me. It wouldn't surprise me in the slightest.

I open my mouth to speak, but he surprises me by pulling me up quickly. Suddenly, we're chest to chest again. Except this time he's brought me even closer to his body. I can feel every inch of his hard stomach against mine.

For a college dropout with no notable redeeming qualities, I'll admit he can dance. He doesn't ever let me take the lead, controlling the pace as our steps fall into perfect rhythm.

He guides us effortlessly around the dance floor, and I wonder where he learned to dance. My parents put me in ballroom classes the instant I could walk, but from what I've heard from Nash, that doesn't sound like something their parents would do. I doubt Aiden went through countless etiquette classes like I did, all before ever hitting puberty. And shortly after my breasts developed and I'd hit my womanhood, I'd been introduced to society with other girls my age. I've known how to dance for as long as I can remember, but I haven't had many dance partners that knew how to effectively lead. Not like this, anyway.

My attention is brought back to the present when he speaks again. "So tell me, Monica," he says, leaning over me. His eyes are serious as they rake over my face. "What in the hell is going on with Roy?"

I pause for a second, wondering how to best distract Aiden and get him off my trail.

"And don't even waste your time telling me some bullshit lie. Nobody likes a pretty little liar," he says quietly, his breath hot against my neck.

It's as if the crowd around us has disappeared. He's commanded my full attention and judging by the ironlike grip he's got on my waist, it'll be a battle to get off this dance floor with him.

Not backing down, I look up at him. "I've never much cared if I'm liked or not. It seems frivolous to care what others think of you. Damned if you do, damned if you don't kind of thing."

He bears his straight white teeth, the grin more wolfish than friendly. "That's definitely something a liar would say. Tell me, does the devil ever miss you in hell?" he says, a slight tease to his tone.

"You can ask him when I murder you later," I fire back.

Shaking his head, he effortlessly transitions into the next song, a slow one. People around us embrace, soaking in the romantic moment with their dance partner. Aiden and I, however, continue with our power struggle.

"I'm waiting," he sing-songs. His arms leave my waist for a fraction of a second. He guides each one of my arms around his neck before his fingers dig into my waist once again.

"I still haven't figured out how I'm going to kill you."

"You can let me know when you figure it out, but that's not

what I meant. I want to know what Nash's label has on him. Or you—or the *both* of you."

We're too close for my liking. I can't even recall the last time I slowed dance with a man—if you can call someone so immature a man. I've never been one to like romance, or the idea of being *swept off* my feet. I've been more worried about my career—not pretending that any man could ever actually make me happy.

"I have no idea what you're talking about," I finally tell him. I've got to give it to the kid, he's bright, despite the cocky attitude he's always showcasing. Somehow he's sniffed out the fact that for the time being, Nash is trapped—therefore leaving me trapped right there with him.

"You see, Monica," he drawls, "that answer just isn't going to cut it for me anymore." He brings his head close to mine. To onlookers, it may look like we're in a sweet embrace, but the hold he has on my waist combined with the look in his eyes is anything but.

"If you're not going to tell me, then I'll have to go ask Roy myself. I feel like after the encounter I just had with him, it may not end well…"

I gasp. "Aiden, listen to me. That would jeopardize everything your brother has worked for. You would never."

He clicks his tongue. "That's where you're wrong, little liar. Because unlike you and Nash, I'm not scared of Roy. In fact, I love ruffling the feathers of that egomaniac. It seems like my brother is already in some kind of shit with them. Could I really make things worse?"

"You could ruin everything we've worked for recently," I lash out, the words tumbling out of my mouth before I have time to think it over.

Oh no. Aiden catches on to my slip-up instantly. "There it is."

I've already made a mistake, given up more information than I wanted to. And by the shit-eating grin on his face, he knows it.

"And what have you been working on recently?" he presses.

"Can you just leave it alone?" I sigh.

"Not in my nature. I thought you were smart enough to know that by now."

"I told you to ask your brother."

"He told me not to worry about it."

I look up at him. "Then he doesn't want you to know about it, Aiden. If you really want to help, you should respect his wishes and stay out of my way."

He takes my hand, guiding me to spin away from him. Both of our arms outstretched, he smiles at me knowingly before tugging on my arm. The movement has me spinning back into him, this time my back presses against his front. He molds his body against mine, leaning over me to whisper in my ear. The hot air against my bare skin has it breaking out in unwanted goosebumps.

"I'm going to figure it out one way or another. It's easier for everyone if you just tell me. Then we can figure out a way to get Nash somewhere else," he says, holding me tight against him.

I step out of his hold, turning around to face him once again. "There is no *we*—ever. I don't need help from some eighteen-year-old."

"Twenty-two," he corrects. "But you knew that already, so let's not play dumb. That's not you, Monica."

My jaw slackens as I look at him in disbelief. I wasn't prepared for his relentlessness. The walls are beginning to close in, and I don't know how to combat his obsession with this.

"Ever heard the saying, *the enemy of my enemy is my friend?*" he questions.

"It makes no sense. An enemy is still an enemy—no matter if they have a common enemy or not." Purposefully, I sidestep incorrectly, letting the tip of my heel dig into the top of his dress shoe. If he feels it, he doesn't let on to it.

"So you're admitting we have a common enemy?"

"I'm admitting nothing. I was just pointing out the flaw in your argument."

"You're making this way more difficult than this needs to be. Tell me what we're up against and *together,*" he emphasizes doing it together, surely just to piss me off after my earlier comment, "we can help Nash get out from beneath the heels of this dickwad. We don't even have to involve Nash—he can keep his hands clean and focus on the tour. I don't mind taking one for the team."

I run my tongue over my teeth, wondering how he knew that I was trying to keep from burdening his brother. To allow Nash to feign innocence if my plan were to go south.

"I don't need you to accomplish what I want," I say.

He shakes his head, pieces of his lengthy hair falling into this face. "I think it's cute you think you don't need me."

"Give me one reason you could actually be helpful. From where I stand, you're only getting in the way."

"Easy, I'm unsuspecting. Whatever you have planned, the freeloading younger brother is the last person anyone will be suspicious of."

"Who says anyone is suspicious?"

He laughs, his Adam's apple bobbing up and down with the laughter. "You're *you*—easily the most intimidating manager in the business. Your ruthlessness and lack of emotion instantly makes you suspicious."

My lip pouts in a tiny frown. He isn't wrong about me being ruthless at times, and I've worked hard to be this intimidating. I just don't like being called out for lack of emotion. I have emotions, I just find no use in over-exaggerating them.

"Keep talking," I say. The music picks up once again. Aiden effortlessly switches our position once again. One hand rests above the curve of my hips and the other takes my hand in his. My free hand finds his shoulder, allowing him to bend my spine so we're in the closed ballroom position.

His excitement is obvious by the large smile spreading across his face. "I can get information from people without them suspecting it. People think I'm dumb, and I can play into it. You'll be shocked at what people will admit when they don't feel threatened by you—when they think you're less than them."

I look over his shoulder as I think his words through. Part of my plan does involve speaking with some of the other artists at Coleman. I'd planned to speak with them myself, but Aiden did have a point. There's a possibility he could get information from some of the artists—information they wouldn't be willing to share with me. I have my suspicions on some of the shady extracurriculars that Roy enjoys, but I need confirmation.

As much as I hate to admit it, I do think these artists would open up to Aiden easier than they'd open up to me.

"You know I'm right."

"*If* I fill you in, you can't speak a word of this to anyone."

"Your secrets are safe with me, little liar."

"Stop calling me that," I hiss.

He licks his lips. "Aw, but it's so fitting for you. I used to call you *evil bitch* in my head, but I thought this was more accurate. I don't like you, but I'm learning there may be more to you than pure evil. The question is, the more I find out, will it be worse or better?"

"Maybe once you grow up you'll realize that not everything is black and white. Adults have to make adult decisions—and I have reasons for the things that I've done."

"I have no doubt you have *reasons*. But the jury is still out on if those reasons were really to benefit Nash."

My feet stop on the dance floor. I'm done with this figurative and literal dance with him. My hand pushes against his chest, giving some space between our bodies. I instantly feel cold, something I don't let myself pay much attention to.

"Everything I've done from the moment Nash hired me has

been for Nash. Soon you'll realize that. I'll tell you what you need to know later—and nothing more. That's my final offer."

His finger traces his bottom lip. It seems like forever that he thinks over my words. Finally, he says, "Deal. Don't make me come find you..."

I nod, somewhat surprised he agreed so easily. "I'll find *you* when I have time to deal with you. I'm busy." I adjust my dress. "As for tonight, stay out of my way."

IT'S BEEN two days since Monica and I came to an agreement and I've barely heard a word from her. She's hardly looked in my direction, and when she actually does, she hides what she's thinking very well.

Yesterday we were cooped up with everyone while traveling to the next stop on tour. The sun was still below the horizon when our plane took off. It was a small jet, but we had it to ourselves. Despite the early departure, Monica still managed to spend the entirety of the flight talking on the phone. Even if she hadn't, there was no way we would have been able to have the conversation I'm wanting to have—not with all the prying ears.

Trying to hide that I was annoyed, I'd spent the flight filling out a crossword puzzle with Lennon. Of course, it wouldn't have taken us the whole flight if she'd let us just *peek* at some of the answers at the back of the newspaper, but she insisted we do it all on our own. She's a glutton for pain, I guess.

Regardless, I played along. I needed a distraction, something to stifle the impulse to rip the Bluetooth earpiece out of Monica's ear and have her tell me what we're up against right then and there.

But now, I've waited long enough. I've bided my time, but

my patience has reached its limit. I need to know what this label has on Nash—and more importantly what Monica plans to do about it.

Getting to go on tour with Nash has been one of the best experiences of my life. I've always known Nash loves music. Seeing him on stage, however, with the woman he loves waiting in the wings, I'm able to appreciate a whole other side of him. He lives and breathes music. It's his life—next to Nora. I won't let anyone take that from him—especially a balding fifty-year-old who is trying to hide the fact that he's aging and can no longer get his dick up.

Nash is halfway into his set for the night. The air in Indianapolis is chillier than at our previous stops. The fans don't seem to care—they go nuts for Nash and his performance. I've seen this same set countless times now, but it's still surreal to see him up there, hearing thousands of fans chant his name.

I've been standing by Tyson, another questionable hire by Nash's team, but only because this guy seems to have rocks for brains. He's spent the last three minutes questioning if eggs should be categorized as dairy or not. I think I've lost a few brain cells listening to him carry on, but I'm trying to keep my eyes peeled for Monica.

I figured during the concert would be the perfect time to corner her, to get information from her lips. My plan has so far been unsuccessful, considering I haven't seen her since well before the show. She was in her element, going over a few pre-concert details with Nash—such as the city we're in and the name of the stadium we're playing. I assumed I'd see her again as soon as the show started since typically she watches most of the show from the sidelines, but not tonight.

Having enough of the dairy debacle conversation, I leave Tyson to ponder life's hard-hitting questions on his own. I go in search of Monica, walking through the tunnel behind the stage in the direction of the dressing rooms.

I hear her before I see her. The sound of heels clacking against the concrete floors mixed with phone notifications gives away her location. Just as I round the corner and find her walking down an empty hallway, she answers her phone.

"Monica Masters," she answers, stopping in the middle of the space. The call must not be too important judging by the way she checks something on the screen while someone speaks to her through her earpiece.

A couple stagehands pass by me, but they barely seem to notice my presence, both of them fully enamored, trying to untangle a wire as they make their way to the stage.

Stepping into the same hallway as Monica, I head toward her. The moment her eyes land on me, she stiffens. She lifts a finger in the air, gesturing for me to wait. I give her some time, but one minute turns into another and it seems like a boring conversation anyway.

Losing my patience, I crowd her space. I reach for her phone, but she swats me away. It looks like her eyes might bulge out of her head as she looks up at me in anger.

"That sounds great," she tells the person on the other line. Her hands go behind her back, protecting the phone from me.

Hang up, I mouth.

She shakes her head.

"Suit yourself," I whisper, lunging at her for the phone. Getting a hold of it, I press 'end' before shoving the phone into the pocket of my jeans.

"Did anyone ever teach you any manners?" she scolds. Her arms are quick as she darts out, trying to get the phone from my pocket. She isn't quick enough. All I have to do is sidestep in one direction until it's out of her reach once again.

I can't help but laugh. "I could ask you that same exact question."

"That was a very important phone call," she says, crossing her arms over her chest. I know others may be intimidated by her, especially when she has the look in her eyes that she's giving me right now. The way her eyes narrow, and her meticulously lined lips form a perfectly straight line shows exactly how upset she is with me. It's a shame I don't give a damn.

"Then you might want to call them back later," I respond nonchalantly.

Closing her eyes, she takes a deep breath. Her lips move as she whispers something to herself. With her eyes closed, I can see the different colors of eyeshadow she's placed on her eyes. I wonder how long it takes for her to get ready in the morning—assuming she even sleeps.

"Saying a prayer?"

Her rage-filled eyes pop open. "No just reminding myself that I have way too much going on today to risk getting arrested for murder."

"I'd love to see you try," I retort.

"Give me back my phone," she says. As if on cue, the phone rings in my pocket. Her eyes dart to the outline of it in my jeans.

I smile. "Stop looking there, little liar."

"Stop stealing other people's things, *little* brother." Judging by the smug look on her face, she thinks she's thrown a jab my way with a nickname of her own.

"You're not going to find anything little down there."

Shaking her head, she grimaces. "You're disgusting."

A group of people walk by us, reminding me that we're in public. I smile at them as they walk by, playing it cool. As soon as they disappear, I look around us. Finding a door a few feet away from us, I grab Monica by the elbow and usher her in that direction.

"What do you think you're doing?" she hisses, trying to claw my hand off her. Her nails are sharp as she scrapes at my skin, but my hold on her doesn't loosen.

My free hand jiggles the handle of the door, happy to find it unlocked. I pull her into the room and slam the door behind us.

For a moment, we're blanketed in darkness. My fingers reach out searching the wall for a light switch. Flicking it up, the room becomes illuminated, showing off a raging Monica in front of me.

"I'm going to scream," she says slowly, her eyes on the door as if she's planning her escape.

"Don't get any ideas," I say, taking in the room. It appears to be some sort of storage closet. There's countless speakers and wires littered throughout. A majority of the floor space is taken up, leaving only about a foot between us.

"Let me out," she demands.

I lean against the door, letting her know she isn't leaving—not yet. "I will as soon as you stick to your word. You said you'd tell me what's happening with Nash. You said I could help."

She mutters something under her breath. Something sounding really close to *relentless asshole*, which makes me smirk.

She's not wrong.

Finally, she sighs dramatically. "I distinctly remember telling you *I* would find *you* when I had time to discuss the matter."

I take a short step to close the distance between us. "I gave you two days. Your time is up."

Her lips rub together as she looks around the tiny room. "You couldn't have picked somewhere a little...*nicer*...to assault me?"

My finger taps at my wrist. "Time's ticking. It's going to be really awkward if we walk out of this closet together after the show."

She throws her arms up in defeat, two simple silver bracelets jingle on her wrist with the motion. "Fine! What do you want to know?"

"Everything."

Her eyebrow arches. "Not necessary."

"We'll see about that," I counter.

Monica lets out one last sigh before beginning.

"A few years ago, before the tour that Nora danced on, Roy approached me with an ultimatum. Nash was being a pain for the label, doing nothing but dragging their name through the dirt. Typically, Coleman Records would turn a blind eye to it, but Nash wasn't creating music during that time either. That wasn't working for them."

She pauses when her phone rings again from my pocket. "Are you going to give that back?" she questions, annoyed.

"Not until I feel like you've told me everything." Just to piss her off, I pull the phone out of my pocket. Thumbing through the countless missed alerts she has, I wonder how one person can get so many messages in such a short amount of time. I can't see what any of them say, it only says their names due to the privacy settings.

"Have I ever mentioned how much I loathe you?" she asks, her eyes trained on the phone in my hand.

"Once or twice," I answer, tucking the phone back in my pocket. "Now keep talking."

She doesn't try to hide the roll of her eyes. "Since Nash wasn't writing music, the label first said they'd have people write songs for him. I'd offered the idea to Nash, desperate to get *something* out of him, but you know him. He said no."

"He's always taken pride in writing all of his own songs since leaving the band."

She nods her head in agreement.

Nash and his friends were discovered by someone in the industry while they performed at a middle school talent show. The band toured for years, they'd become a household name in an instant. It all went great until one of the guys, Nash's best friend, was caught sleeping with Nash's long-term girlfriend at the time. The band broke up and Nash went solo—so did his ex-best friend, but he hasn't had the same success that Nash has.

The album that Nash wrote after leaving the band sold millions of copies. People ate up the story of Nash's broken heart, and the drama that ensued after his very public breakup and betrayal. I remember trying to talk to my brother during that time, but he was in a dark place. And I was just a kid in high school—I didn't know what to do. Especially since my brother was thousands of miles away, doing his own thing in LA. Ever since then, Nash has been adamant that he only performs songs that *he* writes. It's his thing. I can see why he'd turn down the label for suggesting anything else.

"I knew before speaking with him that he would say no. But I had hope, this conversation with Roy and the other label executives was more tense ever. Nash wasn't making them the money he had been at the time. They weren't okay with that. When I told them he wouldn't do it, all hell broke loose."

Her phone rings for the umpteenth time, but this time she doesn't seem to notice, too deep in her thoughts.

"What does that mean?"

She looks back at me. "It means that's when the threats really began. Roy said if Nash couldn't get him an album quickly, Coleman Records would drop him."

"Is that such a bad thing?" I blurt. "I mean, I think any label would take him on, even if he'd been dropped by someone else."

"It doesn't work like that. When Nash signed with Coleman Records, he also signed a contract—one where the label owns all of his masters. Meaning Coleman Records owns every single song Nash has ever recorded with them—everything he's done during his solo career."

"But he'd still make *some* money off the songs, right? Even if he left?"

"Technically yes, he'd make money as the songwriter, but he'd also be lining the pockets of the people who dropped him. He'd also lose control of that music."

"Why would they ever do that? It would still make them money…"

"Because the people at the label—Roy, for instance—are just

terrible, awful people. They care about money, yes, but they're also swimming in it thanks to artists like Nash. If they wanted to be petty, they could—and probably would—block him from ever performing those songs again due to the re-record clause Nash signed in his contract."

"Why would he ever sign something like that?" I question. Nash was still pretty famous when he went solo. Surely he had the ability to get good lawyers, ones that would advise him against signing something like that."

An emotion I didn't expect to ever see washes upon her face. She looks...sad. Almost regretful. Her lips turn down in a frown and she avoids my gaze. "I was there when he signed it. That kind of contract is typical for any artist—well it used to be. At the time, we didn't know any better. We didn't think about how absurd it would be that a label could have control of the sole work of an artist both lyrically and performance wise."

"So if they dropped him, it would mean that everything he's done in his solo career...wouldn't be his? He wouldn't have anything to perform, anything to tour with...nothing?"

Her head nods sadly. "That's exactly what it means."

"So what happened next?"

She cocks her head slightly, looking at me as if it was a dumb question. "You know what happened next, Aiden. It's the thing you hate me for—I hired Nora to break Nash's heart."

16
MONICA

Aiden watches me carefully as my words linger in the air. I give him time to think about everything I've told him so far. For so long, I allowed him to paint me as the bad guy because I was wrong. But I was wrong for mainly the right reasons. Selfishly, I wanted to keep my job. But I also didn't want to see Nash get screwed over by his label.

He runs his fingers through the brown locks of his hair, keeping his hand at the top of his head as he stares at me. His eyes roam over me as if he's trying to plan a way to crawl inside my head and pick away at every thought I've ever had. Just when I think he may not respond, he does.

"Tell me why you did it. What you thought would happen…" his voice is low, and raspy.

"Well quite honestly, I didn't think it would ever work. I thought it was a terrible plan—but it was the only one I could think of. Nash's first album about his ex was some of the best writing I'd ever heard—and I grew up surrounded by music. I thought if I could just give Nash an *ounce* of the feelings he once had for Taylor, that maybe he could get back on track. Back to the thing he loves."

"You wanted to break his heart," Aiden says angrily. "And

you thought the best idea was to let him go through the same pain he'd been through before, knowing just how close he came to drinking himself to death."

"I didn't think Nora would get *that* close to him. She was cute, smart—immensely talented. I'd imagined—even hoped—that she'd catch his eye. I even forced them together by convincing the team they needed to perform a solo together. But I thought they'd have a fling, Nash would lose interest like he always does and then he'd move on, inspired by Nora to at least write a few songs about their brief lust affair."

"But that didn't happen. He fell in love with her. She broke him. He was in rehab for months, Monica. *You* broke him."

"I did," I admit. "When I realized how deeply he'd fallen for her, it was too late. The damage had been done."

"You got what you wanted," he says, finishing the story for me. At least, the parts of the story he knows. There's still more to it, and I know he'll dig deeper to find it out. "You broke his heart, and he wrote you one hell of an album because of it."

All I can do is nod. There's not much else I can say. "I still think a Nash with a broken heart might be better than a Nash that couldn't ever perform—or fully own—his songs again. It seemed like the lesser of two evils at the time..."

And there it is. The choice I made, and the reason I made it. I had to decide between Nash losing everything he'd recorded over the years—losing his identity essentially, or to force inspiration on him so we could appease the label.

I never thought telling Aiden would feel like a relief, but I also didn't expect to feel like I do. He knows the raw, real truth now. If he still hates me, it won't be because he's made up some wild story in his head about how evil and selfish I am. It'll be because the choice I made was *actually* an unforgivable mistake.

These feelings are foreign to me. I've spent years not giving a damn what other people think or how they view me and my decisions. But right now, as he stands just a breath away from me, I'm desperate for him to understand my reasoning.

Neither of us speak. The bass from the concert makes the walls of the storage closet *thump*. If it weren't for the noise, he'd probably be able to hear the pounding of my heart.

I shift the weight on my feet, my arches beginning to ache from being in one position for so long. He takes notice, his eyes shifting down to the floor. When he looks back up, he doesn't look me in the eye. His focus stops just above my collar bone.

Reaching out, he wraps a hand around my neck. I have no idea what he's doing, how things have turned so quickly, but I don't rush to stop him either. Maybe I deserve this.

His other hand follows the same motion until both hands are grasping my throat. His thumbs press hard into the tender skin beneath my jaw.

"You're nervous," he says, looking at where my skin pulsates beneath his grip. "I can feel your pulse racing."

His thumb presses into the spot he's talking about even harder. The pressure slightly obstructs my airway, but I'm too lost in watching him to do anything to stop it.

"Tell me, Monica," he says. "Do I make you nervous?" As if to monitor my reaction, he digs his fingers deeper into the throbbing pulse on my throat.

I look him dead in the eye, managing to shake my head. My eyes water from the pressure, but I don't dare look away from him—I won't back down. I won't let him know that he's the first person to make me feel like this. Not only nervous—but exhilarated.

"You're such a little liar," he says. His hands loosen around my neck, but only just enough for me to catch my breath. He keeps them around my neck, a silent warning—a threat.

One hand moves slowly down to my exposed skin as he flattens it over my chest, right at the location of my racing heart. "Interesting," he says, more to himself than me. "I can feel it here, too. You're nervous. Is it because you're lying to me, and you're nervous I'll find out? Or that you've finally told the truth, and you're scared of how I'll react?"

I refuse to answer him. I'm not lying. Every word I've told him is true. My heart is racing because I'm anxious to hear what he'll make of what really happened—if it changes his opinion of me at all.

"You can deny all you want. It doesn't matter," he whispers. He leans closer—way too close. The bridge of his nose brushes my cheek. His next words are said against my ear. "I'll know the truth."

"Get away from me," I manage to bite out, but there isn't any conviction in my words. My mind tells me to get the hell out of this room, to forget about whatever is happening right now, forever. But my body fails to come to the same conclusion as my head. My feet stay planted, my skin eager to see where he'll touch next.

He laughs, a low rumble from inside his chest. One that vibrates against me with the nearness of his body. "And miss out on the fun? On seeing you squirm? I would never."

The pads of his fingertips from the hand on my chest slide underneath the collar of my blouse. Whatever is happening, I need to stop it.

"You're going to despise me for what happens next, Monica. But I'm so curious to see how far you'll let me go—how far you'll bend."

My eyebrows pinch together. Before I have time to ask him what he means, his hands find my throat again. Roughly, he lifts my chin toward him. Before I have time to process what's going on, his lips are crashing against mine in a frenzy.

I push against his chest, trying to separate him from me. Even if I managed to put space between our bodies, there's no way I could get out of the grip he has on my face. He pins his mouth to mine, sealing our lips together.

His lips press powerfully against mine. The searing tips of his fingers press into my chin hard as his tongue dances across the seam of my lips. He squeezes, making my mouth open to his. He takes the opportunity immediately, his tongue expertly finding mine.

I lose all sense of myself. Angrily, I let my tongue fight his. Instead of pushing him away, my hands fist the fabric of his shirt. Pulling him against me, I play the same dangerous game as him. He wanted to see how far I'd let him go—to see how far I'd bend.

But what if I did the same to him? He's expecting me to stop him—to hate this and resist it. I do the opposite, refusing to give him the satisfaction. Our mouths declare war on one another, fighting to get the upper hand. Tilting my head, I find my bottom lip between his teeth. He bites down, looking at me through hooded eyelids as he pulls his head back slightly with my lip still caught between his teeth.

When I look up at him, he stops. In an instant, his hands drop from my throat. He backs away, a stunned look on his face. I smile, not giving any indication that I felt that kiss all the way down to my toes. The taste of iron coats my tongue. Putting my fingertips to my lips, I dab at them. When I pull away, I see a shade of red darker than the one on my lips.

That asshole bit hard enough to break skin.

I stare at the red on my fingers, looking up at him in anger. He focuses on the tips of my fingers for a moment before he looks up at me. His lips pull into a smile, one that doesn't show humor—one that's more predatory.

"Maybe I don't want to see you bend, little liar," he rasps. Licking his lips he says, "Maybe it's that I want to see you bleed."

"Never again." Using the back of my hand, I wipe my mouth, as if the motion can erase everything that just happened. No matter how many times I scrub, the taste of him—now mixed with iron—remains.

Tilting his head, his smile widens. It's hard to comprehend that I'd allowed those lips on mine moments ago. "Don't tempt me," he says cockily.

Rolling my eyes, I reach for the door. Just as I'm about to open it, he comes up behind me. There's a loud *slap* against the door as his palm flattens above my head.

He doesn't touch me, but his breath is burning hot against my neck. "Be careful, Monica. I don't have to like you to want to do that again." He slips my phone into my pocket.

Reaching over me, he pulls the handle of the door, slipping through it before I get the chance to respond.

I let it close behind him, my forehead falling against the cool wood. Taking a deep breath, I count backwards from ten, calming my racing heart. As the erratic beating slows, I'm bothered by the fact that I can still feel the sear of his fingertips against my throat—and I desperately want to feel them again.

17
AIDEN

Reeling from what just happened, I put as much distance between the storage room and myself as possible, not bothering to look back and find out if Monica is following me or not. I can't imagine that she is, but right now I don't care. Right now I'm putting as much space between her and I as possible.

When I'd cornered her, I hadn't expected for things to unfold the way they did. All I'd wanted to do was find out what Roy had on Nash, and how it involved Monica. I didn't plan on kissing her, or on being kissed back. I certainly didn't plan on not hating it. Having her at my mercy, feeling her racing pulse against my fingers as my grip closed tighter was invigorating. *Too* invigorating.

Shaking my head, my mind returns to Monica's confession. Even if she *was* somehow telling the truth, her actions are still unforgivable. If the people with Coleman Records were threatening Nash, Monica should've told him. He should have been the one to decide his own fate. Instead, she chose the option that made *her* look best. The option that protected her job and her future and threw him under the bus. And yet, as conniving as Monica is, it sounds like the label might be even worse.

Lost in my thoughts and rushing down the hallway, I accidentally smack right into somebody.

"Ow!" a familiar voice whines. I hear the shuffle of movement on the concrete below. Looking down, I find Lennon rubbing her shoulder, a fallen book hanging open at her feet.

Bending down, I pick up the book, handing it back to her as I straighten my posture.

"Sorry, Len." I offer an apologetic smile. "I didn't see you there."

She dusts off her clothes, huffing. "Well that part was clear."

I pull on the end of her long ponytail. "No need to be a smart-ass. What are you doing back here anyway?"

Lennon looks over my shoulder. I follow her gaze, anxious to see if Monica is heading in our direction. Luckily, I'm spared from awkwardly explaining this encounter to Lennon because the hallway is clear.

"I came looking for you," she points out—as if the answer was obvious. Just then her arm jerks, and it's only then that I notice the bouncing puppy at her legs.

Pepper, finally named after what seems like an eternity, barrels toward me, pulling the leash immediately from Lennon's grasp. Bending down, I scratch at the dog's ears. "Hi, sweet girl," I say. She licks my cheek from bottom to top excitedly.

"She was getting restless on the bus, so I thought I'd bring her in," Lennon explains, examining her book for damages.

"No one questioned you bringing her in?" I ask, standing up and grabbing the leash off the ground. This isn't the first time we've brought Pepper into a show, but the first time we *did* sneak her in, she ended up chasing after a poor stagehand that had a bag full of potato chips. The dog *loves* potato chips.

Lennon shrugs, moving to cradle the book in the crook of her elbow. "Sneaking in toward the end of the show pays off. No one noticed me. I typically go unnoticed," she adds as an afterthought, her voice somewhat sad.

"*I* notice you, Len," I tell her. Annoying her by pulling at her ponytail again. She swats my hands away, narrowing her eyes at me.

"Yeah well, I don't care if you notice me or not."

I put my free hand to my heart in disappointment. "You wound me, Lennon Mason."

"You'll get over it," she fires back. Her face changes as it seems she finally takes in the empty hallway around us. Any minute now workers will descend around us, preparing for the end of the show and packing the equipment up all over again.

"Hey, what were *you* doing back here?" she questions.

I look at the empty hallway behind us, grabbing her by the elbow to take us back toward the stage. "Don't worry about it," I answer immediately, pulling both her and the dog in the opposite direction of where I just came. I don't need Lennon seeing Monica leave that room and getting suspicious. I don't even know what the fuck just happened, there's no way I'm going to be able to explain it to somebody else.

What happened in the closet, stays there—at least for now. I'd be lying to myself if I said I didn't enjoy watching her mind and heart race under my grasp, or the power it gave me over her.

"You're acting weird." Lennon pulls her arm out of my grasp, but her steps still stay in line with mine. At least she attempts to, Pepper keeps cutting her off in an attempt to corral us for more pets.

"Says the girl who can't stop pining away after Nash's bassist."

She gasps. "I have no idea what you're talking about."

I laugh, noticing the slight pink tinge to her cheeks. "Keep telling yourself that, Len. Sometimes I wonder when you're reading those romance books if you're picturing Poe instead of one of those lame, unrealistic men in your stories."

Lennon stops in front of me, quickly turning to face me. "For your information, first, I don't *only* read romance. And second, there's no need to ever replace a fictional man with a real man. Fictional men are superior in every way. Always." She holds up her book for emphasis. On the cover, there's a shirtless model looking at the camera as if he hates it.

She taps on the abs of the model. "No one has abs like this in real life. Plus, no one grovels—or is more romantic—than a man in a romance story. And unlike real life, I get to choose if there's a happily ever after or not."

Pepper grows bored at my feet. She starts chewing on one of the laces of my boots. Pulling my shoe away from her, I start to walk once again with Lennon in tow.

Suddenly, the footsteps pattering behind me halt. "And here you are giving me grief," Lennon says.

Confused, I turn around. Clenching my jaw, I see the reason Lennon stopped.

Monica has decided to finally come out of hiding. Unfortunately for me, I wasn't able to get far enough away from the scene of the crime.

Monica looks furious as she approaches us. I'm impressed by the way she's pulled herself together. Minutes ago she was crumbling underneath my touch, but you'd never know that by looking at her now. She's straightened out her clothes, and there's not even a mark on her throat from my hands.

I revel in the thought of her still coming undone on the inside. She can put on a facade but she can no longer hide from me. I felt her racing pulse beneath her skin. I elicited a reaction from her. She was nervous. And now that I'm left with that information, I'm going to continue to mess with her. To see how far she'll let me push her.

Monica stops in front of us. She looks disapprovingly at the dog. "What is that thing doing inside the stadium?" her voice is cold.

"I brought her in here. I'm sorry, she just seemed bored on the bus."

I shoot a look toward Lennon. "Don't apologize to her," I say softly.

Monica doesn't look at Lennon, she pins her gaze on me. I can see the fire inside her eyes. It excites me. I wonder if she hates herself for what she just let happen. I hope she does. I could keep pretending that I did it just to put her on edge, but I had my own selfish reasons as well. Even though I hate how much I loved it, it was a new source of excitement. Different from the thrill I get when pushing her buttons.

"Do I have to remind you of what happened last time you brought that beast?" Monica lectures, reminding us of the potato chip debacle.

At the word *beast*, Pepper pops up, just now noticing Monica. She goes to try and lick her, but I don't give her enough slack on the leash for her to do so.

"We're fully aware. But Pep is a tour dog. She can go as she pleases. Even Nash has said so."

Monica looks to the ceiling, visibly annoyed. "I don't have time for this," she mutters. Looking back at me, she points to the leash in my hand. "Keep that thing on a leash this time." She storms off, the sound of her angry steps a warning to anyone in our vicinity.

"I have so many questions," Lennon says next to me.

"I won't answer a single one of them," I respond immediately.

18

AIDEN

I SLEPT like shit last night. Quite frankly, I've slept like shit for the past week. Ever since that stupid encounter in the storage closet, my dreams have been plagued with the reminder of Monica's lips against mine. The only reason I want to remember anything is because for once, I watched her walls come down. It was only a slightly lowered guard, but it was there. For once in her life, she wasn't in control of a situation.

I'd been the one in control. It wasn't because I had feelings for her, it was the *lack* of feelings for her that drove me wild. The fact I could dislike somebody so much but yet be so turned on by the way her neck felt in my grasp. In my sleep, I'd relived the feeling of watching her relinquish control to me. She'd let me grip at her throat until it was hard for her to breathe.

There was no way I was going to leave that closet without kissing her. I'd always been impulsive. I didn't think too deeply before I'd taken her lips in mine. I had to know how far she'd let me push it.

And to my surprise, she'd let me take it further than I'd expected her to. It should've been something I forgot about the second I left the closet. I should've been more focused on every-thing she'd admitted. I definitely should've been worried about the chokehold Nash's label has on him and his music—and I *am* worried about those things. This thing with Monica is a distraction I don't need now that I know what Nash is up against. But fuck did it feel good in the moment.

Now with a clearer mind, I know the two of us will have to work together to get Nash out of his contract, to ensure that he keeps the rights to every single one of the songs he's written and released. From the first time Roy stepped into the recording studio, I'd gotten bad vibes from him. I just had no idea how right I was. I'm furious that something like that could even happen to begin with. It's ludicrous to think an artist could write and record their own music, but not even own the rights to it.

All the information she'd told me has been swirling around in my mind for days—but so has the memory of the taste of her tongue, the bite of her nails in my forearms as she briefly pulled me in.

The constant reminders of the kiss pisses me off. It was a mistake—an experiment if you will. I wasn't going to deny the opportunity to show her who was in control, to remind her that she couldn't pretend with me. She needed to know that I could read her like an open book.

A furry snout digs into my cheek. The feeling of a wet nose pressed against my neck is enough to get me rolling over in my bunk.

"Not now," I plead with the mass of wiry fur next to me. Pepper whines again, bumping her nose against me even harder. Groaning, I sit up cautiously. The ceiling of the tour bus bunk isn't very high. I've sat up too quickly one too many times, ending up with a smack of the forehead to the wood of the bunk above mine.

As the weeks go by, Pep gets bigger and bigger, meaning sharing a small bunk with her is getting harder and harder. It doesn't help that she loves to sleep on her back with her limbs going in every direction. When she was small, it was adorable. But now it only means that I have less and less of the already small space.

The heel of my hand comes up to rub at my eyes. It must be early afternoon at this point, and Pepper probably needs a bathroom break.

For a dog that lived outside for what I imagine was all her life, she hadn't been too hard to potty train. There were only a few instances that she had an accident—one where she'd peed on Monica's shoes. If only I would've had a camera out to record Monica's reaction to the ordeal. She'd left the bus like a bat out of hell, muttering words under her breath in a sharp tone.

I stretch my legs as far as I can before my feet are pressing against the wall. There's a loud thump as Pepper eagerly wags her tail. She's quickly caught on that when I start stretching it means I'm getting up. She excitedly licks my face until I gently push her away.

"You've got to let me get up," I tell her, pulling the curtain of the bunk. Daylight blinds me instantly. I have to strain to keep my eyes open while they adjust to the bright light.

My feet find the floor of the bus and I can tell we're not moving. I maneuver my way out of the bunk, turning around to grab Pepper after. She's big enough at this point that she could probably jump down from the middle bunk, but out of habit I still grab her. I don't know for how much longer I'll be able to do it. At the rate she's growing she just as well might grow to be the same size as Clifford.

"Good morning, sunshine," Lennon says from a seat at the small table. For once she doesn't have a book in front of her, instead she's scrolling through photos on her phone. Her other hand wraps around a fork as she slowly puts food into her mouth.

"What time is it?" I ask.

Looking up, she smiles. "Oh I wasn't talking to you. I was

talking to sweet Pepper here." The fork drops to her plate as she reaches down to pet the dog on the head. Pep eagerly accepts the pets, her tongue lolling out in happiness at the attention.

Rolling my eyes, I repeat the same motion that Lennon does to the dog, but instead do it to her hair. "Well aren't you just chipper this morning? Does a certain bassist have you grumpy?"

She looks me up and down, not bothering to react to my words. "Did thoughts of a certain manager keep you up all night?"

I almost choke on my spit at her words. "What are you talking about?"

She smiles proudly. "You look like you didn't sleep at all. And if you're going to be a dick then I'm going to be one back."

I make a face at her. "Sometimes you feel like the annoying younger sister I never had."

"We're like the same age," she spits right back.

"You're still annoying."

"And you're still a dick."

I can't help but smile. I hadn't expected to like Lennon so much before going on tour, but she's quickly become one of my best friends. I like that she's okay with silence and doesn't sugarcoat anything. She is who she is, and I admire her for it. I'm just trying to figure out why she's decided to set her sights on a guy who barely seems to notice her—or at least notice the pining glances she throws his way.

"But you love me, regardless," I sing-song to her. My eyes search the bus until I can find my shoes. I find them by one of the couches. Sitting down, I pull one shoe on before starting the next.

"I think love is pushing it," she argues, going back to her food.

"You'd be bored as hell on this tour without me." I grab the leash hanging on one of the knobs of the cabinet. This gets

Pepper's attention immediately. She lunges toward me as I try to wrestle her to get the leash clipped to the collar.

"I'd get a lot more reading in if it weren't for you," Lennon responds to my earlier comment.

"You say that as if it's a good thing."

"To me it is."

My eyes narrow. "I just don't understand."

Lennon shrugs. "You don't have to. Now go let your dog out before she pees on the carpet again. I don't want to hear you getting another lecture from Monica."

As if on cue, Pepper pulls on her leash enough to almost yank my arm out of its socket. I let her guide me toward the stairs of the bus. Opening the door, I follow her out and let her lead the way to where she needs to do her business.

On our way to find some grass, several tour workers stop to pet her. She's become very popular on tour and it's going to her head. She walks the parking lot as if she owns the place. Once she's gone to the bathroom and we've walked around a bit to get her energy out, I finally pay attention to my grumbling stomach. I haven't eaten since last night, and I'm starving.

I guide us toward craft services, making sure I keep a firm grip on her leash. One too many times she's gotten away from me to chase food. I'm not going to let it happen today.

I make friendly conversation with some other staff members as I wait in line for lunch. Many different aromas hit my nose, but I can't quite peg what they're coming together to create. Judging by the line, it must be good because plenty of people wait their turn to load their plates.

When I step up to the table, I'm shocked to find a tray full of aluminum wrapped baked potatoes and different bowls of toppings.

This is what people are having for lunch?

Opening up the baked potato, I find it severely undercooked.

It's still hard in places, and I know that it wouldn't cut near as easily as it's supposed to if I were to run my knife through it.

The toppings are laughable. There's a thing of bacon bits that look stale. Plus the bacon is a strange color. If you're going to make a loaded baked potato, you need fresh, thick-cut bacon. There's also a steaming pot of chili that I'm assuming is supposed to top the potato, but it looks bland as fuck. All I can see is a brown liquid with a few floating beans at the top. There's nothing else even noteworthy in sight.

"This is embarrassing," I mutter under my breath. The girl next to me gives me an odd look as she spoons some wilted chives onto her potato.

"Don't eat that," I tell her. The chives look slimy, the potato looks hard as a rock and I can't even identify the other things she's piled onto her potato.

She pulls the plate close to her chest as she looks at me like I'm crazy. The girl scuttles away with her food, not sparing me another glance.

"Suit yourself," I say. Looking down at Pepper, I try to hand the potato to her, but the dog seems to have *some* standards because she turns her nose up at the food.

"I don't blame you," I laugh. I throw the potato in a nearby trash can and set out to find the person in charge. Someone has to do something about the terrible food they're using to poison all of their hard-working staff. Even if that someone is me.

19
MONICA

The thought flashes through my mind as I sit through yet another session of wedding planning for Nash and Nora. I've never given much thought to tying my life to someone else's forever—not until all of this planning for Nash and Nora started.

When I was a little girl, I wasn't dreaming about who I would marry and what my fairytale wedding would look like. I was dreaming about owning companies and learning how to talk business with men. That's how I was raised.

Since then, my sentiment toward marriage hasn't changed. I haven't had the time, or energy, to devote to any kind of long-term relationship. My thirtieth birthday is approaching and most of my peers from grade school and college have already married and settled down, many of them with children of their own running around. My life is different. I chase a pop star around the world, doing everything in my power to keep him at the top of the heap. And apparently my duties as manager know no limits since I've somehow been roped in to helping plan his wedding now.

After going through every meticulous detail with the wedding couple, I have no desire to plan my own.

Attending the meeting are the future bride and groom along with a few other members of Nash team, with the event coordinators listening in virtually. They're due to get married in a few weeks, and we're going over the logistics of how to make sure the media doesn't catch wind of any details and turn the wedding into a circus. We've been able to keep it all a secret for months now, and I intend to keep it that way.

Tyson convinced the couple to sell a few of their photos from the wedding to *Modern Millennium*, the most reputable magazine in LA, but other than that they've been set on keeping the event private.

I don't blame them. The world has been fascinated with their love story from the very beginning. Paparazzi have been relentless in trying to get someone—anyone—to divulge some information they can sell.

I've worked extremely hard with the rest of Nash's team to make sure that *doesn't* happen. Luckily, the couple chose a relatively unknown ceremony location in Southern California, rather than one of the typical wedding venues for celebrities. Paparazzi tend to stake out the usual hot spots, hoping to get lucky and find a weekend where somebody remotely famous gets married. That shouldn't be the case with their wedding.

The venue is tucked into a small town off the highway. It takes some time to get to, and you wouldn't know it was there if you weren't looking. The ceremony will take place on the terrace of the estate. It has the space to accommodate the growing guest list but still keep the intimate, classic feel that Nora is hoping for.

The reception will take place deeper into the estate where they have lush green vegetation that creates a canopy over guests. If somehow the press were to catch wind of the wedding by the time the reception started, they wouldn't have the ability to fly drones or helicopters over the event to get the photos they so desperately want.

Nash and Nora finish a conversation with the coordinators, some last-minute details they were needing.

Once they're done, I speak up. "Have you decided what you want to do about guests' phones?"

They give each other a look. Nora looks anxious as Nash speaks up. "As controlling as it sounds, we agree with you. We think it's best for guests to check their phones when they arrive."

Nora nods in agreement. I'd suggested the idea to them at their last meeting, but they'd needed time to think it over. They made sure to try and keep the guest list as small as possible in hopes people would keep their nuptials a secret, but you never know who may slip on the details. At least while people are in attendance, they won't mistakenly post details about the wedding or reception while it's still happening.

Guests will also be told to wait until a few days after the wedding to share any photos they'd like from the professional photographers who've been hired.

"I'm glad you came to that agreement," I tell them. My pen scratches against the notebook in front of me as I take notes for myself in relation to their decision. I'm going to have to make sure we have the appropriate amount of people checking the phones, making sure that everything is kept organized. Many celebrities may not be happy with the rule, but they should also be used to it. This mindset isn't something new to people who like to keep things private.

"I just hope no one gets mad at us," Nora pipes up.

I wave my hand through the air dismissively. "They'll get over it. It's pretty much standard for celebrities to do these days, especially with social media being so big now."

"What's the plan for the select people staying at the venue?" Nash asks. His hand reaches over Nora's shoulders, pulling her into his side. He tenderly gives her a kiss on the top of her head as he waits for my answer.

"That's up to you," I begin. There is room at the estate for a select number of people to stay the weekend of the wedding. This includes the immediate family of both Nash and Nora, important team members for Nash, as well as a few friends of the couple. "I'd suggest still asking them to leave their phones in their rooms or they can leave them in the checked area if they desire."

We continue to speak through the details for the next hour. Once we feel like we have a pretty good hold on the last-minute details as well as the wedding security, the group disbands. Everyone clears out except Nash, Nora, me, and Matt.

Once the bus is clear, Nash takes a deep breath. "Fuck am I ready to have this thing over with." He reaches his arms above his head stretching.

"Wow," Nora snorts, "you sound so excited about marrying me."

"I would've married you the day that I proposed if you would've let me," Nash states. He taps the tip of her nose. "But you made me wait and I've never pretended to love wedding planning. I just want to make you my wife already—put a few babies in you."

Nora rolls her eyes. "I blame Zoe for your persistence on wanting a baby."

Zoe is the child of Sebastian and Riley. Sebastian used to be one of Nash's main security guards before he went and fell in love with Nora's best friend, Riley. When they got pregnant with Zoe, Nash insisted on moving Sebastian from full detail to running the security of Nash's home. Sebastian still works closely with Matt on security detail for Nash, but instead of traveling with Nash like Matt and Sebastian's replacement, Monroe, Sebastian runs things from LA.

Nora is getting ready to say something when there's a loud

bang of the RV door. "Nash!" an all too familiar voice yells —Aiden.

"Are you in here?" he continues. The dog comes into view before Aiden does.

"Hi, Aiden," Nash yells from his spot at the table.

Aiden walks toward us with a purpose. The small amount of space from us to the door is eaten up quickly by his long legs.

His eyes flick to me for a moment before he looks back at his brother. The dog makes herself at home. She jumps up onto the couch and curls herself into a ball. I've briefly seen Aiden since the concert—and my temporary lapse of judgment. It's something I'd like to forget, something I hate myself for letting happen. Something I *despise* myself for *not* hating.

He messaged me once, telling me he wanted to talk more about what I'd told him. I ignored it. He knows what we're up against now. I don't need his help bringing Roy down. When—*if* —I do need his help, I'll let him know. Until then, I'm keeping my distance from him as much as possible.

"Nash the food you're serving your team tastes like dog shit," Aiden says, looking down at the dog. "No offense." His hands are on his hips as he focuses on his brother.

"Excuse me, what?" Nash looks to his brother in confusion.

"I was starving, so Pepper and I decided to hit up craft services to get a bite to eat. Imagine my horror when I realized the food you're serving isn't fit for a prison cafeteria."

Nash lets out a sigh and looks over to me. "What is being served today?"

Not knowing the answer to his question off the top of my head, I unlock the screen of my phone to find it. Even though I oversee a lot of Nash's life, I'm not in charge of *everything* that goes on during the tour.

"Don't bother looking," Aiden throws at me. "Today it was *loaded baked potatoes*." His fingers form quotation marks as he enunciates the name of the meal. "And it was the most pathetic excuse for food I've ever seen. I mean really Nash, the potato was nowhere near being cooked all the way and the chili most definitely came from a can that probably expired a year ago."

"I can speak with Tim about where we ordered from today," I say, looking at Nash instead of Aiden.

Aiden scoffs. "Well *Tim* needs to do a better job about finding places to cater in. Even Pepper wouldn't eat it—and she's a dog."

"Okay, so we're trusting the culinary expertise of an animal now?" I bite.

He scrunches his face up at me and flips me his middle finger.

"Mature," I say under my breath.

Nash groans. "Monica, I'll talk to Tim. I don't want to be serving our people *dog shit*," he says, repeating Aiden's eloquent adjectives from earlier.

"Tell Tim if he needs any help that I can be of service."

"That won't be necessary," I say, already thumbing through my phone to correct the issue.

"I wasn't talking to you," Aiden snaps.

Pausing from my phone, I look up to find his gaze pinned on me. His thick eyebrows are scrunched together on his forehead as he angrily looks at me.

"If you want to help find places that will cater in at each stop, I don't see the problem in that," Nash offers.

Aiden looks at me smugly, sticking his tongue out at me like a toddler.

"Nash, you already have a retired chef who has that exact job. I don't see the reason he needs any help."

"Well *I* see the reason," Aiden interrupts. "If he would've been there to look at the food being delivered, he would've known in an instant that it was disgusting."

"Tim doesn't travel with us," I explain. "He does everything from LA, having staff that travels with us to make sure the food is put out on time."

"There's the first problem. He should be here."

Nash finally speaks up again. "Since Tim isn't contracted to travel with us, I think it makes an easy transition for Aiden to help him out, to make sure everything looks good and to even assist in ordering food when needed."

"Plus, *Monica*," Aiden says my name as if it's a dirty word, "weren't you the one who said I should have some kind of job on this tour?"

My eyes narrow on him, hating how he's twisting my words and throwing them back at me. "Well, I..."

He puts a finger in the air, cutting me off. "I distinctly remember you saying something along the lines of how I'm just *mooching* off my brother."

My mouth snaps shut. I did say that, but I didn't expect him to find something he wanted to do on the tour. I thought he was fine with the extra free time he could use to make my life miserable from stop to stop.

Nash claps. "Well this seems settled, and the two of you are starting to give me a headache. I'll tell Tim that Aiden will be assisting him from here on out."

I bite my tongue, knowing there's no use in arguing any further. The decision is made. I rarely eat at craft services as it is. But now, I certainly won't be eating there.

I wouldn't put it past Aiden to poison my food.

20
AIDEN

Monica gathers all of her things in a hurry. Her eyes are cast down as she meticulously places two of the exact same pens in her purse. Next she slides her laptop and a notebook in. Her phone stays in her hand as she slings the purse over her shoulder.

Nash and Nora have already begun to strike up a conversation together. They seem off in their own little world as they pay no attention to either Monica or me.

Monica doesn't bother to even look at me as she turns her body to fit through the narrow walkway to the door. I don't move, purposely making her have to work even harder to make it by me.

She says nothing as she moves right past me and exits the bus. However, it's been too long since we've discussed the sleaze ball—Roy—so I chase after her.

She's already two buses down by the time I make it out the door.

"Monica!" I yell, walking quickly toward her.

"I've had enough of you for one day." She doesn't look back at me, her feet taking her on a mission even though the heels she wears are death traps.

"I don't give a shit," I say, catching up to her. She doesn't give any indication that she's going to stop, so I shove my body in front of hers, blocking her way.

Monica stops before bumping into me. She clings her purse to her side, letting out an annoyed sigh. "Shouldn't you be playing chef? You got what you wanted. Why must you bother me further?"

The whole time she speaks, she won't look at me. She stares at the space over my shoulder. Her tone is bored, dejected, but I can't help but wonder why she can't bring herself to look in my direction.

Reaching out, I grab her chin, directing her gaze on me. "I have more to say."

She slaps my hand away immediately, taking a step back. Her eyes pinball to check our surroundings. Luckily, no one is in the vicinity. That doesn't stop her from taking a few steps until she's hidden between the front of one tour bus and the back of the next.

I follow her. As soon as I'm also hidden in the space with her, she's pointing a manicured finger at me. "Don't ever touch me again, Aiden Pierce."

My cheeks twitch. "Why, Monica? Are you afraid you're going to like it too much like you did the first time?"

She bites down on her lip. Typically, she's got them painted the same red color every day, but today the shade is darker—more brown than red. "Never once did I say I liked it," she says with an even tone.

This time I actually do laugh. "There are those lies again. You might want to be careful, they fall so freely from your mouth you may *actually* believe them."

"It isn't a lie. I think Teddy in the sixth grade kissed better than you do, and he obviously had a lot less practice."

I take one step forward, which in return she takes two steps back. We play the same game until yet again, she's left pinned in a corner with nowhere to go, and I'm left with the upper hand.

"It's okay, you can deny what happened all you want. You can hate yourself for what happened, I wouldn't blame you. I'm disgusted by how good you tasted. But let's get one thing straight, Monica…" I act like I'm going to touch her, and she doesn't move to push me away. My fingertip is just about to trace over her jutting collarbone when at the last second I let my hand drop. "You loved everything about that kiss. Even if it made you hate yourself after because of it."

I back up, needing space away from her before I let the conversation I want to have with her be redirected for the second time. I keep walking backward until my calves are bumping into the fender of the bus across from her. This leaves a good amount of distance between us, but with her, even a battlefield isn't enough space.

"Sometimes I don't understand how anybody can tolerate you," she finally gets out. Her words aren't as smooth as they normally are. It's as if my words got to her, even if only by the slightest bit.

"Funny, I've thought the *same* thing about you. Countless times actually."

"If you're here to talk about Roy, then I've got nothing new to share with you. I haven't heard from him, but I'll let you know when I do."

I click my tongue. "You're not going to get away that easily. You've told me the *why* behind your actions. But you haven't told me the *what* or the *how*. What are you actually going to do about Roy and how are you going to do it?"

She dusts off the front of her dress, buying herself time. Someone shouts something in the distance, but it's too far from us for me to decipher what exactly they're saying.

"I haven't thought it through all the way," she answers. "What I need from you is to make friends with other artists at the label. You won't really have the opportunity to do that until the wedding in a few weeks. Hence the reason I haven't wanted to see your face."

I smile, letting my hand circle my face. "Who wouldn't want to see this face?"

"Charming," she retorts.

I wink just to try and piss her off. "So we're just supposed to sit idly for the next month until the party?"

"That's exactly what *you* are going to do unless I tell you otherwise. I'm going to continue to do some digging and consult with lawyers."

Nodding, I think about her words. I want to be able to do something about it right now, but I understand why this has been a slow game for Nash and Monica. There's a lot at stake here and if I need to wait another month to try and help my brother, then so be it.

I can be patient if it means taking down the asshole who thinks he can steal my brother's music.

Monica pops her head into the pathway between the buses. She looks in one direction then the next before a taking a step out into the clearing.

"And Aiden?" she says, looking over her shoulder.

"Hm?"

"Don't let your brother know about any of this. We want him focused on his upcoming wedding and his music—nothing else."

Nodding, for once I can agree with the she-devil. "Wasn't planning on telling him," I say.

She nods her head once and then disappears between the buses. After she leaves, my mind races with what I could do in the meantime to try and help my brother.

21
MONICA

This was supposed to be a calm evening. I had plans of getting a bit of work done and then possibly doing a face mask while I drink a glass of wine. The tour bus was supposed to be empty, everyone having plans to go out and explore the city. We were all sitting on the bus at the end of the day. It'd actually been a calm afternoon, something we all needed before the wedding next weekend.

Then it became my worst nightmare.

Nora and Lennon were chatting about birthdays. Lennon's is coming up in a few months, and we'll be abroad when it's time. They're discussing what plans they'll make for it when all of a sudden Nora looks in my direction.

"Monica, when is your birthday?" she asks. Her head lays on her sister's shoulder as Lennon looks at something on her phone.

"Not important," I answer dismissively.

This piques her interest. "You'll be turning thirty, right? When is it?"

Nash laughs from where he sits on the opposite couch. He's got a guitar strung around him. Nash, Poe, and Landon have been having a song-writing session as we all went about our separate business. "Her birthday is next week," Nash offers calmly.

The dirty look I give him comes naturally.

Nora gasps, sitting up straight. "Your birthday is next week and you haven't said *anything?*"

Sighing, I shut my laptop. I was trying to finish off an email, but it seems like I'm going to have to explain my disdain for birthday celebrations instead.

"I've never really been into birthdays," I explain. My family wasn't huge on birthdays, at least not the way they should've been. My sister and I always had elaborately themed birthday parties, but they were never about us. They were just another event for our parents to conduct business. I'd only ever enjoyed one birthday in my entire life—my eighteenth.

I was young and naive, thinking I was in love with a boy. I wasn't, but at the time, he was the center of my world. We'd had the best day together. I'd eaten way more sugar than one person ever should, I'd been silly and goofy as we attempted to sit through a movie at the theater. I'd thought the day was perfect, until later that night he'd broken up with me in front of everyone at my own birthday party.

And then, he started dating my sister.

They're still married to this day.

After that, I treated birthdays like another day of the year—equally as unimportant. More time to get stuff done. It's just one date in the span of three-hundred-and-sixty-five days. It's nothing special.

"Monica, you're starting a new decade. It's a big deal!"

"Nora, you're never going to convince her that her birthday means anything," Nash adds. "I've tried for years to celebrate with her. She shoots me down every single time."

Nora throws her hair over her shoulder. "Well those birthdays weren't as important as turning thirty. We're going to celebrate."

Blood drains from my face. "Absolutely not."

My reaction makes Aiden look over. Earlier, he'd been spewing out questions to Nash about what food should be served when we're overseas. He's been relatively quiet the entire day, busy doing his own work for the tour. My luck has run dry, however, because the wide grin on his face lets me know that I'm screwed. "It would be cruel for us to not celebrate your birthday." He makes the words sound sincere, but I know him by now. He's salivating at the thought of making me uncomfortable, loving the idea of throwing an unwanted birthday celebration for me.

Nash looks from Aiden to me. "Aiden, are you actually being nice?"

"Of course not," I say. "He only wants to celebrate because I hate the idea."

Aiden grasps his chest. "Monica, I would *never*. Everyone deserves a birthday celebration."

"Is that so?" Lennon pipes up from her corner.

Traitor. She's supposed to be the quiet one, on my side by default because she keeps her mouth shut and stays out of other people's business.

"We were going to go out anyway," Nora says sweetly. "Now we'll just have something to celebrate!"

"Celebrate Lennon," I offer, remembering their earlier conversation. "Or anyone else's birthday that is relatively soon."

"It's *your* birthday we're wanting to celebrate tonight." Nora's tone is matter of fact. She doesn't make it seem like she's going to let it go, which is a huge problem for me.

"I have plans tonight."

Aiden clicks his tongue. "Staying in doesn't count."

I resist the urge to flip him off. It's entirely un-ladylike and very unprofessional, but it's also incredibly tempting.

Nash sets his guitar to the side. "Monica, it looks like we'll be celebrating your birthday whether you like it or not."

"Or not," I spit. I appreciate Nora's sentiment for wanting to celebrate my birthday, but it isn't needed. I'm perfectly fine pretending it isn't happening. There's no reason for me to be excited about aging another year. I have to work twice as hard in the gym to maintain the same figure I had in my twenties and have to spend triple the amount of money on skin care to pretend that I'm not getting another year older. All things I'm not enthused about celebrating.

"Never in my life did I think I'd be going to a party for Monica Masters," Landon chimes in.

"You'd use anything for an excuse to party," Poe sarcastically responds.

Landon gives Poe a betrayed look. "Celebrating Nash's bitchy manager's birthday is where I thought I drew the line." He winces, as if he's just remembering I'm only sitting a few feet away from him. "No offense."

I shrug, just now noticing a small chip in my nail polish on my thumb. "None taken."

"So it's settled then?" Nora's voice is way too excited. Her sentiment is completely opposite of mine. All I feel is dread at the unfolding plan.

"Oh it's settled." Aiden leaps off his chair, clapping his hands together. "We're going all out for Monica's birthday tonight. First, we need to find somewhere to go."

"I've heard Monica loves karaoke bars," Nash adds, laughing.

"You've got to be kidding me," I groan out, remembering the *one* time Nash convinced me to go to one with him. It was in our early days of working together. We were still trying to figure out our groove, planning how we were going to get him to the top on his own. He'd just released his first single and wanted to celebrate. I'd reluctantly agreed to go out with him. Somehow, Nash had convinced me to do a karaoke song with him.

It had been posted on every media outlet.

Me. Singing.

I sounded like a dead cat performing with Nash. It was silly of me to think that someone wouldn't send in a candid video of a budding solo artist to the media. I'd received a message from both my sister and my father, telling me in their condescending, passive aggressive way that it looked like I was having *so* much success with my new endeavors.

Them seeing the video was worse than the millions of people that saw it online.

Lost in my past embarrassment, I don't hear the rest of the plans that ensue. I tune in just in time to hear Aiden mutter enthusiastically, "Our night is definitely ending at a karaoke bar."

Kill me now.

22
AIDEN

Monica has been over served.

She started the night refusing to take a sip of alcohol, but when we showed up at the karaoke bar, all hell broke loose.

Nora had managed to rent a private room. The only people here are Nash, Nora, Lennon, Landon, Matt, Monroe, Poe, Monica, and me. When Landon got on the microphone, improvising a birthday song for Monica that was titled *Birthday Bitch*, she'd declared she needed a drink.

That was about four drinks ago.

The bartender here must make a strong martini because I've never seen Monica so…normal.

About one drink ago, I'd known she was approaching her limit when she'd finally agreed to wearing the birthday sash Nora had found at the last minute. She'd spent the entirety of the evening—up until then—telling Nora there was no way in hell she'd wear it. Apparently, there *was* a chance, given enough alcohol.

The room we rented is large, clearly intended for larger gatherings than what we've brought tonight. I'm shocked it was even available but leave it to Nora to pull enough strings to make it happen.

There's a large booth that spans the entire far wall, large enough to seat twenty people with its wingspan. On the opposite wall, there's a makeshift stage with a projector screen behind it. Words appear on the screen as both Nash and Nora sing a song together. The rest of our party sit at the cocktail tables in front of the stage, hooting and hollering as a tipsy Nora grinds against Nash. Nash laughs, he's sober as can be, but is still clearly enjoying himself for the night.

I look at Lennon, who watches her sister with a soft smile. She sits at a table on her own, sometimes throwing glances at Poe. Per usual, Poe doesn't seem to notice Lennon looking in his direction. He's too busy telling a story to Monroe to pay her any mind.

Matt sits away from us all, reading a newspaper, seemingly uninterested with what we're doing, but I know otherwise. He's on high-alert with Nash in public. The newspaper is just a farce.

The booth under me lets out a *poof* when a body falls down at my side. Looking over, I find a grinning Monica. The liquid from her drink sloshes from the top as she tries to bring it to her lips. Quickly, I grab the martini glass, handing her a bottle of water instead.

"You're not very fun," she mumbles, working hard to untwist the cap of the bottle.

I let her struggle a few more seconds before I take the bottle from her. Untwisting the lid and handing it back to her, I say, "Never in my life did I think *you'd* be telling *me* I'm no fun."

She hiccups. "Maybe I'm just full of surprises."

"Or maybe you're just drunk."

Shrugging, she looks down at her sash. It's fallen down her shoulder, dangerously close to becoming an oversized belt instead of a sash. Her fingers run over where the sixteen in the *sweet sixteen* has been crossed out, *thirtieth* is written in Nora's neat handwriting above. "Maybe birthdays aren't so bad," she says softly.

The soft tone of her voice unnerves me. I'm used to the bite that is always laced with her words. Right now, there is no hint of that at all.

"Why did you think they were bad in the first place?"

"I had my heart broken on my eighteenth birthday."

Her words catch me off guard. I'd always envisioned Monica without any heart at all. I figured she'd have to be heartless to do what she did to Nash, but as I've gotten to know the situation, my feelings toward her have become complicated. What she did was terrible and I'm not sure if I was Nash I could've forgiven her the way that he did. But the reasons I thought she did it weren't correct at all.

Maybe the heartbreaker actually *has* a heart.

"Monica, I thought you didn't have a heart," I confess.

She adjusts her position in the booth, her arm brushing against my skin. My body lights up at the small touch, becoming all too aware of her closeness.

Why must my body have such a visceral reaction to her?

"Maybe I do, maybe I don't. All I know is at the time, it felt like he'd destroyed it."

"Was it a boyfriend?"

She nods. "Yes. My first. I was young and dumb and had the most beautiful day with him…until it all came crashing down."

I try to picture Monica at eighteen. That would've been twelve years ago. Twelve years ago I hadn't even hit puberty. It's crazy to think about the differences in our lives, the gap in time we have between us. At eighteen, I'd broken my fair share of hearts. It's just hard to imagine her at that age, hard to imagine her being vulnerable enough to have her heart broken.

"What happened?" I finally ask, curiosity getting the best of me.

"He broke up with me in front of every single person at my birthday party."

I wince. "Damn. That's cruel."

She shrugs. The movement causes her jean-clad thigh to press against mine. Looking down, it occurs to me this is the most casual I've ever seen her dressed. I've never seen her in a pair of blue jeans. Paired with a simple t-shirt, I'm realizing that Monica looks better dressed down than I care to admit.

"You probably think I deserved it," she offers, her tone a bit sad.

Probably. At least, I would've thought that when the tour first started. Now I don't know what to think. My hate for her has been muddled with something else...something I don't care to explore or delve into.

"I think it was a dick move of him," I offer, taking a sip of my water bottle.

She lets me off with ignoring her comment. If she was sober, she was bound to have pressed on. But the Monica sitting next to me is different, more unhinged—more honest.

"The real dick move was when my sister started dating him."

My eyes widen. Looking over to her, I find her eyes pinned on the stage. Somehow, Poe has convinced Lennon to get up there with him, and the two of them butcher a popular rap song.

"Your sister dated the guy who broke up with you on your birthday?"

"If we're being technical, she married him."

"You're joking."

She bites her lip, running it between her teeth. "Have you ever known me to tell a joke?"

Holy shit. What kind of family did she grow up with? No wonder she's so cold and callous. It seems like some of her issues may run deeper than I'd expected. I thought she was a bitch just to be a bitch, but I'm slowly learning nothing about Monica is that simple.

"That's entirely fucked up," I finally get out after wondering what other baggage she's carrying around in that head of hers. I shouldn't want to know any of it, it shouldn't matter. But here I am, wanting the backstory on the woman I'm supposed to hate.

"It is what it is. No point dwelling on it. Although, birthdays afterwards haven't really been all that special. I made sure of it."

"Why?"

"Because if something is special to you, it can be taken away and used against you. Better to not create attachments."

"That's a sad way to live." I feel too sober to be having this conversation with her. But I'd told Nash I would go sober with him tonight, and I plan on keeping my word. It feels odd to be next to her, hearing her speak so freely when I know she'll regret every word in the morning.

"Maybe. But it's safe." Another loud hiccup leaves her throat.

"You're going to hate yourself for telling me all of this in the morning."

"Add it to the list of things I hate myself for when it comes to you, Aiden Pierce."

The rawness of her words catches my attention. It makes my stomach do a weird sort of flip, making me feel uneasy. "Well since you probably won't remember this in the morning, I hate myself for so many things when it comes to you, Monica."

I look over at her, finding her already watching me. Her brown eyes are wide. It looks like she wants to say something. I hang at the edge of my seat, wondering what is about to come out of her mouth. My hopes are thwarted quickly, because all too soon she shakes her head, looking in the direction of the stage.

"I still hate you, you know," she says.

I laugh, wondering what the fuck is happening. "I hate you too," I offer.

She stands up, walking toward the stage. Before she gets too far, she turns around. "The reasons I hate you are just far more complicated now." Then she walks away, leaving my head spinning.

23
MONICA

IT ISN'T EVEN ten in the morning and I'm already exhausted. It felt like the day would never come, but finally, it's Nash and Nora's wedding day. During this entire process, I've realized I'd rather help plan a million tours than ever have to help coordinate another elaborate wedding again. Part of that is my fault—I'm too much of a control-freak to leave anything important to the actual coordinators.

The morning started with the florist's van breaking down. I was putting on makeup when I received the call. They'd already been here last night to decorate the entire event space for the wedding, but their trip today brought more decorations and, most importantly, the bouquets and boutonnieres.

I had to quickly find a way for someone to service their van on the side of the coastal highway so they could still make it in time.

My steps are swift as I navigate through a winding hallway on a mission to find Nora. Aside from the one small hiccup, everything is going smoothly, but I still want to check in on the bride.

I knock on the door to Nora's room, waiting for someone to answer. There's a symphony of voices coming from inside as I scroll through my phone. Finally, it swings open. Riley stands on the other side of it. She looks me up and down, giving me a smile. "Well it's been a while, Monica," she says in her typical upbeat tone.

"It's a pleasure to see you, Riley," I respond politely.

"Did you come to see the bride?" Riley asks excitedly, using her hand to gesture inside the room.

I nod. There are a few things I'd like to go over with Nora before she gets too busy with her day. I want her to be fully prepared for everything going on today, so I figured I'd catch her early before she gets swept away in the theatrics of the wedding.

A screech sounds from inside the room. Riley's head spins immediately. "Well she's up earlier than she's supposed to be," she mumbles to herself. Leaving the door open, she hustles inside the room.

I stare at the empty doorway for a moment before walking through it. Inside, I find a flurry of motion that can only be described as chaos.

Riley is in a corner shushing a crying infant. She's not having much luck, however, because the more Riley swings her body back and forth the louder the baby cries. There's a team of photographers in the opposite corner. They're all huddled around wedding invites and a few different accessories, their cameras clicking away with each photo.

In the middle of the room sit four vanity mirrors with director's chairs sitting in front of them. The one closest to me has Nora's mom in it, and next to her sits Lennon. There's an empty chair for Riley, and then Nora occupies the last.

The women in the room wear matching pajamas. Riley, Lennon, and Nora's mom wear emerald green silk sets while Nora wears the same thing but in white. Right now three different makeup artists stand in front of Nora, fussing over getting fake eyelashes on her.

Nora's one eye pops open slightly upon my arrival. She smiles. "Good morning, Monica."

"How are you feeling?" I ask, setting my purse down on a coffee table full of ingredients to make mimosas.

"Wonderful," she says breathlessly. Her body jerks as one of the makeup artists uses a tool to try and fluff the eyelash strip just applied to Nora's eye.

Once both strips are applied, Nora blinks a few times and looks at me. "How's everything going out there?"

I force a smile, trying to make her feel comfortable and at ease. "It's going great." From what I can tell, it *is* going great out there. I've done my best to let the wedding planners handle the rest of the details, focusing mainly on the various members of Nash's team to make sure they're all doing their part to make this day run smoothly and flawlessly.

An ear-piercing wail sounds from the corner with Riley and Zoe. Riley holds the head of the baby as she furiously bobs and weaves while holding the infant. Looking over Zoe's head, Riley smiles apologetically. "Sorry, I don't know why she's deciding to lose her shit. Typically she's an easy baby."

Nora shakes her head dismissively. "You never have to apologize for my sweet niece crying. She can do no wrong. She's perfect."

Riley snorts. "She'd be so much more perfect if she'd let her Auntie Nora have the perfect wedding morning instead of making everyone's ears bleed."

Nora acts as if she's going to get up and help her friend, but one of the makeup artists puts their hand on her shoulder. "You're not ready yet," the girl says nicely. "And we've got a very strict schedule to keep you on."

I nod in approval. In an hour and a half Nora is set to have some bridal portraits done and shortly following that, she will be having photos done with her small wedding party and her family. The couple had decided not to do a first look before the wedding, opting to see each other for the first time when she walks down the aisle instead.

Riley puts the baby on one hip as she rifles through a large bag. Items begin to fly out as she quickly pulls one thing out after another. "I can't find a damn binky anywhere," Riley complains. The baby voices her disapproval by letting out a large wail.

Sighing, Riley looks up at me. "Can you hold her for two seconds while I look for this thing?"

My stomach drops. I don't do babies. I look at the bouncer contraption that Riley just pulled her out of. "Can't you put her back in that?"

Riley's eyes flick to the item before resting on me again. 'I could," she says in defeat, "but then she'll just start screaming again and I don't want my best friend to hear a screeching baby on her wedding day. It'll take two seconds I promise."

"Zoe will love you!" Nora says enthusiastically, she keeps her body still as they line her lids with some shadow. "She's the sweetest."

As if that was all the reassurance she needed, Riley comes over to me and shoves the baby into my arms before I can do anything about it.

"No really," I tell her, trying to push the baby away. "I'm not a baby person and typically babies aren't a fan of me either."

Lennon lets out a soft giggle as someone brushes powder onto her nose. I want to give her a dirty look, but she's got her eyes closed so she wouldn't even see it to begin with.

Even with my persistence, Riley lets go of her child, trusting me to keep ahold of her. Not wanting to start the day off by dropping an infant, I cling to the baby for dear life. I can count on one hand the number of times I've held a baby. As if Zoe can smell fear, she looks up at me with a smile.

"I'm glad you find this funny," I tell her. I try to shift her from one arm to the other, but it's terrifying because she's wiggly and I'm scared she's going to wriggle right out of my grasp.

"She had the stupid thing earlier, but I don't know where it went," Riley explains, taking every item out of the bag. She goes as far as shaking each piece of clothing in the bag to make sure it isn't stuck in any of it.

Zoe begins to wiggle in my arms, her chubby arms trying to push my death grip away from her.

"You're stuck like this," I say, clutching her as hard as I can.

She grunts, her face pinching together in anger. Her tiny hands push against me, and I'm left with no choice but to relinquish a little bit of my hold to let her move.

This experience reminds me why I've never had any desire to have kids. There's a slim chance I'll ever meet a man that's able to put up with me long enough for marriage as it is. I can't imagine having to parent a child—to share control with another human being. Even the thought of being responsible for a pet terrifies me.

Two chubby hands grab at my cheeks. Zoe slaps my face excitedly, amusing herself to the point of hysterical laughing.

"Monica, you're a natural," Nora encourages from her chair.

I scoff, trying to gently shove her drool covered hand away from my own mouth. "Not quite sure about that."

Zoe smiles, pushing her hand right into my mouth as I speak. The smile on her face is precious, it would just be a lot cuter if I wasn't the one responsible for her at the moment.

Riley pokes her head out from underneath a table. "It's like it grew legs and walked away," she mutters.

"Want me to look while you hold her?" I question, but it sounds more like begging. The baby so far has stayed content in my arms, but I know it can't last forever. Any second now, she's going to erupt in a frenzy and I don't have the maternal instincts to know how to shush her.

"Oh shit." She looks up at me in horror.

"What?" I ask, trying to keep a hold on Zoe as she tries to climb up me to pull at the hairpin in my hair.

"I think Sebastian has it."

"Can't you call him to bring it up?"

Riley looks awkwardly over at Nora. "I don't want him anywhere near here. What if he tells Nash what Nora looks like?"

I stifle the urge to roll my eyes. Sebastian does have a big mouth, and I would never depend on him to keep a secret, but I don't see him as observant enough to spoil what the bride is wearing.

Not giving her the option, I hand the baby off to her mother. "How about I go to the groom's suite to track it down?"

Riley gives me a relieved smile. "You'd do that?"

I don't tell her I'd do anything if it meant I didn't have to be responsible for the baby again. I nod. "I'll be right back."

The room Nash and his groomsmen are getting ready in is on the opposite side of the building. It was done on purpose, ensuring that Nash and Nora wouldn't run into one another before the wedding began.

Knocking, I wait for someone to open the door. Other than the baby, it's a lot louder in this room than the one with Nora's party. After waiting a while, I knock again, this time louder. There's music blaring from the speakers, hooting and hollering ringing out from the room occasionally.

Just when I'm about to try the handle, the door pops open. Aiden stands on the other side of it—clearly still getting dressed.

He stands in front of me with only tuxedo pants covering his long legs, and suspenders running over his shoulders. He holds one suspender clip in his hand, fastening it to his pants. The lack of shirt shows off the intricate tattoos that dust his tan skin.

"What are you doing here?" he asks incredulously.

Ever since my makeshift birthday party, one I had *way* too much to drink at, Aiden has been acting differently. He's still cold toward me, but there's less edge to his tone.

"I need to talk to Sebastian." I try to take a step closer, expecting him to move out of the way. Except, he does no such thing. I narrowly miss bumping into his bare chest.

His fingers grasp the edge of the door, not showing any sign of letting the door fall open further. "What do you need with Bash?"

"Does it matter? Just let me in."

"Tell me why first."

Taking matters into my own hands, I dart underneath the open space his arm leaves from holding the door. Before he can stop me, I'm in the room.

What I find is a bunch of men in various stages of getting dressed. The man I'm looking for, Sebastian, stands in a pair of boxer briefs and argyle socks.

Aiden steps next to me. "I tried to stop you. We're indecent in here."

I look over at him. "I don't care. I'll be in and out quickly."

Stopping in front of Sebastian, he looks at me with a humored look. "Fancy seeing you here, Monica," he laughs.

"Riley sent me for a binky. She said you have one?"

The look on his face is one of terror. "Oh no, I think I left it in my pocket this morning." Flying across the room in his underwear, he picks up a pair of shorts from a gym bag. His fingers dig through the pockets. His eyes go wide as he pulls out a pink plastic binky. Holding it up, he looks at it terrified. "Is Riley pissed that I forgot to give it to her?" He walks slowly to me, handing over the item.

"When I left, she was too busy trying to calm Zoe to say one way or the other."

"You're totally going to be in the doghouse!" Landon shouts from where he gets dressed.

Sebastian gives him a look. "I don't need your reminder, asshole." He looks back at me, a crooked smile on his face. "Maybe you could tell her you found it on the floor?"

"I'm going to take this to her now," I say, ignoring his idea. I turn to head toward the door.

"Tell her I'm sorry! And that I love her!" Sebastian pleads.

I'm out the door, making my way back to the other room to fulfill my duties before finding something else to do, when I hear a voice behind me.

"Monica, wait."

Catching me by surprise, I almost trip as I turn around to face Aiden. He stands in the hallway still in nothing but his dress pants. "What do you want, Aiden?"

"Is our plan still the same for tonight?"

"Yes, speak with the artists in attendance that are part of Coleman Records. Just don't make it obvious."

"Got it. And after, we'll talk about what's next?"

I nod, trying not to look at his bare torso. "We will. Goodbye, Aiden."

Turning around, I set out to return the binky to Riley—the binky she's in desperate need of.

Throughout the rest of the day, I manage the small fires that seem to accompany every wedding. All things considered, the rest of it goes off without a hitch. Their vows were beautiful, and somehow we'd managed to keep the location a secret so the media and paparazzi couldn't spoil it. The months of preparation were worth it to see the wedding couple so happy and in love.

It drizzled rain the entire ceremony, something that made Nash and Nora light up with joy.

24
AIDEN

The celebrations for Nash and Nora have been going on for hours now. Even though it rained on us the entire ceremony, the excitement from the bride and groom have been contagious and the guests all seem happy to be here. I allowed myself a brief pause to take in the moment at the beginning of the reception. My brother's happily married now, and I'm thrilled for him.

As much as I wanted to continue to celebrate, I knew I had work to do. I began chatting with anyone that was willing to hold a conversation with me, looking specifically for current or former Coleman artists. After several failed attempts to gain any useful information, I finally found someone with a story to tell. One that I can't help but wonder if Monica already knew about.

People try to stop me for idle chit chat as I make my way toward Monica with the news. I don't hear a word any of them are saying, focusing solely on her.

Her back is to me, her bare shoulders on full display. The open back to the dress shows the fine lines of the muscles on her back. I don't know who she's talking to and I don't care.

As soon as I'm close enough, my fingers wrap around her

elbow. Leaning close, I bring my lips to her ear. "I suspect you've been keeping secrets from me, Monica."

Her shoulders stiffen, but her gaze stays fixed on the person she's speaking to. The bystander takes a sip of their champagne uneasily.

"Excuse us," Monica says through a tight-lipped smile.

As soon as she takes one step away from the person, I'm pulling her through the crowd. She doesn't fight it, probably trying to save face to those who care to notice us.

My fingers dig into her skin as I pull her along. Finally, the string lights above us disappear and darkness surrounds us. I keep going until I've pulled her under the canopy of a large weeping willow. The light breeze stops, partially blocked by remnants of an old stone building nearby.

"Get your hand off me," Monica seethes. Her elbow slides roughly out of my hand.

She has the nerve to look up at me angrily. There's barely enough moonlight for me to see her features, but I can see the glint of rage in her eyes.

"This is not your chance to be mad," I bite, flexing my fingers absentmindedly, wondering why I miss the feel of her skin against mine.

"What's that supposed to mean?"

"It seems like there is a *lot* more to this situation with Nash and the label than you originally let on. Starting with the fact that Roy is using his power—his position—within Coleman to lure young female artists in, convincing them he will make their songs number one if they sleep with him."

"I told you to find out what you could. I had my suspicions, but I didn't have confirmation. Do you?"

My eyes narrow. "I sure as hell do. I was doing what I was told and chatting up guests when I ran into a woman named Chelsea. She came as Roy's date. Apparently, she's also an artist at Coleman, but only recently. She'd had a few drinks, and accidentally mentioned that she and Roy were having a *relationship.*" I say the word relationship with disgust.

Roy didn't give a shit about her. He was doing whatever he could to prey on her all while throwing empty promises her way that she'll make it big. It's not as if he was trying to hide it well, he showed up with her tonight, cockily thinking no one would think twice about it.

"That's what I was afraid of," Monica says quietly, more to herself than to me. She stares at the tree behind me. Its branches fall in every direction, some of them resting atop the stone wall of the building.

"How the hell were you not going to tell me something like that? We've got what we need—we can take this fucker down."

Monica shakes her head. "It isn't enough—not yet. In this business no one is going to blink an eye if they say that the label exec is sleeping with his artists—everyone does that. We need *more.*"

Disgust sits in my stomach like a lead brick. I hate every single word coming out of her mouth, but deep down I know she's right. No matter how hard it pained me to hear that girl— someone who looks *barely* eighteen—talk as if Roy was the best thing that ever happened to her.

"He can't keep taking advantage of these girls."

"No he can't. But we can't show our cards too soon. We've got to take him by surprise. We've got to get more dirt on him— something that will bury him deep."

"This is bullshit," I say, my voice raised. Turning around, I start to make my way to the party. I'm so fucking pissed that this *one* guy has a hold over so many people.

"What are you doing?" Monica's voice has a hint of panic.

"Trying to talk myself out of walking back into that party and putting my knuckles through that fucker's temple."

Her hand finds my back. "Get your shit together, Aiden." She fists the fabric of my suit-jacket hard enough that if I were to try to walk away from her, she'd have a firm enough grasp on me to slow me down.

I laugh, the sound bouncing off the space around us. Catching her off guard, I spin around, yanking the fabric straight from her grasp. "No," I clip.

"Yes," she spits back. Her breath hits my cheek, only then letting me know how close we stand.

"I'm sick of you telling me what to do."

"Then stop making rash decisions that could ruin everything for us."

My blood still boils underneath my skin, but there's something else festering there as well. It's want—desire. My fingers itch to reach out to touch her, to find a distraction in the shitstorm going around us.

I can't control the situation Nash is in, but I *can* control the way her pulse comes alive when I touch her.

A corner of my lip comes up in a smile. "Speaking of rash decisions…" I say slowly. Not giving her time to respond, I grab onto either side of her face and pull her mouth to mine. She shocks me by opening her mouth right away, her tongue striking against mine before I get the chance to do the same. Her fingernails dig into my neck as she claws at my skin, craning her neck to open up for me.

I navigate our bodies through the grass until her back hits the stone ruins. Pulling away, I look down at her. "Tell me how I can hate you but crave you all the same."

"Because you know the truth to my deception."

"I hate the way you lie," I whisper into the darkness. I let my hand fall to her waist, my fingers digging into the cold, gold fabric.

"It's for a good reason." She doesn't push me away as my hand slips down her leg.

"I hate the way you hide things, how I can never tell what you're thinking."

"Lots of practice," she answers breathlessly.

"The only way I know how to get a hint of what's going on in that mind of yours is to push your boundaries. To feel your pulse underneath my fingertips." The bridge of my nose runs over her chin. "You may be able to hide behind that cold, black heart of yours, but it doesn't lie. Not to me." For emphasis I put two fingers to her racing pulse. I can feel the crash of her blood pumping against the tips of my fingers. The beat matches my own racing heart.

Dropping to my knees in front of her, I let my hand drift underneath the fabric of her floor length dress.

"I hate the way that I'm desperate to be in control of your heartbeats, even after everything you've done."

My fingers find the smooth skin of her leg, the feeling of exploring areas of her I've yet to see goes right to my dick. It presses against the zipper of the dress pants, begging to be released.

Ever since that conversation with her at the karaoke bar, all I've been able to think about is her. My thoughts of hating her, my thoughts of touching her...and the memories of what she divulged when drunk.

"I fucking despise how fighting with you goes straight to my cock. Making you rage has become my favorite kind of foreplay."

I push the fabric up her thighs until I'm met with an intricate lace thong.

"Wait...," she whispers, her hands falling to my shoulders but making no effort to stop me.

I look up from my knees, her eyes begging me to continue. "We both know you want this, Monica. I won't get on my knees for you again, I'd much prefer it if it were *you* on your knees. Tell me you want it."

She eagerly opens her legs for me. "Get over yourself." Her body language contradicts her words.

My eyes find the see-through fabric in front of me. The black fabric does nothing to hide the most intimate part of her. There are floral appliqués covering the spot I want most, her arousal glistening from the dim glow of the moon.

"Still such a liar." I hook my thumbs into the fabric and pull them down her legs. She steps out of them, making her lie even more obvious.

"A *filthy* little liar," I add, looking at the wetness pooling between her thighs. Her words hold no weight anymore, I can tell how bad she wants this.

"Do you want to know what I hate most?" I ask, playing with her juices. She bucks underneath my touch, and I haven't even touched the spot where she wants me most.

"I don't care," she pants, her legs trembling as she opens them wider for me, inviting me in.

I can't help but smile. Even as she comes apart before me, she's still trying to pretend that I don't have power over her—that she isn't listening intently.

I lean close to her bare center. My lips are a fraction of an inch away from her clit. "I hate that I know I'll hate myself for what's about to happen, but there's no way in hell I'm going to stop it."

"Aiden...we can't..." Her voice breaks off when my tongue rakes across her clit. Again, her actions betray her words. She arches her hips off the wall, pressing her wet center to my mouth.

She tastes like regret. My mind tries to convince my body that this is wrong, but the urge to devour her wins out. The sweet, warm taste of her is a sharp contrast to the bitter, cold personality she shows the world.

Dealing with her own internal struggle, her mind gets the upper hand briefly. In a futile attempt to push me off her, she nudges at my shoulder weakly. The resistance is short lived, as I press her into the stone wall to keep her still, her body going lax in concession to the pleasure.

I use two fingers to spread her lips open, giving me more access to her swollen clit.

"This shouldn't be happening," she breathes, her other hand finding my shoulder, but not in denial this time. This time, she pulls me toward her to lock me in place and keep herself steadied.

My answer is to grab her leg and put it over my shoulder. Now more of her weight is braced on me as I bury my face into that sweet cunt of hers.

By the way she grinds her hips against my mouth, I can tell that she's close—too close. Too soon. Pulling away slightly, I look up at her. "All you have to do is tell me to stop, Monica. Tell me to stop and you can pretend that this never happened… that I don't make you soaking wet with need. You can go back to pretending you hate me and lie to yourself that you don't want this."

Fire burns in her eyes. For a moment, I wonder if she will resist the desire and tell me to stop and go to hell.

Her head tilts up to the sky as she lets out a defeated sigh. "I can't."

I smile. "Then tell me how bad you want it."

"Never."

I sit back on my heels, letting her leg fall from my shoulder. The movement makes her dress fall back down, covering the spot I've had one taste of and I'm already addicted to. "Then I'm done."

Her mouth opens. "What?"

"If you're not going to admit how bad you want this, then you aren't going to get it. I can have you screaming my name in ecstasy as soon as you'll admit that it's *me* making you dripping wet."

Bending over with an angry sigh, she reaches to grab her discarded thong from the floor. I beat her to it. Yanking the fabric, I bring it close to me.

"These are mine now," I say with a smirk.

She lunges for me, trying to grab the fabric. Clicking my tongue, I hold them close to my chest. "You aren't getting these back until you can admit the inevitable."

"You're being childish."

My only answer is to bring the pair of underwear to my nose, taking a deep breath in. I let the smell of her waft over my senses. I'd much prefer to have my tongue deep inside her right now, but playing this game with her is *almost* as fun.

I stand up and shove the fabric into my pocket. If this were a cartoon, she'd have smoke billowing from her ears. Her shoulders are pulled tight. Her smudged lips puckered in annoyance.

"Ready to admit it?" I ask, taking a step closer to her. Reaching out, I let my thumb run over a smudge of the lipstick. I only smudge it further, but she doesn't have to know that. It's amusing to think of her returning to that party less than perfect.

She knocks my hand away, her brows set in defiance. "No, Aiden. I'm not playing your childish game."

Stepping away from her, I nod in the direction of the reception. "You better get back to the party then. People may start wondering where you are."

She bites her lip. "Seriously?"

My cheek twitches, my face unable to hide the smile that forms. "I'm serious. You want me to make you come? Then you're going to have to ask for it."

"In your dreams."

I shake my finger in the air. "No, Monica, in my dreams, you'd be *begging*."

She scoffs, attempting to fix a few loose flyaway hairs from her tightly spun bun at the nape of her neck. "I'm leaving."

"Be my guest," I answer, taking the panties out of my pocket and spinning them around my index finger.

She looks at them, acting like she's going to make a break for them before deciding otherwise. Her hands run down her dress, smoothing the gold fabric before she heads back in the direction of the party.

Not once does she look back at me. It makes me smile. This game between us is far from over. She can go back to her posh coworkers and keep up her charade of being this effortlessly put-together businesswoman. On the surface, that may be what she is, but underneath it all she's someone who is desperate for a thrill. She needs someone to tell her how to feel, to direct her pleasure. She needs it from *me*.

No matter how much the two of us might hate it, our bodies are desperate for each other. We may have to pretend to play nice so we can take down this bastard, Roy, but that doesn't mean our bodies have to play nice. We can get rid of the sexual tension without having to like one another.

And that's *exactly* what will happen.

I don't want to deny my need for her any longer. I don't like how much I want her, but I won't deny myself either.

She'll come to the same realization I have eventually. And when she does, I'll be waiting.

Until then, I'm left having to free my cock and relieve myself on my own. There's no way in hell I can return to the party before taking the edge off. Tasting her has left me in overdrive.

I still have to give a best man speech. Somehow, I think my brother would be severely disappointed if I gave a heartfelt speech with a hard-on.

My fingers wrap around myself as I stroke up and down my shaft slowly. All I can think about is her. My mind is flooded with memories of the way she tasted—the way her thighs trembled with every punishing stroke of my tongue. I grip myself even harder, imagining what it would feel like to have her smart mouth wrapped around my cock. My hand picks up pace, my balls tightening at the mental image of having her on her knees in front of me, unable to spin any more lies with her mouth full of me.

25
MONICA

The champagne tastes bitter as it rolls down my throat. I stand on my own at the corner of the party. There's an assigned seat for me at a table filled with people I know, but right now I need to be alone.

A breeze passes up my dress every time I walk, reminding me that the little punk stole my panties to prove some kind of point. He can try and prove it all he wants. It'll be over my dead body that I'll ever admit to him how alive my body comes underneath his touch.

Truth be told, I can't remember the last time a man went down on me. When you become as successful as I've become, your work becomes your life, which means all aspects of a personal life go out the window.

But for some reason, when he'd begun to strip me of my panties—I'd let him. He was right, I loathe myself for it. I feel weak letting my body take control of my mind. I'd given him enough control when I let him taste me despite my better judgment.

Leave it to Aiden to not just take the inch he was given. He wanted more, he wanted me to bow down to him—but I don't bow down to anyone, least of all him.

It doesn't mean I haven't been left in even more of a sour mood than my typical one. I was seconds away from an orgasm when he had to stop and become annoying about it.

Speaking of the irritating asshole, he stands at the head table. His arm loops around Nash as he gives his best man speech. I'll hand it to him, his words are sweet, and it seems like he means them all.

Nash seems to eat up every single one of his words. I, on the other hand, can't help but roll my eyes. Everyone in attendance is eating out of his hand, completely unaware that the guy is unapologetically pushing every single one of my buttons.

"It's a wedding. You should try smiling."

Taking a deep breath, I look over to find Matt at my side. I've always liked Nash's head bodyguard. Probably because he's good at keeping his mouth shut and doing his job. Sebastian drove me to the point of insanity, but Nash loved him.

Matt has his hands tucked in his pockets, his eyes trained on Nash like the dutiful bodyguard that he is. I take another drink of my champagne, setting the empty glass on the cocktail table in front of me.

"This is coming from a man I've rarely seen smile." Matt is and always has been all business. It's one of the reasons I've always respected him. He's always done his job and done it well —as good as someone can who is trying to keep Nash safe. Nash has a mind of his own, it hasn't always been easy keeping track of him.

Matt's answer is to let his mouth turn upward slightly. "I smiled the entire time Nora walked down the aisle toward him."

"I think I remember a tear being shed," I answer, remembering the gleeful look on Matt's face. Matt is only a few years older than me, but he's always been like a father figure on tour. His mature, calming demeanor is a stark contrast to the cold and indifferent one of my own father.

Matt lifts a shoulder. "I'll never admit to that."

Shaking my head, I look at the happy couple at the head of the terrace. Nash and Nora stand in front of their guests. Nash's fingers wrap around the microphone as he thanks everyone for coming tonight.

"I can't believe we did it. I can't believe *he* did it," Matt finally says. His voice seems a bit somber.

My eyes find him in confusion. "Did what?"

"That he found happiness," he answers immediately.

I bite my lip, reflecting on everything that's happened in the last few years. There were nights we had pulled Nash out of some pretty rough places. At the time, I hadn't ever thought he'd be in the place he is now. I thought the rest of my days were going to be spent chasing after him, riding the highs and lows of his benders.

But looking at him, the way he looks down at Nora as if she's the only thing in the world—it's clear how happy he is.

And I love Nash as much as I've ever loved another person. I'd do anything for him to keep this happiness, despite my decisions in the past. I've always done what I thought was right for him, consequences be damned.

Now is no different. I'll do whatever it takes to keep Nash this happy. He deserves the girl of his dreams *and* his music. And I'll keep fighting for him to keep that.

"He deserves it," I tell Matt. Looking away from the happy couple, I let my eyes roam until they set on the man that's threatening Nash's happiness.

Roy sits at a table filled to the brim of men in power. Men who have *too* much power. Power that they abuse daily. He laughs without a care in the world. His arm drapes over the woman next to him—the one Aiden spoke with earlier, Chelsea. She giggles at whatever he says, making him smile ever larger. One of his hands brushes the top of her shoulder. She leans in closer to him, totally oblivious that she's flirting with the devil.

I didn't want to invite Roy, but Nash had surprisingly

insisted. "I want that asshole to see me at my happiest," he'd said.

My stomach rolls watching Roy with her. The champagne I've downed in the last ten minutes sits uncomfortably. Tearing my eyes from the scene before I do something I'll regret, I somehow find Aiden's gaze from across the terrace.

He sits at the long head table. Nash was seated to his right, but Nash has been swept off somewhere else, leaving the chair vacant. On the other side of him sits Landon, but he's too enamored in a conversation with Poe, leaving Aiden sitting there alone. On the opposite side of the table, Riley is deep in a conversation with one of Nash's former dancers, and another one of Nora's best friends, Ziggy, if I remember correctly. He'd spent last tour dancing for Nash and was set to come on this one as well, but we had to replace him last minute as he had some emergency to attend to. I look away from whatever conversation Riley and him are having, focusing once again on a person who shouldn't steal this much of my attention.

Aiden.

The fact that no one is speaking with him doesn't seem to bother him. He holds my attention, his usual smirk on his face. Before I can look away, he leans back in the chair, reaching over to drape an arm over Nash's empty seat. His other hand reaches into his pocket, and I stare in horror as he pulls out my panties from earlier. He spins the fabric around his index finger, holding eye contact the entire time.

The gesture infuriates me and turns me on. I want to look away, to see if anyone else has noticed his immature actions, but I'm locked in his stare.

He breaks eye contact, looking down at the black panties for a moment before tucking them into the pocket of his suit jacket.

Looking back up at me, he mouths, "Ready to beg for it?"

I flush, just now remembering Matt is still standing next to me. Luckily, when I look over to him he's busy checking something on his phone, oblivious to the show Aiden is putting on.

My skin feels hot for the next two minutes as Matt and I carry on a conversation about work. The entire time, I feel someone watching me. The side of my face burns from where I know he's watching me. I make a point to not look at him, to not let him see a reaction out of me.

Meanwhile, between my thighs has become warmer, thanks to him. I'm lucky that my dress is long, that no one can see the evidence of my arousal between my legs.

Matt eventually excuses himself, which finally gives me the nerve to look back at Aiden. I find his chair empty, and I refuse to let my eyes wander around the reception to see where he snuck off to.

26
AIDEN

After being surrounded by people until the early morning, my empty room feels too quiet. The reception ended an hour ago, but it took some time for those of us in the wedding party to make it back to our rooms. It'd been nice to sit and talk with some of the people Nash cares about the most.

Sebastian is cool, even if he spent half the night with his eyes glued to a baby monitor. I've already got to know Landon and Poe pretty well through the tour, but tonight they seemed to let loose a little more.

Turning on the lights to the bathroom, I look in the mirror. Nash's typical hair and makeup team assisted with getting the groom and groomsmen ready this morning. The stylist put more gel in my hair than I've ever had. The gel had coaxed my mid-length locks into a semi-styled hairdo. Typically I let my hair do whatever it wants, but today it was slicked back on the side, making me look way more put together than I typically care for.

The jet-black suit jacket still looks as immaculate as when I put it on this morning. Somehow the celebrations didn't wrinkle or crease the expensive fabric at all. Slipping the suit-jacket off, I discard it over a vanity chair in front of the hotel sink.

Next goes the stark white button up dress shirt. The

shirt has tiny little embroidered designs stitched all over the fabric. We couldn't just have plain shirts—not with Nash. Over time, his fashion sense has evolved and he likes to push the envelope a bit with his fashion choices. It's no wonder his wedding isn't any different. I've always opted for more simple, dark clothing that I don't have to fuss over.

As soon as I undo the last button, I pull the shirt open and toss it on top of the jacket. The suspenders from the getup hang limply down my legs.

I twist the knob to the faucet, sticking my finger underneath the water until it's ice cold. When it's cold enough to send shivers down my arm, I lay both of my palms underneath the water. Collecting the water in my hands, I splash the ice-cold liquid on my face.

I keep repeating the action, trying to rid my memory of the taste and smell of Monica. Even after our first kiss, I had an inkling that I'd want to do it again. Her body draws me in like a magnet, the electricity of our disdain for each other only further fueling the fire between us.

I'd spent the entirety of the night—after our encounter— playing with the pair of panties in my pocket. Every time I looked at her, I knew that there was nothing underneath her dress, making my dick spring to attention in my pants. All it would've taken was for me to go up behind her, guide a hand underneath the pleats of fabric and I would've felt her wet warmth all over again.

She tasted much sweeter than I could've imagined and that one small taste has me wanting more. I've never been one to get on my knees for a woman, but I just needed to know what she tasted like—if she'd lose hold on that tightly held control of hers when my tongue met her clit.

Water droplets trail down my neck as I turn off the water. The cold rush to the face has done nothing to help me unwind.

If anything, I'm even hornier and more pissed off than I had been in the first place.

I want to know what it feels like to have her red lips wrapped around my cock. She always has something smartass to say but shoving my cock down her throat would surely shut her up. I wonder if she'd greedily take my dick until it hit the back of her throat, or if she'd be more conservative with it.

My hand is about to snake down into my pants to relieve myself for the second time tonight when there's a loud knock on my door.

At first, I ignore it. It's late and anyone I care about has already gone off to their own rooms. The knocking becomes louder and more irritating.

Sighing, I exit the bathroom and cross the room to the door. When I open the door, I'm shocked to find Monica standing on the other side of it.

Her hand stops midair, like she was about to continue pounding on the door if I hadn't thrown it open.

"What took you so long?" she asks, her tone annoyed.

"I was busy."

Her lips purse. "Let me in."

I stick my head into the hallway, looking to see if anyone is in the vicinity. Luckily, it's late and all of the guests staying have retired to their own rooms.

"Why?"

Ignoring me completely, she shoves her way past me. Her feet pad against the soft carpet as she struts into the kitchen area.

My interest piqued, I shut the door to my room and turn to face her. My weight leans against the door, my arms coming across my chest. I wait for her to say something, but she seems to be too busy looking at every square inch of my living space.

Using the small amount of light coming from the bathroom and the lamp by the bed, I take in her appearance. She doesn't wear the same dress from earlier. She wears some kind of silk nightgown with a matching robe. The nightgown is shorter than something I'd imagine Monica typically wearing, showing off plenty of her tan, toned thighs. It's odd seeing her so dressed down and without accessories. Even the slippers on her feet seem so simple—so unlike Monica.

I'm first to break the silence. "Care to tell me what you want?"

Her eyes find me. Slowly, they drop to my bare chest before popping back up to meet my gaze. A sarcastic laugh bubbles from her throat. "What I *want* is for you to get out of my head."

I taunt her with a smirk. "Can't stop thinking about me, little liar?"

She huffs, looking down and running a finger over the edge of the counter she stands by. "I hate it. I just wanted to go to bed, to get some sleep, but…"

"You realized that you wanted more. That the small taste from earlier tonight wasn't enough to satisfy your desires."

There's something unreadable in her eyes when she looks at me. The bathroom light glows behind her, only giving me a shadowed version of her features. "I don't want more from you, Aiden. I just want to be able to sleep without feeling wound up like a rubber band."

Blood surges into my cock at her words. I smile. "I know a great way to get you to relax."

"One night. And then tomorrow morning we can forget about it and go back to hating one another. It'll be out of our system."

"This isn't some kind of business transaction, Monica. I'm not agreeing to any of your rules. If you want me to fuck you, I've told you what you have to do. You just have to ask for it."

"I just did," she throws out.

I shake my head, slowly starting to stalk toward her. "No you didn't. I want to hear it from your lips. Tell me what you want."

She defiantly shakes her head.

"What *is* it that you envision happening?" I whisper. "I'll tell you what I've thought about…" I brush my fingers along her shoulder, scooting the fabric of her robe so I can see skin.

"I've wondered if those painted red, pouty lips of yours would stain my cock after I bury it in your throat."

An audible gasp passes through her lips. Her body stiffens as I pull the robe off one of her shoulders.

"I've fantasized about what it would feel like to have you gagging on my dick. Tell me Monica, are you someone who likes to give head fast or slow?"

"Neither."

I hum. "You'll learn to do it fast and deep. Just the way that I like it." I pull on the other arm of the robe until the fabric falls to the ground.

My eyes find her peaked nipples through the thin fabric of her nightie. "Do you like it when I tell you what you're going to do to me, Monica?"

She swallows, shaking her head in resistance as she watches me carefully.

Sliding my hand under her gown, my thumb and index finger twist her hard nipple. "These tell me otherwise." I pinch the skin between my fingers, eliciting a soft moan from her. "Your body can't deceive me, little liar."

I take her small breast in my hand, feeling the weight of it in my palm. She's always worn outfits that were just modest enough to hide them underneath her designer clothing, so seeing them now—feeling them—makes my cock pulsate antici-pation. I roll her nipple between my fingers again, kneading the soft tissue.

Her breathing gets heavier, panting as I run the fingertips on my other hand lightly up her forearm. My nose grazes her ear as I lean over her. "You couldn't sleep because you can't stop thinking about this…" Grabbing her hand, I place it on my crotch. Without further instruction, she immediately grabs my shaft tightly.

"Good girl. Now, say the magic words," I whisper, the hand on her breast traveling down the soft fabric covering her ribcage.

"It's not going to happen."

"Then get on your knees and *show* me that you want this," I counter. If she won't use her words to tell me how bad she wants it, then she can use her mouth.

She takes a small step back, her eyes falling to my crotch. Suspenders still lay limply down each one of my hips. My dick strains against the zipper of my pants, begging to be freed. The outline of it is obvious against the tailored pants. While her eyes stay focused on the tented fabric, my fingers work quickly at unbuttoning the pants.

Her mouth falls open slightly as my fingers drag the zipper of the fly down. My fingers slip into my boxers, wrapping around my thrumming cock. I run my thumb over the head before pulling it out.

Looking down, I slowly begin to move up and down my shaft. I can still feel the heat of her eyes watching my every move.

She stands, glued to the spot a few feet away from her. I want her to close the distance to me, get on her knees and give in to the tension between us. But I know her—better than I'd care to admit.

This game of cat and mouse is our thing. So, I take the steps toward her until my body almost presses against hers. The head of my cock is an inch away from her silk covered stomach.

My hand pumps up and down. A drop of cum leaks out, and I know she sees it. It glistens on the tip of my dick. I swipe my index finger over it, transferring the bead of liquid to my fingertip.

The grip on my dick loosens as I raise the finger to her lips. I wipe it on them. At first she doesn't react. All she does is stare into my eyes. If it were only up to the defiant look on her face, I would think she doesn't want me. But her body says otherwise. Her chest heaves in and out as her breaths become labored.

Shocking me, her tongue peeks out and licks the come from her lips. Bringing her tongue back into her mouth, her teeth run over her bottom lip.

It's one of the hottest fucking things I've ever seen, and it's coming from the woman I thought I hated most.

Whatever blood I had left runs straight to my dick. Unable to control myself, I angrily pull her into me. My fingers tangle in her hair as I crash into her lips.

All of my anger is thrown into the kiss. The way my cock throbs between us makes me even more irate. Moving from her lips, I scrape my teeth against her chin. My teeth move on to the delicate skin of her neck. I bite hard enough to leave a mark. I've become obsessed with the thought of doing whatever I can to mar the perfect image she tries so hard to portray.

Tomorrow she'll have to think of me as she undoubtedly covers the proof of the two of us. I hope it makes her blood boil, remembering that I'm the one who makes her lose control.

I ease the sting of the bite with my tongue. My lips find her ear. I nip at her earlobe before blowing air on it.

"Get on your knees, little liar."

27
MONICA

His hand slowly travels up my back until it finds the base of my neck. He's dangerously close to my thumping pulse. My heart beats erratically in anticipation.

Once again, his fingers tangle in the tendrils of my hair. I had my hair perfectly pinned for the wedding, but when I went back to my room I'd pulled the pins out, letting the strands dust the top of my shoulders. There's a sting on my scalp as he grabs a fistful of my hair. He pulls down, not gently, trying to steer me to my knees.

I wince, the sting of his fingers pulling at my hair *almost* too much. My knees lock from the pain. Instinctively, I want to fight it.

His grip loosens a fraction. The warmth of his lips dance across my cheek. "Show me how bad you want this."

The combination of his rough grip on my hair and the gentle touch of his lips on my skin has my knees bending. Between my legs throbs from the direct tone of his voice. I've never been one to like to be told what to do, but for some reason his demands are what turn me on.

The carpet feels rough against my knees as they fall to it. It isn't plush or soft, instead it's rough and itchy. I barely notice though now that I'm face to face with his cock.

Aiden doesn't let go of my hair. Instead, he guides my head so my mouth lines up with the glistening head.

Unable to stop myself, I reach up, wanting to feel it for myself. My fingers slowly wrap around the base. It's larger in my hand than I was expecting. He's younger than me by a number of years, far younger than any man I've ever been with. But holding him in my hands, it's proven that despite how many times I've thrown jabs at him, he's a grown adult.

"Fuck," he says, his teeth grinding as I let my hand pump up and down the shaft once. If I wanted it in my mouth, all I would have to do is lean forward slightly and I'd be able to taste him. For now, I'm enjoying exploring him. I have the sick need to watch him fall apart in the same ways he's made me unravel.

I need to know I'm not the only one whose head is at war with their body from the connection between us.

My fingers work him up and down. I can feel the outline of an angry, pulsing vein against the palm of my hand.

Aiden lets me get away with just touching him for a bit, but it isn't long before he's wanting more.

"It's time for you to suck it," he insists. His free hand takes his cock in his hands. He rubs the tip along my lips. My mouth opens only partly.

Undeterred by me, he smiles. "And remember how I told you I like it." His hips jam forward, pressing his cock against my mouth—hard. I open my mouth all the way, allowing him in. The base scrapes against my teeth as he slowly inches further in before he pulls out again.

When he begins to push inside again, my tongue flattens over my teeth. He tightens his grip on my hair in pleasure.

"That's it, baby," he moans. "Open that throat for me."

His hold on me is tight as he pushes himself as deep as

possible into my mouth. My cheeks hurt having to open wide enough to let him in.

He picks up the rhythm of his hips, shoving himself into my mouth faster and faster. He'd warned me earlier exactly what he likes—and how he wants it. My hand falls from the base of his cock, it's clear I'm no longer in control as he fucks my face. My hands find his thighs to brace myself as I take in as much as I can as he thrusts himself inside of me.

My eyes sting as the pressure at the back of my throat becomes too much. Tears well up in my eyes so I shut them tight, refusing to let them fall.

I'm about to pull away, to tell him it's too much when his thighs clench underneath my touch. His head falls back at the same time his fingers tense in my hair. I can feel the tightening of his cock in my mouth.

Suddenly, a salty taste hits the back of my throat. I rip my mouth away from him, refusing to swallow the evidence of his orgasm. Aiden looks panicked as he quickly grabs his shaft. He pumps up and down, his come emptying all over my face and chest instead.

Once he comes down from his orgasm, he slides one hand underneath my arm and pulls me roughly to my feet. His fingers are tight around my bicep as he holds me close to him.

His eyes are filled with rage and lust. They flick to the spot on my cheek where I feel his cum slowly descending down my skin.

"You think you won by refusing to swallow…but you haven't. Eventually you'll gladly swallow every last drop of me— until then I'll revel in seeing the evidence of you getting on your knees for me all over your face."

Aiden doesn't give me time to respond. Quickly, I'm tossed over his shoulder as if I weigh nothing. I bounce up and down as he walks to the bed in the middle of his hotel room. There's a soft *thud* when my body collides with the mattress.

His fingers wrap around each one of my ankles as he pulls me across the mattress. Crawling onto the bed, he stops on his knees between my legs. Picking up my leg, he lets his fingers skirt on the underside of my calf. It sends tingles all the way up my spine. He bends my leg at the knee, repeating the same motion and finally spreading my legs wide open.

"Keep these here," he instructs, tapping the top of my foot. Then his eyes land on the wet spot of my red panties. "Red is becoming my favorite color." Leaning down he hooks his fingers into either side of my panties, pulling them off in one fell swoop. "But I personally think it looks better on the floor."

Once again, I'm left bare in front of the last man I'd ever expected.

"You're soaking wet for me." He runs his fingertip through my slit before pulling the same finger into his mouth. His cheeks hollow out as he sucks in my juices. The action makes even more wetness pool between my inviting thighs.

Lowering his body, his mouth hovers over me. His breath is hot on my inner thighs. "Your mind may hate me, but your pussy doesn't." He moves his hands so they loop underneath my ass and hold onto the meat of my thigh, pinning me in place.

I close my eyes, hating how turned on I am right now. Hating myself even more for not stopping this way before it ever started. Finally, my eyes still closed, I muster up the bravado to say, "I've always had terrible taste in men."

His body freezes. He looks up from me from between my thighs at the same instant his fingertips dig into my flesh.

"Talk about other men when my face is between your thighs and I will make damn sure this sweet little pussy isn't usable for weeks."

Stunned, my eyes pop open. I hadn't expected my words to strike a nerve, but clearly they had. I lock the information away in my mind to use for a time in the future. There's no doubt that no matter what happens tonight, our distaste for one another will remain. If he throws a jab my way, I'll have something to throw back at him.

He tightens the grip on my legs to show his disapproval of my silence. "Do you understand me?" he says, his voice commanding.

My answer is to let my legs fall open, spreading myself open for him even further.

The movement makes him smirk. "Good girl," he mutters, just before he licks me from top to bottom. His hot tongue presses into me. Just when I begin to climb to an orgasm from the feeling of his licks and sucks, he changes the pace of his mouth. It's like he's punishing me for my words.

When he brings me to the brink of another orgasm before pulling away, I lose my patience. Sitting up on my elbows, I look at him angrily.

He smirks, knowing exactly why I'm angry. He looks down between my legs one more time before he sits up. "The first time I feel you come, it's going to be on my dick."

His words have my muscles tightening. I've been brought to the edge of an orgasm so many times tonight I feel like a rubber band that is seconds away from snapping. It's the reason, against all logic, I showed up at his door tonight.

I've lost all sense of reason around him recently, letting my hormones take control of me. I should be pissed that I blew him to the brink of gagging so he could come all over me, but yet he's edged me so many times I've become pissy. Except, I'm more turned on than angry.

My thighs shake as his mouth trails up my body. His hands push the fabric of my nightie up, while his mouth travels the same path shortly after.

Each press of his tongue against my skin sends my body into overdrive, goosebumps lining my skin. He does kiss any intimate part of me currently and yet my body is like a live wire.

Pulling his mouth away from my skin, he looks me in the

eyes. "Do you trust me?" he asks, inching the fabric of my nightie up over my breasts. Cold air hits my nipples.

"No," I answer immediately. My hips shift on the bed as I try to find some kind of friction on my skin. I'm *so* close to bursting into fire.

He gives me a wolfish grin. One that sends electricity right down my body. "Good," he states, pushing the fabric up my body until it covers my eyes.

In one of his large hands he holds both of my wrists, pinning my arms above my head. His other hand is left free to do whatever he pleases. Which right now is to hold the fabric of my own clothing against my eyes, covering everything around me in darkness.

The sensation of not being able to see what's about to happen has my senses in overdrive. I'm left to anticipate where he will touch next, where his mouth will press against next.

The slightest touch of his fingertip on my collarbone has my back arching off the bed. He runs it along the bone, applying just enough pressure for me to know he's there.

"My cum is still on you," he states matter of factly. "It looks good on this perfect, unblemished skin of yours."

I moan when he roughly pinches my nipples. My head moves from left to right to attempt and move the fabric from my vision, but it doesn't work. I'm left staring into darkness, wondering where he'll be next.

He doesn't make me wonder for long. I feel his breath against my nipple before I feel his mouth. He blows on the hardened peak. My hips buck off the mattress at the same time his teeth clamp down on my tender skin.

I wriggle underneath his mouth, causing him to tighten the grip around my wrists. If he keeps the same tempo, I might come from the way he bites and sucks on my tender breast.

"Aiden," I moan his name as a plea to put his mouth elsewhere, or for him to do as he promised—to take me and make me come all over him.

"It's hot as fuck when you moan my name, little liar," he breathes against my skin.

Moving his mouth from my skin, I'm left wondering where he went. The only current point of contact between us is the fingers around my wrist, and the whisper of his thigh against my inner thigh.

Just when I'm about to voice my frustration, I feel something press against my clit. I know immediately it isn't his finger, it's the tip of his cock.

Another moan falls from my lips. My body is on fire with anticipation. I'm so close to coming undone and I'm *finally* about to get that relief.

He runs the head of his cock up and down me. My legs quake eagerly. He plays with my clit using his tip. Just once he lets the head slip in a fraction of an inch. Liquid pours out from between my legs at the movement.

He's aligned perfectly with my pussy when both of his hands find my breasts. He cups them in his palms, shifting the weight of them in his hands.

Slowly, he pushes inside me. He's not even halfway in and I feel like I could come.

"Oh god," I moan, angling my hips to try and let him in further—to get him to go faster.

He stops, squeezing my breasts another time. "I don't know what would make me hate myself more..." he says thoughtfully, "if I were to fuck you right now and let myself lose control in you. Or if I were to stop this before it begins."

"Don't stop," I demand, my tone more pleading—more desperate—than I'd like. "We already hate ourselves for this enough. We'll let it happen this once and it'll be out of our systems."

His shaft slides out of me quickly as his hands fall from my breasts. For some reason I feel cold at the loss of contact between our bodies.

"I think I'd rather make you wait until you're ready to admit that you feel the same pull that I do," he says. The mattress shifts as Aiden's weight leaves the bed.

I rip the fabric off my eyes just quick enough to see him disappear into the ensuite bathroom. The click of a lock is followed by the sound of running water.

"You're such a fucking prick!" I yell, climbing off the bed in a rush. I rip my discarded panties from the floor, angrily stepping into each leg hole and pulling them up my hips.

I hear a soft chuckle from inside the bathroom. "I can't wait to have you naked and begging, Monica. Until then, have fun while you touch yourself. Make sure to think of me when you have fun with your hand."

There's a pause, then I hear the shower door open and close. I don't bother to stick around, flying out of his hotel room as fast as my feet will take me. Thankfully it's late, and the hallway is clear.

Closing my hotel door, I lean my back against it and bounce my head off the hollow wood.

"Never again."

28
AIDEN

The pounding at my door matches the pounding in my head. A groan escapes my throat. I bury my face into the soft pillowcase, wondering who could need me at this hour. The reception went late into the night, and that isn't even including the unplanned encounter I had with Monica last night.

I'd expected to sleep until at *least* noon. Pepper is with a sitter from the tour crew, which means for once I'm not being woken up by her wet nose.

Another loud bang rings against my door.

"What the fuck," I mumble, stretching my legs underneath the sheets.

Whoever it is, they're not getting the satisfaction of me answering.

The comforter gets stuck as I try to pull it up and over my head. I continue to yank until I finally free it enough to pull it over my eyes. I shut my lids, hoping to block the light and go back to sleep.

My eyes shut and covered by the piece of fabric, I'm brought right back to last night. Brought back to when Monica was almost in this same exact position. The way her body reacted to every small touch of mine.

I'd spent longer in the shower last night than I'd intended, wondering if I should have just fucked Monica out of my system. I'd love nothing more than to show her the best night of her life, ruin her for everyone else, and then go back to hating her. It pisses me off that out of all the women in the world *she's* the one who's got me twisted. But after feeling her unravel underneath me, I knew I'd want more.

It gives me a certain feeling of power to know that behind closed doors, Monica Masters *likes* to give up all sense of control. In the bedroom, she *enjoys* being told what to do. And I'm becoming addicted to watching her lose control and hate herself for it. I just have to be careful not to get consumed by it.

Hard as a rock and unable to go back to sleep, I pull my ass out of bed. Picking up my phone on the nightstand, I check the time. It's only nine in the morning, much too early to be up. I throw my legs over the edge of the bed, reaching my arms to the sky as I stretch.

My shaft throbs inside my boxers. I try to ignore it, annoyed that one of my first thoughts this morning was reliving last night.

We both have more important things to worry about right now. We've got to break my brother free from his label—and expose Roy for the creep that he is.

I dig the heels of my hands into my eyes, trying to wipe the fog of exhaustion from my brain. I make a mental note to find Monica today to try and continue our discussion from the reception last night.

Somehow in the haze of lust I had for her last night, I forgot all about what she'd admitted about Roy. She'd known that he was using his power to seduce young artists. It's wrong on so many levels. There's an uneasy feeling in my stomach knowing that Monica suspected it and hadn't acted on it. But I know there's not much she can do about it now.

I made sure to talk some sense into the young, naive girl at my table. I'd told her she didn't need some shriveled up dick to make her successful. Judging by the way she was hanging on his arm later that night, I don't think she listened.

It was worth a shot.

It's becoming more abundantly clear that this Roy guy has got to go. I had reason enough for what he did to my brother, and what he continues to do to Nash with hanging his music over his head. But this goes deeper than Nash. I know there's so much more to Roy than what we currently know. I'd bet my life that there are more skeletons in his closet, and I'm going to make it my mission to find them.

And I know that I'll need Monica's help to do so.

My phone vibrates in my hand. Looking down, I see a text from Nash saying that they're all having breakfast if I want to join.

At the mention of food, my stomach growls. Standing up, I make my way to my suitcase. I rifle through it until I find something to wear to breakfast. I hadn't expected Nash to be up and socializing. Shouldn't he and Nora be fucking in newlywed bliss all day today?

If I were to ever get married, which is a very large *if,* I know there's no way I'd be letting my wife out of the room the next day. We'd be too busy consummating the marriage to pay anyone else attention. And that's if she's even able to walk the next morning.

As soon as I open my door, the scent of bacon hits my nostrils. It smells delicious. I follow the scent of the meat mixed with sweet smells all the way to a large expansive dining room.

There's a long table in the middle of the room that's mostly occupied by the people who have slowly become like family to me. An assortment of food lines the table. Nash sits at the head, looking way more rested than I'd expected him to be. That being said, he's no stranger to late nights and parties, so he hides exhaustion well.

Nora sits next to him, a soft smile on her face as she listens to Riley talk animatedly about something. Sebastian sits on the other side of Riley, a baby girl perched in his lap. He holds a bottle to her lips as he watches his girlfriend ramble on. Ziggy sits on Nora's opposite side, making faces at the baby.

"Holy shit," Nash says from his spot. He looks at me with a grin. "I hadn't expected you to actually be awake when I sent you that text. It was more of a courtesy than anything."

Groaning, I fall into an empty seat a few chairs down from Nash. Next to Nash sits Landon and then Poe. Poe has his head down on the table, a pair of dark sunglasses over his eyes. I'm not even sure he's awake.

Moving over to the seat next to Poe, I give him a small poke. "Looks like I'm not the one you should be surprised about."

Poe returns my sentiment with a loud groan of his own. He waves his hand in the air, showing at least a small sliver of life.

Nash laughs, looking at his friend. "Poe here had a little too much to drink last night. I don't miss those days at all."

Ziggy chuckles. "I tried telling him that the long island to end the night wasn't a good idea. He told me my opinion didn't matter since I had to bail on the tour."

"We still love you," Nora pipes in.

"I don't want to talk about it. It was a little too much," Poe mumbles, his head still face down in his arms at the table.

"*A little?*" Lennon snorts from her seat next to Sebastian.

My eyes land on her while she stays looking at Poe. The way she looks at him shows a little bit of anger, a look I'm *very* used to seeing from Monica, but never from sweet little Lennon.

I store the information for later, wanting to ask my friend if she's okay once we're alone.

"So what has you up so early?" Nash asks me. He pops a strawberry into his mouth, chewing loudly.

I reach for the serving spoon in front of me, dishing some

hash browns onto my plate. Lennon reaches across the table, handing me a plate of pancakes.

"Someone pounding on my door woke me up. I thought maybe it was you." I answer, stabbing a few pancakes from the plate and handing it back to Lennon.

I continue to place food on my plate.

"Wasn't me, man," Nash defends.

"Oh, what a shame you didn't get to *finish*...sleeping in," Monica chides from further down the table, enunciating the word *finish*.

My mouth stops mid-chew. Eyes narrowing, I turn my sights towards her. Holding my eye contact, she stabs a piece of cantaloupe with her fork. There's a satisfactory smile on her face as she brings the piece of cantaloupe to her mouth and takes a bite. Juices from the piece of fruit run down her chin.

The smug look on her face tells me *exactly* who woke me up this morning.

Bitch, I mouth.

I pick up a sausage link, taking a large bite out of it without breaking her gaze. I'm okay with playing dirty.

"You know Monica, you don't look so good either. You're looking a little...*tense* this morning."

She takes a deep breath and briefly closes her eyes, showing off the shadow dusted across her eyelids.

Not done pushing her buttons, I continue. "You know I've heard an orgasm is *great* at helping someone relax. You should try it sometime."

Nora chokes on her iced coffee. It drips from the corners of her mouth as she tries to swallow it before coughing it all over everything. Nash leaps out of his chair, pounding on her back to get her to stop.

Content with my jab, I lean back in my chair and take in the glorious look of disgust on her face.

"I'm suddenly very uncomfortable," Poe mumbles next to

me. I side-eye him and see he's finally attempted to sit up but hasn't made it far. His cheek rests in his palm as he leans into his elbow on the table.

My hand finds the back of his neck. "That's just the hangover," I offer.

His reaction is hidden behind his sunglasses. "No, it's definitely the thought of Monica having an orgasm."

"What's wrong with a woman having an orgasm?" Riley pipes up.

"Monica isn't a woman she's a..." Poe drifts off as he searches for the right word.

Monica shifts uncomfortably in her seat, clearly not a fan of the conversation. Frowning, she looks at Poe, "Are you even aware of *how* to give a female an orgasm?"

The comment has both Nash and Sebastian doubled over in laughter. Landon follows suit, the three of them try to catch their breath through the deep rolls of laughter.

Unable to hide my smile, I look at Monica. I was hoping my earlier comment would throw her off more, but she seems to have bounced back quickly. If she was still reeling from the effects of being cut off from an orgasm last night, you wouldn't know it this morning. Her blonde hair falls in perfect stick-straight strands around her face.

She looks casual in a v-neck that looks soft to the touch, even all the way from across the table. It reminds me of what she wore the night at the karaoke bar. The night she confessed to things I know she can't possibly remember.

"I'm too hungover for this shit," Poe grumbles. Reaching in front of him, he grabs a bottle of water and chugs it quickly.

Everyone else falls into their own conversations. I continue to empty my plate, satisfying the hunger lingering in my stomach.

Once I'm done, I sit back in my chair and take a deep breath. Looking at my brother I ask, "How's it feel to be married?"

He smiles, looking over at Nora. "Exactly the same as before."

She slaps his arm. "Oh shut up, Nash. He spent all morning telling me *all* about how he's so happy I'm his wife."

"I'm sure he *told* you all night long, too," Riley says under her breath. There's a small *thud* underneath the table. Riley winces, letting out a small yelp.

She looks at Sebastian. "What was that for?"

Sebastian rolls his eyes at his girlfriend. "Our daughter doesn't need to hear about her aunt and uncle's sex life."

Riley sighs, waving a hand in the air dismissively. "Our daughter is a baby, Bash, she doesn't know anything we're saying. Plus, one day we'll have to tell her that she was conceived because we couldn't keep our hands off one another… even though our best friends were broken up."

He coos at the baby in his arms. It's comical to see how soft he's gotten for the tiny human in his arms. Sebastian was a bodyguard for Nash for years. He's intimidating for his size, and knows numerous ways to take a man down, yet he's a puddle of mush for the baby girl in his arms. It's odd seeming him take on such a different role than I was used to seeing him in.

Finally he speaks up, still looking down at his daughter in his arms. "Zoe isn't allowed to know where babies come from until she's twenty-one."

A laugh bubbles from Riley's throat. "Keep telling yourself that, babe."

"I'm with Bash on this one," Nash interjects. "Our sweet Zoe girl isn't allowed to look at boys until she's of legal drinking age."

Nora and Riley share a knowing look.

Sebastian looks between the two of them, a disgusted look on his face. "While it's so much fun talking about when my baby is old enough to have the sex talk," he begins sarcastically, "I'd rather get back to the unexpected tension in the room." He looks at between Monica and I, raising his eyebrows. "Monica? Aiden? Care to share what's up this morning?"

Monica doesn't bother to hide the dramatic roll of her brown eyes. Her chair screeches against the floor as she stands up quickly. "I've got a call to make," she says, not bothering to look back at any of us still seated at the table.

Sebastian whistles, leaning back in his chair. "I have *so* many questions," he chuckles.

I watch Monica's retreating form.

I plan on answering none of them.

29
AIDEN

Nash and Nora are off on their honeymoon, leaving me—mostly—alone. We've pretty much wrapped up the American leg of the tour. There was a gap in the schedule for Nash and Nora to go on their honeymoon. Upon their arrival back home, there will be two LA shows and then we're off to jet-set around the country. At least when the tour starts back up I won't feel nearly as lonely.

Lennon is here too, but she doesn't come out of her room much. I'm wondering if she's nocturnal because I don't ever see her out during the day to eat.

Out of boredom I'm tempted to go knock on her door to give myself something to do, but I don't. If she wanted company, she'd come out of her room.

Pepper follows me out of the guest room I'm staying in. Her nails click against the hardwood floor as I aimlessly wander around.

"What should we do today?" I ask her, heading in the direction of the kitchen. She ignores me, instead choosing to run to her food and water bowl. She happily laps up water as I open one of the kitchen cabinets. I reach in, grabbing a glass out of the cabinet.

"Still talking to the dog I see," a voice says from behind me.

Turning around, I find Monica sitting at the kitchen island. She has a laptop placed in front of her, its screen holding her attention.

"What are you doing here?" I ask gruffly. It's silent aside from the sound of ice cubes falling into my glass from the dispenser on the refrigerator.

"Did you forget the part where I work for your brother?" she deadpans, still looking down at the device in front of her.

"Did you forget the part where he's out of the country?" I throw back at her before taking a drink of my water.

Sighing, she looks at me over the top of the laptop. "I came to see you actually."

My eyebrows raise to my hairline in surprise. Smirking, I lean up against the counter. "Are you finally ready to beg?"

"No, I'm here to talk about..." her words drop off as she looks over her shoulder.

"The only other person here is Lennon," I say. "Well, I *think* she's here, but she rarely comes out of her room so it's possible she slipped out at some point."

Monica nods. When she speaks again, her voice is lower. "I want to discuss what you found out at the wedding as well as some other details. I figured with a gap in the tour this is the perfect opportunity."

I nod my head in agreement. "Alright, let's talk."

Monica shuts her laptop. Standing up, she neatly puts back the items she'd laid out on the counter back into her purse. "I'm not discussing all of this out in the open. Let's go to your room."

"Trying to get back into my bedroom already, Monica?" I joke.

"Can you take this seriously for two seconds?" she says, an exhausted tone to her voice.

I ignore her comment. She knows I take getting Nash out of

his record deal seriously. It's just second nature at this point to try and ruffle her feathers.

She allows me to lead her from the kitchen toward the room I'm staying in even though I'm confident she knows the layout of Nash's house better than I do. The two of us don't talk as we make our way to the room. The only sound is that of Pepper's paws against the hardwood and Monica's heels clapping against the wood.

Luckily, we don't end up running into Lennon. My luck would be that one of the only times I see her while our siblings are enjoying their honeymoon bliss would be when I'm walking Monica back to my room.

Stopping at my door, I motion for her to enter.

She pauses, perhaps second-guessing her decision to meet in here. She stands in the doorway, her feet halfway between the plush carpet of my room and the hardwood floors of the hallway. She stares into the room in front of her. From our vantage point, you can see the large four-poster bed in the middle of the room. Its headboard towers up the wall, taking up a lot of the space.

There are two wingback chairs placed in front of a set of double french doors that lead out to a patio. A few steps away from the patio is an outdoor gym that I've been hitting hard in my boredom as of late.

After she doesn't budge, I slide past her and go into the room. The carpet sinks below my feet as I make my way to the bed, collapsing onto it.

"You can stand there as long as you want," I say casually, crossing my ankles at the foot of the bed. "But if Lennon *does* decide to come down this hallway for some reason, she may find it odd to see you standing there."

"It's not odd because nothing is going to happen," Monica snaps. "We're purely conducting business."

I arch an eyebrow. "Are you going to do business from there?"

"Of course not," she says, taking a step into the room.

She barely looks at me as she makes her way across the space. Her belongings rattle around inside her purse when she sets it on the floor next to one of the chairs by the patio doors.

Her back is stiff as a board as she settles into the seat. One of her manicured hands slips into the purse, pulling out her laptop.

I don't move from my perch on the soft bed, realizing it's probably best to keep my distance from her if we want to make any progress. Seeing her in my own space has my head and body at war with one another. I can't help but picture her hands digging into the suede fabric of the wing-backed chair as I rail into her from behind.

And *those* are the kind of thoughts I can't have happening. Not when she's made the effort to come to Nash's house and to include me in her plans to take down the label.

My cock disagrees with the sound logic in my head. I have to subtly adjust myself, glad Monica is too busy typing away on her laptop to notice me. Closing my eyes, I rub the heel of my hands into my eyeballs, doing whatever I can to get the mental picture out of my head.

"So I went digging into Roy when I had time the other night," she begins. "And I found some interesting allegations against him over the years. I have to hand it to him, his team has worked very hard to keep this out of the press." She makes direct eye contact with me, "But I work harder."

I have to admit, as much as I hate the way she handled the situation with Nash, she is skilled at what she does. She's ruthless in all the right ways—you just have to be on her side to think that. "Tell me more."

"It's not all *business as usual* when he visits their recording studio in Miami. It appears that he's using label money to fund lavish parties there. I think he's using these parties to hunt for starving artists. The way I've heard it, if you catch his eye he invites you to the after party."

"And what happens at this after party?"

She shudders, her lips pursing. "Nothing good from the sounds of it. Apparently he talks these young artists into recording a demo for him, and when he gets them alone he pressures them into doing...favors...for him."

"That's fucking disgusting." I'm glad my stomach is empty. If I had anything in it, it would feel sour at the thought of Roy taking advantage of these young musicians.

He's convincing them he will give them the world, with just a small admission fee.

"How do you know all this?"

"Do you remember the girl you spoke to at the party?"

I nod, words sticking in my throat as I wonder how many artists he's made promises to. How many women have had to learn the hard way that he doesn't give a shit about them...or their dreams? How many have to live with what they were coerced into?

"It turns out he dumped her a few days after you talked to her. Since you'd made a connection with her, she felt comfortable reaching out to me. She confirmed my suspicions, but she says she has more."

"And did you ask her what that is?" I question, wondering what other disgusting shit this miserable excuse of a man has done.

Monica shakes her head. She holds her laptop in the air as she adjusts her legs, crossing one leg over the other. For a brief moment I get a peak of what she has on underneath her skirt, wondering how it would look on my floor.

Stop. Focus.

I blink hard, returning my attention to the conversation.

Placing the laptop back in her lap, she says, "No. She said she wanted to talk to you."

My eyebrows raise. "Me?"

"You made quite the impression."

"So when do we meet?"

"She's out of town until this weekend."

"This weekend it is," I confirm. This seems big. If we can get her to confide in us, we're one step closer to the proof we need. One step closer to taking the fucker down.

Standing up, I walk the short distance until I'm standing in front of the chair across from hers. I fall into it, my knees spread so my elbows can rest on top of them. I lean forward and use my index fingers to prop my chin. "Is that all you came for?"

She stares at my fingers—or is it my lips? I can't tell.

"No," she finally says. "If you're up for it, I still have a lot of research to do on Roy and the rest of the label. We could do it together."

"Together?" I roll the word around on my tongue. If you'd asked me when I started this tour if I would ever be using the word together in conjunction with Monica, I would've laughed in your face. I didn't think there was any way the two of us could've handled having a civil conversation, let alone come up with enough of a truce to work *together*.

Of course, I also didn't think I'd be fantasizing about fucking Monica against every single surface in this room—yet *here we are*.

"I'm happy to do the research on my own," she says, taking my silence as rejection. Sitting forward, she begins to shove the laptop back into her purse.

I shake my head, trying to clear all of the thoughts running through it. I lurch forward, my fingers wrapping around her wrist. "No, stop."

Her skin is cold underneath mine. I can feel the slight, steady tick of the pulse in her wrist underneath my fingertips, and it reminds me of the times I've been the reason that pulse elevates.

We're close enough that I can smell her. She doesn't smell fruity or flowery like most women I've been with. It's more unique. It's earthy and spicy and so unique. I'm wondering how this is the first time I've really noticed her smell.

It's also the first time I'm realizing how intoxicating that scent is. I want to run my nose against her skin, find every place the smell is stronger—the points on her body she sprays it in the morning.

"Aiden," she breathes. I don't know if my name on her lips is a warning or a plea. I don't know if she knows either.

I let her wrist fall from my grip. Going back to my seat, I put some needed distance between us. Whatever that was, I don't want it to happen again.

It didn't feel like the typical sexual aggression between us. It felt deeper—meaningful. Neither one of those things are any good when it comes to Monica.

"I told you I wanted to do whatever possible to help my brother. You aren't doing it alone," I answer, my voice a little more firm than necessary.

Her eyes stay focused on me a little too long for comfort. Her slightly narrowed lids make me anxious.

"Good," she finally says. "Let's get to work."

30
MONICA

Before we know it, the sun sets behind the LA cityscape. Aiden and I have been holed up in his room for the entire day digging into Coleman Records. Occasionally I have to take a phone call or attend to something on behalf of Nash, but for the most part we've been able to spend the entire time doing research.

There's a lot of smoke around Roy, but we've yet to find any actual fire. If we can just get more of his past artists to talk, I know we'll find an explosion just waiting to detonate. At the very least, getting enough people together to tell their stories would create enough attention to warrant some action.

I also want to find a way to dig deeper into the financials of Coleman Records. I have no doubt some of the investors in the label are part of this sleazy thing Roy has got going on, but I doubt *all* of them are. I bet some would love to know that the money that is supposed to help fund Coleman is the reason Roy and his buddies are all able to cheat on their wives in the name of *business*.

"Have you ever heard of Sasha Reed?" Aiden asks from the chair across from me.

I look up from my computer, wracking my brain for the

name. "It sounds vaguely familiar," I admit. "But I can't put a face to the name."

He swivels the laptop around, showing me his screen. "Four years ago she won a singing competition. She was supposed to be the next big thing. Part of her winning was that she landed an album deal with Coleman Records."

I nod, instantly remembering the girl on the computer screen. Nash had made an appearance on the finale of that show. He probably doesn't remember it, being three shots to the wind while performing one of his old songs. I'd spent a majority of the night on pins and needles, hoping he didn't say something we'd have to spend weeks cleaning up in the tabloids.

But I do remember her face—her innocent smile. I remember she was young. She'd gone from waiting tables and singing at her college karaoke shows to winning it all. Yet somehow, she didn't go anywhere after winning.

I hadn't thought much about it at the time—it happens in this industry. But now, I wonder if it had something to do with Roy.

"Did she ever release an album?" I ask, my eyes scanning over the various articles of her on Aiden's laptop.

He shakes his head. "Not from what I can tell. If you search her name on the streaming platforms, the only songs that come up are the ones she recorded from the show."

My teeth run over my bottom lip in contemplation. "This has to be connected, right?"

Aiden shrugs, turning the laptop back in his direction. For a moment the only sound is his fingers typing across his keyboard. "There's only one way to find out," he finally says. "I just direct messaged her Instagram account."

"Let's hope she answers," I say, leaning back in my chair. I'm used to long days, but typically I don't spend the entirety of the day in one spot. My fingers find my temple, trying to rub away the dull headache from staring at a screen all day.

"Think we should call it for now?" Aiden asks. I don't open my eyes, but I can hear the sound of him shutting his laptop.

"I think we've got a good start. We'll see if Sasha messages you back, and then we'll visit with Chelsea this weekend to see what we can find."

He claps his hands together, the noise startling me. My eyes pop open, finding him standing next to the seat he was just in.

"I need some food and to let Pep out."

Aiden doesn't wait for me to give him any kind of response. He opens the door and disappears into the hallway before I can tell him goodbye or formulate some kind of plan for this weekend.

I stare, unsure, into the empty room around me. It's never been like me to feel awkward. Not since my childhood when I'd do all manners of things to get the attention of my parents. But now, I look around the vacant room and wonder if that was his hint that I should leave.

Why are you thinking so deep into this?

I've got the means to text him or find him here if I need to speak next steps with him. There's no reason for me to stay in his messy room. And yet, I haven't moved.

Instead, I find myself looking around the room, taking in every aspect of his personal space. I tell myself it's because I want to be able to give him grief for his lack of organization skills—the unruly pile of cookbooks on the top of the dresser indicating just how unorganized he is. What I don't try to think about is the teeny, tiny need I feel at the back of my mind to stand up and look around his room. To get to know him better— to understand who he is.

If I've learned anything recently, it's that there's more to Nash's younger brother than I originally thought possible. All of the small nuances that make him, *him,* shouldn't matter to me. But against my better judgment, I find myself standing and running a finger along the large pile of books and papers on his dresser.

Picking up one of the pieces of paper, I find small, neat handwriting covering each page. The same handwriting can be found on all of the pieces in the stack, making me believe it has to be Aiden's. His handwriting is neater than I'd imagined. My finger runs over his words, noting how hard he presses into the paper by the indents of his letters on the paper.

Each page has a list of names with different foods noted next to it. I scan over each page, noting that these are all staff members on the tour.

My eyebrows pinch together as I try to figure out what the lists mean. There are so many familiar names with different types of food or dishes next to their name.

My breath catches when I land on my own name. There are a few question marks next to my name that have since been crossed out. Next to the eliminated marks there's a few dishes neatly scrawled out.

Lemon chicken and chickpea salad
Caprese on gluten free toast
Find out what is in the smoothie she drinks

I reread the words over and over again until I realize what these lists are. Somehow he's collected a list of the crew members' favorite foods. There are so many names on here, I wonder if he made an effort to ask every single one of these people what they prefer.

I'm staring down at my name when the door opens. Before I have time to react, that beast of an animal has her freezing cold nose pressed against my calf. My stockings do nothing to protect my skin from her ice-cold nose. The piece of paper drops out of my hands, but not before Aiden can see what I was up to.

He watches me carefully as he shuts the bedroom door

behind him. In one hand he holds a bottle of wine and two long stemmed wine glasses. The other holds a tray of what appears to be different meats and cheeses.

He doesn't say anything as he makes his way deeper into the room. The glasses clink together as he sets them down on the nightstand beside the bed.

"What are these?" I say, motioning to the dresser. Part of me hates that he caught me snooping, but now that he knows, I don't want to pretend like I didn't see them.

His eyes flick to the scattered papers across the sleek wood. He taps one of the piles with his finger.

"Find anything interesting?" he asks, seemingly unbothered by me going through his things. He pops a grape into his mouth, staring me down as he waits for my answer.

"Yes. What are these?" I repeat, holding up the piece of paper with my name written on it.

"My lists."

"Your lists?"

He nods. "I want to know what the people I'm going to be feeding on tour like. In my spare time I've been asking everyone what their favorites are. And wouldn't you know it, not once has someone said a rock-hard potato with shitty toppings."

I trace a finger over the spot where he'd written my name. "You never asked me."

When I look back up, I find him standing right next to me.

He leans in close, closer than he should. "You wouldn't have told me if I'd asked."

"I don't trust you not to poison my food."

He smirks. "I wouldn't dare…"

My eyes roll. "How do you know what my favorites are? Who did you ask?"

"I didn't ask anyone. I just noticed those things seemed to be your favorite."

Inside my chest, my heart does this weird, foreign thing. It almost feels like it stopped for a moment, but logic tells me that is simply impossible.

I'm stuck trying to form a response—to try and find a hidden meaning behind his words. There has to be some plot he's cooking up in his head. Because if there's not, and there's no ulterior motive, it means that Aiden did something thoughtful. For me. It's the simplest of things, taking notice of what foods I enjoy, but it seems much bigger than that.

Someone who hates you shouldn't care about your likes and dislikes. They definitely shouldn't be writing it down on a list full of people they actually like.

I'm wondering what kind of territory Aiden and I are stepping into. We aren't enemies anymore. At least, it doesn't feel like it. But we aren't friends. Perhaps having a common enemy has allowed us to temporarily put aside our differences.

But this gesture doesn't have anything to do with Roy or the label. It's sad that this gesture, one that seems so insignificant, is one I know I won't be able to let go. Hours—and days—later from now, I know I will still be focused on it.

"Stop reading into it," Aiden says, retreating back to the discarded wine and food. "I did it for literally everyone on tour."

I swallow, closing my eyes to purge my thoughts. When I open them, I find him pouring wine into one of the empty glasses.

"I should really get going," I say, taking small steps toward my belongings.

He shakes his head, paying no attention to my words by starting to pour wine into the second glass.

"I've got plans tonight," I offer. It's a lie. I have absolutely no plans other than maybe taking a bath and reading a few chapters of a new book I've been reading about connecting with your inner self. Other women my age are dating, or at least have friends to go have a drink with. I'm not other women. I've always opted to put work before anything socially, and I'd much prefer my own alone time when given the chance.

He sets the wine bottle back down. His hand engulfs the narrow stem of one of the wine glasses. It looks odd, seeing his large fingers encompassing the fragile glass. "Suit yourself. I'll drink this bottle on my own. Or invite someone to enjoy it with me."

He walks across the room, his arm brushing against mine as he passes me. One hand holds his wine glass while the other holds the platter of food. Not bothering to look at me, he uses his foot to open the doors to the patio.

"You're stealing from Nash's private stash of wine..."

He smiles over his shoulder. "I won't tell if you don't tell." Walking across the patio, he stops at the stone wall that overlooks the hills behind Nash's house. He paid a lot of money to get a house in a gated community that still allowed space between him and his neighbors. Aiden's room is at the back of the house, his door leading straight out to the outdoor gym Nash insisted he needed.

A few feet away there's a table and lounge chairs, but that doesn't appear to matter to Aiden. He seems happy standing against the wall, taking in the lights of the city in the distance.

I'm left standing in the room, needing to make a choice. He isn't asking me to stay, yet my feet stay planted. I know that the wise decision would be to pack up my things and leave this room. We've accomplished what we wanted to for the day. There's no reason for me to stay. No reason to complicate things.

Staying would almost certainly mean giving into him. He knows it. I know it. The fact that I haven't already left probably gives him great satisfaction. He's not dumb, he knows my hesitation to leave is answer enough.

I'm so tired of fighting this—hating it. Somehow Nash's little brother has got to me. He holds a power over me that I'm not sure I've ever allowed anyone. I just want to give into it. And it's unlike me.

I eye the wine on the nightstand. It's a dry red—one of my favorites. Nash keeps it stocked for me for when he has dinner parties. I wonder if it's a coincidence that Aiden chose this exact wine, or if it's part of the game he's playing. If he's making a point to show me that he knows me better than I thought—that he *does* hold the power.

"Monica?" Aiden says from the patio.

I don't look at him, all I do is stare at the already poured glass of wine, weighing my options but knowing my decision.

"For once in your life, stop overthinking things. Give in." His words fall short for a moment before he adds, "Stay."

31
AIDEN

I KNEW I had her the second she didn't flee the room when I stepped outside. I'd given her the chance to leave. I wasn't going to beg her to stay. She got what she came for today—more answers on Roy. Yet, when I'd gone to grab food and let the dog out, it didn't feel like the night was over for us.

It felt like it'd just begun. I tried not to read into why I felt pleasure in preparing a charcuterie board for two. I've always loved to feed people, and that stands true—even for someone like Monica.

When I'd walked in the room and caught her snooping through my meal plans, I wasn't embarrassed. In fact, part of me was relieved that she knew how close I'd been studying her. I'd become obsessed with wanting to know everything about the woman who is Monica Masters—including her favorite foods.

They say keep your friends close and your enemies closer. But what happens when you get too close? I feel like I have this insatiable desire to get to know her, fueled by an intense need to get into that head of hers. To see what makes her tick. To get her to give up control and let loose.

It's the reason I asked her to stay. I still want her to be the one that gives in—to admit that her body is as desperate for mine as mine is for hers. But, that doesn't mean I can't help her in that direction.

Staring out at the city lights, my cool exterior demeanor doesn't match the jitters I feel in my stomach as I wait for her to respond.

"This is a terrible idea," Monica says, her eyes pinned on the glass of wine I poured for her.

"Probably. But I'm not going to stop it." Turning to look at her, I see the exact moment she makes up her mind. The small step she takes toward the glass of wine instead of toward the door tells me everything.

She's giving in to this. Somehow, it feels like she's waving her white flag, and I'm hit with the realization that maybe I began to wave mine a while ago.

Maybe this whole time I'd been telling myself that she was the enemy so I could pretend that the obsession I have with her is healthy. Pretend that I'm studying her to protect my brother from more treachery. Now that we seem to be at a ceasefire, I'm faced with the possibility that these feelings in the depths of my heart have developed to no longer resemble hate.

For now, I shove those feelings down deep. I'm not prepared to face this realization. For tonight, I want to get lost in her body—in her surrender—and forget about the rest.

My heart fights against my ribcage as I watch her pick up the wine glass. Standing in front of the nightstand, she brings the glass to her lips. The muscles in her throat move delicately as she takes a large sip of the drink. It reminds me of the way her throat worked when my cock was shoved down it, the way she had to open it to allow me in.

She downs the entire glass of wine, not bothering to sip on the wine the way it was intended to be enjoyed. Quickly, she reaches for the bottle, filling her glass full once again.

Taking a deep breath, and one last gulp of wine, she turns to face me. Her eyebrows inch toward one another on her forehead, creating a crease right at the center. My fingers itch to run a hand over the line and smooth it out.

"What are we doing here, Aiden?" she wonders, her voice full of trepidation. Despite the unease in her voice, her feet slowly bring her closer to me.

I fight the primal urge to reach out and touch her—to feel her skin against mine.

I have to look away from her before I lose the battle with my resolve. There aren't many false pretenses between us. We can both identify what's about to happen here, but I need a moment to really think about her question.

"Everything we shouldn't be doing," I admit to the rolling hills in front of me.

"I'm so much older than you, *and* you're Nash's little brother. We can't do this." I feel the heat of her body as she takes the spot next to me. If someone were to stumble upon us, they'd just see two people looking at the barely visible stars through all of the light pollution of LA. They wouldn't see the friction sparking between our bodies, even though no part of us touch. They'd have no idea that a few months ago, I hated this cunning, manipulative, and selfish woman. They'd be clueless to the fact that she could barely tolerate the sight of me. That it took everything in her to hold her tongue around me.

But now, it's hard to fathom hating her, and hard to fathom not. We're two completely opposite people—oil and water— dancing around each other but too different to be together. Too different to get along long enough to be anything meaningful.

Yet, I've never felt the animalistic need for another human like I do with her. I've never desired the taste of a woman the way I desire hers. I've never felt desperate to control every single one of someone's heartbeats. I no longer want to kiss her just because I want to piss her off, I want to kiss her because the thought of not kissing her drives me mad.

"Does it bother you?" Her voice breaks me from my

thoughts. I finally lose the battle with myself, I look at her, wondering how the features I used to hate about her are the ones I'm attracted to most.

"Does what bother me?"

She sighs, the lips that used to snap rude insults back at me are now pursing in annoyance. Now those lips are something I can never stop staring at. I used to hate that she seemed to wear the same shade of lipstick every day, now that shade of red has become my favorite color. "My age. You've just begun your twenties…I've left mine in the dust."

I shake my head. "Never thought about it. I don't give a damn about age."

I don't know why, but something as simple as Monica sliding off each one of her heels does something to me. It's incredibly mundane, but it seems intimate. She wears heels from sunup to sundown. The fact that she's at ease enough to slip off each one in my presence…it has my mind going places it has no business going.

"I work for your brother," she adds. I still stare at her feet, watching the way she flexes her neatly painted toes inside her sheer stockings.

I set my wine glass on the ledge of the rail, freeing up my hand. Reaching out, I play with a stray piece of blonde hair. Typically she has perfectly styled hair, but it's evident keeping it flawless wasn't at the top of her to-do list today. Sometimes when I'd look up from my own laptop, I'd find her twisting the same strand I play with around her finger. She seemed to do it when she was deep in concentration. Her lips would move quickly as she would read whatever was on the screen to herself, her finger busy twisting and untwisting the strand until it no longer was perfectly straight like its counterparts.

"Are you trying to talk me or yourself out of this?" I let the hair fall to her shoulders. Using both my hands, I push all of her hair back, letting it fall down her back. With her hair gone, I'm left with inches upon inches of bare skin, just begging to be touched.

My finger traces over the curve of her collarbone.

"Me. You." She sighs. "*Both.*"

I let my finger dip closer to the swell of her breasts. The square neckline of her blouse allows me access to so much of her tan, creamy skin. "You won't talk me out of this, Monica."

"Of course I won't. I'm supposed to be the responsible one here," she says breathlessly as I slide my finger underneath the fabric of her shirt. My index finger rubs at the soft skin of her breast gently.

"Don't worry. Out there," I motion to the city behind us, "you can pretend to be emotionless and always in control. But here…" I pause, finally finding the hard bud of her nipple. I flick it, feeling it pebble even more underneath my touch.

Her knuckles turn white from the ironlike grip she's got on the stem of her wine glass. "But here?" she whispers.

"Here, you're none of that." My finger slides out of her shirt and immediately begins to work on undoing the buttons. The fabric molds perfectly to her body, but as I unfasten each button it opens up, allowing me a better view of the hidden skin underneath. When I get to the bottom, I have to pull the fabric from her skirt. The shirt falls open as I get the last button undone.

My eyes rake over the bra underneath. The sheer black fabric is miserable at hiding her raised pink nipples. The wires of the bra lift her perfectly round breasts, the display causing my pants to stir.

"Here, you're not in control," I grit my teeth, angry at how badly I want this, "*I am.*"

In this moment, I can still give the illusion that I hold all of the power and she holds none.

I reach behind her and unzip her skirt in one quick motion. The fabric falls at her feet and I'm left taking in all of the sexiness she'd hidden underneath.

I didn't think anything could turn me on more than the sight of her perky nipples peeking out of her bra, but I was wrong. Her high-waisted underwear is completely sheer. So sheer that she's unable to hide the evidence of her arousal—the fabric glistening with wetness at the bottom.

The bulge in my pants throbs as I finish taking her in. A belt that loops around her narrow waist keeps up two thin straps of fabric, which run down the front of her thigh before two small clips fasten to the top of her stockings.

Monica allows me to take my time marveling over the sight of her. I'm still fully dressed while she stands in front of me in her most intimate clothing.

Air escapes my lips in a whistle. "Fuck, the sight of you of right now is the sexiest thing I've ever seen."

She looks down at her body, shifting from one foot to the other.

I place my hands on the small of her waist right above the fabric of her belt. "Tell me, Monica, did you put this on this morning envisioning that I'd be stripping it off you tonight?"

Her response is immediate. "No."

I laugh. Bending down to her level, I place my mouth next to her ear. "I don't believe you, little liar. I think you picked this out just for me."

My hands trail down her waist, roaming to her back. I let them continue to explore the way her skin feels underneath the lingerie. My fingers are quick at unclipping the garter belt.

"Tell me the truth," I demand, wrapping my arms around her to find the meaty flesh of her ass.

"I didn't think of you at all," she says, her voice shaky.

I look down at her and find her looking back up at me, her chin lifted in defiance. "Is that so?"

She nods, her lips falling open when I suddenly pull at the fabric of the underwear. It slides down her thighs effortlessly, landing on top of her bare feet.

"Aiden, we can't do this out here. Someone might see."

Before she can protest further, I grab her waist and place her onto the railing of the patio, standing in the void between her legs. I take her chin into my hand and pull her face close to mine, holding eye contact. "Good, I want them to see," I say.

Falling to my knees, I spread her legs open. The concrete is hard against my knees, but I barely notice now that I'm eye-level with her bare pussy. I can smell her arousal, the sweet tinge overtaking my senses.

I lift my finger and run it through the wetness. Looking up from the ground, I find her watchful gaze. I place the wet finger in my mouth, sucking the taste of her off me. "Let them see when I finally get you to tell the truth. That you're absolutely as ravenous for me as I am for you. That you're my filthy little liar, desperate to be under my control."

Before she can answer, I latch my mouth to her sweet little cunt. The sudden movement forces her to grip the rail for support. I reach around her hips, gripping her thighs to stabilize her. My tongue licks and sucks at her as I revel in each and every admission of pleasure from her.

Her hands leave the rail and weave into my hair. Once I have her panting and moaning, I pull off a fraction of an inch and look up at her.

"Say the words, Monica. Tell me you put this sexy little number on for me and *only* me. Tell me that this sweet little cunt of yours doesn't drip like this for anyone but me. Tell me, and I'll prove to you how much it's mine."

Her thighs clench together. She throws her head back, letting out a groan. "You win, Aiden. It's for you—only you."

"Good girl," I tell her with a smile. It takes no time for me to stand up and fold her in my arms. I take long strides until we make it to the workout equipment beyond the patio. Laying her down on one of the workout benches, I spread her legs open, placing her feet on either side of the bench. Every inch of her is on full display for me.

As much as I want to linger here and commit this sight to memory, I can't help but go right back to my task from earlier. I pull her body down the bench until her ass is on the very end, perfectly lining up her pussy with my mouth.

One finger enters her warmth while my tongue licks the spilling juices from top to bottom. It doesn't take long until she's writhing underneath my mouth. Her moans bounce off the stone of the patio and echo into the valley below. If someone happens to be within earshot of us, there's no way they won't hear us.

It doesn't deter me, even if it should. The only thing I care about at this moment is bringing her to release. When I know she's close, I stop using my mouth, rubbing her clit gently with my fingers instead to keep her on the edge.

"I'm going to fuck you now, Monica," I tell her. "You're going to cum all over my cock and then you're going to do it again and again until I tell you I'm done. Understood?"

Her back arches off the bench. A frustrated moan passes her lips, voicing displeasure at me stopping her from an orgasm once again.

Reaching to the back of my neck, I pull at the collar of my shirt and let it fall to the ground. I remove my pants and boxers just as quickly. My cock throbs as I run my hand up and down it. "Don't be frustrated, baby," I say, stepping between her legs. "You're going to get your chance, I'll make sure of it."

32
MONICA

THE HEAD of his cock plays with my wetness, setting all my nerve endings ablaze. He's got me so primed and ready that every touch threatens to send me over the edge.

"Tell me you're on the pill or some shit like that," he says through clenched teeth. It's evident that he's holding back right now, that he's dying to enter me and unleash himself.

It's what I want too.

He speaks again before I can answer. "Monica, I want to come inside you—to have you reminded of me hours later when I'm still leaking from you. Tell me you're on the pill, that we don't have to have a barrier between us."

"Of course I'm on the pill." My hips buck to try and align him with my entrance. "Now fuck me, Aiden. Please."

He doesn't spare a second. He shoves inside, giving me no warning as he buries himself inside me. "I told you I'd get you to beg for it, little liar."

My eyes squeeze shut as I fight off the approaching orgasm. I don't want this to end before it begins. Earlier I'd been desperate to reach the brink of release, but now I'm fighting off every sensation to try and make this last a little longer.

The leather of the workout equipment sticks to my back,

holding me in place as he pulls all the way out of me before pushing deep inside again. The quick movements force my tits into a rhythmic motion as my body jolts back and forth on the bench. He repeats the same motion, pounding me deeper against the bench with each thrust.

Strong fingers grasp my jaw. His fingertips dig deep into my cheeks as he straightens my head toward himself. "Look at me when I make you lose control," his voice is rough, strained as he beats in and out of me.

I open my eyes just as our lips crash together. The warmth of his tongue as it circles mine sets my entire body ablaze with an uncontrollable madness. I will my heart to slow enough to reign myself in as his hips thrust in time with his tongue, but I'm unsuccessful. His thick, smooth cock shoves into me rapidly before sliding back out and I feel every inch of his bad intentions for me. He's pushing me, stretching me, sending me spiraling to the brink of ecstasy...and I meet and every thrust with a moan of his name. The movements of his tongue are slow and passionate. He kisses me like he forgives me but plows into me like he's punishing me.

Maybe he *is* punishing me. Maybe he's punishing the both of us for igniting this fire that can't burn forever. I don't care. I gladly meet each and every one of his brutal thrusts, lost in the sensation of the soft kisses mixed with the punishing beat of his hips.

My toes curl as an orgasm begins to build, threatening to send me over the edge at any second.

"I'm so close," I pant. My nails dig into the small of his back in an attempt to find something to hold onto before he fucks me right off this bench.

For a slow, brutal moment he stops. His cock stays buried inside me as he pulls me back down the bench. In one fluid motion he adjusts our position, straddling the bench with me on his lap. My legs come over his hips but aren't long enough to touch the ground behind him. The new position forces him to carry all of my weight. It also puts his cock even deeper inside me, a delicious pain I greet eagerly by wrapping my legs around him.

His hand is hot as it travels up my spine. The tips of his fingers are gentle at first as he tangles them in my hair. Balling his fists, he tugs on the hair, forcing my head backward. My eyes well at the pain in my scalp.

Before I can complain, he eases the pain with pleasure. Placing his other hand on the dimples on my back, he starts the motion up and down on his length.

I wrap my arms around his neck for support, feeling his hot breath against my face. Desperate to feel him move inside me, I rock my hips back and forth. My thighs begin to shake in anticipation of losing control.

His lips find my throat and he bites down on the tender skin between my neck and shoulder. His teeth pierce my skin as ecstasy rips through me. My moans pierce through the silence of the outdoors for the world to hear. I try to stifle them, but it's no use. The waves of the orgasm roll through me as Aiden continues his motion.

"You're so god damn sexy when you lose control," he says, his teeth grazing my throat as he speaks. "I want to see it again and again until you're so spent you can't even walk."

I'm still riding the high of my orgasm when he picks me up by my ass and pulls out of me. Before I can ask him what he's doing, he flips me over so I'm on all fours. I arch my back, feeling like I'm on full display for anyone in the vicinity.

Looking over my shoulder, I find Aiden focused on my core. His stare is hot against it, and I know he can see the juices leaking out of me from my own orgasm.

I want to come inside you, to have you reminded of me hours later when I'm still leaking from you. My thighs clench remembering his earlier words, the thought makes even more wetness drip down my legs.

"We should get inside," I say, moving to step off the bench.

His fingers dig deep into my hips, pinning me in place. He doesn't look up from where he stares between my legs when he speaks. "We're not going anywhere."

I should argue with him. There's no way that Nash or anyone else can find out about us. It could ruin everything. Aiden and I are supposed to hate one another. How am I supposed to explain this to someone else when I can't even rationalize it for myself?

But I. Can't. Say. No.

I can't stop this.

Somehow the danger of being exposed coupled with the taboo of sleeping with Aiden has my brain numb to all reason.

Right now it's just him, his commands, and the night sky around us.

Any thought of stopping this is lost as he shoves back inside me. This time, he strokes slower than earlier. The cold bench makes my nipples stiffen as they gently graze it. He presses my head further into the leather while my hips stay in the air.

"This right here," he pulls all the way out of me before slowly making his way back in. "This is mine. I don't want to fucking hear about anyone else taking what's mine. Do you understand me, Monica?"

All I can do is moan. Lost in the euphoria of our joined bodies, all I want to do is agree. But I've always been a logical person, and neither him nor I are naive enough to think this will transcend to anything more than sex.

We're two people connected at the most primal of levels, unable to deny one of our most basic instincts. But there's a thousand reasons why this shouldn't happen again, why this has always been a bad idea from the start.

He presses a hand into my shoulders, making me sink

deeper into the leather, my back arching to an almost painful level. "I said, do you understand?"

"No," I pant, my cheek pressing hard into the bench. "You aren't my boyfriend, Aiden. This isn't exclusive."

He jabs into me angrily while his palm digs into the spot between my shoulders. "No I'm not your fucking boyfriend. But that doesn't make you any less *mine*. Another man doesn't get to touch you. Not while I'm still having my way with you."

To prove his point, he moves in and out of me at an agonizingly slow pace. His free hand traces over my ass slowly. I'm seconds away from arguing with him, but his finger continues until it moves over my clit, making me forget everything.

It doesn't take long for me to reach the brink of an orgasm all over again. My moans excite him. His pace picks back up. Both of his hands manage to find my hips as he uses the new grip for leverage. He pulls me into him while he pushes inside me.

My cheek slaps against the leather with each one of his thrusts. Even though my arms feel like Jell-O, I manage to push up off them to lift the trunk of my body. My nails dig into the leather as I grasp the sides of the bench for dear life. It's the only way I'm able to steady myself as the orgasm overtakes me.

He grasps the flesh of my hips so tightly I know there's bound to be marks from him tomorrow. His entire body stiffens as he reaches climax, emptying himself deep inside me. There's no escaping him as the two of us ride the waves of our pleasure together.

It's the first time in a long time I've felt completely at peace. My body is exhausted. I'm emotionally and physically spent from what's transpired between us on this patio, but yet the way he's gently pulled my body into his as we came down from what just happened—it melts years of stress and anxiety away.

We aren't cuddling. There would need to be more points of

contact between our bodies to ever be considered cuddling, but it's close to it. Too close for two people like us.

Our skin sticks together, my back to his front. I can feel each and every one of his heaving breaths. They perfectly match my own.

I let myself revel in the near feeling of being held. Something I haven't had in ages. I give myself a few moments pretending that the best sex of my life wasn't with my client's little brother —with the person who frustrates me more than any other human.

In my mind, I envision that he's someone my age. Someone I met at my yoga studio, country club, or business luncheon. Someone sophisticated, established—someone completely opposite of who he really is.

Then the moment stops. I'm brought right back to reality when Aiden says, "I hate that I'm already thinking about doing that again."

I peel myself from him, feeling the loss of his body heat immediately. Even without the sun, it's warm here in LA. The air around isn't cold, but it still feels like I've lost all warmth as I crawl off the workout bench. I walk over to my discarded clothes by the entrance to the house. Snatching my underwear off the cobblestone, I step into each one of the leg holes and pull the delicate mesh up my thighs.

Aiden stands up. "What are you doing?"

I set my blouse and skirt down so I'm able to put my bra on. Sliding on the bra, I look at him. "What does it look like I'm doing?"

"It looks like you're leaving."

"Didn't take a rocket scientist to figure that one out, did it?" I snap. The zipper on my skirt catches. Sighing angrily, I try to force it up but it won't budge.

During my struggle, Aiden slips on a pair of boxers. I feel the unexpected brush of his knuckles as he holds the two sides of my skirt together. He gets the zipper to budge, his knuckle tickling the bare skin of my back as he pulls it up.

"You don't have to do this," he says softly, his tone gentler than I was expecting. Both of his hands lay limply at his side when I turn around to face him.

"Do what?" I ask, adjusting the strap of my bra on my shoulder.

"Fuck I don't know, Monica. Make things complicated?" he says, making it sound more like a question than a statement.

A shrill laugh breaks through my lips. "It isn't complicated. We had sex and now I'm leaving."

His fingers run through his hair in frustration. "So we're going to keep playing this game aren't we?"

"What game?"

"The game where we act like there's not something going on here. That for some sick reason the universe seems to be pushing us together, yet we continue to fight it. I'm tired of fighting it."

"I told you, Aiden. The only reason I wanted it to happen once was so we could get it out of our system. We've accomplished that." My fingers diligently work at fastening the buttons of my blouse.

His eyes widen, his cheeks puffing out in annoyance. "So that's it. I'm just…out of your system, huh?" He rubs his hands together as if he were wiping them clean.

"Yes," I say, the word sounding stronger than it feels saying it.

The world around is silent as he stares at me. I don't know what to do with this version of Aiden. He's never quiet or contemplative. This version of him unnerves me. I'd rather him lash out—insult me like usual. I can take his jabs, it's his silence that scares me.

My eyes focus on the ticking muscle of his clenched jaw, a clear indicator of his frustration with me.

Silently, he walks to his discarded pants. He takes his time sliding each one of his legs through and pulling them up his body.

I watch him carefully, wondering if he's going to say anything else. There's no reason for me to linger, but I'm stuck wondering what's in that head of his. When it remains quiet, I accept that the conversation is over, sliding my feet into my heels.

Right as I twist the handle on the door to his room, he speaks up from behind me.

"I've always known you were a liar, Monica. I just didn't expect for you to be a coward, too."

I muster every ounce of confidence I have. My shoulders push back as I refuse to look back at him. He doesn't need to know that he's right. He doesn't need to know that I'm shuttering at the response my body had to him. Underneath every ounce of pleasure he plucked out of me, there were feelings that I don't want to bother approaching. I don't understand them and I don't *want* to understand them.

I told Aiden it would only take once to get him out of my system.

But now I'm afraid that it won't matter how many times we do this.

It won't ever be enough.

33
AIDEN

Staring at her retreating form, I want to yell, cuss, do *something* to get her to turn around and look at me. I just had what was the best sex of my life and judging by the way she trembled under my touch, I know it was the same for her.

I'd never agreed to her stupid terms of only one time to get it out of her system. I knew the tension between us wouldn't dissipate after one time together. After getting a taste of how it was with her tonight, I want to do it over and over again until both of us feel satiated—if that's even possible.

All I wanted was for her to admit that her body was feeling what mine was. That she felt the undeniable connection that pulled me to her like a magnet. Instead, she'd done what I should've expected from her all along.

She lied.

She looked me in the eye and told me that this one time together was enough. Never did I think that Monica and I needed to be boyfriend and girlfriend or any of that shit. It isn't *us* to define anything. I just want to stop pretending that there isn't something more. Our bodies speak in a language we don't have to understand. We crave each other as much as we hate one another. It's not something that's going to go away with just one encounter. I'm afraid the more access I have to her body, the more I'll want. Furthermore, I'm terrified that the more I get to know her, the small glimpses she allows me, the more I'll be drawn in. We've begun to spiral down a road we won't be able to come back from. At least *I* won't be able to.

And that's why I stand here angry, shirtless, and wondering what the hell just happened.

Never did I imagine asking her to stay. What I'm only just realizing, as the weight of her absence truly hits me, is that I'm pissed off. But not because of anything I would've thought. She's the last person I should want, yet she's the *only* person I want.

I curse myself for these feelings I never asked for. Pure self-loathing courses through my chest at the desperate desire running through my veins. Because below all of this uncharted need I feel for her, I've been burying away feelings for her, too.

And no matter how deep I've tried to bury those feelings, they're clawing their way out from six feet under, refusing to be ignored a moment longer.

The slight thought of her with another man elicits the most violent thoughts out of me. For *Monica*. The person who used to make me violent in a completely different way.

"You know, I called this from the very beginning, right?" a voice mutters from inside my bedroom.

A groan escapes me as I look up at the sky, wondering why the universe hates me right now. Yanking my shirt off the patio, I walk toward my open door.

Lennon is just hanging out on my bed. She sits cross-legged, Pepper's head tucked into her lap. The dog's tail wags lazily as Lennon strokes the top of her head. It reminds me of earlier in the day when I caught Monica giving the dog affection. I'd wanted to comment on it, to let her know that I saw her giving the animal she pretends to despise affection. I kept to myself, going back to my research. For some reason it was refreshing to see her being so tender with the dog. It wasn't something I'd expect from her.

"Don't make this awkward," Lennon says, breaking the silence.

I pull the t-shirt back over my head before diving to the open space at her feet.

"Wouldn't have to be awkward if you'd just pretended you saw nothing," I tell her.

Her eyes roll. "It wasn't necessarily what I *saw*. It's what I heard."

Flipping to my back, I stare at the ceiling. My hands go to cover my face. In the moment, I hadn't given a damn if anyone saw what Monica and I'd been doing. I'd have done it in front of a crowd full of people to keep her reacting to my touch the way she was. But now after the fact, after the stinging pain of her lies and rejection, I wish no one else had to know what transpired.

"I really don't want to talk about it, Len," I say, defeated. I was already exhausted from staring at a computer screen today. Add in everything that just happened with Monica and I'm tapped out for the day.

"Well my ears are scarred forever. I just need you to know that. I didn't want to hear *Monica* moan like that." She shudders, making Pepper stir in her lap.

"God, you're making this so much worse."

"What are the two of you doing?" she asks, her voice softer than it was before.

I turn to my side so I can look her in the eye. My shoulder lifts in a shrug. "Hell if I know."

She tucks her unruly hair behind her ear. Her body settles deeper into the throw pillows on my bed. "How did this even start? You *hate* one another."

I laugh. "My dick and my brain weren't on the same page."

"I wouldn't know," she whispers.

"What do you mean?" I ask, picking at the loose threads on my comforter as I wait for her to give a response.

Pulling one of the pillows from her side, she uses it to bury her face in it. "I didn't say anything."

My arm reaches out, pulling at the pillow until I can see her eyes. Half of her face is exposed, revealing her crimson cheeks. "Tell me," I say. "We're friends, Len. You're the only person who knows about this disaster of a secret I've been keeping. Whatever you want to say…you can say it."

She looks to the ceiling embarrassed. "I just mean I wouldn't know what it's like to just have some kind of uncontrollable *need* to be with someone," she pauses uncomfortably, "on that level."

"Like to want someone for sex?" I ask, trying to clarify what she means.

She nods. "You know what happened in high school with me…and Nora's boyfriend." Her words fall off.

As if Pepper knows that Lennon's mind is going to a dark place, she leans up and gives her a wet lick across the face. Lennon laughs softly, gently pushing the dog away. There's still a soft smile on her face when she talks again. "I'd never done anything with a boy before that, and after…"

"It's understandable why you'd want to be cautious after everything that happened," I offer. I don't know all of the details because I'd never pushed her on it before. Even though we've become friends, I don't need to know all the dark details of her past. I do know that when she was in high school, Nora's boyfriend had drunkenly crawled into bed with Lennon, thinking it was Nora, and had done things to Lennon that no man should ever do to a woman. There was an ugly legal battle afterwards, and I know in the aftermath that Nora and Lennon's relationship was never the same.

It was the reason Lennon had come on the current tour with Nash and Nora. They're starting over, and I'm thankful to have a companion like Lennon the entire time. But even if it seems like she's doing her best to heal, I can't begin to fathom what she still goes through daily after something traumatic like that.

We sit in silence for a while. Finally, she speaks up. "What if I *don't* want to be cautious? All I want is to feel what you mentioned. I want that intense need for someone…for someone to have that for me, no matter what our brains thought of the matter. I just want to know what it feels like to want someone so passionately that you throw all caution to the wind. That you can't stand another second without someone that you can't even move from the public patio outside to the bed inside."

Her answer makes me sad. Before Monica, I'd never felt such an intense desire for someone, but now that I've had it, I can't imagine *not* feeling it. Even if I hate it sometimes. "You deserve that and so much more."

"I tried to find it. I bounced from state to state and then country to country, hoping someone along the way would fill the void but…"

"They never did," I finish for her. At some kind of level, I know what she means. I'd been with countless women before Monica. I didn't realize there *had* been a void back then, but it's clear as day now. I'll just have to figure out how to fill it once our fire eventually burns out—if she didn't already snuff it out.

"Nope," she says, popping the 'p'. "It was worth a shot though. Until then, I'll keep feeling it through my books." She pulls a book from her side, holding it in the air.

"It all makes sense now. That's why your nose is always so buried in a book that you're barely keeping up with reality."

Her eyebrows scrunch on her forehead. "Poe says the exact same thing. He won't let me live it down that I'd rather be with fictional characters than real people."

I playfully shove at her leg, happy for the subject change. "Speaking of Poe. You know my dirty secret, tell me yours."

Moving the pillow from her face, she holds it against her chest. "You know you asking me about Poe isn't going to make me forget that I have *sooo* many questions about you and Monica."

"You know deflecting back to me and Monica isn't going to make me have any less questions about what's going on between you and Nash's sexy, broody bassist."

"Absolutely nothing," she says, a little too quickly for me to believe her.

"It isn't hard to miss the way you look at him. And that sometimes, he's caught looking at you, too."

"Yeah, well, we're just friends. He's made it very clear that he's nowhere near looking for anything—especially with me."

"Then he's dumb as fuck," I throw out there immediately.

She throws the pillow my way, hitting me square in the face. "You're just saying that to make me feel better about the fact that I have a crush on a guy that wants nothing to do with me."

"Well, I'm afraid I might be developing feelings for The Wicked Witch of the Tour so I'm not in a position to give advice."

She shoots up, pillows disappearing behind her with the sudden movement. The jerk also causes Pepper to wake up from her deep slumber. She sighs, standing up and walking across the bed. She circles around and around before finding a new spot, no longer touching Lennon or I in her annoyed state.

"I need more details. Are these like *real* feelings or like *I just want to bang you* feelings?"

"Fuck I don't know," I tell her truthfully. "I don't know anything when it comes to that woman. She's the most infuriating person I've ever met, but also…"

"Also?" Lennon interrupts.

"She's also the most intriguing person I've ever met. I'm left wanting more every time I'm with her. It's a dangerous game. It was supposed to be just sex."

"Maybe nothing is ever just sex."

"Oh it can be. It just isn't with her."

"Sounds like the two of us are just really lame," Lennon says, seemingly done with the conversation by the way she picks her book up from her side. The spine makes a cracking noise as she opens it and sets it in her lap.

I can't help but laugh, finding nothing but truth in her words. I hate the way I'm lying here, pining after a woman that I wanted to ruin not too long ago.

34
MONICA

For some reason, my heart pounds against my chest as I idle in the circle drive leading to Nash's front door. Typically, I'd hire a driver, but I don't want a record of the meeting Aiden and I have with Chelsea today.

I'd almost decided to go alone, but I didn't want to give Aiden the knowledge—the satisfaction—of knowing I was still rattled from the other night.

I was also curious to see if Sasha had messaged Aiden back. If we could get her to talk, I suspect that we would find a lot of things that Roy would prefer to stay hidden.

Checking the time on the dash, I become frustrated. I'd told Aiden I was here more than ten minutes ago. I'm about to say information and pride be damned and head to this dinner on my own.

I'm close to firing off one last angry text to him when the door opens. Aiden steps into the daylight, looking out of place in the bright landscape in his all-black attire. From the worn t-shirt he wears to the shoes on his feet, there's no color on his body. His clothes are vastly different from what I typically prefer on a man. I've always been under the impression that there's nothing like a man dawning a sports jacket but watching him walk to my car has me second guessing myself.

He looks way too sexy in something so casual. It's unfair. He's just a kid. But you'd have no idea watching him walk in my direction with all of the confidence and swagger in the world.

When he nears, I turn to face the windshield. I'm glad for the large pair of Prada sunglasses I have covering my eyes. They're big enough to hide a lot of my features, which will come in handy since I'll be stuck in a car with him for a while.

He goes to open the door, but nothing happens. Aiden pulls at the handle again.

My finger hovers over the unlock button. I know I'm being childish for keeping it locked.

His tan knuckles rap against the tinted window. Leaning down, he looks through the dark glass. I know he can't see me, so I use the chance to stare at his face for a moment before unlocking it.

The door clicks. He opens it immediately, sliding into my passenger seat effortlessly. The smell of him assaults my nostrils—the spicy cologne overtaking my senses.

"Think you're being cute?" he growls while buckling his seatbelt.

My sleek sports car now seems cramped with his imposing figure taking up half the space. I throw the car into drive, pressing hard on the gas pedal to get us on the road.

"I forgot it was locked," I answer simply.

He cuts a glance in my direction. "Just another one of your lies."

"Someone is a gem to be around this morning," I mutter under my breath. I wait for a line of cars to pass so I can turn out of Nash's gated driveway.

"Maybe it's from the fact that I can see way too much of your thigh. I mean fuck Monica, how could you put that on and expect me to not want to run my hand up your thigh?"

His answer takes me off-guard, making me step on the brake a little too hard. The two of us lurch forward. I wasn't expecting him to be so up front. The last time I'd seen him was when I'd left him standing on the patio, noticeably upset with me for bailing as soon as we'd finished.

"Stop," I manage to bite out.

"Stop what? Being honest? You should try it sometime."

The car revs as I navigate between lanes, picking up speed in the direction of the restaurant we're meeting Chelsea at.

"You're supposed to be mad at me, not telling me that you want to put your hand up my skirt."

I don't have to look at him to know he's smirking. I can tell just by the tone of his voice when he speaks that his typical cocky smile is in full force. "Oh I'm furious with you, but it doesn't mean I'm perfect and not distracted by the inches of your skin on display."

His warm hand falls into my lap, making me jump. Tearing a hand from the wheel, I maneuver his hand away from my bare skin.

"I can be mad at you and still want to fuck you," he offers nonchalantly. I used to hate how crass he was. Now it's one of the reasons I can't seem to tell him no.

"We agreed it was a one-time thing."

He laughs, the sound booming off the small space we're trapped in. "No *you* came up with that dumb rule. I, on the other hand, would love to bend you over my knee and punish you for ever thinking such a thing."

My knuckles turn white as I grasp onto the steering wheel for dear life. I need something to steady myself right now, to keep me grounded. The last thing I'd expected from him was for him to get in my car and be like *this*. I'd braced myself for anger, silence, *anything* else.

What I hadn't prepared myself was for his brutal honesty.

His admittance of his lust for me was way worse than any insult he could throw my way.

"Is there a reason you're clenching your legs together?" he points out, bringing my attention to an action I didn't realize I was doing.

My legs relax, my own way of defying him, of trying to prove him wrong.

"We should be talking about what we're going to say to Chelsea. Have some sort of game plan." My attempt at changing the subject works.

Aiden removes his hand from the arm rest between us, running it down the front of his jeans as he adjusts in the seat. "That's fine. We'll continue this conversation later."

I ignore his comment, praying that we never have to have that conversation. I'm not equipped to handle him with the way he's acting. His jabs are still there, they're just accompanied by vulgar truths that I cannot face right now.

"Did you hear back from Sasha?" I question. I try to shift my weight in the seat, uncomfortable with the wetness between my legs.

Pulling his phone from his pocket, he sighs loudly. "Oh yes, I sure as hell did. And did she have a story to tell…"

He recounts the conversation between him and Sasha.

She'd told him that she was in the process of recording her first album when he'd first come on to her. One night he'd insisted that they record a song in private. He told her it would come out better—more raw and emotional—if it was just them.

They were in the middle of the session when he made his move. Playing back her vocals, his hand traveled to her knee. At first, she ignored it. She was so excited to be there recording her very own song and even more thrilled that someone so high up in the label had taken an interest. She was naive enough to believe that he was only interested in her music, that maybe he had just been overcome with emotion listening to her track.

She didn't want to rehash everything but said that he'd tried to force himself on her. She refused, but he wouldn't let up. She'd secretly started recording earlier in the evening, not expecting where the night would lead. She'd set her phone to record just so she could have the memory to look back on one day to remember her first recording session. Little did she know what that video would *actually* catch that evening. Luckily someone else had been in a room nearby and once she told him no loud enough, he let up. Roy made sure no one ever found out. She was too scared to let anyone else see the recording…until now.

"It's so fucking disgusting, Monica," he spits out. "He ruined her entire career because she wouldn't sleep with him. He made sure not one single song she'd recorded ever got released. Made sure no other label would touch her with a ten-foot pole. She's working at a diner now, Monica. Her dreams are over. No one even recognizes her and it's all because that sick fucking pig of a man got ahold of her." He pauses, chest heaving with angry breaths.

"We have to take him down, Aiden." My teeth dig into my lip in anger. My mind races with all of the ways I want to destroy this man.

It started because I wanted to help Nash—to get him out of his contract. But now, this is bigger.

"I don't want to just take him down. I want to burn that fucking label to the ground with every single one of those men who think they're untouchable still inside. And then I want to pluck the keys from their ashes."

He's silent, making me wonder if I said too much. The only reason he joined me on this mission was to help out his brother, but I can feel that this means more to him now, too. After hearing the stories from these women that deserved so much more from someone they sold their songs—their lives—to, it's impossible for this to only be about Nash.

His words break the silence.

"I'll bring the gasoline."

35
MONICA

"Are you ready for this?" Aiden questions from the passenger seat. We're in line waiting for our turn to hand the keys over to the waiting valet.

"I'm more than ready. This is something I've been wanting to do for over a year now. Roy deserves what's coming his way, and I want to be the one to serve it to him." Reaching behind me, I grab my purse from the cramped backseat.

"It's hot when you're vengeful," he says.

I roll my eyes, the valet guy stopping me from saying anything else when he walks up to my window. Not waiting for any other vulgar comments to come out of Aiden's mouth, I open my door, careful to not hit the valet guy.

He takes my keys as I grab a ticket with a number from him. Tucking it into a pocket of my purse, I head toward the entrance of the swanky restaurant. It's far enough from the typical celebrity scene that I don't think anyone we know will spot us here.

A warm hand finds my back. I cautiously look over my shoulder to find Aiden's eyes focusing on the host at the stand. His hand continues to press firmly on my lower back as he guides us to the teenager dressed in a suit a size too big for him.

"Welcome to Lois," he says, staring at an iPad in front of him. Finally, he looks up at us. "Name for your reservation?"

"Ann," I tell him, making sure not to list my actual name. I'd been careful when making the reservation, making sure there wasn't any more proof of us being here than there needed to be. It probably wasn't necessary, but it's in my nature to be overly cautious.

"Table for three?" he glances at the empty space between Aiden and I, clearly noting that there's only two of us.

I nod. "Our other party member should be here in a few."

The host fiddles with a few different menus. Pressing them to his chest, he grabs one last menu and nods his head in the direction of the dining room. "Follow me."

We weave in and out of diners. I'd requested a private table when making the reservation. My request appears to be granted, judging by the direction he leads us in. We stop in front of a square table in the far corner of the room. There's a partition on one side of the table, it's canvas fabric a home for a tumbling vine plant. The long tendrils of green create even more privacy for us from the wandering eyes of other diners.

The host moves to pull out a chair at the table for me. I'm getting ready to take my seat and thank him when Aiden bumps into me. He elbows the poor teenager, moving him out of the way.

"I've got it," Aiden says, his voice rough.

The host puts one hand up in surrender, shaking his head at Aiden.

Not wanting to make a scene, I hang my purse on the back of my chair. My hands slide down the sides of my thighs, smoothing out my skirt before taking a seat. As soon as I sit down, Aiden slides the chair in.

I catch him glaring at the host as he takes his own seat.

The poor kid barely looks at the two of us as he places our

menus in front of us. "Your server will be right with you," he mumbles, scurrying off as soon as the words leave his mouth.

"Was that really necessary?" I ask. He's taken the seat next to me. His large frame takes up a lot of the space, his elbows encroaching into my own personal space.

"I have no idea what you're talking about." His eyes stay downcast as he pretends to look at the drink menu.

"I'm talking about the way that you almost bit the head off of that poor kid for pulling a chair out for me. He was just being a gentleman."

He looks at me from the top of his menu. "I was perfectly capable of doing it."

"You're not a gentleman."

The corner of his lip twitches. "Fuck no, I'm not. If I remember right you weren't looking for a gentleman, you were looking for…"

"Anyway," I say a little too loudly. My eyes track over the people around us, making sure none of them are paying attention to Aiden and his dirty mouth. I know exactly where his words were leading, and they were not things that need to be said in public.

My fingers fumble with the silverware next to my plate, my mind trying to think of what to say next.

"Thinking of stabbing me?" Aiden asks. He nods toward the knife underneath my fingers.

I lift it slightly off the table, unable to hide my smile. "Can't say it isn't the first time I've thought about stabbing you. Not sure a butter knife will do the trick."

"Aiden?" a voice says from behind us.

The two of us turn toward the voice, finding our dinner companion standing a few steps away from us. Her typical bleached hair is hidden underneath an obvious black wig. She'd been well on her way to fame before Roy dropped her, ready for his next plaything. Her face was all over the place for a couple of weeks before people moved on to another budding artist. To play it safe for our meeting, I'd suggested she come in disguise, making sure no one catches wind of our meeting.

Aiden stands up, embracing her slightly before directing her to the open seat across from me. She takes a seat, looking at Aiden for a moment before focusing on me.

"Monica Masters in the flesh," she says coolly.

Arm outstretched across the table, I smile. "It's a pleasure to formally meet you."

She takes it, holding my hand steady as she shakes it. "I've heard *so* much about you."

"All of them terrible I presume," Aiden says, smirking. He returns my dirty look with a wink.

One of Chelsea's thin eyebrows lifts. She looks between the two of us. "It depends on what way you look at them I guess."

Someone comes to our table to fill our waters. All of us are silent as we wait for them to finish the task. As soon as they walk away, I break the silence.

"Well if you were keeping Roy as company, I can't imagine that you were hearing many nice things."

She smiles. "You'd be surprised by the things he says about you."

My lips purse, trying to figure out what game she's playing. I was expecting someone…different. She seems like she can hold her own very well. I'm wondering how someone who doesn't seem to have rose-colored glasses could've possibly been associated with Roy.

We're interrupted again, this time by our waiter. Our conversation pauses as we order ourselves a drink.

As soon as the waiter walks away, I sit up in my seat, leaning toward her. "We wanted to ask some questions about Roy."

She pushes the strands of the wig over her shoulder. "I know. You told me that when setting up the meeting."

"Are you still speaking with him?" The question slips from

my mouth before I can stop myself. I don't *think* she's still in association with the man, but before I divulge too much, I want to make sure.

Anger flashes in her eyes. "Not a chance. That asshole ruined my career because I refused to go to some sort of weird sex party with him."

Aiden and I share a knowing glance. "Sex party?" Aiden pushes, feigning shock.

She sighs, taking a drink of her water. "Yes. *Sex party*. Like a bunch of rich assholes at a house getting their rocks off by letting their wives get touched by other men. Except from the sounds of it, most of those men weren't taking their wives, it was their mistresses."

"So you were fine that Roy was married? And you still dated him anyway?"

Chelsea waits for the waiter to set our drinks in front of us. I tell him that we'll need a few minutes to look over the menu, hoping to buy us time to talk with her further without any inter-ruptions.

She wastes no time getting back to the topic as soon as he walks away. "Look, you can judge me all you want, but I saw an opportunity to follow my dreams and I took it. I've got daddy issues a mile long," she offers passively, as if that was enough of an explanation

Don't we all.

"His wife doesn't care what he does. She turned a blind eye to it all as long as he still funded whatever her newest hobby was. Roy gave me attention—affection. He told me I had the talent to make it big, I just needed someone to help guide me. Never did I think he would fall in love with me or any mushy stuff like that. He could do things for me no one else could. He could make me a successful recording artist."

"But in return?" I ask quietly.

"It didn't seem like that at first," she answers truthfully. "It didn't seem like he wanted much in return other than to bank off the successes of my career. That seemed normal. He was taking me on extravagant dates, introducing me to people I'd only dreamed of meeting. I was doing all of these things while getting promised fame and fortune."

"It seemed perfect," Aiden finishes for her.

She takes a long sip of her iced tea. "It was. Until it wasn't. Until I didn't give him what he wanted."

"What was this sex party?"

"I don't know all of the details. I refused to go, but I do know there's a group of people involved with Coleman Records and with other people in the industry that do these lavish parties. They make it seem like they're promoting the label, but from the sounds of it, the things that go on behind closed doors is…"

"Illegal?" I blurt.

She shrugs, leaning back in her chair. "Sketchy, to say the least."

"I've got a feeling that there are members of the board at Coleman that wouldn't want their money going to these events." Aiden sits back in his chair. His fingers steeple underneath his chin as he works through the information we've been given.

"Why do you want to know all of this?" she questions. She briefly glances at Aiden, but her focus lands and stays on me. "I don't think you called me here to help get my career back, so what's the play?"

"You didn't deserve what happened to you." There's conviction in my voice. None of these artists deserve what's happened to them, but she's right. We aren't here to try and help her, at least not yet. First we have to find a way to stop Roy and everyone else involved in this scheme. After we do that we can talk about reclaiming the voice, the songs, of so many of these artists that have been wronged by Roy.

For the rest of the night, we huddle around the table, Aiden and I prying as much information from Chelsea as we can. I fight the urge to take notes, wanting to remember every single word from her mouth, that way I can look over it tomorrow and in the coming weeks.

The biggest takeaway from the night is that we *finally* may have what we need to topple a giant.

36
AIDEN

"Give those back to me," Monica demands, her voice low and controlled. Her tiny hand reaches into the air to try and pluck the keys from my grasp.

My hand extends even higher above my head, keeping them from her reach. "I'm going to drive us home."

Her eyes dart to the parking attendant a few feet away from us. There are lingering guests and staff members around us, all of them too busy with their own lives to pay much attention to the drama unfolding between Monica and me.

It wouldn't have to be drama if she would just let me drive her car. But in true Monica fashion, she's putting up a fight with just about everything that has to do with me.

"No you aren't, Aiden. It's my car." Her fingers wrap tightly around my forearm as she tries to pull my arm down and closer to her level, but her futile attempt at taking me by surprise doesn't work.

"Afraid of my driving?" I tease, leaning a little closer to her while keeping the keys from her reach.

"Stop being a child." A vein on her forehead protrudes with her anger.

"I wouldn't have to be childish if you would just stop arguing with me and get in the fucking car."

"People are starting to stare." Her arms fold over her chest, making it hard to ignore the touch of cleavage peeping through her top.

I laugh. "Does it look like I care?"

She shocks me by slightly stomping her high-heeled foot. It's a very un-Monica-like thing to do, making it ten times hotter.

Her hips angrily sway as she rounds her car, opening the passenger door more dramatically than what is needed. I'm sure I hear her mumble something under her breath, probably an insult toward me, as she slides into the leather seat.

I hand a tip to the guy at the valet stand before returning to the car and an angry Monica. I can tell she's furious with me by the way she stares angrily ahead of us.

I have to push the seat backward to accommodate my legs. Once I'm in the correct position, I peel out of the parking lot, knowing damn well it'll anger her even more.

"Just when I was beginning to wonder if we'd reached an agreement, you go and make me regret ever working with you."

"You've done a *lot* more than work with me."

"We aren't talking about that ever again," she snaps.

The engine rattles underneath us as I accelerate. "Oh we sure as hell *are* talking about that again," I toss back at her. "As a matter of fact, I think right now is a perfect time to talk about what the fuck happened the other night, and what happens next."

"Nothing happens next. We've got what we need to formulate a plan to take down Roy. We take him and every other shitty person at Coleman Records down and then we get Nash ownership of his songs"

Ignoring her, I begin to mess with the touch screen between us. It's tiny compared to my large fingers, and I keep clicking on the wrong things. I want everything that she wants with the label, and I'm confident we have what we need to get that sleazeball Roy out of the picture for good. But just because we're on the pathway to finishing what Monica and I came together on in the first place doesn't mean I can move on without having additional conversations with her.

"What are you doing?" she asks as I click on the wrong thing once again.

"I'm trying to find the address to your house."

"We aren't going to my house."

"Doesn't look like you have any control over that considering *I'm* the one driving."

"No one is allowed in my space. You aren't coming to my house."

My smile is wide when I look over at her. "Fine. Then I'll find somewhere else for us to have this conversation. But Monica, we're going to have this talk whether you like it or not. I'm guessing you don't want it to take place at Nash's since I know for a fact Lennon is hanging out with Poe there tonight. But if you won't tell me your address, we might just have to make that work."

"Absolutely not," she says immediately. "They can't know about us…they can't see us together."

"Yeah well, too late for that," I say casually.

"*What?*" she shrieks.

I shrug. "Lennon heard you moaning during our little gym rendezvous. Maybe you should work on being a little quieter the next time my cock is inside you. Not that I'm complaining or anything."

Out of the corner of my eye I can see her manicured fingers rubbing at her temples. "You've got to be kidding me. This isn't happening."

"Your place or mine?"

"Tell me you're kidding about Lennon."

I guide the car in the general direction of the city. I have no idea where she lives, but I know that I'll drive in circles if I need to. Whatever it takes to get her to talk to me. To figure out what the hell is happening between us.

"I'm definitely not kidding. After you stormed out the other night, I found Lennon hanging out in my room. She'd told me that she couldn't help but overhear our," I pause, thinking of the right word, "*activities*."

"I should've never let that happen. What was I thinking? If Lennon knows then…"

"Lennon isn't going to say anything to anybody. She doesn't care what you, or me, or anyone does in their spare time. She's good at minding her own business."

"No one is good at minding their own business."

"Lennon is. Your place or mine?" I repeat, moving on from the topic of Lennon. I know for a fact that Lennon won't tell a soul, but I'm not going to sit here and go back and forth with Monica about it.

"You don't have a place. It's your brother's. And since you are relentless, and great at giving me a headache, we can do mine. But nothing is happening between us, Aiden. I can just tell you it'll never happen again from a new house, you can leave me alone and we can finish what we started with Roy and the label."

She's quick at putting her address into the GPS of her car. For the remainder of the car ride, the two of us are silent. I spend the entire ride wondering what exactly it is that I want from her when we get to her house. I'd started this drive just wanting answers from her—clarity.

But now as we get closer and closer to that, I'm wondering if I'm prepared for what her answers will be. Or if I'll even believe them to begin with. I've always known she's a bit of a liar.

37
AIDEN

MONICA'S CONDO looks exactly as I'd imagined. Walking through the front door, everything is neat and perfectly in place. There are small pops of color, but for the most part it's as bland as how I thought she used to be.

"Stop staring," Monica's voice breaks me from my thoughts. She stands next to an entryway table, her purse sitting neatly atop it.

"Why? Does it make you uncomfortable?"

Her eyes travel around the room. "No. I just don't see why you find it necessary to look and touch every single thing in here."

I set down a book that was sitting at the end of the entryway table. It's a hardback biography about a person I've never heard of before. "You don't tell me much about you, so I'm left to put together the pieces of who Monica Masters really is by looking at your personal space."

She scoffs, moving into her kitchen. Opening a small wine fridge, she brings out a bottle of wine. She's quick at opening the bottle and pouring herself a glass. I don't miss how she doesn't offer me one. "Good luck with that," she says, taking a sip of her wine.

"There's got to be *something* personal of yours in here." Walking over to her coffee table, a large round block of wood with different adornments scattered neatly on top of it, I pick up a picture frame. I hold it to my face, inspecting the picture. "You don't have any family pictures. This one looks like store-bought artwork."

"My family isn't one I want to put on display in my home."

My mind latches onto her words. She may not have meant to, but she just gave me a small sliver of insight into who she is. I've gotten to know her body intimately, but I still want a small peek at what goes on in her mind.

"Tell me about them?" I know she won't, but I ask anyway.

"There's nothing to tell. You know how I am. My problems didn't stem from things that happened in my adulthood. My issues run childhood deep." She finishes off her words by taking a large sip of her wine.

I run my hand over the soft fabric of her white couch. I want to ask her more about her family, but first, I need answers to different questions. Maybe once I get those, she'll open up about the parts of her I don't know.

"We need to talk, Monica." I stop looking at every nuance of her living space. Instead, I walk all the way to the kitchen until I'm standing on the opposite side of the counter from her.

"I don't see why," she says, staring down at her wine glass.

I wait until she looks at me to speak again. Finally, her brown eyes reluctantly find my face. "I can't stop thinking about you."

"Well, you need to."

"No."

"Yes," she fires back angrily.

I loop around the counter until I'm standing directly in front of her. She grasps the edge of the counter with one of her hands as if she's holding on for dear life. Her knuckles ghost white from the grip.

"I'm tired of trying to tell myself I hate you."

"Aiden, stop it."

"I'm over the lies. Lying to you, lying to myself. Because the truth is, I don't hate you. I don't hate the way you make me feel. The only thing I hate is that I have no idea where your head's at."

Reaching out, I carefully remove her vice-like grip from the counter.

"What are you doing?" she whispers, staring at where my fingers wrap around her thin wrist.

Bringing her hand up, I place it on my chest. Right over the spot where my heart beats erratically.

"Do you feel that?" I ask, my voice coming out low and gravelly.

She nods.

"For some catastrophic reason I'll never be able to understand, it only beats like that when I'm around you."

"It doesn't mean anything."

"What if it does? What if it means everything?"

Her head falls against me. Her forehead presses right up against my thumping heart. I can feel her warm breath through my shirt. The feeling of her so close, in such a personal moment, only makes my pulse beat faster.

"Aiden..." she pauses, her hands fisting the fabric of my shirt. "We can't."

"Says who?"

A sad laugh passes her lips. "Says *us*. We tolerate each other at best."

"Things change. They evolve." I sigh, not able to put words to what I'm feeling inside. "Fuck, I don't know, Monica. All I know is I'm done hating myself for wanting you."

She lets my hands wander up her sides. They run over the slick fabric of her skirt and then the soft fabric of her top. My fingers seek out the warmth of her neck, my thumbs skirting over the tops of her ears. Cradling her face, I angle it upward.

Her brown eyes used to be one of the things I hated most about her. They always hid so many secrets behind them. Every time I looked at her, I knew she was calculating something behind that manipulative gaze. Now those same eyes don't show a hint of deceit. No proof of scheme. They only give a hint of the war that's going on within herself.

The sad look in her eyes makes my stomach fall. It isn't the look someone gives when they're about to be honest, it's a look that means they're still fighting something within.

"Don't say it. Don't tell me you don't feel this," I plead with her. I brush my thumb over her lips, thinking of the times I've felt them pressed against mine.

I pull her lip down, showing off her bottom teeth. "You can still tell me you hate me. You *can* hate me, fight me, loathe me, I don't fucking care. As long as I have you in some way. Hate is a feeling, and where it's not one I feel for *you* anymore, if that's the only feeling I can get *from* you...then I'll take it."

Leaning in for a kiss, I hover above her mouth. I want to take what I desperately want as mine, but I need *something* from her. If she won't admit that this has amounted to more than hate between us, then the least I need from her is for her to start the kiss. For her to prove to me that her body won't continue to tell me lies.

Once again, she proves to me how solid the walls built around her are. Pulling away, she pushes my hands off her. "I can't do this with you, Aiden. You can go now." I don't watch her leave, instead listening to the sound of her heels on the floor as she walks away from me.

I've told her how I feel, despite everything in me telling me I shouldn't. I've laid it all out, confessing that the hate I had in my heart for her has turned into something different. Something

I don't understand, but something I'm not willing to fight or deny any longer.

And still, she walked away.

When I finally look up, I find her walking down a hallway to what I assume is her room. I could let her win. I could walk out this door and pretend I never uttered the words I did tonight in her quiet kitchen.

But she should know I've never been one to let her get her way. This time is no exception.

38
MONICA

I RETREAT ALL the way to my closet, trying to put as much space between Aiden and I as I can. My closet is the furthest point from the kitchen in the condo, and right now space is exactly what I need.

I was close—too close—to giving in to his words. To believing what was coming out of his mouth. The problem is, we've been so wrapped up in this game of push and pull, attack and retreat, that I can't begin to process what is real anymore and what is still a game.

What if this is all part of some elaborate plan to get back at me? To do to me what I did to his brother?

My feet hit the soft carpet of my closet as I slide each one of my heels off. Bending down, I put them back neatly on the shelf where they belong.

I wish I could do the same with my heart. It would be much easier if I could pull my heart out and set it nicely on the shelf for safe keeping. Then maybe I could focus instead of constantly being distracted by a man I have no business thinking about.

Angrily, I pull each one of my arms out of my blouse and let the fabric fall to the ground at my feet. Staring down, I know I should pick it up and throw it in the hamper at the back of my closet. I never leave my clothes on the ground. But right now, I don't have it in me. My mind is still replaying Aiden's words on repeat.

"We aren't done with this conversation."

I jump, looking up to find Aiden leaning in the doorframe of my closet.

"Didn't you take the hint to leave?"

He crosses his arms over his chest, a clear indicator that he did not. His eyes flick to my bare chest, reminding me that I'm standing in front of him in a bra and skirt, not the appropriate attire for the conversation we're *apparently* still having.

I try to push past him, but his toned arm reaches across the empty space of the doorway, blocking my exit.

Angrily, I take a step back and look up at him. "What else do you want from me, Aiden? I told you, I don't want to do this with you."

He throws his head back, the muscles in his throat rippling with laughter. "What do I *want* from you, Monica? You're fucking kidding right?"

One of my arms wraps around my middle, trying to hide my exposed skin. "No."

Aiden's head shakes manically. His eyes bulging. Ripping his arm from the doorway, he pulls at the hairs at his head. "I want you to fucking admit that you feel *something*. Prove to me that you aren't the evil robot that everyone thinks you are."

"You used to think the same thing about me," I point out in anger. My shoulder brushes against him as I duck under his arm, relieved to be in a bigger room.

"You're right, I did. But then I got to know you, the *minuscule* parts of you that you allowed me to see—and I realized…"

"You realized what?" I interject, bracing myself for whatever insult comes next. I'd deserve it.

"I realized that I know almost nothing about you. But I want to—more than I've ever wanted to know anything about anyone.

And I can't explain why. It's the scariest position I've ever been in because the things I *do* know about you tell me that even if you felt the same, you'd never admit it."

"Then stop wanting me, Aiden!" I shout, losing my patience. "It's easier that way. We will *never* work. Look at us, all we do is fight!"

He paces in front of my bed, his fingers wrapped in his hair. "You don't think I've tried?" he yells. "I've spent nights hating myself for wanting you this bad, Monica. Of course I've fucking tried not wanting you!"

"Try harder."

"No."

"Yes."

"For fuck's sake," he shouts, his voice bouncing off my bedroom walls. "Will you ever not be a stubborn pain in my ass?"

"What happens when you do get to know me and you don't like what you discover?" I never yell, but my words match the same volume as his as they spill out of me in anger.

He looks at me stunned. His hazel eyes wide as he watches me carefully.

My chest heaves up and down. My next words are said softer, my vulnerabilities beginning to pour out of me. "What's your plan then, Aiden? Because we can fuck and ignore all the differences between us, but what you're asking for...you're asking to know everything about me and I'm trying to save you the hurt. Once you get to know me, you won't find what you like."

"I don't fucking care," he says, his voice low. "Try me," he finishes.

I shake my head, hating the feeling of my throat closing with emotion. "I'm as empty as you've always thought me to be, Aiden. I have *nothing* to give you. All of my lies, they're just a cover to hide that I'm hollow inside."

He rushes across the room to where I'm standing, pulling me

into him. I try to retreat, but his arms wrap around me, holding me tightly against his chest. His embrace holds firm as I struggle for a moment, trying to figure out what he's doing.

It's a…hug. A tender embrace meant to be shared by lovers. It seems too intimate for what we are—but maybe it isn't. I don't know the last time I was simply hugged by a man, but I know that his hold on me feels genuine. His grip feels tight enough to hold the two of us together, even if I'm breaking apart inside.

"Then I'll give you everything that I am. I'll give you enough for the both of us. Just stop with the lies, Monica. Give whatever the hell this is a chance…"

"I'll be left with nothing when you realize I'm not capable of giving you what you want from me," I whisper into his chest.

His arms wrap around me even tighter. "I'm just as stubborn as you are, Monica. I'm not fucking leaving."

I look up, trying to get a read of his face. I'm terrified of the feelings bubbling up inside my chest. Somehow in between all of the insults and games, I've given way too much of myself to this man—more than I thought I had left.

I've destroyed bits and pieces of myself through the years to be able to become the image of success that I am. The ruthless manager of Nash Pierce. It started at a young age, ignored by my parents, at war with my sister, I was basically born with a chip on my shoulder. I wanted to prove I could make it in this business. I'd done just that, but it was at the expense of myself.

I have no idea who I am anymore. I don't know what I have left of me, but whatever I do have left, I'm scared to admit it may already be his.

Standing on my tiptoes, I reach up to kiss him. If I can't use words to describe how I feel, I can use my body. We've never been good with words, but our bodies have never had a problem communicating.

The kiss is gentle, soft, unlike all the others between us. His fingers dig into my hips as he pulls me against him. Starving for more of him, I twist my fingers in the hair at the back of his neck. My tongue dips into his mouth as I pull his face closer to me.

His desperation for me must run as deep as mine for him. Lifting me by the hips, he picks me up. I try to wrap my legs around his middle, but the tightness of my skirt doesn't allow it. As if he's reading my mind, he shoves the fabric up until it gathers at my waist, allowing me the room I need to wrap around his middle.

All of this is done without our mouths ever separating. He kneads at the meat of my bottom, pulling me into him harder. Our kiss may have started gently, but we're back to our original ways.

He rips his mouth from mine, quickly putting it on my throat. His lips travel the base of my neck, as he rubs his erection against my burning core.

Aiden continues to explore the exposed skin of my neck as he backs up. Eventually, he makes it to the ottoman at the end of my king-sized bed. He falls down on it, careful to keep a hold of me in the process.

His fingers come around my back. In no time, he has my bra unclasped and pulled off me, discarded somewhere on the floor.

He takes one of my peaked nipples in his mouth, biting down on the tender flesh. "These right here," he says before licking the spot he just bit, "are mine to enjoy."

It doesn't take him long to move on to the next one. He repeats the same motion as before, sending tingles down my spine.

His gaze is possessive when he looks up from his task. "You're mine, Monica," he demands, his tone making it clear there are no arguments.

"I'm not yours," I argue, "I belong to no one but myself," I say while trying to find friction by rubbing my hips along him.

He smiles. "I'd beg to differ." Without warning he's lifting me off his lap. Before I can ask what he's doing, he's placed me in a new position—this time laying across his lap.

He shifts my body until my chest rests against the soft fabric of the ottoman. My hips rest against his lap, his bulging erection hitting my stomach.

"What are you doing?" I ask, trying to lean up. He stops my efforts instantly, flattening his palm against my back and pushing me back down.

"I'm proving to you that you're mine. With a label, without a fucking label, I don't give a damn." He runs his palm over the flesh of my bottom. My skirt still bunches at the small of my waist, allowing him the access he has now. "This right here," he squeezes, "is mine."

Without warning, his hand comes down hard. The only thing that blocks the sting of the slap is the fabric of my underwear.

"Aiden," I pant, wondering why more wetness pools between my thighs at his angered touch.

He caresses the spot he just spanked. "Everything about you is mine, Monica." His fingers hook into the sides of my panties, pulling them down to rest at my mid-thigh. "And I'm going to keep reminding you of that."

I don't expect the next slap either. His palm comes down just hard enough against my flesh to sting. Tears gloss over my eyes at the sting of his skin against mine. Just as quick as the spank came, so does the soft caress of his hand on mine.

"You're so fucking wet," he comments. His finger further proves the point when he runs it through the pooled wetness between my thighs. He spreads the wetness over the spot he just slapped.

"Does it turn you on when I remind you who you belong to?"

My core tightens at his words. Normally something so degrading would have me fuming, but it's always been different with Aiden. Giving him the power to do what he wants with me only fuels my burning desire.

I shake my head, trying to fight the building sensation in my core.

"Liar," he scolds, his hand coming down once again. This time, one hand lands hard against my skin while the other presses directly against my clit. Never could I imagine the sensation of the sting of the pain mixed with him pressing against my clit could elicit so much pleasure.

One of his fingers coaxes inside me. He pulls it in and out of the wetness, bringing me dangerously close to a release. "Say it, Monica."

My teeth clamp down as I try to fight the orgasm threatening to overtake me. My fingers try to find something to hold onto as he expertly works inside me, but there's nothing for me to grab except the edge of the ottoman. I try to escape his touch, but he just holds me harder against him with his free hand.

"Say that you're mine, baby," he says, his voice filled with lust. Turning my cheek so I can see him, I find his eyes focused on where he moves his finger in and out of me.

It's erotic to watch him watch what he's doing to me. A second finger fits inside me, solidifying that I won't be able to fight this much longer.

As if he can feel my gaze, he turns to face me. His teeth bite into his lip as he watches me carefully. His fingers threaten to slow down as I feel the orgasm begin to overtake my body.

"I'm yours," I scream, desperately not wanting him to stop. He doesn't, and my body shakes as an orgasm rips through my body. The pleasure radiates to my limbs, making them numb.

His finger runs down my spine as the final waves of my orgasm wash over me. So tenderly it makes my heart squeeze, he brushes hair out of my face.

"Good girl," he whispers, smiling at me. "And for the record, I'm yours, too."

39
AIDEN

I GIVE her a few seconds to come off the high of her orgasm before pulling her off my lap. Flipping her body, I cradle her against my chest as I climb up on her bed. Once we're in the middle, I set her down.

I commit this moment to memory. Below me, Monica lays, cheeks flushed, waiting to know what is going to happen next.

"We're no longer going to fight this," I tell her as my fingers unbutton my jeans. "Do you understand?"

She nods, watching me carefully as I free my cock. It threatened to bust just at her willingness to concede moments ago, her finally admitting that she was mine as she rode out her orgasm. The sight of my handprint on her ass was just about enough to do me in.

My hand works up and down on my shaft. Monica eyes it carefully, her tongue darting out to wet her lips. Leaning up on her elbows, she reaches a hand out. She's direct with her movements, purposefully moving my fingers out of the way to wrap her own around me.

"Your turn," she demands, pushing against my chest until our positions switch. Now I'm the one laying against her fluffy comforter, her tits dangling in the air as she leans over me.

She's silent as she pushes against my thighs, spreading them to make room for her to rest in between them. Sitting back on her heels, she looks at my cock hungrily. "This time, I'm in control."

My dick, begging for her to touch it once again, twitches at her words. Her eagerness to please me about sending me over the edge, and that filthy little mouth of hers hasn't even had the chance to wrap around me yet.

"Did you hear me, Aiden?" she says, her voice more zealous than before.

I nod, unable to speak. My throat feels gravelly, my body overtaken with lust for the woman in front of me.

She doesn't need anything else from me. Pushing her hair to rest along her back, she leans forward to take my cock in her mouth. Her warm, wet tongue licks from the head all the way down to the bottom of my shaft. Monica repeats the motion one more time, teasing me.

Just when I'm regretting letting her take control, she surprises me by shoving my length all the way down her throat. She gags but doesn't let up. Her head bobs up and down on me at the perfect pace.

"That's it, baby," I say through gritted teeth. My hands reach between us to fondle her bouncing breasts, needing something to do to keep them busy. I'm itching to tangle my fingers through her hair, to guide her head just the way I want it. But she told me she wanted to do it her way, and I'm not going to argue.

Soon enough I'll have her bent over and taking my cock just the way I like it, so for now I'll let her have her fun.

"You remembered just the way I like it," I moan. My spine starts to tingle, my impending orgasm near. As much as I want to make her swallow every last bit of me, I rip my hips from her throat.

There's fire in her eyes when she looks at me. "I wasn't—"

"You're done when I say you're done. And right now, I'm desperate to be inside you. I need to feel…"

"I know," she cuts me off, already crawling up my body. She angles herself directly over me. "I feel it, too." Her hands fall to my chest, the only way she's able to steady herself as I pound into her.

"Mine," I pant.

Leaning down, she plants a kiss against my lips. Her body jerks against mine as she tries to match me thrust for thrust.

"Yours," she agrees, arching her back. The new pose places her perky tits right in my face. I take one nipple in my mouth, nipping and sucking it to drive her wild. Her moans ricochet off the white walls of her bedroom, mixing with the sound of our bodies slapping together.

"I'm going to come again," she moans. Her fingers dig into my chest.

"Do it," I tell her, slowing down, allowing her to set the pace. "Use my cock to make it feel good."

She doesn't argue, eagerly setting the pace that feels the best to her. Slowly, she takes all of me before moving her hips until only the tip of me is inside her. She repeats this movement over and over, making it slightly quicker each time.

Helping her out, I palm each one of her breasts. Her hands come out to cover mine, as she instructs me just the way she wants it. Guiding my fingers to pinch each one of her nipples, she lets out a loud moan.

"Oh god, Aiden," she pants. Her head falls backwards as I twist the peaked buds.

There's a slick sheen of sweat on her body as the orgasm overtakes her. The sight of her taking exactly what she wants sends me over the edge with her.

Her body falls limply against mine. The soft tendrils over her hair spill over my chest as the two of us catch our breath. My fingers run over her back, enjoying the moment of peacefulness with her.

I don't know how long we lay there. Time seems to stand still as we do something I suspect neither one of us are used to. We cuddle, and there isn't a rush for one of us to leave.

There aren't regrets or lies between us. It's just...us.

40
MONICA

MY BODY IS COMPLETELY SPENT. Aiden lays next to me in bed, his finger tracing the slope of my hips with his index finger.

"You didn't tell her?" I laugh into his chest, not at all shocked by the story he's telling me about a girl he once dated.

"Of course I didn't tell her," he scoffs. "I accidentally dumped an *entire* saltshaker of salt into the pasta dish and she told me it was the best dish she's ever eaten. I couldn't get the date over with quick enough, knowing she was lying right to my face to impress me."

Goosebumps pop up on my skin as he tenderly plays with the hair at the nape of my neck. "Poor girl, she just didn't want to hurt your feelings."

He grunts, ignoring my comment and moving on to a new topic. "Your turn to tell me something embarrassing."

Lifting my head from his chest, I narrow my eyes at him. "Are you asking me this so you can have dirt on me?"

His teeth dig into his lip as he smirks. "Maybe…maybe not."

Shaking my head, I place my ear to his chest, comforted by the strong *thump* of his heart. "Pedicures stress me out," I admit.

His fingers pause for a moment. "Like getting your nails done?"

"My toes," I correct. "I'm insanely ticklish at the arches of my feet. Every time they go to scrub them, I just about kick the poor person in the face."

"Ticklish on your feet?" Aiden says, a mischievous tone to his voice.

Before I can react, he's popped off the bed, my face falling into the sheets from his sudden disappearance. He reaches for my leg, pulling it into his chest. I curl my toes, knowing exactly what he's about to do.

"Aiden, no…" I plead, trying to rip my ankle from his grasp.

His fingers are too strong, and to my horror, he digs them into the part of my foot that causes me to squeal. My naked body squirms in the sheets as I try to do whatever possible to pull my foot from the punishing feel of his fingers at my foot. I can barely breathe, laughs bubbling from my stomach despite my desperate attempt to stifle them.

Aiden laughs along with me, relentless with the assault.

Finally, his fingers slow, allowing me time to catch my breath. Letting go, he lets my leg fall back into the sheets. He returns to his spot from earlier, his elbow propping his head up as he looks down at me.

All too quickly, his face drains of all humor. His eyes rake over me, making my toes curl for an entire new reason. It isn't like he's just looking at me, he's looking *through* me, seemingly seeing every single part of me.

He gently moves a piece of blonde hair from my face. "Tell me something else. Something real…something unexpected."

I sigh, knowing exactly what I could divulge to shock him.

"My family owns the director competitor of Coleman Records."

His head tilts. "What?"

"Master's Music, it's the biggest label for pop artists besides Coleman. And it was the last label on Earth I wanted to work for when I began my career."

He pulls me against his chest tightly. "I want to know every-thing," he says against my temple.

So I tell him.

"When I first started out, I was fully aware of all of the dirty details of Master's Music, my father's label. It was the reason I told Nash he needed to go with Coleman instead of theirs when I first became his manager. At the time, I'd known all the seedy things they did to their artists, the corners they backed them into. I didn't want it for Nash. I thought Coleman Records would be a better choice."

I think back to my younger self, how naïve I was. I was under the allusion that it was just *my* family that did sketchy things in the name of music. All I'd hoped was that Coleman, where I'd encouraged Nash to go, would be better. I was wrong, but I plan on making it right—on clearing the swamp and making it safe for young musicians.

Aiden doesn't interrupt my thoughts. Shockingly, he's quiet as he waits for me to continue on. His comforting touch to my naked skin encourages to divulge even more.

"When I'd taken Nash to Coleman instead of Master's Music, my family livid. I found it comical how they thought I had any allegiance to them. They'd molded me into this ruthless person, always in competition with my sister, from an early age. They pitted us against one another so they could decide on who would get the legacy of Master's Music."

"Tell me more about them," he says quietly.

Something like sadness settles deep inside me. Grief for the relationship I *should* have had with my sister, but something my family never allowed for the two of us. "My sister and I were never close. I can't remember a time where it didn't seem like I was competing with her. Instead of giving us the time to be sisters, to grow up and see if running a label was something either of us even wanted, my father always threw in comments on how the things we did were measuring up to who he wanted to leave the label to."

Words spill from my mouth as I let Aiden in on all of the insults I'd heard over the years, straight from the mouths of the people who were supposed to love me most.

You were silent at dinner when people were speaking to you, Monica. How do you expect me to trust you with Master's when you can't even hold a dinner conversation?
Did you see how great your sister did at her piano recital, Monica? She seems fit to run a label one day.
Show more personality, Monica. People will like you more.
Don't show emotion, Monica. People who run companies don't let their emotions run them.

When I'm finished rattling off examples, Aiden takes a deep breath. "Fuck. My parents weren't exactly parents of the year, but at least Nash and I were never pitted against one another so ruthlessly."

I shrug. "Occasionally, I was my parent's favorite. My sister would be on the receiving end of the jabs. It made her hate me. It didn't matter if she was the favorite child that day or not, she did everything in her power to make my life a living hell. So over the years, I plotted. I didn't want a label. I wanted to work for the artists that amazed me with their talent. But I didn't want to ever work for an artist that had anything to do with my family."

"So then you found Nash?"

I nod, exhaustion starting to catch up to me from the numerous orgasms from Aiden and now the divulgence of personal things I choose to keep unknown for a reason.

The silence between is comfortable. I take peace in the easiness of feeling his skin against mine, of simply laying in his arms. Finally, I turn my head to look up at him. "Your turn."

I've never taken an interest in other people's personal lives, especially with someone I've shared a bed with. I'd rather go through the torture of a thousand pedicures, letting someone scrub at my feet until I can no longer stand the feeling of being tickled, than to divulge anything personal about myself. Because of my sentiment, or lack thereof, of sharing about myself, I've also learned to not care about other people's stories.

Yet, I'm laying here desperate to know more about Aiden. Everything in me wants to know about the man who was planning my demise because of my deception.

"There were so many times over the year I'd wished that Nash was just a normal teenager, that his talent was never acknowledged at that talent show...that I'd have known my brother growing up."

I let his words settle in, truly letting my mind try to think about what it would be like to be in his position. "I hadn't thought about what that would be like," I tell him truthfully.

"It's a selfish standpoint, not one I'm proud to admit. Don't get me wrong, I love that the world knows of my brother's talent, but also...I've watched the world tear him down. Stalk him. Insult him. Steal him with his obligations. Sometimes I just wanted it all to go away, for me to be able to see him more than the occasional weekend and holiday."

"So maybe you aren't just the spoiled little brother of arguably the most famous popstar."

He snickers. "Don't tell anyone my secret. Honestly," he lets out a large sigh, "I don't know how Nash does it. The constant spotlight would be exhausting—not something I'd ever want. That's why college wasn't for me, and that was on such a small scale."

I let my fingers trace over the taut muscles of his stomach. "What do you mean?"

"Everyone knew I was Nash Pierce's little brother. They thought if they got close to me, somehow I'd give them an in to get close with Nash. People were always chasing after me, pretending to be my friend or acting interested in me because they wanted to get close to him. I didn't really want the college degree, and I didn't want all of that attention, I just wanted to find a way to cook for people."

I think about his words, wondering if what he's doing with the tour is something that makes him feel like he's fulfilling his dreams.

"If you could do anything, could cook for people in any way, what would you do?"

His answer is immediate. "I'd have a food truck at the beach. I'd get to know locals, tourists—all sorts of people while I cooked from my soul." He gets this wistful look on his face. "Pepper would be laying at my feet, I'd be able to cook whatever I felt like, without parameters, and it would be chill...lowkey."

"It'd be perfect," I finish. I picture him in the scenario he just described. It seemed so *simple* for the little brother of Nash Pierce, yet it seemed to fit him so...perfect.

He slides his fingers down my hips, pulling my body fully against his. His dick pushes into my thigh, Aiden not bashful of his erection. "I have an idea." My back arches as his lips sweep against my collarbone.

"Mmm?" I hum, relishing in the way his fingers dig into my skin.

"You seem filthy," he teases, nipping at my ear. "I think you need me to clean you off."

I stifle a moan as fingers dip into the wetness between my thighs. "Is that so?"

He nods. "You're a dirty girl, Monica. It's time to get cleaned up." Aiden doesn't allow me time to answer, he picks me up in one fell swoop, throwing me over his shoulder as he races toward the bathroom.

Aiden keeps me thrown over his shoulder as he reaches into the shower and turns the nozzle. My feet find the soft material of the rug as he places me in front of the shower door. Steam begins to bellow through the crack in the shower door.

The two of us stand front to front, naked in multiple senses. Not only physically, but emotionally as well. We've both unloaded deeply buried parts of ourselves tonight. I don't know what has my body flushed more, knowing I trust him with what I've told him, or the way he stares at my body like he's ready to devour me.

He nods his head in the direction of the running water. "Get in," he instructs, his focus on my breasts, the two of them heavy with desire.

Doing as I'm told, I open the door and step in. The water is scorching hot against my skin. Aiden steps in behind me, the door slamming behind him.

The foggy air between us from the steam does nothing to hide the lust in his eyes. He carefully tracks the track of the water down my body with his gaze. My core tightens when his tongue peeks out between his teeth, slowly licking his bottom lip.

Keeping his focus on me, he reaches for a loofah hanging on the wall. Grabbing a large black bottle, he squeezes liquid on the loofah and steps closer to me.

"Turn around." His tone is sharp, demanding.

I'm too focused on the way his muscles glisten under the spray of the water. The random array of tattoos splattered on his body appear even darker on top of his wet skin.

Fingertips dig into my hip as Aiden closes the distance between us. Leaning over me, one hand holding the loofah while the other bites into my skin, he smirks. "I told you to turn around," he scolds. He leans in, kissing the top of my nose gently before taking me off guard and forcefully spinning my body around until my front presses against the shower wall. The cold stone feels harsh against my hard nipples.

"Much better," he says, his foot hitting my ankle to spread my legs wider.

For the next hour, the two of us make sure every inch of our skin is *very* clean.

I didn't think twice about it when once we were all clean, he climbed in bed with me. It'd been a long time since I'd shared a bed overnight with another man, and somehow it felt natural to wake up with him next to me.

Well, *almost* next to me. I'd woken up with his face between my thighs—the best alarm clock I'd ever had.

While I ironed my clothes for the day, he stepped out to grab us coffee. I told him to grab us breakfast as well, but he looked at me like I was dumb and left before I'd been able ask him what the look meant.

I'm in the middle of fixing my hair when he walks through the door. One hand holds a drink tray with two coffees and a smoothie, the other holds a grocery bag from the small store across the street from me.

"I got you coffee and a smoothie to hold you over, but I'm not buying breakfast when I can prepare it for you here." He doesn't bother to elaborate. He sets the smoothie and coffee on my marble bathroom counter and then exits the room.

The clanging of pots and pans sound from the kitchen as I finish with my hair. Nash and Nora will be landing from their honeymoon this afternoon. I planned on picking them up from the airport, but a text message this morning from Roy forced me to find other accommodations for them.

The text requested a meeting to discuss Nash and acted as a reminder of everything Aiden and I had worked on recently. We have enough—probably more than enough—to get the solid board members of the label to drop him. I just have to play it cool for a little while longer while I figure the details out.

I'm putting the last touches on my makeup, swiping blush

across my cheeks when Aiden walks into the bathroom. He watches me closely in the mirror.

"I could get used to this," he says.

"To what?" I ask, spraying setting spray on my face.

"To watching you get ready in the morning...making you breakfast. It feels normal. I like it."

I smile. "Well I do have to get going soon. Roy called for a meeting."

His eyebrows rise. "What do you think he wants?"

I shrug, looking in the mirror to touch up my lipstick. "He's probably wondering if Nash has any new music. He wouldn't allow Nash a week off to enjoy his honeymoon."

Aiden is quiet, his knuckle running over his bottom lip as he thinks about something.

Finally ready for the day, I walk around him toward my kitchen. "What's for breakfast?"

He follows closely behind me. "Your favorite. Or at least, I think it's one of your favorites. It's something I've seen you eat often on tour..."

Walking into the kitchen, I find two bowls nicely placed on my kitchen table. More often than not I eat at this table with my laptop out, trying to multitask while nourishing my body. It feels strange to sit down and have someone sitting in the seat next to mine.

"You made açai bowls?" I ask, looking down at the work of art in front of me. The fruit on the top of the bowl is cut intricately. Strawberries are fanned out to look like a flower, and there's a sprinkle of coconut over the top.

Aiden mixes the contents of his own bowl around, a sheepish smile on his face. It's the first time I've ever seen him look shy in the slightest. "It wasn't that hard."

Dipping my spoon in, I take a bite of the breakfast. The flavors erupt in my mouth, tasting much better than any my assistant has ever found for me. The granola isn't overly sweet, and the consistency of the açai is perfect.

For a moment, I almost forget I have to endure a meeting with Roy later.

He watches me carefully. I take another bite, savoring the fruity flavors on my tongue. "It's delicious," I tell him.

Aiden smiles, going to take a bite of his own bowl. "Keep me around and there's more where that came from."

41
MONICA

"Care to tell me what you've been up to Monica?" Roy is seated across from me, he leans back in his large leather chair at the mahogany desk. His hands are folded behind his head, bringing attention to the slight pit stains on his designer button down shirt.

I maintain a poker face, even though my pulse has spiked significantly at his question. "What do you mean?" I ask, feigning innocence.

He grins, showing off his tacky set of veneers. His meaty fingers type something on his computer. It takes him a moment to pull up whatever he's looking for, but when he does, he looks at me with that same smile. Turning the screen toward me, I'm shocked to find a photo of Aiden, Chelsea and I seated together at the restaurant last night.

"You know exactly what I mean," he chides.

A colossal pit forms in my stomach. I keep my gaze fixed on the photo, not wanting to see Roy's smug face.

"Tell me, what could Nash's manager and brother possibly want with one of my former artists? Especially one that tried to sleep her way to the top to make up for her severe lack of talent."

Bile stings my throat. This is how he managed to turn the fault on Chelsea. To make everyone believe she was the villain and ostracize her from the business.

"She's a close friend of Aiden's," I lie, unable to think of any other excuse.

He nods. "Funny, I remember them introducing themselves at the wedding."

Taking a subtle deep breath, I try to regain my composure. "Maybe you had a few too many drinks," I offer patronizingly.

His bushy eyebrows narrow. "I'm not fucking around, Monica. Whatever you're up to, it won't end well for any of you."

He doesn't know everything yet. The realization calms me down a bit. He only has this photo. It's clear he doesn't know what was discussed.

"I'm curious, Roy," I ask, straightening a stapler on his desk. "Why do you have this photo to begin with? Here I was thinking we trusted one another…"

"I want to trust you Monica, I do. But then I see this and I'm questioning if I should."

I shrug off his statement, giving off the illusion of indifference. In reality, I'm wondering how I could be so careless. Of course he had me followed. I should have known. I can't let him figure out what we know—it would ruin everything. Somehow, I've got to find a way to rid him of all of his suspicions. "You're going to be extremely bored at what you find out about my day-to-day activities."

"We'll see. Now, are you going to tell me the real reason you were dining with one of my past…"

"Artists?" I finish for him, plastering a fake smile on my face.

His nod is slow. "Yes, of course," he finishes.

My lips roll together as I adjust myself in my chair. I cross one leg over the other, grimacing. "I wasn't trying to make this awkward Roy, but since you asked."

Roy leans forward in his chair, anxiously awaiting my answer. The look in his eyes tells me he thinks he's cornered me. That he's about to get a confession that matches his suspicions. It's my job to make him think the opposite.

"Chelsea wants to find a way to get back on with Coleman Records." My words taste sour in my mouth. I know that's the last thing she wants, but I need to convince Roy, and he is just egotistical enough to believe it.

He looks surprised. "Really?"

I nod. "She asked if I had a way to get back in your good graces. The only reason Aiden tagged along was because I'm essentially babysitting him while Nash is away."

"Interesting. Go on..."

"I didn't want to make it awkward, since it's clear the two of you have...history...but I wasn't sure what else I was supposed to do."

"You were supposed to call me," he barks.

"Lesson learned," I say. In this case, I believe less is more with what I say. I don't want to over explain my lies and open myself up to questions. The less I say, the better.

I don't know if he believes me, but I didn't have enough time to prepare anything else. Deception is unfortunately becoming a strength of mine—but I usually have more time to carefully plan out my lies. I don't have that luxury here.

My phone vibrates inside my purse. Trying to act as if this is just business as usual, I pull it out. Roy knows I always check my phone. If I were to ignore it, it may put him onto me more than he already is.

Looking down, I find a text chain between Nash and his people letting us know that they're boarding their flight now.

I glance up from my phone. "Did you need anything else from me, Roy? I'm afraid I've got to run," I lie.

His eyes flick to the picture of us on his screen. Luckily, it doesn't seem like he has anything else, but the seed has been planted in his mind, which isn't good for us—at all.

"No," he states, leaning back in his chair once again. "Let Chelsea know if she wants back in, she can call me."

I take my time gathering my things and sliding out of my chair. I don't want it to appear that I'm trying to run out of here.

I'm halfway out the door when he speaks again.

"Oh, and Monica?" he says calmly.

I turn around. "Yes?"

His beady eyes narrow. "If I find out that you're up to something, Nash's career is the first thing I'm ending. I'll make sure no other person in the industry touches him. Then, I'll come after you. Is that understood?"

My breath hitches. I swallow, getting myself together quickly. "That won't be necessary," I answer before leaving his doorway.

I don't make eye contact with a single person as I make my way to my car. The moment I get to the safety of it, I scream.

Roy is undoubtedly onto me. He knows more than he's letting on.

Now Nash's career may be ruined—and it's all because of me.

42
AIDEN

As I approach Monica's condo, I notice her front door is cracked open. My grip on Pepper's leash tightens as I jog the rest of the way, stopping at the entrance. The sound of breaking glass has me throwing the door open. As soon as I make it through the doorway, I slam the door shut and let go of Pepper's leash. This is her first time over at Monica's, but she'll have to wait for a formal tour.

The sound of something else breaking fills the otherwise quiet space. I lunge through the hallway and toward the noise, finding Monica standing in the middle of her office in a fit of rage.

Picking up a pair of scissors, she throws them across the room until they bounce off one the photos hanging on the wall. Next, she picks up a stack of papers, angrily ripping them in half and throwing the shredded pieces in the air.

"What the fuck?" I mutter, my eyes taking in the scene before me.

My words break her out of her frenzy. When she looks at me, I see black streaks running down her face.

"Holy shit, are you crying?" I ask, running toward her.

Monica stops me, holding her hands between us. "I cry when I'm mad."

"Why are you mad?"

She laughs, but not the same laugh as earlier this morning when I'd found the ticklish spot on her abdomen. "Because Roy caught us speaking with Chelsea. I think he knows what we're trying to do, Aiden. He's not going to sit around and wait. He's going to retaliate…I know he is."

"How does he know?"

"Because I underestimated him, and he didn't underestimate me. He's been watching us." She picks up a picture frame from her desk and chucks it across the room, shattering the glass against the wall.

"Does he know anything else?"

She looks at me with tear-stained cheeks. It's jarring to see her in such a vulnerable state. The only time I've seen her come unhinged was because of my touch. I've never witnessed her falling apart in anger, or in fear. "I don't know what he knows, but he knows more than he told me. He's threatening Nash, Aiden. And it's all because I'm stupid and careless and foolish for thinking we'd ever be able to win against that kind of money and power."

I want to reach out, to pull her against my chest and tell her we'll figure it out, but when I try to step forward, she steps backward.

"Monica, wait!" I lunge forward, but it's too late. Her bare feet step over a pile of broken glass from a frame.

She barely winces, despite the large gash on the bottom of her foot. I bend down to examine it.

"I'm fine, Aiden," she says, her voice seeming far away even though she's standing above me. It's as if her mind is somewhere else completely.

"No it isn't. You might need stitches." I try to look to see how deep the cut is, but she pulls her foot from me.

Standing up, I don't give her time to argue. I lift her off the ground, walk out of the office and head toward her bathroom. I don't stop until I'm able to place her on her bathroom countertop.

She stares blankly ahead as I search her cabinets for some sort of first-aid kit. There's no way a control freak like Monica would go without one.

"What are we going to do, Aiden?" she asks as I'm rifling through what has got to be a hundred different hair products in the cabinet underneath one of her sinks.

"Right now we're going to fix this cut."

"I'm bleeding all over my white rug," she states matter-of-factly.

"If you'd tell me where the first-aid kit is, I could stop it," I tell her.

She points over my shoulder to a small closet. When I open it, I find neatly folded towels. One shelf has extra toiletries and the thing I've been looking for.

I pull it from the shelf, setting it down on the counter to find what I need.

A wet nose nudges my leg, reminding me that I brought Pepper.

"You brought the dog?" she asks, her voice void of emotion.

I throw a glance at Pepper sitting at my feet. "We were trying to surprise you," I offer, pulling out the supplies that I'll need.

Pepper, intuitive as always, nudges against Monica's leg. She continues the gesture until Monica reaches a hand down to pet her. The moment Monica touches her, Pepper's large tongue comes out to lick Monica across the forearm.

And as much as Monica pretends to dislike the dog, the smile on her face proves how much she cares for my furry companion.

Monica continues to pet Pepper, her brown eyes a fraction of a bit brighter than they were a few minutes ago. "We've got to do something and we've got to do it soon," she says softly, referring back to the earlier conversation.

She winces in pain when I wipe an alcohol swab over the cut. It isn't deep enough to need stitches, but it's close. I've wounded myself enough in the kitchen to know how to tend to deep cuts.

"Then that's what we'll do," I answer simply.

"I won't be the reason he loses everything he's worked for. I can't handle it…he's the only family I have. The only person I've ever cared about." She looks down, "Well, the only person until *you*."

Her honesty throws me off guard. She hasn't opened up to me much at all yet, but I'm still caught off-guard by the confession.

"What about your family?" I prod.

"My family is exactly like me. A bunch of heartless, career-driven, power-hungry people. I was merely an accessory to my parents—brought out for them to show off as a shiny toy to their business partners but neglected behind closed doors. My sister and I had to compete for a shred of love from our parents. We were pinned against one another from the very beginning."

"You're nothing like them," I demand, placing a bandage over her wound. Standing up, I grab each side of her face. "Do you hear me? You aren't like them. They don't deserve you."

She smiles sadly. "I used to think I was *exactly* like them. You know what I've done, Aiden. Stop pretending that I'm some saint."

"You did what you did because you cared about Nash. It wasn't what I would have done, but I forgive you Monica. You have to forgive yourself."

"It wasn't enough. Not if Roy stays one step ahead of us. All of this will have been for nothing."

I hold her face tight in my hands. "Listen to me right now. We're going to get to Roy first. We're going to make him pay. We'll get Nash out of this, together. Then, we're going to forgive ourselves for every shitty thing we've done in the past, okay? We're going to get through it and we're going to move on. I promise."

43
MONICA

I'd allowed myself one night to be weak. To act completely out of character. For the entire night, Aiden held me and made promises to me he may never be able to keep. But I let myself believe him. I let myself momentarily forget that so much was at stake—that so many artists might be abused if I fail. For a night, I wanted to pretend that Nash's career didn't rest in my hands all over again.

When the honeymooners returned that same night, I wanted to tell Nash every single thing we discovered in his absence. But his hate for Roy runs deep enough already, and I can't be certain he'd maintain his composure if I did. That, and I didn't want to riddle him with anxieties before the two back-to-back nights of his LA shows.

I also didn't want to ruin the post-honeymoon bliss he was clearly in. He's finally *happy.* I desperately want him to hold onto that happiness for as long as he can. No one deserves it more than him.

Nash doesn't need any distractions, especially one this large. He knows that I'm working on getting him out of his contract, but he doesn't know to what extent.

Tomorrow is the first hometown show. It's a sold-out concert and we've sold double the amount of meet and greet tickets than we normally do since it's his local show. He needs to stay focused on performing, and I need to stay focused on my plan for Roy.

Once I'm certain I have everything I need, I'll tell him. I've already made the mistake of excluding him once, I won't do that again.

I'm sitting inside my own tour bus, one I share with other members of Nash's team. I don't enjoy spending time here, but I am fortunate enough to have the larger room at the back. It wasn't something I'd asked of Nash, but he'd insisted I had it for this tour.

Everyone else is out working, leaving the bus empty for once. I pounced on the opportunity to work alone in silence, avoiding any and all distractions as I get everything I need together to finish my plan.

Speaking of distractions.

I'm deep into sending an email when the door to the bus opens, a fifty-pound dog lunging straight for me. I don't have time to react before Pepper is toppling me over.

"Pep! Heel!" Aiden yells, hot on Pepper's heels. He isn't quick enough. The beast of a dog has already climbed into my lap, even though there's no space for her there.

Pepper licks at my face. I swear she gets bigger every time I see her. "You clearly have her so trained."

Aiden smiles. "Her training has been a bit neglected recently. I've been a bit...busy." He winks, insinuating exactly what he's been busy with—me.

I allow the dog to nuzzle into me as my cheeks turn pink. Aiden's right. If either of us have had any spare time, it's been spent with one another. Not that we've had much. He's been diving headfirst into sprucing up the meals for our team. I'd been reluctant to the idea at first, but he's done so much with our craft services, and he isn't breaking the bank by doing it.

We've also been very busy finalizing our plan of attack on Roy. He's been up late with me, sneaking around so no one knows what we're up to. After our late-night sessions compiling everything we know, we spend the rest of our nights unable to keep our hands off one another.

I try not to put too much thought into what will happen next. We can't sneak around forever, and Lennon already knows about us. It won't be long until someone else finds out, too. Aiden is fine with coming clean to his brother, I on the other hand, am not.

I keep putting it off, telling him we can maybe do it...once we get the Roy situation taken care of. I just don't know what I'd tell Nash. *Hey, guess what, I think I have feelings for your little brother?* That conversation seems fun. Aiden and I aren't boyfriend and girlfriend, but he's made it very clear that I'm not to be involved with anyone else. And I feel the same about him. The thought of another woman touching him makes me feral.

I want to keep him but I don't want anyone to know about it.

"Earth to Monica?" Aiden snaps his fingers in front of my face. Pepper's tail thumps against my thigh in excitement at his sudden nearness.

"Yes," I say, blinking.

His lip twitches, his eyes flicking to my lips. "Hi." Slowly, he leans down and lays a chaste kiss on my lips.

"Hi," I say against his mouth.

"Care to share with the class what you were thinking about? You were so lost in your own thoughts that you were actually petting Pep."

I shake my head. "I don't even remember. I told you it isn't that I don't like the dog," I run my hand down the coarse fur on her back. "It's just I think she could use some better manners."

This makes him smile wide. His arm brushes mine as he reaches to scratch Pepper's ear. Leaning in close to her, he whispers, "Did you hear that, Pep? I think we're growing on her..."

My eyes roll. "I don't hate the *dog*. The verdict is still out on *you*."

His hand flies to his chest. "I can think of a few ways to prove just how much I've grown on you…"

"I'm busy."

He leans close, brushing his nose over my cheek. His hot breath against my skin makes me break out in goosebumps. Pepper, suddenly annoyed by the encroachment of her personal space, jumps off my lap.

His fingers are hot as they travel underneath the fabric of my dress. It's warm in LA today, and I knew I'd spend a lot of my time in between my bus and the stage to make sure rehearsals go smoothly. I hadn't expected Aiden to use my light dress to his advantage.

"Take it back," he whispers. His fingers run up my thigh.

"Never," I breathe, leaning into his touch.

"You asked for it." Quickly, he finds the ticklish spot on either side of my hips. His fingers dig into it, making me howl out.

"Aiden!" I yell, trying to squirm away from his touch.

He's ruthless, pressing harder to hold me down.

"Take it back, baby," he says next to my ear. He pulls away, stopping the pressure to allow me to gather my breath.

When I don't answer him, he continues his assault.

"Fine!" I wheeze, trying to gasp for air. "You've grown on me, asshole. You knew that already."

He falls to his knees between my legs. My dress has been pushed up in the process, showing off the panties he'd picked out for me this morning. Even though my tour bus was parked on the lot and way closer than my place, Aiden's been spending the night at my condo. It's been the norm for us. We haven't discussed what happens when we're back on the road.

He kisses the inside of my knee tenderly. "It doesn't mean I don't want to hear it," he answers honestly. "It's hard not ever knowing what's going on in your head. Forgive me for needing to know you haven't grown tired of me yet."

"Not yet." I jump at the feeling of his tongue coming out to lick the inside of my thigh.

His fingers splay out on either side of my thighs. "It seems I need to remind my girl of who she belongs to."

The warmth from his tongue moves further and further up my thigh, getting closer and closer to where I want him most. He runs a finger over the wet spot of my panties.

"Aiden, we have to stop," I pant. He moves the fabric to the side.

He smiles up at me with a devilish grin. "You sure about that?"

A moan leaves my lips when he softly licks me from bottom to top. I know there's a good chance he left the door to the bus unlocked, meaning someone could walk in on us at any moment. I'd told the team exactly where I was going when I broke away from the setup this morning. It wouldn't be hard for them to find me here.

I know all of this, but still I don't stop him. The edge of the table digs into the side of one of my legs, but I hardly notice. I'm too lost in the feeling of his tongue pressed against me.

It doesn't take him long to bring me to the brink of a release. He clamps a hand over my mouth as the orgasm surges through me. I have to bite down to try and stifle my moans. The walls of the buses are thin. If someone were to walk by, they'd be able to hear everything.

Once I'm done, he kisses the inside of my thigh once again. "Are you reminded?" His grin is cocky as he wipes my juices off his face with the back of his hand.

I laugh, unable to hide my smile. "You're something else."

He picks my panties up off the floor, guiding each one of my feet through the holes and helping to push them back up my thighs. "You know what I am?" he asks.

I finish pulling my panties all the way back on. Leaning forward, I wrap my arms around his neck. He still sits on his knees on the floor, my body planted in the chair and arms wrapped around his neck.

"What are you?" I ask, playing with his hair.

He kisses the top of my nose. "Yours."

The heart I didn't know still existed flutters inside my chest. I've never been one to get butterflies in my stomach, yet his words do something to me.

"You may regret saying that one day," I say sadly. Things between us seem to be going *too* well for it to last. Two people that started out as enemies can't possibly be this...normal.

He shakes his head. "Not likely."

The only answer I can give him is leaning in to kiss his lips. I put everything I have into this kiss. I don't know all the answers. I don't know what's going to happen between us. But for now, I don't care. I'm happy with where I'm at with him. He's brought me a peace I didn't know I needed.

But peace can't last forever, and eventually the differences in our lives are bound to catch up with us.

It's only a matter of time.

44
MONICA

The sun has started its descent as I wrap up my work on the bus. It took some coaxing to get Aiden to leave so I could get back to work. He tried to protest, even offering to stop seducing me and let me work. His idea didn't last long thanks to a text from someone in craft services, saying that the lunch delivery was late.

I spent another hour plotting against Roy before deciding I should probably go check on Nash and the concert setup. I've got everything I need on Roy at this point, I just need to figure out how best to expose him. People like him aren't easy to take down. They have too much money and too many connections. I have to be perfect if this is going to work.

I'm hardly paying attention to where I'm walking when I step off the bus and directly into another person.

An overly warm hand grips my bicep tightly. Looking up, I find a beaming Roy. "Where are you off to in such a hurry?"

I look around. Most of the crew is setting up for the concert, leaving the parking lot around us dead. All I can see are rows and rows of parked buses, empty aisles everywhere. "Just working," I answer, pulling my sunglasses down over my eyes.

"Well you were just the person I was looking for. Mind if we step back onto your bus for a chat?"

I stare up at him, wondering what he's doing here. According to his schedule, he's supposed to be at an event in New York for the next three days. I know this because ever since the restaurant incident, I've been extra cautious. If the man sneezes, I've made it my business to know about it.

"Sure," I finally answer. "I've got a few minutes, but then I need to get to where I was going…"

Without hesitation, he reaches around me to open the door to my bus. The smell of his body odor stings my nostrils as I make my way up the stairs. I continue walking until I'm seated at the same table I was at an hour ago, with Aiden doing dirty things to me.

I erase the memory from my mind, knowing I need to stay completely focused for the likely unpleasant conversation that is about to unfold.

"How can I help you?" I ask him.

His eyes are fixated on a magazine left out on one of the couches. Tucking his hands into his pockets, he looks at me. "It's more about how I can help *you*, Monica."

I frown. "My apologies, I'm not sure what you're talking about."

"I wasn't a fan of how we left things last time we spoke, Monica. It really bothered me—kept me up all night."

He turns his attention from the couch over to where I sit, his beady eyes focused on me.

"I was thinking, we used to be such terrific partners, you and I. Look at what we did with Nash. That was *us*, Monica. We turned a playboy addict into the most successful pop star of our generation."

What game are you playing? I try to decipher his words while avoiding looking disgusted.

"And *you*. You've gone from completely unknown to one of

the most successful and respected managers in the business. I don't want to fight with you, Monica. No, no, no. I want you on my team."

"Excuse me?" I blurt, unable to keep from looking surprised.

He smiles eagerly, like he's been holding onto a secret that he can't wait to unveil. "I have a proposal for you. Two, in fact."

He makes his way over to the table, sitting across from me with his hands folded in front of him.

"It's no secret Nash doesn't like me."

A small snort leaves my nose, causing Roy to frown briefly.

"Like I said, it's no secret," his smile returns as he continues. "If he wants to move on—go to greener pastures—who am I to hold him back?"

"What are you saying?" I ask in disbelief.

"Nash is free from his contractual obligations to me. If that is what you both want."

"Why would…"

Roy raises his hand, cutting me off. "In addition to Nash's freedom, I have an offer for you, Monica."

He pauses, as if to add suspense to the unveiling of his offer.

"I've seen the way you handle business. You're cunning, ruthless, and just the type of person we need on the board at Coleman. What you've done in your relatively brief career is nothing short of miraculous. It's time you stopped slumming it as someone's bitch, Monica, you're too talented."

Anger boils in my veins. I'm nobody's bitch. "I work *with* Nash," I answer smoothly.

He waves at the air dismissively, as if my words mean nothing. "You don't need to do that anymore. It's time you move up to the big leagues and take a spot where your talents will be utilized better."

My eyebrows furrow. He'd be giving up his top artist. Roy likes money too much for this to make any sense.

"Nash is one of your biggest assets. And you'd just let him

walk away with all of his music? For *what?* To get me on the board? What's in it for you?"

He holds his index finger up to his temple. "You're always thinking ahead, Monica. It's one of the reasons I respect you. Women often get caught up in the present, in their emotions, and aren't able to think ahead like that."

You misogynistic pig.

He sighs, throwing his hands up in defeat. "You win. I can guess what you've got on me, Monica, and I can't have that information getting out. What better way to make sure it doesn't go public than to give you a piece of the pie—a spot at the head of the table. I'm offering you everything you could ever want. More money and power than you've ever dreamed of."

As much as I hate myself for it, I let myself consider the offer. Not because of the position on the board. Truthfully, I never really wanted to work for a label. Money and power never interested me as much as the ball-busting I get to do on a daily basis working my current job.

I try to consider the offer because for the first time since I started looking into Roy, I finally have a guaranteed way to break Nash's contract. The whole reason I began this crusade in the first place was for the sole purpose of freeing Nash from the tyrannical hold of Coleman Records. I could finally do just that. As much as I can't stand Roy, I would work with him if it meant finally doing right by Nash.

Unfortunately, Nash isn't the only one that needs me anymore. Sasha and Chelsea were brave enough to share their stories with me and Aiden. How many other aspiring artists have a story to tell? How can I be any better than Roy if I turn a blind eye? But then again, there's no guarantee that what I have will make any difference to someone with that much power.

My head spins as I try to analyze the situation.

Taking a deep breath, I decide I won't refuse a deal with the devil—yet. I'll never bargain with a man like Roy, but I need time to process all of this.

"Give me time to think about it."

45

AIDEN

My heart pounds in anticipation as I press my ear to the door of the RV. I eavesdrop on the interaction between Monica and Roy. I'm close to barging in on them, making my presence known so I can tell Roy to fuck off and that his offer is something she would *never* accept.

But she hasn't answered yet.

Her pause is making me anxious.

My ear flattens against the door of the tour bus. I hear her take a long, dramatic deep breath. Her next words kill me. "Give me time to think about it."

The world around me spins. As quietly as I can, I back away from the entrance to the bus.

Part of me wishes I'd never eavesdropped. I hadn't done it to try and get dirt on her. Quite the opposite, I was trying to protect her. I saw Roy as I was headed towards the stadium and decided to follow him. I'd never seen the man at a concert before, so I figured something was up. When he confronted Monica, I had to make sure he wasn't cornering her.

What **an ass** I've made of myself.

She didn't ever need protection. From the very beginning, she's been playing all of us. Roy was never a threat to her. We'd done all of this work, found all this dirt. For what? The girls—what he'd done to them, they didn't mean anything to her.

It was never her intention to help them. I don't even know if it was ever her true intention to help Nash. Maybe all along, these were excuses to get exactly what she wanted...to spite her father...and to take a position with the main competitor to her family's company.

She made a fool out of me.

These women had trusted me. They'd shared their stories with *me*. And in return, I trusted Monica to help me—to help them.

The asphalt crunches underneath my shoes as I get as far away from the bus as possible. As far away from *her*.

I'd known from the start she's nothing but a liar. I knew all about her schemes and deception before I'd ever met her. And yet...I allowed her to seduce me—to pull me in. I fell for her conniving games.

To think I'd been so close to barging up the stairs to defend her.

Give me time to think about it.

Her words ring in my head over and over. She's actually considering his offer. Of course she would. Every time she has the opportunity to do something selfless, she chooses herself.

I've always called her a little liar. I've known all along.

Bracing myself on a bus far away from hers, I take in as much air as my lungs will allow.

Her betrayal hurts far worse than I could've imagined.

I have to tell Nash.

But before I do, I have to get my head on straight. I have to figure out how I'm going to admit to my brother that the woman who plotted against him is the same woman whose bed I was climbing into at night. I need some time to think. I need to find a way to get back at her.

Fool me once, shame on you.

Fool me twice, shame on *me*.

I don't take well to being made into a fool.

<hr>

"WHERE DO YOU THINK YOU'RE GOING, LITTLE LIAR?" I yell through the narrow aisle of buses.

Monica, just stepping out of Nash's tour bus, looks up at me in shock. Her eyes widen, looking at the few people around us. "Aiden," she says coolly. You'd never know all the lies she's hiding beneath the calm tone of her voice.

"What were you doing?" I demand, looking over her shoulder at Nash's tour bus. Once I'd finally gathered my thoughts, I'd texted him asking where he was. He'd responded that he was in a meeting on his bus, but that we could talk after.

Who knew the meeting was with the bitch of a liar standing in front of me?

"Talking to Nash." Her answer is simple. She looks at me, confused. She reaches out to touch me, but I back away.

"Don't you fucking dare," I seethe, looking down at her in disgust. "Don't ever fucking touch me again."

Tucking her hair behind her ear, she grimaces. "What's going on, Aiden?"

I laugh, throwing my hands up in the air. "You're really going to play dumb aren't you? God, I'm so fucking embarrassed that I actually fell for it."

"Maybe we should talk somewhere more private," she says, biting the inside of her cheek. Someone walks past us. She gives them a forced smile, trying to pretend that everything isn't up in flames right now.

"Why? So everyone doesn't know how much of a bitch you are? How much of a liar?"

I look around me, raising my voice. "Well guess what, they should all know. Monica Masters is a cold-hearted bitch. But we all knew that already didn't we? It's just *me* who'd thought otherwise."

"Aiden...whatever you were told..."

"I didn't have to be told anything. I heard every single word of your conversation with Roy." My teeth clench. "Every. Last. Word."

For once, she looks panicked. What a great actress she's turned out to be.

"Tell me, would no one else fuck you? That's why you had to spin your web of lies to get me to do it?"

Her mouth hangs open. "Aiden, it isn't what you think."

"Oh so you weren't needing time to think about betraying the women you've claimed to care about? You weren't thinking about working with that *pathetic* excuse of a man?"

"There's more to the story..."

"You didn't need more time because it was your fucking plan all along. You'd blackmail Roy, get a spot on *his* board to get what you want. Nash, these girls...me...we were all just collateral damage. You don't give a fuck about any of us."

"I'm going to tell him no. I just needed to buy time!" she yells, having to talk over me to get a word in.

Shaking my head, I look at the woman I'd fallen for, despite every single one of the warning signs in my head. "I don't fucking believe you. You're abandoning these women who *trusted* you to tell their story. I trusted you." It seems like the world is falling apart at my feet. From the very beginning I *knew* what she was capable of, but I was blinded by lust. I would have believed anything that came out of her mouth.

Not anymore.

Her bottom lip shakes. "You know me. Aiden, I would never."

I close the distance between our bodies. Like in the very beginning, she tries to back away from me, ending up cornered against a bus.

"That's the thing, Monica." I brush a piece of hair from her face. "Everything I know about you tells me you *would*. That you *did*."

Her chest heaves up and down. "That's it? You overhear small fragments of a conversation and *everything* you've seen me do for Nash, for these girls, in the last few weeks just goes out the window?"

"Your deception knows no bounds."

I watch as the hurt in her eye's morphs to anger. She's no longer able to keep the innocent mask on, her true colors are beginning to seep from her pores. The mask is slipping, giving me a glimpse at the real her...the one I'd known about all along.

"I'm glad you think so low of me. I remember you telling me that you're mine just this morning."

"You were a decent fuck, I guess my mind was caught up in that, saying things I didn't mean. You'd know how that feels, wouldn't you?"

Taking me off guard, she shoves against my chest. She puts enough power into it to put some space between us. "I didn't fucking betray you or Nash or anyone!" she shouts, waving her hands frantically in the hair. She's completely unhinged, her hands aggressively slicing through the air. "But you're never going to believe me, Aiden. Deep down, you've had this idea of me from the very beginning. You were never going to get rid of it, no matter how many times I tried to prove to you that I care. I care deeply about these girls, about their stories being heard... I care about Nash...and I care about *you*."

"You don't care about anyone but yourself."

Rolling her eyes, she wipes at her cheek.

Is that a tear?

I blink, knowing my mind is playing tricks on me. There's no way she's crying. Or maybe she is, at this point I don't know how far she'll go to get what she wants.

"Go fuck yourself, Aiden," she shouts, walking away from me.

I'm left watching her go, wishing like hell I hadn't let her in. Wishing I hadn't fallen for her lies.

Most of all, wishing that it didn't hurt so bad to watch her walk away, even after all the pain she's caused.

46
AIDEN

The next day, I woke up to a string of missed calls from Nash, asking where I went. In my fit of rage last night, I'd forgotten that I told him we needed to talk. I'm regretting it now.

Today is the first of two LA shows, and Nash hasn't had a moment of silence all day. I've tried to tell him I need to speak to him alone—that it's important—but he won't listen.

Sitting in his dressing room, just minutes before he's set to take the stage, I've finally been able to talk to him, but he keeps dismissing me.

After all the progress we've made in our relationship, this is the absolute worst time for him to revert back to treating me like a child.

"You need to do something about her," I tell Nash. He sits in a makeup chair, his team having just left to give him some quiet before the show.

At least he thought it'd be quiet, but I'm not done having this conversation with him.

"It's being handled, Aiden," Nash says, his tone exhausted. "Monica's handling it. She has a plan, but I don't have time to tell you everything before I have to go on stage. Just trust me."

Monica must have lied to him, too.

"How can you be so sure? She's lied to you before. What if she works with Roy? Keeps all of this dirt hidden?"

"She won't."

I sit up angrily on the couch. "How do you know that? What aren't you telling me?"

Nash opens his mouth to speak, but before he can get any words out, Roy bursts through the door.

A sinister grin covers his face as he focuses on Nash. "Did I interrupt something?"

"I'm busy," Nash clips, not bothering to look over at Roy.

Roy looks like a fucking kid in a candy shop. His smile is too wide, too creepy. "Oh I won't take long, I just came to gloat. To share the good news…"

Nash doesn't humor him with words, but I can't help myself. "And what's that?"

Roy turns to me, his eyes narrowing. "The little brother, still riding his big brother's coattails…"

"My name is Aiden."

"That's right. Well, *Aiden*, I came to share with Nash personally the news that Monica has ditched him. That she's going to take a more dignified position at Coleman. I'm afraid she'll no longer have the time to babysit you."

My heart sinks. Even though I knew in my head she was a liar, my heart still held onto hope that she would refuse his offer and do the right thing. It feels like the last piece of my soul has been ripped out of my body.

"Monica wouldn't do it," Nash points out matter-of-factly. My eyes turn to my brother. Why doesn't he seem surprised? Roy just confirmed everything I told him. Why is he letting this asshole barge in here and gloat? And how could he possibly think Monica wouldn't do it? *Of course* she'd do it.

"I'm finally getting rid of you once and for all. I can't say I'm sad to see your annoying pop star ass go. You were always more difficult than you're worth."

Nash stands up, walking to stand in front of Roy. He stares him down, looking unfazed. "The feeling was mutual, Roy."

The two of them stare eye to eye, neither backing down. Finally, Roy breaks eye contact, backing away in the direction of the door. He pauses before opening it.

"Oh, and before you go I have one more surprise to leave you with," he says cockily.

Outside the room, you can hear the sound of the crowd beginning to cheer Nash's name. "I have a show to get to," Nash says, seemingly unphased.

Roy's face lights up. "That's the surprise, Nash. You don't have a show anymore."

"Excuse me?" Nash asks, his voice low.

"That's right. We're canceling your shows—both of them. It makes no difference to me anymore what your fans think of you. You've made me look bad so many times, it's time I return the favor."

Finally, I see emotion from Nash. "That isn't possible."

"It isn't? I pay for these shows. I can cancel them as easily as I can put them on. But if you don't believe me, go see for yourself. We have someone going on right now to cancel it."

Shoving past Roy, Nash, and I both take off. He goes toward the stage, I go to find Monica.

I need to talk to her, to see if somehow she has it in her cold, black heart to stop Roy from doing this.

47
MONICA

Standing in the wings of the stage, my eyes dart around, wondering where the hell Nash is, my mind reels with the possibilities of why he's late. He was supposed to be up here by now.

One of Roy's people walks onto the stage. At first, the crowd erupts in cheers, thinking it's Nash walking out to start the show.

Their voices die down when they realize it isn't him.

My heart hammers against my chest. Any moment now, there will be a group of people I've gathered here to meet Nash, but for that to happen, I need him here.

"Good evening, LA," the man says into the microphone. Nash's band is already on stage behind him. Poe looks to the side of the stage confused. He walks over to Landon to say something, but all Landon does is shrug.

No one knows what's going on. What's about to take place.

"I've got some bad news," he continues on stage. "The show tonight has been canceled."

The crowd erupts in madness. He tries to talk over them, to explain what's happening, but they don't give him the chance.

I'm beginning to panic when Nash runs up to me. "They actually canceled it?" he says, breathless.

I nod, grabbing the mic pack I was holding in my hand. "Apparently. But it doesn't matter, you're going out there no matter what. To hell with the consequences. What took you so long to get here?" I add, trying to take a deep breath. I wasn't expecting Roy to try and cancel the show, but the plan can still go accordingly.

He turns for me, allowing me to fasten it to the back of his jeans. "Roy found me in my dressing room."

I run the wire underneath his shirt, pulling his earpieces out the top of his shirt. "Does he suspect anything?"

Nash turns to face me, placing the earpieces in his ears. "No, not a damn thing. But Monica, Aiden heard it all…he's looking for you. And he's pissed."

"He can be pissed. Right now we've got bigger things to worry about."

"Did you do it?" Nash asks.

I nod, knowing exactly what he's talking about. "It's done."

"You're a fucking mastermind, Monica." He manages to smile, something I'm unable to do with all of the nerves passing through me.

Looking over his shoulder, I find who I've been waiting on. "I've got some people for you to meet," I tell Nash.

He turns around, coming face to face with two of the artists whose careers were ended because they put their trust in Roy.

Chelsea smiles, holding a guitar in her hands. "We heard you were sticking it to the man. Mind if we join?"

Nash turns to me, shocked. A wide smile on his face, he nods his head. "Fuck yeah you can. Let's go show the world your talent."

They don't need anything else from me. Nash, Chelsea, and Sasha all walk out to the stage.

Some fans are already making their way to the exits when

others begin to notice the trio of artists. The guy at the microphone turns around, looking confused as Nash shoves him out of the way.

"You're not getting rid of me that easily, LA," Nash says into the microphone. The crowd erupts, breaking into a wild frenzy and rushing back towards the stage.

"Give them hell out there," I whisper to myself, feeling proud to see the girls standing out there, ready to try again despite all the wrongdoings that have been done against them.

I turn around to go deeper backstage. We're ready for the next part of the plan. I weave in and out through different equipment until I find Matt, Monroe, and Sebastian. I wasn't planning for Sebastian to be in on this tonight, but he'd shown up to support Nash, and he wasn't going to miss out on what happens next.

"Are you ready?" I ask the three of them, taking a deep breath.

"Fuck yeah," Sebastian answers for the three of them. "My night just got so much more interesting."

"Are you sure about this?" Matt, always the voice of reason, asks.

I nod. "It's already done. There's no turning back now."

"Monica!" Roy yells from down the hallway.

Right on queue.

He stalks toward us, fists clenched. Nash's three bodyguards take their spots behind me, letting me face Roy on my own.

Red in the face, Roy stops in front of me. "Monica! Why the hell is Nash on stage right now?"

The acoustics from the concert speakers bounce around the concrete walls of the stadium and make their way back to us. Perfectly on time, Nash's voice rings around us. "I'd like to introduce you to these incredibly talented artists around me. You may remember them, their names may be familiar. But they trusted the wrong man…"

Roy looks down at me. "What is he doing? Make him stop. Right now!"

Over his shoulder, I notice Aiden barreling around the same corner Roy came from. I ignore him, looking right back at Roy. "Why would I do that?" I question, cocking my head.

Nash continues on stage, "These women trusted someone they thought would help their careers. Instead they were taken advantage of, their life's work snuffed out because they decided to set boundaries with their label owner—with Roy Goodman."

Roy's eyes go wide. "You didn't."

I smile at him. "But what if I did?"

"Then your career is over, Monica Masters!" he yells. Spit flies from his mouth as he angles his body over mine.

I don't flinch. Holding my hand up to my ear, I direct his attention to the crowd going wild for the performers on stage—to the ones who took him down by being brave enough to share their story and get on stage tonight.

"You know Roy," I say confidently, "I actually think it's *your* career that is over."

He lunges for me. "Fuck you, Monica."

His red laden face is inches from mine. Before he can grab me, anger turns to shock as he is pulled backwards.

Aiden's hand grasps the back of his collar, pulling Roy away from me. Matt and Sebastian both take a step forward to grab Roy, but Aiden doesn't give them the time to intervene. "Don't you fucking touch her," he yells, spinning Roy around and smashing his fist into the middle of Roy's face.

The blow sends Roy to his knees, blood spurting from his nose, staining his neatly starched shirt. Aiden stands over him, winding up for a second blow and hitting Roy in the jaw before Sebastian can pull him off.

"That's enough, tough guy," Sebastian mutters, holding onto a rabid Aiden.

"I'm not fucking done with you yet!" Aiden growls, trying to break free of Sebastian's grip.

Matt and Monroe each take one of Roy's arms, pulling him to his feet. "Get off me," Roy snarls. He spits a wad of blood onto the concrete below our feet.

"No can do," Matt says to him, his grasp on Roy's arm tight. "We've got clear instructions to take you to the police waiting outside."

Roy's face turns to panic. Eyes wide, he looks at me. *"Police?"*

It's my turn to speak up. "Yes, Roy, police. I think they'll find everything you've been up to very interesting. Underage girls, blackmail, embezzling. You've been a busy little criminal. It's time you pay for it."

His eyes are angrily pointed at me. "You can rot in hell, Monica. I'll get you back for this."

I take a step closer to him, feeling confident in the hold Matt and Monroe have on him. "You know Roy, I hope you remember my face as you rot in jail for what you've done. I hope you remember my face, Nash's face, and the face of every woman you thought you could take advantage of."

Turning around, I don't give him time to respond. There's nothing else that needs to be said.

We pulled it off.

48
AIDEN

"MONICA, WAIT," I plead, running after her retreating figure. She left Nash's bodyguards with Roy to hand him off to police. I was so caught up in watching everything unfold that she'd managed to get a head start on me.

She gives no indication that she plans on stopping. Finally catching up to her, I step in front, cutting her off. "We need to talk." The words come out harsher than I'd intended, but after everything that just went down, I'm still trying to screw my head on straight. "Please," I add, softer, hoping she listens.

Monica doesn't even look at me. She stares over my shoulder. "We have nothing left to talk about, Aiden."

We have everything to talk about.

"I beg to differ." I have to speak up to be heard over the concert taking place on the other side of these concrete walls.

When her eyes do land on me, they're angry, exhausted, but what sticks out to me most is the hurt in them. It's enough to make me feel like the biggest piece of shit in the world. "You've said plenty, Aiden. There's nothing else to say."

I shake my head. Reaching out, I try to lace my fingers through hers. "I fucked up. Big time."

It's the understatement of the year. When I'd overheard her

conversation with Roy, I lost all sense of reasoning. I was cata-pulted back in time to when I thought she didn't care about anything but herself. I said some damaging things, and now all I can do is take it back and hope she'll hear me out.

She pulls her hand away from me, sticking it behind her back. "We don't have to do this, Aiden. I've already set up a meeting with Nash and the remaining board members. Once they get all of the drama of Roy's departure from the label settled, they'll draw up a new contract that'll allow Nash to own all of his music. We got what we wanted. Let's leave it at that."

A sinking feeling builds in my chest. The things that I said to her yesterday were unforgivable. I was blindsided by what I thought was her betrayal and lashed out in the worst way possi-ble. "I can't just leave it at that. What I said yesterday was..." My voice breaks.

There's no emotion on her face. "It's how you feel. It was honest. I don't care to speak about it any further."

"It isn't how I feel though," I argue.

She sighs, shaking her head at me. "Aiden, I don't know what we ever thought we were doing. It's clear this was never going to work. You don't trust me. I tried to give you everything I had to give to earn that trust...it wasn't enough."

"If you would've just told me your plan..."

"You didn't even give me time to explain!"

"You went to Nash instead of me, even after everything we worked on together."

"He needed to be onboard with the plan—it was his concert. I was going to tell you after, but you never gave me the chance before you..."

"Ruined everything?" I say, cutting her off.

"You said it yourself, Aiden. I was just a decent *fuck*," she emphasizes the word, her tone laced with biting anger the longer she goes on. "I'd spent weeks proving to you that Nash was the one person I cared about. Him and," her voice gets softer, sadder, "*you.*"

"I should've believed you."

"But you didn't. There's nothing left to discuss between us, Aiden. Forget it all and leave me the hell alone."

She turns to walk away. But this is what we do—she runs, I chase. I will continue to chase this woman until I can win her back, to prove to her how deep my feelings run, no matter the stupid shit I've said that I regret.

"I said those things because I was upset!" My heart thumps against my chest in desperation. What I say now could seal our fate, and I won't let her walk away from me again until I've said everything I need to.

"I gathered," she yells, not bothering to look over her shoulder.

I know there's people around us, that the more she walks away, the louder I'll have to yell what I'm about to say. People will hear this. At this point, I don't give a shit who hears me. All I need is for *her* to hear the words.

"I was upset because I felt deceived." I pause, taking a deep breath. "I felt deceived because I've fallen in love with you!"

She stops. Her eyes are wide when she turns around to face me. I continue, knowing she may not wait for long. "There it is, Monica. I love you. I felt so deceived, so blindsided because it's you...you've become my everything and the thought of you not feeling the same wrecked me. The thought of you deceiving Nash...deceiving me, when my heart was so clearly yours, it was more than I could handle."

Neither Monica nor I look away from one another. Time seems to stand still as she stares at me, her eyes traveling over my face. My heart on the line, the wait for her to respond seems like an eternity. Her narrow shoulders rise and fall in a sigh. "The things you said, the way it felt like you meant them, that's not love, Aiden." She laughs bitterly. "I'm no expert when it comes to love, but this, whatever has happened between us, isn't it."

Stepping forward, she presses her hand to my cheek. "It's over, Aiden. I'm no longer going to waste my breath trying to convince you of who I am and who I'm not. You can't have love without trust, and you've convinced me that I'm not the kind of woman you'll ever fully trust."

Her hand slips from my face, and for once, I let her walk away from me.

Tonight is not the night I'll prove my love to her, but one night will be. I'm stubborn, and I won't stop until she knows she's mine.

49
MONICA

My mind replays Aiden's words over and over as I wait for Nash in his dressing room. Toward the end of the meet and greet, I'd told Nash I needed to speak with him privately after the show. Sitting here alone, I wonder if it would've been best to stay in the company of others so I wouldn't have been left to my own thoughts.

The silence causes Aiden's confession to ring in my ears. He told me he loves me. It was the first time in my adult life that a man had told me he loved me, and I couldn't believe him. If I was the same naive girl I was as a teenager, I would've jumped for joy at his admission.

Life has changed me over the years, it's made me more callous—more realistic. Realistic enough to know that there's no way Aiden can love me. You can't fall in love with somebody you don't trust—somebody you used to hate. We're proof of that. He made that clear when he abandoned ship the moment doubt was introduced. Past lies wounded him too deeply, it isn't possible for love to bloom from the scars.

I'd confided in him more than I've ever confided in anyone else, and it still wasn't enough.

Aiden had come into my life, rattling every single one of my nerves from the very beginning. Somehow, along the way, I let my guard down enough to let him in. I relinquished control to him. The passion had been too much for me to ignore, eventually I had to give in. I just hadn't expected my heart to get so involved. I never would've thought I'd develop feelings for my enemy…but I did.

Now I'm reminded of why I guard my heart. It's the same reason I hate birthdays. If you allow something to feel special, it can be used against you.

I don't want to recognize this gut-wrenching feeling in my stomach. The betrayal and hurt that I feel is because despite it all, I fell for him, too.

The door swings open, ripping me from my thoughts. A sweaty Nash walks through. "I'm beat," he sighs, falling into the couch with a satisfied smile.

I hand him a water bottle, knowing after performing the entirety of a show and speaking with fans that his vocal cords will be shot.

"How did the rest of the greet go?" I ask, settling deeper into my chair across from him.

"It was incredible. The fans loved being able to meet Sasha and Chelsea. So many of the people tonight were already talking about how they were looking forward to new music from them."

Something like relief, or maybe it's pride, settles in my chest. "You did right by them," I tell him.

He sits forward, setting the water bottle aside. "*You* did right by them, Monica. I didn't have to do much. All I did was bring them on stage with me, everything leading up to that was all because of you."

I shrug, feeling uncomfortable with the sincerity in his words. "It was the right thing to do."

He nods. "True, but it doesn't mean that everyone would've

gone through the trouble of doing it. You could've got me my songs without helping these women."

"They're talented. They deserve to show that talent off, not be stifled because they fell for the lies of some seedy man."

Nash nods. "They're both *so* talented. I told them that as soon as I get back from our international leg I'd love to sit down and do some writing sessions with them."

"That's a great idea."

"By then they should be good to go in the studio, finally getting what they deserve and able to put music out into the world. I want to help them as much as possible."

"They deserve it all," I agree with him, "and Roy deserves everything coming his way."

"Tell me how he took it," Nash says, clapping his hands together. "God, do I wish I could've seen his face when we outed him. What did he do when we brought them on stage? I need every single detail."

I laugh. "Oh he was pissed. I don't think he thought we'd ever actually do it."

"What did he say?"

"He told me to rot in hell," I answer nonchalantly.

Nash busts out with laughter. "That was the best he could come up with?"

I shrug. "Apparently. It wasn't very impressive if you ask me."

"What happens with Coleman now?" Nash asks, the conversation turning more serious. Even though Roy is getting what he deserves, we still have to ensure that Nash gets all of the rights to his own music.

"Now, the board has some decisions to make. They're going to have to hire new people, a new label head. They're already working out a deal to get you to stay with them…and you'll own all of your masters. Call it an apology."

His eyebrows raise. "They'd do that?"

I shrug. "They aren't all bad over at Coleman, and the ones that are left want to keep you with them."

"You could probably join the board, you know," Nash offers. "I wouldn't blame you in the slightest."

My eyebrows narrow. I look at him, trying to read his face. *He can't be serious.*

"That's never been my desire, Nash," I tell him.

"You could maybe even run it. Can you imagine the look on your father's face if *you* became his biggest competitor? I would pay money to see that."

It would rattle my family if somehow I got the position they'd always held over my head, just with another company. Younger me may have jumped at the chance to grab a spot at the top. It would be a poetic twist to my story, to the war I've waged with my family for years. My sister would be furious. She'd always gloated that she was the one to get everything my father had established. The more she bragged, the less they got to me. Until eventually one day, I realized it was never my intention to run a label.

It was always my intention to be on the other side, to represent the artists. They're the true heart and soul of a label.

"Are you trying to get rid of me?" I reflect on who I was when I first met Nash. The two of us were lost souls, trying to find our place on our own in this industry. He'd just left the boy band he'd been a part of for years, and I'd just told my family to go to hell. When I first approached him, he'd turned me down. He was looking for someone with a track record, someone with clients. I argued, asking him why he'd want someone who wasn't able to solely focus on him—on making his solo career take off. It took some convincing, but eventually we came to an agreement.

Years later, I can't picture myself doing anything but working with him. We've been through so much together. That's assuming he still wants me. He's about to embark on a new journey in his career, so it wouldn't be out of the realm of possibilities that he'd want to find someone different for it.

His silence makes my stomach turn. I can't picture what my life would look like if I wasn't working with him, having to watch him grow from the sidelines.

"Things haven't always been easy between us, Monica. But there is nobody in this world who has fought harder for me than you have. I'd keep you as my manager for all of my days, even when I'm old and reliving my glory days on a throwback tour. But I'm not sure staying with me is what's best for *you…*"

"It's a good thing that isn't your decision then, isn't it?" I say, a bite to my voice. I want to shut down this conversation immediately. I'm not going anywhere. I've been his biggest fan for years now, and I don't plan on stopping soon.

Nash was the brother I never had. He drives me insane, and I've done things to him I regret, but I can't imagine him not being a constant in my life for a long time to come.

He throws his hands up defensively. "Easy, tiger. If you want to slum it with me still, I'm all for it."

"Deal." I sit up straighter, giving him a smile. "But to keep me, to afford me, you need to get this next album out."

He laughs, shaking his head at me. "*There's* the Monica I remember. I will, boss, don't worry."

Nodding, I stand up. "Good. I'll let you get to your wife now. She's probably wondering where all of this came from."

"It's Nora, she'll understand."

I'm pushing against the door to leave when Nash speaks again.

"Hey, Monica?" he asks, his voice sounding unsure.

I look over my shoulder at him. "Yeah?"

"If you ever want to talk about what's going on between you and my brother, I'm here."

My heart races at his words. Nash is insinuating that he knows more than I'd anticipated. I guess after the last few days, and Aiden's outbursts, it isn't hard to fathom that Nash might be onto us.

Sadness washes over me with my parting words. "There's nothing to speak of. Goodnight, Nash."

50
AIDEN

Even being in a different country doesn't stop Monica from ignoring me completely.

The international leg of the tour started two weeks ago, and she's barely uttered two words to me in the time we've been on it.

It isn't due to lack of trying on my part. Every morning, no matter where we are, I make sure she has one of her favorite breakfast items. It means I've had to wake up hours earlier than I used to, even with the shifting time zones we're jumping between. No amount of jetlag will stop me from trying to prove my feelings to her.

I wait outside her bus now. The schedules she hands out to crew members has become what I live by. It's the only way I know what she has planned for the day, since she's made it clear she has no desire to speak to me.

After studying the schedule for her day, I know that she's just getting out of a meeting with Nash's PR team. He's been able to sneak in a few recording sessions recently, and they're working with the label to sort out what to do next with those songs.

The door opens, Monica stepping out of it. Her eyes land on

me immediately. The loud, dramatic sigh that leaves her lips shows her sentiment on seeing me waiting for her, yet again.

"Good morning," I say, way too chipper for it not even being seven in the morning yet.

Ignoring me, and the smoothie in my hand, Monica bends down.

"Hi Pepper," she says sweetly, petting the dog at my feet. Pepper eats up the attention eagerly, trying to lick Monica's wrist as Monica pets the top of her head.

Every morning, Monica pretends that I'm not even here. She gives Pepper attention and leaves me in the dust. It doesn't deter me. Today I'm feeling bold, running to catch up to her when she starts to head toward the stadium.

"You forgot your smoothie." I shake the smoothie in front of her. "It's your favorite."

She stops, narrowing her eyes. "Can't you catch a hint, Aiden? I don't want it. I don't want anything from you."

I smile. "Can't *you* catch a hint, Monica? I fucked up, and I won't stop until I prove to you that I meant it when I said I'm yours." Sticking the straw of her drink in my mouth, I take a long draw of the fruity flavors. Moaning dramatically, I wink at her. "This smoothie's *delicious.*"

She rolls her eyes at me. "I'll take your word for it."

And then she walks away, like she always does.

And like I always do, I yell after her. "One day I'll prove to you I love you." I take a breath, "I can't wait for that day," I mutter to myself.

WE WOKE UP IN CANADA THIS MORNING.

I stood outside of her hotel room with a special ordered egg white omelet.

She'd ignored me.

As always, I made sure she started her day knowing that I love her.

THIS MORNING, MONICA SAID MORE THAN A FEW words to me.

It was only because Pepper had accidentally tripped me as I held her acai bowl. In a complete accident, I'd come tumbling down, the bowl flying out of my hands. It landed at her feet, dousing her pants in purple liquid.

Nothing out of her mouth was nice, but it was a step up. She uttered more than a sentence.

As she returned to her room to change, I'd made sure she still started her day knowing that I love her.

IT'S BEEN A COUPLE OF WEEKS SINCE WE TOOK OFF for the international leg of the tour. We've traveled from different provinces and territories in Canada and then over to Great Britain. In a few days, Nash is playing in Glasgow, but we've got a few days to settle in before Nash performs.

Like always, I wait for Monica outside her room. The buses came to Canada with us, but we didn't bring them overseas. Instead, all of the tour equipment is shipped via shipping containers, and we get the luxury of staying in hotels every night. It means a lot of moving my stuff, but the beds are always nicer than the small bunk I'm used to sleeping in.

I hadn't realized I was leaning on her door until it opens, making me lose my balance. I'm able to catch myself before I fall into her, luckily not spilling the food container in my hand. This morning, I was able to get into the kitchen of the hotel. The chef in charge was kind enough to show me around, to help me make a specialty of theirs for Monica.

"This is getting really old," Monica says, her lips tight. She wears a turtleneck sweater and a pair of leather pants. Her hair is pinned to the top of her head. I wasn't expecting Glasgow to be so cold, or windy, but it seems she came prepared.

I hold the container in the air. "I made this for you this morning. It's a Glasgow specialty."

"Then I'm sure you'll enjoy it." She tries to shoulder past me, but I don't let her by easily.

"We could enjoy it together," I offer, eyeing the privacy of her hotel room behind us. I'd do anything to catch her sole attention for a few moments, to have the opportunity to fall to her feet and apologize for every stupid thing I said.

"Never again." Her words sting, but I try to let them slide right off. I deserve every rude comment she gives me. If I want to win her back, I can't let her insults deter me.

"All I need is five minutes. If you don't want to talk to me after those five minutes, then I'll leave you alone."

She stares at me, and for an instant I wonder if she's going to take the bait. I may have told a small white lie. If she hears me out for five minutes and still doesn't give me the time of day, I'm not going to let her go that easily, but she doesn't need to know that for now.

I've become desperate, one little lie isn't going to hurt.

It doesn't seem to matter, because she looks up at me, annoyance written all over her face. "No. Goodbye, Aiden."

I'm getting used to watching her leave. Opening up the box of the food I'd so carefully prepared and plated, I pick up one of the potatoes I'd roasted, tossing it back in the container. Every time I watch her walk away, I feel a little more defeated.

With everything in me, I wish I could take back what I told her when I overheard her speaking to Roy. I wish for once in my life, I wasn't impulsive, that I'd thought before I lashed out. If I would've taken a step back from the situation and really thought about it, I would've known that Monica wasn't selling out Nash. Deep down, I knew she wasn't the person I first thought her to be.

As she disappears around the hallway, I wonder if maybe I did lose her for good.

Maybe it wasn't her deceiving me that ruined us before we ever began, maybe it was me and my inability to trust her.

51

MONICA

I BLOW hot air into my fists in an attempt to warm my hands. The stone walls of the restaurant do nothing to trap in the heat. I'd wanted to ignore going out with the group all together, but Nash had insisted I come out with them. He wanted a dinner to celebrate his new record deal, which included full ownership of his previously recorded songs.

We did it. The leadership at Coleman agreed to sign over the tracks to Nash, and in return he would stay with them under new management. His next four albums will be with them, but this time in a true partnership. One where the artist owns their songs, and the label is still able to profit off the success.

Normally I like to avoid parties, but for this one I'd made an exception. This was several years in the making, and something worth celebrating. I wanted to be here for Nash, but not necessarily everyone in attendance.

I didn't want to have to be around his brother.

I'd done my best to avoid Aiden at all costs, but he's absolutely relentless. Every single morning, like clockwork, he waits for me with one of my favorite breakfast foods. Every morning he'd tell me he loved me and ask for a chance to talk.

And every morning I shoot him down, even though it takes everything in me to do so.

I desperately want to believe him. He brought back to light every reason we shouldn't be together. Each day I remind myself it would never work, even if some days I don't entirely believe it.

Our group gathers around a large wooden table in the center of a private room. The fans here in Glasgow have been tamer out in public than the ones we're used to back home, but we still didn't want to risk dining in public. Not with the size of our party tonight.

Everyone on tour came out to help celebrate Nash and his win. All of his bandmates, his family, and other crew members fill the private dining room. We take up multiple tables to account for all of the bodies.

In the commotion of claiming seats, I'm left sitting next to Poe on one side, Tyson on the other. It must have been chaos, because for once Landon and Poe aren't connected at the hip to each other. Landon sits on the opposite side of the table, oddly enough by Lennon.

"Fancy finding you over here," I tell Poe, my eyes roaming the menu. "Typically you and Landon are a package deal."

Poe looks at me from the corner of his eye. He lets out a long sigh. "Landon seems to be doing *just* fine."

I look to where Landon whispers something in Lennon's ear. She smiles up at him, rolling her eyes at something he says.

"I'm not even going to ask," I mutter, looking away from Landon and Lennon. Whatever is going on, I don't want to know anything about it. I've got enough drama of my own, I have no desire to get involved with someone else's.

"For once, I actually like you," Poe breathes. He shoots a dirty look in the direction of his best friend. "And I need a fucking drink."

I look over my shoulder, our waiter hasn't come around to

take our drink orders yet, and I don't see them anywhere near us. "I'm going to pretend you didn't say that, and I hate to break it to you, but you may be waiting awhile."

Sitting back in his chair, he crosses his arms over his chest. "Why is it so damn cold in here?"

"I was just thinking the same thing!" I came prepared in a sweater, but all Poe wears is a thin shirt. It has sleeves, but they only come down to his forearms. Skin peeks out underneath the sleeves, showcasing an intricate ocean tattoo on his right arm.

A pair of tennis shoes come into my peripherals, signaling our waitress has arrived. Before we get a chance to order our own drinks, Nash steals her away and orders champagne for the table.

Poe and I have idle conversation while we wait for the champagne to arrive. For someone I've known for years, I know almost nothing about him. All I really know is he's one of Nash's best friends, will always call Nash out on his shit, and he's always with Landon. This is easily the longest conversation we've ever had, and I'm glad I'm finally getting to know him.

Poe is explaining to me where he grew up on the coast when the waitress returns with a tray full of champagne. Each one of us takes a champagne flute. Once everyone has a drink in hand, Nash stands at the head of the table. Even while standing, he keeps his hand on Nora's shoulder.

"I wanted to take a moment to thank every single one of you for coming out tonight to help me celebrate. Today a deal was made, one not many artists get the luxury of having." He makes eye contact with me from across the table. "I give everything I have to the songs we perform each night, and I'll never take for granted everything that was done to make sure those songs are truly *mine*."

Nash pauses briefly as he looks at everyone sitting in this room. "This tour so far has been a blast, and I'm so psyched for the rest of this leg. Thank you, all of you, for embarking on this journey with me. I'm the luckiest son of a bitch alive." Lifting a water cup in the air, he finishes by saying, "Cheers!"

All of us echo his cheers, lifting our flutes in the air and taking a drink.

Nash sits down and everyone returns to their earlier conversations.

But then, Aiden stands up.

He dramatically taps his knife against his champagne glass. "If I could have everyone's attention for just a moment."

Nash gives his brother an odd look from two seats down, but doesn't make an effort to stop him, so Aiden proceeds with whatever nonsense he's up to.

"I've had the pleasure of getting to know many of you throughout the course of the tour so far, and I'm grateful that you've welcomed Nash's baby brother into the crew with open arms."

Not like we had a choice.

"If you've got to know me as well, even in the slightest, then you know I can be a bit," he pauses, glancing at the ceiling before looking back at those seated around us, "impulsive."

A bit?

"Recently, I did something so impulsive, that it lost me someone I care deeply about."

Oh no.

No no no no.

"And I've tried multiple times to make it right, but I can't seem to get through to her. So I was hoping, with an audience tonight, that I might have *one* more chance to right my wrongs."

Is he doing what I think he's doing?

Aiden's eyes land on me. My stomach plummets. Under his stare, I want to crawl behind my chair and hide from him and all of the odd looks being thrown my way.

"Monica," Aiden begins. The entire party looks in my direction. I wish this chair would swallow me whole. There's no way in hell he's about to be this stupid.

Or maybe he is.

"Aiden," I say, my voice filled with warning. I try to fake a smile, but I know it comes off lackluster due to my fear and embarrassment.

"I've tried to apologize, but you wouldn't hear me out," he explains. "So now I'm left to embarrass myself in front of all of these people so I can finally get these words out to you."

My hands fold uncomfortably in my lap. I have too much pride to leave the conversation before it begins. Not with everyone watching.

"I've lost count of the dumb things I've done in my life. It's typical for me to speak before I act. It hasn't caused me much trouble...until you."

Everyone is silently watching us, but it's like he's the only one here. Ignoring the onlookers, my focus is solely on his apology.

"It's no secret, to you or I, or anyone at these tables for that matter, that we didn't get along at first."

All I can do is nod. He was never secretive about his feelings toward me before or after he'd joined the tour.

"From city to city, I found myself being drawn to you more and more. You had this magnetic pull that I couldn't fight. Eventually, I stopped trying to fight it at all. It seemed that the hatred between us was misplaced."

He takes a deep breath before continuing. "It was easier to pretend that I hated you when in reality, I was falling for you. Madly, deeply, without any sense of what we *could* be. I was coming to terms with the feelings I had for you when it all came crumbling down. It took what I thought was complete deception for me to realize that I love you. But I do, Monica, and I don't think I can stop."

My bottom lip begins to shake. I do everything in my power

to stifle the feelings bubbling up in my throat. I was raised not to show emotion, especially in public. I won't cry in front of all of these people.

But the way he says these words, in front of everyone, makes me *want* to believe him.

"I was so furious because even in my darkest moment, when I thought the absolute worst of you, I couldn't stop loving you."

Poe shifts next to me, but I ignore it. Aiden is looking at me like I've never been looked at by a man—like he's channeled every bit of love and suffering over the past couple months into this one moment.

"I didn't handle things right at all. I was fortunate enough that you allowed me in. And I ruined it. I should've known you'd never do what I thought you did. But know, with every fiber of my being, I trust you, Monica Masters. I trust you so much that my heart is so fucking yours. I'll make an ass out of myself every day if that's what it takes for you to know how sorry I am, for you to know how much I love you. So what do you say?" he asks with a sheepish smile. "Can you begin to forgive me so I can prove to you just how in love with you I am?"

52
AIDEN

The room is silent. All eyes are on Monica as my question lingers in the air. She stares back at me for a few agonizing moments before looking down.

Her chair loudly scrapes against the stone floor of the restaurant. Like a punch to the gut, she stands up and walks away from the table, not bothering to look back at me once.

The silence is deafening as everyone processes what just happened.

Again, she walked away from me.

This time seems more final than any other time.

Maybe this is really it.

Nash speaks up from his seat. "Aiden," he says, his voice filled with sorrow. "Are you okay?"

I ignore him. Embarrassed and hurt from the reality of losing the woman I love, I excuse myself from the table. I make my way to the door she just exited from. Squeezing through the patrons in the normal dining room, I find the door to exit the building completely.

The moment fresh air hits my face, a body flings against me. Two small hands reach for my face, angling it downwards. Monica stands below me, gazing back up at me.

"It took you long enough to get out here," she scolds.

I open my mouth to speak, but she places her finger against my lips. "It's my turn to talk. I just refuse to do it in front of all of those people."

Hope begins to build in my chest in the form of my racing heart.

"I love you too, Aiden." Her smile is wide as she looks up at me. "I don't know how it happened, but I've fallen for you and I can't pretend I don't anymore. It took a lot for you to forgive me for what I did in the past." She brushes my cheekbones with her thumbs. "It's only fair that I return the favor."

"Do you mean it?" I ask hopefully. All I want is for her to forgive me. For us to move on from the hurt we've caused in the past and look toward a future. There's no future for me that doesn't have her in it, I just need to know that she's on the same page.

"Of course I mean it," she says confidently. "Although I may *never* forgive you for making a scene in front of all of those people."

I tuck my hands into the back pockets of her jeans, bringing her hips toward me. "It did the job, didn't it?"

She shakes her head, lifting up on her tiptoes to bring her face closer to mine. I lean down, our foreheads now pressed against one another's.

"Will you say it again?" I ask.

"I love you," she whispers immediately.

"Again," I demand, pressing a kiss to her cheek.

"I love you."

"One more time."

Her head shakes against me. "I hate you," she laughs.

My hands move from her pockets to the sides of her face. "Not what I asked," I tell her.

"I love you, Aiden Pierce."

"Not as much as I love you," I tell her before gently pressing my lips to hers.

Pulling away, she looks up at me. "Aiden?" she asks.

"Yes?"

"Kiss me like you hate me."

"Always," I promise, leaning down to ravish her mouth the way I wanted to the first time I kissed her moments ago.

EPILOGUE
AIDEN
2 Years Later

"I still can't believe I agreed to this," Monica mutters from my side. She reaches up and adjusts the pearl headband atop her head, all the while staring down the couple making out a few seats away from us.

I laugh, putting my arm over her shoulder and pulling her into me. "Personally, this is the best idea I've ever had."

She gives me a look before resting her head against my chest. "The verdict is still out on that. I might still run."

"You would never," I say, softly kissing the top of her head.

It's been two years since Monica told me she loved me, so when I found out she had a business trip in Vegas, I thought it would be the perfect opportunity for us to get married. At first she'd scoffed at my idea, saying only drunks and washed-up celebrities get married in Vegas. But once we got here, I worked my charm and was able to change her mind.

Once we figured our shit out, things got serious quickly. It was easy to fall into a committed relationship with each other—especially because we were constantly together. The rest of Nash's tour went by in a blur. If we weren't working, we were spending time getting to know one another. Each day I fell more and more in love with her.

It was when we returned back to LA, when things settled down, that I knew one day I would marry her. She'd been honest on her sentiment toward marriage, that it wasn't at the forefront of her mind. It hadn't been on mine either, but as time went by, I wanted to call her my wife.

Just like I'd told her every day when we weren't together that I loved her, I began waking up each morning, making her breakfast and telling her I wanted to be her husband.

Sometimes, she'd drop by the food truck I established to grab a bite to eat and I'd remind her then—one day, I wanted to be her husband.

And now, that one day will be today.

"Are there no courthouse weddings here?" Monica asks, her eyes still trained on the couple playing an intense game of tonsil honkey next to us.

I narrow my eyes at her. "People don't come to Vegas and do a courthouse wedding."

She straightens, no longer lounging on my shoulder. "People like us don't do a Vegas wedding. Period."

I nod my head to the door. "If you really want to, we can leave."

She eyes the door for a moment before looking down at the bouquet of flowers in her lap. We'd stopped at three different florists looking for what she deemed a suitable bouquet. One florist had offered a bouquet of roses, to which Monica scoffed at. She'd told the lady she wasn't that cliche. Finally, she'd settled on a bouquet of orchids, stating they were a more sophisticated flower.

Her finger runs over one of the delicate petals. "No, I want to do this. I just never imagined an Elvis impersonator officiating my wedding."

"Well, they said their Elvis may be all booked up so I don't even know who'll be doing it."

Monica shakes her head. "You're the only person in this world who could get me to do this, Aiden Pierce."

My hand runs down the smooth skin of her thigh. The dress she'd chosen for today was short, allowing me to touch so much of her tan skin. "Have I told you I love you today?" I ask, my fingertips pressing into her skin.

She places her hands over mine. "Only a few times."

I remember waking up next to her this morning. She was already awake when I'd rolled over to face her. There weren't many mornings that I woke up before her. In the years we've been together, I've become more of an early riser because of her —and Pepper. Pep used to sleep in with me a little, but the moment Monica and I moved in together, Pepper switched to the dark side. Monica quickly became her favorite person, and surprisingly, Pepper grew on Monica. One night I got home late from the food truck to find Monica and Pepper spooning in the bed. Up until then, Monica had sworn the dog wouldn't even be allowed in the bedroom.

Now Pepper sleeps with us every night, curled up perfectly at Monica's feet. It also means that when Monica gets up in the morning to read whatever weird non-fiction book she's into that week, Pepper also wakes up and doesn't allow me to sleep without her.

I wouldn't trade it for the world.

This morning, instead of waking up to her reading a book, I woke up to her watching me. Her hands had been folded neatly underneath her cheek, her eyes hooded as she looked at me. She looked so beautiful, so at peace, the first words that had left my mouth had been, "Marry me."

Monica had rolled her eyes, reaching out to run her hand over my bare chest. It was something I loved about her, the way she'd always reach out to touch me, preferring for our bodies to always have some kind of contact. When I asked her again, she surprised me by agreeing to it.

I only asked her about a million times, as we were getting ready for the day, if she's sure about marrying me. We spent the afternoon shopping the strip, buying what would be our wedding clothes. I wore a simple black suit, it was the only one I could find that fit me properly. Monica could wear anything and look stunning, but what we chose for today took my breath away.

"Pierce wedding?" An older lady who must've drowned herself in perfume this morning asks.

Monica and I stand up at the same time.

"Right here," Monica says. She fusses with the hem of her dress, getting it to cover a few extra inches of her leg. It cuts straight across her chest, showing not a hint of cleavage, but even her naked shoulders and exposed collarbones has me just as turned on. The cream fabric balloons around her biceps before gathering at her elbow and running all the way down her arm. The dress is short, cutting high up on her thigh. She wears a headband in her hair in place of a veil.

I stare at the masterpiece of a woman that is about to be my wife as the two of us follow the elderly woman through a hot pink door. When we walk in, there's a man standing in front of a few church pews. He waits at the end of the small aisle for us. He isn't Elvis, but he still wears a suit that looks like it was stolen straight from a thrift store in the fifties.

"Marty here will be officiating your wedding. Did you get all of the paperwork filled out?" Monica nods, handing her the clipboard with the papers we filled out together.

The woman's eyes look over the paper thoroughly. If she knew anything about my future wife, she'd know that it isn't necessary for her to comb over it so carefully. Monica doesn't miss anything. We spent forever filling out the paperwork together, all while the couple in the waiting room with us dry humped one another.

Looking up, the woman finally smiles. "This is perfect.

Thank you." She begins to head toward the door she just led us through. Right before she walks through, she turns around. "Congratulations."

When she disappears, Monica and I glance at once another before turning to face the man who will officiate our wedding.

He grins. "Are you ready?"

Monica reaches out to grab my hand. Her fingers squeeze my palm tightly as she nods her head. "We are," she says confidently.

I squeeze her hand back, bringing our joined hands up to lay a kiss on her skin. "More than ready," I complete, in awe that I'm about to marry this woman.

Marty points to a small archway off to the side of the room. Vines and sheer fabric hang from the arch. "Monica, you will go into that room. When you hear the music from your song of choice, feel free to come down the aisle whenever you're ready."

"Got it," Monica whispers.

He looks between us. "Do we have any family joining us today?"

The two of us shake our heads. Monica had insisted she wouldn't invite her family even if we'd decided to have a big wedding instead of eloping. I love my new tour family and the friends we've created on our journey, but this feels right. I want to share this moment with Monica and Monica alone.

"Just us," I clarify.

His hand finds my shoulder, squeezing tightly. "Then we're ready to get this started. Monica, when you're ready…" His head nods in the direction of the room.

Monica turns to walk toward the archway, but I stop her before she can get too far away. Tugging on her arm, I pull her toward me until her body is pressed against mine. My hands find both of her cheeks. "I'm so ready to marry you, Monica Masters."

She smiles, biting her lip. "I'm ready, but you have to let me walk away first."

I shake my head at her. "As long as you'll be walking straight back to me after."

Even in heels, she has to stretch on her feet a bit to reach my lips. Her red lips, a color I insisted she wear even today, press firmly against mine. "Always."

I watch her walk away and disappear into the room, wondering how I got so lucky to call her mine. Marty leads me down the aisle, gesturing for us to stop in front of an altar.

"Ready to get married, young man?" Marty asks, sliding on a pair of glasses.

I nod. "I've never been surer of something in my entire life."

This makes him smile, a warm inviting smile that eases the small bit of nerves I still had left. "That's when you know she's the one."

I laugh at him. "If only you knew how long it took for me to realize that."

He pulls out a small book from a pocket inside his jacket. Opening it up, he makes eye contact with me. "Son, that's when you know it's worth it."

He's right. Everything that led to this moment, to us getting married in Vegas with a stranger who only half looks like Elvis, was worth it. If someone would've told me that I'd be marrying the woman I'd set out to ruin—when I first insisted that I go on tour with Nash a few years ago—I would've never believed it.

She was my enemy. I hated her fiercely. I didn't think there was a single redeeming quality about her.

All it took was time, and getting to know her, to realize that everything I thought I knew about her was wrong.

My body knew it was hers first, followed by my heart.

I'm happy with how our story played out.

It all led me to *her*.

Music fills the room. Time seems to come to a halt when Monica steps into view.

She holds the bouquet in both her hands, the flowers resting in front of her chest. Her steps are slow as she makes her way down the small aisle. The entire time, her eyes stay locked on mine. Before she stops in front of me, she mouths, *I love you.*

I'm mouthing it right back when she comes to a halt in front of me. Marty takes the flowers from her, placing them on a small table behind him.

He starts some sort of speech, but none of the words register to me. I'm too busy locked on the brown eyes of the women who will be mine forever. My former enemy turned accomplice turned lover.

I've always heard the saying *keep your friends close and your enemies closer.* I took that to heart when I fell in love with Monica Masters.

"Do you, Monica Masters, take Aiden Pierce to be your husband?" Marty's words break through my thoughts.

Monica nods, squeezing my hands tightly. "I do."

"Do you, Aiden Pierce, take Monica Masters to be your wife?"

"I guess," I joke, winking at Monica. "I do," I say after pausing.

She rolls her eyes, mouthing, "Sometimes I hate you."

I pucker my lips at her, not having the chance to respond before Marty begins to talk again.

"Then I now pronounce you husband and wife. Aiden, you may now kiss your bride."

Not needing to be told twice, I bring her face close to mine.

Right before I kiss her, Monica asks, "Kiss me like you hate me?" It's something she's been saying for years now, reminding us both where we started and how far we've come.

"Always," I promise, giving everything to the kiss. Our first kiss as husband and wife.

We probably look just like the couple from earlier as we kiss way longer than what Marty is used to. Or maybe it's *exactly* what he's used to, because when we finally break apart, he looks completely unfazed.

"I have the pleasure of now presenting you as Mr. and Mrs. Pierce," Marty declares, handing Monica back her bouquet.

I take the hand of my wife, walking us down the aisle for the first time as a married couple.

When we filled out the paperwork, I'd assumed she'd want to keep her last name. Hell, I was prepared to take *her* last name if it meant I finally got to make her my wife. Monica took the clipboard from me immediately, crossing out her last name and writing mine. When I'd asked her why, she said she had no allegiance to her family name. She wanted mine.

Walking out of the building and into the hot Vegas sun as Mr. and Mrs. Pierce, we head toward our car. We don't make it far before I push her against the brick wall, my lips finding hers instantly. I kiss my wife, my hands running all over her body.

"Aiden?" she breathes, pulling away slightly.

My eyes open, finding her lipstick smeared. "Yes?"

She reaches into the side of her dress, showing off a pocket I didn't know was even there. She fists something in her hands, moving it from her pocket and placing it inside my tux.

"There's nothing underneath this dress."

My eyes widen as I look between her legs. All I'd have to do is slide the fabric up a few inches to have her totally exposed to me. Reaching into the pocket of my tux, I find the familiar feeling of her lace underwear. It reminds me of many moons ago, when I stole her underwear just to piss her off.

"Don't tempt me to take you right here." I lean in, kissing down her neck as I let my hand travel down her hips.

"Take me back to our room, husband."

"If I can wait that long, wife."

I grab her hand, rushing her down the sidewalk in the direction of our car.

I can't get us back to the room quick enough. I practically throw her inside our rental car when we finally reach it. She giggles and I smile, knowing I'll get to hear that sound for the rest of my life.

As I speed toward the hotel room, ready to make love to my wife, I know that there is nothing I'd change about our story. It may not have been the most traditional love story, in fact sometimes it seemed impossible, but I think that's what makes it feel so special now. Monica and I didn't have love at first sight. We didn't even have *like* at first sight. But we're proof that love can find even the most unlikely couple. That with a leap of faith, sometimes the most epic of love stories can stem from a relationship that was founded on deception.

ACKNOWLEDGMENTS

Founded on Deception was only possible because I'm fortunate enough to have some of the best humans in my life cheering me on. Releasing a book is no joke, and this story was no different. I had so many people pick me up along the way when I thought it wouldn't be possible to finish Aiden and Monica's story. For them I'm forever grateful.

To my husband—my person. There will never be enough words for me to be able to thank you for your constant support. You do so many behind the scenes things and never once bat an eye doing it. This book is what it is because of you. Thank you for always supporting my dream. I love you.

To my kids. Baby girl, you've thankfully held on in the belly until this book's release. Thank you for hanging out a bit longer so I could release before you make your entrance into this world. Decker, I hope you have twenty years until you even contemplate reading this book. I love you both.

Ashlee, you're everything I didn't know I needed in a friend. Because of you, I know that soulmates can be in the form of best friends, too. We're completely opposite, yet the same in so many ways. Thank you for understanding me and loving me even when I don't respond for 7-10 business days. My chaos fits with your chaos so well. I love you and like I've said before, you're stuck with me forever.

Tori, working with you has been a dream. Thank you for knowing exactly what I want to say, even when I don't say it well. I appreciate all of the hard work you put into Monica and Aiden's story to make it what it is now. I appreciate you so much.

Stevie, thank you for dealing with me even when I drop off the face of the earth and make your job even harder. My life would be a mess without you and I'm so grateful for all of the behind the scenes things you do so I can write. Love you!

To my betas. Erica, Amanda, Heather, Brianna, I don't know what I'd do without you. You've stuck with me through multiple books now and your feedback is everything to me. Your attention to detail is unmatched and I adore reading through all of your comments that make me giggle. Thank you for always giving me your real, honest opinions and helping me make my stories better. I love you and stay with me forever, okay?

To the authors I've gotten to know along the way in my author career. I'm in awe of your talent and the fact that I get to call you friends.

To the bloggers, bookstagrammers, booktokers, and people in the community that share my books. I'm so eternally grateful for you. I've connected with so many amazing people since I started this author adventure. I'm appreciative of the fact that you take the time to talk about my stories on your platform. I notice every single one of your posts, videos, pictures, etc. It means the world to me that you share about my characters and stories.

You're the lifeblood of this community. Thank you for everything you do.

To all the ladies at Give Me Books. Thank you for supporting me through the release of Founded on Deception!

I have the privilege of having a growing group of people I can run to on Facebook for anything—Kat Singleton's Sweethearts. The members there are always there for me and I'm so fortunate to have them in my corner. I owe all of them so much gratitude for being there on the hard days and on the good days. Sweethearts, y'all are my people.

Lastly, to you—the reader. If you've made it this far, I wish I could give you the biggest hug ever. THANK YOU for taking the time to read my words. Because of you, I'm able to do this author thing full time now. I wouldn't be able to follow my dream and release books if it wasn't for your support in reading my words. There are numerous amounts of amazing, badass, breathtaking books out in the world. The fact that you chose mine from all of the options out there is incredible! I hope you continue to tune in to the many more books I have planned.

ABOUT THE AUTHOR

Kat Singleton is an author who developed a passion for reading and writing at a young age. When writing stories, she strives to write an authentically real love story for her characters. She feels no book is complete without some angst and emotional turmoil before the characters can live out their happily ever after. She lives in Kansas with her husband, her baby boy, and her two doodles. In her spare time, you can find her surviving off iced coffee and sneaking in a few pages of her current read. If you're a fan of angsty, emotional, contemporary romances then you'll love a Kat Singleton book.

ALSO BY KAT SINGLETON

THE AFTERSHOCK SERIES

Volume 1: The Consequence of Loving Me

www.books2read.com/TCOLM

Volume 2: The Road to Finding Us

www.books2read.com/TRTFU

THE MIXTAPE SERIES

Track 1: Founded on Goodbye:

www.books2read.com/fog

Track 2: Founded on Temptation:

www.books2read.com/fot

Track 4: Founded on Rejection

You Can Preorder Here:

www.books2read.com/FOR

LINKS

THE MIXTAPE SERIES

Founded on Deception Pinterest:

https://bit.ly/FODpinterest

Founded on Deception Playlist:

https://spoti.fi/3ro4F2d

CONTACT

Facebook

Facebook Reader Group

Free Download of The Waves of Wanting You

Goodreads

Instagram

TikTok

Website

If you enjoyed *Founded on Deception,* **please consider leaving a review on the platform of your choice and Goodreads.**

My major focus since the announcement I was a princess had been learning how to act like a lady. To be the best princess I could be. This confrontation counted as neither of those. Inner disappointment drilled deeper. Queen Dahliadew had been so patient with me and I didn't want extra attention from Gardenia. Especially since I was so close to being introduced to the Grand Council and getting accepted into the wand guild. But I also couldn't let this guy get away with his terrible actions.

"Go ahead and tell the princess." *Just don't tell the queen.* Of course, saying that out loud would be waving a red flag. Instead, I bent down to the brownie and snapped my fingers. A wet cloth and a fiddleleaf appeared in my hand. "Are you okay?"

The brownie glanced at me and his master. Keeping his head low, he responded, "Yes, miss."

My body warmed as I remembered talking to my good friend Tos. "One of my best friends is a brownie."

Mr. Not-Perfect-At-All choked.

I ignored him. Using the cloth, I wiped the blood off the brownie's head and pressed the fiddleleaf against the wound. "My friend's name is Tos. What's yours?"

Gardenia had believed it best that Tos and Hokima return home before the noblets arrived and the Grand Council meeting began. I missed them already.

"Tagh." He spoke so quietly I almost didn't hear.

Another sign of fear and possible abuse. I couldn't accuse anyone without proof though.

Standing, I helped Tagh to his feet and faced Mr. Not-Perfect-At-All. "While at Queens Academy I expect you to treat our servants and yours with respect."

Spluttering, he tried to stand taller than me. Which he couldn't do because he was shorter, although not by much. "Who are you to tell *me* what to do?"

I wasn't about to tell him anything. Holding a laugh back, I flicked my whip and it recoiled around my waist. "I'll be watching you."

"Then the jerk hit his brownie servant." I used my anger to slash at Stone with a broad sword. Not my weapon of choice, but one he insisted I learn to use.

Without magic.

Our human enemy owned special technology to freeze magic. Tech I'd personally experienced.

"And of course, you said something." Raising his muscular arm, Stone used his bulk to fend off my attack with ease. Half human and half giant, he didn't possess magical powers.

I huffed and glanced around the clearing in the forest outside the grounds of Queens Academy. The tall trees shot up into the sky, creating a canopy of secretiveness. The thick undergrowth discouraged hikers or passersby. The pine scent and the crisp air kept me alert.

No one could discover our secret training sessions. I'd been trying to be the best version of myself. To do all the right things a full fairy princess would do so the fairies would continue to approve of me. The only times I disobeyed was sneaking off for weapons training with Stone and communicating with Rye through the orb. Worry returned, flipping in my stomach.

"I couldn't let the jerk get away with treating the brownie poorly." With indignation boiling in my blood, I took a pass forward and lunged. Sweat poured down my back. We'd been training for over an hour without a break. I needed the exercise and the distraction the night before the Grand Council meeting.

"What if the guy had recognized you and reported you sneaking out of the castle?" Stone's long blond hair swung with his actions. His bulky form didn't slow him down. "That would give the wrong impression."

"Especially if they found out I was sneaking out to meet a hunky Captain of the Guard." Winking, I took advantage of his surprise and completed an empty fade before charging again.

He deflected my charge, knowing me too well. "If I'm so hunky, how come you picked someone else?"

My movements stiffened. I'd thought we'd tied up our relationship in a tight friendship bow. "Stone, are you okay with everything?"

He'd been acting strange since I arrived. Double-checking the clearing, setting up parameter wards, and his wooden conversation. "Tense with the noblets arriving."

Whirling his blade, he pressed the hilt against my neck and held me against a thick tree trunk. His arm pressed harder and I heaved in defeat.

An imaginary blow landed on my chest and weighed me down. "Are *we* okay?"

"A distraction technique." Stepping back, he wiped his face with his sleeve. Tonight, he wasn't wearing his majik army uniform. He was dressed in black, highlighting the bulging muscles in his forearms. "And it worked."

I tugged on my leather jacket and stared. "Are you sure?"

"Yes, I'm sure." His chiseled chin and carved cheekbones appeared harsher. "The Connected Crown Prophecy foretold you and Prince Zacharye would be together."

My heart pumped a note of sadness through my bloodstream. "If only that were true."

The prophecy stated we'd retrieve the orb together and it would unite us. Physically, we were separated by miles and a war. Especially now the communication device on his replica orb had stopped working, we couldn't even talk. His uncle was in the news vid spotlights and he hated majiks. Rye never appeared on the vids. It was as if he'd disappeared.

My stomach flopped in the other direction. "I'm worried about Rye."

Stone placed a hand on my shoulder. "I know."

"The orb's not communicating with him, Regent Theobald has taken complete control—not even pretending to pass the crown—and Rye is nowhere in public view."

Stone grabbed his cup and took a long drink of water. "At least the regent hasn't crowned himself king yet."

I slapped his arm. "Don't say that."

Worry gnawed at my gut. Something was wrong and the troubles in the kingdom kept getting worse. "Have you heard of any progress to join the majik leaders together in battle?"

"Might have." Stone's expression went blank.

His discretion rubbed against my already raw emotions. I understood he was a warrior and a covert agent. He was also one of my best friends and supported me with secret training. I wished he'd share more. "Thanks for risking getting in trouble with your superiors to secretly train me."

His gaze shifted to the grassy ground. "I won't be able to do this for much longer."

"What? Why?" This was my favorite time of the day. Or should I say night? I could be myself and say what I wanted. "Has someone discovered us?"

My question sounded like we were having a tawdry affair. With my spirits already at a low point, I didn't want anyone thinking that or for him to get in trouble.

"No one has found out." He pursed his lips together and stepped closer to me. "I'm leaving for an undercover mission."

Anxiety scraped down my spine. "Where? When?"

He shook his head. "Things I can't disclose."

"I'm the princess." I never pulled rank with him, but I needed to know where he was going and whether he'd be safe.

"Sorry, Princess." He smirked the last word, reminding me of when I'd thought it was a nickname. "Let's continue training while we can. You have a lot to learn."

"Ha." I raised my sword and charged.

He easily blocked each and every attack. His teasing and encouragement kept me going. Someday I'd be as good as him.

A branch cracked.

We both paused. My pulse hammered in my ears.

An owl hooted and crickets chirped. Wind stirred through the branches.

"What was that?" My tense muscles scrambled for release. I should run. I couldn't get caught the night before the Grand Council meeting and my wand test for entrance into the Guild of the Wand Supreme.

Stone hunched, waiting for an attack, and his gaze darted around. "Wait here."

His whispered words triggered my nerves. He edged toward the forest and stood by the trunk of a tree. It was too dark. He wouldn't see anything.

I tiptoed behind him. Flicking my fingers, I created a ball of light.

"Elle, no." He covered the light with his large hand.

Swift and pounding, feet ran. The light had alerted whoever had been watching. "Elves' bells."

Stone sprinted after them.

It sounded like one person or an animal and he could handle it. If we found them, I needed to explain why I was out here in the middle of the night. Putting out the light, I tried to follow behind. I came upon Stone, one hundred yards away from our original spot, bent over and panting.

"Who was it?" I landed next to him, bringing my wings to my side.

"I don't know, but they were fast."

"Only one?"

"Yes."

I didn't appreciate his short answers. "A deer or a brown hare?"

"Nope." He lifted his head to stare at me with incredulity. "She was blond."

Jolted, I teetered, not knowing what to think. He meant a human. A really fast human if Stone couldn't catch her. And so close to Queens Academy when we were at war against them. "She must be a spy."

Chapter Two

"The Bombardment Attack Battalion is stationed on Drage Mountain awaiting orders." Commander Gardenia, my fairy godmother and the queen's righthand advisor, sat opposite the queen in her private sitting room. Magical fighting figurines marched across maps spread on the desk.

So cool. I hadn't seen Gardenia's war strategies before. The magical figurines marched into the positions she'd assigned.

"We're sending back up by redirecting the Bregab Squadron here." She flicked a long finger and another group of figurines moved on the three-dimensional map.

Standing in the doorway, I hovered silently using my wings to keep from making a noise. Sometimes the way to find things out was to eavesdrop. The fairies were a secretive bunch. I wanted to know what was happening with the war and if they'd gotten word about human spies in the area. A blond spy in particular.

Between not talking to Rye and seeing a human in the woods last night, I was concerned.

Queen Dahliadew's sitting room was part of her large suite of royal rooms including her bedroom. Uniformed guards let me into her inner sanctum with no announcement, as they had since I'd returned with the Divinity Orb and been officially recognized as the lost princess.

"What about the new recruits?" Queen Dahliadew used her wings to rise from the highbacked chair. Her free-flowing pink dress shifted with her. She paced from the magically plunging waterfall from the castle roof to the open floor-to-ceiling window where birds and butterflies and lightning bugs flew in and out at will.

Gardenia shook her head, flinging her long white hair back and forth. "They're not ready. And we're trying to find a lieutenant leader."

"What about Stone?" The queen flicked her wrist and brought up an image of my friend.

I leaned closer. The photo must've been taken before we first met. He seemed young and less battle wary. Concern wove through my system. Had my adventures caused the change?

"He's..." Gardenia pivoted in her chair and glared, her laser-sharp hearing or sight discovering my hiding place.

My pulse raced as I held my breath. Since I'd been caught, I might as well come out strong. I flew into the room. "What about Stone?"

He'd taken risks for me in the past. Under the human palace when he'd disobeyed orders and helped me blow up the auraguillotine—a machine that sucked out majiks' powers. On our hike to Aristos Sanctuary, where he'd searched for days after I ran away with Bee the Betrayer. And now, with our covert training.

"You know more about Stone than me." Gardenia raised a suspicious brow. "Don't you?"

Guilt walloped my ribcage. Did she know about our secret rendezvous? I didn't want to get him fired or demoted.

Shrugging, I ignored the question. "I want to know about the Bregab Squadron. What happened to its last leader, Colonel Grayray?"

Gardenia shot a look at the queen. They hadn't expected me to know the colonel's name.

"What?" I stuck up my chin. "I study and I listen."

"Spy more like." Her chastising tone brushed off me.

"I'm the princess. I should be informed about important decisions." Determination hardened in my bones. I'd be ruler someday, although hopefully not soon. The queen had completely recovered from an earlier poisoning and she was strong. She'd live a long time and I planned to learn and rule beside her.

"You should be focusing on royal etiquette for the Grand Council meeting later today." Queen Dahliadew lifted her arms, and I went into them for a hug. Her natural scent of mist and citrus soothed. She might be queen, but she was my grandmother too.

"What about the wand test?" Nerves twisted in my midsection.

She laughed. "I have no doubt you'll do well there."

Her confidence eased my tension. My magical skills had improved so much from the accident-prone power I couldn't control when I'd first received my magic at sixteen. I wasn't even seventeen yet, but my capabilities had improved to the point the queen recommended me for the wand guild. If I'd lived in the fairy world my entire life, I'd have possessed my wand earlier and had much more practice.

My grandmother understood the diplomacy and etiquette training would take longer. I needed to behave perfectly for the noblets to trust me because of my human heritage.

I tugged at the uncomfortable dress with a high collar and flowy purple skirt, feeling no emotions from the material. And this was a simple princess day dress. The outfit for the Grand Council meeting was more intricate with hand-sewn sequins weighing a ton. Good thing I could sit during the meeting.

"Have you tried on the dress for the council meeting?" The queen either read my mind or saw me fussing with my current garment.

"Yes." I held in my grimace. When the queen lifted a brow in question, I didn't tell her the only outfit I felt comfortable in was the warrior outfit from my mentor. "It's a little tight."

And constricting.

Gardenia flew around me. "You're taller than the average fairy."

One of the many ways I stood out. My cheeks warmed. I couldn't change my height. I'd already changed my hair, wearing it in a tight bun every day instead of the free-flowing tresses of regular fairies. My clothes were more formal. I'd even been trained how to flit my hands similar to a fairy instead of direct pointing. And they'd tried to strike certain words from my vocabulary because they were deemed too human.

Gardenia was trying to make me look as fairy as possible to make up for my human half. Except it was part of me. And everyone in the kingdom knew my background and my heritage. She was trying to make them forget or, if I appeared more regal and more fairy, accept me.

The queen took hold of both my hands. "Ellery is beautiful as she is."

I glowed. Queen Dahliadew's opinion meant so much to me. I'd spent hours with her talking and learning. Impressing her was more important than impressing the Grand Council. Although since that was important to her it was important to me, too.

"And she's learning her fairy lessons, practicing her etiquette, and acting with the utmost integrity." She sounded proud and loving. Her green gaze softened. "She's above reproach."

Squirming, I tried to keep a pleasant smile on my face instead of displaying my guilt. The Divinity Orb was supposed to be used for predicting battle movements and attacks, not as my own personal communication line to Rye. Of course, it wasn't working so I wasn't guilty even though I tried. She and Gardenia didn't realize how often the prince and I spoke until communication broke down. And then there was the whole sneaking out at night for weapons training.

"Acting is the right word," Gardenia murmured, low enough for me to hear.

I sucked in a breath and shifted my head to beseech her with my gaze not to speak up about my indiscretions.

My best friend Arbor flew into the room. Her small smoke sprite wings fluttered back and forth as she buzzed around the space. She'd added multiple colors to the strands of her short haircut. We'd met before I knew I was the princess, and she was my best friend until I discovered the smoke sprite worked for Gardenia and had been ordered to befriend me. But we'd discussed the situation and made up. Now even though Gardenia would prefer us not hanging out all the time because it wasn't princess-like, we did. I didn't care if Arbor wasn't royal.

She landed on my shoulder in a familiar position. "She's here."

"Who's here?" Lately, strangers arrived every day at the castle.

The once regal castle had been changed into a school when majiks were no longer allowed at human schools. Now, the castle was also the headquarters for the majik efforts in the war. There were a lot of different majiks coming and going all the time. The noblets with their uppity families, servants, and assistants arrived *en mass* making the castle staff overworked and nervous. For example, Mr. Not-Perfect-At-All from last night.

"We have a surprise for you." The queen grinned with a twinkle in her eye.

I wasn't a huge fan of surprises. There'd been too many in the past year.

A troll in a hooded, long red robe stood in the doorway. Her gloopy eyes glanced around and landed on me. Her bulbous nose flared, and her large mouth lifted into the biggest smile I'd ever seen.

"Watu!" My spirits bloomed and I ran to her. "What're you doing here?"

"Elle." Her thick arms wrapped around me as we hugged. Her body stiffened, and she took a step back. Her nervous gazed darted to the others in the room. She awkwardly bowed to me. "Princess Ellery."

Horrified, I grabbed her arm and tugged her to stand. "Stop. You don't need to bow to me."

"She does." Gardenia's lower lip pouted. "Everyone does."

I wriggled my shoulders in discomfort, wanting to stick my tongue out at her. Watu had saved my life after a dragon dropped me on the side of Drage Mountain. She'd nursed me back to health and taught patience and insight. I'd gotten my wings while I stayed with her.

"Bring your friend forward." Queen Dahliadew's command was softened with a smile. "I've heard much about her from my mother."

"Grandmother, this is my mentor, Watu." Holding her thick hand in mine, I brought her forward. I really wanted the two of them to like each other. "Watu, this is my grandmother, Queen Dahliadew."

Watu bent at the waist and bowed less awkwardly than to me.

The queen nodded in greeting. "I'm so glad you were there to take care of Princess Ellery."

"Mine was the pleasure." Watu had an unusual but endearing pattern of speech.

"Watu will be one of your advisors." The queen's announcement caused my eyebrows to gather.

"Advisors?" I didn't understand the need. Plus, she was a troll and Gardenia had sent my other troll friend home before the council meeting.

"Even as queen, some things are out of my control." Queen Dahliadew's expression clouded for a moment. "Tradition, history...alliances long past." She sighed and placed a thin hand on my shoulder. "As royals, some we accept, some we fight."

The cryptic message unsettled. What was she, and—in context—I, accepting?

⫷⫸ ⫷⫸

"What do you think of the dress for your first Grand Council?"

At Arbor's question, I stared in the tall mirror in my bedroom and examined myself. Was that me underneath the glitz and glamour?

Flat heels so I wouldn't tower above the members of the council. A deep green silk dress with natural stone beading weighted my body. The skirt of the dress flourished out in wisps of netting material. The waist pinched me, and the corset top squished my breasts, making it difficult to breathe.

Or was that the regal image reflected back at me?

I didn't resemble me. Not the servant at Milford house or the waif in the dungeon rescuing my friend or the soldier fighting for her place and competing for the Divinity Orb.

My lungs expanded and I stood tall. This was the new me. The me I'd worked so hard to become. To be polished and professional. To be royal. To be fit for my place wearing the crown.

Glancing at the shiny purple, flower-shaped gemstones in the tiara on my head, I noted the skewed angle revealing it didn't fit right on the whitish blond strands of hair on my head. A sign of things to come?

A lot had happened in my sixteenth year, and who knew what would come next.

One step at a time. Impress the Grand Council and pass the wand test to join the Guild of the Wand Supreme. Throughout history, every member of the royal family belonged. It was another way to prove my right to rule.

"Do you like it, Watu?"

My mentor stood in a corner afraid to touch the nice furnishings she was surrounded by. "I like what doesn't matter."

I grinned and hoped I translated correctly. She liked me for the reality beneath the glamour.

"Remember Arch Noblet Oakton prefers to be addressed as *The* Arch Noblet." Arbor screwed up her expression. "And many of the other noblets follow his opinions, although they don't always agree with him."

Nodding, I tried to keep everything, the etiquette and various bows and titles and rules, straight. It was good to know about the personalities of the court. "So if I impress *The* Arch Noblet, everyone will approve."

Arbor tugged at a strand of my hair, loosening it from the bun. The strands softened my face. She sprinkled sparkling dust across my cheeks, giving me an ethereal glow. I wished Rye could see me dressed as a real princess.

"*The* Arch Noblet's son arrived last night." Arbor continued to tug on the dress and straighten the material on the skirt. "He might be a few years older, but his lineage is impeccable, and he has a stellar reputation."

"Worry not about others." Watu's sage wisdom calmed my nerves. "Worry about yourself."

Her wisdom and loyalty were what I needed now. "You're right." I was who I was. I couldn't change my parents, my past, or most of my appearance. "Thank you."

Arbor opened the door. "It's time."

"Strength is within and uniqueness is your strength."

Watu's words were tattooed on my soul. I knew I'd face adversity. My entire life I'd faced adversity. Here, I needed to prove I belonged.

One second, I was listening to advice as they fluffed my dress and reminded me of etiquette practices as we walked down the grand hall. And suddenly, I stood in front of the imposing double doors, ready to make my entrance alone.

My heart rattled. I tried to shake out the tingling in my fingers. I'd practiced for this. I'd proven myself by bringing back the Divinity Orb. I was ready and I possessed authority because I was the princess. I'd be working with the council on policies for the fairy kingdom and our relationships with other majik fiefdoms. The war would also be part of our discussions. I'd play an important and essential role.

If the council didn't like me, it might make my job more difficult, although not impossible. I understood the queen ruled, but she did so with guidance from the council. They crafted policies and she approved them. I wanted to help with the fairy kingdom's direction. I wanted to write policies which included other majik factions. I knew this would go against the biases of the council. If they approved of me, I'd be able to wiggle my beliefs into the discussions and win them over to my way of thinking.

A gong sounded and reverberated into my bones.

It was time.

Magically, the double doors swooshed open.

I froze in place, even as my pulse skyrocketed.

The large ballroom seemed to get larger, farther away. The glass wall and ceilings of the huge atrium had been darkened for security purposes, making the atmosphere somber. No trees or flowers showed through the glass. The green vines wrapping around the Doric columns had withered.

The empty queen's throne chair floated above the proceeding. The queen entered the meeting last, according to tradition.

The noblets sat at an oval-shaped table made from gleaming wood. The table appeared higher and the fairies sitting around it grew taller in stature. I recognized none of them. Stark aloneness hollowed my gut.

I picked out details like a man's tall orange top hat and a woman's colorful scarf made of live butterflies draped around her neck. Not one friendly expression. They sat stone-faced, unwelcoming, hostile.

I'd faced hostile crowds before. For example, under the human palace when I'd gone to rescue Arbor, there'd been the majiks who hadn't trusted me because I pretended to be human and the guards who imprisoned me. At Queens Academy when I'd first arrived, no one knew I was the lost princess and because I was half human and didn't have wings, they'd treated me poorly.

That was school antics. This atmosphere was different. It crackled with tension and a thick fog of animosity wafted toward me, sizzling with contempt.

Holding my head high, I took a step into the room. I hadn't expected applause, but the room went dead silent.

The hairs on my arms rose expecting an assault. With my past fighting experience, I knew this wasn't going to be a tea party. This was going to be a battle.

A battle of words and personality. Just as tense and just as deadly.

The man in the top hat peered down the long room. He didn't stand or bow or do anything resembling a display of respect. Instead, he volleyed the first shot, "There's the half breed now."

CHAPTER THREE

I choked and halted my progress. My legs quivered and I wrung my hands together. Not quite the introduction I'd expected.

I'd expected resistance and dislike, not pure hatred. Brushing off the attack, I remembered who I was, why I was here, and how I'd faced worse slurs.

Holding my head higher, I refused to show intimidation. I placed a neutral smile on my face and continued forward. I didn't regard anyone. My feet, wearing the stupid flat shoes so I didn't make the noblets uncomfortable, stepped up and down. The noblets obviously didn't care how they made me feel.

Heat swamped me with each step. My stomach's contents tossed and turned, and I felt seasick. Even with their blatant animosity, I forced myself forward at a slow, regal pace. In long drawn out seconds, I stood at the head of the table by the chair closest to the queen's.

The chair that was appointed to me, designed in the same purple and green colors with the royal insignia similar to the throne chair.

Except my seat was taken.

Stunned, I didn't know what to do, how to react. My chair was filled by the man wearing the silly orange top hat. The same man who'd called me half breed. His graying red hair puffed out from beneath the hat and his glowing complexion had wrinkles hiding beneath his perfect-skin glamour.

At that age, his skin would not be so smooth. He'd used magic to conceal his wrinkles and spots.

Standing tall, I waited saying nothing, doing nothing, waiting for the man in my chair and the noblets to make the appropriate gesture. Rightness fought with unworthiness in my chest. Rightness won.

I'd been taught etiquette and not only should this noblet not even be sitting in my chair, every noblet should've bowed. I wasn't going to ask them to do it or pretend I didn't know the etiquette behind the bow. This was a silent battle of wills and respect, and I planned to win.

The silence ticked on. My heart pounded against my ribcage, surely bruising the bones. Sweat formed on my upper lip and my belly roiled. This was a small thing. I didn't even enjoy people bowing at me. Except I knew if I wanted them to respect what I said, they needed to respect my person. Plus, I was literally taking my place at the ruling table. I needed to take my actual place. Not make excuses and sit somewhere else. Not request the man get up. He knew what was expected and I'd wait.

My fear evaporated and left the glowing shine of honor.

A couple of the noblets appeared uncomfortable, shifting in their seats or peering away from us. The woman wearing the butterfly scarf perused the table. The butterflies flew off from around her neck and circled her head, similar to a cartoon character. A man's multi-colored mustache twitched. One man at the end of the table transported back his chair to stand and bow, until another gripped his arm stopping him.

I waited.

Counting seconds seeming like hours in my head, I remembered the announcement at my entrance. It had been said to make me skittish and uncomfortable. All the noblets had agreed or gone along with this spectacle, possibly even practiced it to put me in my place.

I knew my place. It was next to the queen's throne chair. Next to the queen.

Pulling my shoulders back, I kept my expression serene and my gaze empty. Refusing to put up a fit, refusing to ask permission, refusing to let the meeting continue until they'd greeted me and accommodated me as proper.

My back was ramrod straight. I stared at the group. Waiting. Who would blink first?

Queen Dahliadew said I'd bring a fresh perspective into the stuffy room. I was half human and had lived in the human world most of my life, I'd befriended other types of majiks, and I'd confronted our enemy. She'd spoken of old prejudices and grudges and how I could make a difference.

I wanted to make a difference.

The man in my chair cleared his throat. His muddy brown eyes flashed with anger. With a hand flick, he moved the chair back and stood. "I was keeping the chair warm for you."

I forced myself not to nod or acknowledge. I knew I had to exhibit no weakness when dealing with the noblets. Especially this one who'd called me half breed. "Thank you."

Stepping in front of the chair, I refused to sit down. They knew what was supposed to happen next. My breathing stayed even. My heart beat at a normal pace. These noblets would not rile me again.

The man from my chair shoved the man to my right aside. He made a quick and awkward bow before taking the seat. The man he'd pushed bowed and conjured an additional chair. One by one the other noblets stood, bowed, and retook their seats.

"Thank you for such an interesting greeting." I hoped I kept the sarcasm out of my tone. Tucking my wings back, I smoothed the skirt of my dress and sat down. "You *know* who I am. I'd like to know who you are and where you're from and if you hold any special titles or roles in the Grand Council." I wanted to construct a good working relationship. I didn't want every moment to be a conflict. My gaze cast around the table, noting how the man who'd sat in my chair tilted forward eager to speak.

"Let's start at the far end of the table." A slight smile snuck onto my face. Annoying the man might be fun. He deserved it for the way he'd treated me.

The man who'd tried to bow early stood up. His suit had a narrow tail centered down the back. His natural cotton shirt had deep wrinkles. He'd been sitting for a while. "I'm Noblet Rainbowfly. I represent the Fae Forest region where fairies and elves live in harmony."

"Mostly." The noblet beside him stood and made a perfunctory bow. He was the one who'd held the first man down. "I'm Noblet Firo."

The woman with the butterfly scarf stood. "This is ridiculous. We've known each other for years and don't need an introduction. You're the *unknown* at the table."

I sat perfectly still, even though her butterflies had somehow landed in my stomach. Without changing my expression, I leaned forward, hoping to appear aggressive. "And your name?"

I indicated I was taking notes to kick butt later. I'd be lucky if I remembered any of them. All my brain cells worked toward making me look strong and competent, not presenting any of my human side, including using human words and not throwing up on the table.

"Noblet Mangowort." Her voice trembled.

Nodding graciously, I hoped, I signaled to the next fairy. And on down the line it went. I wished I could speed this up. One of my royal lessons said a princess never acted rushed or in a hurry. I wanted my grandmother to arrive and take her place on the throne chair to mediate the meeting.

Finally, we got to the troublemaking man who'd sat in my chair.

I sat up a little straighter. His name I'd remember.

Huffing, he stood and straightened his silk cravat. "I'm *The* Arch Noblet Oakton."

Ah. This was the man causing trouble and inconveniencing others.

He flashed his hand, showing a jeweled ring on every finger. "Your mother and I—"

The royal gong boomed, signaling the queen's arrival.

Every noblet stood and faced the doorway. Respect mixed with a little bit of fear shined in their expressions. My grandmother could be intimidating.

With a flick of the wrist, I magically shuffled my chair back and stood.

Queen Dahliadew floated to the center of the room. Her green silk gown flowed behind her and her crown circled her gray hair. Her regal-ness and her magical-ness changed the atmosphere. The sun streaked through the darkened windows warming the room. Colored prisms from the trees and flowers on the other side of the glass tinted the table and floor. She brought light and color into the proceedings.

Each and every noblet bowed deep. No hesitation, no disre-spect.

Sticking my chest out, I bowed as well. The thought that she was my grandmother and loved me boosted my sagging spirits.

The queen floated in front of her chair and waited for the accolades to end. With a quick wink in my direction, she sat in the throne chair.

"Thank you for attending the annual Grand Council meeting." Queen Dahliadew's voice broadcasted into the room, even though she spoke with quiet dignity. "And a special welcome to my grand-daughter, Princess Ellery."

I stood a little taller. In her way, she was telling the council they should respect me. I hoped they listened.

"Excuse me, Queen Dahliadew." *The* Arch Noblet Oakton straightened his black and brown jacket. "While we're on the subject of your...granddaughter." His nose flared with distaste. "Do you think it's appropriate she sit for the full council meeting? She's young, and inexperienced, and not a full fairy."

Or half breed, as he'd stated earlier.

I bristled while trying to appear placid, keeping my mouth shut. Why didn't he use the term half breed in front of the queen? I raised a single brow in challenge.

The queen's expression remained calm although a small tic materialized in her cheek. "She's the princess and will be ruler someday."

Murmurs came from the council.

"If anyone has something to say, speak up now." Her tone rose and the tips of her wings fluttered.

You go, Grandma.

Noblet Mangowort raised her hand. "Of course, I trust your judgement that your granddaughter is ready to be part of the council, Queen Dahliadew. But the girl looks so...human." The woman pursed her lips together, as if tasting something sour.

The sourness went down my throat and I gagged. I clamped my lips shut and glanced down at myself. I'd done my best to appear the part of full fairy princess. I wore the clothes, carried myself with comportment, studied fairy history and policy. I had my wings and my magic. What more did they want?

Annoyance built up inside me, stone by stone, blocking common sense. Jumping to my feet, I couldn't stay quiet and let the queen speak for me. I could speak for myself.

"I have wings." I fluttered my wings and lifted off the floor. "I have magic." I flicked my fingers and a flame danced in the middle of the oval table without scarring the wood. "I have fairy blood, *royal* fairy blood, running through my veins."

The queen nodded, approving of my speech.

With additional confidence, I continued, "I might've been brought up as human, but that will help us in our just cause. I'm familiar with how humans think and act. I—"

"You could be a spy, for all we know," *The* Arch Noblet Oakton interrupted. He never would've interrupted the queen or any other full royal fairy.

My skin heated and steam should've risen out of my head. I licked my lips.

The room went silent as his words rang in my brain. Tension poured from my pores. Would they ever accept me? They really didn't have a choice.

Firming my muscles, I let my determination to create change make me stronger. "I'm the princess and future ruler of the fairies."

"We'll see," he muttered, and I wasn't sure if I heard correctly. If so, the words could be construed as a threat.

I chose to ignore him. We *would* see. And I'd show them all.

Queen Dahliadew used magic to sound the gong and end the current discussion. "We are not here to discuss Princess Ellery's succession to the throne. We have more immediate and pressing matters. If we don't solve our problems and win the war, there won't be a throne to rule."

The sobering declaration had me taming my feistiness. The fairy way of life, the majik way of life was at risk. Because of Rye's evil uncle. I wished I could talk to him through the orb, find out what was really going on.

The discussions continued with the queen mostly listening. The noblets spoke of the loss of fairy life, although they didn't mention other majiks who'd died. The battles the fairies had won or lost and the reasons why, which mostly involved blaming other majiks. The best way to end the war with the fairy kingdom intact.

"My son has arrived at Queens Academy." *The* Arch Noblet Oakton sat up higher. "He's put together a fairy delegation to travel to the human palace in Lindenhamn to discuss a treaty."

"We can't make a deal with the regent and force the other majiks to agree." Queen Dahliadew leaned forward slightly—a telling sign of disagreement. "We need a delegation of representatives from every majik faction."

"The ignorant trolls will never agree." Noblet Firo pounded his fist on the table.

I sucked in a sharp breath at his comment. Watu was a royal troll and now my advisor. They'd be seeing a lot of her around the castle. I didn't care why the queen thought I needed an advisor. I was glad she was here.

"And the brownies don't understand the significance of a compromise." Noblet Mangowort chopped her hand at her scarf and the butterflies scattered again. "They're always smiling and cheerful."

Which she clearly was not.

"The elves are smart and fierce fighters." Noblet Rainbowfly rubbed his chin. "I've had talks with their leaders."

"That's one decent majik faction." *The* Arch Noblet Oakton scrunched up his face.

The noblets talked between and over themselves and the volume of the room rose. They fluttered their wings aggressively.

Lost in the crowd, I let their words spew around me. The raised, angry voices, the accusing gestures. These arguing noblets advised the queen, yet they couldn't agree.

"Quiet." Queen Dahliadew did not raise her voice. Still, everyone listened. "Noblet Oakton, I've already agreed your son may travel to the human palace as arranged to discuss a possible peace treaty."

She must've spoken privately with *The* Arch Noblet. Although she didn't call him by his full title.

The murmurs twittered with excitement. A delegation traveling to the human palace was a novelty. It hadn't happened since Regent Theobald took control of the kingdom and banished majiks from the palace. Rye's palace. My heart bumped. I'd talk to the queen privately about joining the delegation. I could search for the prince.

"I'm also working with other leaders to put a contingent together of representatives from each majik faction to work together for our future. They must agree to the peace treaty with the humans."

At the queen's statement, *The* Arch Noblet Oakton furrowed his brow and frowned.

Could this be Stone's covert assignment? Even though he'd worked for the fairy commander for years, could he represent the giants? Gardenia and the queen trusted him implicitly.

"A two-pronged approach will work best." The queen considered the angles. "Your son will work with the humans to reach a peaceful agreement. The contingent of majik representatives, once assembled, will approve the deal."

The Arch Noblet Oakton's frown deepened. His gaze slitted and he glared in my direction. He believed this development was my fault.

"The other majik factions should not have equal say," the woman at the end huffed, "because they don't have equal worth."

My eyes widened and I stared down the table at her. I opened my mouth to object.

The queen must've sensed my intent because she shot me a scowl. "That is not part of this discussion."

Did she allow everyone to vent and then do what she wanted? The action seemed a waste of time.

She nodded at *The* Arch Noblet Oakton. "Why don't you bring your son into the meeting so he can explain his plans."

With a flick of his fingers, he sent a smoke message. Seconds later, the doors to the ballroom swished open and in sauntered Mr. Not-Perfect-At-All.

Why didn't their relationship surprise me?

Aversion stuck in my throat.

The son sauntered forward at a dignified pace, a royal pace, as if he deserved to be in the room with the rulers. His entrance provided more pomp and circumstance than my own arrival. The noblets were riveted by his confident strut and his perfect, white-toothed smile. He wasn't wearing a snarl like he had last night.

He bowed to the queen and peeked at me. His gaze flickered over my face again and both his red brows rose in sharp arches.

I couldn't stop the smirk from forming on my lips. He recognized me from last night.

The Arch Noblet Oakton waved his hand in introduction. "My son, Bracken Oakton, I'd like you to meet Princess Ellery."

The corners of my lips twitched higher as I remembered his statement about telling the princess about my antics.

Taking his time, Bracken bowed deeply. Was he demonstrating respect or trying to figure out what to say?

His father glanced at the queen and smiled too brightly. "Princess Ellery, I'd like you to meet your fiancé."

Chapter Four

The introduction ping-ponged from one ear to the other and then rolled around in my head. My eyes popped and my jaw dropped to the floor. "Excuse me?"

I wanted to say more, but I could only form two words.

"Bracken is your fiancé." *The* Arch Noblet Oakton repeated the lie.

My numb lips prickled as the information went from rolling around my head to becoming a gigantic rock smashing into pieces of anger spewing out. "Impossible. I just met this man. Like a second ago."

Except for last night. I bit down on my prickling lips and peered at the queen. Her expression didn't change, neither confirming nor denying the statement.

My breath came out in panicked pants. "I'm too young to get married."

Especially to this man, Mr. Not-Perfect-At-All.

My heart jangled and emotions clattered in my veins. *I love Rye.* I kept this last point to myself. "This is ludicrous."

"Don't speak back to me with that tone." *The* Arch Noblet Oakton whipped off his orange hat and his grayish-red hair stood up in tufts. "The two of you are engaged."

Fairies couldn't lie. The stark truth slapped me.

"Grandm—Queen Dahliadew," I gritted my teeth, forcing panic back. I had to be calm and reasonable. "Tell him he's crazy. There's no possible way—"

"The details have not been finalized and the engagement was not to be announced." Her quiet tone didn't show her displeasure, yet I could see it in the flash of her green eyes.

A shattered breath escaped my lungs. Not a denial exactly. A confirmation there'd at least been discussions. "This is stupid. I didn't agree to anything. I don't love—" To make my point, I pivoted to my supposed fiancé. "Excuse me, what's your name?"

He titled his pointy nose in a snooty way. "Bracken Oakton." He spoke loudly, boastfully, believing I should've remembered the first time.

Maybe I should have. I could've kicked him out of the castle last night.

Noblet Mangowort waved her butterfly scarf in front of her face. Her gaze had gone soft and her lips pursed, as if awaiting a kiss. A couple of the other noblets nodded and smiled in an approving manner.

"Love?" His father sliced the word, suggesting it was an imaginary term. "A human notion. Fairies, especially royal fairies, don't marry for love."

I might've stopped using human terminology, like the word doctor, but they'd never take the notion of love away from me. Love mattered, whether I could be with Rye or not. All kinds of love. The love for my dead parents, for my grandmother, for Arbor and Watu, and my other friends.

"That's sad for the fairies." Crossing my arms, I wondered how they'd lived and loved and formed partnerships. The man had a son. Surely, he loved the woman who'd born him. I glanced at the queen, hoping she'd back me up. She must've loved her partner because she'd had three daughters with him and spoke of their time together in an adoring way. "I will only marry for love. And when I'm ready."

"Negotiations are ongoing." Queen Dahliadew stared straight ahead, refusing to look at me. "An old contract wasn't fulfilled on our side."

Hurt dripped through my bloodstream. We'd spent hours together every day. She'd never mentioned anything about an unfulfilled contract or an engagement.

"Your mother was supposed to marry me." Controlled rage spit from *The* Arch Noblet Oakton's mouth. His fatty cheeks turned red and his gaze narrowed as if I was the target. He didn't act heartbroken. He acted similar to a kid who'd had some toy taken away from him. Or was it the power my mom, a princess, possessed?

My poor mother. No wonder she'd wanted to escape the castle and marrying this man. And then she'd met my father and fallen in love. Real love.

My dad had told me the stories. How they'd met in a forest near his home, how my mom had been bathing in a river and he'd stumbled upon her. He hadn't noticed her nudity or her wings. He'd noticed her bright green eyes. She'd covered herself and they'd talked, and he'd discovered her intelligence and warmth.

Tenderness softened my spirits. Love at first sight. How I'd felt with Rye.

My mother had been the third princess with no expectation of becoming the ruler. While I, on the other hand, would rule the fairies someday. Mr. Not-Perfect-At-All didn't want to marry me. He wanted to marry into the ruling family.

Bracken Oakton was taller than his father, but not taller than me. His fancy clothes fit his slim form nicely. His thick, red hair complemented his gleaming white skin. He was handsome for a fairy, possibly too handsome. His manners today had been impeccable. While last night, he'd been atrocious.

Who was the real man?

After my years of servitude, I knew.

My chest tightened, straining my ribs. He'd seen me on my late-night rendezvous. The information would not go over well with the queen or the Grand Council. If they found out about my misbehavior, of actions unbecoming a perfect princess, they wouldn't trust me at the table. Bracken knew my secret. I knew his secret as well. How he treated the castle servants and other majiks. Although the information might not be held against him. The council treated him as if he was Mother Earth's son, while they treated me like a pariah.

"Princess Lily eschewing her responsibilities should not be placed on the shoulders of her daughter." Queen Dahliadew's rigid tone revealed where the negotiations stood on her end.

"A contract is a contract," Bracken's father blustered. "The terms must be satisfied."

Shock pelted my mind and bruised my pride. "What if I was a boy?"

Indignant, I wanted to fight my own battles. Except maybe not in a public setting.

"You wouldn't be in line as a future ruler."

"Aha!" That was what was important to him.

Fairy royalty was passed through the females. Very rarely did a male rule, and every time it had happened the fairies suffered in some way. Whether it be fire or drought, or humans kicking them out of their homes. Pain shot through me. Before they'd known I existed, my male cousin Perry had been next in line for the throne. He'd been killed at Aristos Sanctuary.

"Excuse me, Queen Dahliadew, Father." Bracken made a big show of bowing to my grandmother, trying to impress her no doubt. "May I take Princess Ellery for a stroll? I believe it would be good for the two of us to talk."

My body tensed. This must've been as much of a shock to him. We could sensibly talk and let the council, including his father and my grandmother, know neither one of us was interested.

His father's face scrunched up about to deny the request.

I jumped from my seat. "I'd love to."

The queen's eyebrows rose and *The* Arch Noblet Oakton smirked with satisfaction. Did the man think I'd succumb to his son's charms?

Bracken put his arm out, suggesting I was a helpless waif. I'd learn to fight the important battles, so I slipped my arm through his. There were no tingles at his touch. No sparks of attraction. No nothing.

Strolling out of the room, pleased nods followed us. The noblets approved of us being together. The guards at the door bowed deeper to him and opened the door.

As soon as the door shut, I slipped my arm from his. "Bracken, I—"

"Wait. Please."

Had the please been added as an afterthought? He seemed like a guy used to demanding.

I smashed my lips together as we walked through the corridor with colorful stone and flowers sprouting from the walls. I was the princess. He shouldn't be telling me when to talk. "I think we need to talk about this ridicul—"

"Here we are." He pushed aside a heavy velvet curtain and indicated I should step inside. "One of my favorite places when I was younger."

The circular room reached high into the sky with a round stained-glass window colored with objects of nature. It must be situated in one of the lower globed turrets. Curvy stone benches lined the room with mosaic glass decorations creating flowers and trees and the sky and clouds above. The benches were covered in cushy moss and the intimate atmosphere suggested hours of relaxing reading or artists creating sonnets and poems.

I twirled around in the center, surprised Bracken enjoyed a room with this atmosphere. I hadn't known this room existed. It was hidden away and would be great for spying on the council if I wasn't invited back. "You're familiar with the palace?"

"Yes." He smiled, displaying perfect white teeth. It wasn't similar to Rye's mischievous grin, but I could appreciate Bracken's male beauty and luring qualities. "I spent many months here as a child."

"Why?" I took a seat on a bench and ran my palm over the springy moss.

"You know, royal connections." Waving his hand, he laughed self-consciously, which made me like him a little. He wasn't as bad as his father. "You didn't know your mother was supposed to marry my father?"

"No." Sadness wove through my veins. Being in my mom's childhood home brought back more memories of her. She'd probably loved this room. "She died when I was a toddler and didn't talk much about her life before my dad."

"When your mother...left fairy society, my father married my mother and they had me. When my mother died—"

"I'm sorry." Immediate sympathy pinged inside. We'd both lost our mothers.

"Father brought me to the palace because Princess Daria had recently lost her husband."

I slumped back on the bench. Were princesses so interchangeable? I swallowed. Possibly still were. "Were they supposed to marry?"

"Yes."

His father had said marriage wasn't about love and his actions proved it. Going from being engaged to my mother, to marrying someone else, to then planning marriage with my mother's sister. I shivered. "What happened?"

"You don't know your own family's history?" A tinge of something in his voice made me feel uncomfortable or less somehow.

"I'm learning." I was learning fairies were secretive, and my family in particular kept things hidden. I wanted to discover their secrets. Well, except for this engagement contract one. That secret could stay buried.

"Princess Daria died before my father had the chance to marry her." Bracken sat down on the same bench about a foot away. He must realize I wasn't ready to be cozy with him. I never would be.

"The reason why the marriage contract terms haven't been met." And now those terms somehow applied to me.

"Yes." He swallowed the tough pill well. Taking hold of my hand, he rubbed a smooth finger on my skin. He must never have done manual labor in his life. "I want to apologize for what you witnessed last night."

Distress slithered across my skin. I didn't want to be rude so I didn't yank my hand away. I was a princess and I needed to act like one. I placed a stiff smile on my face.

Sighing, he rubbed my skin harder. "I was tired from traveling and we'd run into trouble on the road."

The war, the spy, and the trouble at the pub jumped into my head. "Nothing serious?"

"Nothing I couldn't handle." His indulgent smile made me believe he felt I was too delicate to hear the gory details. Little did he know the battles I'd fought. "This isn't an excuse. I've been handling delicate negotiations with the humans and it's been stressful."

Sounded like an excuse to me.

He hung his head, expecting me to feel sorry for him. It didn't work. "I'll be traveling to Lindenhamn shortly and everything needs to be in place before I leave."

I sat up straight and slipped my hand from his. "You'll be going to Prince Zacharye's palace?"

"Regent Theobald's. He seems to be the one in charge." Bracken's hard-to-believe-it tone had me warming toward him. Maybe I'd found an ally against the regent. "Anyway, I gave the brownie a few days off."

My gaze narrowed. "You mean, Tagh?"

"Yes, Tagh. And a bonus." Looking at me, Bracken must've realized I wasn't impressed with his supposed generosity. "I'm embarrassed by my behavior and I hope you won't mention the incident to anyone."

He sounded sincere. Maybe his treatment was a one-time thing because of travel and stress as he'd suggested.

And there was my little indiscretion to discuss. "I won't say anything about it, if you don't say anything about seeing me."

His red brows gathered together, as if he was plotting. "Agreed." He spoke slowly.

I blew out air. Things were settled about that night. Now, we had to discuss how to get out of this preposterous engagement.

He picked up my hand and kissed the back of it. His cold lips caused a shudder that I tried to control. I wasn't used to courtly gestures without meaning. Rye always made me feel something when he kissed my hand or my lips. This was probably similar to the old-fashioned handshake in the human world.

"Where were you sneaking off to?" The way the question slid into the conversation had me stiffening. His hand held mine a little tighter.

"Nowhere." My cheeks heated. He might've promised to keep one secret, but if the council found out I was continuing my weapons training they wouldn't be happy.

His lips tilted into a smarmy smirk. "Is that why you were so upset about news of our engagement? You were sneaking off to be with another man."

"No." Horror washed through me. Stone was only a friend. And since he was going off on a spying mission, did the secret meetings even need to be confessed to? And certainly not to Bracken, a complete stranger. "Nothing like that."

"Good. Then I have no reason to be jealous."

"What do you mean jealous?" Confusion threaded through my mind. "We left the room to discuss getting out of this absurd engagement."

He gripped my hand tighter, hard enough to hurt. "There's nothing absurd about our engagement. I can't wait for our wedding."

CHAPTER FIVE

I yanked my hand out of his and took a step toward the door. "You've got to be kidding. We don't even know each other."

"You're a princess and I'm of noble birth. There's a contract." He didn't care about love. To him, this was a business transaction.

Disgust had me curling my lip. "I didn't sign anything." Shoving the velvet curtain aside, I stormed out into the hallway.

He rushed toward me and grabbed my arm, yanking me in close. His wet dirt scent was suffocating. "Contracts are similar to a binding promise. Do you know what a binding promise is?"

My stomach dropped. I sure did. I'd made my own binding promise to assassinate Prince Zacharye when I'd been naïve. I wouldn't make the same mistake twice. Good thing the Dagger of Justice had deemed Rye unworthy of being killed.

"Glad to see the two of you getting along." Gardenia sounded pleased as she tucked her wings in and walked toward us in the corridor.

Getting along? My brows arched. What was she talking about? Bracken and I had argued and when I'd tried to leave, he'd yanked me to his side. Except that wasn't what she saw. She saw him holding me close with his arm circling my waist, mimicking cuddling. His position and expression had changed from anger to adoration.

Gross.

"No." I pulled away and shivered, trying to get the feel of his touch off me. "This is not what it looks like."

He turned my rejection into a smooth move of his own, picking up Gardenia's hand and kissing it. "Commander Gardenia."

She actually blushed and a giggle erupted out of her mouth. "Looks fine to me."

Why does everyone fall for his practiced charm? The women on the council, Gardenia. Sure, he was handsome and polite and possibly smart if he'd negotiated a visit with the regent. He wasn't the guy for me. He treated his servants horribly and I loved someone else.

I grabbed Gardenia's arm. "Can I talk to you? In private." I spoke through gritted teeth.

"Of course, Princess Ellery." She wasn't normally so formal with me. Was she putting on a show for him? Trying to make me appear more important? "If you'll excuse us, Bracken?"

Bracken? Gardenia knew him that well?

"Of course, I have to return to the Grand Council meeting." The urgency in his tone increased, as if he were desperately missed from the meeting while I was not.

Which was probably true. My lungs deflated and a sense of unease settled over me. I'd never be appreciated for who I truly was. Which was too bad. I appreciated me. So did Rye and Stone and Arbor and Watu.

He bowed. "Princess Ellery, I look forward to getting to know you." He pivoted on his heel and sauntered down the hallway knowing we both watched.

Gardenia sighed. "You have such a nice young man."

"He's not my young man." Fisting my hands, I let the slow burn of my anger vent. "You knew about this...this...preposterous engagement?"

"Most in the court did, dear." Her condescension rubbed against my outrage.

"Why didn't you tell me?" Lost, I blinked back the telling prickling sensation in my eyes. I felt stupid, vulnerable, and hurt.

Huffing, she pulled me behind the velvet curtain. "Oh, Bracken's favorite room as a child. He pretended to read. I knew he spied on the council."

It was becoming my least favorite room. She knew more about him than me. "You're *my* fairy godmother. You should be on my side."

"He's perfect for you." She sounded dreamy, *actually* dreamy.

Everything inside hardened. My lips firmed and my nose flared. "Prince Zacharye is the guy for me."

"He's human." Her flat tone spoke volumes. She didn't believe he was appropriate for a fairy princess.

Too bad. "I'm half human."

"You're a fairy princess." She flicked a long pointy finger at me. "And Bracken is the perfect complement to your, shall we say, liability. He knows how to act. He knows our history. He knows about fairy royals and the court."

In other words, he would've been a better future leader of the fairies than I.

My muscles slackened and pain sawed my midsection. I thought she believed in me. It's why I'd been working so hard to be the perfect princess. I knew I could do the job when it was time. "You and Grandmother don't have confidence in me to lead?"

"We have confidence you'll make the right decisions when you learn everything." Gardenia placed a conciliatory hand on my arm. "Bracken will be by your side and teach you. He's respected in royal circles and by the Grand Council. He's a perfect partner for you."

Perfect.

How I hated the word. I wanted to be the perfect princess. For Queen Dahliadew and the fairies. Did that mean marrying someone with an impeccable pedigree?

Did that mean giving up my independence? Giving up my love?

"Can you believe it?" Back in my room, I recounted everything to Arbor.

My best friend would take my side. She'd been with me from the beginning. She'd gone against Gardenia's wishes to stay my friend. And I'd rescued Arbor from the dungeon.

Ensconced on my pillow, she beamed in an insipid way. "He is handsome and has powerful magic. His family is noble."

Her betrayal sliced deep and agitated me into action. Pacing the luxurious room, I went from the four-poster bed carved from trees, passed the door to the large bathroom, to the sitting area and returned to the bed. I squeezed the post with the twinkling lights letting the bulb poke my skin.

"He's pompous and arrogant and treats..." I'd promised not to mention his treatment of Tagh. "Never mind."

Sitting up, she twitched her wings, exhibiting discomfort. The small guard uniform she wore had been modified with interesting cuts and color. "Because your father was human, you don't fully understand male fairies. In the fairy realm, females rule which sometimes causes males to act smug and in control, as if they're more important than they are. Once you get to know him—"

"Well, Bracken is not in control of me." I stomped toward the bed and picked up a pillow, smashing it against my chest. I'd asked Arbor to meet me in my room so I could gain her perspective, not get another lecture. I needed to calm down before the big wand test.

Another step to show the fairies I was a leader. I shook my hands at my sides. Wasn't bringing home the Divinity Orb good enough?

"Bracken Oakton is the most eligible bachelor in the fairy world." She waved her hands in front of her face. Was every fairy in love with him?

I threw the pillow onto the bed. "I'm not going to marry some stranger."

She flew to my shoulder and landed. "Make it a long engagement."

"Life-long," I muttered, not caring if she heard. I'd never marry him. Her belief I should wed rankled.

"The two of you can take your time and get to know each other." She fluttered off and buzzed in front of my face. "After the delegation trip to the human palace, he'll be living at Queens Academy permanently."

I hated the idea. Always having him underfoot, restricting my movements even further. Of course, Stone wouldn't be around to secretly train me because he'd be gone. I hoped he'd assign one of his soldiers to continue working with me. And the Divinity Orb wasn't communicating with Rye any longer, so I didn't have to hide the activity. I'd have nothing fun to distract.

"You'll have time to get to know him better when he returns." Arbor flew toward the window and peered out in the courtyard. She swung around to face me. "Promise me you'll give Bracken consideration."

"Hmmm." My mind tickled with an idea and sent my thoughts whirring with possibilities. If I used the excuse of getting to know Bracken, I could suggest joining the delegation and find out what happened to Rye.

A knock on the door stopped my thoughts.

Watu entered wearing a more formal outfit than before. Shimmers threaded through her tunic with seamed hems and large pockets. "It's time for your wand test with the Guild of the Wand Supreme."

My earlier thoughts and schemes tumbled into a tangled bunch of nerves and dropped into my gut. What I should've been thinking about, and practicing for, was the wand test. Not Bracken.

Already, he was ruining my life.

I scudded out of the room with Arbor and Watu beside me, flanking me. The corridors blurred as we traveled by. Marble columns wrapped with green vines, trees reaching the cathedral ceiling, colorful mosaics and stained glass. It was like a kaleidoscope of hues. What was normally comforting and uplifting made me sick. The moving effect combined with my nerves contorted and curled in my stomach. I needed to relax and focus.

Opening an arched door, I stepped into a room I'd never seen before. Big surprise. The castle was large, and I'd never taken the time to wander. I'd always been too busy and hurrying from one place to the next.

The room had rows of tightly packed chairs. The chairs were full of fairies tittering with excitement. A small stage sat front and center and at the back of the stage sat a grouping of larger chairs behind a black wood table with intricate designs carved into the legs. Queen Dahliadew, wearing a more spiritual dress of flowing robes and wide bell sleeves, sat in the middle chair. Commander Gardenia sat to her right, wearing a similar outfit with less ornamentation. A third woman, someone I didn't recognize, sat to Gardenia's right. The last chair was taken by Noblet Mangowort.

I held back a shudder.

The three of us approached the stage. Bracken, who was sitting in the front row by his father, stood and took my hand helping me onto the stage as if I was a delicate flower. I wasn't. I could probably take him down in a fight with my secret training.

Watu and Arbor took seats on the other side of him.

A fairy who sat behind Watu shifted his chair further back. Murmurs from the crowd grew louder. I picked out a few words from the general din. *Stupid troll* hit me the hardest.

If I could hear, she could too.

Watu didn't flinch. Her expression stayed blank and focused on the stage. Yet, I could sense her embarrassment. Not for herself. For the rude fairies.

I opened my mouth to speak.

"Noblets and guests." Bracken wheeled toward the audience. I couldn't see his face, but his father smirked beside him. "Watu is a distinguished guest. She is a Priestess of Aristos Sanctuary, noble by birth, and the savior of my fiancée's life."

My dislike of him softened. He might've been mean to Tagh due to stress, but maybe he didn't always treat other majiks as lesser.

Twisting around and taking his seat, he gave me a slight smile. I mouthed the words *thank you*.

Commander Gardenia floated upwards to get everyone's attention. "Let me remind everyone, you are observers to this process. Queen Dahliadew, myself, Posy Purplecloud, and Noblet Mangowort are the scoring judges."

The noblet had already judged me in the Grand Council meeting. Tilting my chin up, I knew I could handle this test. I'd practiced and practiced and practiced. I could do the compulsory figures in my sleep.

"Let us begin." Gardenia indicated a spot on the stage where I should stand and handed me a wand.

An immediate sense of loss engulfed me. This wasn't any wand. It had been my mother's and if I passed the test, it would become mine. It glimmered at my touch, recognizing where the wand belonged. Varying colors swirled around the wand and ended in a tiny orb at the top shaped into a heart. I'd found the wand in my mother's old trunk. I'd played with it as a child and had hid it from my greedy stepmother.

"Start with number one and go through each compulsory figure." Gardenia retook her seat.

The wand slipped lower in my sweaty hands. I pinched it tighter, knowing I couldn't drop the wand or lose control. Taking a deep breath, I ignored the audience to my left and didn't stare at the judges to my right.

I started with a simple circle. There was a series of ten figures and each one needed to be performed with precision in order to receive the highest score. In this section, there were no opinions on the scores, which would work to my favor. I had to make the figures perfect.

My fingers stumbled. There was that word again.

The crowd's murmurs picked up. I could catch an odd word here and there but couldn't tell who spoke.

Focus on your task, Elle. This was only the first part of the test.

"...father was human, and she lived with *them* until recently..." The phrase caught my attention.

The man was talking about me. I tried to ignore the gossip and performed the three-turn which included a change in direction of the wand.

"She was a servant in a human home." *The* Arch Noblet Oakton was informing others about my past.

Baffled, I pressed on with the pattern. The man didn't need to confirm rumors about my upbringing. He'd been told about my past and my indiscretions because of his position.

"A servant!" a voice trilled and broke my concentration.

Stalling, I licked my lips and continued to the next figure. Hopefully, none of the judges noticed my distraction. Twisting my wrist, I performed the counter turn which included an intricate flourish in the middle.

"The smoke sprite is her best friend." A woman pointed at Arbor. "As a princess, she could do better than a smoke sprite."

How could Arbor not hear the insult? She was closer than me. My lungs contracted and I wanted to jump off the stage and defend my friend. In the past, that hadn't always been the case. Arbor had stood by me through everything. If I reacted or attacked, I'd be the one judged lacking in manners. I had to keep control of my emotions.

"I heard the princess went beneath the human palace to the dungeons to rescue the thing." A woman sitting by the first one visibly shivered.

I bet those two women weren't true friends. They probably talked about each other behind their backs.

"And she made friends with other majiks." The obvious distaste in a man's voice carried even higher.

How much more verbal abuse could I take? Anger blazed through me. They were talking loudly. They must have known I could hear. Were they trying to make me fail? Possibly. I tried not to listen and concentrated on my rocker turn, a movement where the compulsory figure started and ended on opposite sides.

"I saw her with a brownie and a troll a few days ago." The first woman lowered her voice, but it still carried far. "She took them with her to Aristos Sanctuary."

With Commander Gardenia's approval. Why didn't she say something about the audience's rudeness? My already tight muscles contracted further. This must be part of the test.

"And they got Perry Moss killed."

My eyes burned. *I* got Perry killed. He was defending me from Bee, my betrayer. I thought Bee was my full fairy friend. Really, she was half human and hated fairies, hated me. She'd tried to steal the Divinity Orb and disappeared. She hadn't been found.

"Was the troll one of them?" With disgust dripping from his tone, a man pointed at Watu with his wand.

How rude. Pointing with your wand was considered impolite and a threat.

They thought Watu was dirty and uncouth, except she wasn't rude and she wouldn't betray me or say mean things behind my back. She'd taught me life skills and helped me get the Divinity Orb through her teachings. Anger seared my entire body, causing my fingers to shake and sweat. I executed the bracket figure with a wand flip in the middle, even though I wanted to flip my middle finger.

"That troll recently arrived," *The* Arch Noblet Oakton pivoted in his chair and informed the gossipers. "Can you believe Queen Dahliadew allows it? First a half breed princess and now a troll as a marriage advisor."

My temper spiked and traveled from my fingers, up my arm, and to my heart. These fairies were terrible to me and to poor Watu. Oakton was trying to start an uprising against Grandmother because of me.

"Your poor, handsome son." A woman placed a hand on Bracken's arm. "If something happens to the princess, my full fairy daughter is eligible."

The daughter could have him. Nausea rose in my throat. Swallowing, I tried to steady my hand as I performed a figure eight.

What they said wasn't important. This test was important. I was the princess, and they could never change that fact.

"She did bring home the Divinity Orb with their help," Noblet Rainbowfly said defensively.

Finally, someone I liked on the council.

"Can you believe our half breed princess spent time in the troll's cave?" The voice was the same woman who'd offered her daughter. "Imagine the debauchery. She was probably despoiled."

My ears prickled. I'd kissed two people in my life, Rye and Stone, and neither of them had taken advantage of me.

Between the prejudice and the hate, the insults meant to injure and distract, and the lack of concern for me and my friends, I could no longer contain the explosion building inside.

Fuming, I swung my wand to point at the last commentator. "You rude cow!"

Chapter Six

"Watu has more knowledge and class in her clawed finger than you have in your entire pea brain. She's smart, compassionate, and patient enough to teach me. Not only did she save my life, she saved my future." I took a breath to emphasize my point. "She saved the fairies' future."

My final word echoed and hung on complete silence.

No one moved or spoke. Not even a twitch. Everyone had been shocked and struck dumb.

My entire body tensed. I'd gone too far. Said too much of what I believed. The perfect princess act was finished.

The uproar exploded into flurry and sound. Everyone talked and yelled at once. Certain shouts caught my ear.

"She speaks like a human."

I cringed.

"She shouldn't talk to her betters in that way."

I gasped, horrified. The prejudice against me was real.

"How will we ever contain her?"

Contain me? In what way? I was practically a prisoner in the castle. I was wearing clothes I didn't want and learning etiquette I didn't care about. I winced and my whiny thoughts stopped. The betrayer Bee had accused me of whining.

"How dare you!" *The* Arch Noblet Oakton's voice raised above the others. He flew onto the stage and grabbed the front of my dress in his pudgy hand. "You half breed, you're not fit to be a royal princess. How dare you treat a troll with more respect than the noblets."

My eyes widened, taking in the large mole on his nose. I was that close to his face. Alarm bells rang in my head. He raised his other hand, ready to smack me. Fear scorched through my bloodstream. Not even my evil stepmother had hurt me physically.

"Oakton." Gardenia flew in front of us, trying to get between. "Let Princess Ellery go or I'll change you into a toad."

With her command, my alarm waned.

Two guards charged into position behind her. They were there to back her up. Would they back me up? Even though I was the princess, I had no authority.

My tension slackened and my body drooped. I'd proved myself loyal and worthy. What more did they want from me? Just because I didn't agree with their hateful opinions didn't make me less.

Seconds slowed. Oakton's nose crinkled and his gaze narrowed into slits. He wanted to harm me. I tensed back up again. I refused to accept physical abuse. I'd give him ten seconds to release me before making a move. I'd left my whip and dagger behind because I'd been told they weren't appropriate accessories for a princess. I could take the wand I held and use it against him magically.

Or I could shove it up his large nose. That would break his grip.

My dangling arm twitched, and I tightened my grip around the wand.

"Father." Bracken stepped beside the tense group. He placed a hand on his father's shoulder. "Now is not the time. Let Princess Ellery go."

My fingers relaxed around the wand, but not too much. When would the time be for his father to attack? A question I'd need to ponder at a less intense moment.

Oakton grunted and let go of me. He brushed off his clothes, suggesting I'd contaminated him.

I stumbled back and my tension let up. Why did he want his son to marry me if he hated me? If he believed I was a half breed? I was the heir, of course. My gaze narrowed. If we were married,

Oakton would try to take control from me, similar to what Regent Theobald had done to Rye.

"The show has ended." Gardenia ordered her guards to escort both Oaktons off the stage. She used her magic to open the doors to the room. "The entire show is over. Everyone out."

Guards ushered fairies toward the exit. They protested.

"Does she think she's special and deserves privacy for the test?" a man complained.

My jaw dropped. I was being treated differently, not special.

From my understanding, these tests were open to viewers. Usually no one came. The fact I had a packed audience said something. They wanted to see me fail.

Watu slipped around a guard. "Appreciation. Stand up for a troll many wouldn't. A fine leader you will make."

My heart softened. This troll, this woman, was the mother of my soul.

"I agree." Queen Dahliadew rose from her chair, flew over, and hugged Watu and me. "You stand up for what you believe in and you won't let the noblets crush your spirit."

"Thanks?" Where had she been during the chaos?

"I hope you understand, as queen, I won't always be able to speak up with you or for you." She winked in Gardenia's direction. "But I have my ways. Many different ways."

Nodding, I stared at the ground. Queen Dahliadew couldn't show favoritism because she was my grandmother. I'd have to fight my own battles. And that was okay. As long as she trusted me to lead.

"I'm sorry, Watu, you'll need to leave the room." Gardenia's respectful tone demonstrated her understanding of Watu's status.

"Your training you will remember." She bowed to me. "Confidence in your head and in your heart."

I soaked in her words of wisdom as I watched her leave. The empty room echoed. Only the judges were left.

"Shall we begin?" Noblet Mangowort wrinkled her nose. The current scarf was made from wasps. A more fitting accessory for her stinging comments. "The disruption took enough of our time."

Still unsteady with slight trembling in my arms and legs, I would now have to face the harder part of the test.

"We shall give Princess Ellery a minute to collect herself." Queen Dahliadew flew back to her chair and sat down.

Blowing out slowly, I closed my eyes and tried to soothe my nerves like Watu had taught.

"There's no time to collect yourself during a magical battle." Posy Purplecloud had been silent through the commotion.

My eyes popped open. I thought the fairy was on my side. Her orange dress clung to her narrow frame.

Gardenia's gaze darted to the queen. "I'd say this was a special circumstance."

"Because she's a princess?" Noblet Mangowort's tone dripped with sarcasm, reminding me of betrayer Bee's harsh criticism.

"Because she was emotionally and physically attacked by The Arch Noblet." Queen Dahliadew sniffed in a dignified manner. She wasn't making excuses but explanations.

"After she verbally attacked every fairy in the room." Noblet Mangowort brandished her wand in a circular sweep.

Smashing my lips together, I wasn't sure how to respond. Justify myself or stay silent?

"She wasn't attacking. She was defending." Gardenia whirled on the noblet. "Believe me, I know the difference."

I let out a low sigh. I didn't have to defend myself. Gardenia was doing it for me. Even though we'd had our own arguments, I knew she was on my side. She'd found me in the human world and forced me to face my true identity. Now, she stood beside me. I might not always appreciate her controlling my life, but I appreciated her now.

"Thank you, Gardenia."

"Whenever you're ready." Posy Purplecloud relaxed into her chair and examined her wand.

She seemed to be accommodating me, though something felt off.

Gathering myself, I knew I didn't have all day. Better to get this done so I could celebrate later. I didn't want to take advantage of the respite. I had to prove I could pass the wand test and be the perfect princess. I wanted to show the queen what I could accomplish. Then, after I proved I was an ideal princess, I could start speaking up about the inequities between the fairies and other majiks. "I'm ready."

With feet shoulder-width apart, as Stone had taught me to fight with weapons, I waited for the first attack. The judges would take turns casting spells and I had to counteract them. I'd practiced with Gardenia for hours, her throwing everything she could think of my way.

"Queen Dahliadew will go first." Gardenia beckoned to the queen.

The queen rose and flew to a space in front of me. Her blank expression gave nothing away. I didn't know if she'd go easy on me or not. She raised her wand.

I tensed. Anxiety wove through me, causing my skin to itch. I had less than a second to figure out the spell and respond. Extra points were allotted if I shouted out the name of the spell and the defensive spell I casted.

The queen made her move.

Her wand tilted to the right and switched to veering left. The variety of color blasting from the wand tip signaled a multi-pronged attack. *Sizzle, sizzle, sizzle.* I recognized the sound. This was a spell we'd practiced. A tickle of excitement wiggled through my limbs.

"Frenzy of Senses." I jiggled my wand up and down to counter. "Clarity Wave."

The waves of sparks from my wand wove through the queen's spell, stopping it.

Smiling, I relaxed a little. One down and three to go.

"I'm next." Gardenia's fierce expression displayed in her narrowed gaze and furrowed brow.

"Don't take it easy on her because you're her fairy godmother," Noblet Mangowort called out.

She hadn't said anything to my grandmother and queen. Would Gardenia's attack be harder because of the taunt?

"As if." A shaft of light came from her wand with no warning. It arced up and then blasted downward.

Shrieieieieieieikkkkkk.

I froze at the noise and light. It was a missile.

"Thunder Missile." I'd read about this spell in my magic book and knew I had a split second to defend. "Force Barrier."

My wand created a wall of magic. The magic missile hit the dense wall and absorbed the magic with a prolonged pop. The missile couldn't penetrate.

Rolling my shoulders, I let out a puff of relief.

"My turn." Posy Purplecloud leapt from her seat with an evil grin and attacked. Her wand whipped into a zigzag. Flames shot into the air and heated my skin.

"Dragon Bolt." A difficult spell, but since I had a little experience with dragons... "Tranquility Charm."

The charm calmed the anger of the bolt by dancing around the fire.

"Very good." Posy Purplecloud jerked her head down in a nod.

Satisfaction streamed through me and caressed my skin. I had one test left.

Noblet Mangowort flickered her wings to stand in position. Her face went hard, and she snarled.

Dread weighed me down. This was going to be my hardest test. She hated me.

She spun and twirled her wand. The dark flare from the tip went right, left, up, and down. It was pure chaos.

Aha.

"Savagery of Chaos." A spell not in any schoolbooks and only whispered in the halls. My mind whirred, running through magic books and rumors. I couldn't believe she'd cast a difficult, and borderline illegal, spell. I hadn't been allowed to learn how to cast it. How was I supposed to defend against it?

The chaos blasted toward me.

Kaboom! Tchtchtch! Kerplot! A whistling so sharp it tormented my ears. Streaks and flashes and strobe effects of dark and light, mostly dark. The different effects stung my eyes, causing me to tear up.

I couldn't see and couldn't hear. My lungs shredded and panic spiked down my spine. Milliseconds slowed to a life or death moment for me.

"Interruption Aura!" It was difficult magic for a novice to perform. And I was definitely a novice. Focusing my energy into my fingers, I used my internal royal magic passed from my grandmother to project into the wand, giving it additional strength.

Sparks spurted from my wand in colors of lightness. Yellow and orange and pink and lime green. A sparkler trying to ward off the dark. Or the dark forces. The colors swirled into a large, multicolored cloud. The cloud puffed around the chaos coming from her wand. The puff suffocated her spell.

My counter spell worked. I wobbled on my feet. The darkness faded into nothingness inside the cloud.

"That wasn't on the list of approved spells, Noblet Mangowort." Queen Dahliadew's displeasure vibrated in her tone.

Mangowort grimaced. Something dark flashed on her face. She tossed another spell.

Stunned, I jerked upright. *Elves' bells.* This was not how the wand test was supposed to work.

Her wand swirled in an angry storm, hurtling right and left, taking everything out in its path. Wanting to take me out.

"Noblet Mangowort, stop!" Gardenia's voice roared through the whirlwind.

My pulse jolted. My hair tore free of the restrictive bun and tangled. The skirt of my dress molded to my legs. Throwing an arm up to protect myself from the spell decimating me, I ran through the scenarios I'd practiced. If her first spell hadn't been approved, this one probably wasn't either.

A tornado of destruction spun around the room. Similarly, panic spun around my ribs and I gasped. The empty audience chairs whipped and circled, the clattering and clashing adding to the noise.

Posy Purplecloud screamed and ducked.

A tree column wavered and crashed to the floor. Decorative real flowers ripped from their stems. Mother Earth cried. The natural adornments were devastated by the wind.

Devastation. Destruction. And...and...

"Aura of Decimation." Yelling over the commotion, I put a name to the devilish spell.

Something about the *D* words drilled into my head. That had to be the answer. The counter spell had to be another *D* word.

Think, think, think, think...

"Spectral Disruption," I shouted in triumph.

Now, if I could cast the defensive spell. My nerve endings tingled.

A chair flew at me and I dove to the floor. My gaze darted to the queen. She used magic to create a barrier around herself. She was still in danger. The others couldn't cast the termination spell because the spell had been specifically directed at me and their wands had been tethered and restricted so they couldn't interfere.

With my stampeding pulse, I wanted to run out of the room. Instead, I scooted to a crouched position.

The illegal spell wasn't anything I'd been taught, but Watu had trained me how to bend things to my will. Maybe this was the time. Concentrating, I thought about the title of the counter spell.

Disruption, disruption, disruption. How could I disrupt the evil spell?

Rubbing my now-numb fingers together, I regripped my wand. Determination rammed through my veins. Again, using my internal energy, I forced more magic into the wand. I called to the trees and plants and flowers being destroyed to assist me with

Mother Earth's gifts. I wasn't cheating. I was using everything at my disposal. Mother Earth's gifts had helped Rye and I retrieve the Divinity Orb. The human prince had helped me to access the earth's powers and I'd healed a tree.

Mother Earth settled the winds. The trees stopped bending and the flowers stopped ripping from the dirt. The chairs fell to the floor.

I firmed my shoulders. Now to stop the actual spell.

Sparks flew from my wand and twined together to create a magical whip. Perspiration formed on my upper lip. Similar to the Silver Snare, I cast the magic whip back and lassoed the dark flare coming from the noblet's wand, tying it down. It crashed and crackled. Her wand fizzled and the dark light went out.

My real whip had given me the expertise to cast precisely.

Exhausted, I crashed to the floor with a loud thud. My breathing went shallow and sweat pooled on my lower back.

"Noblet Mangowort." The queen's angry voice went low and deep, clearly disapproving. "That is not how this test works."

Those *D* words were stuck in my head. A side effect of the spell?

"You and Commander Gardenia threw soft spells at her." Mangowort's nose stuck up and her indignant tone told me she didn't care about rules. "That's not fair to our status as Guild of the Wand Supreme."

"The Thunder Missile is not an easy spell to counteract." Gardenia flourished her wand, ready to cast a spell on Mangowort.

"Still, the girl is half fairy and we need to make sure she's of the same quality as the rest of the guild." She huffed and stormed to her chair. "The other guild members should've been present to test her."

The floor grew colder with the woman's words. The sweat morphed to ice against my skin. I understood what she was really saying. I needed to be better and work harder to be equal to a full fairy.

Not fair. I'd already worked more and studied harder. I'd changed my appearance and done what had been asked.

"We tried to get the others in the guild here on time. It was imperative Princess Ellery get her wand status right away." Gardenia's wings flustered and she returned to her chair. "Besides, only four casters take part in the testing and there are four of us."

The Guild of the Wand Supreme was an all-female guild for the best wand spellcasters. From my reading, the group was prestigious, and every female royal has been a member. So it was important for me to be a member too.

Queen Dahliadew stood and raised her wand. "Shall we vote?"

My stomach twisted and tangled. Her tone made it seem as if I had her support. I struggled to sit, even though I didn't have the strength to stand. Mangowort would never vote for me.

"The girl's hand was a bit shaky during the compulsory figures." Noblet Mangowort held out her wand, not touching it to the queen's, still undecided.

My chest rattled. To vote, they tapped their wands together and a specific color came out for either yes or no.

"Where did she go wrong?" Gardenia was defending me. "I didn't spot one mistake."

"Her hand was shaking." Posy Purplecloud nodded.

"So would yours if you had fairies shouting around you." My fairy godmother leaned forward.

"Ladies, a vote please." The queen tapped her wand to Gardenia's.

Noblet Mangowort and Posy Purplecloud exchanged a glance.

My body tensed. The combination of magic and anxiety messed with my mind and body.

Sparks lit from the bunched wands. Every sparkle was purple.

Everyone had voted the same way. That had to be good. Gardenia and the queen wouldn't vote against me. I held my breath.

"Congratulations, Princess Ellery. You've passed the wand testing." The queen gave me a regal nod.

I wanted to shout with joy. I jumped to my feet and hugged the queen and Gardenia. Glancing at the other two members, I halted.

Smiling, I nodded at both of them. "Thank you. You won't regret this decision."

Their despondence couldn't stop my excitement. Their down-beat expressions became a parade in my soul. Music wove through my head and my heart.

"Hold your wand this way and swish when you respond." Gardenia mimicked the action.

"Do you, Princess Ellery, agree to uphold the principles of the Guild of the Wand Supreme?"

Biting my lip to stop my huge grin, I swished my wand. "I do."

The wand heated in my hand and glowed for a second before returning to its normal color. Even though I'd been using the wand to practice, it was similar to a learner's permit. Now, the wand registered that I was its official owner. Purple sparks shot from the tip. The sparks exploded into colorful fireworks.

"As queen of the fairies, and leader of the guild, I Queen Dahliadew, welcome Princess Ellery into the Guild of the Wand Supreme."

Gardenia clapped loudly. The other two women put their hands together in a polite, singular don't-really-mean-it clap.

I jumped up and fluttered my wings, floating around the room. Lightness filled me and for this one moment I wouldn't worry about being perfect or the future. Giggling, I did the backstroke, swimming around the room.

Queen Dahliadew laughed. Noblet Mangowort sneered and bent her head. Did she think I might hit her with my swimming antics? I didn't care. She wouldn't ruin this moment. I'd worked hard to achieve this status. It was another way to prove to the fairies I was worthy of being their princess. Another trophy on the shelf.

I wiggled and danced in the air. I flicked my wand and colorful balloons fell from the ceiling. Tapping at the balloons, I watched the colors boogie and float. I couldn't wait to tell Arbor and Watu. Telling Rye would have to wait.

"May I have a moment of your time?" Gardenia asked the queen and they huddled in the corner.

Officially dismissed, I twirled happily and headed toward the door with my ordained wand. I glowed. My mother's wand. Flying ahead of me were Mangowort and Purplecloud.

"I hope Bracken can finalize the details for the delegation and get approval from the nasty regent soon." Noblet Mangowort talked to Posy Purplecloud. "He needs to return to Queens Academy and get *things* under control here."

Was the thing she referred to me and this terrible idea of a marriage?

My spirits deflated, mimicking balloons. Landing on the floor, I tucked my wings to my side. So much for not thinking about the future. Disquiet darkened my outlook.

I needed to find a way to get out of this wedding. The sooner the better.

CHAPTER SEVEN

At my slight touch, the Divinity Orb lit up and swirled with colors greeting me. Shades of red, purple, and orange eddied inside the globe and settled with my mind. I concentrated as I'd been taught.

A fairy battalion waited on Drage Mountain. Another squadron of majik troops marched in formation toward their destination. New soldiers trained in a nearby encampment as well as inside the castle walls. The hospital wing overflowed with injured.

The Divinity Orb showed me things happening right now, and possibilities for the future. Although I hadn't learned how to interpret the future yet. The views would be helpful with the war.

The circular Illuminate Turret securing the orb had windows on every wall. In the day, sunlight brightened the space. At night, or early morning, like now, stars shined. A large moss-cushioned chair sat to one side and, in the middle of the room, a stand carved from a willow tree held the Divinity Orb.

I picked up the orb and held it in my palms. Heat from the orb's glow ignited through my body. The magic didn't bring comfort. I was desperate to get word from Rye especially now that I might be engaged to someone else. The human prince had won my heart and we'd been separated ever since. The Divinity Orb provided our only form of communication, especially since we were on opposite sides of the war.

I hadn't been able to sleep with the excitement from the day and the worry about tomorrow. I'd decided to try again to communicate with Rye to tell him about the wand test and how Mother Earth had helped defend me. I'd hoped this new power would help me communicate.

Had his uncle, Regent Theobald, discovered the prince had brought back a fake-twin orb? The man would stop at nothing to rule the Kingdom of Alandaska, even kill his nephew—the true ruler.

A tremor ran down my spine. Rye was in danger.

Focusing, I attempted to initiate contact through the magical artifact. Like a celltab, the Divinity Orb communicated with its twin replica between me and Rye only. We'd retrieved the orb together, but he'd given the real orb to me to bring back to Queens Academy, understanding the powerful artifact would support my new position as fairy princess.

Guilt curdled in my stomach. I shouldn't have accepted such a precious gift. His uncle had demanded Rye bring the orb back if he survived a quest against majiks. But neither of us wanted the orb to fall into his evil uncle's hands.

The Divinity Orb was safer at Queens Academy, where it was protected by guards and magic.

My fingers wrapped tighter around the globe, trying to strangle it into compliance, trying to feel even a slight vibration. "The orb isn't working."

When Rye was near the twin orb, it would shake in response, our way of knowing we could orb chat. My chest constricted. Several weeks had passed since I'd last heard from him.

Prince Zacharye had declared his love for me at Aristos Sanctuary before we'd parted. I never got the chance to tell him I felt the same and telling him through the orb hadn't seemed appropriate. Then, war had been declared, majiks and humans were dying, and now we couldn't communicate at all. Plus, I couldn't forget about the Bracken complication.

A fizzle of frustration gurgled in my gut. I sank onto the chair and bonked the back of my head against the wall. Stupid to try again.

I closed my eyes and bonked my head again. Tiredness flowed through my body. I'd sit for a minute...

A creaking startled me.

Too tired to open my eyes, I analyzed the crick in my neck and the sharp item poking my ribs—the arm of a chair. I was not in my cushy bed. I'd fallen asleep in the turret room.

The creaking came again. A loose paving stone or the door swinging open. The scent of mud tickled my nose.

Not many fairies had access to this room. My gaze flickered.

The orb's comforting glow cast light around the center. Early morning light glared through the windows. The creaking got louder and longer.

I jerked to a sitting position and stared at the door opening on its hinges.

A nicely dressed man backed into the room. His wings were tucked in tight and he hunched over, trying to make himself appear smaller, which I knew didn't work because I'd tried the same tactic several times. He snicked the door closed and spun.

"Bracken?" I tugged at the collar of my nightgown.

His brown eyes widened, and he froze in place. Redness crept up from his neckline and his lips pursed in disapproval.

Of me?

"What're you doing here?" Only a few were given access to this room because it held the precious magical artifact.

Standing straighter, he tugged on his four-leaved bow tie and smoothed his expression. Whatever had flashed across his face was gone, replaced by calmness and smooth skin.

"Princess Ellery?" He smiled, showing his perfect teeth. "What're you doing in the Illumine Turret so early in the morning?" He arched a suggestive brow. "Or should I say, very late at night?"

My cheeks heated, remembering the first time we'd met. Glancing down at the nightgown, I understood why he might think I'd been out all night. I smoothed the material and stood.

"Nothing so indecent." I huffed. In a way, it was. Gardenia had warned me to stop using the Divinity Orb to communicate with Rye, which was why I always snuck in at night. I couldn't tell Bracken anything about my relationship with the human prince. "I came here to see if after passing the wand test, I'd have a stronger connection to the orb. I must've fallen asleep."

"What connection?" Bracken treaded closer, inspecting the glowing orb.

I smirked. Someone else didn't know the full capability of the orb's power. "When I retrieved the Divinity Orb from the Reflection Pool, a connection developed between me and the orb."

He ogled the orb with lust and adoration as he never looked at me. Which was okay. I didn't want him to want me.

"I have that connection." The brag tasted bitter on my tongue. I might have a power connection, yet I'd lost the communication I craved with the prince.

"What does the connection do?" His gaze darted between me and the orb. He didn't believe me.

With his father's connections, I was surprised he wasn't versed in fairy history and lore. "The priestesses of Aristos Sanctuary can use the prediction powers of the Divinity Orb. Only those connected to the orb can actually see events taking place somewhere else." I picked up the orb and the glow morphed into colored swirls. "See?"

"The priestesses have secrets of their own." His brow furrowed in a contemplative expression. "Regent Theobald insists I bring the Divinity Orb with me to the peace negotiations. The man wants to confirm we have the real orb."

My heart stopped and then ticked faster and faster. The statement confirmed the regent knew the orb in his possession was fake. Rye was in trouble, possibly in prison. The ticking sped up, about to explode. I smothered the sensation, refusing to think about anything worse.

Which made going to the human palace more urgent.

"The orb won't work the way the regent expects for anyone except me." And Rye. I needed to use that to my advantage and convince Bracken of my plan. Even though I didn't want to get closer, I hooked my arm conspiratorially through his. "Which means I should be part of the delegation traveling to the human palace."

His body stiffened. "I'm not sure I have the authority to demand you accompany me."

As princess, I should have the authority. I didn't. My thoughts tumbled. When would the fairies trust me? I couldn't wait that long.

"We can convince the council together." I needed his help and he needed the orb. "When does the meeting start?"

"I'm headed to the Grand Council meeting to discuss the delegation now."

Things could work out for me if they needed me to go. I could find Rye. "Perfect. I'll come with and help persuade them."

Flicking my wand, I changed from my nightgown to a respectable yellow dress. I didn't worry about my hair or face. The council already thought I was a hideous half human.

"I guess you can come." Bracken agreed because he didn't think the council would approve my request. He didn't know I had my points thought out in advance.

Walking through the castle corridors resembling a couple, I didn't take notice of the stares or nods of approval. My focus was on one thing: convincing the council I should go with the delegation for the best interests of the fairies.

The thick wooden doors swung open and Bracken and I stepped over the threshold. The noblets did a double-take, seeing the two of us together. Everyone stood and bowed deeper as we passed. Tilting my chin up, I understood the respect was more for him.

My wings ruffled and I forced a smile to stay on my face.

The Arch Noblet Oakton sat in my small throne chair again. He jumped to his feet and bowed. He offered me *my chair.*

Narrowing my gaze, I noted neither Queen Dahliadew nor Commander Gardenia were present. This couldn't be an official meeting if there was no royal representation.

"Good morning." I took my seat and straightened my dress. "I wasn't aware the Grand Council meeting was starting early today."

Bracken's father's cheeks puffed. He flung the tail of his jacket behind him and took the chair next to mine. "We didn't want to bother you with pesky details."

"Maybe I'm mistaken." I wasn't. "Technically this can't be a Grand Council meeting without the presence of a royal or a royal representative."

Several of the noblets nervously glanced around.

The Arch Noblet Oakton narrowed his gaze at his own son. "Bracken was planning to be present."

"Bracken's not royal, even if we might be engaged." I played innocent, betting they'd planned the early start time so they could discuss things without a royal present. "Good thing I'm here."

Murmuring, everyone took their seats. There were no welcoming greetings. They weren't happy I was here. Too bad.

The Arch Noblet snarled and smashed his elbows onto the table. "Why don't we start with discussing what happened at the wand test since we were kicked out."

Pushing the negativity down, I flourished my wand. I needed them on my side for this discussion. "I passed."

The noblets started talking, louder this time.

"Says you." He pounded his fist, imitating a judge's gavel. "You're half human. You can lie."

The intended insult punched me in the gut. I could lie. That was better than being honestly rude.

Loud gasps exploded from the Grand Council members and I wished I had a gavel to silence them. I wanted to yell and confront everyone, yet I forced myself to stay calm and sit perfectly still like a good princess. I would not be drawn into a shouting match about whether I lied or could lie. Whether I passed or hadn't. Whether I was worthy or not. My word should be the gold standard.

Once they realized they were arguing with each other, they went silent and glared at me.

"The others will vouch I passed, including Queen Dahliadew, Commander Gardenia, Posy Purplecloud, and…" I glowered across the table at the noblet who'd used an illegal spell to test me, "Noblet Mangowort."

She stared back, trying to stay defiant. Her buzzing scarf made of flies swarmed around her head. Her cheeks reddened, and her chin dipped.

"In fact, the noblet gave me extra credit." For the illegal spell and the extra surprise attack. My gaze challenged her. "Isn't that right, Noblet Mangowort?"

Her chin rose higher and shook more. Did she want to deny the truth? Except as a fairy she couldn't lie. "The girl passed."

I relaxed back in my seat, not even taking exception to the term *the girl*.

Bracken's father's lips twisted into a crooked line. "Let's move to more important matters."

I leaned back further. The man was the one who brought the test up and now he dismissed it as unimportant. Folding my hands together, I squeezed to stop myself from speaking out.

Using his wand, *The* Arch Noblet Oakton summoned a folder. "While Commander Gardenia is taken up with the war, we need to be planning for the future. For the war's end."

It was ridiculous to be planning for what would happen after a war that just started. Although if Bracken's idea for a peace treaty worked, the war would end sooner and with less loss. Everyone could return to a better life. No more fighting or death. No more taking advantage of majiks or humans crushing and limiting them.

"When we win," the man continued.

Nodding, I liked that he thought positive. I had my doubts though. The regent was treacherous and prejudices against majiks were ingrained. Once the fighting ended, there'd still be battles to change humans' minds about us. Regent Theobald had been poisoning humans against us since he had taken power almost sixteen years ago.

"We will need to reorder the various majiks." His words made my stomach queasy.

With the way they spoke about other majiks, I could imagine his sinister scheme.

"If the humans win..."

The other noblets reacted to the unpopular opinion. They roared and waved their hands dismissively.

I didn't want a winner or a loser. I wanted a truce, kind of like Bracken. Maybe he wasn't all bad.

The Arch Noblet Oakton used his hands to signal them to be quiet. "The fairies will have to come to an agreement with the humans."

He had left out a very important part. This might be a council of fairies, but we had to work with other majiks no matter the outcome of the war. Wasn't that the mission Stone had been sent on? I couldn't stay silent. "What about other majiks?"

His chin dropped into his hand. "No matter the outcome, the fairies will rule the other majiks just as our royal court represents them."

Horror scratched my lungs. The fairies treated other majiks as if they were lesser, similar to how the humans treated us. Could they not see the double standard?

Most of the other noblets held their heads high, agreeing with the man. Noblet Mangowort nodded with enthusiasm. Noblet Rainbowfly glanced down. If he disagreed, he wasn't willing to speak up.

I remembered how the student fairies at the academy had treated Tos and Hokima when they'd arrived to train with me before our mission to Aristos Sanctuary. They'd come back heroes but were still treated as the enemy. That had to change. Conviction fortified my nerves. I opened my mouth to say something but then snapped it shut. Speaking up about their bigotry wasn't going to change their minds. They didn't like or trust me. Going on the peace delegation was the most important thing at this point. I had to convince them to let me go and take care of majik equality later. Once I rescued Rye and became more respected, I'd present my viewpoint.

"My son's upcoming delegation to Reximus Palace in Lindenhamn will start the process, showing the humans that fairies are reasonable and open to negotiation." He proudly contemplated Bracken and bent down to whisper, "Did you get the final object?"

"There's been a complication." Bracken whispered back and his gaze darted to me. He straightened, realizing I could hear everything they said. Clearing his throat, he spoke loud enough for everyone. "The Divinity Orb has a connection to the fairy who retrieved it from the Reflection Pool at Aristos Sanctuary. And while others, mostly the priestesses, can use the orb to predict a possible future, they can't see what's happening right now in other places."

I huffed. He appeared smart when he'd repeated what I'd told him. Pushing my irritation aside, I realized he fell right into my personal plan.

"Bracken brings up an excellent point." I smiled and made sure my gaze touched each of the decisionmakers. "You know I was the one who retrieved the Divinity Orb." Hopefully, they hadn't heard about the Connected Crown Prophecy. The prophecy foretold the way to raise the Divinity Orb was through two royals with different blood who were united. The priestesses had planned to keep the prophecy secret. I'd learned about it when Rye and I had retrieved the orb. We both had a connection to the Divinity Orb. But there were spies everywhere as I'd learned the hard way with my ex-friend Bee. "I'm the one with the special connection to the orb. The one who can use it to its full potential."

Bracken's expression tightened. He knew where I was headed.

"And as you have pointed out multiple times, I am half human." The noblets' murmurs sounded negative.

I didn't care. Lying could be an advantage in schemes and negotiations.

"I grew up in Lindenhamn." My pulse flitted as I remembered my home. I'd loved the house and the younger years with my parents. Once my father remarried, it had become a jail. Since moving to Queens Academy, I'd given up my right to inherit the house. With a little magic, my stepfamily didn't even remember my existence. "And I've been to the human palace. I know many of its secrets."

Like the dungeon, and the magic suppression, and that the prince was in trouble.

I kept my voice steady. "I believe I would make an excellent addition to the delegation."

Objections exploded.

"No!"

"We can't trust her!"

Heat rolled through me at each insult.

"Settle down, everyone." Bracken stood and got everyone's attention. "Princess Ellery has a good point."

He needed me and the Divinity Orb. The reason he spoke on my behalf.

"She's familiar with human etiquette and tradition."

Way to point out what they'd consider flaws.

He hurried to my side and took hold of my hand. "Traveling together will give us a great opportunity to get to know each other."

Inside, I squirmed, wanting to slip my hand from his. I forced myself to stay put. He helped me now. I'd never love him.

"One second." His father held up his hand. "I need to consult with my son, the head of the peace delegation."

The two of them stepped a few feet from us and whispered back and forth. This time, I couldn't hear. I leaned forward.

Stepping back toward the council table, Oakton announced, "I think it's a fine idea."

My jaw dropped. How had he gotten his father to agree so quickly?

"Bracken will be at Princess Ellery's side to protect her and her being at his side with the Divinity Orb will prove to the humans we're trustworthy."

The council table erupted again. Most of them weren't convinced.

"I know we'll need to have a private vote." Bracken's father silenced them with a raised hand. "But keep in mind the princess can show the regent that the orb works. And when she leaves it behind, it won't help him see what we are doing."

I sucked in a sharp breath. I wasn't leaving the Divinity Orb behind with the regent. Now, if Prince Zacharye were in complete control of the throne, I'd consider it. And he could use the orb.

"And when Bracken and the princess return, their wedding will take place immediately." His father winked obnoxiously. "After all, they'll have spent many days and...*nights* together."

My entire body felt on fire. Flames shot from my toes and singed my body, overheating my face. Did the man think I'd sleep with Bracken just because we were thrown together? Shuddering, I held in a negative response.

Noblet Mangowort stood and pounded on the table. "She's not worthy of representing us in negotiations."

And with that, the excellent points for why I should go with the delegation collapsed.

Chapter Eight

"The man basically said I'd have to marry his son!" I slumped onto the floor of Arbor's tiny bedroom.

"The Grand Council is considering allowing you to go. That's good news." Arbor fluttered above me and tickled my nose.

"On their terms." I slammed my fist into the floor. Mangowort's assertion that I wasn't worthy played into the negotiations and the final vote which wouldn't take place until tomorrow afternoon. "If I go, *I'm to represent royalty by being silent during the negotiations.*" I held my fingers up in air quotes.

Female queens ruled the fairies, yet princesses had no respect. Princess rules were archaic and strict.

Arbor landed on my stomach. She blinked her mossy green eyes a few times. "Are you going to go with those conditions?"

"I'm going. Even if they say no, I'll find a way. And I refuse to be silent or placed in a compromised situation." I'd rescue Rye. I'd negotiated a fair treaty for majiks. And hopefully, I wouldn't get caught in a compromising position with Bracken.

"What do you have planned?"

A half-hysterical and half-scheming giggle erupted out of my mouth. "Since Watu is my marriage advisor, I've asked her to be my chaperone on the trip."

Arbor's body smoked into a lime green color. One of the smoke sprite's tendencies was to show emotion through colored smoke. "What about me?"

"Gardenia needs you. Plus, Watu is a troll. She'll repel Bracken away from me."

Arbor's wings drooped. "I feel as if we never spend time together."

"Me, too." Slowly sitting up, I held out my palm so she'd land there. My palm and shoulder were her favorite places to perch. "I'll be leaving the day after next as long as the vote goes in my favor."

Her tiny feet dug into my skin. "Stone left too."

My shoulders dipped. He'd told me he'd be leaving soon, not exactly when. Arbor knew because she worked for Gardenia and so did Stone.

"He never said goodbye." Sadness and worry swam through my veins. Stone was on an undercover mission. Arbor was busy working on battle plans with Gardenia. Tos and Hokima had returned to their homelands. Perry, Bim, and Keltie had died. Bee had betrayed me. And Rye was in danger. The only one who would be with me was Watu. Everyone else on the trip would be Bracken's ally.

I shook off the melancholy. "When I get back, we'll have lots of time to be with each other."

Arbor could help me make new friends in my classes. She'd be able to tell me who liked me for me or who wanted to be with me because I was the princess.

"Except you'll be busy with the wedding."

My midsection clenched. "There won't be a wedding."

"What's wrong with Bracken?" Her face went soft and her body limp. "He's handsome and polite."

I snorted. She acted similar to other female fairies taken in by his fairy good looks. I twisted my lips in sarcasm. "Because that's exactly why you should marry someone."

"He'll help you secure your position as princess. He'll garner you respect." She sat up on my shoulder, no longer a slumping mass of hormones.

"Will he?" I raised a thoughtful eyebrow. "Or will he be the one securing his position?"

"You're first in line to the throne." Arbor fluffed her wings.

"True." A crack formed inside my heart. Maybe marrying Bracken would be a necessary evil. It might be the only way the fairies would accept my rule. Marrying Bracken would make me the perfect princess for the fairies.

But if I gave in and gave up, would I be perfect in my own eyes?

"Lastly, we will discuss magic sources." Professor Sands tapped with his wand on my desk. "Princess Ellery?"

I snapped my attention back to the teacher. "Excuse me?"

The class laughed.

It was hard to pretend to pay attention when his teaching was as dry as his name. And not get noticed when I was the princess, and all eyes were on me. I'd had a restless night and had so many other things on my mind. This class was boring compared to flying class, which was next. And I had to pack for the peace delegation trip. If I got to go. There'd been many negative reasons why I shouldn't be allowed on the trip mentioned at the meeting yesterday.

The professor tapped his finger against his dimpled chin, drawing the class' attention to his gorgeous face. "The royals have an instinctual burst of power passed down from generation to generation. What is it called?"

"Burst of power?" I jolted straight up in my chair, remembering when I'd held the queen's hand when she'd been poisoned and Gardenia had thought she'd die.

"Glad to see I've finally piqued your interest." The professor had known I hadn't been paying attention the entire time. My face heated as he continued to lecture me. "As princess, you're supposed to be a role model. A perfect student."

The word grated against my nerves. Perfect princess. Perfect student. Perfect wife.

I threw up in my mouth.

He continued to talk about the power. "Regiis Enhanced Imperium is a natural burst of power handed down from queen to queen. Because the queen is female..."

Obviously.

"She needs the enhanced or superpower to control the male fairies."

My eyebrows arched. Magic wasn't like physical strength. Male or female, any fairy's magic could be more powerful than the other. The more practice the more skill.

Professor Sands lifted his bare arm and flexed. "The enhanced power gives the new queen an extra burst of magic."

It explained the charge of power I'd received right before I left for Aristos Sanctuary.

The professor swiveled in front of the classroom and placed his palms on my desk. His bright white teeth gleamed. "Isn't that right, Princess Ellery?"

I didn't want to answer the question. The fact I'd received the extra burst of power was a state secret. "You're the professor. Why don't you tell us?"

His gaze narrowed and he shot daggers at me.

Blanching, I waited, expecting a real attack.

The bell rang and I jumped from my seat, looking forward to the freedom of flying class.

"Princess Ellery, may I have a word with you?" It wasn't really a question.

Watching the other students leave, I waited by his desk. I tapped my foot, fretting my insolence would get me in trouble.

He flew to my side and sat in his chair, swishing his long blond hair. A strong chin and dimples had the girls drooling. And some of the boys. Professor Sands knew it. His arrogance as he posed in the classroom got sighs from many. "I know you're hoping to leave with the peace delegation tomorrow."

"You know?"

"So I'll forgive your distraction." He flicked his fingers and the door slammed shut. "My point is, Queen Dahliadew already bestowed the Regiis Enhancement Imperium to you. My job is to teach you how to control the power."

He'd been told. Which was okay if he could teach me to control the royal power.

"This is an important lesson you need to learn and I advised The Arch Noblet Oakton and the rest of the council you weren't ready to leave castle grounds without learning techniques to control your special magic."

I slapped my hands on my hips. "You can't tell me I can't go."

"I can give my opinion to the Grand Council." The professor firmed his lips in a static expression. "And I have."

He couldn't ruin my plans. I had to find Rye.

"Teach me how to control it."

The professor guffawed. "Humans."

I huffed. I'd been called half breed enough times. "What's that supposed to mean?"

"You're impatient."

Watu had taught me patience; I just didn't always get it right. "I don't think that's only a human trait."

"Directness."

I shook my head. "Again, not only human." It was unfair my bad qualities were assumed to be from my human side while my good qualities were assumed to be from my fairy side. "Besides, directness is not a negative quality. Only direct rudeness."

The professor paced the room. His frown told me he didn't want to help. "Let's move on, shall we?"

"Yes." I crossed my arms. "Or is that too direct for you?"

"You think you're so important because you brought home the Divinity Orb. Well, those powers can be transferred with a simple spell."

Unless the queen wanted those powers, I'd be keeping them for myself because it was the only way I could communicate with Rye.

Or at least, I used to be able to communicate. The reason I needed to go on the trip.

Professor Sands fingers strangled his wand. "To control the extra magic inside, you must blow a puff on the tip."

"Sounds easy." I held my wand up and thought about a spell to try, wishing I could cut his arrogance down.

"The puff must be exactly on the tip with the exact amount of air at the exact second before casting the magic. It must be perfect."

I stilled and clamped my mouth shut. The word perfect was like an alarm ringing in my mind.

The disapproving shake of his head suggested he believed I was helpless. "It will be much easier when you're surrounded by superior fairies."

Raising my brow, I waited for him to tell me who these superior fairies were.

"Never mind." His wary tone insulted me. "At least give it a whirl. That way, I can say you tried and failed."

I glared. The man didn't like me and didn't want me to go with the peace delegation. I'd show him. I wanted to get this right on the first try. I remembered how he'd done a short puff of air to demonstrate.

Holding my wand up, I noticed my hand trembling. What if I screwed up? For sure, he'd tell the Grand Council. What if he was lying about the control remedy? Except as a full fairy, he couldn't lie. He could just make things difficult. I blew on the tip right before casting my wand forward, pointing at the cold liquid in the cup on his desk. The liquid started to steam even though I could've easily made it boil.

"I did it." I'd passed an extra difficult wand test and I'd learned how to control my royal magic.

"You certainly did." He didn't sound pleased.

"I've got this royal magic thing handled in a snap." I snapped my fingers.

The liquid boiled and bubbled over his cup.

My face heated. "Oops."

He used his wand to clean up my mess. "Your destiny will be assured once you marry Bracken Oakton—"

"I never said I'd marry him." Why does every conversation I have come back to my supposed fiancé? Was he this alleged superior fairy?

"We'll see."

After my altercation with Professor Sands, I hurried to change out of the constricting princess dress and into the red outfit for flying class. This class was held in the courtyard with new students who'd recently received their wings. At almost seventeen, I was the oldest in the class.

And now I was late.

A group of ten fairies flew around in a circle above the training ground. Their multi-colored wings were a moving rainbow in the blue sky. Their lighthearted laughter lifted my spirits. They'd gone through the warmup drills and landed on the ground around the professor. I edged in between a boy with a rip in his shirt and a girl who appeared a lot younger than the minimum age.

The professor whirled around and bowed with her wings dipped. Standing in front of me on the ground, she flipped her long red tresses back. "Alright, you first years and Princess Ellery."

My cheeks baked. I didn't want special attention drawn to me. I already stood out because I was the oldest and the tallest.

"Today, we will learn the appropriate way to dive and do some free flying."

My pulse quickened. I loved flying. The freedom and the beauty of sights from above. No one could watch me from the sky.

Everyone spread their wings and took off. The wind brushing my wings gave me tingles. The fresh air on my face had me taking deep breaths and pulling the oxygen into my lungs. My entire body felt lighter and freer. From up here, you could see things from a different perspective.

The professor called out a flying formation and the students would shift. Left and right. Up and down. I believed I did better than the others because I had experience. I'd received my wings during my mission to Aristos Sanctuary and while Watu had taught me the basics of flying, I'd used my wings a lot on the journey and Perry had trained me in fighting maneuvers.

"Class, I'll be right back." The professor spread her wings and took off. "Continue free flying."

Everyone flew into their favorite positions.

I floated on my back and swung my arms, swimming in the sky. Today would be my last day in class for a while if I went to the human palace. I should probably be practicing something important. Shifting into a position with my feet down and my wings at a slight angle, I took out the dagger at my waist and practiced striking positions as I'd been taught.

"You're not allowed to do The Perry maneuver in Flying 101." The boy with the ripped shirt flew next to me.

Choking, I remembered when Perry had taught me the move and dubbed it with his name. I thought he'd been joking. Yet this kid knew the maneuver's name and had chastised me for using it.

I straightened my wings and held my sad memories at bay. "Perry Moss taught me the move himself."

A girl who'd been flying near skidded to a stop. "Whoa. You knew Perry Moss?"

My eyes prickled with moisture and I blinked a few times. I'd known him. He'd died defending me.

Another kid flew above. He glared. "My older sister says the princess caused his death."

Feeling as if my own dagger stabbed me, I lost my concentration and my wings fluttered faster. I started falling.

My breath whooshed out. I backpedaled with my feet and spread my arms trying to get my wings to activate. Where was my cockiness now? Why wasn't my royal magic helping me?

My wings caught air and I lifted. My body straightened and I was in recovery mode. A pain flashed in my head and my wings numbed. I started to fall again.

The three kids watched. Their expressions were more curious than scared. No one helped or even screamed. I didn't know if they hated me because of Perry or because I was the princess and only half fairy. Or maybe they were afraid to help. They were new fliers.

Air rushed by me, no longer comforting. My wings wobbled like an old kite, completely useless. The ground was getting closer. My thoughts disappeared except for one: I wasn't going to die. I was going to be seriously injured.

Injured enough where I wouldn't be able to go with the peace delegation. I wouldn't be able to rescue Rye.

A scream built in my throat.

Chapter Nine

My speed downward stopped.

It was similar to hitting a hammock and slowly floating down. Arms wrapped around me. Bracken. My body tensed for a second and then relaxed because he'd saved me.

He tucked his wand away. "Are you okay?"

I didn't know how to respond. "Thank you." I felt nothing in his arms except gratefulness.

The other students flew closer, watching. The girls had a dreamy, longing expression while the boys seemed in awe, probably wishing they could be like Bracken when they were older. Why did fairies believe good looks were so important?

"Isn't this some traditional human marriage thing? Carrying one's beloved over a threshold." His joke shoved down my throat. His fancy suit had an obnoxiously bright print of leaves and branches today. Finely cut and fitting him perfectly.

Struggling, I wriggled, trying to get down. I could use my own wings. "Put me down."

With a twirl, he flew down and stood. He set me gently on my feet and took hold of my hand. Bowing, he kissed my hand. "Princess Ellery. There's an urgent matter needing your attention."

Lately, nothing ever needed my attention.

"I'm in flying class." I gritted the words because this was a beginner's class, and at my age, I should have been in more advanced classes. Gardenia had insisted I start from the bottom and advance. Which made sense. I didn't want to miss something important.

"Were going to be spending many days," and nights, as his father so indelicately put it, "together. Can't we talk then?"

"There might not be a *then*." He bent his head toward my ear and whispered, "The Grand Council is having a secret emergency meeting to discuss your joining the peace delegation."

"What?" I grabbed his arm and tugged him to the side of the large training ground. The vote wasn't supposed to happen until later today.

"There hasn't been a vote yet, and there have been...complaints that perhaps you're not prepared for the trip and you're too precious to travel to the human palace." He kissed my hand again. "I agree with the precious part."

His words meant nothing. "You don't think I'm capable of going on the trip?"

He winked, resembling his father. "I think you're able, willing, ready."

I crossed my arms and stared at his expression, wanting to see the truth on his face. "Then why did you say you thought I was precious?"

He pressed my hand against his chest. "I meant you are precious to me."

I yanked my hand away. "You don't even know me."

"I will." He pursed his lips and made this love-sick expression until his smile went flat. "We should get to the meeting now."

I gazed down at my warrior priestess outfit. The Grand Council would never approve. "Like this?"

"There's no time to change, not even with magic." He grabbed my hand and flicked his wand.

"But—"

The world turned like a kaleidoscope. It was comparable to being on a ferris wheel or a roller coaster after eating too much. My stomach churned and I lost my objection. My eyes glazed, making me feel dizzy. Realizing he was apparating and taking me with him, I squeezed his hand tighter. If I let go, who knows what would happen.

The one reason students weren't allowed to apparate inside Queens Academy was because we weren't experienced. Things could go wrong.

My feet hit the stone pavement outside the throne room's double doors. I wobbled and stuck my hand out to balance myself. My belly roiled and perspiration coated my back.

The double doors swung open and Bracken pulled me inside before I could tell him to give me a few minutes to compose myself. Between the warrior clothes and being dizzy, I felt unfocused and unconfident. Was Bracken trying to make me look bad in front of the council?

Except he'd told me about their current discussion and believed I needed to be there to defend myself. He'd also saved me from a disgraceful fall. I wouldn't be advancing to the next flying class any time soon.

The noblets of the Grand Council swiveled in their seats, startled at the interruption. Their expressions changed from surprised to disgusted when they realized it was me. Narrowed gazes and frowns lined the faces at the table. They peered at me expectantly.

The perspiration on my back chilled with the frigid reception. My roiling stomach cramped.

Bracken dropped my hand and slinked to a spot by his father. He might've told me about the meeting and voting, but was he going to help me?

My nerves buzzed and I bit my lower lip. "I'm sorry for interrupting. I've been informed you're discussing not allowing me to go with the peace delegation." Dizzy, I tried to focus my mind on the issue. The vote was supposed to take place this afternoon and I'd been planning to approach specific noblets to convince them to vote my way.

The Arch Noblet Oakton stood and narrowed his gaze. "Young lady, it's clear you are not a diplomat."

Squirming on the inside, I kept my body stiff. I refused to show him how uncomfortable he made me.

"You should stay here and be quiet and try to be pretty." His voice rose at the end, suggesting I wasn't pretty at all.

"And learn to fly." Bracken snickered quietly to his father.

Not quiet enough.

Whose side was he on? My brow furrowed and I thought back to flying class. I'd started to recover from the initial fall when a pain had shot through my head, causing me to lose focus. Had he caused the fall so he could rescue me? He told me about the meeting but left me floundering on my own. Was I a pawn to some unknown game he was playing?

I brushed off the insults and insecurities. How any of them thought I looked wasn't important. Gathering my courage, I stomped toward my throne chair. "I might not be the fairy vision of pretty. That doesn't matter. I'm smart and I'm cunning and I'd be an asset to the team."

Noblet Rainbowfly raised his hand. "I don't understand why we're discussing this again. She made her points very well yesterday. She's half human, is familiar with the city, and has been to the human palace."

I stood taller. At least he was solidly on my side. "I'm also royal and would bring importance to every meeting I attend."

"I'm practically royal." Bracken stood up so fast his chair flew backwards. "Of...of course, that's through you so your attendance will be critical."

What was going on with him? One second, he pedaled forward and the next back. Was he trying to help me or help make me appear a fool?

Taking an unnoticeable breath, I vowed to stay composed and diplomatic and royal. "Again, besides being the princess, I'm half human, which will be my greatest asset."

I could lie. I wouldn't point that out, although it would be an excellent reason for me to be involved in negotiations. Humans could lie to the fairies to make their positions stronger. Fairies did not have that advantage, although they could twist the truth very convincingly.

Sidestepping to stand beside Bracken, I forced myself to place my hand on his arm. "Again, traveling and working together will give Bracken and I a chance to get to know each other."

I wanted to puke, even though what I said was true. Although I did want to get to know him so I could figure out what game he was playing and stop the wedding at the end of the trip.

The females on the council looked moonfaced and sappy at my declaration. The men nodded with approval. Playing the falling-in-love card might work.

Bracken tucked my hand under his arm. Our stance mimicked a walk down the aisle. "I'd be thrilled to have Princess Ellery on my arm."

As if I was a decoration.

"And her title and her half human side..."

Did he wince slightly?

"...will give us a distinct advantage."

I didn't care if he did wince. He argued for me.

"She won't actually be part of the important negotiations." He dug himself a deeper hole on the wrong side of me. "And as her fiancé, I will be able to protect her by always being at her side."

Raising a brow, my gaze ran down his short stature and thin frame. The glitzy and decorative sword hanging at his side had a dull blade that probably couldn't cut melted ice cream. If there was trouble, I'd be the one protecting him.

"Let's take the final ballot." Bracken's father held his wand up.

Everyone else put their wands up, including Bracken. I held my wand up.

"You don't get a vote." *The* Arch Noblet Oakton's lips distorted in a sneer.

I strangled my wand, picturing his neck. The man didn't say anything about his son having his wand up and voting when Bracken wasn't on the council either.

"Does the queen get a vote?" Although she might not be onboard with me traveling to the human palace. As her heir, it might be dangerous and she knew my feelings for Rye.

"The queen is not present and she will approve our decision."

I let Oakton get away with the call.

White sparks shot from one wand and then the next.

Holding my breath, tension threaded through my body. I didn't know what the white meant.

The white sparks continued down the line until every wand but mine flared white. Either everyone voted yes, or everyone voted no.

Bracken's father held his wand higher. "Let the record show the vote was unanimous to allow Princess Ellery to travel with Bracken Oakton and his peace negotiation team to the human palace."

Euphoria spiraled inside me, counteracting the dizziness. I was going to Reximus Palace. Rye's home, and I bet, current prison. I'd been given the opportunity to find him.

⤛⤜

That night, I couldn't sleep. My bags were packed, and I'd made arrangements with my professors to study while I was gone. Even so, I tossed and turned in my bed with my thoughts churning. What if Bracken purposely put us in a compromising position to get caught? I guess for princesses, propriety was still a thing. He wanted to marry me not for love, but for power.

Anxiety bubbled in my stomach. I wanted to start this trip as soon as possible. I wished we could leave right now in the middle of the night. I'd done that before.

The sooner we got to the human palace the sooner I could find Rye.

Thinking Bracken might screw up the peace negotiations drilled into deep worry. He didn't understand how dangerous Regent Theobald was. And why were the fairies willing to give up the Divinity Orb?

A knock sounded at my door.

"Come in." Sitting up in bed, I expected Arbor or Gardenia.

Watu entered carrying a tray. She wore the same old cotton shift she'd worn in her cave, even though I'd offered her silk. "My tea for you."

My eyes drifted closed. The mention of her tea made me sleepy. "I'm not injured."

I remembered the wild dreams the tea had given me when she'd made me drink it after being attacked by dragons.

"Sleeping trouble you are having." She moved quietly for someone with such large feet.

Backing up further on the bed, I made room for the tray and her. I didn't question how she knew I couldn't sleep. She tended to know things. "Yes. What's in the tea?"

"My own special ingredients." Her sharp-toothed grin should've been scary, except I knew her too well. "Help you sleep, dream."

I shook my head. "I don't need any crazy dreams. I have enough crazy thoughts."

"Yes." She sat on the edge of my bed, calm and listening.

"I'm afraid if I go on this trip, I'll be forced to marry Bracken." My chest ached and felt full at the same time. I wanted to burst with my thoughts and contradictions. "Even though I know it will help with my fairy reputation, I don't love Bracken. I don't trust him." I sniffed as the loneliness of a loveless marriage hit me, especially when I loved someone else. "I love Rye and I never told him. I have to go on this trip so I can find him."

"Missing the young human prince is."

Stated as fact, my fear for him spiked.

"The Divinity Orb isn't communicating with Rye anymore." I quickly explained how the head priestess had given a replica orb to Rye. "I'm worried he's injured...or worse. I have to rescue him or...or..."

My heart pounded, echoing in my head. My imagination was running through various horrible scenarios of what happened to Rye. I definitely did not want to drink the tea and have pictures in my head of those same scenarios. One dream I'd had during my healing had been Rye being dragged to a tower. Now, I wondered if the dream was a prediction and could be happening right now.

She handed me the tea. "Representing all majiks, you are. Not just fairies."

I gritted my teeth. "If they even allow me to speak in the meeting."

Watu smiled in a strange, knowing way. "Maybe saving your prince will save everyone."

Chapter Ten

Morning finally broke and the castle bustled with servants and courtiers rushing about. Luggage and boxes were shifted and transported both by the fairies and magically. Talking, shouting, and clattering filled the hallways. My stomach jumped and twirled with more anxiety than excitement. I couldn't wait to be on the way but I worried about Bracken and his planned policies and antics.

Watu and I strolled into the courtyard where the podships awaited and clear blue skies greeted me. The podships in the front and back appeared similar to other podships transporting large amounts of troops or goods. I'd ridden in a smaller version when we'd left for the mission to Aristos Sanctuary.

The transport in the middle wasn't a podship. A rounded carriage floated off the ground. Brown and black decorative curlicues coiled around the carriage, resembling dead vines wrapped around a column. A man in Bracken's livery colors sat on the outside bench seat with a wand in one hand and a whip in the other. Attached to the front of the carriage, a single dragon pawed at the ground.

A Wyvern dragon.

The dragon's mouth was harnessed, smashing its jaws tightly closed so it couldn't shoot fire, eat, or breathe through its mouth. Horror yanked my lips. The harness doubled as a torture instrument.

"Elves' bells." I shuddered, watching the dragon struggle to take in air through flared nostrils in its large orange snout. "What is that? Why is the dragon tied up?"

Bracken sauntered to my side wearing leather riding breeches. Did he plan to ride a horse or the dragon? "Do you like the carriage? It's an Oakton family heirloom sure to impress the regent."

Of course, I didn't like it. I hated it. He didn't want to hear my real opinion. "The dragon isn't really going to pull the carriage, is he?"

While I'd almost been killed by a dragon, I'd also been saved by one. The huge dragon pulling the carriage was not my young friend. Thank Mother Earth.

"We've used magic to train them." Bracken's boast gave the impression he'd personally done the work. I doubted it. He'd had a pretty easy upbringing and wasn't the type to work hard. "The lead trainer keeps the dragon in line."

Tortured him.

"Your luggage has been loaded and I've added a couple of extra things." His pleased-with-himself smile didn't please me.

Frowning, I doubted I'd enjoy his surprises. "What kind of extra things?"

"Oh, you know. Normal things a fiancé would give his princess." He held out his hand. "Let me take the heavy bag you're holding."

"Watu will take it." Signaling at her to come over, I handed her the bag. The bag held the Divinity Orb, and she was the only one I'd trust with it. The reason I'd agreed to bring the orb was because I hoped it would help me find Rye. No way was I giving it to the regent.

Bracken's nose crinkled when he glowered at Watu. "It's good of her to see us off."

She arched her bushy brows, realizing I hadn't told him about her coming along. Her slight frown demonstrated disappointment. I rolled my shoulders. I hadn't wanted to fight with him about her presence and if he didn't know he couldn't say anything to stop me. With a final scowl, she climbed into the carriage.

"Watu is my advisor and is coming as my ladies' maid." I forced myself to sound pleasant, not combative. "And my chaperone."

His red eyebrows flew upward into a shocked arch and his chin dropped. I held in a laugh, expecting his reaction. He tugged my arm and pulled me closer to the front of the carriage by the dragon.

The acrid smell of burnt embers choked me. The huge dragon's scales glimmered in the sunlight. Getting closer, I saw the dragon's large pointed teeth were bigger than my fists. Its fire-red gaze glistened, probably embarrassed tears. I hated how such a grand animal was being treated as a domestic donkey. I wanted to stroke his shiny scales and show him love.

The trainer cast back his whip and lashed the dragon's back. I jerked. The dragon screeched and reared. The trainer lashed again.

The slashing noise sliced through my ears. I cringed, trying not to yell at the trainer. In the future, I'd outlaw this type of treatment.

"I don't think the regent will appreciate a troll in his palace." Bracken ignored the treatment of the dragon, still stuck on Watu.

"It's Prince Zacharye's palace." I hoped.

"I'm negotiating with the regent."

"Why?"

Angling his head, Bracken studied me and frowned when he spotted breeches and boots under the full skirt. "The regent is the leader of the kingdom."

"He shouldn't be. Prince Zacharye is the next in line and he's old enough to rule."

"Don't share your sentiment around the regent." Bracken reeled away and ordered people about, not giving me the opportunity to respond with the reasons why Rye should be in charge.

The castle guards flew into formation around the three vehicles. The black and brown liveried servants finished carting luggage into the back podship and climbed inside. The brownie, Tagh, was one of the last to enter.

"Princess Ellery." A female castle guard bowed in front of me, dipping her wings in a perfect salute. "I'm Captain Clover and the head castle guard escorting the podships."

"Nice to meet you and I'm sure you will keep us safe."

"There will be four guards in front and four in the rear. We have two guards rotating between the two groups, and two guards, myself included, taking position by the Oakton Family carriage." Clover's short stature was made up by her muscular build. Her long, flowing brown hair reached her waist. "The guards will be staying in the human guard quarters. Because we're fairies, the regent is not allowing us inside the palace."

Concern threaded through me and pulled tight. Another way the regent was controlling negotiations from the start. "What about protection for the negotiators?"

We had magic, but the regent had instruments of torture and magic suppression systems.

She smiled with a twist to her lips. "I hear you can protect yourself with weapons and magic."

My hand glided across the spot where the Silver Snare hid beneath my skirt and patted my head where my dagger acted as a hair ornament. I'd been told it wasn't princess-like for me to carry weapons, but I'd been in too many tight places and knew I should be prepared. "Where did you hear that?"

"A friend of mine, who when he left, told me to keep an eye out for his important friend."

The coded message was simple to figure out. She was a friend of Stone's and he'd told her to watch out for me.

I leaned closer, caution giving way to concern. "Have you heard from our mutual friend?"

"No." Her raw voice scraped against my nerves, doubling my concern.

"Princess Ellery." Bracken didn't acknowledge the captain. He treated her similar to how he treated his servants. "Let's not dawdle."

As if I was the one holding us up. He'd gone off to yell at his servants about his multiple pieces of luggage, reminding me of the night we'd first met when he'd hit Tagh.

Bracken helped me into the carriage.

Inside the carriage, two cushioned bench seats were placed across from each other. A table, which probably had been used to hold food and drinks, now had technical equipment installed, including radar. It was a mix of old tech and even older luxury, combining fairy grandness with human tech. Where had he gotten the equipment?

"Does she need to travel in the carriage with us?" Frowning, he glared at Watu sitting on one of two bench seats.

"Watu is my chaperone. I wouldn't want anyone getting the wrong idea." Arranging my skirt over the breeches, I went to sit next to her.

"Sit here, facing forward." He spun me around so I landed on the second cushioned bench seat and he sat down next to me. Swishing his wand, he must've given a magical signal because the carriage lurched into the sky.

Taking a deep breath, I appreciated I was finally on the way. I'd begged and cajoled to go on this trip, and I was in charge of finding what I wanted most: Rye.

Sitting on the edge of my seat, the silence oppressed my excited mood. I didn't know what to talk about with Bracken and anything I'd want to talk about with Watu, I wouldn't say in front of him. He sat back with his arm spread out behind my back. His legs were crossed, and he jiggled his foot with nervous, annoying energy.

Watu barely moved. She didn't want to be noticed. I felt bad for dragging her with me, but she was one of few I trusted.

Searching for a topic, I asked, "How close will we fly to the dome?"

The dome had hidden the Kingdom of Alandaska since Concealment Day, protecting us from the rest of the world's troubles. The kingdom had enough troubles of our own. At least, right now.

"Not close at all." Bracken's sharp tone told me he thought my question stupid. "Why?"

"Someone once told me there were cracks in the dome." The information had come from Bee the betrayer. I couldn't believe anything she'd said.

He chuckled and then stopped short. "Humans have the funniest notions."

A knock thumped against the carriage door.

He slid open the curtain and pressed a button for the window to go down. "What do you want?"

Captain Clover flew right outside the door. There was no reason to be rude to her.

I tilted forward. "Hello Captain Clover."

"Princess Ellery." She bowed with her head. "We're flying over a beautiful part of the Daska River and I wondered if you'd like to stretch your wings."

I glanced at Watu to make sure she was okay with me leaving for a few minutes and when she nodded, I said, "I'd love to."

"What? No." Bracken's sternness made me want to escape even more. "You can't fly out there alone."

"I won't be alone. I'll be with Captain Clover." Sliding the dagger out of my formal bun, I slipped it to Watu beneath our full skirts. He didn't need to know about my weapons.

"You're a princess." His flabbergasted objection caused me to beam.

"Correct. I'm a fairy princess. I have wings." I shifted to the door and opened it. "I can fly."

"Can you?" The sarcastic comment didn't ruffle my feathers. He could make fun of the one fall if he wanted. "Captain, keep Princess Ellery safe or it will be your life."

His threat strangled my joy at flying. "I'll be fine. Why don't you fly with us?" I didn't really want to invite him. But I needed to stay on his good side in order to convince him I should take part in the actual negotiations.

"No, thank you." He spoke as if flying was beneath him. He'd rather have a dragon pull him around.

Or maybe when you've had wings your entire life it wasn't as exciting. "Okay. You can keep Watu company."

His expression darkened.

Giggling, I flew off, enjoying the unconstrained freedom for the first time in days. Maybe if I annoyed him enough, he wouldn't want to marry me.

Smirking, Captain Clover flew beside me. "Are you sure Watu will be safe alone with him?"

"Watu can take care of herself." I'd seen her toughness in action.

"Then, let's fly." The captain flew higher and I followed.

The wind caressed my wings and stroked my face. Strands of hair tugged out of the elegant bun and I didn't care that I didn't look perfect. I loved flying.

The deep green forest where Queens Academy had hid for centuries thinned out near a river winding down from the hills. To our far right was Alandfjell, the mountain range where the city of Lindenhamn and the palace were located. The mountains rose high and almost grazed the invisible dome we'd just discussed. The dome had been erected using a combination of tech and magic in a time when humans and majiks worked together.

"This way." Captain Clover veered left. She pointed at the river and flew around a bend.

The river dropped into a beautiful lake with varying shades of blue from turquoise to sky to midnight. Tall trees surrounded the lake, sentinels guarding nature. They must have been some of the oldest surviving trees in the kingdom and I sensed their strong energy reaching out to me.

"Amazing."

"The reason I asked you to fly at this point in the journey." She pointed to an open field. "We'll take a break there for lunch before edging around Alandfjell and landing at Reximus Palace."

We circled back and trailed the podships as they landed in the field. The two of us landed right after them.

Bracken jumped out of the carriage and hurried to us. "Flying is dangerous and inappropriate for a princess." He must have thought of more reasons why I shouldn't fly while he'd been cooped up in the carriage.

His assaulting words pounded against my head. He berated and belittled my choices, an emotional abuse I'd have to tame or endure if we married.

"I was perfectly safe."

"You'll ride in the carriage for our arrival at Reximus Palace." He stomped off before I could respond, going to yell at someone else probably.

This argument was less about safety and more about controlling me. If we married, he'd try to manipulate and master everything I did or said.

After eating a light lunch, I used the facilities the guards created magically and tried to do something with my messy hair. Watu had given me my dagger back and it flopped in the inelegant bun I created. I wished Arbor were here to style the tangled strands and to give Bracken a piece of her mind, except she seemed infatuated by the man.

Whistles split the air, which meant we were getting ready to depart. Another step closer to finding Rye.

Hurrying back to the carriage, Tagh tugged on my long skirt. He bowed. "Princess Ellery."

"Hello, Tagh." I smiled at the brownie. "I heard you got a couple of days off. I'm glad you're traveling with us."

He angled his tiny head and his thin brows gathered. "I need to tell—"

"Princess Ellery, we're on a tight schedule." Bracken hurried to my side and glared at his servant.

Tagh lowered his head and backed away.

"We'll talk later." Frowning, I hated how he acted beaten and I planned to seek him out once we arrived to discover the real situation.

With Bracken behind me, I climbed into the carriage and then stopped. "Where's Watu?"

He slammed the carriage door. His smarmy expression told me he was up to something. "She's riding in the back podship with the servants."

My pulse galloped. "She's not a serv—"

The carriage jerked upward, and I slammed onto the cushioned seat next to Bracken. He was too close.

Nerves jittered in my stomach and swished across my skin. I shifted away from him. The uncomfortable silence dragged. I pressed my palms into the seat cushion. Emotions from previous occupants swamped me. Fear and terror, disdain and greed, and the overall emotion of superiority. I'd been distracted during the earlier part of the trip and hadn't used my hands to touch the seat. Now, one of my unusual powers walloped inside of me. I sensed the emotions of the multiple fairies who'd at one time sat in the carriage.

I yanked my palms off the seat and rubbed them together. I knew the superiority had come from the current occupant and his father. What had triggered the other emotions? What had happened in this carriage?

"Are you okay?" A strange tension radiated from Bracken. He let his arm move from the seat and drop onto my shoulders.

"I'm fine." I didn't plan to tell him about this power and had nothing else to say. Twisting, I let his arm fall and peered out the window.

The edges of the city were below, and I pressed my nose against the window, trying to spot familiar places. A warren of narrow streets with dilapidated buildings seemed familiar, although I knew I'd never been this far west of the city. Larger homes dotted the hillsides leading up to the palace. Would we fly by my old home, Milford House?

Bracken's front pressed against me as he angled closer. I shuddered, trapped. His torso pressed against my back while one arm was stationed on the back of the chair and the other planted on the windowsill. My breathing stalled and I blew out short puffs.

Trying to hold onto my dignity and not give in to the panic, I shifted further into the cushion. "What're you doing?"

His arms barred escape. "We should have our first kiss seeing as we're engaged."

My lungs deflated. Between my whip and dagger, I could easily gullet this guy. That wouldn't help the perfect princess act or trying to prove I wasn't a threat. "We're not engaged."

"My father has the contract signed, sealed, and delivered." His face moved closer to mine.

His puffy, dry lips had tiny cracks in them. *Bleck.* He planted his mouth on mine and his lips lugged against my mouth, the dry cracks rubbing like sandpaper. Repulsion ricocheted from my mouth to my heart. I'd kissed two guys before and both had meant something to me. Rye's kiss had curled into me and ignited a connection I hadn't experienced since. Stone's kiss had been between friends.

Bracken's hands mauled my body, trying to scar every inch of my skin. Thank the priestesses the dress material was heavy and covered most of my body.

Placing my hands on his chest, I shoved him away. I could never tolerate his sweaty caress. I didn't want to make him angry either. "Stop. We shouldn't. I don't have a chaperone."

I hoped pleading innocence bought me time.

"The point of getting rid of the troll." He pounced again and I turned my head. His mouth puckered against my forehead.

He was prejudiced against other majiks. I should've known by the way he treated Tagh. I'd been trying to give Bracken the benefit of the doubt. My repulsion doubled and ended in another shudder.

He yanked up the skirt of my dress and his hand slid up my leg covered by breeches.

The air strangled in my throat. His nails scratched sending frozen shivers of disgust straight to my heart. I should grab my dagger and slice his hand off. How would I explain the injury to the others?

My belly dropped.

No, my entire body dropped. And Bracken's.

The carriage was falling from the sky.

"Ahhhh!" Bracken screamed and released his hold on me.

The carriage careened out of control. The wind roared. An intense heat infiltrated the small cabin.

Or was I sweating from fear?

The heat and the acrid smell reminded me of the forest fire I'd set raging out of control. This was much worse. Closer, more cloying.

The door to the carriage ripped open and Captain Clover held out her hand. "Get out of the transport vehicle. We need to get you away."

"What's happening?"

"Dragon attack!"

Chapter Eleven

My feet were rooted to the carriage floor and my mind flashed back to when I was attacked by a dragon. Oxygen swooshed out of my lungs. The dragon had picked me up by digging its claws into my shoulders. I'd bobbed from his claws until he'd smashed me into the side of the mountain and left me for dead.

Watu had found and healed me.

I didn't want to experience the puncturing pain again. We should stay in the carriage. The vehicle would protect us from the claws and the flames and the putrid breath. Before I could speak, Bracken yanked open the other door and dove out, not even considering or helping me.

My mouth dropped open. So much for him being my hero. Had my fall in flying class been on purpose? Staged?

The dangling door ripped off from the force of the falling carriage.

Leaning forward, I peeked out to see how much further I had to fall. Trees and bushes and grass appeared so close I could see the insects. The ground seemed to be meeting me halfway. My pulse kicked into high gear. There wasn't much time left or I'd be smashed to pieces with the carriage. The front end of the carriage was higher and two new dragons surrounded the original one.

One of the new dragons let out a stream of hot flames, melting the harness attaching the original dragon to the carriage. The second new dragon gripped the metal between its sharp teeth and chomped.

They were trying to free the enslaved dragon.

This wasn't a dragon attack. It was a dragon rescue.

The smaller of the two dragons turned its head, noticing me. Its bright red eyes peered at me, fascinated.

I leaned further out the carriage door. "Drago?"

His head raised and he continued to stare.

The second dragon roared and sent fire in my direction.

I shrank back into the carriage. No time to worry whether the one dragon was my old friend. I had to get out now. Grabbing my bag, I took a flying leap and jumped from the carriage. I hoped the dragons wouldn't follow.

Clouds of dark smoke swirled around. The heavy smell suffocated, and I coughed. I kept flying further away.

"Princess Ellery!" Captain Clover's shout reached me through the darkness. "This way."

I followed her voice and emerged from the dark cloud. Sucking in clean air, I checked behind to make sure none of the dragons followed. They hadn't. Twisting around, I wanted confirmation that Drago was alive and safe.

"Thanks for finding me." I flew toward the captain. Someone had cared enough to wait. And it wasn't Bracken.

"It was my honor." Angling her head, she grinned. "You did fine on your own."

Except for the part where I'd panicked and froze, thinking about another time and another dragon.

She flew toward a large park where the two podships had landed. So had Bracken. Now I was glad Watu had been in one of the podships and not the carriage. She couldn't fly and I didn't know if I could've carried her. Bracken would've been no help.

Clover and I circled in the sky.

The harnessed dragon broke away from the falling carriage and flew upwards, its wings spreading wide, and circled around its saviors. The other dragons roared and shot flames upward in celebration.

My smile bloomed. The dragons' joy twirled inside of me. The harnessed dragon was free and back with its friends.

The carriage broke away and crashed to the ground, smashing into pieces. An iron wheel broke off and rolled free, another wheel bent in half. The glass windows shattered, and the ugly black and brown vines charred with the fire the dragons had set.

The three dragons flew upwards and kept flying further and further until they were spots in the sky. If we hadn't used the historic carriage pulled by a dragon, we never would've been attacked.

Clover and I flew to where the two podships were located and we landed.

Watu rushed forward and hugged me. "Worried about you I was."

"Is everyone okay?" I stopped a guard. "Anyone injured?"

"No, Princess Ellery." The guard bowed. "The podships landed without harm. The carriage driver flew away. Only you and Nobletive Bracken were in danger."

My spirits plummeted. Ever since finding out I was a princess, there'd been danger. Actually, even before the discovery, there had been danger. "Where is Bracken?"

"Over there." Watu pointed to him flying over the wreckage of the carriage.

While flying, he fisted his hand and waved it around. He shouted something I couldn't hear and probably didn't want to. He threw up his hands in disgust and zoomed forward, landing near me. "Bloody fungus! Those stupid dragons attacked my family's antique carriage."

He was more upset about the carriage than my welfare and for some reason, that didn't upset me. It proved his priorities.

"I did point out the flight plan took us close to a dragon habitat." Captain Clover's expression stayed blank. "The dragons are family-orientated and will save each other."

Anger crackled in my veins. He'd known the danger and gone ahead with the plan.

"It's ruined!" he shouted in the captain's face. "Your job was to keep me safe."

Stepping closer to Clover, I tried to insert myself between them. I'd seen how he treated majiks who worked for him. Defending herself, she'd risk her position.

Her lips smushed together, holding in a smirk. "And you're standing here. Safe."

"No, thanks to you." He stomped around, getting out of her face. "I flew out of the falling carriage myself."

And didn't worry about me.

"Bracken." The tone I used would've been appropriate for chastising a small child. "Everyone is safe. That's what matters."

His nose scrunched and his lips sneered. It was an ugly expression, and it ruined his devastating handsomeness. If his admirers could only see him this way. "My father is going to kill me. He was so proud of the carriage."

It was too bad his father would think a carriage more important than his son. Having met his father, I understood Bracken's fear. Maybe that was the reason why he was such a jerk. "I'm sure your father will be glad you're alive and everyone else is okay."

Then again, his father had sold him on a loveless marriage to gain power.

He twisted his lips in disbelief and confusion. Smoothing each perfect proportion into place, he said, "Of course, Father would."

"As leader of the delegation, you should double check everyone is okay and make plans to continue on." I'd already done the first part, but it would make Bracken appear more of a leader and get his mind off his loss. Although why I was helping him, I didn't know. Mostly, I wanted to continue to Reximus Palace.

"Fine." He pivoted and stomped back toward the majiks gathered around the two podships. He yelled useless orders like *everyone get back on the podship*.

That's not what I'd meant. He sounded abusive, not like a leader.

"I'll need to let my father know about the carriage." He whipped his wand around, writing his message in the sky. The message would travel to the appropriate destination. "He'll send someone to see if the historical artifact can be repaired."

Curling my lip, I couldn't stay quiet. "The carriage was cruel to dragons. You should bury it."

He paused in writing his message and his entire body stiffened. He whirled around and stalked toward me. His eyes flashed, resembling a thundercloud. His nose flared and he raised his hand to strike me.

I leaned back and reached for my whip. If he tried to hit me, I'd stop him with the Silver Snare. I'd done it the night we met.

As if realizing what he was about to do, he pulled his hand down to the side and trundled away from me. He shouted at everyone else again, taking his frustration out on them.

The getting-to-know-my-fiancé excuse for joining the delegation had the opposite effect of what the noblets wanted. I despised Bracken more.

Everyone filed into the two podships and he insisted we fly together in the front vehicle with the other negotiators and senior guards. Watu was designated to the back podship. Since the flight wasn't long and there'd be others in the front podship, I let it go.

The podship sat about two dozen. Large enough for an entire army troop. Two nicely dressed fairies sat up front, playing an electronic game. A handful of castle guards sat in the center podship. And a few similarly dressed fairies, which had to be servants for the two well-dressed fairies, lingered in the back.

"Go further back." Bracken shoved a fairy wearing a fancy suit. "The princess and I will need the entire front row."

"Why?"

He ignored my question and shooshed the two males back. Were they his negotiating team? Why would he treat his partners as lesser? He hadn't even introduced me. He dropped into the middle seat and patted the one next to him. Why push everyone away if we were going to sit next to each other?

"I'd enjoy looking out the window." I chose the chair against the window of the podship.

The podship lifted smoothly and jetted forward. Much faster than our original pace. The carriage must've slowed the entire caravan down. Another reason for hating the atrocious vehicle. I was glad it was ruined.

The park we took off from was near my old home and the central part of the city. I peered out, desperate to get a glimpse of Milford House. A red roof sloping a specific way caught my attention and I bit my lip. We traveled too fast for me to confirm if it was my old home. The home I'd given up to stay in the fairy world.

Domescrapers stretched toward the kingdom's dome filled with hi-tech companies, modern-apartment living, and fancy stores and restaurants. The view of the city from above was amazing. I wished I'd had wings when I'd lived here, except by the regent's decrees I wouldn't have been allowed to live here. Or fly.

So much had changed since Regent Theobald took charge. First prejudice against majiks, then fear, then restrictive laws, and now civil war.

Bracken scooted over to peer out the window. "What's that?"

He pointed to the moving sidewalk weaving throughout the central part of the city between the tall buildings.

"It's the skywalk. It transports people from one part of the city to the other."

He tilted his head in confusion, as if he didn't understand why the city would need such a thing.

"Humans can't fly." I wanted to add a *duh* but held myself back.

"The reason it's called a sky*walk*." Nodding, a satisfied smirk landed on his face. "What's that?"

He pointed to a large, squat building with a pointed roof. His awe and fascination were obvious by his wide-eyed expression.

"It's the mall. A place filled with shops and restaurants humans go to buy things and socialize." I'd tried to buy a dress for Rye's Presentation Ball there.

Tall glass spires reached into the sky and I remembered my dream about Rye being imprisoned in a tower. "There's Reximus Palace."

Bracken pushed in closer, blocking my view. That was okay. I'd seen the palace before.

I leaned back in my seat, remembering the first time I'd arrived here. I'd been late for Prince Zacharye's Presentation Ball and traveled in a podship Gardenia had made from an ugly orange chair. Terrified of being discovered, I'd barely been able to climb the grand stairs leading to the palace doors. I wasn't at the ball to dance. I was there to save Arbor and assassinate the prince. I'd fallen in love with him instead. My heart bumped. And now, I was desperate to find out what had happened to him. My stomach churned and my ribcage squeezed as we flew closer to the palace. I had to find Rye.

We landed in the grand front courtyard, like I had nine long months ago. Instead of a line of humans dressed in fancy ball attire, the crowd greeting us were uniformed SCUM. Their hard expressions and stiff stances told me this wasn't a welcome party. They were an intimidation team.

Standing, I straightened my dress and made sure the dagger in my hair displayed just the decorative handle.

"We should come out last as befitting our station." Chiding me, Bracken tugged on my arm to hold me back. "It's a negotiating tactic. Make them wait."

I fisted my hands, trying to control my frustration. The humans waiting for us outside were not important to the negotiations. Plus, I wanted to run straight into the palace and find Rye. I tapped my foot.

After everyone in our podship shuffled by, Bracken peeked out the window. "Everyone is gathered below. Let's go." He held out his arm for me and I reluctantly slipped my hand through.

After ducking under the podship doorway, I stood next to him at the stop of the stairs. He held me tight. Did he understand I wanted to hurry? Or was it fear?

Right below the podship stairs, our group gathered like cattle, fairy guards and castle servants, Bracken's liveried servants including Tagh, and Watu. They were scared with pale faces, hugging themselves or standing completely motionless. The SCUM surrounded them with their anti-magic weapons pointed at the group.

This was not the greeting I'd expected, and yet I shouldn't have been surprised. I wasn't involved in setting up this meeting and from what I learned about Bracken during our day of travel, he probably didn't worry about details such as the safety and security of our delegation.

"I'm Nobletive Bracken Oakton, son of The Arch Noblet Oakton, and leader of the fairy negotiation team." Bracken used a broadcast spell to make his voice loud. He let go of my arm and flew into the sky.

Multiple weapons clicked and pointed toward him and me.

I froze. Didn't Bracken realize his action would be considered combative by the trigger-happy SCUM? He probably didn't know what the acronym stood for. I did: Security Collectors of Unique Magic. The acronym was more accurate. They marched to the regent's orders. They enforced and arrested majiks based on even a suspicion of not following the new decrees. They hated majiks.

"Land with your hands raised." One guard used a bullhorn with advanced options that squeaked in a high pitch, hurting my ears with splitting pain.

I cringed and my shoulders lifted, trying to protect my ears. I was afraid to use my hands to cover them in case it was construed as an aggressive act.

Bracken fluttered his wings. "I'm the leader of the fairy negotiation team. Do not point your weapons at me."

"Land with your hands raised."

Bracken lifted his hands up and landed in front of the guard who'd spoken. So much for negotiation tactics. He'd disclosed how affable fairies were. Well, I wasn't. I'd keep the information to myself for now.

Another guard patted down Bracken for weapons and took his decorative sword.

He blustered. "Now see here—"

"Listen up, fairies. My guards will search each of you for weapons and wands before you enter the palace." The lead guard's fierce expression matched the darkness of his uniform. The hat with the broad bill shadowed his face.

My gaze darted to my waistline where the Silver Snare hid beneath my skirt and my head itched at the spot where the dagger poked through my hair. I hoped the guards wouldn't find them. Dressed as a princess, they'd probably assume I didn't carry weapons. Many fairies didn't because they had magic. Most didn't know the humans had technology to take away our powers as well.

"Negotiators," the guard shot a smirk at Bracken, "and servants will be taken round to the back entrance."

My muscles tensed. I knew what the back entrance meant. It was the place where majiks were taken to the dungeon never to be seen again.

"The fairy guards will be taken to the army barracks for the duration of your stay."

I gaped at Bracken, our supposed leader. He said nothing, not disagreeing with this peon in the army. I knew the rankings of the human guards and I knew processing us in this way could be a tactic of the regent. Or pure prejudice. Either way, I wasn't going to put up with this treatment.

"Excuse me, private?" With tight lips, I addressed him with the lowest rank. "Perhaps you were misinformed by your general." I continued down the stairs at a slow, regal pace. "I am Princess Ellery."

His eyes widened. Did he recognize my name?

"Myself, Nobletive Bracken Oakton, my chaperone Watu, and the other negotiators will be entering through the front entrance as is befitting our station."

I didn't let him speak.

"Our servants will be coming with to assist us."

"The regent—"

"Where is Regent Theobald and Prince Zacharye?" I used the demanding voice I'd learned from my human stepmother. Hard to believe she was the one helping me now. "Well?"

"I'm sorry, miss—"

"*Princess* Ellery."

"Yes, Princess Ellery." The guard half bowed. "The regent said we needed to check for weapons and wands and mist you with a Magic Blocking Fixatif in the tunnel."

I knew what he was talking about. I'd been sprayed with it before.

Bracken paled and wilted in stature. Did he expect the regent to trust him not to use magic on him? With Bracken as our lead negotiator, the majiks were in trouble.

Nodding, I lifted my hand to let them check me for weapons. "And what about your weapons?"

"Excuse me?" the guard sputtered.

"Really? Who is in charge here?" I used a droll tone to push my point. "We've been traveling all day, had a slight accident with one of our transports, and we're treated like criminals on our arrival. Not an auspicious beginning to peace negotiations."

The guard stood there and said nothing.

"We are leaving." My muscles tightened with my pivot. Leaving would be one of the hardest things.

"What?" Bracken's jaw dropped.

I'd wanted the guard to call my bluff, not him. "This will go down in history as the shortest negotiation ever."

"Wait, wait." The head guard held up his hand. "I received a comm. Regent Theobald is on his way to greet you in the throne room."

My body relaxed. Spinning back around, I grimaced. "About time."

"Wonderful." Bracken's expression became animated. "I'll gather the delegation members for introductions."

Closing my eyes for a second, I hoped for patience. He pandered to the humans and regent again, admiring them.

"You'll have to turn in your wands and weapons and go through the magic block tunnel before greeting the regent." The guard pointed to the machine in a tunnel shape.

This must be some new demeaning device. I'd been sprayed with Magic Blocking Fixatif from a weapon, but not through a tunnel. It didn't hurt. The guard's insistence on the point annoyed me. I knew I could only push so far. I'd gone for sixteen years without magic and I could handle being without it for a few days. I'd been trained with weapons and spying, thanks to Watu and Stone, and I could handle myself.

Bracken, I wasn't so sure about.

He lined up his two male delegates behind him and they handed over their wands. Identical to Bracken in dress and demeanor—young, spoiled fairies who'd been taken care of by their rich parents. One sported a goatee and both had long, flowing blond hair. They resembled fashion models more than serious negotiators.

He'd never introduced them to me. Either they weren't deemed important enough or I wasn't.

Scrutinizing the machine, he shifted to acknowledge me. "Ladies first."

Ha. He was afraid of going through the mister and was willing to sacrifice me. No surprise.

I held out my wand to the guard. My mother's wand. My fingers automatically wrapped tighter around it. "Don't lose this." Putting a threat in my voice, I slapped it into the guard's hand.

He jumped.

Shaking my head, I stepped in front of him and into the machine. I knew this wouldn't hurt. If it was similar to the spray, it was more degrading than painful. The machine dampened a majiks' magic. It was nothing like the auraguillotine the regent had constructed in the palace dungeon, which sucked out powers permanently.

The machine turned on and misters shot from tiny holes throughout the arch. The mist smelled of chemicals and cold. The opposite of the natural scents fairies were associated with.

Emerging on the other side, I tapped my foot while Bracken, the other two negotiators, and even Watu were forced to walk through. She didn't even have magic. Humans didn't understand majiks even though they were engaged in a war against us.

"This way." The head guard bowed to me and led us up the grand staircase.

I was tempted to fly. It was more important not to display the abilities they hadn't taken away.

"I wish we'd had time to clean up before meeting Regent Theobald." Bracken's excited tone rubbed against my nerves.

The regent wasn't important. Rye was.

As we waited for the grand doors to open, I waved for Watu to join me up front.

There was no DNA detector at the door. I guess the humans knew what we all were. Or did they? Did they know I was half human? Had Bracken informed the regent ahead of time or could I use my half human status for leverage? From what I'd seen, Bracken had charm and little negotiation skills. I hoped one of the other negotiators took the lead because I planned to be absent so I could sneak around the palace while the regent was busy.

The room didn't seem as massive as it had the first time I stepped inside. The actual size hadn't changed, which meant I had. Confidence made me stronger. I now lived in a castle and would be the future ruler of the fairies. I wasn't a servant girl trying to hide from my stepmother and stepsisters.

Rows of Roman-inspired columns reached up to the frescoed ceiling. Not as nice as the open-air experience of Queens Academy's ballroom. We ambled toward a large raised area where a single velvet and gold chair sat. I heaved a breath. Last time, I was here there were two chairs: one for the regent and one for the prince.

Bracken and his friends pushed ahead, wanting to meet the regent first. If only they knew I'd already met the evil man.

My heart stopped while my pulsed raced forward. I'd met Regent Theobald when I'd been blowing up the auraguillotine. I hadn't expected him to be involved in the day-to-day negotiations.

Would he recognize me?

Chapter Twelve

My muscles tensed and I tried to exhale and inhale slow and calm. If Regent Theobald remembered who I was and what I'd done, I'd be back in the dungeon and the peace negotiations would end now. But I'd been dressed as a palace guard and he'd run out of the room as soon as there was trouble. Still...

"Watu," I whispered.

She tilted in closer.

"The regent has seen me before. What if he recognizes me?" My whisper was filled with worry and fear.

She ran her gaze from head to foot over me. "Dressed like a princess you were?"

"No."

"An image fools a man." With her hands clasped in front of her, she portrayed serenity.

"Are you saying I'm dressed as an image?" Or I was an image?

I didn't feel comfortable dressed in princess finery, although I was getting used to it. Bracken and his father and most of the other members on the Grand Council didn't believe I did a good enough job projecting the image they preferred.

I might dress differently for them, but I wouldn't change inside. I refused to be something I wasn't.

Horns blared announcing what should be the king. I knew it wouldn't be Rye. That would be too easy.

Everything inside me hardened. It was too late for me to leave now.

Regent Theobald strolled in wearing black pants and a white ruffled shirt. The royal red robe swished behind him as he sauntered. His heeled shoes *tap-tap-tapped* on the stage. His large stomach stuck out of his short frame and his blond hair tufted to the side with more baldness showing than actual hair. Flinging the robe behind him, he sat on the royal throne chair.

I gasped and quickly covered my mouth. From royal etiquette classes, I'd learned the throne chair wasn't merely a nice chair. It was a symbol of leadership. Only the king or queen could sit on it. Biting my lower lip, worry gnawed at my midsection and crawled up my throat. Where was the prince? I knew I couldn't ask the question. If I did, I'd ruin my chance to find out what really happened to Rye and ruin the fairies' chance for peace.

Bracken shoved his men aside to be closest to the regent.

I took a step back, okay with being forgotten.

Bracken bowed low and introduced himself and his role in the delegation. "I must apologize for our appearance. We just arrived."

The man obsessed over his clothes and his looks.

Regent Theobald studied him through slitted eyes. His frown exhibited disapproval. "If you had time to make yourself look better, would you have cut off your wings and pointy ears?"

I sucked in a stinging breath. A tremor started at the tips of my wings and traveled to my soul. How rude.

The negotiators glanced at the ground and shuffled their feet. No one else spoke and the silence stretched.

Bright red spots sprouted on Bracken's cheeks. His Adams apple bobbled. "May I introduce you to the other negotiators?"

Royal etiquette dictated I should be introduced first. I was okay with not being introduced at all.

"Fine. Fine." The regent waved his beringed hand, indicating he didn't care and didn't want to be present.

"This is Sequoia." The man with the goatee stepped forward and bowed low.

"Like the tree?" The regent chortled. "And Bracken? What does your name mean?"

"It's a leaf, sir." His cheeks puffed red as the regent continued laughing. "And this is Cedar."

The other negotiator stepped up and bowed, his long hair falling in front of his face.

At least I knew their names too, knew who was on our team. And both of them were named after trees.

Bracken shoved his friend aside and took my arm, tugging me forward. "This is Princess Ellery, my fiancé and princess of the fairies."

He spoke as if the fiancé was the more important part and it wasn't even true, except in his and his father's minds.

"Step forward." The regent didn't bow or stand.

I stayed where I stood. I might not be used to people bowing to me, but I'd learned to wait for the courtesy. The regent wasn't royalty and I held rank above him.

Bracken pushed on my back and I stumbled forward. I thought he said he knew royal etiquette. Obviously, he didn't know negotiation tactics either.

I refused to bow.

The regent leaned forward, not in a bow. "You look familiar."

My pulse pounded through my bloodstream, creating a blockage in my throat. I choked and licked my lips, trying to think of an excuse. "I...um..."

"I know I've never met a fairy princess before." He waved his hand around. "I mean, why should fairies have royalty? I'm the true leader of the Kingdom of Alandaska."

Fisting my hands at my sides, I clamped down on my lower lip, forcing myself not to shout out that Rye should be the ruler. I spoke calmly and informatively. "The fairy kingdom has been around longer than Alandaska."

"Whatever." He angled forward in his chair and squinted. "There's something about you."

My pounding pulse heated my skin. Sweat formed on my upper lip. I dipped my chin, trying to get out of his harsh spotlight.

"Excuse me, sir. You must've seen holograms of her on the news vids." Bracken bowed again in a subservient manner. "It was a big deal, finding the lost princess. And she's half human."

He whispered the last part, not thrilled with my pedigree. Impressed and fascinated by humans unless they were half something else.

"Ah, yes." The regent relaxed back in his chair and waved a limp arm. "Welcome to Reximus Palace."

My abs clenched. He didn't want us here and could barely take the time to greet us. I didn't speak up. I didn't want to make waves as I had more important things to accomplish.

Dozens of cyborgs rolled into the room and issued orders. They handed out identification badges we were told we had to wear for access to certain parts of the palace. The servants would be allowed in the servant area and the rooms of the people they worked for. We were told some places in the palace were strictly off limits. Which meant I wanted to search for Rye there.

The two male negotiators, Bracken, Watu, and I were led out a door. I'd had to explain she was not a servant, she was a chaperone, and must stay with me.

The cyborg led us through wide hallways decorated with gold filigree moldings, murals painted on ceilings, and mirrors in most of the picture frames. A crystal chandelier hung every ten feet. We turned right and left and then left again. Door after door lined the passageways.

"Your suite of rooms Nobletive Oakton and Princess Ellery," the cyborg announced in an electronic voice before placing its glass eye in front of a retina scanner. The door opened and the cyborg rolled inside.

Stopping, I froze. A tremor ran through my body.

"Excuse me," I called from outside the door. "I require my own suite of rooms."

The cyborg rotated toward me with no expression. "As requested, the suite is assigned to both of you."

"Ellery." Bracken smiled in his standard charming way. He hadn't realized his smile didn't work on me. "Don't be difficult."

My body went rigid. "We are not married. My chaperone and I must have our own bedroom."

"Two bedrooms." The cyborg rolled across the living room toward a series of doors. "One living room and small butler pantry."

"Oh." I edged into the room to take a peek. "This isn't appropriate. I want my own room."

My tone and request reminded me of how Bracken had demanded his rooms be corrected in the middle of the night at Queens Academy. I didn't want to be anything like him. I'd never hit a servant to get my way.

"Don't be silly, Elle." Bracken flung open one door and then the other leading to the two bedrooms. "You can have this room because it has a nanny room. I'll take the master."

I cringed. Just friends called me Elle. And, I couldn't believe his hubris in claiming the master bedroom. He believed he was more important.

"What about Watu?"

He glared at my friend. "She can sleep in the nanny room attached to your bedroom."

That sounded better. I wouldn't be sleeping in the same room with him. We'd be sharing a living room. And Watu would be close.

He stepped closer and took my hand, kissing it. His lips were ice. "Don't you trust me?"

I forced myself to smile back. "It isn't about trust. Royal etiquette states a fairy princess should not be left alone with an unwed male."

Fairy etiquette had been used as one of the reasons I shouldn't practice weapons training with Stone, which was why I'd had to sneak out.

The cyborg bowed to me again. "I'm sorry the negotiating team picked out very specific rooms at Lord Bracken's request. There is no place else."

Doubtful in a palace this large. If I acted more easygoing, maybe they'd pay less attention to me and the cyborg would leave. I tugged my hand out of Bracken's grip. "Very well."

The cyborg revolved toward his bedroom. "I will unpack for you."

"No." His sharpness stopped the cyborg. "My servants will bring the luggage and unpack. You did say they were allowed in their master's rooms?"

"Correct. I will unpack for Princess Ellery."

"No, thank you. I'm tired from our journey. Watu will help me later."

"If there is anything you need, there's a button in the butler pantry. Press it and someone will arrive to help you." The cyborg headed to the door.

"Thank you." I wanted to get out of their presence, search my bedroom for electronic surveillance, and start my real mission, finding Rye. My heart pumped harder. "I'm going to rest for a bit."

"Don't forget, we have a late dinner tonight with the human negotiating team." Bracken's reminder annoyed as he'd sent me a schedule with the parts he expected me to attend.

Watu followed me into the room and I dropped onto the comfy bed. The decoration in the room was simple. The small bed was built for a child. I was okay as long as Watu stayed near. A bedside table held a lamp, and a comfortable chair was next to it. Three other doors were in the room. One to the bathroom, one a closet, and the third to the nanny's room. Hopefully, it wasn't too small.

"Is there a song vid player? I'm feeling in the mood for music." I pushed off the bed and whispered, "Loud music."

Nodding, she went to the comm center and found the correct button. Music blared into the room.

The obvious cameras were in the ceiling light and the comm center. Knowing the hi-tech available in the palace, I'd planned for surveillance and brought fake vid screens to show prerecorded views of the room and our actions I wanted the palace security to see. Watu and I covered the lenses with the screens. We could turn them on and off depending what we wanted them to see. For example, I'd record myself sleeping so the vids could be used while I was out at night.

"Here's one." Watu used a hi-tech sensor to find electronic signals being sent out from the room.

Even though they'd taken away our magic, we had technology too. Watu might've lived in a cave, but she was experienced with hi-tech and had suggested bringing several devices which I'd put in my Necessary Bag. The small bag with the Divinity Orb either Watu or I had carried the entire journey.

Working together, we went around the room, covering the electronic surveillance. At times, we'd let them hear and see us. At others, they'd see prerecorded vids. Once the luggage arrived, I'd record myself in several outfits to make the vids appear real.

Once completed, I sighed with relief and took off the badge hanging around my neck. Another royal etiquette Bracken ignored or didn't understand. Princesses did not wear badges. They wore jewelry. "Can you fix our badges so we can go where we want?"

"I'll fiddle with them now and make additions once I'm more familiar with their security and the layout of the palace. If you're okay on your own with...him." She made a face in the general direction of Bracken's room. "I'll snoop around."

"Thank you." I sat back on the bed. "I'll wait for my clothes to arrive so I can start recording vids."

I wished I could go with her. I couldn't be impatient. I was in Reximus Palace—the same building as Rye. And I'd find him.

A timid knock sounded at my door.

If I thought it was Bracken, I would've feigned sleeping. His knock would be loud and obnoxious. If he even knocked. My luggage had arrived minutes after Watu left and I'd shooed the cyborg servants away afraid they'd use the opportunity to plant more surveillance devices. I'd taken one item out at a time and filmed myself pretending to read, sleep, pace, or peering out the window.

Feeling trapped, I hadn't wanted to explore the living room of the suite, afraid I might run into Bracken.

"Come in." I straightened my gown and stood.

The door opened. "Pardon me, Princess Ellery." Tagh stood by the door. "Would you appreciate help unpacking?"

"Have you finished in Bracken's room?" I didn't want the brownie getting in trouble.

"Yes. He decided to keep most of his clothes packed and ordered new suits from the palace tailor."

"I'd love some help and some company." I waved at the small bag I brought, which was mostly empty, and the trunk Bracken had brought for me. "I didn't have the energy to put those dresses and shoes and coats away."

After sorting through the items Bracken had brought, I figured they could stay in the trunk.

"Happy to help, Princess Ellery."

"Please call me Elle."

"That would be inappropriate."

"You called me Elle the first night we met."

"I didn't know who you were."

"I'm the same person and my other brownie friend calls me Elle." I put up my hand. "It's an order."

"Yes...Elle." Tagh pulled out a hideous, bright orange gown with ruffles. He held it up. "How would you prefer these arranged in your closet?"

"In the back." I faked a shiver. I would never wear his dresses. I'd wear the few I brought. "Arrange them however you believe is best."

The brownie hung one ugly dress up after the other.

I helped by putting the foolish accessories, hats, gloves, and silk stockings away. "How long have you been in service to Bracken?"

Tagh stopped his action for a second before answering. "His father gave me to him."

"Gave you?" I fell back against the bed. Was that legal in fairy society? Another thing I'd change. "You're a person, not a possession."

"My family owed the Oakton family a great debt." His serious voice dropped an octave. "I'm happy to serve the great Oakton family."

He didn't sound happy. His words struck as a rehearsed line.

"What is it like working for Bracken?" How someone treated their servants said so much. I knew because I'd been a servant.

Again, the brownie halted his movements before jerking back into action again. "It's a pleasure."

Inside, I guffawed. Impossible. Brownies could lie. I pulled out a ridiculous hat and put it on. "Does he ask nicely or does he yell, like the first night I met you?"

Tagh smashed his lips together apparently trapped by my question. "That night was an exception. We'd arrived late because we stopped to visit..." Panic flashed on his face. "Anyhow, he had an argument earlier with someone and was in a foul mood."

I wanted to get to know the man everyone wanted me to marry, what he was truly like and not the charmer he presented to most of the world. The information would be used as evidence against him. "Being in a foul mood doesn't excuse treating anyone poorly. Especially over a piece of luggage."

He patted my arm. "Don't worry Princ...Elle. Bracken would never treat you poorly."

"Why do you say that?"

"After you're married, he won't spend a lot of time with you because he has a girlfriend."

I gasped, not out of jealousy but disbelief. "He's courting me with a girlfriend in tow?"

"He's promised to move her into Queens Academy after the wedding."

My gaze hazed over. Shock traveled through my veins in an electrical current. I didn't care that he had someone else. I was upset he thought he could marry me, control me, and still be with the person he loved. While I could not.

I refused to be treated as second.

"And right now, his girlfriend is staying at the palace."

Satisfaction quenched my anger. He'd be so busy spending time with his girlfriend, he wouldn't even know I'd be out searching for Rye.

Chapter Thirteen

Pretending to be asleep, I counted down until my bedroom door flung open right on time. Bracken had been antsy and excited to see more of the human palace and meet with the other negotiators at the late dinner.

"Are you ready to go?" He stood at the doorway dressed in glittery pants and matching short jacket, a silk shirt, and a tie that would normally spin in circles. Without magic, the tie drooped against his chest. It was a fancier suit than normal. He was trying to impress someone with the elegant fairy threads. His new suits must not be done yet.

"Oh." I rolled on my side. "Is it time for dinner already? I fell asleep. I was exhausted from traveling."

"You've had hours to recover." He crossed his arms and glared.

"I had to unpack and freshen up." Plus, the issue of taking care of the fake security vids.

He inspected the room, searching for any item out of place. Or a certain item. "There are servants for unpacking."

"I didn't bring my own servants." He'd probably never unpacked in his life and I wasn't going to tell on Tagh.

"You have Watu."

I jerked to a sitting position. "Watu is not a servant. Is that clear?"

Bracken held up his hands and took a step back. "The cyborgs could've helped."

Traditional fairies believed robots had been corrupted by evil. It goes back to a time when fairies couldn't touch metal. I'd been around robots and metal devices my entire life. They'd helped me clean my old home, but I could play on the fairy prejudice now. "You really wanted me to stay in the company of a cyborg longer than necessary?"

His expression steeled. He held his head in a stiff position and his mouth and cheeks didn't move. Not even the frown lines around his lips moved. "They're here to serve us. Take advantage of it."

I wasn't going to win this battle. It wasn't important. "Either way, I'm not ready and I'm really tired. I wouldn't be great company tonight."

"This dinner honors our arrival."

"It's a dinner honoring the delegation team's arrival. You're the leader of the team. They're honoring you." Since I couldn't play into his prejudice, I'd play into his ego.

His shoulders straightened. "They will be expecting a princess."

Smashing my mouth together, I controlled the spike of pain in my chest. I was just a title. A princess. Any princess would do.

And if he wanted a princess, I'd give him one. Using my most arrogant tone, I said, "Make my apologies and promise them I will be at the meeting in the morning, fresh and excited to begin work."

His chin pulled in. Maybe he hadn't expected me to attend the meetings. He wanted me as a showpiece. My original plan was to drop in now and again during the important meetings to get direct knowledge of the specifics of the treaty while using the rest of the time for my personal reconnaissance mission.

"Very well." Bracken bent forward to kiss me.

I plopped flat on the bed and rolled away from him, facing the opposite direction. "Goodnight, Bracken. I'll see you in the morning."

My muscles tensed. Would he take my curt dismissal or force a kiss?

Seconds ticked by and I sensed him staring at my back. I forced myself to close my eyes and not react. To stay motionless and pretend I drifted to sleep easily. The click of the door closing had me peeking to confirm I was alone. My tension relaxed and I sat up and got the fake sleeping vid from a drawer. I slipped the vid into the device controlling each security camera and muted the sound.

Then, I went to my Necessary Bag and took out the Divinity Orb. The orb still had magic which lit at my touch. Purple, orange, and green swirled and glowed from within.

The orb created prisms of color throughout the room, flashing on the walls, furniture, and bedding. At Queens Academy it had been in a charm protected room, and yet Bracken had gotten inside. Here, besides hiding it in the Necessary Bag, I had no other way to secure the orb and I couldn't carry it everywhere, especially while sneaking around. What if I got caught and was searched?

I swirled my hands around the orb, palming the heated glass and letting it sense our connection. In my head, I thought about what my goal was for tonight. "Find the replica orb. Find your duplicate orb."

The colorful prisms flared out, rotated, and turned into a single shot of light on a blank wall. The colors eddied into a whirlpool of lines, pinpointing a location. Excitement swirled with confusion. That was where the replica orb was hidden, except I didn't know what the lines represented.

When reviewing troop positions, I could easily distinguish the landscape by a mountain or a lake. The whirling and curving lines made no sense pointing to a spot on my wall. How was I going to find the duplicate orb if I didn't understand where the colors were leading?

A knock at the door interrupted my thoughts. I quickly lost the connection with the Divinity Orb and shoved it under the blanket.

A cyborg rolled into the room. "Excuse me, Princess Ellery. I thought you'd be at the welcome dinner hosted by Lord Frederick."

Which meant the cyborg had come to spy. I definitely needed to find a good hiding spot for the Divinity Orb. My eyebrows rose.

Was my fake sleeping vid not working or were the cyborg servants not connected to the security system? They had to do whatever job they were programmed to do and report.

I stretched my arms above my head and stepped to the side of the bed. "I was too exhausted to attend the dinner. I was going to go to sleep."

"I will assist you in preparing for sleep." Did the robot's red eyes have camera lenses planted inside?

"Assist?" I wished I could read the expression on the cyborg's metal face. "No. I'm fine. Thanks."

"I will draw a bath." The cyborg rolled into the bathroom.

I pulled the covers more carefully across the orb and followed the cyborg to the bathroom.

A smart mirror recognized and greeted me upon entry. "Good evening, Princess Ellery. What can I help you with?"

The mirror changed light based on skin coloring. Above the sink, electronic arms pointed out, ready to put toothpaste on a toothbrush, grab a cloth to wash your face, or use a comb to smooth your hair.

With a single command, the tub could fill and heat to the correct temperature. Nozzles provided bubbles and music played from the speakers built into the side of the tub. Why did I need help from the cyborg if I wanted to take a bath?

The shower was even more of a miracle. One stepped into the glass cubicle and the shower did the cleaning for you, automatically dispensing shampoo and soap and washing your hair and body with brushes that reached every part of your back.

The single mundane thing in the room was the shiny marble floor.

"I already took a bath." Flicking my fingers, I used magic to spread water droplets in the tub so it proved my lie. Except, it didn't work. I sucked in a breath. Oh yeah, they took away my magic at the door. And my wand.

Okay, don't panic. Water was natural.

"Oh?" The cyborg's mechanical gaze swiveled to the tub and back to me. It didn't believe me.

I scanned the room, trying to find a natural element nearby.

A small potted plant sat on the nightstand. Mentally, I reached out, trying to pull water from the plant's roots or the dirt in the pot. My muscles tightened and I focused on the water inside the plant. A tiny droplet tugged out of a leaf, and another, and another. Using my connection to Mother Earth, I flung the water from the plant into the tub.

"Yes, I already took a bath. It was a while ago." My nervous chatter probably made me look more suspicious.

The cyborg rolled toward me. "I will turn down the bed."

I rushed around the robot and sat on the bed on top of the orb. "That's okay. I prefer everything in a particular order." I used my snooty voice. "Watu will arrive soon to arrange my bedding just so."

My cheeks heated because I'd told Bracken she wasn't a servant and here I was saying the opposite.

"If you're certain?" The cyborg bowed.

"I am. Thank you. That will be all for tonight."

"Very well, Princess Ellery." The cyborg wheeled around and left my room, closing the door behind it.

I let out a sigh of relief, positive the cyborg's spying mission had been unsuccessful. Flipping back the blanket, I slipped the orb out and swirled my hands over it. I had to figure out what the images meant and where it pointed to. The colors projected out again and whirlpooled into the same image. An image that didn't make sense.

The door opened without announcement.

I clutched the orb to me, tried to shut down the prisms of color, and hide the orb behind my back. I needed to get a lock for the door.

Watu stood at the entrance, wearing a simple brown shift. She pulled out a folded canvas from her large pocket.

"Oh." I collapsed onto the bed and placed my palm against my chest. I was going to have a heart attack. "It's you."

"Me just." She shut the door and lumbered into the room. "You're doing what?"

I pulled out the orb and connected with it again. The prism of colorful swirls displayed on the wall. "Finding where Rye's orb is located."

"Have you?" The stiff fabric crinkled as she unfolded the canvas.

"Kind of." I pointed to the midpoint of the swirls on the wall. "The orb is right there. Unfortunately, I don't know exactly where that is."

"Help you I might." She held the brown wrinkled canvas against the wall. It looked like a map. "Old friend who worked in palace gave this."

"What is it?"

"Three-dimensional architectural layout of the palace."

I held up the other side and the colors swirled against it. "Is the map the right way?"

"This way move." She took her edge and lined it up with the ground and the edge I held switched to the top. "No. Angle to shift."

We switched the map positions again and the colors swirled, pinpointing an exact spot.

"It's right there." My tone trilled with excitement. "In that room." Rye could be in that room. Memorizing the details, I figured out which floor of the palace and the approximate location. "I need to change."

Letting the map slip from my fingers, I sprinted into the closet and pulled out the red warrior outfit Watu had given me when we'd first met.

"Your plan is what?" She folded the map. Her calm action should've soothed me. Instead, my nerves jittered.

Scurrying around, I dressed in the outfit, slipped my dagger onto the belt, and attached the Silver Snare—the whip was my favorite weapon. "I'm going to go where the duplicate orb is and find Rye." A trill sang in my bloodstream. I could be seeing him in minutes.

She tutted. "Unprepared you must not rush off."

"You're right." I smoothed the red leather vest over the tight red shirt.

She'd taught me patience and planning when I'd been recovering from wounds made by a dragon. I had to follow her lead. "I could say I was lost."

"Like that dressed?"

"I'll think of something. I need to start my search." The need to move, to find Rye, was like an internal itch.

"Remember, no magic have you."

Nodding, I remembered the tub incident.

"You find what if?"

My hopes soared at her question. What would I do if I found him? Kiss him, for sure. What if he was heavily guarded? Or too injured to transport? "I want to find his location. Once I know where he is, and his condition, we'll work out a plan to rescue him."

Patience. One step at a time.

"Gone too long don't. Early morning meeting you have."

Groaning about the thought of sitting through a boring meeting, I snuck out the bedroom door, through the living room, and into the hallway.

According to the map, the duplicate orb was located two floors up from where my suite was situated. Not in the high glass towers and, thank the elves, not in the basement with the prison and secret dungeon. From Watu's research, I could use a side set of stairs to the next level. To get to the upper floor, I'd have to be creative.

The corridor outside my room was empty. I easily wended from there to the next hallway, taking a right. My muscles pulled taut like a spider's web, except I was the one who didn't want to get caught. Where the curlicue moldings connected the ceiling to the wall, I scanned for cameras. This was the older part of the palace and while I suspected there were cameras, they weren't as plentiful. If I moved fast and kept my head down, I hoped to be a blur or at least unrecognizable when security viewed the vid feeds.

I reached the stairs and went up two at a time. A rushing sensation brushed my skin. I had to hurry. While the fake security vids showed me sleeping, Bracken or another *helpful* cyborg might check on me.

The urge to use my wings to fly up the stairs was natural to me now. I kept them tucked in tight. If I flew, security would know I was a fairy. Best to keep my activities stealthy.

Arriving at the top of the stairs, I took a right. The dark corridor was lined with antique cabinets and portraits of long-dead rulers. The more impressive décor told me I'd entered an important person's domain. My heart bumped. Was I headed to Rye's bedroom? Would I find him right now? I hurried silently on the cold marble floor.

Footsteps reached my ears.

I halted while my pulse charged ahead. Frantically, I searched for a place to hide. Spotting a large statue, I dashed to the backside and pressed myself against the cold marble. The life-like statue represented Regent Theobald's bulk and I was small enough to fit behind it, which would help me with my spy work.

The footsteps marched right by me.

My muscles relaxed and I took a second to control my breathing. I peeked around the massive statue. No one was around. Crawling from behind, I stayed low. The room I wanted to cut through was to the right.

Putting my ear to the thick wooden door, I heard nothing. There was no retina scanner. I wrapped my hand around the knob and twisted. I cringed at the loud click. Pausing, I waited. When no one questioned or shouted and no alarms went off, I scooted into the room closing the door behind me. The room was lined with shelves filled with books. A few tables scattered around the room. A library. I crossed the room to the window, opened it, and leaned out. The room with the orb was right above me.

No light spilled from the window above. Taking it as a good sign, I slipped on my gloves, another gift from Watu. My gut hardened with fortitude. This is why I'd come. Using my arms, I planned to climb to the next level. Similar to the stairs, my wings would be too noticeable. Flying was a last resort.

I hoisted myself out the window and stuck my hands higher on the wall. The starry night held a crisp scent. Holding my breath, I tested the adhesiveness of my gloves by leaning back and peering down. The ground swirled at my feet making me dizzy. Looking down was a mistake.

"Focus, Elle." I beheld my target.

Using my feet, I pushed off and scrambled to find purchase against the wall. I wheezed. Next, I stretched first one arm and the other, sticking and unsticking the palms of my glove, pulling myself up. My feet scrambled against the wall, pushing me higher. I crawled up the exterior to the window above.

Grabbing onto the window ledge, I peeked inside the dark space. The room appeared empty and eerily familiar.

I took a simple tool out of my bag. Arbor had given me the glass and wire cutter before leaving Queens Academy. She'd taken it from a captured human soldier. The sharp edge etched a circle into the glass. I used my fist to punch the glass through and reached inside to open the old-fashioned lock.

Now, for the security wires.

Spotting the wires around the edge of the window, I reached inside again and grabbed hold. Then, using the sharp edge of the device, I cut the wire. Scrunching my shoulders, I waited for a blaring alarm.

An alarm didn't sound.

I let out the breath I didn't know I'd been holding.

Sliding up the window, I climbed inside and took a moment to get my bearings.

The large room had the trappings of royalty. Intricately carved floor to ceiling bookshelves, sitting area with royal insignia embroidered on the material of the chairs and couch, drink and food station featuring the best China and crystal, and an overbearing large desk sitting near the window. The desk held expensive knickknacks and modern computers.

My gaze swung to the vent in the ceiling I knew would be there.

I'd seen this room before, from the vents above when I'd been escaping the prison beneath the palace. This was Regent Theobald's office.

My stomach dropped. I'd been hoping to find Rye with the orb. If it was in the regent's office, he must've taken it away from Rye. Where was the prince?

I hoped the replica orb would have clues to answer the question.

Starting in the most obvious spot, I opened the top drawer of the desk. Nothing. I yanked on the second drawer. It was locked. I wanted to slam my fist against it. I controlled my anger and used another tool to easily open the lock.

There, sitting front and center, was the replica orb. Turmoil roiled in my belly. Excitement and disappointment churned inside me. I'd found the orb in the worst place possible. Locked in the regent's desk.

I picked it up and the orb flared to life with colors. The duplicate orb wasn't broken, it had been held by the wrong person. The regent. Just like the real Divinity Orb, the replica orb only worked for Rye and me. Since I'd been unable to communicate with Rye for more than a month, it meant he hadn't been around the replica orb for the same period of time.

My shoulders slumped so low I thought they'd graze the floor. The orb wasn't going to help me find Rye.

I placed the replica back in the drawer, wanting to slam it shut. Instead, I slid the drawer shut quietly. Peering at my father's watch, I noticed the time. If I was going to be up in time for the meeting, I needed to get a few hours' sleep.

The door clicked open.

My body froze and panic rushed through my veins in chunks of ice. My taut body moved like an iceberg. I ducked behind the long curtains by the window I'd climbed through.

The open window.

A breeze filtered through the curtain, drawing attention to it and me.

Light footsteps crossed the carpeted floor. The footsteps paused and I pressed myself closer to the wall. If I were discovered in the regent's office, no lie would get me out of it. My ribcage constricted around my lungs. I'd be sentenced to the dungeon.

A muscular male hand reached around the curtain and grabbed my arm.

Terror shrieked through my muscles. My training kicked in and I lunged for the Silver Snare at my waist.

The assailant's other hand flattened against the spot where I kept my whip. "I know every move you've got."

CHAPTER FOURTEEN

The voice. The grip. The way he professed to know my every move.

"Stone?" I hesitated. How was that even possible? My friend was on a secret mission.

The iron grip tugged me out of the curtain, and I tumbled against his torso. "Hello, Elle. What're you doing in the regent's office?"

His long blond hair was now short and brown. His distinctive green eyes were less sharp as if in a fog. Baggy clothes hung on his frame suggesting he'd gotten smaller and chubbier at the same time.

"What happened to your hair?" A stupid first question. I couldn't believe he was here. "What're you doing here?"

"Rescuing your cute butt again."

Wanting to giggle, I instead took a step back from his large chest. "I don't need rescuing. I'm fine."

"And if someone else had come into the room? What then? How would you explain Princess Ellery dressed as a warrior priestess?" His tone edged with fear.

Not for himself. For me.

"I wouldn't." I huffed because I didn't have an appropriate bluff. "I wouldn't have gotten caught."

He chuckled. "I easily found you hiding behind the curtain. Rookie technique."

"It was the closest place to hide. Besides, you have superior instincts over a human guard."

"I have superior instincts over everyone." His pleased-with-himself smile told me he'd forgiven me for my un-smart action. "What about a cyborg security guard with extra sensory receptors?"

"They have those?" My brows rose before I realized he'd baited me. "I would've ripped the cyborg apart."

"Which would've sent an alarm signal to the palace communication center." He shook his head, clearly disappointed. "You would've been surrounded in seconds."

I jerked my chin toward the open window. "I would've been gone in seconds."

"Flying?" His question went higher in disbelief. Flying would be a dead giveaway.

"No." I raised my gloved hand to his cheek and rubbed the sticky palm against his skin. "Climbing."

He laughed, merrier this time. "You always surprise me."

"You always surprise me." He always found me in the strangest places. An underground tunnel, a lake high in the mountains. "What's up with those clothes?"

The expertly tailored jacket hung on his frame. The tie around his neck was twisted too tight. The long pants dragged on the floor and his shiny shoes reminded me of something a human lord would wear.

Stone glanced toward the door. "This isn't the best place to talk."

"The entire palace is bugged so nowhere is good."

"I'm impressed you noticed." His lips pursed together. "I can help you with the surveillance."

"Watu and I have taken care of my bedroom." I stiffened. "Is there surveillance in here?"

"Not right now." He placed his arm around my shoulders. "Let's get you out of here. I'll walk you to your room."

He ushered me toward the door, and I stopped. "You never answered me. What're you doing here?"

"It's part of my undercover mission." His face went hard.

"Who are you supposed to be?"

He paused in front of the door. "Lord Vitor. I can't tell you everything and certainly not now."

That explained the clothes. Why were they so big and why had he colored his hair? Or was the brown natural?

Walking through the corridor and down a side set of stairs, we kept silent while my brain whirled. Was Stone a real lord or was he acting as one? If he wasn't, how would he get such a prestigious cover? He'd gone undercover before as a guard in this very palace. My mind and my mouth wanted to burst with questions. Every time I opened my lips to speak, he'd shake his head or a guard or cyborg servant would pass.

Each time someone approached, I lowered my head so I wouldn't be recognized.

If he were undercover in the palace, he'd been here for about a week. My hopes darted in varying directions. He might know what happened to Rye. "I was looking for—"

"I know who you were looking for." Stone peeked around a corner and tugged me forward. "We can't talk now. The regular security sweeps will be taking place soon. Every hallway, corridor, nook, and cranny. You need to get back to your room."

I tensed. "Is there a specific time for the sweeps every night?" Good information to have for my next secret outing.

We arrived at my suite door.

"I'll leave you here. Wouldn't want Oakton to see us together." He kissed me on the cheek. "I suspect we will meet again very soon."

And then he left. Left me to wonder how he knew about Bracken, how he knew where my room was located, and how he knew I was even in the human palace.

Most of all, I wondered what Stone was up to. He knew I was searching for Rye yet hadn't told me anything about the prince.

Why? My heart fractured and cracked. Was it bad news?

"What're you wearing?" Bracken's greeting the following morning stopped me short when I stepped out of my bedroom. He sounded horrified, as if I'd stepped out wearing beggar's rags.

I inspected the modern suit with angular hems and slim-fitting top. "Clothes."

"It's disgusting. You're a princess, not a prostitute." He stormed toward me. "Take it off."

"This is a human outfit." I crossed my arms. I'd thought I looked nice. It was something my stepsisters would've worn when they got dressed up. "It will help me fit in."

"You're half human, that should make you fit in enough." Disgust braided his voice and he tugged at the sleeve of my blouse. Yet, his clothes appeared more human this morning with the suit and long, thin tie. Must be one of the new ones he'd ordered from the palace tailor. "I brought you several dresses to wear. Perfect princess dresses."

His touch creeped me out more than his authoritarian tone. I didn't want to fight with him about my clothes or his attitude or his girlfriend. Not yet, anyhow.

"I'll make a deal with you." I patted his hand on my arm and slipped from his grasp. "I'll change into one of your dresses if we keep the information about our engagement discreet."

"I already told the regent."

"He probably won't care or remember."

"I might've mentioned it to the human negotiators last night. And of course, my negotiating team knows."

Firming my lips, I tried to throttle my disappointment and frustration. The more people who knew about this stupid engagement, the harder it would be to disentangle. "You can't keep a secret."

"I keep lots of secrets. I just can't lie like you." He tossed the insult, mimicking a grenade.

If I asked him outright about having a girlfriend, what would he say? "You can obviously lie about loving me."

"Who said anything about love?" He grabbed hold of my hand and squeezed tight, not lovingly but in dominance. "We are engaged. We will get married."

His statements churned in my stomach. Not if I could help it. I'd do everything in my power to stop this wedding as soon as we returned to Queens Academy. "The details have not been worked out."

"Father promised to have the deal signed and sealed by the time we get back to Queens Academy."

I gulped. Maybe I shouldn't have come on this trip. I could've been arguing on my behalf to cancel the engagement. Finding Rye was more important. When I finally found him, he'd become ruler of the kingdom and no peace negotiation would be needed.

"Well, it's not official so I'll wear what I want." Now and in the future.

Parading toward the door to the hallway, I couldn't imagine a future with Bracken.

"Wait." He grabbed my arm again. "As my fiancé, you'll embarrass me wearing the human garment."

"Then, don't tell anyone else we're engaged." I raised a brow. "And your clothes are more human-appearing than usual."

"You win." He dropped his hand from my arm and his defeated expression did not make me feel bad. He held out his arm.

Deciding it was best to present compliance so he wouldn't make my life more difficult when I complained about a headache or other made up things keeping me from the meeting and us apart, I slipped my hand through his arm. We headed out of our suite where a cyborg waited for us.

"I will escort you to the meeting." The mechanical voice of the robot held no opinion.

"Guard us, you mean," I murmured to myself. Noting the cameras hidden in the crystal chandeliers, I kept my head averted. The less vids they had of my face the better.

"What?" Bracken must've heard me.

"Nothing." Shaking my head, I let my gaze wander along the walls, taking in the artwork from the various periods.

The Renaissance nudes, Impressionist dots, Cubism shapes, Abstract Minimalism, and the newer Anti-Conceptualism art. The decorative trim went from the older section of the palace to the more modern. Throughout, small hidden doors led to passages for the cyborg servants.

I'd been in some of the passages in my past, running away and then toward my destiny. I might be a princess and not an escapee, but I was still a prisoner in this palace. Constantly being watched and listened to. It was a different type of captivity.

A captivity where protesting outright wouldn't work. I had to pretend and, yes, lie. I had to sneak and I had to spy.

"Were you escorted last night to dinner?" I made my voice casual, even though I was digging for information.

"Yes." His bland answer made me want to knock his head sideways.

"You don't think it's suspicious?"

"It's a big palace. We're guests. They're helping us find our way."

I rolled my eyes. He didn't understand the cyborgs were part of the surveillance. I whispered, "With the cyborgs reporting our every action, the humans will know everywhere we went and everything we said, and the negotiators could use it against us."

"They wouldn't. They're good people. Friends." Bracken worshipped his new friends, Regent Theobald, and the human way.

We turned a corner, and the corridor grew wider. It went from resembling a hotel with door after matching door to more individualized entrances, arched doorways, and glass.

"Elle, you need to remember my team and I are the official negotiators. You're only here to lend leverage with your title." He spat the last word, annoyed I had something he didn't.

Something he wanted.

I gave a noncommittal nod and kept walking.

The corridors resembled some of the high-rise office buildings nearby in the city. Glass doors, conference tables, and cubicles.

"And it wouldn't hurt for you to throw me a compliment once in a while."

Holding in a choked snort, I wanted to strangle him, not compliment him.

The cyborg stopped in front of a steel and glass door and used a retinal scanner to let us inside. Did the cyborgs have access to every room with their retinas? Something to think about and consider.

Stepping into the conference room, I scanned the walls and furniture. The room was dominated by a thick, glass, oval-shaped table. A chandelier made of sharp metal and glass hung from the center. Squinting, I spotted cameras and microphones in every direction. Comfortable leather chairs ringed the table and each spot had an electronic tablet. Would Bracken even know how to use one? And if he did, would there be spyware inside the device?

A side counter had been filled with refreshments, including breakfast dishes, coffee, tea, and summer wine. Only the fairies were served alcohol.

Vid screens lined one wall. A tiny green light blinked on and off at the top of each blank monitor.

"This is Lord Fredrick Larsen." Bracken pronounced his title with importance as he introduced the man wearing a slim fitting black suit. "And this is Princess Ellery, my—" I shot him a glare and he stopped before continuing. "She will be listening to our discussions."

I placed a fake, almost flat smile on my face. I didn't even rank as one of the negotiators in Bracken's mind.

"Nice to meet you." Frederick held out his hand. His dark eyes held no emotion. His short, dark wispy beard and his black straggly strands of hair didn't impress.

Staring at him, I kept my hand clasped to my sides.

"You're supposed to bow." A deep, familiar voice entered the room from the door behind me.

A true smile burst on my face. I didn't realize Stone would be in on the negotiations. I was glad to have a friendly and familiar face.

I smushed my lips flat, trying not to show delight. I couldn't let on that I knew him.

"Oh, sorry." Frederick gave a short bow.

"He's only used to bowing to Regent Theobald." Stone bowed to me with respect.

According to etiquette class, there was no standard for bowing to a royal representative like a regent. Bracken and his buddies—Cedar and Sequoia, the Trees—had when we'd met the regent upon arrival.

"What about Prince Zacharye?" My heart stopped beating while awaiting a response. I shouldn't push the issue so soon, although I desperately needed an answer.

The faces of Frederick and the other human male near the food whitened and went blank. If they knew, they weren't going to tell me.

Frustration and fear bubbled to the surface. I wanted to yell at them to tell me, but knew it would do no good. I had to be patient.

"We haven't seen the prince in a while." Stone spoke through gritted teeth. Too bad. He hadn't let me ask the question last night. "I'm Lord Vitor."

"Nice to meet you." I tried to speak in a bored, neutral tone, even though I wanted to ask a million questions.

"And I'm Lord Henrik Hansen." Holding a tray of eggs and bacon, the other male human gave a quick bow and avoided my gaze, but not before a spark lit his blue pupils.

Interesting. Neither of these two men respected me. They didn't want me here. Which meant maybe I'd need to take a place in a few of the meetings to find out what was going on.

"Help yourself to the food and drinks before we get started." Frederick held out his hand to indicate the food and the seats. "There's summer wine I received as a gift from an old fairy friend of mine."

"Wonderful." Bracken poured three glasses for himself and his negotiators. As an afterthought, he asked, "Elle, would you enjoy a glass of summer wine?"

We had serious business to discuss. Drinking wine would not help their negotiating skills and I bet Frederick knew that. I pinched my lips together, not wanting to make waves. Yet.

"*Princess* Ellery would not." Giving the impression of a total prude, I checked my father's watch. It was early morning, and they should not be drinking.

"Would you like something to eat, Princess Ellery?" Stone spoke with respect and kindness. He held out a chair for me, not at the top of the table, which is what I deserved as the highest rank. He sat me near the window.

Why? Stone did everything for a reason.

"Yes, thank you." I took the seat offered and scanned outside.

Troops had gathered in formation in the side courtyard on a dreary, cloudy day. They weren't practicing drills or weapons training. They waited. It was similar to what I saw out my own window at Queens Academy, except instead of all humans, I saw every type of majik working together.

I glanced at Stone and he frowned.

"Bracken and I have been communicating for several weeks." Once everyone had filled their glasses and plates, Frederick began speaking. He sat at the head of the table, giving himself the position of power.

The other human negotiator, Henrik, was to his right. He slouched in his chair as if this was a social event. His blond hair was dark at the roots. Did he dye his hair like Rye had been forced to do?

Stone sat to his right. He appeared relaxed, yet his gaze never stopped assessing the situation. Bracken sat across the table from Stone. My supposed fiancé had filled his plate and his cup. The Trees sat opposite each other. They enjoyed the summer wine, quickly draining their glasses.

I would've arranged the seating differently, fairly. It should've been three humans on one side and three fairies on the other. Plus, me somewhere. Except I didn't seem to matter as they continued their discussion around me. I pinched my lips again. The humans avoided my eyes, although I'd catch a sly glance from Stone every once in a while.

He was half human and half giant and blended into this environment easily. The barely noticeable greenish tint to his skin was covered by something. The baggy clothes made him less impressive, which was probably on purpose. A lord, no less. How had he gotten this deep undercover?

"We have. And I think the fairies are going to be happy." Bracken glared pointedly at me.

Nodding, I pretended to adore him when, really, I threw up a little in my mouth.

I peered outside again. The contingent was growing bigger and they were setting up something. Why were they building up their army if we were days away from signing a peace agreement?

"We have an outline we've both agreed to and we need to finalize the details and arrangements." Frederick droned on.

That sounded good. If we agreed to a truce, the war would stop. We wouldn't stay in this human palace of glass and metal and they wouldn't be able to watch my every move. Of course, I had to find Rye first. I'd thought about ditching this meeting. Watu had reminded me how first impressions were important. At lunch, I'd plead a headache and snoop around.

I noted the cameras swiveling around, trying to get a good view of what was happening in the room. Angling my head away, I peered out the window again.

The large, unadorned gate swung open. A large truck and a crane slowly drove into the side drive. A large tarp partially covered a machine.

"First, we've found a way for the fairies to control the other zaubers—"

My head jerked up, offended at the term. Every majik in the room should be offended. "Excuse me?"

The two humans, and more slowly, Stone pivoted in my direction. Their gazes weren't friendly.

My heart thudded. Stone was half giant. He should be offended too. Of course, he was playing a role as human nobility.

I tilted my chin higher. My job was to defend all majiks. I didn't want to ruin negotiations though. "Zauber is an offensive term." I toned down my complaint.

Why hadn't the other fairies explained the slight?

"Elle, it's just a word." Bracken's shut-up timbre went down with a chill.

I wouldn't shut up. If they didn't respect us, the peace negotiations would never work. "It's not just a word. It's an insult."

Frederick gave Bracken a look. His phony smile didn't fool me. "Princess Ellery," His condescending use of my title rubbed against my nerves. "We need a way to distinguish fairies from other...majiks."

"Why?"

My question had Frederick and Henrik exchanging confused glances with each other. Bracken hadn't allowed me to review any of the documents or communications about the treaty.

"Bracken, can you explain to your princess?" Frederick spoke as if I was stupid when I was beginning to learn my fiancé was the ignorant one.

Bracken's mouth dropped open. The other two fairies stared at him for guidance, believing he could control me somehow.

My muscles bunched.

He took a large sip of his summer wine. Buying time or getting drunk? "Elle."

Frowning, I hadn't chastised him the first time. I would now. If he wasn't going to defend me, why should I appear besotted? This wasn't a love match, and it didn't even resemble an equal partnership. "Excuse me?"

"Princess Ellery," he dutifully said my title and correct name. If I could cow him easily, he was going to get stomped on by the human negotiators. "Frederick and I have been working on this for weeks. You waltz in here at the last second and ask questions we've answered a while ago."

The bunching muscles got tighter and twisted. My anger built into a blustery storm. Over their treatment of me like I was a fool, the use of the slur with no complaints from Bracken and the Trees, and their disrespect from the second I entered the room. I rolled my shoulders, loosening my limbs. Then again, I was the one who sat here half listening as they nattered about wording of the treaty.

I stood up to leave and then my gaze caught the activity outside.

The large tarp had been taken off and the crane had been connected to the large, round machine. The metal glinted in the sun and I blinked. Silver tanks aligned around the largest portion of the machine and on top of the tanks, different colored lights blinked. Wires and electrodes stuck out from the main frame and attached to the tanks.

Pain ripped through my chest. It couldn't be. The machine seemed familiar but different. Except, we'd destroyed the terrible thing several months ago.

A portion of the rounded side was made of glass so you could peer inside to watch the torture. Another form of inhumanity. The tanks were large and able to hold more majik power. The slow-moving sidewalk was gone, replaced by a quick conveyor belt.

Majik after majik after majik would be sucked in and tormented.

My blood ran cold. This was a bigger, better auraguillotine. An improved torture machine that sucked power from innocent majiks. Power that could then be used by the regent to control all fairies. All majiks.

My dead friend Keltie's yell as she was sucked into the old auraguillotine to die echoed in my head. Echoed her suffering and her agony. Echoed the demise of majiks everywhere.

Chapter Fifteen

"Princess Ellery? Are you okay?" Stone handed me a glass of water. "Drink this."

His blank face expressed no emotion, but I saw concern in his eyes. He'd wanted me to see the auraguillotine. To know. Was the machine the purpose of his undercover mission? I had no idea.

Easing out a slow exhale, I tried to control my raging feelings about the past. The original version of the terrible machine had killed hundreds, if not thousands, of majiks. My friend Keltie had died saving Arbor, who had been about to be sucked inside. My chest fissured, spreading pain through my entire midsection. Keltie had taken her place. And I never got to tell her how I felt about her and her sacrifice.

Stone and I had blown up the machine and Rye had been caught in the damage.

I swung back to Stone.

His expression gave nothing away. He was good at his spy job. While I was frantic, a frenzy building inside, wanting to come out in the form of screaming questions.

Taking another sip, I couldn't express my past hurt or my current confusion. Except for Stone, none of the humans or fairies in the room knew who'd destroyed the first auraguillotine. Did they know about this new machine? About the damage the machine could cause?

Observing the others, I hoped none of them had noticed my reaction. They hadn't been sitting by the window and seen what was brought into the palace grounds. If we were close to a resolution on the peace treaty, why would the humans need a new auraguilliotine?

I blew out another breath, trying to slow my pulse and my impulse to start jumping to accusations. Maybe the machine had been contracted before the negotiations had gotten so close. Either way, I had to find out what the humans' plan was for the terrible machine. My muscles hardened and everything inside me calmed. I would not let Keltie die in vain.

I slammed down the glass of water and put my hand to my head. "I'm feeling a little faint. Would you gentlemen mind if I returned to my room?"

Playing the helpless victim was not my style, but it was the one ploy I could think of at the moment.

"Not at all." Frederick waved me away. My absence wouldn't be noticed by him and I had to wonder why.

Bracken stood. He didn't offer help. Typical. "Do you know how to find our room?"

His emphasis on the word *our* sent a cold shiver across my skin.

Frederick and Henrik's eyes widened and the leader grinned. A ton of filth poured over me. Sequoia and Cedar smirked lasciviously, as if they were in on a tawdry secret. The Trees appeared to be more muscle than brains.

My cheeks heated, embarrassed at what Bracken had hinted at. Fairies could lie in their own way.

"I'll show her to her room." Stone gathered his papers and shoved them into a folder. He picked up the celltab by his spot and shoved it into a pocket. Efficient and controlled. I understood there was more to his movements. "I need to check on the matter we discussed earlier, Lord Frederick."

A satisfied simper landed on his face. "Fine, Lord Vitor. Report back as soon as you've heard."

"Will do." Stone saluted smartly and held out his arm to me.

Bewildered, I slipped my hand through his arm. I felt like I was in a play and didn't know my lines.

Once the door closed, I dug my nails into his arm. "Is that what I think it is?"

"Yes." He kept his expression blank. "The regent had another auraguillotine built. This one is stronger and easier to use."

All the oxygen evacuated my lungs. "Why? We're working on a peace treaty."

Stone angled his head and quirked a brow. "Have you been involved with the negotiations?" When I shook my head, he bent down to whisper, "The treaty isn't what you think."

My confusion multiplied. A peace treaty was a peace treaty.

Two cyborgs rolled up the hall toward us.

He straightened away from me and placed my hand on his arm in a less familiar way. "I'll escort you to your room, Princess Ellery."

I knew the cyborgs watched everything we did, as well as the cameras placed in the hallway in inconspicuous places. Probably listening devices too. I couldn't act too familiar with my friend. I should be good at acting. I'd been doing it since I decided to become a perfect princess.

Because I knew I wasn't perfect.

Stone turned right and took another left. He knew where he was going.

I'd studied Watu's old map of the palace and I knew how to get to most places, except the newer wings and towers which weren't displayed.

We reached the corridor where my room was located.

He glanced my way, breaking his stoic expression for a second. "Sorry about your room situation." His shrug was an ask for forgiveness. "The request came from the lead of the fairy contingent."

"Bracken." I screwed up my face. "Did you hear about the"—I swallowed—"engagement?"

"Yes." Stone's conciliatory voice proved he was on my side. "I'm sure the queen and Commander Gardenia will get you out of the marriage."

"I wish." My hand tightened around his arm. "Gardenia is in love with Bracken. She'd marry him if she could. So would Arbor and half the females in the kingdom. Even some males. He's held as the perfect fairy specimen."

"What about you?"

"I see his fake charm, his lack of intelligence, and his father's power-hungry scheming."

Stone smiled. "I like how smart and intuitive you are."

Pleased with his assessment, my step lightened, and I whispered, "Why are you here masquerading—"

"Hold on." He took out a small electronic device and flicked a switch. "Okay. Go ahead."

"What's that?"

"It's a human-made device that blocks conversation from being heard. Can't use it too long though, or the listeners will notice the dead silence."

"Cool."

"You were asking?" He flashed his trademark sexy smile. The one that would put Bracken's fake smile to shame.

"I was asking why you're in Reximus Palace masquerading as a human lord? Is the peace treaty part of your mission?" It would be nice to have a plant on the other side.

"Technically, Lord Vitor is my real identity."

I stumbled. "You're human nobility?"

How could that be? He was a specialized guard at Queens Academy. A captain, no less.

"On my father's side."

"Nobility." Shaking my head, I tried to put the pieces together. That explained his regal attitude even as we strolled through the enemy's palace. A lord, no less. Hurt wavered through the belief in our friendship. Why hadn't he told me?

"I wasn't part of the peace negotiation until Frederick pulled me into it. It's cutting into my spy mission." Stone's real mission wasn't the treaty.

Neither was mine.

"I understand." I wished I could spend all my time searching for Rye. "Do you know where Rye's rooms are?"

"Yes, and he's not there. I looked."

I'd been hoping for a quick lead. "Any idea where he is?"

"No. But he's not dead."

The harsh word slashed my heart and then eased, giving me hope.

Stone bent his head and watched my reaction. He was worried about me. "If the prince was...gone, Theobald would've declared himself king."

We walked a few more steps both in our thoughts.

"The replica orb is not in Rye's rooms either."

"I brought the real Divinity Orb, and it located the duplicate in the regent's office." I was glad I could offer a little return intel.

My friend nodded as we strode. "I'll continue to poke around and keep my contacts searching for Rye. I'll be leaving the palace soon to attend an important meeting for Commander Gardenia. In the meantime," Stone stopped outside my door, "I have one more thing to help you."

He took out an antique perfume bottle with etched swirls in the small, round base.

"How sweet. Perfume." Not something helpful and not something a platonic friend should be giving me. The image of my mother's perfume bottle spiraled in my head. This was similar to that bottle, and that bottle held magic. "What is it really?"

"It can restore your magic for short periods of time."

This was a great gift. "Thank you." I stood on tiptoes and kissed him on the cheek.

He slipped me a piece of paper. "Here are the instructions. Use it wisely."

"I will." My brain whirred with what I could accomplish with access to my magic. "Where did you get this from?"

"Not everyone at the palace hates majiks." He placed his hand on the doorknob and leaned on it heavily.

Tilting my chin, I studied him. Worry pinged through my bloodstream. "When will I see you again?"

"It depends on when I leave for the meeting." His expression went bleak. "Stay safe, Elle. Everything is not as it seems."

My pulse thumped.

The glass slipper sat beneath a pile of dark socks in the top drawer of Rye's armoire. My glass slipper.

The piece of furniture was the last place I'd searched in the prince's entire suite of rooms, including his sitting room, office, and bedroom, for clues to where he might be. I'd searched here last because I knew it would hold personal items and undergarments.

And I'd been right.

My eyes stung as I took out the single shoe. My high heel from the night we'd met at his Presentation Ball. I'd lost the shoe and he'd found it when he followed me into the dungeon beneath the palace. My heart softened and I pressed the shoe against my chest. He must've kept it as a memento through the past few months. This proved he'd experienced the same connection I had from the moment we met.

Gardenia had given me the shoe made of elfin glass to help evade detection my first time in the palace. That night had changed my life. I'd rescued Arbor and other majiks, met Stone, destroyed the first auraguillotine, and fallen in love with the prince.

Realizing a grin had crept onto my face, I chided myself. I couldn't stand here dreaming about the past. There were too many worries for the future.

Putting the shoe back, I stepped out of the closet and scanned the bedroom. There were no clues here about when Rye had been taken or where he had gone. My entire night had been a waste of time and a waste of the single spritz from Stone's perfume bottle. I'd used the magic to make myself invisible and it made me smell like rotting vegetables.

Stone had said he'd checked the prince's rooms for clues and found nothing. Yet, I'd had to see for myself, believing I might notice some small thing out of place or a hint about what had happened to Rye.

Climbing out the window, I used the stickiness in my gloves to crawl across the heavily fortified stone wall. By studying the map, I figured out the best way of avoiding those annoying doors with retina scanners, was by going out a window in a hallway and climbing the wall outside before slipping into the prince's apartment. I followed the same path to leave. I was invisible, but still solid and couldn't pass through doors.

Dropping onto my feet through the lower-level window, I checked in both directions. I easily found my way back down two flights of stairs to the corridor where my room was located.

A blond girl backed out of one of the side doorways.

I inhaled sharply and hid around the corner. The door led directly to the master bedroom in our suite. Bracken's room. This must be the girlfriend Tagh had warned me about.

The girl's hair went past her shoulders. No wings poked out of her too-tight shirt. She wasn't a fairy. I couldn't see the shape of her ears since her head was turned. Could she be human? We were in the human palace. Except Bracken despised the human side of me.

A noise caught my attention, and I swiveled. Nothing was there. I turned back to examine the short, curvy girl more carefully. She was gone.

My mouth dropped open. If she was human, how had she moved so fast? Unless she'd gone back into Bracken's room. That must be it.

Tiptoeing to the front door of the suite, I hoped I didn't run into him. I wasn't jealous. I also didn't want to be part of a three-way relationship. The fact he had the nerve to flaunt the affair while we were guests in the human palace was another point against him. Resentment burned inside me. I'd have to figure out a way to use the girlfriend information to get out of the engagement. What I needed was proof.

I crept through the dark living room to my bedroom door. My room didn't have a separate entrance. Opening the door and slipping inside, I let myself relax against the door.

"Back you are."

I jumped and covered my mouth, muffling a yell.

Wearing pajamas, Watu sat in a chair by my bed. "Find anything did you?"

"No." I shrugged away from the door and headed toward the bathroom. An image of the glass shoe flashed in my mind and I couldn't stop a small smile. I'd found something proving how much Rye cared about me. I needed to find him to tell him I loved him. I'd waited too long.

I set down my weapons and slipped off my jacket and belt.

"Trouble any?" Watu followed me into the bathroom. Her clawed fingers twisted together, exhibiting her worry. She cared about me too.

I hugged her. "No. Stone's perfume bottle restored my magic for the entire time so I stayed invisible." I took the perfume bottle out of a drawer and measured its contents. "I can't spend every night searching rooms hopelessly. Do you know how big this palace is?"

"Four hundred and twenty-five thousand square feet." She'd done her research.

I weighed the bottle in my hand. "I can't waste Stone's gift on unsuccessful missions where I sneak out and find nothing." I flopped into the chair she'd vacated. "I have no idea where to look for Rye next."

Her hands clasped together, and her expression appeared resolute. "Help I can. If you are willing."

"Willing to do what?" At this point, I'd try anything.

"Dreamed you did when you drank my special tea."

"I had vivid nightmares. Although not last time." I'd slept well the night before the journey to Reximus Palace. "I thought your tea only healed."

"Here." She patted her leg and arm where I had been injured most, and then her head. "And here."

"So the tea helped me dream. How are dreams helpful?" I rubbed my forehead, remembering the pain and the visions. One had been of my now-dead cousin Perry claiming the fairy throne. It could've happened if they'd never discovered me. One had been of Rye being beaten up. And last time, I hadn't dreamed at all.

"Dreams or visions?" Her mysterious smile and unhelpful question set me on edge.

I leaned forward, wanting a guarantee. "The tea will make me dream of where Rye is located?"

She waggled her head. "Depends on what is here." She tapped her chest.

Weighing my options, I didn't see any better choice. I loved Rye and my heart might help with visions of him. It was worth a shot. "Okay. Let's do it."

She left the bedroom to go to the butler pantry. While she boiled the water, I changed into my pajamas and sat back on the bed. Worry and remembered dreams wove through my head.

Watu returned with a steaming mug and took off a pouch hanging around her neck beneath her shirt. She took dried herbs from the pouch and sprinkled them into the hot water and stirred. She handed the cup to me. "Dreams sweet, dreams accurate."

I took a small sip, remembering the taste from last time. Nothing, yet something. Not bitter or sweet. Swirling my tongue around my mouth, I noted an additional strange taste. "Is something different in the tea?"

She pursed her lips. "Something more potent."

I listed back, a bit wary, but I trusted her so I kept drinking. My eyelids grew heavy and I blinked several times, trying to stay awake. The fast-acting tea was already affecting me.

My body fell back, and she grabbed the mug from my hand. I flopped onto the mattress. My bones lost their strength and I felt like a slug on the bed. My eyelids slammed shut and I couldn't force them to reopen.

"Sleep. Dream. See." She'd said something similar to me in the past. Except the last word was new.

A sharp buzz went through my brain and everything went dark.

An orb glistened in the distance. The familiar sight comforted me. Multiple colors flared out from the orb, casting a shadow on another round object behind it.

A second orb. The replica orb that had once been in Rye's possession.

I followed both orbs in my dreamscape.

The orbs showed a small, dismal room with a pointed ceiling. A tower of some sort. Bright light filtered in through the point made of glass. The flat, gray walls circled the small space and chains with cuffs were attached to the wall.

"Are you sure about this?" Henrik's speech floated into my head and he materialized in the vision. He forced someone's cracked hands into the two cuffs.

I didn't know if he was talking to his prisoner or someone else in the room.

"Yes." A familiar voice sounded rusty as if he hadn't spoken much in a long time.

Henrik stepped back and I saw his prisoner's face.

Rye.

I melted into a puddle.

His dark hair was matted to his head and a trickle of dried blood stained his forehead. His bloodshot eyes sported both shadows and bruises beneath. His lips were cracked, his cheeks sallow.

The ends of his mouth lifted in a faint smile. "You know why."

Why? *I screamed in my head.* What was happening?

Henrik swung a fist forward. He socked Rye's chin and Rye's head jerked back from the force.

No! *The scream inside me didn't echo in the room. Neither of them turned my way. Because I wasn't there. Was this real?*

Is this how Rye was being treated? Disgust and anger mixed in my stomach.

Henrik picked up a tray with an empty bowl on it. Without checking on Rye, he left the room, locking the steel door behind him. The orbs followed Henrik down a narrow, circular staircase and into a restricted glass elevator.

Go back! *I didn't want to see him. I wanted to see Rye. Make sure he was okay.*

I jerked awake. Sweat poured from my skin and pooled on my lower back. Opening my eyes, I perused the gilded ceiling above my bed in the palace. The blankets were twisted around my feet. I hadn't traveled anywhere. I hadn't left my bed. My gaze flickered closed.

The orbs continued to follow Henrik.

I didn't care about him. I cared about Rye. The orbs didn't listen to my plea. The dreams or visions always began by following the orbs.

The orbs followed Henrik out of the tiny elevator into the main part of the palace. He took another elevator down and returned to the meeting room where the peace negotiations had taken place.

Bracken and the Trees sat at the table drinking again. The dark sky showed through the windows. I hadn't been told about this late-night meeting.

Frederick poured another glass. "We are celebrating. You're late."

"I had a task I needed to complete." Henrik rubbed his fist, showing the bruises.

How many times had he punched Rye?

"Vitor is missing, too." Frederick handed a glass to the newcomer.

"He sent me a message about urgent family business." Henrik lounged in a chair. "What are you celebrating?"

"We've finalized the details of the agreement and all we need are signatures from the regent and the princess." Frederick's grin appeared sinister. "The fairies will be self-ruled, while the humans will control the other zaubers."

Dread leached through my body, making my skin ignite and my head hurt. The treaty sacrificed all other majiks.

Frederick raised his glass. "Bracken has assured me he will obtain the princess' signature, and once they're married, he will rule the fairies and continue to help us."

Over my dead body. The orbs had led me to where I needed to go. I needed to learn of this travesty. Bracken hadn't been negotiating for the good of all majiks, he'd been negotiating for the good of himself.

I wasn't going to sign anything.

Chapter Sixteen

Glaring down the table at Henrik, I tried to hold my hate for the man inside. Had he really punched Rye in the face? If so, the man was a traitor. When I'd been in the dream or vision, I'd believed everything I'd seen. Now, I had doubts. Once I rescued Rye, I'd find out the truth and see Henrik locked up. Right now, I had to listen to him and Frederick and Bracken drone on about details for a treaty I wouldn't sign.

Acid burned my gut. Actually, all of the men in this room were traitors if what I'd learned about the treaty was true.

The civil war was humans against majiks. The fairies fought with, and for, other majiks. By cutting them out of the treaty, they'd betrayed them. The acid climbed to my throat and spread throughout. They'd betrayed me.

Because I believed all majiks were equal. To each other and to the humans.

The Trees didn't contribute much. They were happy drinking free summer wine and making lewd comments, which I tried to ignore.

"All the manual labor humans have to do." Sequoia lifted his glass and took another sip after one of the humans had brought up a point about tasks. From his delicate hands and fine clothes, it was clear he'd never worked a day in his life.

Similar to Bracken. Although, Bracken was working now.

Working to betray his majik heritage and slaughter every majik, except fairy.

Fisting my hands, I had to hold in my knowledge. It might've been a dream or a possible future vision. I didn't know for sure that Bracken had betrayed majiks and Henrik had hit Rye. It had seemed real.

I peeked at Henrik's fists and noted the bruises. My gaze narrowed and incinerated him.

"I mean, I know you have your technology." Cedar waved his full glass around, spilling summer wine on the table. He didn't notice. "You still have to design the tech, make sure it works."

Frowning, I thought about the auraguillotine. Human tech meant to kill majiks and steal their power. I hadn't seen Stone to ask more about it. He wasn't present at the meeting today. I wanted to ask Frederick where my friend was but didn't want to draw attention to him when I knew his spy mission was critical.

I firmed my muscles. My spy mission was critical too. To both majiks and humans.

"Which is a form of labor." Bracken sipped from his glass. Maybe he was smarter than I'd thought, although he'd drunk plenty in my dream. "We snap our fingers to get what we want."

Which might be why the fairies had a spoiled upper class.

"I miss my magic." Bracken flicked his fingers and nothing happened. "What about you Elle? Do you miss magic?"

I froze. No possible way could he know I had a perfume bottle that restored my magic. Plus, it had only been a few days since our magic had been blocked when we entered the palace. "Unlike you, I wasn't surrounded by magic for most of my life. I grew up in the human world as a human and lived right here in Lindenhamn."

He leaned toward me and whispered, "Not something to brag about."

Frowning, I stood. I wanted to emphasize my point. "As you know, I'm half human."

"Elle, sit down." He tugged at my hideous, old-fashioned princess fairy dress.

"I won't sit down and quit calling me Elle." My patience fractured. The fairies didn't respect an honest day's work and the humans didn't respect me. "I'm Princess Ellery. When I lived in the human world, I was a servant in my own home. I cooked. I cleaned. I did the laundry."

Frederick's eyes popped out. Henrik's jaw gaped. He didn't seem as surprised. He had a distinct light of knowledge in his gaze.

I pushed the thought aside.

"Work builds character and an inner strength." Something the three male fairies in the room didn't understand. "And I, for one, am proud of my background."

Silence greeted me.

Bracken scrutinized me. The Trees' cheeks imploded about to laugh. Frederick looked anywhere but at me. Henrik slightly nodded his head.

"Princess Ellery," Bracken jerked to his feet and grabbed my hand pulling me toward the door, "may I have a word in private?"

His words came out through gritted teeth and I could tell he was embarrassed at my outburst. I didn't care. He was spoiled and wanted me to sign the worst treaty in history.

"Let's take a fifteen-minute break." Frederick relaxed back into his chair, wearing a slight smirk. "I'll have lunch brought in."

"Come with me." Bracken opened the door and dragged me outside. He slammed the door behind us, and I jolted. "What do you think you're doing?"

I opened my mouth to speak.

He kept talking. "Your story about when you were human and lived in the city is putting us at a disadvantage in the negotiations."

"How?" Hadn't he put us at a disadvantage by capitulating and fawning over the humans? By dressing similar to them? By drinking and allowing his two other negotiators to drink during the meetings?

"Because we need to prove we're better than them and yet our princess, the next person supposedly to sit on our throne, is half human and reminiscing about living with them."

Supposedly? The word carved into me. I'd be sitting on the throne after my grandmother passed. There'd be no supposedly about it. I let the word slip by not wanting to draw attention to my knowledge. "Relatability is important in negotiations."

"So is superiority."

I placed a hand on my hip and tilted toward him. "How are you proving fairies are superior? By having your negotiating partners get drunk?"

His high cheekbones reddened. "It's summer wine. Fairies can't resist."

"I can."

"Which displays another way you're not a full fairy."

"I don't want the negative fairy traits. For example, drunk and arrogant."

"You think I'm arrogant?" His tone rose in a challenge.

"Yes." I stayed calm. Arguing with Bracken wasn't going to help the situation. "These negotiations are important. A peace treaty will be best for everyone. *Every* majik."

Emphasizing the last point, I watched his reaction.

He peered down the hallway.

Doubts pitter-patted across my chest. How much of my vision had been true? Was he selling out the other majiks? I needed to make a claim to these negotiations to see what the draft treaty said and to put my mark on the future.

"I'd like to read the treaty."

"It's legal jargon. It'll bore you, Elle."

"Sitting in a meeting without knowing the terms is boring." I knew I couldn't get what I wanted from him. "I believe the scales are off balance. The majik team has a fairy princess in attendance at the meetings." I smoothed my skirt down. "Yet the human team has no royal taking part in the negotiations."

"Regent Theobald is a busy man."

"What about Prince Zacharye?" I held my breath, waiting for an answer. Was it possible Bracken would know more about what was happening to the prince?

"Frederick keeps saying he's busy too." Bracken angled his head, considering my proposal. "Maybe you're right."

I let the breath go. He'd actually admitted I was right.

"I'll push Frederick to get a royal representative to attend meetings in the future. There won't be many left before we sign the treaty."

Forcing myself to smile, I nodded. "And as leverage, I will not attend a meeting until a human royal does."

Which meant missing out on hearing what the exact wording to the treaty was. I'd find a way to read the entire document before signing. And I could spend the meeting time finding and rescuing Rye.

❧ ❧

The buzzing from the microphone buster Stone gave me was like a gnat in my ear. I ignored it. "If I use the perfume spritzer to become invisible, I can go through here," I pointed at the map spread across the table, "and take these stairs to get up to the highest level."

It was after dinner and I'd claimed to be tired. Bracken had wanted to stay and socialize with his friends. Or maybe he was seeing his girlfriend. I didn't care. I had more important things to do.

Watu sat in a chair at the table. Her serious expression showed her thoughtful concentration. "Idea good. Because of guards, elevator avoid."

Between the microphone buster and the fake vid of me taking a nap on the couch, we could talk freely in the living room area of the suite. The palace guards must think I slept a lot.

"Based on my dream last night, Rye should be somewhere around here." I stabbed at the spot with my finger, remembering Henrik punching him in the jaw. "I'll have to use these two elevators. I don't have a choice. I'll go in, search the top tower room, and find Rye."

She stroked her chin. "Rooms how will you get in?"

Most of the closed rooms had retina scanners to unlock the doors and I couldn't climb the outside wall of the tower.

"I can't use magic to go through the door sensors." I'd tested it out after Bracken had dragged me out of the meeting room this morning and he'd gone back inside. While waiting for my cyborg escort, I'd spritzed myself and tried using magic to unlock the meeting room door. It hadn't worked. When the cyborg had arrived, it used its eye lens to deliver a lunch tray to the meeting room before escorting me to my suite. It used the eye scan to unlock my door too.

"Climb on outside towers you can't." Watu had done several reconnaissance missions, playing the innocent lost servant or chaperone to gather intel. "All day, all night, spotlights shine on crystal towers. Guards watch."

I remembered the spotlights from when I'd lived in Lindenhamn and how they highlighted the palace and the advances in human tech. She was right. I couldn't climb up the crystal spire.

The door clicked open. I grabbed the map and tucked it behind my back. My muscles tightened.

A cyborg servant rolled in. "I'm sorry, Princess Ellery. There's something wrong with the acoustics in this room."

"Acoustics?" Ah, the cyborg meant the surveillance microphones. The security team must've realized the microphones weren't working.

"I would hate for the buzzing to hurt your sensitive ears."

Reaching up, I smoothed my slightly pointed, and now heated, ears. I was sensitive about their shape, especially when I remembered the regent asking about cutting ears off. An idea formed in my head and I followed the robot to the butler pantry.

"Before you fix the acoustics, would you mind helping me with a project?" I scanned the room, trying to find something for the cyborg to do. The room was kept spotless, plus neither Bracken or I spent much time here. Probably because neither of us wanted to see each other. "I'll be hosting a gathering and every piece of China, serving tray, and glass needs to be hand-cleaned right this second."

"Certainly, Princess Ellery."

I stepped beside the cyborg behind the counter leading to the butler pantry. I remembered what Stone told me about dismantling a cyborg. "Can you call your manager or whoever you report to so they know you'll be occupied for a few hours?"

Watu gave me an odd look. She didn't say anything.

"Certainly, Princess Ellery." Text typed across the robot's display screen on its midsection. "Message sent."

"Thank you." My fingers itched with caution and anticipation.

I stepped closer, blocking the cyborg. Flapping the cloth map, I wrapped the map around the cyborg's head. None of this could be recorded for the security team. I signaled to Watu and had her move closer.

"This does not compute. Light circuits are not out, but everything is dark." The cyborg swung its arms back and forth.

One of its arms whacked me in the face. The accidental punch stung.

"Sorry." Even though the cyborg had no feelings, I felt bad for what I'd done and what I was about to do.

With nimble precision, I grabbed the cyborg's head and twisted, hoping to stop any emergency communication. I opened the panel in the back and yanked on several wires. The wires broke free and the humming of the cyborg's electronics went silent.

I wrestled with the lifeless metal body. "Watu, get my Necessary Bag."

She jogged into the bedroom and hurried back with my bag. "Your plan is what?"

Thinking about the tools I'd need, I reached my hand in the bag and pulled out pliers, wire cutters, and a screwdriver. "I'm going to borrow this cyborg's eye."

Clamping the pliers around the cyborg's lens, I popped out the glass piece and then used the screwdriver and wire cutters to disconnect the eye. The dull red lens didn't have the light projected from the minicomputer in its brain.

"Work how will?" Watu leaned forward to watch.

"I'm hoping the lens will open doors." Similar to an all access key. I reached into the bag again, pulled out a flashlight, and shined it in the eye. "Hope this works."

"Do with that what are you?" She pointed to the lifeless cyborg.

I glanced around the room again. "The security team won't expect this cyborg back for hours. Can you switch it on again and have her clean the dishes? Security won't notice a missing eye if the cyborg is moving."

"Can I." She picked up the metal body. "You doing what?"

"I'm going to find and rescue Rye." After I found him, together we'd figure out the best way to approach the regent. I spritzed myself with the liquid in the perfume bottle so I had magic. "Wish me luck."

I became invisible and slipped out the door.

Following the path Henrik took in my dream backwards, I went from the meeting rooms to the large elevator. This late at night, I saw no one. With anticipation tingling inside me, I made myself visible and held the cyborg lens up to the retina scanner and placed the flashlight to the back of the lens.

Ding.

The elevator arrived and the door swished open. A trill lit up my veins. Stepping in, I pressed the button for the highest floor and used the lens and flashlight to pass the security check. This thing was going to come in handy.

My stomach roiled as I went up and up and up. The elevator took seconds. For me it seemed a lifetime. I didn't know what I'd find on the other side when the doors swished open.

A troop of guards. A concrete wall. Another security feature I wouldn't be able to open. My gut clenched. Rye.

The doors opened and, becoming invisible again, I stepped out.

Bringing the image of the map to mind, I realized this was where the map ended. The crystal spire was a newer addition to the palace. I remembered the spires from when I'd lived in the city. Whoever had drawn Watu's map had lived here a long time ago.

I edged forward, searching for the narrow elevator Henrik had taken down after visiting Rye. Two right turns and I came to a dead end. I tensed. Swiveling, I headed in the other direction. I didn't know how long my invisibility would last and I didn't want to spritz myself again.

A cyborg rolled past me and I froze. It carried an empty tray, and I remembered the tray Henrik had took from Rye. Maybe tonight he'd been visited by the cyborg and not a traitor who'd punched him.

I fisted my hands and continued on.

Two guards, wearing standard uniforms, sat in front of a narrow gold door.

The elevator. It had to be. I could easily sprint past the guards in my invisible state, but if I pulled out the cyborg eye and opened the elevator door, they'd notice.

Refusing to give up, I skimmed the area. What I needed was a distraction.

My fingers twitched. There was one thing I was good at now. I rubbed my fingers together and started a fire a couple of yards down the small hall, away from the elevator entrance.

"I smell smoke coming from there," Guard number one said. "Go check it out."

Guard number two snapped to attention and marched around the corner. "Fire! It's a fire!"

"I'll get the fire extinguisher." Guard one jerked toward a cabinet near the elevator.

Anxiety crinkled my skin. Too near.

"Hurry!" The other guard's voice carried down the hall.

Yes. Bring your buddy the fire extinguisher. I stretched on tiptoes, waiting for the first guard to leave.

He grabbed the red extinguisher from the cabinet and rushed around the corner.

Neither could see me. Now was my chance.

Making myself visible, I held the cyborg eye and flashlight up to the retina scanner and clicked the flashlight on.

The elevator door swished open and dinged.

"What was that?" the first guard asked. His voice grew louder as he approached the elevator.

I stopped breathing knowing I was visible, knowing they'd recognize me in seconds, knowing I'd be caught. I couldn't get caught. Too much was at stake.

"Hey!" he yelled at me.

"Hmmmmm," I hummed and stepped into the elevator. Humming calmed the average human. "You're not seeing me." My suggestion was a command from Mother Earth, something I'd learned from Arbor when I'd believed I'd spent the rest of my life as human. I became invisible again. "You'rrre noooott seeeeeeing mmmeeeee."

The elevator door closed, and I became visible and held the cyborg eye to the retina scanner and then pressed the top floor. The elevator rose.

Slumping against the wall, I took several puffs of air. The suggestion with the humming should work. My belly lurched with the movement of the elevator. Seconds seemed like hours as the elevator climbed to the top of the crystal spire.

The door opened and I was afraid to get out.

What if I didn't find Rye? What if he was in worse shape than in my dream? What if the guards followed me?

If the princess of the fairies was caught sneaking around the human palace, the peace treaty would be thrown out. Which might be a good thing. But what would happen to me?

Pressuring myself to advance, I stepped out of the elevator and into the hall. The winding stairs were right beside the elevator, similar to my dream. Soothing my nerves, I pushed forward, climbing the steps one at a time. With each step, anxiety once again frazzled my nerves, shooting small pulses down my back.

What if I was wrong? What if Rye wasn't here? What if he was dead? My imagination ran wild with possibilities.

I should've flown up the stairs.

Arriving at the top, I recognized the steel door. My gaze widened, scanning to confirm. This was it. Either he'd be here or he wouldn't.

I patted my hair and checked to make sure I looked okay. After months of separation, I didn't want Rye to see me at my worst despite the severity of the situation. The red warrior priestess outfit appeared sleek and mysterious. The perfect image I wanted to project.

I took out the cyborg lens and the flashlight and pressed it to the retina scanner.

The lock clicked and the door swung open.

Anticipation mingled with fear. Open to the future or open to despair.

Making myself invisible again in case he wasn't alone, I stepped into the room.

"Who's there?" Rye's question hit a chord in my soul. He didn't sound afraid. More like wary. "Quit joking around. Who's there?"

Just like in my dream, his wrists were cuffed in metal chains attached to the wall. A red, puckered scar ran the length of his muscular chest and I wanted to kiss the wound into healing. Other healing, or partially healing, injuries marked his skin. His once-nice dress pants now featured tears, rips, and stains. The pants hung around his slimmer waist. His hair was darker than before, crusted with dirt and blood. Dirty strands hung in front of his face.

But it was him. I'd found Rye. Prince Zacharye.

My heart twisted with love and rage. Tears burned, blinding me to everything except Rye. After all these weeks, I'd found him.

Chained, bloody, and thin, but alive.

Chapter Seventeen

I saw stars.

Not explosions. Fury burst through me. Regent Theobald had ordered the imprisonment. Who had beaten Prince Zacharye? Henrik? Others? A purple bruise had formed on Rye's chin right where Henrik had punched him in my dream.

My hatred for the man dug deep. "I'm going to kill him."

"Kill me? On whose orders?" Rye's voice sounded stronger than he looked. He yanked at the chains holding him to the wall. A fierce light shined in his silver gaze. "Quit hiding behind the door and show yourself."

His demand proved he had fight and spunk. Pride in him made me stand taller and I made myself visible.

Rye's expression went from hard and fierce to soft and disbelieving. His eyes went wide and sparkled. His mouth opened slightly. He stopped struggling. "Elle? Is it you or is this a mad vision?"

"Mad vision?" I rushed to him and wrapped my arms around his bare waist, like I'd dreamed of doing a million times. "It's me."

The smell of sweat and dirt rising from him wasn't as bad as I'd expect from someone being held prisoner for weeks when we'd been unable to communicate. His ribs protruded from his normally muscular chest and the scars on his back were new. Renewed horror clawed through me. He'd been whipped.

"Why did you find me?" He didn't sound thankful. He sounded crazy.

Why? I stepped back to take in every single inch of him. His once shiny black hair hung from his head and crusted with dirt. His smooth skin had creases of mud and red slashes. Lips, that had once kissed me with passion, were dry and bloodied.

And yet, even with the signs of distress and abuse, he appeared entrancing and attractive and right for me. Our gazes locked and our connection sparked. The earlier explosions morphed into fireworks.

Using magic, I released the shackles around his ankles and the cuffs pegging him to the wall. The metal torture devices clanked as they hit the concrete ground.

He stumbled forward at the unexpected release. Easily balancing himself, he stood straight. No bend in his back or neck from being held in that odd position for so long. His expression went from disbelief, to wonder, to concern. "Elle."

I hugged him again, unable to get enough of him. "I can't believe I found you."

His arms wrapped around my waist. "What're you doing here?"

"Rescuing you." My smile bloomed. My mission was complete. I'd found Rye and would help him escape.

"No, you can't. I can't." Letting his arms drop from around me, he took a step back and rubbed the red spots on his wrists where the handcuffs had chafed. "I have to stay here."

I analyzed him. He must be going crazy from being shackled for so long. "Why would you even say that? I'll make you invisible and we'll walk right out of the palace. Then we'll figure out how to confront your uncle."

"I can't leave." His deep voice grew stronger, more stubborn. "How did you get your magic back?"

How had he known about my magic being blocked? How did he know I was at the palace? "You aren't shocked to see me."

His dry lips lifted in a smile. A smile displaying his intelligence and empathy. A smile that warmed me. If he could smile in his current condition, he was a guy I could depend on forever. "I've got sources. I knew you arrived with the peace negotiators, knew the fairies' magic was blocked and their wands taken away."

"Why didn't your sources get you out of here?" Like I was doing. Sarcasm leaked from my tone.

"Elle," He took my hand. His rough skin rubbed against the softness of mine and sent shivers down my spine. Good and bad shivers. He'd been through so much and now we were together. It didn't matter what he knew and why. The magical connection we'd had from the moment we met sparked with our entwined hands. Not magic magic, but love magic. "My uncle locked me up when he found out I was trying to negotiate treaties of my own with the majiks. He also found out the orb was fake."

My shoulders dipped. "This is my fault. You never should've given me the real Divinity Orb."

"It's not your fault. You needed the orb more."

"I'm not the one in a prison cell." I ran my fingers through his hair.

He backed away and grimaced. "You don't want to touch me. I haven't had a shower in days."

Dirt and stink didn't matter. We were reunited.

"I don't care. I already hugged you." I leaned in to kiss him, needing his lips on mine. Wanting his comfort and his passion.

"Elle, no." He grabbed my arms and held me back. Desire combined with agony swirled in the silver depths of his eyes. His cheeks stained red and he stared at the ground. "I'd love to kiss you and hold you but not now. I wasn't expecting you yet."

I straightened and tugged my arms free. Disappointment threaded through my bloodstream. "You're right. There will be plenty of time for kissing once we're out of here."

He crossed his arms and stubbornness was stamped on his face. "I'm not leaving, Elle. I need to stay locked in these chains."

My chest tightened. "Why? What's going on?"

"Did you get the message I sent?"

"No."

His lips twisted in a grin. "Obviously you didn't get the message because you're here."

"What message?"

"I sent it through one of my lieutenants who I trust and who is taking care of me while imprisoned."

Taking in his injuries, weight loss, and dirtiness, I couldn't help but criticize. "He's not doing a very good job of taking care of you."

"I can't look well-fed and clean when my uncle visits." Rye rubbed a crusted wound on his arm. "The regent believes I'm interfering with ruling the kingdom and the war. And he'd be right."

Confusion whirred in my mind. "You mean you want to stay locked up?"

"It's part of the plan." He paced the cell with a limp. "I've got troops on the ground, lieutenants in every force, and spies throughout the palace. I know what's going on everywhere."

Did he? He knew I was in the palace and my magic had been blocked. Did he know about the terrible peace treaty being negotiated? And if the treaty were signed, it would be terrible for all majiks, except fairies and maybe even them. Did he know Frederick? Because I didn't trust him. "Do you know what's going on with the peace treaty?"

"Which one?" Rye's lips twitched, indicating he had a secret. Several secrets.

"What do you mean, *which one?*" My brow furrowed.

Bracken had bragged this was the best treaty ever and he was responsible for it. He might not get to sign the deal, I or my grandmother needed to be a signatory, but he'd be applauded for the treaty's contents.

"I have so many balls in the air. Spies and counterspies." Rye surveyed the corner and my gaze followed.

Air whistled out of my lungs. I'd been so excited to find Rye that I'd forgotten to check for cameras. "A surveillance device."

"Don't worry. I switched it off when you appeared." He glanced again at the device. "Which means we don't have much time before a guard comes to check on me." His voice sped up with his worry. "You have to get out of here, Elle. You can't get caught."

"I'm not leaving without you." A chill went down my spine when I spotted the shackles. I imagined the weight around my wrists. "Why would you willingly stay here?"

He took hold of my hand and caressed the top with his other. Sparks of love danced on my skin. His understanding smile didn't help. I didn't understand. "Elle, you have to go and leave me here and not say anything to anyone. I have a plan and I have to stick to it for the good of the kingdom, for humans and majiks."

His timbre deepened with authority and purpose. It made me want to be strong for him. To follow his lead and help him succeed.

"How long is it going to take? How long will you be imprisoned?"

"A while." His lips twitched.

"What's the plan?"

He sighed. "I don't have time to explain. Just believe in me."

I did believe in him. He knew what he was doing. I had to trust him and I needed to help. "Am I allowed to heal you?"

He tilted his head, considering my offer. "Internally. Nothing on the outside."

"You want to stay ugly?" I joked because I wanted to cry.

"Will my ugly scars turn you off?" His tone rose in a tease while holding an edge of seriousness.

"You know they won't." I placed my palm against the worst wound on his chest. "You know I don't care about a person's looks or position."

I liked him before I knew he was a prince. And my best friends were a troll, a giant, a brownie, and a smoke sprite.

"Which is why I love you."

His words melted into me and started an internal fire. Gnawing my bottom lip, I tried to gather my nerves to tell him I loved him too. This wasn't an appropriate place. I couldn't even kiss him if I said the words for the first time now.

Atmosphere didn't matter as long as the sentiment was real. "I—"

A pounding came from the stairs.

"Can you visit me again?" He spoke fast, knowing we didn't have time.

"Yes." The single word sang.

"When it's safe to come for a visit, I'll send you a message."

"Like you did last time?" I smirked, trying to lighten the goodbye. The temporary goodbye.

"This time, I guarantee you'll get my message." He lifted my hand off himself and kissed my palm. "Now, turn invisible and go."

Pleasure rippled up my spine. Every caress of his was significant. "I'm not happy about leaving you here."

"Believe me, it's not a picnic staying." He bent and picked up one of the shackles for his leg. He snapped it around his ankle and the click reverberated in my chest. He snapped the second ankle shackle in place. "For the kingdom, I have to stay and pretend I'm not a threat. Will you lock my wrists?"

My limbs deadened. I hated being part of locking up Rye. Yet, I wanted to be part of the right solution. He sacrificed himself for the cause so I could do this little thing. Pulling the first cuff hanging from the wall, I kissed the red welt on his wrist before slipping the cuff on.

"Elle," he groaned. "You're making this difficult."

"Good." I kissed the other wrist before putting the second cuff on. "I want you thinking about me while you're hanging around."

"I'm thinking about you all the time." His low voice sent a rolling tremble across my skin.

My heart tumbled. I'd wanted to lighten the atmosphere with my joke about hanging around. His response made it impossible.

A clicking came through the door. The guard had arrived.

Panic flashed across his face. "They're here."

I scowled at the door and back to him.

"Go, Elle." His expression hardened. "If you got caught because of me, I'd die."

The cell door creaked open.

Swirling my finger, I became invisible.

Rye stared at the spot as if he could still see me. And I wanted to be seen. My skin ignited and my pulse sped.

"First a fire and now the cameras are out." The guard with the fire extinguisher swaggered in. He glared, blaming both on the prisoner.

Rye hung his head, pretending not to be a threat. He didn't rattle the chains or put up any kind of protest. He acted meek and weak, which proved he was the opposite.

⟫⟫⟫ ⟪⟪⟪

Wearing pajamas, I stumbled into the living room of our suite to speak with Bracken the following morning. "I'm too tired to attend the meeting today."

Tired from lack of sleep caused by worrying about Rye and angry because I didn't know if I could sit at the same table as Henrik and not strangle him.

Bracken's eyes went cross, and he tugged on his very fine pin-striped jacket. The attire was more formal and human than usual with a pink silk shirt and matching handkerchief in his pocket. "You have to come. Regent Theobald is coming today."

The way Bracken spoke indicated the man was his hero.

My stomach revolted. The regent was the exact opposite of a hero. Knowing he was the reason Rye was locked in a cell, I didn't know if I could look the man straight in the face. "I didn't sleep well and—"

Bracken grabbed my arm, pinching my skin. "The regent is coming to the meeting because of your stupid request. Now get dressed and be ready to go in five minutes."

Yanking my arm out of his grip, I thought about using magic to put him in his place, but I couldn't reveal the secret. He treated me like a possession, not a person. As if I was beneath him even though I was the one with a royal bloodline. I'd give up my claim to the throne before marrying him.

Now wasn't the time to take a drastic action or state my opinion. I'd get dressed, attend the meeting, and listen to the men talking. They didn't want or listen to my comments. I'd meet with the regent and try not to commit murder.

I should've asked Rye how I could help with his plan. He said he'd contact me about meeting again, and once he did, I'd demand to be told everything.

A short time later, I was in the meeting room with Bracken, the Trees, and the humans Frederick and Henrik. I glowered at the latter and fisted my hands. I wanted to punch him. The regent wasn't here.

I was tired and in a terrible mood thinking about Rye's treatment and the ineptitude of Bracken and his negotiating team. Tapping my foot on the wood floor, I couldn't believe I'd hurried getting dressed so I wouldn't be late for the regent and yet he'd kept us waiting. Typical royalty.

I was royalty too, a higher position than the regent. I could be uppity too. "Where is Regent Theobald?" I made a point of peering at my father's watch and tapping the glass face.

"He's a busy man, Elle." Bracken's weak smile accompanied the excuse.

An excuse saying I wouldn't understand because I was a woman and not important in the grand scheme of things. Except I did understand and knew my signature on the final document was important.

"I'm a busy woman." I could be visiting Rye and learning his plans.

"That's a beautiful antique watch." Henrik's compliment wouldn't dissuade me from my hate. "You know the saying. Patience is a virtue."

I huffed, reigning in my need to confront him.

"Where did you get the watch?" His interested tone had me answering.

"The watch was my father's." I veered away and took a seat at the head of the table. Henrik was the last person I wanted to befriend.

Frederick's gaze narrowed, watching me take the position of power. "I'm sure the regent will be here shortly. We should begin negotiations."

Bracken took his normal low-on-the-totem-pole seat. "I was talking to...someone and she suggested since we're so close to signing the deal that we should celebrate with a ball."

I shifted in my seat, wondering if this someone was his girlfriend.

"A masked ball." Henrik's enthusiasm rocked through me.

"We are in serious negotiations." Frowning, I kept my voice stiff. "I don't think a frivolous ball would set the right tone when we have those on both sides fighting a war. Casualties and death."

My heart was wrapped in black. Did they not realize majiks were fighting against humans? Fighting and getting injured and dying? People on both sides were losing their loved ones.

"Let them eat cake." I quoted a historical figure who had done frivolous things in the middle of a revolution.

"Come on, Elle," Standing, Bracken chided me. "The fighting will end soon."

He probably believed he could associate with his girlfriend at a masked ball and I'd never know. Maybe I could catch him and get proof that he already cheated on me and stop the wedding. I smirked. Maybe I could sneak Rye into the ball and finally get my dance.

A dance with Rye wasn't worth the frivolity.

Bracken dropped his hands onto my shoulders and his fingers dug into my muscles, a poor attempt at a massage. "A masked ball would be fun and loosen some of our stress."

Cringing, I shook his hands off. His fingers didn't relax or excite. They irritated and pressed down, an unwanted burden. "What do you have stress about?"

I had stress. Fending off his pawing and being careful not to get stuck alone with him. This upcoming marriage I didn't want. Now that I'd seen Rye, I worried about him even more. And I worried about the fate of all the majiks, not just the fairies.

Trumpets blared.

Everyone's chair slid back, except mine. They stood and waited for the regent's arrival. I stayed seated, clasping my fingers together. I was of higher rank and wouldn't be cowed by his horns and his pages rushing alongside him.

Regent Theobald entered the room, sliding his feet along the wooden floor, resembling a skater. His shiny black pants shimmered with the movement, suggesting he wore them for that effect. A white, ruffled shirt peeked out from underneath the red royal robe. His neutral expression didn't show whether he'd meant to be late on purpose or if he even wanted to be present. His head tilted to a regal angle, as if he was having a hard time balancing the large jeweled crown on his head.

Frederick and Henrik dropped into a deep bow from the waist.

Bracken, Cedar, and Sequoia followed them, bowing even deeper.

I clasped my hands tighter and flattened my lips to a neutral position, looking neither pleased nor displeased. Even though I was displeased. Extremely.

Regent Theobald dressed like a king. He strutted and used the trumpets and the pages like a king. He wore a crown like a king.

"Your Majesty, thank you for attending." Frederick even addressed him *like* a king.

I wanted to scream, *The regent is not a king!* Rye should be standing here, ruling the country, having courtiers bow to him. He shouldn't be locked away. I kept my calm. I had to stay regal and keep my emotions in check.

Regent Theobald spotted me sitting in the chair. He studied me.

My midsection churned. Was he glaring because I didn't bow? Or because I'd taken the head position at the table? Or was he trying to remember where he knew me from? I couldn't let him figure out the latter.

"Regent Theobald." I trilled my voice higher, using an insipid tone. Inclining my head slightly, I beamed and clapped my palms together, trying to become a perfectly trite representation of a princess interested in silly things. "We were discussing a masked ball."

"Yes. We thought a celebration would be in order since the treaty is almost complete." Frederick signaled the page to pour a glass of wine for the regent.

The page poured a glass, took a sip to taste, and handed the glass to the regent.

Interesting. The regent was afraid of being poisoned.

He took a long drink. "I love a good soiree. Yes, a ball would be wonderful." He pointed at the page. "Let's find a date and arrange it as soon as possible."

One word from him and everyone jumped to do his bidding. An angry sensation burned in my gut. I wanted to ask why Rye, the true leader, was imprisoned. I clamped my mouth shut.

"I've been told the negotiations are coming along satisfactorily." Regent Theobald's twisted grin gave me the creeps.

Had he been told about the injustice of the deal? That was probably why he was smiling.

"The negotiations are going very well, Your Majesty." Bracken bowed again, proving his incompetence and his lack of a backbone.

The regent ogled me again and I tensed. Seconds passed and no one said a word. I held my breath, waiting for him to rat me out or demand my head on a platter. I needed a distraction. Clapping my hands together, I tittered, "Let's talk about the ball some more."

Bracken gave me a curious glance. "The treaty is more important."

Said the man who'd requested the ball.

Regent Theobald handed his wine glass to the page. "Fabulous news on the treaty. I'll have people plan the ball. Now, I must get back to doing royal duties."

Then, he was gone. I collapsed into the chair. Approving a ball was more important to him than negotiating a peace treaty.

The tension seeped out of the room and the men visibly relaxed. Bracken and the Trees poured themselves more summer wine before taking their seats. Frederick and Henrik whispered among themselves.

"I expected the regent would be part of the negotiations. Why didn't he stay?" Why was I stuck here when he could come in, say a few words, and leave?

Frederick sighed. He didn't believe he needed to answer my annoying question. "He will sign the final version, making the treaty law in the kingdom."

Even knowing I shouldn't, I couldn't stay silent. "Wouldn't Prince Zacharye be the authority to sign?"

Henrik straightened. "The prince has given complete authority to the regent."

His claim sounded stiff, practiced, fake.

I glared, knowing he lied. Something flickered in his eyes before his expression went blank. If I could use magic, I'd force the truth from him. I had to play it cool. Find out what Rye's plan was and help him.

"Let's get back to the treaty." Frederick tapped a stylo on his celltab. "We should try to be done by the time of the ball."

"It will take a while to plan a ball. I don't know if we'll even still be at the palace." I hoped we weren't, and yet I knew I'd have to stay for Rye.

"Not on the regent's orders. I'm guessing the ball will take place in a day or two."

I sat back in my seat and half listened to the discussions as the men talked around me. I knew I needed to pay attention, but I was so tired. My eyes flickered closed and the orb gleamed in front of me.

Jerking upright, I realized I was about to drift off into a dream. Like the dream about Rye being locked in the tower. My dream had been correct. Was the second part of the dream accurate as well?

I listened more intently.

Bracken talked about fairies and humans respecting each other. Frederick agreed when humans were hunting, they'd go around the ancestral fairy homes.

What about the ancestral lands of the trolls and the brownies? I leaned forward, unease slithering through me like a snake. And the snake was Bracken.

Frederick pulled up a map on his celltab, showing the fairy homeland and its borders in bright red.

Blood red.

He pointed his finger around the area. "When we're hunting zaubers..."

The hateful term sliced through me.

"...we'll not enter the fairy zone." He held up his hands. "And as ruler of the fairies, you will make sure no fairy leaves the area."

My heart dropped into my stomach. Frederick talked as if Bracken was already in charge. My entire dream had been correct. Bracken was creating freedom for fairies at the expense of the other majiks.

The throbbing in my gut created an answering beat.

Helping Rye was not enough. I had to stop this treaty and save all majiks from this terrible deal.

CHAPTER EIGHTEEN

Pacing my bedroom floor, I fisted one hand into another. A message had been slipped into my belt, asking me to visit Rye tonight. I'd found the note when I'd changed clothes before dinner. The note could've been planted on my person any time during the negotiations, at lunch, or when I walked the halls.

"Not a trick are you sure?" Watu's wise question had my belly doubling in pain.

It could be a trick. A way to trap me and Rye. I wrung my hands tighter. "The note said something about how I make his time a picnic. Rye said something similar last night when I'd found him. It has to be from Rye or at his direction."

"What if listening someone was?" Her advice never came as a direct lesson. She hinted and asked questions.

I'd thought the same thing. But why send me a note when they could've arrested me if they'd known I'd visited before? "Maybe. I'm going anyhow."

"You are of course." Her stoic expression exhibited she knew me better than I did myself. "Consider others you must."

My ribs constricted. I wouldn't endanger others. "No one knows you're involved. You'll be fine. And Bracken will disavow me if I get caught. He'll save his own neck."

"Not me worry." She tapped her shoulder to emphasize her point. "Majiks. All majiks. Need you."

I titled my head. "What do you mean?"

"Dream vision hinted and I hear." She brushed the rough skin by her ears.

"You hear what?" Uncertainty bubbled. What had she heard? And from who at the palace? Was it a reliable source?

"Not good these peace negotiations." Her harsh tone told me she believed what she heard. "Not good for all majiks."

I lurched back. The truth hit me harder coming from her. She was right about the peace negotiations being unfair, terrible really, for all majiks except fairies. I'd seen it in my dream, and I'd heard Bracken and his fellow negotiators talk about fairies' rights. Not other majiks.

Her stare unnerved me.

I knew I had to do something. Speaking up in the meeting wasn't a wise idea. I had to be more cunning and smart.

Slumping onto a chair, I threw up my hands. "You're right. I shouldn't even go and meet Rye."

"Prince Zacharye is close to your heart." She placed a fist on her chest. "Together discuss issues you must. Engagement tell him and negotiations you are learning. Tell him you love him."

Heat coiled through me. How could I tell him I loved him in one breath and tell him I was engaged in the next? Determination reamed through and straightened my spine. I would tell him I loved him tonight. No excuses. "I will."

"Conversation important very." Her tone grew serious and less soft. "Aristos priestesses have seen it foretold."

Great. Another prophecy. The first one, The Connected Crown Prophecy, foretold two royals would bring up the Divinity Orb. *Check.* That part had happened. The prophecy also said Rye and I would be together, and that hadn't come true. Especially with Rye locked up and me engaged to another man.

"Important most, discussion of deal and future of all majiks." It was the most straightforward thing she'd said.

I knew I needed to do more than listen to the treaty negotiations. I needed to shape the deal. Bracken and his gang might think they were almost done. Although after hearing what they said today, I wouldn't sign anything. I'd broker a new peace deal with my conditions. This wouldn't be between fairies and humans as Bracken expected, but between humans and all majiks.

"You're right, Watu." Pride surged through me. "While I'm gone tonight, can you find a copy of the draft deal on Bracken's tablet?"

She nodded and knowing how tech savvy she was, I didn't doubt her success.

"I'm not going to be a royal figurehead who does what I'm told. I'm not going to be perfect. I'm going to take charge of my own destiny and the future. I'm going to rewrite the peace treaty so no majik will suffer."

Her crooked grin lit up the room. "You will be the savior for humankind and all majiks."

"I don't know about savior." Warmth rose in my cheeks and my head steamed. "I'm not only here to rescue Rye like originally planned. I must ensure the safety of all majiks."

⇒⇒⇒⇒ ⇐⇐⇐⇐

I rubbed my clammy hands against the pants of my red warrior priestess outfit. My pulse jolted and my stomach roiled. Nervousness at seeing Rye again rumbled through my system. Or maybe I was nervous because I planned to tell him I loved him, and I couldn't sit by and watch the negotiations proceed in their current direction. Rye said he had a plan. Him still being locked up didn't prove it was working.

Standing outside his cell door, I realized this time I passed fewer guards. Good or bad omen? Watu had implanted the idea this could be a trap, and so my anxiety was high. I didn't want to believe it. Even so, my nerves quivered and the hairs on my arms stood at attention.

Pushing open the door, I expected either Rye hanging from his chains or an entire regiment of guards with anti-magic weapons. My gaze popped. Neither of those things greeted me.

Rye stood tall in full dress uniform complete with short jacket and gold braids. His clean, dark hair had been combed and styled. A plaid blanket was spread out at his feet with a picnic basket and summer wine. He held a bouquet of daisies.

My nerves rolled off in waves and my smile flourished. "What is this?"

"A date." He handed me the bouquet tied with a blue ribbon.

"Thanks." I sniffed the flowers to hide the sudden prickling in my eyes. "I didn't dress up."

"I like the warrior outfit. It's sexy." He took hold of my hand and helped me to sit on the blanket.

"How did you arrange this?" Amazement rang in my voice. "You're a prisoner."

"Only because being a prisoner helps with my plans." He sat beside me and poured a glass of summer wine. "Surveillance is off. The guards on duty are on my side. We have a short time to be together."

"Thanks." I still had to sneak back to my room. I couldn't make any mistakes because my new agenda was too important.

He poured himself a glass of human wine. Since I was half human, both drinks would affect my judgement. He held up his glass. "To us."

"To us." My heart thrummed with love. I clinked my glass against his. "To peace."

"To peace." He understood peace was more important than the two of us.

"And equality for humans and all majiks." This was what I'd be working for from this point forward.

"To equality." His somber tone told me he understood my intentions.

We both sipped our wine, and the silence wasn't tense. It was anticipatory. We were alone for the first time since being at Aristos Sanctuary. There was no pretense or doubt.

Skimming the room, I couldn't wrap my head around the scene. Stars shimmered through the slitted windows near the pointed ceiling. "Are you sure about the guards? Where did you get every-thing?"

"Yes. I told them to give us an hour. I wish it could be more." His secretive smile tipped up on one side and he winked. "I have ways of getting things, but I can't tell you or I'd have to—"

"Kill you?" I finished the corny line.

"Kiss you." He leaned toward me and his lips softly brushed against mine.

Tingles ignited from my mouth all the way to my toes. My body warmed and shivered at the same time. This kiss felt different then the few others we'd shared. More intense, more knowledgeable about each other, just more.

His silver gaze stared back at me, telegraphing the intensity of emotions.

Closing my eyes, I touched my lips to his, a light caress. Tingles exploded like magic and my entire body throbbed. Hot quivers raced across my skin. He placed both his hands on my cheeks and tilted my head so his mouth could fit precisely against mine. Perfectly. I sighed against his lips, knowing this was the first time in a while that I was okay with the word perfect.

His tongue nudged against the seam of my mouth and I opened to him. Opened physically and emotionally. I wanted to share his kisses and his innermost thoughts. I wanted to be together and kiss him whenever the temptation struck. I wanted to tell him I loved him.

Placing my palm against his chest, I broke the kiss.

"I love you." My voice came out strong and positive. I held my breath, waiting and watching for his reaction.

He opened his eyes slowly, and the ferocity of the silver pupils grew stronger. The connection between us sparked and magne-tized, drawing me closer.

"I love you too." His manly lips tilted into a smile again. "No reason to stop a good kiss."

My cheeks heated and my wings fluttered. "You thought our kiss was good?"

"I thought our kiss was amazing."

For seconds, we peered at each other. My chest shifted up and down with the rhythm of my heart, my attraction, and intense emotions. Love, desire, caring, and respect. I felt those things for him. I believed he reciprocated.

"I can't block the surveillance for long so let's eat." He picked up a bite of chocolate and held it up to my mouth. "Royal Alandaska chocolate."

My lips wrapped around the sweet and the chocolate melted on my tongue. "Delicious."

We were back to a normal date. Or as normal as a date could be between a prince and princess, where one of them was locked up. Where did he get the food, and the tech to block surveillance? I had so many questions and yet didn't know where to start and didn't want to waste our time together talking about practical things until the end.

I wanted to enjoy our date together. I wanted to get to know the real Rye, not the guy pretending not to be a prince when we'd first met, or the competitor for the Divinity Orb. I wanted to see Rye laughing, talking about mundane things, kissing. I never wanted the night to end, but also knew too much was at stake.

"This was so great. Such a respite from my new normal routine." Getting to his knees, he began packing up the food and wine into the basket.

My pulse dragged. The signal that our time together was up. The time to ask tough questions.

I stopped his hand from putting the last glass into the basket. "Tell me something. You said you stay locked up to not appear a threat to your uncle?"

"Yes." He took hold of my hand and kissed it.

Shaking my head, I tried to understand. "If you have troops and secret lieutenants, you could fight for your throne outright."

He got to his feet and held out a hand to help me stand. "And the people's blood would be on my hands. I've got a plan to take back the throne without spilling too much blood. I need you to be patient. Patience is a virtue."

The old saying clicked a memory. I couldn't put my finger on it. Shaking the feeling, I scanned the gloomy interior. "What happens to the food and the clothes?"

"And the toothbrush?" He waved his hand in the direction of a small metal sink attached to the wall, next to a half door with a toilet. "My trusted lieutenants brought everything to me, and they'll take it away after you leave. Can't let my uncle realize I'm not suffering as much as he thinks."

I couldn't believe this was how a prince lived.

"What is your plan?" Hope lightened my outlook. Hope he could end the regent's reign without death and we could be together.

"I have agents who have traveled to the homelands of all majiks. They're talking to their leaders."

"Like my grandmother?"

"Yes." He jerked his head down.

I waited for him to say more. Gardenia had similar plans. When he didn't share details, I asked, "What about humans? Do you have any of them on your side?"

"I do. And once all majik factions have agreed, they will come together, and I will confront my uncle." His solemn statement was a promise. "Hopefully without too much bloodshed."

My stomach curdled with my own complicity. "What about the treaty the regent's negotiators are discussing now?"

"I was hoping you could delay the signing." He grabbed my hand and tugged me against his warm chest. "Will you help?"

How could I refuse with him holding me so close? With his heart beating against my own chest?

"Of course, I will."

He didn't even need to ask.

"It's a terrible and unfair treaty. I was going to refuse to sign."

His brow furrowed. "Don't refuse outright. Delay." Concern threaded through his tone. "Be careful. I don't want to put you in more danger."

"The full treaty has been drafted and we need the signatures of Princess Ellery and Regent Theobald to make this complete." Frederick's suit had been tailored to a precise fit. He must use the same palace tailor as Bracken.

I'd taken the head position at the table. This time, I wasn't bored with the meeting. This time, I was interested and planned to make a few changes to the document. No, not a few changes. Many many changes.

And delay, delay, delay.

Watu had borrowed Bracken's celltab when he'd been out carousing, probably with his girlfriend. When I'd returned from my date with Rye, I'd spent the rest of the night reading the final draft. I'd expected to fall asleep reading the diplomatic nonsense, instead I'd jerked alert at each awful clause and paragraph.

"Excuse me." I scanned my notes on the celltab in case, in my tiredness, I imagined intent where there was none. With a quick reread, I determined every unimaginable, horrible detail had been accurate. With what little sleep I'd had, vivid enduring nightmares based on what our world would resemble if this document went into effect haunted me.

I wouldn't let on how much I knew. I'd take it slow, hint at the changes, even if I had to play stupid. I'd let Rye's plan roll out. "Maybe I'm wrong. I believe the treaty says there'd be forced repatriation of zaubers? What exactly does that mean?"

The men in the room exchanged uncomfortable glances, confirming what I knew to be correct. Other majiks in the fairy zone would be forced back to their homelands or enslaved.

Bracken bent and gripped the celltab. He tugged, trying to take it away. "Where did you read the treaty?"

He understood in the five minutes I'd been in possession of this conference room celltab, I couldn't have read the entire thing.

"I read a copy...somewhere." I waved away his question as he did so many of mine.

"You must've read an old draft." His fingers whitened as he gripped the celltab where the words blared in front of our faces.

Peering at my notes, even though I'd memorized every line, I stated the version and yesterday's date. "Are you saying this isn't the latest version?"

A few more uncomfortable glances. Frederick frowned at Bracken, believing he could control his fiancée. *Hah.* I held in a smirk.

"The treaty is a complicated document, Princess Ellery." The lead human negotiator took a sip of water. "You don't need to worry about the specifics. Know Bracken represented the fairies well."

By selling out the other majiks.

I wasn't an idiot. I could read.

Clenching and unclenching my hands, I tried to control my rising temper. They didn't understand I held sway. "If you want my signature on the treaty, we'll go through the document point by point."

"We don't have time." Bracken's face scrunched up in a petulant snarl. "The ball is in a few hours."

I raised a brow. My supposed fiancé thought a ball was more important than majik lives.

"Patience is a virtue." Henrik, who'd been silent, finally spoke up in a cryptic way.

Stilling, I repeated the phrase in my head. It was an old cliché. Enough people said it in normal conversations for it to go unnoticed. Except he'd said those same exact words before and so had Rye. Was the man on Rye's side? One of his secret lieutenants?

"We should start going through the document now. We'll read it section by section and line by line." That should take several days. "Let's begin with Section One, Paragraph One. Bracken why don't you read?"

They greeted my suggestion with groans.

Bracken tossed his hands up. His cheeks reddened. "Elle, this is ridiculous."

"You don't want to read out loud the words you've agreed to?" The force in my voice hopefully had an impact on him. "I'll read them, shall I?"

The Trees slumped into chairs, akin to school children having to listen to the teacher. Frederick grabbed a sausage from the serving dish and chomped on it. Bracken's gaze darted between me and the others. He appeared afraid of what I might expose. Henrik perched on his chair, the only one interested.

"Humans have the right to engage zaubers in manual labor." I paused to make a point and scrutinized each one of the men. "By manual labor, you mean slaves, correct?"

Everyone froze. Not a blink or a twitch of lips. They knew what the document said and weren't shocked.

"If a zauber is caught using magical powers, their powers will be stripped and they will be put to death." I gasped. This clause referred to the auraguillotine machine, where majiks powers were sucked from their souls.

Again, no reaction from the men. They resembled statues, most of them staring at their own celltab. They might not be listening, focusing on something else on their devices.

My fingertips turned white on the celltab. I read a few more clauses before banging the device down on the table. What was the point? They knew what was in the peace treaty. "Do I need to read further, or should we discuss this section first?"

My stomach roiled and boiled, imagining the terrible things which could happen to any majik except a fairy. My head pounded and wanted to burst. My friends Tos and Hokima were in danger. Even Watu, who'd accompanied me to Reximus Palace.

"Bracken, you agreed to this filth-filled, traitorous document?" I didn't wait for him to answer. "I disagree with everything written. The Kingdom of Alandaska is not made up of just humans and fairies." My voice grew stronger and bolder. This was my new truth and my new passion. These men needed to value my opinions. "All majiks need to be treated fairly and this treaty doesn't do that. My job as princess of the fairies is to protect *all* majiks. I refuse to betray them in this way, letting them be hunted, used, and killed while the fairies live in peace."

"You're right, Princess Ellery." Henrik's confidence oozed.

There were decent humans like him and Rye. There had to be others.

"What?" Frederick snarled at his partner. "We've been working on this for weeks."

"Patience is a virtue." Secretly smiling, I let Henrik know I understood whose side I believed he was on.

"Elle, can I talk to you? In private." Bracken spoke through gritted teeth. Standing up, he waved his hand at the door.

"If you'll excuse us." Grinning with satisfaction, I flounced out the door. My goal had been to rouse things up a bit, to let them know I wouldn't be a pushover, and to take up precious time. I'd succeeded.

Bracken slammed the door closed behind us. Wrinkles formed on his nose, displaying his disgust. "I'm the lead negotiator and this is the best deal we can get. I'm saving fairy lives."

His superior and sacrosanct attitude doused my satisfaction and riled me up again. He didn't care about anyone but himself.

"I'm saving majik lives. The current war is between humans and majiks. Trolls, brownies, ogres, giants are fighting on our side with fairies. For us. We can't sell them out."

I knew there was another plan. Rye's plan as well as a scheme Gardenia and Queen Dahliadew worked on with royals from other majik factions. Without full magic, I couldn't get a message to them so the plans could be combined. I had to worry about things I was informed about and things I could control. I refused to go along with Bracken's inferior peace treaty. And if I delayed the signing, the other treaty, the treaty between all majiks, might already be a done deal.

He leaned into me. His gaze went dark, threatening. "Quit being a pain in my ass, Elle."

A cyborg servant rolled up. "Nobletive Oakton, I have a message for you from Miss B."

The robot had saved him from receiving a few truths.

He snatched the note card and unfolded it, reading it while the cyborg rolled away. He forgot about me and his threats.

Studying him, I wondered if Miss B was his girlfriend. His expression softened and his eyes lost the fierce intensity. He certainly read the note quick. "Are you going to continue seeing your girlfriend *if* we get married?"

His gaze rose above the notecard. He glared while assessing what to tell me about his girlfriend. He couldn't lie. Glancing around the hallway, he leaned closer to me again. "Yes."

He didn't care that I knew about the female.

I gave him a tight-lipped smile. "Then I'm going to continue being a pain in your ass."

CHAPTER NINETEEN

"What do you think of this?" I swirled around in a bright red ballgown.

One spritz from the perfume bottle to create a dress lasting the entire night. The question was which dress? There was no mall to go shopping at for inspiration.

"Inspired by the designer Lavender? How about?" Watu stepped out of the bathroom in a simple silver sheath, holding a hooded mask which would cover her entire face with slits for her eyes. She'd insisted on the hooded mask so she wouldn't be recognized as a troll. She had covert matters to attend to and didn't need the extra attention.

"You know Lavender is a fairy, right?" I cocked my hip in the tight silk. It was funny that most humans who wore the famous designer's clothes didn't realize she was a majik.

I twirled around and changed the dress from red to purple, then switched to green. Tugging on the skirt, it morphed from tight to flowing to pleated. I'd slid in the fake recorded vids in the surveillance system and muted the microphones so I could use magic and speak freely. Although not for too long. I couldn't show them I knew about the surveillance, I still had to be cautious.

"Why is deciding on my dress so hard when creating yours was easy?" I waved my hand and changed the skirt from pleated to a hemline shorter in front and dipping longer in back with a slight train.

"Not a princess am I." She smoothed a large hand down her dress. Her gloopy eyes took on a shiny sheen.

Tears, possibly?

I grabbed her thick hands. "You look like a princess tonight."

Her green skin turned gray on her cheeks. Could trolls blush? "Determined by beauty, a princess is not. Though thank you."

Spinning around, I added ruffles to the sleeves. "This?"

"No."

I changed the color to an atrocious yellow with a daisy imprinted on it. At my first ball, Prince Zacharye's Presentation Ball, I'd worn a natural green dress with a rip away skirt and shorts underneath.

In case I'd had to run. And I'd had to.

This ball was different. There'd be no running away. Every muscle and tendon firmed. I'd make my stand.

"Definitely not." She shook her head.

"Its nature based." I didn't want to hide the fact I was a fairy. I'd be the lone female fairy at the ball.

Watu tugged at the hemline. "Color favorite?"

"Purple."

"There start."

Imagining the deep richness of a purple pansy, I replicated the exact color in a chiffon. The sleeveless bodice resembled an old-fashioned corset with velvet strips at the sides and ruffles down the middle. A lacy peplum gathered around my waist. The skirt dropped straight down, giving me room to maneuver and hide my weapons.

A princess always had to be prepared, especially a warrior princess.

Posing in front of a mirror, I examined my reflection. The purple color was natural yet bold. My wings fluttered behind me in a smooth motion. The dress didn't constrict my flying ability. Satisfaction oozed through me. For the first time since being told I was a fairy princess, I felt like a real princess. Making my own decisions and forging ahead with my plans.

"Sophisticated you are." She grinned.

"I look so different compared to the first ball I attended at this palace." That night, I'd been a terrified girl. Tonight, I was a confident woman.

Squealing, I spun around. Well, maybe a bit of a girl. "I wish Rye could see me dressed this way."

She slipped her own hooded mask on her head. "What about a mask?"

"Purple, of course." I flicked my fingers, creating a lace chiffon mask with an elaborate spray of lace and tiny jewels above the holes for the eyes. Slipping the mask on, the piece above the nose fit comfortably. Peering at my face in the mirror, my green gaze sparkled from beneath the half-mask. Which reminded me...

"What happened to the cyborg I stole the eye from?"

"Reported it I did." She nodded. I couldn't see her face, but I heard the smile in her words. "Guards found it in a hallway on the other side of the palace."

"No questions asked?" I found it hard to believe they didn't immediately suspect Watu. She was a troll and shouldn't have been on the other side of the palace.

"Questions yes. Answered."

Which meant I could keep the eye for future quests. Although between the men's anger when I left the room and Rye's plan to gain the throne, hopefully I wouldn't need it for long.

"I guess we're ready."

Our plan was for her to stick to the edges and listen and learn, gather intel about people and plans. Anything of use. I'd push Frederick for more concessions about the treaty and try to avoid dancing with Bracken.

Confidence soared inside my veins and I strutted out of the bedroom similar to a model on a catwalk. Even though guilt ticked in my muscles about the frivolous ball, I'd use tonight to forward my goals.

Bracken leaned against a counter in the living room, wearing a beautifully tailored suit. With the starched collar and long tails, the outfit appeared more human than fairy, suggesting he wanted to be Frederick's twin. He sipped summer wine.

"Where did you get the gown?" He gawked and I wondered if I had something on my face or if my elaborate hairdo had come down. "It's not one of the ones I bought for you."

Déjà vu. He disapproved of my clothes.

"Where did you get the suit?" I countered.

There must have been slots for his wings to come out through the back of the light wool pinstriped jacket. Matching pinstripes on the long pants grazed the top of his leather shoes. Fairy men usually wore breeches.

He brushed his fingers through his trimmed hair and his hand flailed, expecting the hair to be longer. The ponytail most fairy men sported was gone. "None of your business."

I pasted on a fake smile. "Then my dress is none of your business."

Telling him I had access to limited magic would never happen.

Escorted by a cyborg, of course, we left together for the ball with Watu trailing behind. I'd rather be walking beside her. Excitement and dread combined in a weird tango in my gut. My hero wouldn't be at the ball because he was locked in a cell. And my anti-hero gripped my arm as if I was his prisoner.

Stepping down the same grand staircase I'd traversed before, this time I wasn't afraid for myself. I was afraid for the future. There'd be no hiding behind the Roman-inspired columns and avoiding people. This time, as the only female fairy present, I'd be the center of attraction.

I stepped onto the marble floor and glowered at the ceiling. The same images of a human king greeting majiks of every kind. The historic art represented history. The current regent wouldn't greet all majiks. The man barely tolerated me and the fairy negotiators. A shiver ran down my back as I remembered the stark words of the treaty.

The one raised platform held the single throne chair. No fighting cage tonight like the one that had shocked me at the Presentation Ball.

Bracken led me through the crowd, acting above them even though he wasn't flying. He became more animated once he was with the negotiating team. I don't know if it was because the Trees were his friends or if he enjoyed Frederick and Henrik's company. Heralding the negotiators as if they were buddies and not the opposing team, Bracken shook hands and slapped backs, imitating a human politician. Fairies didn't operate that way, or maybe they did, and it just wasn't something they taught a princess because our positions were secure.

Or were they?

My insides squished together remembering the hatred from the noblets. I had to wonder sometimes with the way I'd been treated by the Grand Council.

Each member of the group greeted me as well. Even with the masks, I could tell who everyone was. Henrik with blond and black hair gave a deep bow. Frederick with his know-it-all attitude gave a nod trying to show respect yet not achieving it. And Sequoia and Cedar, whose wings fluttered, gave a snicker. Each of them had a glass in hand.

"After I left the meeting, did you discuss my new terms for the treaty?" I needed to know their objections so I could continue the fight.

"No." Frederick's single word made me more suspicious.

"What did you discuss then?" I indicated their almost identical outfits. "What you were going to wear tonight?"

Another man joined the group. His broad stance, tall height, and the way he held his shoulders told me exactly who he was even wearing a mask. Stone. His dyed brown hair appeared longer than before, and blond stubble grew on his cheeks.

My muscles relaxed and I calmed the constant spot of worry in the back of my mind. I was glad he'd returned safely from the mission.

He gave a deep bow. "Princess Ellery."

"It's nice to see you again, Lord Vitor." Questions ran rampant through my head. Where had he been? Had the mission been successful? What had he accomplished for our accord? Did it align with Rye's plan?

"I'm sorry I couldn't continue to attend the peace treaty meetings." Angling his head, he gave a sly wink.

"It's good you've returned at such a crucial point in the negotiations."

"Elle, this is a party." Bracken spoke between tight lips. "Let's not talk business."

My mouth dropped. They'd been discussing the treaty until we walked up.

"If I may, Nobletive Bracken," Stone bowed to him, even though the man didn't deserve respect. "There's a professor I think Princess Ellery would enjoy meeting. Do you mind if I steal her away for a few moments?"

My spirits lifted. Getting private time with Stone, I could ask a million questions and tell him everything that happened while he'd been gone. How I'd found Rye and the disaster Bracken had been passing off as a peace deal.

Bracken's relieved expression made me laugh inside. "Of course, Lord Vitor."

With neither Bracken or I wanting to be together, or even liking each other, our marriage would be a lonely relationship. But marriage was never going to happen. I'd convince the queen to let me be free.

Stone placed my hand on his arm and led me away. He respected me and my opinions. He cared for me as a good friend. I felt comfortable and not always on alert in his presence.

"You're back." I squealed in a whisper once we left the group.

"Not for long." His clipped tone told me he couldn't say much.

I opened my mouth to ask a question. Before I could say anything, he stopped in front of an older man. "Princess Ellery I'd like you to meet Professor Nilsen. He's an old friend of my family and resides at the palace."

Even bent with age, the man bowed with respect. His bushy gray hair circled his head, resembling a halo, and a matching mustache gave him a professorial appearance. "It is an honor to meet you, Your Highness."

"Princess Ellery is a close friend." Stone scanned the room, always on alert or searching for something or someone.

"It's nice to meet you, Professor."

"The professor provided the perfume bottle you received as a gift." Stone lowered his voice.

My brows rose. This man was on my side, our side, and had possession of a fairy artifact. Which was technically against the law. "Thank you so much. The scent is quite amazing."

"It is." He chuckled. "Have you enjoyed your stay at the palace?"

Loved finding Rye. Hated the negotiations. I needed to be diplomatic. "Yes and no."

"Understandable." Small lines crinkled when he smiled. "This palace must be quite different from your own castle. I've visited Queens Academy."

If he'd been invited inside the castle, this man had a deep understanding of the fairy culture. Impressed, I studied him closely.

"This palace has changed even in the short time since I attended Prince Zacharye's Presentation Ball." For example, Rye was not being celebrated. He was imprisoned.

"It has." The professor sounded forlorn and I wanted to reach out and comfort him. "And I should know since I live and work here."

"How long have you lived here?"

A sad sheen covered his gaze. "Too long. Alas, I must prevail."

Confusion wrapped around my mind. I opened my mouth to ask another question.

"Would you like to dance?" Stone took hold of my hand and squeezed in a warning. "This song is a particular favorite."

I never thought of Stone as a dancer. I hadn't known he was a lord either, though.

"I'd be happy to." Although I'd wanted to ask more questions. He must be aware of surveillance or eavesdropping nearby and wanted to stop me from digging more deeply.

"Professor, if you'll excuse us." Stone shook the man's hand.

"Yes, of course." He nodded his head. "I'll continue looking for her...the item we discussed."

"Thank you." Stone's dire tone spiked into me. Something was going on and I didn't think he'd share details.

He swung me onto the dance floor and took me in his arms. His smooth move and guiding hand had me taking the right steps. He was a good dancer. His feet shuffled with confidence and his strong arms navigated us across the floor. He scanned the area as we waltzed.

"I like your friend." I wondered if his parting comment had anything to do with Stone's restlessness.

"If you need assistance, he'll help out."

Stress alleviated a bit more. Another ally.

"I forgot. I have something for you." Stone dug into his pocket and took out a slip of paper. "It's old but, I think, important."

I took the paper and opened the note. The message, scrawled in Rye's familiar handwriting, explained his current circumstances and told me not to find him until he sent word.

Laughing, I crumbled up the note and gave it back to my late messenger. "I found him myself."

"Of course, you did." Stone sounded proud of me. "I'm staying in the palace tonight. My mission had a setback and I'm going back undercover."

My pulse slowed. "Are you in danger?"

"Don't worry about me." He kissed my cheek below the mask. "You need to be careful. While I love you speaking up for yourself and what you believe with regards to the treaty, it puts you in more danger."

"How do you know about my speaking up?" Doesn't matter. There were more important things to discuss. I leaned in closer and whispered, "Did you know Rye has a plan to unite all majiks and humans?"

The song ended.

"Yes. I must go." Stone bowed to me and he wended his way through the crowd. He hadn't fully answered and I hadn't the chance to say goodbye or good luck.

A little lost and sad, I stood by myself in the middle of the dance floor. I slipped off my mask and rubbed the spot where he'd kissed me.

"Ellery?" The familiar voice bubbled up from years of nagging and teasing.

With dread pooling, I wheeled to face my stepsister Ingrid.

Her red hair had been sleeked back into a more sophisticated style than usual. Her fair skin shined, displaying a trail of freckles on her cheeks.

She shouldn't remember me. Gardenia had done a powerful spell to erase the memories of both my stepsisters and stepmother. Except when I'd returned to Milford House, my father's ancestral home, to retrieve my father's watch, Ingrid had said something about visiting a fairy palace and learning I was a princess.

Since I wasn't supposed to be at my old home, I'd never mentioned it to Gardenia. Then again, I'd never expected to see anyone from my human past again.

A big yellow caution sign flashed in my mind. Ingrid's correct memories could cause a lot of trouble.

Chapter Twenty

Ingrid waved her hand high and strode forward at a fast pace. Her pink dress softly hugged her curves. No silly hairpiece at this ball. "Elle? It is you."

Frozen, I couldn't run. Running would bring more attention than my stepsister parading through the crowd with her hand up and waving. And if I told her she was mistaken, she'd make a bigger scene.

"Um, oh." If I chatted with her, it wouldn't create a big show, except I didn't know what to say. "Hello, Ingrid. How're you?"

"How am I? How're you? You disappeared and Mother and Ilana don't even remember who you are." Her eyes grew wider and she began to talk faster. "You have wings."

I shrugged. "Well, I am a fairy."

"Half fairy," she whispered.

Choking back a dark chuckle, I fluttered my gossamer wings. "The secret is out."

"I still feel terrible that my mother wouldn't allow you to attend Prince Zacharye's Presentation Ball." Ingrid indicated the crowd dancing around us. "Yet, here you are at the most important ball of the year." She leaned in conspiratorially. "Probably the last ball."

Shifting my feet, I'd expressed my thoughts about how this ball would look to those fighting on the front line. Decadent and a waste of money that could be used for more important things. "Y-y-yes."

"Wow! Your dress looks like a Lavender original." Her voice rose and she arched a brow. "How can you afford a dress this extravagant when you gave the house to my mother?"

In the past, I hadn't been allowed a new dress to attend the ball even when my stepsisters and stepmother had gotten new and expensive clothes. My thoughts turned murky. I'd been ignored and put down. Exactly how Bracken treated me.

Scanning the people around us, I didn't want everyone to know about my past. With the current situation, our relationship could put Ingrid, her sister, and her mother in danger. I also couldn't confess how I used magic to make this dress. "My mother's family has...um...connections."

"Are fairies at the ball?" She scanned the people, trying to determine if other fairies were present. "I mean, of course fairies are at the ball, you're at the ball. And the party is to celebrate a treaty between humans and fairies."

Even my sister knew who the treaty was between and how other majiks were excluded. My thoughts morphed darker, more somber. I didn't want to discuss politics with her in the middle of the dance floor.

"Why are you at the ball? Is Ilana or your mother here?" Dread dropped in my stomach with the need to know. I never wanted to see them again. At least Ingrid had been nice.

"They wish." She smirked. "My girlfriend's brother is Lord Henrik."

A couple of people peered at us.

"How fun for you." I slipped my mask back on. "How are all of you doing? Do you live in Milford House?"

Less than a year ago, Milford House was the one thing I'd wanted. Now, I realized there were so many more important things. For example, saving the majiks from the regent and saving Rye.

"Yeah. It's not as nice as it used to be. My mother's boyfriend is living with us but refuses to marry her. They're always fighting."

"Maybe it's best if they don't marry." Sounded similar to how my marriage to Bracken would turn out if we were forced into the contract.

"He's working as a guard at the palace. Maybe you'll see him."

I hoped not. "What about Ilana?"

"She didn't pass Continuum and will end up at tech school. She'll never meet the prince there." Ingrid giggled, suggesting her sister had finally gotten what she deserved.

Ingrid wouldn't meet the prince here either.

Glancing around, I realized I'd spent too much time with her. I'd been curious about my former family and home. Talking to her could put her in danger. "It was great talking to you, Ingrid."

"Princess Ellery," Sequoia fluttered his wings beside us, creating a breeze. "Regent Theobald demands to talk to you."

My chin jerked up. Princesses didn't go to regents at their request. It should be the other way around.

"Princess Ellery?" Was Ingrid remembering when Gardenia had told the family I was a princess?

"Excuse me." I gave her a flat smile and let Sequoia lead me to the regent. I didn't want Ingrid asking too many questions or anyone asking about her. It was best I leave.

Bracing myself, I strolled toward Regent Theobald sitting on the throne chair without a mask. He wanted everyone to know who he was, or at least who he was supposed to be. He'd never be my ruler.

Had he heard about my disagreements with the negotiators? I arched a brow. Did he want to discuss things with me personally?

His pages stood beside the chair, one holding a wine goblet and the other holding a tray of food. Guards circled near the back of the stage. The regent had a skinny leg thrown across the arm using the throne as his personal fainting chair. He didn't stand or even sit up at my approach.

Contempt for him had me fisting my hands. I wanted to reprimand him. He shouldn't be sitting in Rye's chair and he should greet me properly.

His gray eyebrows arched as he waited for me to bow to him. He could lock me up before I'd take such an undignified action. We could stand here for the entire ball and stare until one of us concedes. It wouldn't be me.

Justness had me standing straighter. I refused to quiver or waver.

The pages and guards surrounding him shifted their feet and stared at the ground. Frederick, who sat on a short stool near his feet, set his glass down and placed his hand on the small knife hanging from his waist. As if the small blade could stop me.

I stayed as immovable as the new, ugly statue at the back end of the stage. The carved marble depicted the regent standing proudly with more hair on his head than he actually possessed and majiks kneeling at his feet, comparing them to slaves. My outrage roiled at the depiction.

The tension grew thicker. The pages became more uncomfortable. The atmosphere extended to the partygoers in the immediate vicinity.

"Bring Princess Ellery a chair so we can talk." Regent Theobald broke the deadly silence.

A small victory. And since I was curious about what he wanted, I'd oblige and sit.

A page ran to do his bidding and came back with a smaller version of his chair. This resembled the tiny chair Rye had sat on as a child next to the regent to give the man legitimacy. I clearly remembered vids of Rye sitting on this dais with his dyed blond hair sticking out of a too-big crown, appearing sad and confused. The regent had taken hours to conduct the royal business and had forced the toddler to sit next to him the entire time.

Taking a seat, I pressed my hands against the red velvet, hoping to feel some of the younger Rye's emotions. Perceiving nothing from his past, I kept my chin tilted at a superior angle and my lips in a straight line.

Regent Theobald slipped his leg off the arm of the chair and leaned closer to me. Too close. His hot breath smelled of liquor and I wanted to slant away. "I understand you've screwed up our peace treaty."

Refusing to cower, I didn't back up or back down. "The document doesn't deserve to be called a peace treaty." Forcing my voice to stay even, I pushed down my boiling anger at his bullying. "It gives permission to annihilate every majik, except fairies."

"You're a fairy and a human. What does it matter to you?" He winked.

My mouth wanted to drop to the floor. I kept my lips clamped shut. The man was callous and cruel. How could Rye grow up with this man and be so honorable?

"It matters because all majiks matter," I practically shouted.

Frederick waved at Bracken. He wanted help to change my reasoning.

I knew yelling would get me nowhere. Questions and superiority might. I prodded deeper. "I don't know why I'm discussing this with you. You're not in line to rule."

Regent Theobald's mouth pinched together, and his gaze narrowed to thin slits. His cheeks puffed and turned a ghastly red color.

If I could get under his skin this easy, it was time to push harder.

"Where is Prince Zacharye?" I wanted the response to be public. "Is the prince at the ball?"

I knew the answer. I wanted the regent to show his real stripes and I wanted to know what he was telling everyone about the prince. How was the regent explaining Rye's absence?

Regent Theobald leaned back in his gilded chair. "The prince is indisposed."

The man didn't care about his nephew's health. But for me, worry about the prince spiked.

"Indisposed how?"

"He's sick, very ill." The regent shook his head, trying to display a modicum of concern.

I knew this was a lie. Humans could lie, which put fairies at a disadvantage.

Except for me. "I should visit him to exhibit the fairies' good wishes."

"No. No." The regent's immediate answer proved his anxiety about my pressing, which made me want to push harder. "My nephew is very contagious. I wouldn't want you to expose yourself and get sick...or die."

Beatings aren't contagious.

Oh, how I wanted to respond in that way. Then, the regent would realize I knew the truth. My muscles stiffened. I understood the threat in the regent's words. If I continued to press on this matter, I'd find myself in the same condition as Rye. Locked in a cell.

"Fairies don't get human illnesses." I never got sick as a child.

"Ah, yes. But since you're half human, you might." Regent Theobald sang the words, indicating he'd won this discussion.

Maybe he had. I could push him about how Prince Zacharye would need to sign the treaty because he was old enough to rule the kingdom. This didn't seem the right time or place. I didn't want to show my knowledge and conviction. Plus, Rye had a plan of his own. He'd asked me to delay, not confront.

I'd delay as long as possible. But at some point, I'd have to prod and push and challenge.

Standing at the edge of the dance floor, I watched the couples swish past me. Bracken danced with a buxom girl with curly blond hair. I couldn't see her face because of the large mask she wore. She didn't have wings so she must be human. She resembled the girl I'd seen sneaking out of his room.

This must be his girlfriend. I could confront him now, make a scene so there'd be plenty of witnesses that he'd cheated on me. The Grand Council probably wouldn't care. They approved of him more than me.

"Why is such a beautiful girl frowning?"

My heart fluttered and my middle transformed into a pile of goo. The familiar voice soaked into my skin and made me happy.

Spinning around, I wanted to reach out and touch Rye. Wearing a plain gray mask, his silver eyes sparkled at me. A trill burst inside. His plain gray suit blended in with the other dancers. He didn't want to stand out.

"What're you doing here?" Happiness and worry collided like two objects in space, creating kinetic energy between us. Being here was risky for him. His enemy sat in the throne chair, watching everyone. Guards stood at every door.

"A masked ball is the perfect opportunity for me to sneak around and stretch my legs." His deep timbre held an edge of warmth. He held out his hand. "I know you've turned me down once before, but will you dance with me?"

A teasing smile tickled my lips. "I turned you down twice."

"Ouch. You wound my soul." He pressed his fist to his chest, although I heard the grin in his tone. "Please."

I remembered the please too. It had almost stopped me from my mission to rescue Arbor. I put my hand in his. "I'd love to, if you're sure it's not too dangerous."

"I live for danger."

"And punishment apparently." I firmed my mouth, unable to banter back. He'd been seriously hurt in captivity.

We shuffled onto the dance floor and disappeared among the whirling couples. Could we ever disappear? Right now, he was anonymous. But people would recognize me with my glamorous gown, floral tiara, and wings. People would know I was the princess and they'd be watching. Nervousness crushed my enjoyment.

"Henrik told me you were magnificent in the meeting today."

The compliment caused my anxiety to unfurl and my heart to bloom. "I thought he was one of your men."

"I didn't realize you both were attending the treaty meetings until recently." Nodding, Rye tucked me closer.

The heat from his body eased into me and I relaxed for the first time this evening. His sandalwood scent wove around me, creating fantasies in my head of what it would be like to be together as the Connected Crown Prophecy had foretold.

"I finally got your first note from Stone."

"Your friend Stone is a good guy." Rye's tone lifted on the word friend as if it was a question. He knew I'd kissed the man and I wanted to reassure him.

"Stone is a friend. That's all." I wanted to be clear on that aspect. "I didn't even know he was here." I pressed my lips to Rye's ear. "He's on a secret mission."

"I know," Rye whispered back. "We can't talk about it here."

We both laughed. The few seconds of merriment soothed. Being normal felt so good, even if it was about something so mundane as jealousy. When he succeeded and took the throne, we could be together openly. Rule in concert. Someday marry. "We should discuss the weather."

"What?" He swirled me in a circle with a strong guiding hand pressed to my back.

My skin ignited at his touch. "It feels good to be normal. Two regular teens dancing."

"You could never be normal." His voice dropped low and tingles spread from my toes to the tips of my wings.

"Neither could you." I tilted in closer, wanting to kiss him.

"I could be dead."

My heart dropped into my stomach in a pile of dread and terror. "Don't say that. I thought you had a plan."

"We've had setbacks. The clandestine meeting of my representatives and the majik representatives was busted up. People died and some were imprisoned."

I shivered and he enfolded me in his arms. "Imprisoned where?"

He snorted. "In my dungeon. Unfortunately, I don't have control of the prison right now."

I took in oxygen, needing to sound hopeful. "You will."

His gaze seeped into my soul. "I want to kiss you." He spoke my earlier thoughts.

"Me too." My pulse raced.

"We can't."

"Too many people watching." I sighed, never wanting this moment to end.

Even though I'd thought the ball wasteful and frivolous, the event had given me this short time in Rye's arms. We deserved a happy moment before facing the challenges ahead.

Because there would be challenges. Even after he took control of the throne, there would be prejudice. Would humans want me with their prince and ruler? How would the fairies react?

"May I cut in and dance with my fiancé?" But Bracken didn't ask. He ordered.

Ordered the prince of the kingdom to release me.

My lungs deflated and I struggled to breathe. Cold invaded my limbs. My body stopped swaying and froze. Rye and I had been caught and our moment of happiness ended. He could be recognized and we'd both be imprisoned.

Worst of all...

Bracken had told Rye—the love of my life—I was engaged to another.

CHAPTER TWENTY-ONE

My body swayed. Pain scraped through my lungs. This horrific scenario could not be happening.

Rye's cheeks sunk beneath his black mask. His frown deepened. And his silver eyes disintegrated into a cloudy gray.

My ribcage tightened, barring my heart from reacting on the exterior. "No, it's not tru—"

Bracken yanked on my arm, pulling me out of Rye's embrace.

"Wait." Wheeling around, I broke free to explain.

Rye was gone. The pounding in my chest grew louder. The second my back was turned he must've faded into the background.

Standing on tiptoes, I tried to spot him in the crowd. To no avail. I flitted my wings, ready to fly.

"Don't you dare fly away from me." Whispering, Bracken gripped my arm tight and pinched my skin. "And don't you dare embarrass me by using your wings at the human ball. Or ever in a human's presence."

As if they were superior to us. As if he wanted to be human.

"I don't plan to be in a human's presence for much longer." I yanked on my arm.

It was best Rye retreated. For him and his safety. Still, I wished I could explain Bracken's statement.

Bracken's fingers dug into my skin harder creating white spots. I'd probably bruise. He leered into my face. "You'll always be in a human's presence. You are half human."

"I don't understand you. You seem to love the humans you're dealing with." I'd noticed how he'd praised Frederick and Henrik and simulated how they acted and dressed. Bracken's girlfriend was human. Yet there was something about me he hated. "Why do you despise me so much?"

"Because you're a halfling. A half breed." His face contorted with ugliness and a dark pall hung above him. "You're not pure."

"If you hate me, why did you stop me from dancing with someone else?" It definitely wasn't jealousy. So why did he care that I'd finally gotten one moment of levity?

"Was he a stranger?" His gaze shimmered with venom, even while he twirled me into a dance step. "You accuse me of having a girlfriend while you have someone on the side as well."

The truth tickled my tongue. I'd love to come out and tell him the man I danced with, the man I loved, was the prince of the Kingdom of Alandaska and the true ruler of the land. I couldn't. I couldn't give up Rye's secret even if it made my life more difficult.

I'd deal with Bracken. "You didn't have to spit out we're engaged."

"When a guy is leaning in to kiss my fiancé, I have every right to claim you." He confirmed what I'd believed all along. He thought of me as a possession, something that would give him a position of authority.

"I'm not your possession and I will never marry you, no matter what the old contract says." I jerked out of his arms and dashed off the dance floor with as much dignity as possible. My eyes stung with unfallen tears. I was engaged to a monster who resembled an angel, at least to the other fairies.

I pushed through the crowd with my head down. Men inspected me and women analyzed my clothes and wings as I rushed past. It was hard not to be noticed with my wings flapping behind me.

What was Rye thinking after the big reveal? I should've told him about the forced engagement when we'd last met. He must know how much I cared for him. I'd told him I loved him. Doubts dodged around inside me. Of course, he knew I could lie. Just like him.

Pushing the door to the bathroom open, I ignored the surprised stares of the women in fancy gowns using the facility. They'd see my blotchy face and know I was upset. A cyborg servant opened a stall door. Instead, I dashed to the last stall, needing my privacy.

I slumped against the closed door, wanting to sink to the ground, and took a deep, shuddering breath. Loneliness swamped me and I fought the urge to give in to the tears. I couldn't sit in the stall for much longer. I had to salvage the rest of the evening because the treaty was the most important thing. I needed to delay and block the treaty signing. For Rye.

A tap on the stall door.

"Elle?" Ingrid's soft voice.

I groaned quietly. I couldn't deal with my ex-family now. The girl knew I was a fairy princess. What did she want from me?

"Elle, are you okay?"

"What do you care?" Harshness flew out of my mouth.

She'd gone along with her mother and sister's cruel treatment of me. She treated me as a slave.

"I care. I always cared. I was just afraid to show it in front of my mom." Her timidness floated over the door.

Ingrid had been the nicest of the three. She'd slip me extra dessert or sneak me her old clothes to wear. She wasn't as cruel as her sister.

Swiping at the wetness on my cheeks, I opened the stall door. "I know. I'm sorry."

I noted the blotchy skin and red eyes staring into the mirror. I wished I could use my magic to make myself look better. Turning on the faucet, I splashed water on my face.

"Are you really a princess?" Her tone went dreamy.

"Yes. A fairy princess, so, in your mother's book, it doesn't count." I remembered her disdain of Queen Dahliadew.

Ingrid shook her head, slightly bemused. "So I didn't dream up going to your castle?"

"No." I took a cloth from the cyborg and patted my wet face.

"What's it like? Being a princess?" Her eagerness indicated immaturity.

I'd been similar once.

Being royal had hardened me. It had been a nightmare since discovering the truth. Well, mostly. There'd been good parts. I wouldn't whine. I'd been accused of using the poor princess act before.

Once I'd accepted my royal position, making an effort to be perfect had gotten me nowhere. The Grand Council was trying to marry me off to Bracken. At Reximus Palace, I'd tried to mind my own business, complete my own quest to find Rye. Impossible. Not once I learned about the terrible deal Bracken negotiated. I had to step in, even though they weren't taking me seriously.

Ingrid peered at me expectantly.

I had to give her an answer and I wanted to be truthful. "Being a princess is like being an overdressed prisoner. Being a princess is not a fairytale."

Before she could question further, I marched out of the bathroom and into the crushing atmosphere of the ball. Straightening my shoulders, I wasn't ready to face the human crowd, my enemies, or my fiancé.

I wished I could find Rye and explain. Or that I could sneak away from the ball to his cell and resolve any miscommunication. I had to trust he believed in me and our love.

Keeping to the edges, I scanned the area. Frederick sat by the regent up on the stage. Henrik wasn't to be seen. Sequoia danced with a human girl, fluttering his wings and his eyelids. He flirted with her. Cedar watched from the side with a crowd of girls gathering around him. One girl flipped her hair. Another took hold of his hand. A third ran a hand across his wings. Each move became more aggressive. Obviously, Bracken's friends enjoyed human girls too.

I didn't spot Watu. Maybe she'd left. Stone and his friend, the professor, weren't in sight either.

Now would be a good time for me to take off too. Rye must have gone, and any enjoyment I'd had left with him. I wanted to remember the few minutes we'd had together. I didn't want to argue or discuss anything about the treaty after the negotiators had been partying and drinking. Maybe they'd be hungover in the morning and my persuasive arguments would work.

Reeling down a dark corridor, I didn't want to be escorted to my room by a cyborg. Everything inside me firmed. I wasn't a prisoner. I could find my room on my own and do a little spying on the way.

The narrow hallway had enough room for two cyborgs to pass.

And a couple making out.

A silhouette of a guy and girl with their bodies pressed against each other and their arms wound around each other's necks. The male had wings.

I sucked in a sharp breath. The only male fairy I hadn't seen in the ballroom was Bracken. And I didn't want to see him now, especially when he was shoving his tongue down this girl's mouth.

Pivoting, I went to leave the way I came.

"I can't believe I have to marry the half breed to gain power." Bracken's bitterness stabbed me in the back.

I paused, spun around, and flattened myself against the wall behind a large service cart.

The female ran a hand through his hair. Her tight dress emphasized her curves. "It's only for a short while." Her articulation came low and sexy. She slid her fingertips around the edge of his wing and he visibly shivered.

What had she meant by "for a short while?" There was no divorce in the fairy world.

"She's screwing up the treaty process giving fairies freedom and power."

Interesting Bracken mimicked the regent's words.

"We'll have to do something about it." The girl sounded cutthroat and familiar.

"Locking Elle in her room?"

"Too good for her." The girl's hard tone hinted at a personal vendetta against me.

Stumbling, I backed further against the wall. Her voice needled just beyond reach.

"We should force her into a quick marriage at the palace by having you and her found in a compromising position." The girl's suggestion was similar to Bracken's father's comments.

My skin crawled. I wasn't going to do anything more than shake his hand. Unbelievable that his girlfriend would suggest such a disgusting thing.

"I don't want to marry her. I want to marry you." Bracken was a spoiled child.

The girl's giggle mimicked a sinister chuckle. "After the marriage, we'll kill her."

Chapter Twenty-Two

My viewpoint twirled like a kaleidoscope.

Everything up went down. Everything to my left veered to my right. My head spun. My emotions crashed. Happy to see Stone. Angry at the regent. Thrilled to dance with Rye. And now, to overhear a mortal threat.

It wasn't my day or my night.

I backed away from Bracken and his human girlfriend. They were both my enemies. My head hurt and my lungs shriveled. I had to keep my wits about me. Get away without being noticed. Find room to think.

Slipping back into the crowded ballroom, I again scanned the room, searching for someone I knew and avoiding those I didn't want to confront. Music and laughter attacked my ears. My mouth tasted dry as dust. Varying scents of flowered perfume, food, and sweat caused my stomach to churn. My eyes burned and I squinted, trying to keep the tears from falling. I had to get out of here and I had to appear normal.

The crowd thinned toward the stage. I headed that way.

Ingrid stood in a group of regular teenagers, laughing and flirting. How I wished I could fit in. I'd never fit in. Not even when I pretended to be human. I'd always been an outcast.

Wending my way through the crowd, I pressed a hand to my belly, trying not to get sick. A man leaned toward me and his sweaty scent stung my nose. I covered my mouth with my hand. Weaving around the stage, the brassiness of a trumpet assaulted my ears and split my head with pain. I normally loved music. Not tonight.

A back exit behind the stage beckoned. If I could sneak out unnoticed, I could pretend to be lost. Anything to get away from the people and the noise and the scents. I pushed open the door and let it slam behind. Reveling in the silence, I slumped against the wall and breathed.

A mechanical buzz caught my attention and I peered up. A camera. Stiffening, I should've known. In this palace, one was never truly alone.

Flashing a fake grin, I straightened away from the wall. I'd have to knock the camera out if I wanted to sneak out this way.

"You're not supposed to be back here." A man wearing a guard uniform placed his hand on the weapon at his waist. His gaze roved up and down my body, taking in my dress, my wings, and my crown. His hand shook and I was afraid he'd accidentally shoot me. He knew who I was.

Wary, I couldn't even act afraid. "I needed respite from the crowd." True. I wasn't going back to the ball and this man was going to help me. He just didn't know it.

I'd planned to take the perfume bottle out of my bag and use magic. But I couldn't demonstrate my tricks to the camera. There was something else I could use. Something that would calm the guard.

"Hmmmmmmmm."

"What're you doing?" He snarled the question.

"I'mmmmmmmm hummmmmming." I kept my voice soft and low. "Hmmmmmmmm."

"Why are you humming?" He clutched the gun at his waist and then released it.

I continued to hum. "Hummmmmmminnnnnnng is very ssssooooooooothing. Donnnnnnn't you thinnnnnnnnk soooooooooooooo?"

Both his hands flapped at his sides and his gaze was dazed. "It is."

The calm humming made me more tense. Would this work or wouldn't it? "Cannnnnnnnn you uuuuuuse your celltab to turn-nnnnnn off this cammmmmmmeraaaaaaa?"

"Yes." He took the celltab out from his pocket.

"Pleeeeeeeeeese turnnnnnnnnnn the cammmmmmmmmera of-ffffffffff."

Before I'd pledged to live in the fairy world, Arbor had taught me that humming calmed the average human. Since then, I'd realized it also persuaded them.

"Tell mmmmmmmmeeeeeeeee the beeeeeeeeeeest waaaaaaaaaaaaay to leave throughhhhhhhhh a back exitttttttt."

The guard pointed to a small door behind an old stand-up piano.

Giving him a smirk, I hurried through the door and out of the room. The camera feed would only display my presence and my humming until he switched it off. I could easily explain my need for a moment of peace. I couldn't explain leaving through the back door.

Once in the hallway, I checked for more cameras and when I found none, I took out the small perfume bottle and sprayed myself. I used the magic to make myself invisible. With the new information I had about Bracken forcing me into marriage and killing me, plus needing to explain to Rye about the engagement in the first place, and needing his comfort, I knew where I wanted to go.

My heart led the way.

Between studying Watu's map and the deep grooves in the concrete from the cyborgs, I followed a trail leading to the large elevator, only passing an odd-placed small podship. Two guards were stationed out front of the elevator doors and when they moved, I hit the button and slipped inside.

"Did you open the door?" one guard asked.

"No. Did you see anyone?" The second guard peered at the open doors.

Grinning, I watched the elevator doors close on the perplexed men. I'd passed one hurdle.

When the doors opened at the top, I waited a second before slipping out between those guards. They glanced at each other and shrugged. Neither used their celltabs to communicate with anyone else. So far so good.

Turning down the next hallway, I kept to the wall and didn't pass anyone. No guards stood by the second, smaller elevator. A cold tingling sensation crawled up my spine. Eerie almost.

I forced myself to push the button and step into the elevator. The entire ride up, I tapped my toe and shook out my hands. I was going to explain to Rye about Bracken and the death threat, find out Rye's full plan and timeline to take back his throne, and how I could help more than delaying the treaty. And of course, kiss him.

Yet, everything felt wrong.

The elevator clanked to a stop and the doors slid open on silent hinges.

I peered outside. No guards here either.

The crawling sensation morphed into shivers. My muscles tensed and I reached for the whip at my side. I edged outside the elevator.

Had Rye been caught at the ball? Had our dance caused him to be punished or, gulp, murdered?

Not caring if it caused a windy draft, I spread my wings. I was invisible and my wings would be too. I flew up the round staircase to the top floor. With the whip in one hand and the cyborg eye in the other, I edged around the corner. The heavy metal door was open.

My lungs labored, even though I'd done nothing athletic. I paused in my mad dash. What if it was a trap? Bracken and his girlfriend wanted to kill me. Maybe others did too.

I flattened my body against the wall and shuffled to the open doorway. Holding my breath, I peered into the cell.

The empty cell.

Shock rocketed through me. Rye wasn't here. Neither were any guards.

The metal shackles hung empty on the wall. A bowl of mush had been spilled and spread across the floor. A pile of rags sat in a corner.

Maybe he hadn't come back. Although I hadn't seen him in the ballroom again. Maybe he'd snuck off to go to an important meeting. Maybe he'd finally escaped to fulfill his plan.

My inspection stopped on the torn gray mask. He'd returned to his cell.

Only to be discovered and taken in a struggle.

My organs scrunched and twisted. That had to be the case. I'd lost Rye again. Terror shredded my ribcage and I struggled to take in oxygen. I took several long breaths, soothing myself.

I'd found Rye once. I'd find him again.

⇝⇝⇝ ⇜⇜⇜

Arriving back at my room, I used the cyborg eye to open the outside door. I didn't want to become visible in case Bracken was back and I didn't want to use my scan because there'd be a log of my entrance. The door clicked open. The living room was empty.

Phew. No Bracken to worry about forcing me into a compromising position requiring marriage.

I tiptoed across the room, in case he was in his bedroom, and opened the door to my room, and then closed it quietly.

"Watu?"

No answer. She must not be back. Worry threaded through my raging emotions. I hadn't seen her at the ball either.

Studying the doorknob, I knew there was no way to lock it. I'd been interrupted by cyborgs plenty of times. Without her here, I had to find a way to protect myself.

I grabbed the chair and shoved it beneath the door handle. It wouldn't stop anyone for long. It would serve as a warning and give me time. I slipped in one of the fake surveillance vids and flopped onto the chair.

Now what?

I didn't know where Rye had been taken or where Watu might be. I didn't know when Bracken would return and if he'd bring his girlfriend with him.

My brain clicked and I sat up straight.

The Divinity Orb.

Even though it couldn't communicate with Rye, it might help me see things I needed to know.

My private classes on forecasting with the orb had just begun. But I was a quick learner and I'd figure something out. I pulled the orb from its hiding space and ran my fingers over the globe. Colors swirled and I peered into the rounded surface. "Show me Rye. Show me Watu."

The orb's colors twined into mud. Something must be wrong. It wasn't even giving a clear picture of my current surroundings, let alone the future.

Shaking the orb, I held it a little tighter, pressing my skin against the surface. It recognized me yet wouldn't show anything. Anyone. Why wasn't it working?

Shaking it harder out of frustration, I tried again and again and again.

Tossing the orb onto the bed, I headed into the bathroom to wash my face and brush my teeth. Exhaustion and stress weighed heavily on my body and I wanted to rest for a while. Then, I'd try the orb again. Without changing, I went back to the chair holding the door closed and got comfortable. I took out my dagger and whip so they were both within reaching distance, in case Bracken decided to attack.

I'd close my eyes and relax. And wait.

Bang, bang, bang.

The pounding against my head startled. I jerked to a sitting position and rubbed my face. Daylight shone through the window. I'd slept all night and now someone was knocking on the door.

I hoped it was Watu. She hadn't returned. My constant worry increased with a thud in my stomach. My eyes itched and my body ached. I'd fallen asleep. The night had been restless, not restful. Nightmares about what had happened to Rye in the cell had tormented my mind.

"Elle!" Bracken pounded again. "It's time to go to the meeting. Are you ready?"

My wrinkled ball gown wasn't ready for anything. This meeting was important though. So important they'd scheduled it the morning after the ball. I couldn't miss it. I'd finally made progress with my demands and today, I'd push harder to demand justice for all majiks.

"Just a minute." Urgency shot through me. I jumped to my feet and grabbed my bag and took out the perfume bottle. One spritz and a wave of my wand and I was cleaned and dressed.

I placed the almost-empty bottle into my purse. I'd have to use the rest wisely.

I shut off the fake vids, pushed the chair into place, and yanked open the bedroom door. "I'm leaving for the meeting, Watu. I'll see you later."

In case Bracken got any ideas about taking advantage of the fact we were alone.

He tugged on a long tie hanging around his neck. Another new human suit with slits cut out for his wings. He glowered. "You slipped out of the ball early."

"I'm surprised you noticed." My snippiness boomed sharp in my ears. I had to act normal, calm. I couldn't let him know I knew his devious plans. "You were so busy with Frederick and Henrik."

And making out and plotting with your girlfriend.

He pursed his lips in a sneer. "It's called schmoozing, Elle. I'm surprised you haven't heard of it, seeing as you're half human."

The put-down didn't put me down. Regent Theobald tried the same tactic. I'd learned to accept both sides of myself as good, to protect all, and to work with the right leader of the humans to end the war.

That meant Prince Zacharye. Not the regent. And not Bracken and his blond bombshell.

Arriving at the same meeting room, I noted the difference. The lighter atmosphere in the room pressed down. The tension coming off Frederick and the Trees set off alarms in my head. Instead of summer wine, champagne chilled in a silver bucket.

Henrik wasn't present so I couldn't read his friendly face.

"What're we celebrating?" Uneasiness skittered down my spine.

"We've taken into consideration some of your requests." Frederick pulled out a chair and indicated I should sit. When I did, he shoved a stylo in my hand. "It's time to sign the peace treaty."

There was no question in his voice. No sign of weakness.

My nerves frayed, one string at a time. I examined the stylo. Were they going to force me to sign?

I refused to be pressured and arched a brow, doubtful they'd rewritten the treaty overnight. "This is a new document?"

"Yes." Frederick nodded and gave a stiff smile.

"Sign it, Elle." Bracken had known what awaited me. He wouldn't have let me sleep in or come later. He wouldn't have pounced to force marriage. To him, signing the treaty was more important.

I thought I'd have time. Time to press my points and pressure change. Time to delay for Rye. I didn't.

Not exhibiting my tension, I relaxed into the chair. I crossed my legs at the ankles as I'd been taught in princess etiquette lessons. "Of course, I'll read it first."

A few groans filled the room.

"That will take a lot of time." Bracken's complaint dug the deepest. As a majik, he should care about other majiks. He didn't care about anyone but himself.

"Isn't it worth taking the time to make sure everything is right?" *Patience is a virtue* drummed through my head. I wished Henrik were here. He'd signal I was doing the right thing.

Starting to read, the first line sent a chill through me.

The purpose of this agreement is to develop peaceful relations between humans and fairies and to constrain other zaubers as vassals under King Theobald.

Surprise dove into me and uneasiness swam in my bloodstream. This wasn't good. I didn't know what to say so I kept reading and reading and reading.

"How's it going?" Frederick stood by my shoulder.

"I'd love a cup of tea." I didn't. I just didn't want him standing over me as I read. I hoped inspiration would hit.

"This is ridiculous." Bracken's petulance grated on my already frayed nerves. "We don't have time for the four of us to stand around and do nothing."

Lifting my head, I frowned. "Then go do something useful."

What he thought of as useful probably wasn't.

"Fine." He stormed out of the room.

Relaxing, I continued to read. I found the use of the term zauber offensive. The document agreed to maintain the respect and integrity of the fairy homeland, not the other majiks. I tried not to cringe or show emotion while reading.

When I'd seen enough, I set the celltab down on the table with a clink. "There's barely a change."

"You must've missed paragraph thirteen, clause five." Frederick twisted open the cork on the champagne bottle. "Instead of forced repatriation, any zauber found in the fairy zone will be dealt with by fairy authorities."

"Dealt with?" My tone went colder, and my temper boiled. "Other *majiks* are our partners."

The door to the meeting room burst open and Bracken stumbled in. "He's coming. The regent is coming."

Horns blasted down the hallway.

Security guards scrambled inside, making sure the room was secure. A red-haired guard peered under the table. Another made sure the windows were locked. Sad the regent wasn't safe in his own palace.

Because it wasn't his palace.

Regent Theobald paraded into the room. He wore a large crown with colorful jewels circling the gold. His robe flowed behind him as he walked, displaying his large paunch tumbling beyond his belted pants. His shirt was open, displaying a flabby midsection.

"The celebration of the signing of the Regent Theobald Peace Treaty may begin." He waved his hand, combining a parade wave with a salute. "Where shall I sign?"

I rolled my eyes. He'd named the treaty after himself, even though he'd had no part in the negotiations.

Frederick bowed again. "Princess Ellery hasn't put her signature on the document."

"Yet." Bracken placed his palm on my shoulder and pressed.

The pressure weighed on me physically and emotionally. I wouldn't back down. "I refuse to sign this permission slip to slaughter."

I'd said something similar to the regent at the ball. If I signed, Watu could be arrested and killed immediately. Maybe she already had. My lungs flamed and I held in a choking cough. Other majiks in the city would be rounded up. My friends and their families in their homelands could be taken into custody. Every single majik, except fairies, would be at risk.

Their deaths would leave scorch marks on my soul.

Bracken pressed harder on my shoulder. "It's a suspension of hostilities on mutually agreed upon terms."

I was surprised he knew those big words and what they meant.

"A suspension of hostilities between the humans and the fairies. What about the other majiks, Bracken? We'd be selling them out." I tried to appeal to his compassion.

The regent ripped the stylo from my fingers and signed the document with a flourish. "See, I've signed. It's easy. Now it's your turn."

He stabbed the point of the stylo at my face. I didn't flinch. I'd been bullied my entire life by my stepfamily and kids at school. This little man didn't scare me. Crossing my arms, I glared at the room in general.

"We will force you." Bracken grabbed my arms and tried to physically pull them apart.

My chest heaved and my hope shattered. I wanted to reach in my bag and spray the perfume on myself to show who was in charge. I didn't even need magic. I could best him in a fist fight. "You are a traitor to all majiks, Bracken."

"You're a monstrosity to all fairies. An aberration."

The cruel words didn't slice and burn. I didn't care what he thought. Words could wound, they couldn't kill. I'd been called many names. I was more concerned with his threat to force me to sign. I had to find a way to delay the inevitable. To delay for Rye.

"A peace treaty is signed between the leaders of the two factions. You're not the leader." It was a direct challenge to the regent. I'd danced around the issue at the ball. I couldn't afford to wait any longer. I had to push and use whatever was at my disposal, including threats. "Where is Prince Zacharye? He's of age. He should be signing the document."

"I told you, he's sick!" The regent shouted his lie.

I'd known it was a lie last night when I believed Rye was in his cell. Now, I didn't know where he was. If Rye had been killed, surely the regent would say he was dead.

Standing, I launched into my points. "Illness doesn't matter. I know human laws and the order of succession. Prince Zacharye is of age. He doesn't need a royal guardian or a regent. He's rightfully the ruler of the Kingdom of Alandaska."

Regent Theobald's gaze flashed with fury. His blond-gray hair stood straight out. His cheeks blushed red with rage. Then, he smiled. A calm and creepy grin. A fake smile not hiding his insincerity. "You're right."

"I am?" I fell into my chair. Had my threat worked? "This document isn't valid without his signature, as well as mine."

I'd won. Everything inside me lightened. The regent would release Rye to sign the treaty. I'd know if he was okay and he'd share his plans to take back the throne. Everyone in the room would know he was alive and well and ready to rule.

"Unless, of course," Regent Theobald's fake smile became sinister, "the prince committed treason."

A chorus of surprised *ohs* came from the others in the room.

I didn't believe it. Rye would never betray his people.

"You see..." Regent Theobald paced to the window and back. A guard shadowed him. The regent's brow furrowed. He was either pondering the situation or making up a story. "Prince Zacharye was sent on a very important mission to Aristos Sanctuary."

I sucked in air. The regent expected Rye to die competing against majiks, including me. The man really didn't understand majik ways and laws or the sanctuary's purpose, even though retired human royals resided there.

"The prince was supposed to return with a powerful artifact." Regent Theobald swiveled and faced me. "I believe you're familiar with the Divinity Orb."

I sucked in a second sharp breath and held it.

"The prince returned with a forgery." The regent shifted and angry red slashes decorated his cheeks. "I found out it was fake when an...an associate of Bracken's brought it to my attention."

Associate? Couldn't be Sequoia or Cedar. They weren't smart or wise enough. It must be Bracken's girlfriend. She was human and had access to the palace and probably the regent.

"Because of my nephew's treachery"—I could see the wheels revolving behind the regent's eyes—"he's been imprisoned."

At least I knew Rye wasn't dead.

No one else reacted to the news that the prince had been imprisoned. They'd known.

"You're not surprised, Princess Ellery." Regent Theobald's fat fingers pinched my chin and jerked my head up.

I tried to keep my expression blank and give the impression of no emotion. Inside, disgust flared from his touch and his lies. I jerked my chin out of his grip. "Nothing you do surprises me."

"Or did you know because you are in possession of the real Divinity Orb..." The regent straightened and leered. "...and charmed the orb away from my nephew. And I don't mean magically."

My pulse charged. He knew I'd met Rye, that we'd spent time together. Who told him?

"I've been informed of the real orb's capabilities."

Last night it hadn't been capable of much. The orb hadn't helped me find Rye or Watu.

"She brought the Divinity Orb with her," Bracken volunteered, wanting to score points with his future overlord.

Displeased, I tilted my chin and glared.

"Ah, so maybe you already know what's going to happen." Regent Theobald gave a friendly tease. He knew the Divinity Orb could predict possible futures. "And because you're so insistent to have the true rulers' signatures on our peace treaty..." He paused dramatically. "I will crown myself king after I put my treasonous nephew to death."

The pronouncement rung through the room in a death knell.

The death knell of my love.

My heart crushed and crumbled. My throat went dry while tears scalded. My demand to negotiate and have the prince sign the document had signed his immediate death warrant.

Blackness cloaked my spirit. I'd sacrificed Rye in order to stop the treaty.

"Arrest her!" The regent pointed his stubby hand at me. "Hold the princess until my coronation as king."

His gesture sliced through my chest like a knife. My body froze while wild thoughts careened through my mind. I reached at my waist for my whip. It was gone. I heaved. When I'd magically gotten dressed this morning, I'd changed so fast I'd left the whip behind.

"I have diplomatic immunity. I'm here on a peace mission." I refused to shout or scream. I might be shocked, but I'd be dignified.

Two guards grabbed my arms in a vice grip. They yanked me to my feet, lifting me off the ground. Cuffs encircled my wrists, resembling terrible jewelry. One guard took my bag. I cringed, knowing the perfume bottle, dagger, and cyborg eye were inside. The other guards' metal guns pointed in my direction and clicked.

For me, this couldn't get any worse.

"With your permission, Your Majesty," Bracken bowed in front of the regent, the future king, thanks to me, "your coronation day will be the perfect day for a wedding. A wedding between myself and Princess Ellery."

I was wrong. Things could get worse.

Chapter Twenty-Three

The guards uncuffed me, shoved me inside my bedroom, and slammed the door shut. I tumbled forward, tripping on the chair I'd moved earlier, and landed in a pile on the carpeted floor.

My mushy bones couldn't move. My shaking limbs couldn't stand. My mind couldn't comprehend. What had happened?

"Watu?" I didn't sound like myself. Despair rushed through me and it was probably a good thing she wasn't here. If she'd been here, they would've thrown her in the dungeon. Maybe they already had.

My entire body quivered uncontrollably. I'd been subjected to a body search by one of the guards. Good thing I hadn't had my whip on my person. They'd dragged me out of the meeting room to Frederick and the regent's laughter. Bracken had given an insipid protest and promised to control me once we were married. The guards pulled me through the halls where others had watched the spectacle.

A fairy princess facing total humiliation.

I flushed, remembering the stares and jeers. I didn't care about them. At least I wasn't locked in a cell. The room seemed darker than before. Or was that my new outlook?

The door clicked and clanged on the other side of the wood. A guard had said they'd made a special lock to hold a fairy inside.

I stumbled to my feet and darted to the window.

Idiots. Fairies could fly.

I threw open the curtains, planning to crash through the glass and fly away. To make my escape.

Metal plates covered the exterior of the window.

With my hopes dashed, my entire body drooped.

I hurried to the next window and the next, throwing open each of the curtains and finding the same metal wall. At the last blocked window, I bunched up the material and yanked the curtains down. The purple color swirled around my feet. The room had seemed darker because it was. Light wasn't the biggest problem at the moment.

Rushing back to the door, I banged on the thick wood, trying to work out my frustration and get their attention. "Why don't you lock me up in a cell?"

No one answered.

This was almost worse. Having the decadence of my nicely appointed bedroom but not having the freedom to leave. Having my fancy but ugly clothes and having nowhere to wear them. Having the sumptuous bed and knowing I couldn't sleep.

The bed.

Pivoting, I scrambled to the covers. Sure, they'd had time to install a special lock and metal window coverings, and yet no time to make the bed. A good thing. My fingers swished through the silk sheets and heavy blankets. Nothing. I picked up the comforter and shook it. Nothing fell out. I tossed the comforter to the ground and searched through the blanket and, finding nothing, tossed the blanket to the ground too. I dug through the sheets.

My hands came up empty. And so did my hope.

The Divinity Orb was gone.

My chest hollowed.

After hiding it there yesterday, I'd fallen asleep on the chair and Bracken had rushed me out the door this morning. Wariness filled the hollow hole. Had he known they'd planned to lock me up?

Grabbing hold of the sheet, I lifted the material to my nose and took a deep inhale. I rubbed the sheet between my fingers, trying to catch a whiff of emotion. The emotion of the person who'd stolen the orb. One of my unusual fairy talents.

Hateful thoughts and feelings invaded my mind. The person hadn't held the sheet for long. Even so, I picked up hate and revenge.

My arms and legs went weak from the dark emotions. I flopped onto the bed, similar to how I'd tossed the orb on the bed last night. A short pant escaped my mouth. Then another. The precious fairy artifact had been stolen. I wouldn't panic. Only Rye and myself could activate it.

Maybe Watu had come back this morning and hidden the Divinity Orb. She would've realized it was a mistake to leave the orb out. Except the black emotions I'd experienced weren't those of Watu. I knew her too well.

What about my whip?

The dagger was gone with the perfume bottle and the cyborg eye because the guards had taken my bag. When I'd changed this morning, I'd magicked the ball gown off and the Silver Snare with it. The gown I'd left lying on the floor in the corner of the closet.

The bit of hope soothed my wheezing. I jumped off the bed and went to the closet. The gown had been moved and the whip gone. Yanking open one of the large suitcases, I dug to the bottom hoping I'd find anything useful. I found nothing but ugly clothes. I plunged to the floor, letting my body be consumed by the extravagant dresses.

Panic crawled up my back and tapped at the hairs standing at attention on the back of my neck. Had something happened to Watu?

No. I couldn't think that way. When she came back to our room, she'd find the door barred and locked. My pulse stopped and raced ahead. Would they arrest her? She wasn't a fairy and not protected by the terrible treaty. The guards wouldn't care that she was with me. They'd arrest her and murder her, possibly put her in the auraguillotine.

It was best if she stayed away. I hoped it was her choice.

"Watu, if you have any type of telepathic connection"—after all, she'd known to search for me when the dragon had dropped me on the side of a mountain and seemed to be able to read minds at times—"please stay away from our room and get out of the palace." I sent up a hopeful prayer. "Warn Queen Dahliadew that Bracken is a traitor."

To the fairies. To me.

A shadow crossed my soul. I'd known he didn't love me or care about me. I'd thought he'd represent the majiks well. He only thought of himself and his status. Which was why he wanted to marry me. I'd known since the moment the engagement was announced, but I'd expected a little respect, a little caring.

"And the regent is going to execute Rye." I wailed and gulped the scream down.

How did my arrest interfere with his or his people's plans? He'd been counting on me to delay the treaty negotiations.

Regent Theobald had agreed to host and preside at the wedding right after his coronation as the ruler of the kingdom. How long did it take to plan a coronation? Or had it been in the works this entire time?

Like my bedroom prison.

Suspicion clambered through me.

Rye was missing, possibly already on his way to a firing squad. Watu hadn't returned. Stone was on a mission. I couldn't count on my friends to help because they weren't nearby.

I'd need to rescue myself.

The suspicion made me stronger. I stood and scanned the room. How?

I had no weapons and no magic.

A piece of red caught my attention. My warrior priestess outfit. At least wearing the clothes would boost my confidence.

I picked up the pants and the angry burn of hatred seared through me. Whoever had searched my bed had touched this outfit. Forcing my fingers to stay clasped, I held up the pants. Raged-torn slashes ripped through the entire garment as if clawed by an animal. Pain that the garment experienced raked through me.

The red had become strips of swaying fabric. Dropping the pants, I skimmed the room and found the top and the jacket. The same treatment had been applied.

Who had the strength to rip leather into tiny pieces? And why?

The suit wasn't a weapon in and of itself. Why would some stranger do this? It felt like a personal attack. Ruining something I'd prized.

A personal vendetta.

I'd thought the same thing about Bracken's girlfriend's tone when I saw them making out in the hallway at the ball.

I picked up the pieces of the outfit and took them into the bathroom. The rips would make the outfit more rebellious as long as the material covered the appropriate places. I'd feel competent and strong wearing it, more so than this terrible human royal dress. Quickly, I stripped off the offending dress, put the outfit on, and stood in front of the full-length mirror.

My stature grew. I stood taller and my shoulders pulled back. My blond hair was in disarray from the struggle with the guards. The messiness made me appear wild and strong. My chin pointed with determination. My wings fluttered on their own, ready for a fight.

I was ready for anything. I'd grab the first opportunity. To escape. To fight. To win.

Stepping out into the main part of the bedroom, I heard voices through the door. I better be ready. I put my ear against the wood.

"Was the Divinity Orb working when your *pretty, pretty, phony princess* brought it to Reximus Palace?" The female sneered at the nickname she'd given me.

Her familiar voice grated against my nerves. Familiar because I'd heard her threat last night.

"I don't know." Bracken's frustration came out in his tone. "Elle kept lots of secrets. For instance, she has a boyfriend."

He didn't sound jealous, more peeved I cared about someone else. And no one could describe Rye with such a mundane word as boyfriend. My heart cracked. I didn't even know if he was alive. The crack grew longer and wider and I wondered if I'd ever heal.

"That wasn't *just* her boyfriend she danced with. It was Prince Zacharye." The female's scoff told me she knew more than I'd thought.

A shiver traveled the length of my spine. What else did she know?

"How did he get out of a cell to dance?" Bracken had known the prince wasn't sick.

Which proved he'd been part of the conspiracy.

"I don't know. What's important is the Divinity Orb."

If she didn't know, maybe Rye had escaped. I could hope.

"The Divinity Orb looked different when I saw it at Queens Academy. It was glowing and colorful."

Had he been trying to steal the orb that early morning he'd snuck into Illumine Turret where I'd fallen asleep?

"Only Elle or the prince can make the Divinity Orb work. They retrieved the orb together." Bracken's girlfriend's tone curled in disgust. "And the besotted fool...the prince gave the orb to her."

How did the girl know this? She called me Elle, suggesting familiarity. Had one of the human priestesses betrayed Rye and I by giving up our secret? The replica orb had been created to keep Rye safe from his uncle.

"We need Elle's cooperation." The threat in the girl's voice told me she'd force me.

When the fairy forest froze over. I'd never help them, no matter what they tried.

"So we confront her?" Bracken sounded uncomfortable with the action. "Don't worry, I can control her."

His tacked-on brag made me snicker. He didn't know my train-ing. Even without weapons, I could defend and attack. If they opened the door, it would give me the opportunity to escape the room. I was familiar with the hallways. I could find a window, jump out, and fly.

"Sure, you can, honey. Sure, you can." She said one thing, but her tone said the exact opposite. "Let's talk to her."

She seemed in control of me and the situation. A slight quiver of worry went through me. A human girl with no powers?

The locks clicked and clanged and whirred.

I took a step back and hid behind where the door would open. My feet shifted and raw energy lit up my veins. I could take an unmagical gentleman fairy and a human girl, even if she was a weightlifter. I fisted my hands and braced myself. At the last second, I grabbed the lamp off the side table.

"Since you can handle her, you go in first." The doubt in the girlfriend's tone hung in the air. She didn't believe he could handle me. Still, she let him go first, letting him take the risk of an initial attack.

She might be wise about hand-to-hand combat.

"You got this, honey."

I heard a smack of lips on skin.

A quiver wracked my body. *Ew.*

The door opened and Bracken sauntered in.

I raised my arms and slammed the lamp down on his head.

Thump. Crash. Tinkle.

The lamp broke over his head.

He collapsed to the floor. Blood gushed. Glass scattered across his hair and face and the floor.

Immediate triumph was tempered by anxiety. Now, it was me and the girlfriend.

An arm reached in through the open door. An unbelievably long arm. Who was he dating? A monkey? The arm wasn't hairy though. It was completely smooth. No hair. No freckles. No tan. Perfect to the point of fake.

I stretched to grab the arm and flip her over. I wouldn't even need to hurt the girl. Just take her out and run.

Before I could get a grip, a second arm telescoped out. Narrow fingers wrapped around my wrist, almost crushing my bones. Sharp pain ricocheted out from the grip, as if there was an electronic force. The hand twisted and forced me to my knees.

As I went down, I looked up.

She had long, perfect legs. Again, no blemishes or freckles or hair. She must be tall. Of course, she was human so being tall made sense. Her short skirt emphasized wide hips and a slim waist. Her breasts fell out of her blouse. Long, curly blond hair accented her heart-shaped face. Her smooth skin was unnatural. The familiar smirk cut into me.

My stomach dropped and rolled. The injury in my arm contorted to my chest. My eyes widened and my gaze blurred with memories. She'd befriended me at Queens Academy. She'd convinced me to take her on the mission to Aristos Sanctuary. She'd killed my cousin Perry. She'd lied and betrayed me.

"Bee." Fury curled in each letter.

She reached in a pocket and tossed up the Divinity Orb like a toy ball. "Hello, Elle. Nice outfit."

Chapter Twenty-Four

B linking, I tried to get rid of the vision.

Except it wasn't a vision. Bee stood before me, holding the Divinity Orb in her hand and she'd shredded my warrior outfit.

More memories crashed into me. She'd lost the fake wings and jumped out a high window at Aristos Sanctuary. She should've died. Neither her broken body nor any trace of her had been found. She'd told me she was half fairy and half human, similar to me. It was one of the reasons I'd trusted her so easily. She'd convinced me to leave camp at night and scurried across boulders without tiring. With her strong grip and telescoping arms, she must be something else. Something different.

Her fingers pressed harder and the tips dug into my muscles. My tendons cramped. No human or fairy had so much strength.

Disbelief mingled with the anguish. "That's why you're so fast and strong." I tried to jerk my arm free. "You're a cyborg."

With the façade of a human. She was so real-looking.

She glanced at Bracken's knocked-out body. His eyes were closed, and he hadn't moved since I'd hit him with the lamp. Glass fragments scattered around his face and the carpet. Blood poured from the wound. Bee didn't seem concerned.

"That's why you're so slow...slow-witted." Bee pinched harder and agony shot from my arm.

My skin would puncture, and I'd be bleeding soon. "How did you become a cyborg?"

"Part cyborg." Her quick response told me she didn't appreciate the mechanical part of herself. The inner workings of the hand holding me became visible. Wires and metal plates and integrated circuits.

Fascinated, I studied the anatomy of her hand beneath the fake skin.

"Fairies hurt me when I was a child. I almost died. Human scientists experimented on me, fixed me. They gave me a reason to live." She paused for dramatic effect. "Revenge."

A flicker of a tea-induced dream came back to me. A blond girl in a wheelchair. I'd felt sorry for her. "Cyborg."

Bracken's gaze wavered and he tried to lift himself off the ground. "Did you say cyborg?"

Bee dropped the orb into a large pocket and clunked his head with her iron fist. He passed out again.

I jerked at her cruel action. The pain in my arm increased tenfold.

She must've kept the cyborg part secret from him. Why was Bee acceptable as a half fairy and half human when I was not? He'd called me an aberration because of my half breed status. And yet, he was besotted with Bee.

She chuckled at Bracken, indicating he was a sorry idiot. She didn't care about hurting anyone.

Remembering past betrayals, renewed agony throbbed throughout my body. I tried again to yank my arm free. "You killed my cousin Perry."

"If you had retrieved the orb when I'd asked, he wouldn't be dead." Her simplistic explanation and blaming me for my cousin's death ripped through my head and exploded with torment. "And Prince Zacharye wouldn't be about to die. It's your fault, Elle."

Guilt stabbed through me and worked into a mad frenzy.

Licking my lips, I tried to soothe the fury raging in my system. Which meant Rye wasn't dead. I had time. And Bee didn't care what Bracken thought about her. She was going to do something drastic. "Nothing will stop the regent."

Bracken moaned on the ground. How much was he hearing?

Her knowing grin hacked through me. "Regent Theobald wanted to get rid of the prince from the moment his parents were murdered."

Murdered? I thought the king and queen had died in an accident. Had she just admitted Rye's parents had been killed?

"Theo always planned to take the throne." She crooned the regent's shortened name.

My belly roiled and nausea crawled up my throat. Was she attracted to the regent?

"The plan was for me to marry the prince and get pregnant, with either his or the regent's child. Theo preferred it be his child, with the people of the kingdom believing it was the prince's. One of the reasons he made the prince dye his hair."

I remembered the vids of Rye with blond hair. At his Presentation Ball, he'd had midnight black hair. His natural color.

Bee had relationships with the regent and Bracken and planned to have one with Rye. He must've refused to marry Bee, so they wanted to force me to marry Bracken. Then, they'd kill me to control the fairy world? It didn't add up.

"Disgusting that you're with the old regent." How had she ensconced herself into the man's life? Into Bracken's life?

"I'm older than I appear." She puckered her face, concentrating. Her smooth skin morphed. Wrinkles formed around her mouth and eyes. Dark spots scattered across her cheeks and they weren't freckles. She looked old. "Robotics can take twenty or thirty years off your face."

I sucked in oxygen, shocked by the change. Bracken moaned and writhed on the floor. He couldn't see Bee's transformation from young girl to hag. "Does Bracken know your age or your relationship with the regent?"

"He doesn't know anything." She switched back to the young version of herself and smiled with glee. "That's not why I'm here."

Bracken moaned again. His hands cupped his head.

"You're here to force me to use the Divinity Orb. You want to know the future."

"Are you part elf too?" She smirked, knowing elves had good hearing.

"Are you part anything else?" My sarcasm meant to offend. My words were my only offense. I couldn't move and my arm throbbed. Her iron grip would break a bone soon. "You told the regent the orb that Ry—Prince Zacharye possessed was fake. How did you know?"

"I don't have wings." Her voice edged with gladness or jealousy. Maybe a bit of both. "I couldn't fly away from the Sanctuary. I hid and I watched and I listened."

She'd seen the entire competition play out. She'd known Rye and I were the finalists and how we'd retrieved the orb together. She probably knew about the Connected Crown Prophecy.

"Now." She yanked me closer and piercing pain sliced through my arm. "Turn on the Divinity Orb." She held out the orb and pressed it closer.

"There's no on and off switch. It's not a light socket or a cyborg." If I goaded her, maybe she'd make a mistake.

My insult was a direct hit. Her fake cheeks reddened, and her eyes flashed. Using her single arm, she pinched my arm tighter and picked me off the floor. My feet and my heart dangled. Breathless, I knew I was going to die.

Her arm flung out and my body flopped with it. She tossed me forward like a rag doll onto the bed. The soft landing did nothing to stop the torture.

The torture of helplessness.

"Make jokes. I'm used to it." Her bitterness was combined with a touch of hurt. "I'll be the one laughing last." She brought the orb closer.

Laying on the bed, I didn't have anywhere to escape. I ducked my head and tried to keep my hands away. "Where's my whip and dagger? Did you steal those too?"

"I have no idea. The guards gave me your bag. Thanks for the intel. I'll check." Too strong with her mechanical parts, she pressed the palm of my hand onto the orb.

The Divinity Orb lit up. Colors swirled in the globe.

"I'm not going to help you do anything with the Divinity Orb." She could kill me before I'd assist her or the regent.

"Right now, I needed proof this was the real orb." Her wicked smile cut like a knife. "It is." She kicked Bracken with her foot. Hard. "Get up, honey."

Her sugar sweetness made me sick.

When Bracken didn't move, she kicked harder. His body jerked and she said, "Be nice to your fiancé, Elle."

As if I could kick him from atop the bed. "We're not getting married. Not ever."

Bracken got slowly to his feet with a dazed expression. He rubbed the spot where she'd kicked him. "Our wedding is tomorrow."

Bee gripped his chin and tugged him close. Her lips landed on his mouth and she gave him a passionate kiss before veering to me. "The same day as Regent Theobald's coronation." She crowed with triumph. "You'll be giving the real Divinity Orb to the regent as a gift."

"As you said, the orb only works for me or the prince." I kept my tone hard. I refused to admit my fear. And I'd die before marrying Bracken.

"You haven't done your homework." Bee smirked again.

True. I'd barely started classes before being sent on the mission to retrieve the orb. When I'd returned, I had so many other things on my mind. Rye, my wand test, and meeting the Grand Council.

"There's a transfer spell which you will be performing at the coronation." Her confident attitude filled me with dread.

Loathing coated my tongue and a sour taste slid down my throat. This Bee was so different from the girl I'd first met and the girl who'd betrayed me. Harder, crueler, more vicious. I hated this version the most.

"The surveillance vids will suffice as proof the two of you have to get married." She took out cuffs from her pocket and flicked one around my right wrist. She took the second cuff and connected it to the bedpost. She ogled. "Make it look good, Bracken."

Swiveling, she left the room and closed the door behind her. The locks clicked and clacked into place. She left Bracken and I alone.

The dread stockpiling in my stomach since realizing I'd need to keep my distance and never be alone with Bracken thunked and piled higher.

He held his body stiffly and disgust threaded across his expression. His confused frown changed into a snarl.

Like he was a dog, and I was his dinner.

CHAPTER TWENTY-FIVE

"Bracken." My voice came out hoarse, afraid. Using my feet, I scrambled into a curled position on the bed. "You don't want to do this, fake things that never happened. You don't even love me."

Fear ratcheted up my spine. He wasn't going to do anything to me, just make it seem bad.

"Nothing to do with loving." He took off his jacket in his first action of undressing. With care, he folded the garment and placed it on the chair, implying he had everything under control. He didn't. Blood poured from the wound in his head. "Everything to do with power."

My head spun. "Please, Bracken. Why would you do this to force me into marriage? I'm an aberration. A half breed."

I tossed the insulting words he'd used against me, trying to get through his thick skull and dizzy mind.

Not saying anything, he stepped away from the chair. His stiff movements displayed his discomfort. He moved like an automaton. Or a cyborg. I choked on a hysterical giggle. Bracken gave the impression of a perfect fairy gentleman.

He wasn't.

Panic shredded my lungs, leaving them in strips similar to the warrior outfit I wore. I didn't know what he had planned. Vids of both of us undressed and on the bed together. Him, holding me in his arms. Something worse? I twisted around, searching for an exit. My arm cuffed to the bed pulled from its socket. The strong cuff would never break. How could I make him stop this attack?

"Why are you listening to Bee? Do you know who she is? What she is?" My tone went high, pleading. Anything to make him stop. Well, not anything. I'd refuse to transfer the Divinity Orb and I wouldn't sell Rye and his friends out. "She's...a...cyborg."

He paused with his hands on his belt.

"She's part cyborg and part human." My mind whirled as I tried to find what to say to reach him. He detested halflings. Half any-things. My mind clicked. "Bee is half fairy too. Did you know?"

His white skin paled. "What?"

My brain buzzed. He didn't know. He didn't know his girlfriend was a half breed. A tri-breed, if you counted the cyborg parts. He hadn't had his eyes open when she'd presented her innerworkings and her real age.

"That's right." I'd finally hit on something to shake him out of his trance. "Bee is half fairy and half human."

"No." He shook his head back and forth and undid his belt buckle. The sharp snap of the buckle fractured through me.

I wheezed and panted. I had to keep my wits about me. "Yes. She's a half breed, like me."

I wasn't embarrassed by this fact any longer. I'd accepted myself a while ago.

"No. She's human with a...little bit of...of...robotics." He didn't appreciate the last part either.

I scrunched my face. Unbelievable. He believed she was cyborg and yet not about being half fairy. Although he'd woken up and heard when she'd confessed to the robotics part.

"No, Bracken she isn't." Calming myself, I poured emotion into my declaration, trying to make the truth believable. "She was a student at Queens Academy with me. That's how I know her."

"She doesn't have wings or magic." He yanked on his belt and it slithered through the hoops.

A shudder rocked my body, distracting me. I had to keep convincing him. "True, because she was in a terrible accident and was in a wheelchair for years." The dream about the blond child in the wheelchair fuzzed around my memories. At the time, I didn't realize the dream had been about Bee. I'd felt sorry for the child, not this adult Bee. She was evil. "It's why she's got robotic parts. Humans took her and healed her and—"

"Healed her?" He shrieked. He obviously hadn't known before and didn't accept the fact. "They made a monstrosity out of her, if what you say is true."

"It *is* true." I wished there was a way to prove to him I wasn't lying.

"She lives in Reximus Palace." His voice cracked and a sheen shone in his gaze. "Regent Theobald wouldn't let a half breed live at the palace."

Bracken spoke as if this palace was the most wonderful place on earth. It might be beautiful on the outside and plush on the inside, but it was rotten at the core. The regent's core. Like a glistening apple that had been eaten away by a worm on the inside.

"Maybe the regent doesn't know." Which I found hard to believe. She was having a relationship with the man. I didn't want to use the information unless I had to. Bracken would never believe me. He idolized the regent and was besotted with Bee. I could knock down only one of them at a time. "Bee tricked the regent. She tricked you."

"Impossible." His tone deepened with arrogance. He pushed the top button through the hole and unzipped his pants, causing my pulse to pace erratically. "Bee loves me. She said so the first night we met accidentally at the pub near Queens Academy."

"Was it accidental on her part?" Dark thoughts entered my head. How long ago had they met? Was it the night Stone and I chased a blond in the woods? "I met Bee accidentally, too. She claimed to be my best friend. I believed her."

Bee was using Bracken just as Bracken used me. Both needed to advance their schemes. They were both calculating to the point of cruel. They deserved each other.

He flopped onto the chair, crushing his jacket. Tears ran down his cheeks and his face flushed red. His muddy scent clogged my nose. With his pants undone and his legs spread wide, he didn't resemble a fairy aristocrat. He resembled a fool.

"You believed her too, didn't you?" I used a gentle tone. Bee's betrayal still stung. "She's a very convincing liar."

"No!" He jumped to his feet and his wings flitted with agitation. "Bee loves me. Unlike you. Once you and I get married and you're...gone..." He glanced away and swiped his tears with the back of his hand. "She's going to marry me. We're going to live here at the palace. I'll rule the fairies from a distance with help from my father. It's planned."

My eyes grew wider and wider, trying to take in his fairytale.

It was an impossible story. Regent Theobald would never allow a fairy to live at the palace. He barely accepted our visit. The man had plans and a personal relationship with Bee. Whether he cared about her or not, he wouldn't let her marry Bracken.

"Bee told me a different plan." I had to use all the information at my disposal. I spoke with conviction, softening my tone because Bracken was in for a rude awakening. "She's having an affair with Regent Theobald."

"No!" Bracken shouted and slashed his arm. "She loves me! That's gross. The regent is twice her age."

My stomach roiled. She'd fooled Bracken, too. I could relate. Once I'd realized her betrayal, I'd never denied it. I needed to convince him of the truth, using care so he didn't lash out against me. Do the exact horrid act I was trying to prevent.

Licking my lips, I stayed curled in a ball so he believed I posed no threat. "No, Bee is the regent's age. She fooled you and everyone."

"I don't believe you. As half human, you can lie." He gripped the waistband of his pants.

My pulse pounded. "You're right. I can lie and so can Bee, because she's half human too. The surveillance cameras can't." I indicated the cameras with my free hand. Vids, which Bee had wanted to use against me to force me into marriage, would prove what I said was true. "Go view the footage from when you were knocked out. She showed me her true age and her cyborg parts."

He froze, standing there with his pants undone, his hands on his waist, and his wings drooping. His head was down, and I couldn't see his face, couldn't see his reaction to my challenge. My nerves tingled and my roiling stomach churned faster. Bracken couldn't lie, which was why he was being taken advantage of by Bee. Why would he believe me?

His chin trembled. Without a word, he zipped up his pants and grabbed his belt.

A shaky breath whooshed out of my mouth. "Go look at the vids." It was the one thing that would save me. At least from Bracken.

Scowling, he grabbed his jacket and used a special electronic key to open the door.

Jerking on the cuff locking me to the bed, I wanted to follow. Bracken wasn't going to assault me or force me into marriage with faked photos of us being together. At least not yet. He was going to check out the vids and see the truth. My taut tendons relaxed.

"If I'm right and told you the truth, you should set me free!" I shouted before he slammed the door closed.

I'd pinned my escape hopes on a man who wanted to force me into marriage. I had to come up with another plan.

Click. Clang. Clang.

I tried to roll over on the mattress at the noise. My arm pulled and I winced. Jerking fully awake, I realized I'd fallen asleep while cuffed to the bed.

The door snicked open.

My body tensed. Had Bracken finally come to set me free or was Bee here to torture me?

I surveyed the window. The metal coverings were still in place. I had no clue what time of day it was. I'd sat cuffed to the bed for hours with my gaze glued to the door. Bracken hadn't returned. Feeling creaky, I'd laid on the bed to get more comfortable. If I was stiff, I couldn't fight.

No one had come to help.

Finally, I'd dozed, hungry and alone.

My pulsed raced, bringing my limbs back to life. Someone was finally at the door. My hands fisted. I was ready for the fight of my life...for my life.

A servant cyborg rolled into the room, carrying a tray of food. The door closed behind it and my chance to escape diminished.

"Sorry to wake you, Princess Ellery."

The cyborg greeted me politely, not surprised to find a fairy princess chained to her bed.

"I've brought your dinner." She set the tray on the side table.

My stomach growled. I hadn't eaten the entire day. "Can you unlock this handcuff? I have to use the bathroom."

I knew the interaction was being recorded. Possibly watched by a security team or Bee. I wanted to stick my tongue out at the camera, but I pretended not to know about the surveillance. Yes, I'd blown the façade when I'd told Bracken to find the vids. Hopefully, no one had watched that tape except him.

Shivering, I put a placid smile on my face. "I've been locked here all day."

"Patience is a virtue." The cyborg's voice changed, became less mechanical and more real.

My heart stopped. "Excuse me? What did you say?"

Lights flashed in the cyborg's pupils readjusting. "I will give you the cuff key once the room is secure."

My head spun. How was that even possible? "What? What do you mean?"

Pivoting, the cyborg headed for the door.

My lungs shriveled, my hope exiting. "Wait! What about unlocking me? What did you mean about being patient?"

The door clicked and clanked and opened. The cyborg rolled outside, rotated, and peered back at me. Its arm extended longer and longer. Similar to Bee's. A silver key dangled from its metal finger.

Flopping forward, I stretched my arm out. My other arm socket pulled. "Ow." I wiggled my fingers, trying to make them go farther.

The cyborg stayed in place. Not moving. Not closing the door.

What was going on? Was the cyborg my rescuer? The saying Henrik and Rye had both used echoed in my head. If they'd sent the cyborg, why didn't they let the thing hand me the keys?

Grunting, I rolled onto my stomach and stretched further. My fingers connected with the ring and wrapped around the metal. I held on tight.

I raised a proud fist. I had the key to the cuffs, the door was open, and I could escape.

The door closed. The locks clicked and clanged into place.

My shoulders sagged and I hung my head off the edge of the bed. There'd be no escape. I could unlock my wrist, use the bathroom, and eat. I could try to find a way out on my own. I could think about the cyborg's claim that patience is a virtue.

And I could wonder if the statement was true.

"The red gloves are a good luck charm for fairy weddings." Gulping, I waved the red gloves from my warrior priestess outfit, hoping the cyborg or its controller believed the lie. The gloves were the one part of the outfit Bee hadn't torn apart. Having them with me would bring confidence on this terrible, awful day.

My blood pumped slowly and sadly through my veins.

I hadn't seen Watu since we'd left for the ball two nights ago. I hadn't seen Bracken either. I'd hoped he'd come back some time in the middle of the night to let me go. I'd tried to escape by using the cuff key in the door lock, by using a piece of the bedframe to pry off the metal plates covering the window, and by running at the door with my shoulder. To no avail. All I had to show for my efforts were bruises and bleeding fingertips.

Another good reason for the gloves.

"I have no orders about gloves." The cyborg forced a comb through my tangled hair.

"What do your orders say? Who gave them?"

"The information is confidential." The cyborg yanked on a strand. "You must be dressed for combination coronation and wedding."

I choked. Neither sounded appealing.

The cyborg piled my hair into an elaborate bun and shoved a gold crown on my head. Fairies didn't wear gold. Her metal fingers wrapped around my waist and forced me to stand in front of the full-length mirror. "You're ready."

"No. I'm not." I'd never be ready.

The only plan I had was to let the cyborg dress me, lead me out the door, and find a chance to run away. If I got to the coronation with the hundreds of guards, I'd never escape.

The wide white skirt mingled tiny pearls with small blinking lights. White wasn't the normal color for fairy wedding dresses. A more natural color like green or brown was usually worn. In the few weeks I'd spent at Queens Academy, I'd watched a wedding from the balcony and asked Arbor lots of questions. I'd been fantasizing about my wedding to Rye.

The tight waistline and bodice restricted my movements. The waistline glinted gold. The gold at the waist edged the low V in the front, displaying more than a fairy bride would deem decent. Ringing my throat was a gold and pearl choker, resembling a collar. The leash would come with the wedding ring.

Between the amount of fabric, the pearls, and the lights the skirt weighed a ton. I found it difficult to move and impossible to run. Good thing I had wings.

My heavily made up face covered the shadows under my eyes and the redness of my cheeks. Bright lime green lip color and eye shadow made me appear more cyborg than fairy.

A gold crown with red rubies sat on my head. "This isn't my fairy crown."

"The regent insists."

My wedding day and I chose nothing. Not even the groom.

The door clicked and clanged, and the noise grated against my nerves. Everyone could come in and out of my room except me.

Bracken strolled into the room wearing a traditional male fairy suit of light brown. Breeches and a short jacket over a white silk shirt. He wore a bandage wrapped around his head and a reddish-yellow oozed through it. He was accompanied by two human guards. The guard on his left had lots of medals and gold braids, while the guard on his right had two stripes and a name tag.

Ackerman. I knew the name.

My body stiffened. This was my stepmother's SCUM boyfriend. Ingrid had said he worked at the palace.

He leered at my chest and I swung away from him. He hadn't been with Sybil and my stepsister's when they'd visited Queens Academy. Magic hadn't been used on him to make him forget me. Between him and Bee, old enemies haunted me.

"It's time," Bracken proclaimed with woe, suggesting we were attending an execution, not our wedding.

A lump the size of my heart caught in my throat. Rye was going to be executed. Or he already had been. My eyes burned and I blinked several times to keep the sadness away. I would not let Bracken, or the regent, or the humans attending this charade of an event see me cry.

I had to ask, "Has the prince been executed?" I held my breath, waiting for an answer.

"Elle," Bracken admonished with his tone and peeked at the cameras.

I didn't care what the security team heard. A whisper of a chance settled in my gut. "You believe me about the cameras. Did you see the vids of Bee? Who she is? *What* she is?"

It wasn't my prejudice, but I could play on his.

"Do you mind leaving us alone?" he asked the two guards.

"Yes, we would." The higher up guard fingered the trigger on his weapon. "We're to escort both of you to the coronation. There's a larger group from the security team outside the door."

Bracken sniffed, peeved at not getting what he wanted. He swiveled back to me. "I saw the vids." His expression changed to one of disgust with a scrunched nose and frown.

Hope flickered to life. "So you believe me. Bee is half human and half fairy and part cyborg. And old."

He flicked a speck of dust off his suit. Not a human suit. Was he no longer influenced by Bee? "Yes. Doesn't change anything for you."

"What do you mean?" My hope was doused by his statement. "This changes everything. You don't approve of half breeds. Do you still care for Bee?"

"Doesn't matter what I feel." His gaze hardened. His lips straightened. The skin pulled taut on his cheeks. "I'm not giving up this opportunity to rule the fairies. We're getting married today."

My spirits sunk. He wasn't giving me a choice. There was no way to contact my grandmother, the queen, to stop this travesty. Once married, we'd be stuck together forever.

"And after the wedding?" I raised my chin to stare at his expression. "Do you plan to kill me?"

"Together, we will return to Queens Academy." Nodding, he smoothed every disgusted wrinkle on his face, resigned to his future. "I will be the true ruler and you will sit by my side, agreeing with everything I say. It's what I appreciate about the human world. Males dominate."

Yeah, and look where the world was now with mostly male heads of state.

My brows arched. "What about Queen Dahliadew?"

"She doesn't have much time left to live." He spoke breezily, as if the death of a fairy queen was no big deal.

I couldn't decide if it was a threat or a guarantee. Remembering how someone had poisoned her recently before knowledge of my role in royalty was well known, I couldn't stop my suspicions. Marriage to Bracken meant danger for my grandmother.

I had to get word to her. Unfortunately, I had no magic and no one trustworthy to ask for help. I couldn't imagine my grandmother gone, sitting by his side remembering his and his father's attitude toward me, and their belief in their superiority over other majiks. "What about the peace treaty with the humans? I'll never agree. Never."

Bracken chortled. "You'll agree and you'll sign. Or the second after we're married, you'll have a deadly accident."

"You planned this all along." Anger more than fear had me tugging at the ugly dress. "You even packed a wedding dress for the occasion."

"I didn't buy the dress." He scrunched his nose, examining me. "It's a gift from the regent."

I shivered with disgust.

"Let's go." Ackerman held the door open wide. Not in invitation, a demand.

With shaking hands, I lifted the skirt with my gloved hands. The red reminded me of the blood I'd have on my hands if I was forced to sign the treaty.

Now, I hated the dress even more. I didn't want anything from the man who ordered Rye's execution and was about to crown himself king.

Chapter Twenty-Six

Taking a deep breath, I stepped onto the stage in the palace ballroom and faced the hundreds of curious eyes. The nerves in my stomach fluttered just as my wings wanted to. I held the wings back so I wouldn't stand out more than I already did. The crowd watched Bracken too, as he held my arm. He held his wings out, as did Sequoia and Cedar who sat on a bench at the back of the stage near the terrible statue of the regent with majiks represented as slaves.

But I was the only fairy wearing a wedding dress and crown.

I lifted my chin higher and stared back, refusing to let them intimidate.

There'd been no opportunity to fly away. A contingent of guards waited outside the suite door. They'd circled us as if they were guarding the crown jewels.

"This way, Princess Ellery." A royal page flung his arm, covered in a puffy sleeve, forward.

I wheeled the other way.

A guard stepped in front, blocking my exit and the page grabbed my arm to pivot my direction. He forced me to a spot near the throne chair.

I'd been given a front row position to watch the coronation.

A gray-haired man stood on the other side of the throne chair. His long, embroidered robe indicated his religious position. The padre must be here to perform the coronation and my wedding to Bracken. I wanted to hate the man, even though he had a kind face.

A steel stand next to him held the largest crown I'd ever seen. The solid gold crown must be heavy for anyone to wear on their head. Decorated with green and purple and mostly red gems, the jewels glittered.

"Nobletive Oakton." The page took hold of Bracken's arm and led him to the back bench with Cedar and Sequoia. Frederick joined them.

My gut tightened. No Henrik. Another sign Rye's support team had suffered a major setback.

The Trees were dressed in their best fairy suits with their wings spread out behind them. Frederick wore a somber black suit.

"I should be by the side of my fiancée, Princess Ellery." Bracken's expression morphed into mulish. He'd gone along with the regent's instructions about the wedding and the coronation and the peace treaty. Why was a position on stage so important?

"Regent, soon to be King, Theobald wants you to sit here." The page spoke with force. A tone Bracken wouldn't argue with in front of the humans.

Guards on the edge of the stage lifted their weapons in a threat. They circled the stage and wore a ceremonial uniform. Their weapons were meant for business. Ugly pistols and long tasers meant to kill.

Additional guards were stationed behind the stage, including the escorts from our room, and even more were positioned in the front row. I scanned the crowd to pick out other uniformed guards situated in the middle of the crowd, the back entrances, and the balconies. My chances of making an escape grew slimmer.

From my viewpoint, the light in the ballroom grew dimmer.

The cyborg's stiff message from last night flashed in my head, providing a glimmer of hope. Except no one had come to unlock my door. I had to stay the course until the last second. Patience might be a virtue, but time was getting short.

I glanced at my father's watch and spotted a blond backstage.

Bee.

Everything inside me went dark.

She wore a formal tight dress as if she were a secretary or an assistant, not a mistress. Her breasts popped out of the low-neck cowl and her hips jutted, with one hand signaling the page and the other holding the Divinity Orb.

I scowled, wanting to wrap my hands around her neck and physically steal the orb. As a fake student at Queens Academy, she'd displayed her body openly. She was proud of how the robotics made her appear. Young and sexy.

Bracken's expression changed when he spotted her. First, his eyes softened, and his mouth pouted, clearly infatuated. Then his gaze narrowed, and his lips firmed into a hard line. He might love her, but he still wouldn't forgive her for lying. And still might be disgusted that she was a half breed, plus.

She glared at the page before handing him the dull orb.

With two hands on the Divinity Orb, he pivoted and walked in my direction. Bee smirked when she caught me watching. She believed she'd won and fooled both me and Bracken.

The darkness deadened my soul. She'd definitely fooled us. Had she won?

The page stopped in front of me and held out the orb. "For you to present to the king."

Even through the red gloves, the Divinity Orb lit up like a bunch of lightning bugs at my touch. A multitude of colors swirled.

Oohs and *aahs* came from the audience. Did they understand the significance?

"He's not a real king," I muttered.

The page hurried to get away. He didn't want problems and he realized I could cause trouble. He took his position next to the older man.

Holding the orb in front of me, I stared straight ahead at the audience. I'd lived among humans for most of my life. Instead of worrying about them, I'd remember them. Because when the right side won, I wanted to know who'd supported Theobald.

My soul sparked back to life.

They judged me now. I'd be judging them in the future.

The front row was made up of soldiers, guards, and SCUM in their simple uniforms and long-billed hats. Ackerman had taken a position at the end of the row. I imagined him telling my stepmother the details of the coronation and a fairy wedding.

With her memory of me gone, she wouldn't know who he talked about.

Behind them sat the aristocrats, men wearing colorful suits some with blinking electronic lights and women wearing even more ridiculous outfits. Clothes made of silk and electronics, tall hats with lace and intricate designs.

An older gentleman caught my attention. His fuzzy gray hair was wilder than it had been the night of the ball. Stone's friend, Professor Nilsen. His gaze connected with mine and he gave a slight nod. I didn't know if it was encouragement or fortitude.

My pulse rushed and I searched for Stone. Could he be nearby?

My gaze stopped at a woman in the crowd who had similar features to Clover, the fairy guard. A man with a tall hat caught my attention. The hat contained the shape of a small fairy inside, a smoke sprite. I held in a huff. Did humans think that was fashionable or had he done it to honor me?

Dishonor me, more like.

The hat shifted and my gaze narrowed. Was he using a captured smoke sprite, or were they making cyborgs imitating majiks?

Revulsion shuddered through me. I continued to stand perfectly immobile.

Near the man with the hat was a woman wearing a wide, cloak-type dress. The large hood shadowed her small head. Her face resembled Tos in a much taller body. Shaking my head, I tried to clear the vision. I was so desperate to see my friends I was imagining them in the crowd.

Observing the padre in the hooded robes, I wanted to plead with him to stop this fiasco. The coronation and the wedding.

I could tell him I was being forced into marriage. Surely, he'd respect my wishes.

The crown winked slyly at me. The intricate goldsmithing must've taken weeks to fashion. How long had Theobald been planning to crown himself king? It wasn't the old king's crown and Rye wouldn't be caught dead wearing something so gaudy.

My heart hitched. Rye could be dead. The only way for the regent to crown himself king was if Rye was dead.

My eyes burned and I blinked, fighting the tears. Pursing my lips, I blew short, shallow pants, trying to calm myself down. Even once I married Bracken, I'd fight on the right side. Fight for all majiks' equality. Equality to humans.

Trumpets blared, assaulting my ears.

I jerked, knowing it meant the regent had arrived.

First scantily clad women danced in and tossed gold flakes onto the ground. The women settled at the feet of the throne chair and watched with adoration, waiting for the regent's entrance.

A group of four guards marched in backward. They wore new uniforms made primarily of red. Another item that would take planning to make in mass quantities. More proof Theobald had been planning the coup for a while.

The guards' gazes were trained on the carried gilt chair with Theobald on top, higher than everyone else on stage. Above the guards' heads, he raised his hand and waved to the audience. Passing Bee, he didn't even glance in her direction.

Her eyes narrowed and she frowned. She'd expected at least acknowledgement from him. Not everything was idyllic in their tawdry romance.

More guards marched in behind the chair. Each of the guards' weapons pointed down. Not at the ground but beneath the regent's chair.

What was dangerous beneath the chair?

I leaned forward yet still couldn't see. The guards' legs blocked my view.

The crowd bowed, followed by the page, the padre in robes, Frederick, the Trees, and Bracken. I stood straighter, refusing to bow even when he was about to be crowned king. A fake king.

The chair was hauled closer and I spotted who carried the chair. Majiks.

Dizziness overloaded my system. I gasped and my senses couldn't connect with what I saw.

A troll, an ogre, an elf, and a giant. Chains surrounded their ankles, wrists, and necks. Open wounds dripped with their colored blood. They'd been beaten and wore tattered rags. The shorter elf struggled with the back corner of the chair, raising his skinny arms high. If he dipped slightly, he was kicked or punched or whipped.

Horror scraped my throat in a silenced scream. Already, the majiks were being subjugated.

The chair stopped beside me. The elf squealed. My fingers itched to help. Two guards perused me, as if knowing my thoughts. The Divinity Orb weighed heavy in my quivering hands.

Regent Theobald angled across his etched golden chair. He ogled me from head to toe. A shudder took root in my feet and worked its way up my body. I calmed myself and stared at him. He would never make me cower.

"You look lovely, Princess Ellery." He signaled for the chair to be set down right in front of me and he stood. "I knew the dress would be fabulous on you."

I didn't say anything, didn't react. I spotted the troll farthest from me. *Jayunja?* I blinked a couple of times. How was that possible? He'd gotten free the night of the Presentation Ball, and he'd never dare come close to Reximus Palace. Unless he was captured again and imprisoned.

"Bow." The first guard behind the chair lashed his whip.

The four majiks dropped to their knees and pressed their foreheads to the floor. The subservient position had been taught through torture.

My earlier silenced scream ignited into fury. If I had my whip, I'd teach the guard a lesson.

"I'm happy to see the Divinity Orb is working." The regent's greedy gaze watched the colors swirl. "Where did you get those hideous red gloves?"

"A gift from a friend. A *troll* friend." I wanted him to get angry about my disrespectful tone.

"I have another gift for you as well." Tossing his fur robe behind him, he gestured to the guards near Ackerman.

A curtain to the side of the stage opened. The crowd murmured and craned their necks to see the reveal.

I knew whatever it was, it wasn't going to be nice. It never could be coming from him.

Guards pulled on strong cords connected to a machine. Not any machine. *The* machine.

The auraguillotine.

My horror and fury dropped into the pit of my stomach. A pit of despair. The glinting silver tanks hurt my eyes. The wires and electrodes tangled around the machine. So much closer, I could peer in the side made of glass and imagine the torture.

"W-w-what is it?" I knew yet needed confirmation.

"It's called an auraguillotine and it sucks the zauber's magical powers." His explanation and terminology made me cringe. "Would you appreciate a demonstration?"

"No!" The pit in my stomach sunk further. I didn't think he meant me. Still, fear for others had me peering around. I noticed everyone was still bowing, including Bracken and his friends. The regent could demonstrate on Bracken or the Trees or the captured majiks prone on the ground.

Regent Theobald chuckled darkly. "Later. We have more important things to get to."

"Like a false coronation and a forced fairy wedding," I snapped back, unable to contain my tongue.

He smiled. The joy didn't reach his eyes. This man held no joy. "Something like that."

Strutting toward the throne chair, he flipped the fur robe to one side, revealing gold pants and a bright red silk shirt. A gold slash decorated with meaningless medals hung on his frame. He sat on the throne chair and pulled a microphone forward.

Large screens dropped down from the balcony and his face leered from around the room and broadcasted across the kingdom.

It was the interception of the old and new world. High-tech with medieval decorations. Magic and technology.

Theobald held up his arms. "Arise and greet your soon-to-be king."

The audience rose to their feet. Bracken and the Trees rose as well. As did Frederick, the padre, and the page. The guards were already standing. "Hail Theobald the Benevolent. Hail Theobald."

Benevolent, my wings.

"Welcome citizens of the Kingdom of Alandaska to my coronation and wedding," Regent Theobald greeted his people.

My ears twitched. He meant *a* wedding. He must've forgotten the *A*. It would be a fairy wedding, probably something they'd never seen before. Would a fairy wedding be legal if performed by a human? My personal despair lightened. Possibly the way out of marriage to Bracken.

"When I become King Theobald and officially and decisively rule, I will transport the kingdom into a mighty empire, introduce the world to Alandaska."

His words knocked me back into the present problem, not a future one. Alandaska was a secret island kingdom. No one outside the shield knew about us for our safety.

The audience murmured louder. Frederick and Bee appeared smug. They'd known the regent's plans.

"There will be no more hiding for our nation." Regent Theobald stated with conviction. "Other countries will bow at our feet."

My ribcage constricted.

The murmurs of the crowd grew louder.

"If other countries don't do what I say, they will experience our advanced technological might and our magical powers." The regent waved in my direction, indicating they'd be using my powers.

I listed back, shock gluing my feet to the floor.

I'd never use my powers to help him or to punish others.

"The world will know and understand and bow to our power or they will see our wrath!" He shouted the last part, wanting everyone in the kingdom to hear. And everyone outside the kingdom's dome.

Welcome to the end of our kingdom as we know it.

Imploding, everything inside me shattered.

Regent Theobald didn't want to just rule the kingdom. He wanted to rule the world.

Chapter Twenty-Seven

Theobald planned to open the dome shielding Alandaska from the world and its problems. He planned to expose our technology and our magic—not his magic but the majiks' magic—to the world, putting us at risk while doing his dirty work. He planned to attack other countries if they didn't do what he wanted.

I gripped the glowing Divinity Orb in my trembling hands, fearing I'd drop the precious artifact. The regent would try to force me to use its predictive powers to know his enemies' plans.

Dazed, I wavered on my feet, trying to re-find my bearings.

The audience talked and murmured. They shifted positions. They were shocked by the regent's announcement, uncomfortable even. Professor Nilsen was so upset that he talked to his wrist. Many of the guards' and soldiers' faces had paled. They knew who'd be fighting these battles, and it wasn't the regent.

Alandaska's reasons for hiding from the world applied today. We'd fought in their wars and the majiks' special attributes had been taken advantage of. The rulers were tired of our citizens dying in battles we didn't care about. So, using our magic, we withdrew from the world. The dome protected us. Without wars to fight, our best minds worked on advancing health and technology. And we'd succeeded. Now, Regent Theobald wanted to turn the tables and use our advanced culture and magic to wage war on everyone outside the dome.

Bracken froze in place. He hadn't realized bringing the Divinity Orb to the regent would spell disaster. He didn't know by negotiating the treaty, he'd be stopping a war against the humans only to sign the fairies up to fight with the humans against other countries.

Beside him, Frederick stood taller. The smug quirk of his lips proved his advanced knowledge. He was finally able to lay his cards out and prove he'd conned Bracken and the Trees.

No kidding.

"Some of you are surprised or, shall I say, shocked by my announcement." Regent Theobald addressed the audience.

Shocked was a good word. Tremors shook my hands, going up my arms into my soul.

He raised and lowered his hands, trying to quiet the audience.

The humans spoke amongst each other, showing their confusion and distress.

"This has been in the works for a long time. Our scientists," he pointed at a group near the front of the stage, including the professor, "have been working on this for a long time."

Dread sunk from my midsection to my feet. Professor Nilsen was supposed to be a friend of Stone's. Had the scientist betrayed my friend? Could he betray me? Maybe he was a double agent like Henrik? Except Henrik was gone and the professor stood before the regent.

"We've engineered cracks in the shield." The regent's statement jiggled a memory. Bee had told me about the cracks on our mission to Aristos Sanctuary. No one had believed her claim. At the time, we didn't know she had direct access to the regent. "And we've sent explorers out into the world to research the current situation."

There'd been rumors majiks had been sent outside the dome when arrested. Which I now knew was untrue. The government, the regent, had killed them and tried to steal their powers with earlier versions of the auraguillotine.

"I even sent my nephew Zacharye." The regent didn't deserve to use his name. And he didn't use his title of prince. "Which comes to my next announcement..."

My heart quivered and my hands shook more violently. I tried to control the shaking, not wanting anyone to notice my upset.

"Prince Zacharye betrayed me." Regent Theobald raised his hand with a dramatic flair. "Betrayed our Kingdom of Alandaska."

My body tensed. He was going to announce Rye's execution. The quivering expanded, agitating my torso and my limbs.

The crowd shifted and talked. A loud cry came from someone in the middle. The people of Alandaska loved Rye. Would they believe the regent's lies? Would they have a choice?

Regent Theobald raised his hands to quiet the crowd. "After my nephew returned from outside the dome, he was sent on a mission to bring back the Divinity Orb and brought home a fake. He lied to me. He betrayed me."

Everything was about him. The regent believed he was the center of the universe. That he was always right and never accepted responsibility. He blamed others for his failings and bullied those who disagreed.

Rye had brought home a replica orb to help me.

My hands shook more violently. My disturbed thoughts must have been causing a reaction in my limbs. Although, my legs didn't wobble.

Regent Theobald put his hands together in a prayer position. "For the good of the kingdom, Prince Zacharye has been executed."

My world spun on its axis. I didn't notice the crowd's reaction or the reaction of the people on stage. There was too much misery in my entire body to be aware of what was going on outside myself. My heart crushed into tiny pieces and dropped into a pile of dust. The void in my chest curdled to black, as black as my soul. I clutched the orb tighter as the shaking in my hands and arms grew to earthquake proportions. The rocking caused my entire body to tremble. I wanted to collapse to the floor. I knew I couldn't. I refused to show weakness.

I kept the torment inside, except for the shaking. For some reason, I couldn't control my hands.

"I know the young ladies in the kingdom will be disappointed..."

Will be? I perked up at the use of the tense. It wasn't past. Was Rye not dead, or was it wishful thinking on my part?

Regent Theobald covered the microphone and swerved to me. "Especially one young lady."

A jagged pain went through my empty chest. Did he know I loved Rye? I glanced at Bee. Of course, the regent knew. Bee had told him everything.

"But today is a joyous occasion." Regent Theobald fake grinned. "Today, I will become your king."

Polite applause followed his announcement.

"I will sign the King Theobald Peace Treaty with the fairies, uniting the entire kingdom before our upcoming battle with other majiks, and eventually any country in the world who doesn't bow to our might." He ogled me again and I stared at the ground. I couldn't even look at the man. "And I'll seal the deal with a kiss."

Ew. I shivered, and not from my quivering hands. Kissing to seal a deal was not a human or fairy tradition. Was he going to kiss Bracken?

I peeked at my fiancé. His brow furrowed and he appeared confused.

Maybe the regent had meant by marrying Bracken and me, we'd kiss, and the kiss would top off his treaty and joyous celebration. My shoulders dropped. I highly doubted that. Regent Theobald was too much of a narcissist to care about someone else's wedding.

My hands shook harder again, as if trying to get my attention. I wrapped my fingers tighter around the Divinity Orb. I didn't want anyone seeing my upset or fear.

"I told you today would be special." The regent giggled. He seemed to have a secret he wanted to reveal.

The day had been the exact opposite of special. It had been tragic, and he made the future sound even worse.

"I have one more announcement before the proceedings begin."

This must be the big secret reveal. How much worse could it be? So far, he'd announced he was crowning himself king—a false one, he killed his nephew—the true ruler, and he was going to go out into the world to wage war in a sad attempt to conquer.

My hands rocked back and forth. The effect forced my arms to quake and my body to shudder. I needed to get a grip. I needed to set the Divinity Orb down so I could control myself. Glancing at the orb, I noticed the colors swirled frenetically, trying to tell me something.

"After I'm crowned King of Alandaska, the padre will immediately perform the wedding ceremony."

Marrying Bracken had become more of an annoyance. I'd deal with breaking apart our marriage later. I'd find a way.

The regent grabbed my waist and tugged me closer. "The wedding of Princess Ellery and King Theobald."

My ears rang. I must've heard wrong.

Two guards grabbed Bracken and dragged him away past Bee standing backstage. Her cheeks flagged red. Her gaze flashed with fury. Her mouth curled into an ugly frown.

Neither Bracken nor Bee had a clue about the double con.

A wedding. And not to Bracken.

Finally, the announcement hit me as if a dragon had been dropped on my head. My ears rang and my head exploded. It wasn't me and Bracken getting married today. It was me and the regent.

It was too much to take in. Tugging away from the regent, I collapsed to the floor, dropping the Divinity Orb. "Nooooooo!"

Chapter Twenty-Eight

Grabbing my head, I rocked back and forth on the floor. The ugly wedding gown swallowed me. I wished I could disappear. I should've realized it sooner. From the human wedding dress to the position on the stage to the way the regent ogled me. Greedily. Suggesting I belonged to him.

I'd lost my home, my love, and now I'd be forced to marry this old man. The only thing important to him was my title. Panting, I had to pull myself together. A few seconds of weakness was acceptable. I was a Milford and a princess, and I would fight on.

I had friends, family in the queen and Gardenia, and maybe, just maybe, I had Rye. I couldn't let the hope leave me.

Lifting my head, I stared at the crowd. A few people appeared sympathetic to my cause. Most were curious, as if this were a play and I was the main actor.

I glared at the regent. The torn pieces of my heart tangled in my chest. He smirked at me. This had always been the plan. The way Frederick had dangled the peace treaty meetings if he brought the Divinity Orb, knowing the orb only worked for me. They'd known about my feelings for Rye too.

Similar to how Bee had endured multiple surgeries, they'd operated on me, too. They'd used my love for Rye to lure me to the palace and kept us separated, permanently, through assassination.

The treaty wasn't important. It was me. They'd lured me. The regent wanted me to come to Reximus Palace so he could force me into a union.

Two guards grabbed beneath my arms and yanked me to my feet.

Mortified, I struggled but knew breaking free of the guards would not help me.

"Release my bride," the regent ordered. "She won't go anywhere with the future of the fairies in my hand."

His sinister hand.

I steadied myself, slowing my pulse, and lifting my chin. My hands weren't shaking anymore, even though the situation was more dire than before. Which was odd. The red gloves and my father's watch reminded me of who I was and how I needed to act. I'd figure a way out of this situation and I'd do it in a dignified manner. I wouldn't besmirch the fairies. I'd be a perfect princess.

Until I had to fight. Then, I'd be a perfect warrior.

Clutching my non-shaking hands, I sighted the Divinity Orb lying dully on the floor. No lights because I wasn't touching it. And no trembling. Something triggered in the back of my mind.

"I understand you have non-fairy friends." Regent Theobald reached out to take hold of my hand and stopped. He hated the red gloves. Something I'd have to remember if we ever got to the point where I was alone with him. "You've read the treaty and how non-fairy zaubers will be dealt with."

"Ethnic cleansing," I spat the words.

He gave a short, evil smile. "If you want to negotiate, possibly save your non-fairy friends, you will marry me without a struggle. For my wife, I might be lenient and give the zaubers more favorable terms."

My emotions roiled between hate and hope. It was emotional blackmail. He knew I wanted and had a responsibility to protect all majiks. And even if I agreed, he could change the terms again.

"Guards!" He tapped an impatient foot on the floor and signaled to bring the auraguillotine forward. "Let's give the princess a demonstration of how the machine works."

Terror raked through me. I'd seen how the old machine worked and didn't want or need a new demonstration.

The guards pulled the machine into position in front of the stage. A guard grabbed a prisoner. Jayunja. The troll stumbled forward and fell off the stage to the floor below. Another guard by the machine yanked him near the suction intake. I'd seen Keltie sucked into the machine. Her scream echoed in my head.

"No!" I bit my lip tasting the tanginess of blood. "I mean, yes. I'll marry you."

I couldn't watch an innocent majik suffer.

"Do you promise?" Regent Theobald said it in the same tone my fairy godmother Gardenia once used.

That time it had been a binding fairy promise. This time it wasn't magical, but there would be a bond. A royal bond as long as he didn't break the contract. Trapped, I had no choice. "Yes, if you never hurt a majik again. Those are my terms."

"Very well." The corner of his mouth lifted, and he gestured again. "*I'll* never hurt a majik."

The guard dropped Jayunja to the floor.

I licked my lips, not believing him. My body sagged with relief for my friend. I straightened and my pulse charged. My body quivered or *vibrated* like when I'd been holding the Divinity Orb—also like when Rye was trying to communicate with me using the replica orb. My gut tightened. The only one who could communicate with me that way was Rye.

I held my breath while my brain inspected the evidence. My hands hadn't been shaking uncontrollably earlier. The orb had been vibrating. My heart fluttered, tickling my ribcage and my memory. Which meant Rye was trying to communicate with me.

Which meant he was alive.

The word reverberated in my head and in my heart. Rye had to be alive.

I jerked my head up to peer around. Had anyone noticed the change in my demeanor. That I'd had a revelation?

The crowd tensed, wondering what would happen next in the drama unfolding on stage. I scanned every row, searching for Rye.

Could he be out there? Surely, he'd stop the fake coronation and forced wedding.

Bending down, I went to retrieve the Divinity Orb from the floor, wanting to experience the vibration again. To confirm he'd tried to communicate with me.

The regent clamped a hand on my arm, thinking I was going to run.

"I'm picking up the Divinity Orb." I regarded him and his suspicious frown. Marriage or not, the man would never trust me. And I'd never trust him. And never ever marry him. I'd find a way out of the royal promise. "It's a special fairy artifact and my gift to you."

His distrusting expression changed to triumph. He believed he'd won. Nodding, he agreed to let me pick up the orb.

At my touch, the orb lit up.

It did not vibrate.

My fingers slackened and my head lolled. Had I imagined the vibration before? The regent and everyone else stared at me and the glowing orb. If Rye tried to communicate again, someone would notice. But if it had been a sign or a message, how long did I have to wait? I wasn't known to wait for someone to rescue me. I also didn't want to blow Rye's plans. He'd said he had a strategy to take back his throne without hurting his people.

I'd wait as long as possible. After all, patience was a virtue.

"My coronation will take place first." Regent Theobald ogled the gold crown. "Padre, now."

No please or thank you. Just do this. How could anyone want to marry this man? How could Rye grow up with him and emerge so wonderful?

The padre minced toward the regent. He picked up the gold container with small holes hanging from a thick gold chain around his neck, similar to a thurible.

"Are...you...willing...to take...the Royal Oath?" The padre spoke slowly and haltingly.

"Of course, I am. I mean, I am willing." The regent's response proved his urgency and knew the lines he was supposed to speak.

Confusion irritated my head. If Rye was alive, how could he allow this sham coronation to proceed? I scanned the grand ballroom, hoping to spot a hint of defiance.

He'd wanted me to delay. Which meant I'd have to do something to stop this mockery myself.

The padre lifted the thurible and waved it over the regent's right shoulder. "Will...you...solemnly promise...and swear...to govern...the peoples...of the...Kingdom of Alandaska...according to...the respective...laws and...customs?"

The last part meant according to the laws and customs of the various majik factions. For example, the fairies had their own set of laws and customs which included their own royalty. With this man as king, he'd make new laws and force them on majiks or kill them. He wouldn't respect other practices.

"I solemnly promise I do." The regent spoke as fast as the padre spoke slow. The man was impatient to become king.

I tapped my foot. Where was Rye? What was he waiting for? He needed to stop this ceremony. My foot stalled. Maybe I'd been wrong. Maybe the orb hadn't been vibrating. Maybe Rye wasn't coming.

The padre lifted a trembling arm and waved the thurible over the regent's left shoulder. "Will you, to the utmost...of your power, cause law...and...justice, in mercy, to be...executed...in all your...judgements?"

Executed. The word sliced through my chest.

"I will." The regent sounded giddy. "Hurry up, you fool."

He was so close to succeeding in stealing the throne. Tension spread across my body, tightening my muscles. Even my skin went taut.

The padre waved the thurible over the regent's right shoulder. "Will...you, to the...utmost power, maintain...the laws...and the true...guiding...principle of...Alandaska?"

"I will." Regent Theobald stretched to grab the crown.

"There's more." The padre gazed up towards a balcony on the far side and the wrinkled skin around his eyes smoothed for a second.

My brow furrowed. Was he trying to slow the ceremony? I had to stop it before it completed. I couldn't let the sinister regent become king.

"Go on, go on." Theobald spoke through gritted teeth.

Maybe this was the reason why Rye's secret code was about patience. He was patient while the regent was not.

The padre touched the regent's left shoulder. "Do you...Theobald Bjorn Vegard Reximus...Uncle of Prince Zacharye Reximus...and brother to King Jostein Zacharye Reximus, promise...to uphold...the—"

"I do. Now give me my crown." Theobald clawed his fingers, about to strangle the padre.

The padre bowed inch by inch. He pivoted, mimicking a turtle, and placed his hands around the base of the gold crown.

"I can take it from here." Regent Theobald pushed the man out of the way.

If the crown was placed on his head, Theobald would become king. I had to stop this tragedy. I couldn't stand by and watch this injustice. I'd already pledged to marry the evil man. What else could he do to me?

I grabbed the mic hanging between the two men. "You can't declare yourself king when Prince Zacharye is alive."

Alive...alive...alive... My words echoed through the ballroom.

Regent Theobald and the padre froze in place. Frederick and the guards were stunned by my outburst. The prone majiks on the floor peered up. Bee scowled and gripped the dagger at her belt. She wanted to kill me.

The audience gasped.

The regent yanked the mic from my hand and covered it. "As soon as I find him, he'll be dead."

My ribcage constricted. I was right. Rye was alive. The pounding rushed through my elated bloodstream and flowed to my chest. He wasn't captured or under the regent's control. He'd escaped and he was out there...somewhere.

Theobald used his hands to indicate silence. "Calm down, everyone. Now!"

Guards around the ballroom snapped to attention. They understood the regent's tone. The crowd quieted, even while murmurs erupted around the room. People shifted and moved. A few tried to head for the exit. Others pushed forward to get a better view.

"Declare me king. Declare me king this second." Regent Theobald shoved the crown on his head.

"You didn't finish the oath." The padre tugged on the gold thurible.

"I don't care." The regent slipped a small pistol from his pocket. "Declare me king now."

"No. I can—"

The regent shot him. The padre fell to the ground, his robes rippling around him.

Horror washed through me followed by sadness. My pulse slowed and my mind couldn't comprehend. The regent, the supposed king, had killed an innocent man.

"I'm king. I'm king. I'm king." Theobald stomped his foot.

The crowd gasped. A few people turned and ran. Chaos erupted in the crowd.

"Guards! Guards! Lock the doors!" Theobald shouted orders. "Take control of this situation and find someone else to marry us."

My jaw dropped. He was still determined to marry me, even if the official coronation hadn't been completed. And I was still bound by my royal promise. I studied the padre to confirm he was dead. It would take time to find someone new to perform the marriage.

Steam rose from the padre's body. A magical mist. His body shrunk and his face transformed. He wasn't a human.

"The padre was a shapeshifting ogre." My astonishment caused my voice to rise. If the man wasn't an official, the coronation didn't count. "He wasn't human, and he wasn't official. You're not the king."

Theobald's face paled. His neck scrunched, suggesting his crown was too heavy. "What? How did the zauber get inside the palace?"

The strangling sensation I'd experienced since agreeing to marry the regent loosened. The padre was a majik. According to our royal promise, if Theobald killed one innocent majik, I'd be free. I figured he'd have majiks killed under his orders, not by his hand so he wouldn't break the promise. Except he'd shot the ogre. The strangling horror alleviated with the realization. I stripped the gold and pearl choker off my neck and tossed it to the floor. "You broke our royal promise. The agreement to marry is off."

"Good." A masked man dropped from the balcony above the stage. "Because I love you."

My spirits swelled at Rye's deep timbre. Alive and well and standing in front of me.

He slipped off his mask and his silver eyes gleamed with passion. My heart filled with love and became whole once more. He appeared the same, but different. A couple of new scars, a more determined jawline, passion pouring off him. The passion wasn't only for me, it was for his kingdom. He'd planned and schemed, and now it was time to implement. He'd fight his uncle for what was right.

Theobald waved to his closest guards. The guards paced forward, surrounding him.

Men and women dressed in black dropped from the ceiling as if they had wings. Rye's warriors. I did a doubletake. They didn't have wings, they were human. But something magical had helped them propel down and surround the regent.

"Thanks for giving away my secret, Elle." Rye winked at me before grabbing the mic. He wore black similar to his warriors, yet he wore it better. At least to me. "Rumors of my death have been greatly exaggerated."

The crowd cheered and shouted. Good and bad. There were some regent loyalists in the audience. Shoving and pushing and running ensued as they tried to get out of the ballroom knowing this wouldn't end with Rye's announcement. The gold flake-scattering women darted behind the backstage curtain.

Guards raised their weapons. They didn't shoot because they didn't know who the target was. Some must've believed in the regent's right to rule, or they believed in his sinister plan. Others appeared confused, not knowing whether to believe Rye. It was a tense standoff.

"I'm Prince Zacharye, the true heir and ruler of the Kingdom of Alandaska. My uncle set me up, had me imprisoned, and planned to kill me."

With the spelling out of the regent's atrocities against Rye, a single tear fell from my eye. He'd had a terrible childhood.

"He's an imposter!" Regent Theobald yelled and waved his hands around, emphasizing his lie.

Rye pulled a tarnished crown from a large bag he had strapped around his neck. "Theobald betrayed the fairies working on the peace treaty." Rye took a silver coiled rope out of his bag and tossed it to me.

I caught my whip and held it high in a fisted hand. The Silver Snare. My favorite weapon. He or someone from his team had been in my room before I was locked in.

"Stop, right now!" Theobald yelled and pointed the same gun he'd killed the padre with at Rye.

Fear struck and I didn't think, I reacted. I cast my whip back and forward toward the regent. The tail of the whip snaked around the gun. I yanked the whip back, taking the man's gun away.

"Thanks, Elle." Rye returned to the microphone and the business at hand. "The regent who tried to steal my crown planned to slaughter other majiks. He planned to put the people of Alandaska at risk by opening our protective shield." Rye pounded on his chest with his fist. "I promise to protect you. To be fair and equal to all our citizens. To justly rule."

He waved me to his side. "I know everyone won't agree with my policies. However, I will do what is right. I will unite and equalize the humans and the majiks." He tugged on my hand and I fell against him. "Starting with a relationship between the fairy princess and myself."

His lips landed on mine in a passionate kiss. I responded with equal desire. Happiness and ecstasy thrummed through my veins. We were together, we were in love, and we were going to be successful in our fight.

Together.

Fireworks burst in my head and echoed in my heart.

"To think I knew them when they didn't even know each other's names." Jayunja's grumpiness sounded less grumpy and broke through the passionate haze. "There's a battle taking place and kissing is not appropriate."

His words and another explosion rocked me out of the rapture. Our lips broke apart.

"Kissing is always appropriate." Rye gave me a quick peck on the cheek. "Especially with the person you love."

I wanted to melt. Now wasn't the time. Chaos had broken out in the ballroom. Instead of dancing, there was fighting. Instead of instruments, there were guns and lasers.

And magic?

Sparks flared across the room. The sparks weren't gun blasts.

A guard lunged forward and Jayuna tackled him in front of Rye and me. Using pure strength, he fought the guards who would've attacked us.

"It's time." Rye raised a fist and swirled it around.

A major explosion rocked the room. The wall to the right of the stage crumbled into pieces and fell to the ground. More black clad warriors charged into the ballroom.

"My army." He quirked a grin. "Told you I had a plan."

I raised my whip to join the fight. I'd worried so much in the past hour, in the past week, in the past few months even. He'd said he had a plan and I tried to help and be patient. "Next time, let me know the entire plan."

His lips twitched. "Will there be a next time?"

I hoped not.

Chapter Twenty-Nine

"Kill the traitor prince! Grab the princess!" The regent commanded as he cowered behind the throne chair. A group of loyalist guards surrounded him pointing out their weapons.

I tried to take in everything happening. Rye's sudden arrival. Regent Theobald's threats. My heart skipped a beat with every twist and turn.

"The regent is the betrayer. I'm the true heir." Rye used the mic before dropping it, reeling toward the throne chair and raising his weapon. "Theobald is mine."

Rye's group of black-clad warriors moved in unison with him. They stalked toward the loyal guards to go after his uncle. This was personal.

Nerves bounced around in my stomach. Even though the regent wasn't magical, he always had evil tricks up his sleeve. I took a step to move with Rye and his fighters. The heavy wedding dress slowed my pace.

"Elle!" Arbor buzzed above my head.

Joy leapt inside me and I opened my palm for her to land in. Using my fingers, I gave her a hug. "I thought you stayed at Queens Academy." I paused for a second, an image needling at my brain. "Were you hiding in a hat?"

"Were you kissing the prince?" Her quick wit made it seem like old times when the fate of the kingdom wasn't at risk.

Jayunja's large body flew by and he landed on the floor.

I jerked and lunged toward him. He needed more help than Rye. I helped Jayunja to stand. "Are you okay?"

"Fine." He stumbled before returning to battle.

Which is where I needed to go. To fight.

How was I going to fight in this dress?

"Here." Arbor sprinkled dust on me. "It will give you your magic back."

"How did you know about my magic?" Each speck of dust landed on my skin and burst into a small firework. The contact didn't burn. It tingled. "What was that?"

"I'm not sure." She landed on my shoulder, a quizzical arch to her brow. "I've never seen a reaction like that before. Did the queen ever transfer her royal power to you?"

The transfer was a state secret. Professor Sands had known though. "Possibly."

"That must be why the fairy dust acted so strongly." Arbor's explanation made sense.

Right now, it wasn't important. I had my whip and my magic which added to my confidence. My dagger and wand were missing. I'd fight without them.

A guard lunged, causing adrenaline to charge through me. I cast my whip back and forward. The Silver Snare circled his body entwining him and yanked back. The guard fell to the floor. Using a spell, I knocked the guy out.

One down. Dozens to go.

Scanning the chaos in the ballroom, I decided where the best spot was to jump in while using my newly restored magic to change the ugly, fluffy, heavy wedding gown into a simple white jumpsuit. "What're you doing here, Arbor?"

"Prince Zacharye sent a message to Queen Dahliadew about his plan to take back the throne."

I huffed. Everyone had known his full plan except me.

Fighting beside his injured warriors, Rye battled against the guards protecting the regent. Three guards laid on the ground. Several of Rye's warriors had injuries and were bleeding. Surprised he hadn't snuck away, the regent cowered behind the throne chair with a few guards.

Rye needed my help. Joining at his side, I cast my whip forward and took out a couple of the guards. With the two men on the ground, I used magic to bind their legs, arms, and mouths.

Rye's warriors took down two more and I bound them up. Satisfaction flowed through my bloodstream like royal chocolate. We made a great team.

Regent Theobald was left.

"It's you and me, old man." Rye's tone darkened. He approached his uncle with steady, menacing steps.

The regent stuck his hands up. His large eyes broadcasted his fear. "I surrender! I surrender!"

A determined gleam flashed in Rye's gaze. He continued to stalk forward. Did he hate the man so much he'd kill him in cold blood?

My chest pounded, tormented with his pain. Rye had every right to kill the regent after what the man had done to him over the years. Committing murder wasn't his personality though. Rye's men stood back, seeing he had the situation under control.

"Rye?"

He loomed above the regent and raised his weapon. Seconds passed in silence. I tensed and held my breath.

He dropped the hand with the weapon. "You're not worth it."

My body slackened. There'd be enough death with this battle and by not killing the regent, Rye had proved his character.

"Thank you, nephew. I'll be good from now on and help you rule."

"You'll help me do nothing." His face scrunched with disgust. "You'll spend the rest of your years in prison."

Rye scanned the area, searching for a way to contain the regent. Now that the regent wasn't a threat, his warriors jumped off the stage to fight others.

"Let me." My lips twitched, imagining the terrible things I could do to the man with my magic. I wiggled my fingers and remembered Rye's self-control. I wouldn't hurt the man, but I could have fun.

Spotting the terrible statue at the back of the stage, I twirled my finger. Tiny sparks ignited from the tip.

Regent Theobald lifted off the ground and flopped in the air. "What? Oooh!"

Now he understood how it felt to not have control.

"What're you doing?" Rye's surprised expression held trust.

"Binding the regent so he can't get away." I flicked my wrist and pointed my finger at the ugly marble statue. The urge to slam the regent against the marble twittered through me. I held back and set him gently against the stone.

Not against the tall likeness of himself. No, I pressed him against the brownie—the smallest majik representative. I wanted him to know where his place would be in the new order. Below everyone.

Using a strong, magical thread, I wrapped the invisible cord around him and the statue several times, binding him against the marble.

"Will it hold?" Rye's question offended.

"Of course, it will hold." My shoulders rolled. I'd had my magic for less than a year and was still learning. "Just to be sure."

Sequoia and Cedar stood near the back of the stage, protecting themselves with their muscles. Not fighting. Not helping. They'd probably run if they could. Wasting Rye's warrior's skills to guard a tied-up man didn't make sense.

I flew to the Trees' side. "Are you willing to help Prince Zacharye's side? *My* side? Which will be the fairies' side." I emphasized the prince and I and fairies were in this together.

They glanced at each other. If Bracken were here, they'd let him speak for them. But my fiancé wasn't here. He was locked up somewhere which was probably for the best. He couldn't cause trouble.

"Well?" We didn't have all day.

"Yes." Sequoia nodded.

"Whatever you want." Cedar put his hands together in a pleading action. "As long as you give us our magic back."

"If you complete this task successfully, we can talk about getting your magic back." I led the Trees to the statue. "You will both guard the regent. Do not let any human help him escape."

The only possible way for the regent to get free was to move the massive marble statue.

"Yes, Princess Ellery," they chimed together.

Rye raised his eyebrows. "You trust two of your fiancé's friends?"

"Only magic can undo the binding around the regent and the Trees don't have any." I paused thinking through his entire question. We hadn't talked about my engagement. "Let's talk about Bracken later."

Rye grabbed my hand, tugged me close, and whispered, "Just know, bracken leaves are poisonous to humans. And you are half human."

A shiver traveled down my spine. The warning had been spoken in a sexy timbre, not as a threat. I'd always understood Bracken was dangerous to me. I kissed Rye's cheek. "I only want you at my side."

"Good." He kissed my lips in a short caress. His gaze narrowed at the Trees. "Watch my uncle. Don't let anyone rescue him."

"Yes, sir." Cedar saluted.

Rye took my hand. "Let's battle on."

"Battle on."

Together we jumped off the stage and into the chaos. I used my wings to land gently and he analyzed the first fight he came upon, found the weakness, and joined in. His smart strategy and decisiveness made him an excellent warrior and would serve him well as a ruler.

Professor Nilsen fought off two loyal guards with fists to defend himself. I flew to his side and used my whip to cast the aggressors down.

"Are you doing okay?" I was glad he was on our team.

"Fine, fine." He pushed back his disheveled gray hair.

"Where's Stone?" As a half giant, I thought I could easily spot him in the crowd. I hadn't seen him since we'd danced at the ball.

"He's not here. He has his own battle to fight." The professor's seriousness indicated he wouldn't tell me anything more.

I bolstered my flagging, fighting spirit. I couldn't let anxiety about my friend distract me from the battle going on in front of me.

Using magic, I created a gun and handed it to him. "Take care of yourself."

A guard flew past, and he didn't have wings.

My eyes popped. I peered to see what had the force to throw the heavy man so far. "Watu!"

She was okay. I'd worried about her since she hadn't returned from the ball. She wore human men's clothes and a long floppy hat.

"Elle, finally glad battle joined." She wrapped a strong arm around my neck and pulled me close. "Careful be."

Letting me go, she dashed after the guard she'd thrown.

My gaze dazed. The entire ballroom was a blitz. Guards fighting black clad warriors. Majiks popping up to fight the guards. How many majiks had joined Rye's battle plan? A brown-haired fairy flew above the crowd using the height to her advantage and wielding her wand and a sword, resembling a soldier. Clover. She fought in a similar style to my cousin Perry, who'd taught me how to fly and fight.

Flitting my wings, I rose above the crowd and flew to her.

"Clover." Another person I was happy to see healthy and fighting. The fairy guards had been banished to the outside guardhouses for the entire diplomatic visit. "Are the fairy guards okay?"

"Yes. We're fighting with the prince."

Pride had my shoulders pulling back. Rye had put together a coalition of humans and the various factions of majiks. He'd be a wise leader of the kingdom, and his viewpoints aligned with mine.

All majiks, all humans, were equal.

"I have something for you." She held out my wand.

I clasped the wand in my hand. The only weapon missing was the Dagger of Justice. "Thank you."

"I stole back everyone's confiscated wands. When you see Nobletive Oakton and the others." She patted her pocket.

"Sequoia and Cedar are on stage guarding the regent. Don't give them wands." I didn't fully trust them.

I circled back to the fighting. At this point, dozens lay on the ground, wounded, captured, or dead. Dozens more continued to fight. There was more black in the crowd than red.

I headed for a group of red—guards loyal to the regent. From above, I used my whip casting out and around two guards. They knocked into each other and shrieked, having no clue what happened. I used my wand to place an immobility spell on them and left them laying in the chaos.

Where else could I help most? I flew above the crowd taking in the fighting. I shifted back to a spot with a large troll and a small brownie and landed beside them.

Disbelief had me shaking my head. "Tos? Hokima?"

"Elle!" They both shouted my name with happiness, and we hugged.

Distracted, they didn't notice a guard approaching with a gun. I easily took him out, still stunned by my friends' arrival. They'd been told to go back to their homelands before the fairy Grand Council had convened. "I don't understand...How?"

"Rye sent a diplomatic courier to both of our leaders and asked us to fight alongside him to take back the throne. He promised equality for all." Tos clapped her hands and jumped.

Hokima pivoted and punched a royal guard in the face. He rotated back to me and arched his brows. "Rye will keep his promise, won't he, Elle?"

"Yes, he'll keep his promise." I had no doubt. Scanning the area, I noticed more brownies and trolls. "Did you bring friends?"

Several fairies flew above, guarding our reunion. I waved to them.

"We each brought an entire contingent." Hokima stuck out his large chest.

Tos continued to clap her hands. "When Rye is king, we'll be equal."

"Princess Ellery." Another brownie bowed. He straightened and I recognized Tagh wearing the brown and black livery. He peered at my friends, lingering on Tos. "All of Nobletive Oakton's servants are fighting for you, Princess Ellery."

"Thank you Tagh, and call me Elle." I high fived his tiny hand. "These are my friends. Tos is the brownie I was telling you about."

"You talked about me?" She blushed and tilted her head, acting shy.

"You're Princess Ellery's brownie friend." Tagh took her hand and kissed it.

"She's a friend. Not brownie or majik. Just a friend." I wanted to be clear there'd be no distinctions.

"Oh boy." Hokima stomped on the ground, clearly uncomfortable.

Grinning, I noticed the attraction between the two brownies and so had he. "I'll invite you both to Queens Academy at a later date. For now," I gathered my whip and prepared to fight on, "there's a battle taking place."

"Yeah, not a love match." Grumpy Hokima used a knife to fight off an attacker.

I used magic to knock him out. Tos and Tagh used a rope to tie the guy up.

Teamwork.

Advancing toward another fight, I spotted Ingrid and another girl fighting beside Henrik. Ingrid was on my side. Her new friend, Henrik's sister, must've influenced her for good.

My spirits rose. Human opinions could change. They would change with Rye on the human throne and myself on the fairy throne. And us being together. I needed to find him. I wanted to fight beside him.

I knocked two more guards unconscious and continued on in Ingrid's direction. Spotting Rye, a magnetized pull tugged me toward him. I wanted to melt in his arms, even though I'd told Tagh and Tos that now was not the time for romance.

Rye dove behind Henrik's back blocking an attack with a sharp sword. I sucked in air. Adrenaline lit up my insides. I flew to the action. Before I could get there, Henrik revolved and grabbed the attacker's weapon. Ingrid and her girlfriend grabbed him and slapped cuffs on the guy. Rye laid on the ground. My heart fluttered like my wings and I hurried to his side. Rye stood up. He was okay. Not a scratch on him.

He was a hero. My hero.

I wished I could know my friends would be okay at the end of the battle, that Rye would get his throne back and the kingdom would be at peace.

I gasped. I could see the future.

Except I'd left the Divinity Orb lying on the stage floor. I had to get it back before it fell into the wrong hands. Swirling toward the stage, I flew above the battles. The backstage curtain had been drawn around the statue with the regent. I couldn't see the Trees guarding the man. Had they done that to protect themselves?

Others were on stage. Tingles of anxiety hurried my pace.

A group of Rye's warriors fought off a larger group of guards. The warriors backed them up on the stage curtain. One of the guards stumbled on the orb and fell.

The orb rolled back toward the curtain.

I cringed. The Divinity Orb was a precious artifact. I'd dropped it, and with Rye's arrival and the battle forgotten it. I couldn't leave the orb lying on the floor any longer to get damaged or broken.

Scrambling onto the stage, I dashed toward the orb. No cracks. I went to scoop the orb up. My attention caught on a nicely tailored suit dashing behind the stage's heavy curtain.

Frederick was sneaking backstage to where the Trees guarded the regent. I suspected trouble. Frederick deserved to rot in prison with the regent.

Zooming in a low flying pattern, I followed him behind the curtain. No way was I going to let him get away.

Someone grabbed me from the side. Two more arms wrapped around my legs and pulled me down.

For a second, numbness invaded my limbs. Shock held me in place more than the arms strangling me. "Aiea!" My scream woke up my fighting instincts. I kicked and struggled and twisted to fight.

A spray came at my face, blinding me. The mist landed on my skin. I swiped a hand across my face so I could see. Sequoia had his arms wrapped around my waist, pinning my arms to my side. Cedar held onto my feet so I couldn't fly away. And Frederick held the anti-magic mister.

Dread pooled in my veins. I was caught like a lightning bug. My power was gone. No magic and no escape. We were hidden behind the curtain so no one could see us. The Trees had betrayed me. The elf in the marble statue had been busted into pieces. The magical bind couldn't be broken, but the statue could. Chunks of marble lay on the ground.

Where was the regent?

A wrinkled hand yanked the Silver Snare from my grip. The regent smirked into my face. "You, your title, and your powers belong to me."

CHAPTER THIRTY

Horror clawed through me. Ragged breaths rasped out. Who was strong enough to bust the statue and free the regent? Not Frederick.

I'd come so close to getting what I wanted. Instead, I was being dragged away from the fight because of my title and my powers. It wasn't me Regent Theobald wanted. And I certainly did not want him. Disgust shivered across my skin.

I refused to let him win.

My back went straight. My muscles firmed. Determination soothed the horror. "Aiea!"

I tried to break free. Kicking and twisting my body, adrenaline rushed through me. I might not have my whip or my magic, but I had grit and courage.

One of the Trees held me down while the other handcuffed my wrists together.

I yanked my hands apart, trying to sever the device.

"Thanks for your assistance." Frederick raised a different weapon. A real gun meant to kill. He tossed cuffs at Cedar. "Cuff your buddy."

"How could you do this? Why would you betray the majiks this way?" My questions were a plea. Now, the Trees were prisoners as well.

Cedar cuffed Sequoia's hands. "Frederick promised if we broke the statue to get the regent free, he'd free Bracken and let the three of us go."

The regent's lackey lied with as much conviction as the regent himself.

Frederick cuffed Cedar as well.

"And give us gold coins." Sequoia struggled with his hands behind his back.

The blow of betrayal hit hard. The Trees were fairy representatives and I'd sort of trusted them. They'd been bribed with freedom and money and an escape route out of the fairy homeland.

If we got out of this, when we got out of this, they'd be punished.

"Excellent." Regent Theobald tugged me closer. The stench of his nervous sweat made me gag. "If the large and muscular fairies don't do what we demand, we'll put them in the auraguillotine and steal their power."

My lungs hitched. I wouldn't want anyone to suffer that fate, including the Trees.

"Let's move." Frederick pointed the deadly weapon at them.

The heavy backstage curtain shifted.

A light of hope beamed across my outlook. I crossed my fingers behind my back. Hopefully, it was Rye or one of his warriors. Anyone on our side. I yanked on the cuffs again.

The regent wrapped his wrinkled and bony fingers around my upper arm. "I've got a second, human padre lined up to marry us immediately."

"You promised you'd marry me once I became pregnant." Bee stepped from the other side of the curtain. She'd seen and heard everything.

I balanced on the balls of my feet. How would a scorned girlfriend play out?

Her normally bouncy blond curls were limp. Colored makeup smudged beneath her eyes and ran down her cheeks. I remembered her saying she didn't care whose baby she became pregnant with, Bracken or the regent's, she planned to pass it off as Rye's. Once Rye was executed, the regent could claim to be raising the next king or queen.

"Plans change." Regent Theobald squirmed under Bee's intense glare.

I squirmed inside.

"Plans didn't change. You lied to me about your true scheme." Her cheeks punched red and her gaze flashed. I'd seen Bee angry once before—when she killed my cousin. "You always planned to marry Elle. That's why you told me to tell Bracken he should bring her and the Divinity Orb."

Without moving my neck, I gazed around. Where was the orb?

Regent Theobald snarled. "You might be an abomination, but you were always smart."

Her expression fell at the insult. She'd believed his lies. I actually felt sorry for her.

He jerked his head, indicating the weapon Frederick held. "Smart enough to know if you want to live, you'll step away and pretend you didn't see any of this."

Tension knifed through the backstage area. Everyone stiffened waiting for her response. Waiting to see whether there'd be a battle or a retreat. I wanted Bee to fight. It would delay our departure, create a distraction, and attract the attention of others, hopefully Rye.

I also wanted her to fight for women who had been lied to and abused.

"Well?" Frederick's question was addressed to Bee and the regent.

"Bee, please help. We were friends once," I pleaded, even though it had been one-sided because she'd been pretending. "I was your friend. We had fun together."

She stepped right up to me, leaning toward me in a threatening way. "I never liked you."

Old hurt resurfaced and rubbed against the emotional scars. She brushed my wrists and a sliding-tingling sensation burned at my back near my waist. A new wound or a new attack? I was afraid to check.

Titling back, she smirked with an ugly, payback expression. "You deserve to be with Theo."

She spoke his name with affection. She cared about the man. Unsettled, I tried to figure out what had happened. The pressure at my waist subsided.

"I expect payment for the work I did for you, Theo." She backed away behind the curtain and disappeared.

The men relaxed and the regent's smile broadened. He believed he'd won.

Bereft she'd abandoned me, I scanned for any sort of help, any escape. If the regent got me out of the ballroom, I'd be a goner. Married or killed or both. No matter my objection, if I was forced into marriage, the regent would find a way to take control of the fairy throne too. I had to do something. Panic throbbed in my head and rushed through my body.

"I've got a secret transport hidden in the back hallway of the ballroom." The regent jerked me forward. "Once we're in the podship, it will be clear sailing."

Clear escaping. My thoughts turned dark.

The Trees were in the lead with Frederick pointing the gun at them. He believed they were more of a threat than me. *Hah.* The regent walked beside me, gripping my arm. With my hands behind my back, I played with the cuff.

Click.

The noise was a boom to me, yet no one else reacted. I stilled my hands on the cuffs and poked my finger at the lock.

It was undone. The lock was unlocked. Dazed, I couldn't believe Bee had helped. I could get free.

Hope flickered inside me similar to a tiny firefly. I kept my expression schooled. I couldn't alert anyone. I had to figure out a plan before we reached the transport.

Keeping the cuff around my wrists, I bent my arm to touch the spot at my waist. Bee had definitely made contact there and done something. I'd worried she was poisoning me. If she'd unlocked the cuffs, maybe she'd helped me in other ways.

My fingers encountered bumps and ridges, a handle of some sort. The handle felt familiar. I slid my fingers further down. The cold metal of steel chilled and the sharp edge shivered. A knife.

Thank you, Bee.

She might not have stuck around for the fight, but she'd helped.

I gripped the handle and the ridges dug into the palm of my hand. It must sport decorations or jewels. The hilt fit perfectly in my hand.

The Dagger of Justice.

The weapon had been in my bag with the perfume bottle and cyborg eye when I'd been arrested. Tightening each finger around the hilt, I grasped the blade with a steady hand. I needed to take out the regent and Frederick holding a gun. I took a deep breath. I'd have one chance to kill or maim. One chance at escape.

I slipped the dagger from my waist a millimeter at a time. The metal sliding against fabric sounded like a freight train.

The cuffs clattered to the ground.

Frederick quirked his head. The regent glanced behind me.

Now was my chance. Raising the knife, I twisted my body and grabbed the regent, placing him in front of me. I put the blade to his neck.

"Ack." The regent's Adam's apple moved up and down against the blade, showing his fear.

Frederick jerked and pointed the gun at me. "Let the king go."

"He's not a king." Everything hardened inside me. I felt nothing. No fear. No anxiety. No remorse.

This was my life and my future. There was no one else to rule the fairies after my grandmother passed, except for Bracken and his prejudiced, pompous father. There was no one more capable of ruling the kingdom than Rye.

Killing the regent would be best for both of us.

If the regent lived, there'd always be someone loyal to his cause. A terrorist organization would sprout. Continuing battles and fighting in the streets. The entire kingdom would be affected, and we'd never know peace.

Killing the regent would be the best option.

I swallowed. I wasn't a killer. I wanted to be a peacemaker.

The regent quivered in my arms. The Trees stood motionless in handcuffs, stupefied. Frederick's glare sent dark shivers through me. He'd kill someone outright. He'd kill me.

"Drop the weapon." My voice steadied even as my body quaked. I hadn't decided what to do next. Kill the regent or use him as my own hostage.

Frederick squinted and leaned forward. A nervous tic showed in his cheek. His finger trembled on the trigger.

If I killed the regent, Frederick would kill me. But I could easily fight one man.

He repositioned his hands on the gun. His gaze grew more intense. He flattened his lips into a determined line.

I gripped the regent tighter. "If you shoot me, you'll kill the regent."

He lifted the weapon high and charged toward me. He wasn't going to shoot. He was going to fight.

Reacting, I swung the regent around and tossed him to my right. The man tumbled to the ground. I spread my legs wide and took a defensive position. Adrenaline pumped through my bloodstream and prickled across my skin.

Frederick swung the weapon, ready to bring the barrel down on my head.

The Trees stood there, gaping.

I didn't have time to think about them or even think. Dropping my dagger, I grabbed the long, metal barrel. If it went off, I'd be directly in the bullet's path. He jerked the gun back. I held on, twisting and tugging. Frantic terror gripped me, and I yanked harder. I needed to get him to let go of the gun.

He pulled and I yanked. He contorted his hands to get me to release. I gripped tighter.

His hands inched up the barrel. If he pulled the trigger, we'd both jerk and the shot would go wild. The bullet could hit the wall, the Trees, or even the regent.

Which gave me an idea.

Pivoting, I placed my elbow over the barrel. With my back to his front, I kicked back, resembling a donkey and aiming for his crotch.

"Ahhhhhh!" Frederick screamed and bent. His hands fell off the weapon.

With the reverse of trajectory, I lost my grip. The weapon clattered to our right. Too far to reach.

Desperate, I scrambled to my knees and seized the dagger by my feet.

Frederick grabbed me from behind and yanked me up. The dagger fell out of my hand and flew further. Alarm bells rang in my head. I had to get the knife.

Tussling with him, I stretched my arm, trying to get my dagger.

The regent kicked the dagger with his feet.

The knife slid further away.

Heaving a couple of deep pants, I gathered myself. "I can fight without weapons or magic."

I reached behind and grabbed Frederick around the waist. Using momentum, I flipped him over my back and tossed him to the ground on the far side of the regent. Frederick's head hit the floor. He struggled to get back up.

Emotionally wrecked and physically tired, I bent at the waist and tried to catch my breath. This wasn't the end. A glint under the curtain caught my attention. I scurried and grabbed the Divinity Orb. As Frederick stumbled to his feet, I smashed the orb over his head.

He crumbled to the ground.

For a second, I let relief flow through my veins. I'd done it. I'd escaped.

"Put your hands in the air."

I peeked up from under my tousled hair.

The regent lay on the ground, pointing the gun at me. The deadly gun.

My chest squeezed, pressing on my ribcage. I assessed the situation.

The regent was laying down while holding the gun. His entire body shook, and he had no leverage. He didn't know how to fight, and he was injured. If I could beat Frederick when he had possession of the gun, I could certainly beat this old man.

A laugh built inside, a hysterical giggle. I shoved the laugh down and got ready to fight.

"Woohaaaweee!" Rye swooped in, hanging from a rope used to lift the stage curtains.

A smile burst on my face and my heart swelled with love.

Grasping the rope, he bent low and snatched the weapon from the regent's weak hand. Rye landed on his feet. "Are you alright?"

I nodded. I was great now that he was here.

A group of his warriors surrounded the regent.

"Lock him up." Rye tossed the weapons to one of his warriors and hugged me. "What do you want to do with the fairies?"

"The Trees?"

Rye chuckled and the tinkling soothed everything inside and outside of me, including the bruises. "Is that what you call them?"

I placed a hand on his shoulder. "Cedar and Sequoia betrayed me, betrayed us by accepting a bribe from the regent. They should be locked up until their trial. Is Frederick dead?" My voice shook a little.

"Yes." Rye placed his fingers on my chin and forced me to not stare at the body. "Are you sure you're okay?"

The shaking of my voice agitated in my head and traveled down my spine. My own personal earthquake. I'd killed a man.

Rye's caress comforted me, slowing the aftershocks. The man had been attacking me.

I'd had to defend myself. It had been a fight to the finish. "I've trained for this."

"Doesn't make it easier." He brought me in closer and wrapped his arms around me. "When the fight had just about ended, I panicked when I couldn't spot you in the ballroom. I thought you'd been killed."

My body trembled, a good type of tremble. I leaned back to see his face and touched my palm to his cheek. "I love you."

"I love you too." His silver eyes blazed with emotion. "It's time for us to make a statement."

Taking my hand, he led me to the podium. The ballroom was in tatters, a wall missing and another caved in. Bodies were strewn across the floor and puddles of mixed colors of blood formed. A group of loyal guards were gathered to one side with the black-clad warriors pointing weapons at them. They cuffed them before taking them to the prison.

I shivered, remembering being down there.

At least the fight had been contained to the ballroom. No one outside the palace had been hurt.

Rye grabbed the microphone. "The battle is over."

Cheers went up from the warriors. I scanned the crowd, searching for my friends. My chest lightened when I spotted each and every one of them.

"Regent Theobald has been captured." Rye signaled to his men backstage to bring the regent out. "My uncle has done some terrible things. It is not up to me to be judge and jury. It's up to the citizens of the Kingdom of Alandaska."

The crowd cheered again.

"To those of you who have fought against us, who were loyal to the pretend king, I offer amnesty." His tone rose with passion, firm and assertive. A leader. His arms spread wide, encompassing the ballroom, encompassing the people.

"How do we know you are who you say you are?" one of the royal guards shouted. He sat in a cluster of guards who were being watched by Rye's warriors.

I firmed my lips, trying to control the anger at the men and women who worked for Regent Theobald, who must know in their hearts he was wrong for the kingdom. Taking the microphone from Rye, I cleared my throat. "Let me reintroduce myself. I'm

Princess Ellery of the fairies." I gazed at Rye because I wanted to. "I can vouch this is Prince, soon to be King, Zacharye. I've known him since his Presentation Ball. He's a good man and will be a great leader. He believes in justice for all. All humans, all majiks."

Silence greeted my pronouncement.

My tension rose and I didn't dare breathe.

Professor Nilsen, who had a scratched face and a bloody nose, raised his fist. "Long live King Zacharye."

Others followed suit. Cheering and clapping and calls of "Long live King Zacharye!" echoed through the ballroom.

Watu and Clover cheered. Tagh and Tos hugged. Hokima raised a fist. Ingrid and her girlfriend cried and jumped. My friends had survived.

Success filled my soul. We'd won.

Henrik jumped on stage and grabbed the microphone from me. "The real padre is here and ready to perform the coronation." Grinning, he winked at us and covered the mic. "And a betrothal ceremony?"

Rye dropped to his knee and took my hand. "Princess Ellery, Elle, will you marry me?"

Chapter Thirty-One

Of course, I said yes.

After his proposal, everyone worked together to lock up the prisoners for a fair trial, treat the wounded, and remove the dead with dignity. Sadness wove through my bloodstream. A proper burial would come later.

Today, this moment, was about celebration.

I stood on the stage wearing the white jumpsuit I'd created with magic. Red and green and brown bloodstains adorned the stark white material in a gruesome reminder.

Rye knelt by the throne chair while a real human padre placed a crown on his head. Not the large, gaudy crown the regent had created. His father's simple crown. He spoke his vows with passion and determination. His serious face made him more handsome.

While behind bars, he'd forged a contingent of humans and majiks. The coalition had worked together and defeated Theobald and his cronies. They'd build a better kingdom. We'd build it together.

My lungs expanded and tears glistened. I watched him take his oath with pride. I was part of his success. Me and my friends.

I spotted my group of ragtag friends. Arbor flew above Watu's shoulders. Watu had been wounded and her arm was wrapped in a bandage. Hokima kept a supporting arm around her waist. Tos and Tagh stood on the stairs leading to the stage. The two brownies held hands. Ingrid and her girlfriend also held hands. They stood beside Henrik right in front of the stage. Clover stood proudly with the other fairy guards. Their uniforms were dirty and tattered, yet they smiled. Professor Nilsen leaned on a crutch, a bandage wrapped around his head. He'd been wounded badly but had wanted to attend the coronation and betrothal ceremony.

My heart squashed. One of my friends was missing. Stone. Worried nibbled at my happiness. He was strong and capable and was on an important mission for the queen.

Even though we'd won, the regent had loyal followers. Those that didn't want Rye to succeed. Those that hated majiks. Those that had lost with the regent. There'd continue to be trouble in the kingdom.

I didn't want to dwell on those things. I wanted to celebrate and glow in mine and Rye's love.

"With the authority vested in me, I declare King Zacharye. Long may he reign," the real padre declared.

I beamed and joy spread through my veins. He'd finally ascended and followed in his father's footsteps. Pride and respect and love shined through me, causing an external glow.

The audience erupted in cheers. Shouts of "Long live King Zacharye!" People and majiks hugged and cried and celebrated.

"Thank you for your support. Forgive me for not having a speech prepared. Things have been a bit crazy."

Everyone laughed.

He went to run his hand through his hair in a nervous gesture and stopped when his fingers hit the new crown. "I promise as king to make Alandaska a fair and equal kingdom for everyone. We have a lot of work to do. It will take time. I promise you every day will get better."

My heart liquified and reformed into something stronger and deeper. We'd talked before the coronation ceremony and he'd asked if I minded having a long engagement. He'd told me he needed to focus on putting the kingdom back together, aligning the lords, and rooting out those loyal to his uncle. He promised when we married the kingdom would be under control so he could focus on me.

I understood, we were young and had time. I had to return to Queens Academy and form a new and true Grand Council. I'd work with Queen Dahliadew to make the right decisions.

"My first act as king will be to destroy the auraguillotine and burn the plans." Rye raised a fist. "Many in the kingdom don't believe in equality. Many are afraid of certain citizens having powers."

The regent had encouraged hatred for majiks and it would take time and intervention to change humans' minds.

"In the past, under my father and grandfather's rule, humans worked with majiks to make our kingdom special. We will once again work together, and we'll start with my betrothal to Princess Ellery."

Pressing my lips together, I squealed like a little girl internally. Our future would be bright.

The crowd clapped and cheered. I heard Arbor yell, "It's about time."

"I want to make one thing clear." Rye paused. "Elle and I are not engaged to bring the humans and the majiks together. This is not a political arrangement or stunt." He reached for me and I placed my hand in his. "I love Elle and she loves me."

My face heated and my lips twitched. He'd made a declaration of love hours ago. This one seemed more formal.

"Do you want to add anything?" The way he smiled made my knees give out.

Straightening and strengthening my legs, I stepped in front of the microphone. "As princess of the fairies and a majik representative, I will be working alongside Pri—I mean King Zacharye." The title combined with his name tingled on my tongue.

I'd come from a simple background, a servant in my own home, and now I was princess of the fairies and engaged to the king. I believed in myself and my value and had made many loyal friends. Rye and I would work together even while I lived at Queens Academy and he lived here. Once married, we'd rule the entire kingdom justly and fairly.

I tilted my chin. "I will represent all majik interests, even though I know the new king believes in our rights."

Smiling, he squeezed my hand. His strength, support, and love gave me even more power. "As Mother Morningmist, my great grandmother, said: *Love is more powerful than magic.*"

CHAPTER THIRTY-TWO

With Rye beside me and my friends behind me, I slammed open the doors to the Queens Academy ballroom. Justice and right gave me strength.

The noblets shifted to watch the intrusion. Their expressions changed from surprised to perturbed to disbelief. Their somber clothes reminded me of a funeral. Or possibly a trial.

I huffed. There'd be a trial eventually and it wouldn't be mine.

"I see the Grand Council is meeting once again without royal representation." Marching into the room, my friends and I spread out in a circle around the gleaming wood table. "Don't worry, your princess is here, and I've brought King Zacharye from Reximus Palace."

The noblets murmured to each other. Their shock displayed in raised brows and dropped jaws made me smirk. Their chairs scraped back, and they stood before executing a bow. A human bow. The respect was for Rye, not me. I was okay with that. The noblets still didn't know me. When they did, they'd respect me and listen.

I was getting ahead of myself.

Arbor fluttered above my shoulder. Watu stood to my right. Henrik stood on the other side of Rye. Tos, Hokima, and Tagh were next to him. Clover was near the back with two other guards. Between them were Bracken and the Trees. We wore the same battle-stained clothes from earlier in the day and the same battle-hardened expressions. With Queen Dahliadew, Gardenia, and my powers, we'd apparated everyone to Queens Academy and decided on our strategy.

The Arch Noblet Oakton stepped away from my chair. His suit clung to his heavy frame. "While we welcome his majesty's presence, why are these *others* with you? They're not fairies and they're not noble."

His words used to slash and tear at me. Now, they just made me mad. "They are more noble than any of you sitting here on your butts. They are friends and patriots. They rescued me and they helped Ry—King Zacharye take back his throne."

"They're heroes," Rye finished my thoughts.

We were on the same wavelength and he'd understood the importance of coming here with me to show a united front. He took my hand and pressed it against his chest. His heartbeat paced with mine. The move was a demonstration of love and strength.

"You're interrupting a private meeting." Oakton tilted forward and peered toward the end of the table. "Is my son with you? Well of course, he's welcome to the meeting. He is your fiancé, and we can plan the wedding."

"There will be no wedding planning." My strong voice stomped on this man's shenanigans.

"At least not between Elle and Bracken." Rye's deep timbre soothed my anger and warmed me. In a grand gesture, he lifted my hand and pressed his lips to my palm. A large diamond ring sparkled on my finger. "Princess Ellery and I are engaged. We held the betrothal ceremony at Reximus Palace today, right after my coronation."

Oakton raised his wand and jabbed at Rye. "She's engaged to my son, Bracken."

Protective instincts spiked. The magical threat had me tugging my hand free and stepping in front of Rye. My fingers twitched on my wand.

Gardenia and Queen Dahliadew apparated in a puff of power. The queen sat on her floating chair, intimidating everyone.

After apparating, I'd met with them to introduce Rye, before barging into the council meeting. They'd known of the secret council meetings and monitored what was said. The two women agreed I should be the one to confront Oakton and the council and they'd apparate when it was time.

It must be time.

Confidence inched out in a short grin.

Upon seeing the queen, the other noblets bowed.

Magic flashed from Gardenia's fingers and she took Oakton's wand. "Don't point your wand at the King of Alandaska or any other royal."

Queen Dahliadew's face softened, and she smiled at me and Rye. "I have given my approval of the engagement between Princess Ellery and King Zacharye. Not only will it be a strategic partnership, it's also a love match."

I ignored the murmurs in the crowd. It didn't matter if they agreed or not, or even if we had the queen's blessing. This engagement was what Rye and I wanted. We went to stand by the queen.

Oakton pounded a fist on the wood table. His tall top hat flopped. "I have a contract. The girl must fulfill her mother's obligation."

Before doubt might've wiggled into my nerves. Not anymore. I knew nothing would break Rye and I apart.

The queen's chair floated forward, and she loomed over Oakton. "Royals do not marry traitors."

Noblets in the room gasped.

"What? Impossible. Lies!" Oakton pushed his tall hat back and gaped.

Clover shoved Bracken and the Trees forward.

"Bracken, what's going on? What's happening?" Oakton's speech rose with each question.

Shaking his head, Bracken lowered his gaze to the ground. His hands and mouth were magically bound.

Smashing my lips together, I held back my anger at Bracken, sad he'd followed his father down this treacherous path.

"I'll tell you what's happening." I used my wand to project images onto a wall. "Bracken and his negotiating team sold out the other majiks. The treaty they constructed," I displayed a close up of the document, "was between fairies and Regent Theobald's imposter government. The document gave permission to slaughter other majiks."

"Oh my!"

"What!"

"No way would fairies betray other majiks."

The grunts and comments from the noblets around the table proved everyone wasn't involved in the evil scheme. My tension lightened a bit. The struggle wouldn't be as steep. I wasn't going to explain the harsh details now. The noblets could read the full document later or hear it at the trial.

Oakton waved his empty hand around. "Bracken is a fairy. He was representing *fairies*. Other majiks are free to make their own deals."

The twisting of the truth spiraled through my anger. The fairies had a queen and the royals of the other majiks were similar to the noblets. I understood the fairy responsibilities to other majik factions. I'd learned it in my history lessons. Why hadn't he?

"Fairies rule and protect all majiks." Queen Dahliadew spoke with more calm than I could have mustered. She barely shifted in her chair. "It's been our responsibility since forever."

"Which is why I sent out agents to secure treaties with other majik factions." Gardenia flicked her wand to show a map of the homelands of the brownies, ogres, trolls, and elves. "And I authorized helping King Zacharye."

"Let my son Bracken speak," Oakton groveled. He put his hands together in a pleading action. "Let him explain."

"Nobletive Bracken will have a fair trial." Gardenia spoke with authority.

Oakton's face paled. Then, he smirked. "Trial for what? Working on a treaty that was never signed?"

"Poisoning the queen." My voice shook, imagining if the plot had come to fruition. "And a second plot of attempted assassination."

"You have no proof." He jabbed his stubby finger at me. His wings went rigid in an angry stance.

"Bracken shared his plans to kill me after we married. He plotted murder with his girlfriend. He said Queen Dahliadew wouldn't be around to protect me because she'd be dead." I glanced at Bracken whose muddy brown eyes had drooped more. I refused to feel sorry for him. "He said he would rule the fairy kingdom with help from his father."

Every one of the noblets gasped except for Oakton. Flapping his wings, he shot into the air, trying to make a break.

My pulse skyrocketed and my gaze followed his deceitful actions.

"Arrest Oakton," Gardenia ordered the nearest guards.

I didn't wait for them. My hand grasped the Silver Snare at my waist, and I cast the whip forward. The silver coiled out and clipped the corner of Oakton's wing.

Rye slipped the weapon from his waistband and pointed it at the escaping fairy. He pulled the trigger and a fine mist sprayed in Oakton's direction. "*The* Arch Noblet Oakton no longer has magic. He can't hurt anyone."

Guards poured through the doors and, at Clover's orders, they arrested Oakton and tethered his wings. The guards led him, Bracken, and the Trees out of the room.

Gardenia sent a green spark toward the ceiling, getting everyone's attention.

"Now that the nonsense has been dealt with, I'll be meeting with each of the noblets in person to discuss where their loyalties lie." Queen Dahliadew's sharp gaze took in Noblet Mangowort. "In the meantime, since we have my granddaughter and her fiancé present, let's celebrate their engagement."

The queen flicked her fingers and colorful flower petals fell from the ceiling. Doves circled the room. Summer wine glasses materialized in everyone's hands.

She lifted her glass. "Congratulations to King Zacharye and Princess Ellery! Long may they reign! Long may they be happy!"

Everyone joined in the cheers.

My heart flowed with joy. Everything had come together and ended happily. I lifted the glass to my lips and stared at Rye across the rim. We each took a sip, beaming at each other.

"Kiss! Kiss!" Arbor flew around our heads.

"Kiss! Kiss!" the crowd chanted.

Rye bent his head and pressed his mouth to mine. I welcomed the caress of his lips and responded. The sweet kiss made my head light and my wings shiver in a good way. He caught me in his arms and the simple kiss became more passionate.

For now, we'd each be living in our own castles, but I knew our love was strong and we were united. I'd been given permission to apparate between Queens Academy and Reximus Palace at any time. I didn't need the Divinity Orb to tell our future.

An acrid smell tickled my nose and my eyelids flicked open.

Rye and I broke off our kiss.

A smoke message swooshed through the room straight to Gardenia's fingers.

A warning sizzled across my skin. By my stinging eyes and nose, I knew the news was bad.

She conferred with the queen and waved us over. "Bad news, I'm afraid. I've had word from one of our agents."

"Stone?" I glanced at Rye.

Gardenia angled her head. "Yes, Stone."

"I'm sorry, King Zacharye. This matter concerns you." Queen Dahliadew placed a comforting hand on his shoulder.

"Is Stone okay? He was helpful with the strategy to take back the throne." Rye gripped my hand and squeezed. He understood my friendship with the half giant.

"He has a...situation." Gardenia did not confide more, which left an unfinished taste on my tongue.

"The message was for you, King Zacharye." The queen's somberness foretold terrible information. "Your uncle has escaped his cell."

Shock reverberated down my spine. My head echoed with memories of the man's cruel deeds. I clutched Rye's hand, wanting to provide him strength. His struggle had become more difficult.

Rye jerked his head in a nod. His shoulders straightened and he stood taller. "I have to get back to the palace."

I couldn't stop the streak of disappointment. I'd been hoping we'd have more time together. "I understand."

He had major responsibilities. He had to organize his cabinet and weed out the non-loyal nobles. He had to structure and implement his plans for the kingdom. And now, he had to find his uncle and put down a possible rebellion.

"I'll apparate King Zacharye to his palace." Gardenia understood the urgency. She commanded the fairy troops.

"Thank you." His serious expression wounded my spirits. He was so young and had so much on his shoulders. I was lucky I had my grandmother and fairy godmother to guide me. "Give us a minute."

Taking my hand, he led me out of the room. Once in the hallway, he held me in his arms. His chest went up and down in a deep breath. "You understand I have to find my uncle. He'll start an uprising based on lies and prejudice."

"Of course, I do." I'd help in whatever way possible, including giving him the Divinity Orb.

I'd be busy at Queens Academy dealing with the trials, continuing my education, and learning to rule.

Rye pulled back and peered into my eyes. "I love you, Elle." His deep timbre dropped further displaying emotion.

My heart ba-bumped, and I snuggled closer in his arms. "I love you too."

We poured our emotions and hopes into the goodbye kiss. We'd become great rulers and bring the majiks and humans together. We'd help each other and work together to form a strong union.

Love was more powerful than magic. And love could conquer prejudice.

That was my hope for the world.

Where is Stone?
Turn the page for a sneak peek of the next story in A Glass Slipper Adventure series: Snow Wicked White.

SNOW WICKED WHITE

**The exciting new trilogy in
A Glass Slipper Adventure Series...**

**Snow Wicked White
A Glass Slipper Adventure Book 4**

**She chooses to stay out of the fight. But when she's forced
to help the enemy, her betrayal wakes a sleeping giant.**

Destiny Snow is the last known banshee in the kingdom. Or she
fears she is because her grandfather has disappeared. Humans and
majiks alike discriminate against her because of the banshee wail
of death. That's why she and her grandfather have always lived
as hermits and never joined the majik resistance movement. Until
royal guards knocked on her door.

Under the regent's orders, Destiny is held in an overcrowded cell with seven other criminals while she's forced to track majiks to steal their power.

Except she's never been trained and has no magic. When she makes a major mistake, several important resistance leaders are captured, including her childhood crush, Stone.

Can the bad news banshee convince her cellmates that she can be trusted and help them escape the dungeon before they're all tortured to death?

Snow Wicked White is the first book in the Snow White trilogy and the fourth book in the captivating fairytale series A Glass Slipper Adventure. If you like feisty heroines, twisted fairytales, and secret identity stories, then you'll love Allie Burton's spellbinding novel.

Buy Snow Wicked White to escape with the daring rebels today!

"And that ending, oh my I need the next book!!" – Reviewer

Excerpt:

"You!" The single furious word drilled into me and I tensed.

As if I'd conjured him, the giant from the cave stood in the cell doorway. And of course, his name was Stone. He resembled a muscular boulder.

Chills skittered up and down my spine. Fear or possibly the fading results of the chemical used in the cave. The giant moved fine even with the chains holding him. He should still be affected by the chemicals.

Everyone in the cell went silent.

"Look at me, you traitor!" He glared and I took a step back.

So much for making friends.

Short for a giant, he still dwarfed the three human guards holding him in chains. Fury thundered on the harsh planes and angles of his face. Messy blond hair and furious green eyes made my knees quiver. A swollen eye and a fat lip couldn't hide his rugged beauty.

My heart hammered. Just because I appreciated his handsomeness did not take away the fear. Thank the elves the guards had him chained.

He jerked his arms out of the guard's grips and lunged. The chains rattled. "I'm going to find you and kill you."

The words *find you* echoed in my head. I'd heard him say those exact words. When? The cold inflection did something to me, stabbing like a knife at the same time piercing my deepest soul. A strong tug pulled me forward, similar to when I'd been running away and headed toward the cave. I thought it had been natural self-preservation, but maybe it had been tracking instincts.

I fought the need to go to him.

His fur-lined cloak hung on broad shoulders. The tunic he wore stretched across his chest with leather straps crisscrossing, probably holding weapons until his capture.

I took a step back.

Laughing, the guards released Stone from the chains and left the cell. The metal door clanked, locking in the majiks.

Locking in me with Stone. Without the chains, he was free to murder me.

My throat closed. I held up my hands and took another step back.

Growling, Lukas stepped in front of me. "What's going on? Who is this giant, Destiny?"

The giant's intense glare penetrated deep inside me. My lips trembled and I couldn't speak.

"You got us captured, *Destiny*." Stone squawked my name as an insult. "Several dead. The entire counsel captured."

He spoke as if these majiks were important. As if he was important.

Shivering, I lifted my gaze to face his anger. The snap of recognition I'd experienced in the cave came through with full force. Gripping the rusty frame of the bunk bed, I let the sharp metal cut into my skin. "I didn't know you would be there. That anyone would be in the cave."

"The guards said you led them there." He snarled and punched a strong fist into his other hand. "A majik. A wicked banshee."

I stiffened at his cruel tone. Any recognition or memory must be false. This giant hated me.

"What's going on?" Lukas held up his strong fists. His brown eyes gleamed yellow. "Let's discuss this."

The last thing everyone needed was a werewolf trying to protect a banshee from a giant. In such a small space every inmate would end up getting hurt.

I held up my trembling hands. "Be reasonable. We're both majiks."

The giant leaned around and got in my face. "Watch your back. I'll be waiting for you when your boyfriend's not around."

I jerked, breaking free of his captivating glare. "He's not my boyfriend."

Yeah, because that was the most important thing to say.

"Good. It will make killing you easier." He stomped his foot hard, quaking the concrete floor.

My skin went taut, and I searched for an escape or a place to hide. I was in a cell, in a dungeon prison. If I could escape, I would've found a way sooner. "Let me explain."

He pointed a strong finger. "You directed the SCUM to our secret meeting place."

He punctured holes in my chest. It was my fault. I hadn't meant for the raid to happen.

The others in the cell stopped as if they'd been frozen by the guards' special chemicals. Lukas winced. Now, everyone knew why I'd been brought here. To help the SCUM and the regent.

I wasn't a traitor. I hadn't picked a side, even though I'd wanted to go to the palace with Grandfather.

My lungs shattered. "I didn't know you'd be there."

"That *he'd* be there?" Lukas again glanced between, trying to put the two of us together. "Do you two know each other?"

"Of course not. I don't know you and I don't want to know you." The giant's voice grew louder, more frigid. "You might have skin as white as snow, but your soul is dark and evil."

And don't miss the trilogy's exciting conclusion!

A Note from Allie Burton

I hope you enjoyed Princess Ellery's continuing three-book story. Please consider giving this book a rating or review at your place of purchase. In this brave new book world, the only way for a good story to find its way into the hands of other readers is if the people who loved it let others know. I appreciate any little bit of help you can give, and reviews encourage me to write faster.

The adventure doesn't end. Stone is the hero in the next three-book series starting with Snow Wicked White. (See excerpt above.) To get information about the continuing series, A Glass Slipper Adventure, join my newsletter and receive a free book. You can join at www.allieburton.com.

I love to hear from my readers! If you have any questions or comments, or just want to say "hi," please feel free to email me at allie@allieburton.com or connect with me on www.twitter.com/@allie_burton and www.facebook.com/AllieBurtonAuthor and www.instagram.com/allieburtonauthor.

If you're interested in my other young adult series, below is additional information. Thanks for reading CINDERELLA SPY!

Allie

SNOW WARRIOR WHITE

A GLASS SLIPPER ADVENTURE BOOK 5

She longs to find others like her. But it might cost her the one she loves.

Destiny Snow planned to fight in the battle with the prince, until she's kidnapped by a secret banshee clan. The banshees don't want to hurt her. They need her to take her place at the side of the future leader of the clan. Destiny believes there's safety in numbers and she's finally found other banshees, except they're nothing like her.

Ruled by the Grand Lord Justicar, the secretive banshee clan holds her incapacitated grandfather hostage. Destiny needs to remember her past and take possession of all her magic to heal her only living relative. But when she comes into her full powers, it releases a cataclysmic force no one can control.

Can a reluctant banshee control her shocking powers and give up the guy she loves to save her grandfather?

Snow Warrior White is the fifth book in the twisted fairytale series A Glass Slipper Adventure. If you like powerful heroines, family secrets, and cursed lovers, then you'll love Allie Burton's new installment in this spellbinding series.

Buy Snow Warrior White and leap into a magical quest!

SNOW WITCHING WHITE

A GLASS SLIPPER ADVENTURE BOOK 6

She must learn to control her unusual magic or risk destroying the kingdom, and her friends.

Destiny Snow hates blackmail, especially when she's the victim. Yet, the threat leads her to what she's always wanted—family. With family though, come demands. A requirement to attend the witch academy, where she's immediately an outcast. A call for her sacrifice. A claim on her heart.

The loyal friends that followed her are outsiders who can't handle the toxic atmosphere adjacent to the underworld. Now, Destiny is caught in the

middle of a power struggle between witches and warlocks. Both sides fight over the greater force controlling the devilish double-dealing. A force so powerful the entire coven could be ruined. A force that works against her and will take Destiny away from everyone she loves. A force that prophesized she'd destroy the kingdom.

Can a powerful mixed majik stop the prophecy written about her before it comes to a Wicked End?

Snow Witching White is the sixth book in the twisted fairytale series A Glass Slipper Adventure. If you like magical heroines, split family loyalties, and ill-fated lovers, then you'll love Allie Burton's new installment in this spellbinding series.

"Well-written, amazing characters to keep you hooked." - Reviewer

Buy Snow Witching White and magically fly into jeopardy!

A Glass Slipper Adventure Series continues with exciting new stories! Sign up for my newsletter to get the latest release information and other book news at www.allieburton.com.

Atlantis Riptide
Lost Daughters of Atlantis Book 1

When a girl runs away from the circus...

For all her sixteen years, Pearl Poseidon has been a fish out of water. A freak on display for her adoptive parents' profit. Running away from her horrible life, she craves one thing—anonymity. But when she saves a small boy from drowning, she exposes herself and her mutant abilities to Chase, a budding investigative reporter.

Now, he has questions. And so do the police.

Once Pearl discovers her secret identity, she learns she's part of a larger war between battling Atlanteans. A battle that will decide who rules the oceans. A battle raging between evil and her true family. Will she find a way to use her powers in time to save a kingdom she never knew existed?

This is the start of a young adult fantasy action-adventure novel series. "Sweet summer young adult paranormal with death-defying underwater rescues." Reviewer

Other books in the Atlantis series: Atlantis Red Tide, Atlantis Rising Tide, Atlantis Tide Breaker, Atlantis Dark Tides, Atlantis Twisting Tides, Atlantis Glacial Tides.

ALSO BY

A Glass Slipper Adventure-Young Adult
Cinderella Assassin
Cinderella Soldier
Cinderella Spy
Snow Wicked White
Snow Warrior White
Snow Witching White

Lost Daughters of Atlantis Series-Young Adult
Atlantis Riptide
Atlantis Red Tide
Atlantis Rising Tide
Atlantis Tide Breaker
Atlantis Dark Tides
Atlantis Twisting Tides
Atlantis Glacial Tides

Warrior Academy Series-Young Adult
Warrior's Destiny
Warrior's Chaos
Warrior's Prophecy
Warrior's Curse
Warrior's Rising

Castle Ridge Series-Contemporary Romance
The Romance Dance

The Christmas Match
The Flirtation Game
The Playboy Switch
The Billionaire's Ploy
The Heartbreak Contract

Find all of Allie's books on her website https://www.allieburton.
com

ABOUT AUTHOR

Allie Burton has always been a reader and writer. She wrote her first novel at the age of twelve when she was stranded at a hospital by a snowstorm. Receiving her first romance from her grandmother, she fell in love with the genre. As an adult, she read young adult books with her own teens and was excited to find something fresh and new. Now, she writes both.

Having so many jobs as a teen and adult became great research material for the stories she writes. She has been everything from a bike police officer to a mascot escort to an advertising executive. She has lived on three continents and in four states and has studied art, fashion design, and marine biology.

Allie is a member of several writing organizations. She loves to ski, golf, and run. Currently, she lives in Colorado with her husband and two children.

* 9 7 8 1 9 5 1 2 4 5 1 7 7 *